Nora Roberts is the number one *New York Times* bestselling author of more than one hundred novels. With more than 300 million copies of her books in print, and over 150 *New York Times* bestsellers to date, Nora Roberts is indisputably the most celebrated women's fiction writer today.

Visit her website at www.jd-robb.co.uk

J. D. Robb Omnibus

RAPTURE IN DEATH

CEREMONY IN DEATH

J. D. ROBB

piatkus

PIATKUS

This omnibus edition first published in Great Britain in 2010 by Piatkus

Copyright © 2010 by Nora Roberts

Previously published separately:
Rapture in Death first published in the United States in 1996 by Berkley Publishing Group,
A division of Penguin Group (USA) Inc., New York
First published in Great Britain in 2003 by Piatkus Books
Paperback edition published in 2003 by Piatkus Books
Reprinted 2009
Copyright © 1996 by Nora Roberts
Ceremony in Death first published in the United States in 1997 by Berkley Publishing Group,
A division of Penguin Group (USA) Inc., New York
First published in Great Britain in 2003 by Piatkus Books
Paperback edition published in 2003 by Piatkus Books
Reprinted 2004, 2005, 2007, 2008 (twice), 2009
Copyright © 1997 by Nora Roberts

The moral right of the author has been asserted.

A CIP catalogue record for this book
is available from the British Library.

ISBN 978-0-7499-5396-6

Typeset in Times by Palimpsest Book Production Limited,
Grangemouth, Stirlingshire
Printed in Great Britain by Clays Ltd, St Ives plc

Papers used by Piatkus are natural, renewable and recyclable
products sourced from well-managed forests and certified
in accordance with the rules of the Forest Stewardship Council.

Mixed Sources
Product group from well-managed
forests and other controlled sources
www.fsc.org   Cert no. SGS-COC-004081
© 1996 Forest Stewardship Council

Piatkus
An imprint of
Little, Brown Book Group
100 Victoria Embankment
London EC4Y 0DY

An Hachette UK Company
www.hachette.co.uk

www.piatkus.co.uk

Rapture in Death

But I do nothing upon myself,
And yet am mine own Executioner.

JOHN DONNE

There is rapture on the lonely shore

LORD BYRON

Chapter One

The alley was dark and stank of piss and vomit. It was home for quick-footed rats and the bony, hungry-eyed felines who hunted them. Red eyes glinted in the dark, some of them human, all of them feral.

Eve's heart tripped lightly as she slipped into the fetid, damp-edged shadows. He'd gone in, she was sure of it. It was her job to follow, to find him, to bring him in. Her weapon was in her hand, and her hand was steady.

'Hey, sweetcakes, wanna do it with me? Wanna do it?'

Voices out of the dark, harsh with chemicals or cheap brews. Moans of the damned, giggles of the mad. The rats and cats didn't live here alone. The company of the human garbage that lined the sweating brick walls was no comfort.

She swung her weapon, crouched as she sidestepped a battered recycling unit that, from the smell of it, hadn't worked in a decade. The stench of food gone over smeared the humid air and turned it into a greasy stew.

Someone whimpered. She saw a boy, about thirteen, all but naked. The sores on his face were festering; his eyes were slits of fear and hopelessness as he scrabbled like a crab back against the filthy wall.

Pity stirred in her heart. She had been a child once, hurt and terrified, hiding in an alley. 'I won't hurt you.' She kept her voice quiet, barely a murmur, kept her eyes on his, maintaining contact as she lowered her weapon.

And that's when he struck.

He came from behind, a roar of motion and sound. Primed to kill, he swung the pipe. The whistle of it stung her ears as she whirled, dodged. There was barely time to curse herself for losing her concentration, forgetting her primary target as two hundred fifty pounds of muscle and mean sent her flying to the bricks.

Her weapon flew out of her hand and clattered into the dark.

She saw his eyes, the glint of mayhem heightened by the chemical, Zeus. She watched the pipe raised high, timed it, and rolled seconds before it cracked against brick. With a pump of her legs, she dived headfirst into his belly. He grunted, staggered, and as he reached for her throat, she brought her fist up hard, smashing it under his jaw. The force of the blow radiated pain and power up her arm.

People were screaming, scrambling for safety in a narrow world where nothing and no one was safe. She spun, used the impetus of the turn to deliver a roundhouse kick that shattered her adversary's nose. Blood fountained, adding to the sick miasma of odors.

His eyes were wild, but he barely jerked at the blow. Pain was no match for the god of chemicals. Grinning as blood poured down his face, he smacked the thick pipe on his palm.

'Kill you. Kill you, cop bitch.' He circled her, swinging the pipe like a whistling whip. Grinning, grinning as he bled. 'Break your head open and eat your brains.'

Knowing he meant it pumped her adrenaline to flash point. Live or die. Her breath came in pants, the sweat pouring like oil down her skin. She dodged the next blow, went down on her knees. Slapping a hand on her boot, she came up grinning.

'Eat this instead, you son of a bitch.' Her backup weapon was in her hand. She didn't bother with stun. The stun setting

2

would do little more than tickle a two hundred fifty pound man flying on Zeus. It was set to terminate.

As he lunged toward her, she hit him with full power. His eyes died first. She'd seen it happen before. Eyes that turned to glass like a doll's, even as he charged her. She sidestepped, prepared to fire again, but the pipe slipped from his fingers. His body began that jerky dance as his nervous system overloaded.

He fell at her feet, a mass of ruined humanity who had played god.

'You won't be sacrificing any more virgins, asshole,' she muttered, and as that wild energy drained, she rubbed a hand over her face. Her weapon arm dropped.

The faint scrape of leather on concrete alerted her. She started her spin, weapon rising, but arms clamped her, lifted her to her toes.

'Always watch your back, Lieutenant,' the voice whispered just before teeth nipped lightly at her earlobe.

'Roarke, goddamn it. I nearly zapped you.'

'You didn't even come close.' With a laugh, he turned her in his arms, and his mouth was on hers, hot, hungry. 'I love watching you work,' he murmured and his hand, clever hand, slid up her body to cup her breast. 'It's . . . stimulating.'

'Cut it out.' But her heart was thundering in reaction, and the order was halfhearted. 'This is no place for a seduction.'

''On the contrary. A honeymoon is a traditional place for a seduction.' He drew her back, kept his hands on her shoulders. 'I wondered where you'd gone off to. I should have known.' He glanced down at the body at their feet. 'What did he do?'

'He had a predilection for beating the brains out of young women, then eating them.'

'Oh.' Roarke winced, shook his head. 'Really, Eve, couldn't you have come up with something a little less revolting?'

'There was a guy on the Terra Colony a couple of years

3

back who fit the profile, and I wondered . . .' She trailed off, frowning. They were standing in a stinking alley, death at their feet. And Roarke, gorgeous, dark angel Roarke, was wearing a tuxedo and a diamond stud. 'What are you all dressed up for?'

'We had plans,' he reminded her. 'Dinner?'

'I forgot.' She tucked her weapon away. 'I didn't think this would take so long.' She blew out a breath. 'I guess I should clean up.'

'I like you the way you are.' He moved into her again, took possession. 'Forget dinner . . . for now.' His smile was slow and irresistible. 'But I do insist on slightly more aesthetic surroundings. End program,' he ordered.

The alley, the smells, and the huddle of bodies winked away. They stood in a huge, empty room with equipment and blinking lights built into the walls. Both floor and ceiling were glass-mirrored black to better project the holographic scenes available on the program.

It was one of Roarke's newest, most sophisticated toys.

'Begin Tropical Setting 4-B. Maintain dual control status.'

In response came the whoosh of waves, the sprinkle of starlight on water. Beneath her feet was white sugar sand, and palm trees waved like exotic dancers.

'That's more like it,' Roarke decided, then began unbuttoning her shirt. 'Or it will be when I get you naked.'

'You've been getting me naked every time I blink for nearly three weeks.'

He arched a brow. 'Husband's privilege. Complaints?'

Husband. It was still a jolt. This man with the warrior's mane of black hair, the poet's face, the wild Irish blue eyes was her husband. She'd never get used to it.

'No. Just an—' Her breath hitched as one of his long-fingered hands skimmed over her breasts. 'An observation.'

'Cops.' He smiled, unfastened her jeans. 'Always observing. You're off duty, Lieutenant Dallas.'

'I was just keeping my reflexes sharp. Three weeks away from the job, you get rusty.'

He slid a hand between her naked thighs, cupped her, watched her head fall back on a moan. 'Your reflexes are just fine,' he murmured and pulled her down to the soft white sand.

His wife. Roarke liked to think about that as she rode him, as she moved under him, as she lay spent beside him. This fascinating woman, this dedicated cop, this troubled soul belonged to him.

He'd watched her work through the program, the alley, the chemical-mad killer. And he'd known she would face the reality of her work with the same tough, terrifyingly courageous determination that she'd possessed in the illusion.

He admired her for it, however many bad moments it gave him. In a few days, they would go back to New York and he would have to share her with her duties. For now, he wanted to share her with nothing. With no one.

He was no stranger to back alleys that reeked of garbage and hopeless humanity. He'd grown up in them, escaped into them, and eventually had escaped from them. He had made his life into what it was – and then she had come into it, sharp and lethal as an arrow from a bow, and had changed it again.

Cops had once been the enemy, then an amusement, and now he was bound to one.

Just over two weeks before, he had watched her walk toward him in a flowing gown of rich bronze, flowers in her hands. The bruises on her face a killer had put there only hours before had been softened under cosmetics. And in those eyes, those big brandy-colored eyes that showed so much, he'd seen nerves and amusement.

Here we go, Roarke. He'd nearly heard her say it as she put her hand in his. *For better or worse I'll take you on. God help us.*

Now she wore his ring, and he hers. He'd insisted on

that, though such traditions weren't strictly fashionable in the middle of the twenty-first century. He'd wanted the tangible reminder of what they were to each other, the symbol of it.

Now he picked up her hand, kissed her finger above the ornately etched gold band he'd had made for her. Her eyes stayed closed. He studied the sharp angles of her face, the overwide mouth, the short cap of brown hair tousled into spikes.

'I love you, Eve.'

Faint color bloomed on her cheeks. She was so easily moved, he thought. He wondered if she had any idea how huge was her own heart.

'I know.' She opened her eyes. 'I'm, ah, starting to get used to it.'

'Good.'

Listening to the song of water lapping on sand, of balmy breezes whispering through feathery palms, she lifted a hand, brushed the hair back from his face. *A man like him*, she thought, *powerful, wealthy, impulsive, could call up such scenes at the snap of a finger.* And he'd done it for her.

'You make me happy.'

His grin flashed, making her stomach muscles curl in delight. 'I know.' With easy, effortless strength, he lifted her up and over until she straddled him. He skimmed his hands idly up her long, slim, muscled body. 'Are you ready to admit you're glad I shanghaied you off planet for the last part of our honeymoon?'

She grimaced, remembering her panic, her dug-in-at-the-heels refusal to board the transport he'd had waiting, and how he had roared with laughter and had tossed her over his shoulder, climbing on board with her cursing him.

'I liked Paris,' she said with a sniff. 'And I loved the week we had on the island. I didn't see any reason for us to come to some half-finished resort in space when we were going to spend most of our time in bed anyway.'

6

'You were scared.' It had delighted him that she'd been unnerved by the prospect of her first off planet voyage, and it had pleasured him to keep her occupied and distracted for the bulk of the trip.

'I was not.' *Boneless*, she thought. *Scared boneless.* 'I was justifiably annoyed that you'd made the plans without discussing them with me.'

'I seem to recall someone being involved with a case and telling me to plan whatever suited me. You were a beautiful bride.'

It made her lips curve. 'It was the dress.'

'No, it was you.' He lifted a hand to her face. 'Eve Dallas. Mine.'

Love swamped her. It always seemed to come in huge, unexpected waves that left her flailing helplessly. 'I love you.' She lowered herself to him, brought her mouth to his. 'Looks like you're mine.'

It was midnight before they had dinner. On the moon-washed terrace of the towering spear that was the nearly completed Olympus Grand Hotel, Eve dug into stuffed lobster and contemplated the view.

The Olympus Resort would be, with Roarke pulling the strings, completed and fully booked within a year. For now, they had it to themselves – if she ignored the construction crews, staff, architects, engineers, pilots, and other assorted inhabitants who shared the massive space station.

From the small glass table where they sat, she could see out over the hub of the resort. The lights brightly burned for the night crew, the quiet hum of machinery spoke of round-the-clock labor. The fountains, the lances of simulated torchlight and rainbows of color running fluidly through the spewing waters, were for her, she knew.

He'd wanted her to see what he was building and perhaps to begin to understand what she was a part of now. As his wife.

7

Wife. She blew out a breath that fluttered her bangs and sipped the icy champagne he'd poured. It was going to take some time to understand just how she'd gone from being Eve Dallas, homicide lieutenant, to become the wife of a man who some claimed had more money and power than God.

'Problem?'

She flicked her eyes over his face, smiled a little. 'No.' With intense concentration, she dipped a bit of lobster in melted butter – real butter, no simulation for Roarke's table – and sampled it. 'How am I going to face the cardboard they pass off as food at the Eatery once I'm back on the job?'

'You eat candy bars on the job in any case.' He topped off her wine, lifted a brow when she narrowed her eyes.

'You trying to get me drunk, pal?'

'Absolutely.'

She laughed, something he noted she did more easily and more often these days, and with a shrug, picked up her glass. 'What the hell, I'll oblige you. And when I'm drunk' – she gulped down the priceless wine like water – 'I'll give you a ride you won't soon forget.'

Lust he'd thought sated for the moment crawled edgily into his belly. 'Well, in that case' – he poured wine into his own glass, teasing it to the rim – 'let's both get drunk.'

'I like it here,' she announced. Pushing back from the table, she carried her glass to the thick railing of carved stone. It must have cost a fortune to have it quarried, then shipped – but he was Roarke, after all.

Leaning over, she watched the light and water show, scanned the buildings, all domes and spears, all glossy and elegant to house the sumptuous people and the sumptuous games they would come to play.

The casino was completed and glowed like a golden ball in the dark. One of the dozen pools was lighted for the night and the water glimmered cobalt blue. Skywalks zigzagged between buildings and resembled silver threads. They were empty now, but she imagined what they would be like in six months, a year: crammed with people who shimmered in silks, glowed with jewels. They would come to be pampered within the marble walls of the spa with its mud baths and body enhancement facilities, its soft-spoken consultants and solicitous droids. They'd come to lose fortunes in the casino, to drink exclusive liquor in the clubs, to make love to the hard and soft bodies of licensed companions.

Roarke would offer them a world, and they could come. But it wouldn't be her world when they filled it. She was more comfortable with the streets, the noisy half world of law and crime. Roarke understood that, she thought, as he'd come from the same place as she. So he had offered her this when it was only theirs.

'You're going to make something here,' she said and turned to lean back against the rail.

'That's the plan.'

'No.' She shook her head, pleased that it was already starting to swim from the wine. 'You'll make something that people will talk about for centuries, that they'll dream of. You've come a long way from the young thief who ran the back alleys of Dublin, Roarke.'

His smile was slow and just a little sly. 'Not so very far, Lieutenant. I'm still picking pockets – I just do it as legally as I can. Being married to a cop limits certain activities.'

She frowned at him now. 'I don't want to hear about them.'

'Darling Eve.' He rose, brought the bottle with him.

'So by-the-book. Still so unsettled that she's fallen madly in love with a shady character.' He filled her glass again, then set the bottle aside. 'One that only months ago was on her short list of murder suspects.'

'You enjoy that? Being suspicious?'

'I do.' He skimmed a thumb over a cheekbone where a bruise had faded away – except in his mind. 'And I worry about you a little.' *A lot*, he admitted to himself.

9

'I'm a good cop.'

'I know. The only one I've ever completely admired. What an odd twist of fate that I would have fallen for a woman so devoted to justice.'

'It seems odder to me that I've linked up with someone who can buy and sell planets at a whim.'

'Married.' He laughed. Turning her around, he nuzzled the back of her neck. 'Go on, say it. We're married. The word won't choke you.'

'I know what we are.' Ordering herself to relax, she leaned back against him. 'Let me live with it for a while. I like being here, away with you.'

'Then I take it you're glad you let me pressure you into the three weeks.'

'You didn't pressure me.'

'I had to nag.' He nipped her ear. 'Browbeat.' His hands slid up to her breasts. 'Beg.'

She snorted. 'You've never begged for anything. But maybe you did nag. I haven't had three weeks off the job in . . . never.'

He decided against reminding her she hadn't had it now, precisely. She rarely went through a twenty-four-hour period without running some program that put her up against a crime. 'Why don't we make it four?'

'Roarke—'

He chuckled. 'Just testing. Drink your champagne. You're not nearly drunk enough for what I have in mind.'

'Oh?' Her pulse leaped, making her feel foolish. 'And what's that?'

'It'll lose in the telling,' he decided. 'Let's just say I intend to keep you occupied for the last forty-eight hours we have here.'

'Forty-eight hours?' With a laugh, she drained her glass. 'When do we get started?'

'There's no time like—' He broke off, scowling when the

10

doorbell sounded. 'I told the staff to leave the clearing up. Stay here.' He snugged together her robe, which he'd just untied. 'I'll send them away. Far away.'

'Get another bottle while you're at it,' she told him, grinning as she shook the last drops into her glass. 'Someone drank all of this one.'

Amused, he slipped back inside, crossed the wide living space with its clear glass ceiling and feather-soft carpets. He wanted her there, to start, he decided, on that yielding floor with the ice-edged stars wheeling overhead. He plucked a long white lily out of a porcelain dish, imagining how he would show her just what a clever man could do to a woman with the petals of a flower.

He was smiling as he turned into the foyer with its gilded walls and sweeping marble staircase. Flipping on the view screen, he prepared to send the room service waiter to perdition for the interruption.

With some surprise he saw the face of one of his assistant engineers. 'Carter? Trouble?'

Carter rubbed a hand over a face that was dead pale and damp with sweat. 'Sir. I'm afraid there is. I need to speak with you. Please.'

'All right. Just a moment.' Roarke let out a sigh as he flicked off the screen, disengaged the locks. Carter was young for his position, in his middle twenties, but he was a genius at design and execution. If there was a problem with the construction, it was best to deal with it now.

'Is it the sky glide at the salon?' Roarke asked as he opened the door. 'I thought you'd worked out the kinks there.'

'No – I mean, yes, sir, I have. It's working perfectly now.'

The man was trembling, Roarke realized, and forgot his annoyance. 'Has there been an accident?' He took Carter's arm, steered him into the living area, nudged him into a chair. 'Has someone been hurt?'

'I don't know – I mean, an accident?' Carter blinked, stared

11

glassily. 'Miss. Ma'am. Lieutenant,' he said as Eve came in. He started to rise, then fell weakly down again when she gave him a quick push.

'He's in shock,' she said to Roarke, her voice brisk. 'Try some of that fancy brandy you've got around here.' She crouched down, kept her face level with his. His pupils were pinpricks. 'Carter, isn't it? Take it slow.'

'I . . .' His face went waxy now. 'I think I'm going to be—'

Before he could finish, Eve whipped his head down between his knees. 'Breathe. Just breathe. Let's have that brandy, Roarke.' She held out a hand, and he was there with a snifter.

'Pull it together, Carter.' Roarke eased him back onto the cushions. 'Take a swallow of this.'

'Yes, sir.'

'For Christ's sake, stop sirring me to death.'

Color came back into Carter's cheeks, either from the brandy or from embarrassment. He nodded, swallowed, let out a breath. 'I'm sorry. I thought I was okay. I came right up. I didn't know if I should – I didn't know what else to do.' He spread a hand over his face like a kid at a horror video. He hitched in a breath and said it quickly. 'It's Drew, Drew Mathias, my roomie. He's dead.'

Air exploded out of his lungs, then shuddered back in. He took another deep gulp of brandy and choked on it.

Roarke's eyes went flat. He pulled together a picture of Mathias: young, eager, red hair and freckles, an electronics expert with a specialty in autotronics. 'Where, Carter? How did it happen?'

'I thought I should tell you right away.' Now there were two high bruising red flags riding on Carter's pasty cheeks. 'I came right up to tell you – and your wife. I thought since she's – she's the police, she could do something.'

'You need a cop, Carter?' Eve took the snifter out of his unsteady hand. 'Why do you need a cop?'

12

'I think – he must have – he killed himself, Lieutenant. He was hanging there, just hanging there from the ceiling light in the living room. And his face . . . Oh God. Oh Jesus.'

Eve left Carter to bury his own face in his hands and turned to Roarke. 'Who's got authority on site for something like this?'

'We've got standard security, most of it automated.' Accepting, he inclined his head. 'I'd say it's you, Lieutenant.'

'Okay, see if you can put together a field kit for me. I need a recorder – audio and video – some Seal It, evidence bags, tweezers, a couple of small brushes.'

She hissed out a breath as she dragged a hand through her hair. He wasn't going to have the equipment lying around that would pinpoint body temperature and time of death. There would be no scanner, no sweepers, none of the standard chemicals for forensics she carried habitually to crime scenes.

They'd have to wing it.

'There's a doctor, right? Call him. He'll have to stand in as the ME. I'll get dressed.'

Most of the techs made use of the completed wings of the hotel for living quarters. Carter and Mathias had apparently hit it off well enough to share a spacious two-bedroom suite during their shift on the station. As they rode down to the tenth floor, Eve handed Roarke the palm recorder.

'You can run this, right?'

He lifted a brow. One of his companies had manufactured it. 'I think I can manage.'

'Fine.' She offered a weak smile. 'You're deputized. You hanging in, Carter?'

'Yeah.' But he walked out of the elevator into the hallway on ten like a drunk trying to pass a competency test. He had to wipe his sweaty hand twice on his slacks to get a clear reading on the palm screen. When the door slid open, he stepped back. 'I'd just as soon not go in again.'

13

'Stay here,' she told him. 'I may need you.'

She stepped inside. The lights were blinding bright, up to full power. Music blared out of the wall unit: hard, clashing rock with a screeching vocalist that reminded Eve of her friend Mavis. The floor was tiled in a Caribbean blue and offered the illusion of walking on water.

Along the north and south walls, banks of computers were set up. Workstations, she assumed, cluttered with all manner of electronic boards, microchips, and tools.

She saw clothes heaped on the sofa, VR goggles lying on the coffee table with three tubes of Asian beer – two of them flattened and already rolled for the recycler – and a bowl of spiced pretzels.

And she saw Drew Mathias's naked body swaying gently from a makeshift noose of sheets hitched to the glittering tier of a blue glass chandelier.

'Ah, hell.' She sighed it out. 'What is he, Roarke, twenty?'

'Not much more than.' Roarke's mouth thinned as he studied Mathias's boyish face. It was purple now, the eyes bulging, the mouth frozen into a hideous, gaping grin. Some vicious whim of death had left him smiling.

'All right, let's do what we can. Dallas, Lieutenant Eve, NYPSD, standing in until proper interspace authorities can be contacted and transported. Suspicious, unattended death. Mathias, Drew, Olympus Grand Hotel, Room ten thirty-six, August 1, 2058, one hundred hours.'

'I want to take him down,' Roarke said. It shouldn't have surprised him how quickly, how seamlessly she'd shifted from woman to cop.

'Not yet. It doesn't make any difference to him now, and I need the scene recorded before anything's moved.' She turned in the doorway. 'Did you touch anything, Carter?'

'No.' He scrubbed the back of his hand over his mouth. 'I opened the door, just like now, and walked in. I saw him right away. You . . . you see him right away. I guess I stood

14

there a minute. Just stood there. I knew he was dead. I saw his face.'

'Why don't you go through the other door into the bedroom.' She gestured to the left. 'You can lie down for a while. I'll need to talk to you.'

'Okay.'

'Don't call anyone,' she ordered.

'No. No, I won't call anyone.'

She turned away again, secured the door. Her gaze shifted to Roarke's, and their eyes held. She knew he was thinking, as she was, that there were some – like her – who had no escape from death.

'Let's get started,' she told him.

Chapter Two

The doctor's name was Wang, and he was old, as most medicals were on off planet projects. He could have retired at ninety, but like others of his ilk, he had chosen to bump from site to site, tending the scrapes and bruises, passing out drugs for space sickness and gravity balance, delivering the occasional baby, running required diagnostics.

But he knew a dead body when he saw one.

'Dead.' His voice was clipped, faintly exotic. His skin was parchment yellow and as wrinkled as an old map. His eyes were black, almond shaped. His head was glossy and slick, lending him the appearance of an ancient, somewhat battered billiard ball.

'Yeah, I got that much.' Eve rubbed her eyes. She'd never had to deal with a space med, but she'd heard about them. They didn't care to have their cushy routine interrupted. 'Give me the cause and the time.'

'Strangulation.' Wang tapped one long finger against the vicious marks on Mathias's neck. 'Self-induced. Time of death I would say between ten and eleven P.M. on this day, in this month, in this year.'

She offered a thin smile. 'Thank you, Doctor. There aren't any other signs of violence on the body, so I lean toward your diagnosis of self-termination. But I want the results of the drug run. Let's see if it was chemically induced. Did you treat the deceased for anything?'

'I cannot say, but he looks unfamiliar. I would have his records, of course. He would have come to me for the standard diagnostic upon arrival.'

'I'll want those as well.'

'I will do my best to accommodate you, Mrs Roarke.'

Her eyes narrowed. 'Dallas, Lieutenant Dallas. Put a rush on it, Wang.' She looked down at the body again. *Small man*, she thought, *thin, pale. Dead.*

Pursing her lips, she studied the face. She'd seen what odd tricks death, particularly violent death, could play with expressions, but she'd never seen anything like that wide, goggle-eyed grin. It made her shudder.

The waste, the pathetic waste of such a young life made her unbearably sad.

'Take him with you, Wang. Get me the reports. You can shoot his basic paperwork to the tele-link in my suite. I need the next of kin.'

'Assuredly.' He smiled at her. 'Lieutenant Roarke.'

She smiled back, showed her teeth, and decided she didn't want to play the name game. Standing, she put her hands on her hips as Wang directed his two assistants to transport the body.

'You find that amusing,' she muttered to Roarke.

He blinked, all innocence. 'What?'

'Lieutenant Roarke.'

Roarke touched her face because he needed to. 'Why not? Both of us could use some comic relief.'

'Yeah, your Dr Wang's a chuckle a minute.' She watched the doctor sail out in front of the dead boy on a gurney. 'It pisses me off. It fucking pisses me off.'

'It's not such a bad name.'

'No.' She nearly did laugh as she rubbed her hands over her face. 'Not that. The boy. A kid like that tossing out his next hundred years of life. That pisses me off.'

'I know.' He reached out to rub her shoulders. 'You're sure it was suicide?'

17

'No sign of struggle. No additional insults to the body.' She shrugged under his hands. 'I'll interview Carter and talk to some others, but the way I see it, Drew Mathias came home, turned on the lights, the music. He drank himself a couple beers, maybe took a VR trip, ate a few pretzels. Then he went in, stripped the sheets off his bed, made himself a rope, fashioned a very precise, professional noose.'

She turned away, scanning the room, letting the scene into her head. 'He took off his clothes, tossed them aside. He climbed up on the table. You can see the smears from his feet. He tied the rope to the light, probably gave it a good tug or two to make sure it was secure. Then he slipped his head into the noose, used the remote to raise the light, and choked himself to death.'

She picked up the remote she'd already bagged for evidence. 'It wouldn't have been quick. It's a slow ascent, not enough to give him a nice clean broken neck, but he didn't struggle, didn't change his mind. If he had, you'd see scrapes from his nails on his neck and throat from where he'd tried to claw free.'

Roarke's brow knit. 'But wouldn't it be instinctive, involuntary to do just that?'

'I don't know. I'd say it depended on how strong a will he had, how much he wanted to die. And why. Could have been cruising on drugs. We'll know that soon enough. The right mix of chemicals, the mind doesn't register pain. He might even have enjoyed it.'

'I won't deny there's some illegals floating around here. It's impossible to regulate and supervise every staff member's habits and personal choices.' Roarke shrugged, frowned up at the gorgeous blue chandelier. 'Mathias doesn't strike me as the type for a habitual, even an occasional user.'

'People are a constant surprise, and it's an unending wonder what they'll pump into their bloodstreams.' Eve jerked her own shoulders in turn. 'I'll give the place the standard toss

for illegals, and I'll see what I can find out from Carter.' She
dragged her hair back with a hand. 'Why don't you go back
up, get some sleep?'

'No, I'll stay. Eve,' he said before she could argue, 'you
deputized me.'

It made her smile a little. 'Any decent adjutant would know
I need coffee to get through this.'

'Then I'll see that you got some.' He framed her face in
his hands. 'I wanted you away from this for a while.' He
let her go and walked into the adjoining kitchen to see about
her coffee.

Eve stepped into the bedroom. The lights were low and
Carter was sitting on the side of the bed, his head in his hands.
He jerked straight when he heard her come in.

'Take it easy, Carter, you're not under arrest yet.' When his
cheeks paled, she sat beside him. 'Sorry, bad cop humor. I'm
recording this, okay?'

'Yeah.' He swallowed hard. 'Okay.'

'Dallas, Lieutenant Eve, interview with Carter – what's your
full name, Carter?'

'Ah, Jack. Jack Carter.'

'Carter, Jack, regarding the unattended death of Mathias,
Drew, Carter, you shared suite ten thirty-six with the deceased.'

'Yeah, for the past five months. We were friends.'

'Tell me about tonight. What time did you get home?'

'I don't know. About twelve thirty, I guess. I had a date.
I've been seeing someone – Lisa Cardeaux – she's one
of the landscape designers. We wanted to check out the
entertainment complex. They were showing a new video.
After that, we went to the Athena Club. It's open to the
complex employees. We had a couple of drinks, listened
to some music. She's got an early day tomorrow, so we
didn't stay late. I took her home.' He smiled weakly. 'Tried
to talk her into letting me come up, but she wasn't having
any.'

'Okay, so you struck out with Lisa. Did you come straight home?'

'Yeah. She's just over at the staff bungalow. She likes it there. Doesn't want to close herself up in a hotel room. That's what she says. It only takes a couple minutes on the glide to get back here. I came up.' He drew a breath, rubbed a hand over his heart as if to calm it. 'Drew had the door secured. He had a thing about that. Some of the crew leave the locks off, but Drew had all that equipment, and he was paranoid about anybody messing with it.'

'Is the palm plate coded for anyone but the two of you?'

'No.'

'Okay, then what?'

'I saw him. Right away. That's when I went up to you.'

'All right. When's the last time you saw him alive?'

'This morning.' Carter rubbed his eyes, trying to visualize the normality of it. Light, food, mumbling conversation. 'We had some breakfast.'

'How was he? Upset, depressed?'

'No,' Carter's eyes focused then, and were for the first time animated. 'That's what I can't get through my head. He was fine. He was joking around, yanking my chain about Lisa because I haven't – you know – scored. We were needling each other, just friendly shit. I said he hadn't scored in so long he wouldn't know it if he did. And why didn't he get himself a woman and come along with us tonight to see how it was done.'

'Was he seeing anyone?'

'No. He always talked about this babe he was hung up on. She wasn't on the station. The babe. That's what he called her. He was going to use his next free cycle to pay her a visit. He said she had it all, brains, beauty, body, and a sex drive that wouldn't quit. Why should he play with lesser models when he had state of the art?'

'You don't know her name?'

20

'No. She was just The Babe. To be honest, I figure he made her up. Drew wasn't what you'd call babe material, you know. And he was shy around women and really into fantasy games and his autotronics. He was always working on something.'

'What about other friends?'

'He didn't have many. He was quiet around a lot of people, internal, you know?'

'He use chemicals, Carter?'

'Sure, your basic stimulant if he was pulling an all-nighter.'

'Illegals, Carter. Did he use?'

'Drew?' His tired eyes popped wide. 'No way. Absolutely no way. He was a total arrow, straight as they come. He wouldn't mess with illegals, Lieutenant. He had a good mind, and he wanted to keep it that way. And he wanted to keep his job, move up. You get tossed for that kind of shit. Only takes one time on a spot check.'

'Are you sure you'd have known if he decided to experiment?'

'You know someone you hang with for five months.' Carter's eyes went sad again. 'You get used to them – habits and everything. Like I said, he didn't hang with other people much. He was happier alone, fiddling with his equipment, diving into his role-playing programs.'

'A loner then, internal.'

'Yeah, that was his way. But he wasn't upset, he wasn't depressed. He kept saying that he was onto something big, some new toy. He was always onto a new toy,' Carter murmured. 'He said just last week that he was going to make a fortune this time, and give Roarke a run for his money.'

'Roarke?'

'He didn't mean anything by it,' Carter said quickly, defending the dead. 'You've got to understand, Roarke – to a lot of us – well, he's ice, you know? Solid ice. Rolling in credits, mag clothes, outstanding digs, power plus, sexy new wife—' He broke off, flushing. 'Excuse me.'

21

'No problem.' She'd decide later if she was amused or flabbergasted that a boy barely twenty considered her sexy.

'It's just that a lot of us techs – well, a lot of people altogether – sort of aspire. Roarke's like the epitome. Drew totally admired him. He had ambitions, Mrs – Lieutenant. He had goals and plans. Why would he do this?' Suddenly his eyes swam. 'Why would he do this?'

'I don't know, Carter. Sometimes you never know why.'

She led him back, guided him through, until she had a picture of Drew Mathias that gelled. An hour later, there was nothing left for her to do but put together a report for whoever would be transported in to close the case.

She leaned against the mirrored wall of the elevator as she and Roarke rode back to the penthouse. 'It was good thinking to put him in another room on another floor. He may sleep better tonight.'

'He'll sleep better if he takes the tranqs. How about you? Will you sleep?'

'Yeah. I'd turn it over easier if I had a glimmer of what was troubling him, what pushed him to it.' She stepped out into the corridor, waited while Roarke disengaged security to their suite. 'The picture I've got is of your average tech nerd with grand aspirations. Shy of women, into fantasy. Happy in his work.' She lifted her shoulders. 'There weren't any incoming or outgoing calls on his 'link, no E-mail sent or received, no messages recorded, and the security on the door was engaged at sixteen hundred hours by Mathias, disengaged at oh thirty-three by Carter. He didn't have any visitors, didn't go out. He just settled in for the evening, then hanged himself.'

'It's not a homicide.'

'No, it's not a homicide.' Did that make it better, she wondered, or worse? 'Nobody to blame, nobody to punish. Just a dead kid. A life wasted.' She turned to him suddenly, wrapped her arms tightly around him. 'Roarke, you changed my life.'

Surprised, he tipped up her face. Her eyes weren't wet, but dry and fierce and angry. 'What's this?'

'You changed my life,' she said again. 'At least part of it. I'm beginning to see it's the best part of it. I want you to know that. I want you to remember that when we get back and things settle into routine, if I forget to let you know what I feel or what I think or how much you mean to me.'

Touched, he pressed his curved lips to her brow. 'I won't let you forget. Come to bed. You're tired.'

'Yeah, I am.' She skimmed her hair back from her face as they started toward the bedroom. Less than forty-eight hours left, she remembered. She wouldn't let useless death mar the last hours of their honeymoon.

She angled her head, fluttered her lashes. 'You know, Carter thinks I'm sexy.'

Roarke stopped. He narrowed his eyes. 'I beg your pardon?'

Oh, she loved it when that lilting Irish voice turned arrogant. 'You're ice,' she continued, circling her head on her tensed shoulders as she unbuttoned her shirt.

'Am I? Am I really?'

'Solid ice, which is, as Mavis would say, mag. And part of the reason you're ice, in case you're wondering, is because you have a sexy new wife.'

Naked to the waist, she sat on the bed and tugged off her shoes. She flicked a glance over at him and saw that he'd tucked his hands in his pockets and was grinning. Her lips curved as well. It felt very good to smile.

'So, ice man' – she cocked her head, lifted a brow – 'what are you going to do about your sexy new wife?'

Roarke ran his tongue over his teeth, then stepped forward. 'Why don't I demonstrate?'

She thought it would be better, facing the trip back, being flung through space like a kid's ray ball. She was wrong.

Eve argued, using what she considered very logical reasons why she shouldn't get into Roarke's private transport.

'I don't want to die.'

He laughed at her, which had her eyes kindling, then he simply scooped her up and carried her on board. 'I'm not staying.' Her heart jittered into her chest as he stepped into the plush cabin. 'I mean it. You'll have to knock me out to get me to stay on this flying death trap.'

'Mmm-hmm.' He chose a wide, scoop-shaped chair in buttery black leather, kept her in his lap and, moving quickly, strapped her in, trapping her arms to limit any possible reprisals.

'Hey. Stop it.' Panicked, she struggled, wiggled, swore. 'Let me out. Let me off.'

Her snug butt jiggling on his lap gave him a solid clue as to how he intended to spend the initial hours of the trip. 'Take off as soon as you have clearance,' Roarke ordered the pilot, then smiled at the flight attendant. 'We won't need you for a while,' he told her and engaged the locks on the cabin doors the moment she made a discreet exit.

'I'm going to hurt you,' Eve promised. When she heard the hum of engines gearing up, felt the faint vibration under her feet that signaled imminent takeoff, she seriously considered gnawing at the safety harness with her teeth. 'I'm not doing this,' she said definitely. 'I am not doing this. Tell him to abort.'

'Too late.' He wrapped his arms around her, nuzzled her neck. 'Relax, Eve. Trust me. You're safer here than you are driving through midtown.'

'Bullshit. Oh Christ.' She squeezed her eyes tight as the engine let out a powerful roar. The shuttle seemed to shoot straight up, leaving her stomach flopping on the ground below. The g's slapped her back, plastering her against Roarke.

She was barely breathing by the time the ride smoothed out and she discovered that the pressure in her chest was caused

24

by the fact that she was holding her breath. She let it out in a whoosh, then sucked in air like a diver surfacing from a great depth.

She was still alive, she told herself. And that was something. Now, she would have to kill him. It was then she realized that not only was she unstrapped, but her shirt was unbuttoned and his hands were on her breasts.

'If you think we're going to have sex after you—'

He merely swiveled her to face him. She caught the glint of humor and lust in his eyes just before his mouth closed cagily over her breast.

'You bastard.' But she laughed as pleasure speared into her, and she cupped her hands behind his head to urge him on.

She'd never take for granted what he could do to her, do for her. Those wild floods of pleasure, the slow, thrilling glide of it. She rocked against him, let herself forget everything but the way his teeth nipped, his tongue licked.

So it was she who pulled him onto the thick, soft carpet, she who dragged his mouth to hers. 'Inside me.' She tugged at his shirt, wanting that hard, muscled flesh under her hands. 'I want you inside me.'

'We have hours yet.' He dipped to her breasts again, so small, so firm, already warm from his hands. 'I need to taste you.'

He did, lavishly. The subtle variety of flavors, from mouth to throat, from throat to shoulder, shoulder to breast. He sampled with tenderness, with finesse, with a quiet concentration focused on mutual pleasure.

He felt her begin to tremble under his hands and mouth.

Her skin grew damp as he roamed to her belly, easing her slacks down, nibbling his way between her thighs. His tongue flicked there, making her moan. Her hips arched for him even as he cupped them, lifted them, opened her. When

25

his tongue slid lazily into the heat, he felt the first orgasm rip through her.

'More.' Greedy now, he devoured. She would let go for him as she had for no one else, he knew. She would lose herself in what they made together.

When she was shuddering, when her hands lay limp on the carpet, he slid up her body, slipped into her. Mated.

Her eyes fluttered open, met his. Concentration was what she saw there. Absolute control. She wanted, needed to destroy it, to know she could, as he could destroy her.

'More,' she insisted, hooking her legs around his waist to take him deeper. She saw the flicker in his eyes, the deep, dark need that lived inside him and, pulling his mouth to hers, scraping her teeth over those beautifully formed lips, she moved under him.

He fisted his hands in her hair, his breath quickening as he rammed himself into her, harder, faster, until he thought his heart would burst from the ferocity of it. She matched him, beat for beat, thrust for thrust, those short, unpainted nails digging into his back, his shoulders, his hips. Delicious little bites of pain.

He felt her come again, the violent contraction of her muscles fisting over him like glory. *Again*, was all he could think. *Again and again and again*, as he hammered into her, swallowing her gasps and moans, shuddering from the thrilling sound of flesh slapping wetly against flesh.

He felt her body tense again, revving toward peak. As that long, low, throaty moan slipped through her lips, he pressed his face into her hair, and with one final thrust, he emptied himself.

He collapsed onto her, his mind fuzzed, his heart thundering. She was limp as water beneath him but for the rage of her heart against his.

'We can't keep this up,' she managed after a moment. 'We'll kill each other.'

26

He managed a wheezing laugh. 'We'll die well, in any case. I had intended a bit more romance – some wine and music to cap off the honeymoon.' He lifted his head, smiled down at her. 'But this worked, too.'

'It doesn't mean I'm not still pissed off at you.'

'Naturally. We've had some of our best sex when you're pissed off at me.' He caught her chin between his teeth, flicked his tongue along the slight dent in the center. 'I adore you, Eve.'

While she was adjusting to that, as she always did, he rolled off, got lightly to his feet, and walked naked to a mirrored console between two chairs. He laid his palm on it, and a door slid open. 'I have something for you.'

She eyed the velvet box with suspicion. 'You don't have to get me presents. You know I don't want you to.'

'Yes. It makes you uncomfortable and uneasy.' He grinned. 'Perhaps that's why I do it.' He sat beside her on the floor, handed her the box. 'Open it.'

She imagined it would be jewelry. He seemed to thrive on giving her body decorations: diamonds, emeralds, ropes of gold that left her stunned and feeling awkward. But when she opened it, she saw only a simple white blossom.

'It's a flower?'

'From your wedding bouquet. I had it treated.'

'A petunia.' She found herself sentimentally teary-eyed as she picked it out of the box. Simple, basic, ordinary, one that might grow in any garden. The petals felt soft, dewy, and fresh.

'It's a new process one of my companies has been working on. It preserves without changing the basic texture. I wanted you to have it.' He closed a hand over hers. 'I wanted both of us to have it, so we could be reminded that some things last.'

She raised her eyes to his. They had both come from misery, she thought, and survived it. They had been drawn together through violence and tragedy, and had overcome

27

it. They walked different paths and had found a mutual route.

Some things last, she thought. *Some ordinary things. Like love*.

Chapter Three

Three weeks hadn't changed Cop Central. The coffee was still poisonous, the noise abominable, and the view out of her stingy window was still miserable.

She was thrilled to be back.

The cops in her unit had arranged for a message to await her. Since it was blinking slyly on her monitor when she walked in, she figured she had her old pal Feeney, the electronics whiz, to thank for bypassing her code.

WELCOME BACK, LIEUTENANT LOVEJOY
Hubba-hubba

Hubba-hubba? She snorted out a laugh. Sophomoric humor, maybe, but it made her feel at home.

She glanced over the mess on her desk. She hadn't had time to clear anything up between the unexpected closing of a case during her bachelor party and her wedding day. But she noted the neatly sealed disc, competently labeled, sitting atop her stack of old work.

That would be Peabody's doing, Eve concluded. Sliding the disc into her desk unit, she cursed once and slapped the drive to cure the razzing hiccups it emitted, and saw that the ever-reliable Peabody had indeed written the arrest report, filed it, and logged it.

It couldn't, Eve mused, have been easy on her. Not when she'd been sharing a bed with the accused.

Eve glanced at the old work again, grimaced. She could see she had court dates stuffed and layered together over the next few days. The schedule juggling she'd had to do to accommodate Roarke's demand for three weeks away had had a price. It was time to pay up.

Well, he'd done plenty of juggling as well, she reminded herself. And now it was back to work and reality. Rather than review the cases she would soon give testimony for, she bumped up her 'link and put out a search for Officer Peabody.

The familiar, serious face with its dark helmet of hair fizzed onto her monitor. 'Sir. Welcome back.'

'Thank you, Peabody. My office, please. ASAP.'

Without waiting for a reply, Eve switched off the unit and smiled to herself. She'd seen to it that Peabody had been transferred to the homicide division. Now she intended to take it a bit further. She engaged the 'link again.

'Lieutenant Dallas. Is the commander free?'

'Lieutenant.' The commander's secretary beamed at her. 'How was your honeymoon?'

'It was very nice.' She felt a quick flush of heat at the gleam in the woman's eye. Hubba-hubba had amused her. This dreamy look made her want to squirm. 'Thank you.'

'You were a lovely bride, Lieutenant. I saw the pictures and there were several news runs on the event and the gossip channels were full of it. We saw clips of you in Paris, too. It looked so romantic.'

'Yeah.' *The price of fame*, Eve thought. *And Roarke*. 'It was . . . nice. Ah, the commander?'

'Oh, of course. One moment please.'

As the unit buzzed, Eve rolled her eyes. She could accept being in the spotlight, but she was never going to enjoy it.

'Dallas.' Commander Whitney's grin was an acre wide, and he had an odd look on his hard, dark face. 'You look . . . well.'

'Thank you, sir.'

'You enjoyed your honeymoon?'

Christ, she thought, when was someone going to ask if she'd enjoyed being fucked around the world and into outer space? 'Yes, sir. Thank you. I assume you've already read Officer Peabody's report on the closing of the Pandora case.'

'Yes, very complete. The PA is going for the maximum on Casto. You ran a close one there, Lieutenant.'

She was very well aware how close she'd come to not only missing her wedding day, but the rest of her life. 'It stings when it's another cop,' she said. 'I was rushed, sir, and only had time to give you my recommendation for Peabody's transferral, permanently, to my unit. Her assistance, in this matter and others, has been invaluable.'

'She's a good cop,' Whitney agreed.

'I agree. I have a request, Commander.'

Five minutes later, when Peabody stepped into her crammed office, Eve was tipped back in her chair, scanning the data on her monitor. 'I've got court in an hour,' Eve said without preliminary. 'On the Salvatori case. What do you know about that, Peabody?'

'Vito Salvatori is being tried for multiple murder, with the added circumstance of torture. He is an alleged distributor of illegal substances and stands accused of the murder of three other known dealers of Zeus and TRL. The victims were burned alive in a small rooming house on the Lower East Side last winter – after their eyes and tongues were cut out. You were primary.'

Peabody recited the data matter-of-factly while she stood at attention in her shipshape uniform.

'Very good, Officer. Did you read my arrest report on the case?'

'Yes, Lieutenant, I did.'

Eve nodded. An airbus boomed by the window, spewing noise and displacing air. 'Then you know that before I

31

restrained Salvatori, I broke his left arm at the elbow, his jaw, and relieved him of several teeth. His lawyers are going to try to fry me for excessive force.'

'They'll have a rough time of that, sir, as he was trying to burn down the building around you when you cornered him. If you hadn't restrained him in whatever manner was possible, *he'd* have been fried. So to speak.'

'Okay, Peabody. I've got this and several others to go over before the week's up. I need all the cases on my court schedule downloaded and condensed. You can meet me with the requested data in thirty minutes, east exit.'

'Sir. I'm on assignment. Detective Crouch has me chasing down vehicle registrations.' Only the faintest sneer in her voice indicated Peabody's feeling about Crouch and the garbage assignment.

'I'll handle Crouch. The commander's cleared my request. You're assigned to me. So pass off whatever grunt work that's been dumped on you and get your ass in gear.'

Peabody blinked. 'Assigned to you, sir?'

'Your hearing go bad while I was away?'

'No, sir, but—'

'Have you got a thing for Crouch?' It delighted Eve to see Peabody's serious mouth drop open.

'Are you kidding? He's—' She caught herself, stiffened up. 'He's hardly my type, Lieutenant. I believe I've learned my lesson about romantic attachments on the job.'

'Don't beat yourself up over that one, Peabody. I liked Casto, too. You did a hell of a job on that one.'

It helped to hear it, but the wound was still raw. 'Thank you, Lieutenant.'

'Which is why you are now assigned to me as my permanent aide. You want a detective shield, Officer?'

Peabody knew what she was being given: the opportunity, the gift out of nowhere. She closed her eyes a moment until she had her voice under control. 'Yes, sir, I do.'

'Good. You'll work your ass off for it. Get the data I requested, and let's move.'

'Right away.' At the door, Peabody paused, turned back. 'I'm very grateful for the chance you're giving me.'

'Don't be. You earned it. And if you screw up, I'll bust you down to traffic.' Eve smiled thinly. 'Air traffic.'

Court testimony was part of the job, and so, Eve reminded herself, were high-class weasels like S. T. Fitzhugh, attorney for the defense. He was slick and he was savvy, a man who defended the lowest of lowlifes – as long as their credits held out. His success in assisting drug lords, murderers, and molesters into slithering out of the grip of the law was such that he could easily afford the cream-colored suits and hand-tooled shoes he affected.

He made a dashing figure in the courtroom, his melted-chocolate skin a fine contrast to the soft colors and fabrics he habitually wore. His long, aesthetic face was smooth as the silk of his jacket, thanks to the three-times-weekly treatments at Adonis, the city's top enhancement salon for men. His figure was trim – narrow at the hips, broad at the shoulders – and his voice was the deep, rich baritone of an opera singer.

He courted the press, socialized with the criminal elite, owned his own Jet Star.

It was one of Eve's small pleasures to despise him.

'Let me try to get a clear picture, Lieutenant.' Fitzhugh lifted his hands, bringing his thumbs together to form a bracket. 'A clear picture of the circumstances that led to you attacking my client in his place of business.'

The prosecuting attorney objected. Fitzhugh graciously rephrased. 'You did, Lieutenant Dallas, cause my client great bodily harm on the night in question.'

He glanced back at Salvatori, who had costumed himself for the occasion in a simple black suit. Following his attorney's advice, he had skipped his last three months of cosmetic and youth restoration treatments. There was gray in his hair, a sag to his face and body. He looked old, defenseless.

The jury would make the comparison, Eve imagined, between the young, fit cop and the delicate old man.

'Mr Salvatori resisted arrest and attempted to ignite an accelerant. It was necessary to restrain him.'

'To restrain him?' Slowly, Fitzhugh walked back, passing the recorder droid, moving down the jury box, drawing one of the six automated cameras with him as he laid a supporting hand on Salvatori's thin shoulder. 'You had to restrain him, and that restraint resulted in a fractured jaw and a shattered arm.'

Eve flicked a glance toward the jury. Several members of the panel were looking entirely too sympathetic. 'That's correct. Mr Salvatori refused my request to exit the building – and to put down the cleaver and acetylene torch in his possession.'

'You were armed, Lieutenant?'

'I was.'

'And you carry the standard weapon issued to members of the NYPSD?'

'I do.'

'If, as you claim, Mr Salvatori was armed and resisting, why did you fail to administer the accepted stun?'

'I missed. Mr Salvatori was feeling pretty spry that night.'

'I see. In your ten years on the police force, Lieutenant, how many times have you found it necessary to employ maximum force? To terminate?'

Eve ignored the jitter in her stomach. 'Three times.'

'Three?' Fitzhugh let the word hang, let the jury study the woman in the witness chair. A woman who had killed. 'Isn't that a rather high ratio? Wouldn't you say that percentage indicates a predilection for violence?'

The PA surged to his feet, objecting bitterly, going into the standard line that the witness was not on trial. But of course she was, Eve thought. Cops were always on trial.

'Mr Salvatori was armed,' Eve began coolly. 'I had a

warrant for his arrest in the torture murders of three people. The three people whose eyes and tongues were cut out before they were set on fire and for which crime Mr Salvatori now stands accused in this courtroom. He refused to cooperate by flinging a cleaver at my head, which threw my aim off. He then charged, knocking me to the ground. I believe his words were, "I'm going to cut out your cop-bitch heart," at which time we engaged in hand to hand. At that time I broke his jaw, knocked out several of his teeth, and when he swung the torch in my direction, I broke his goddamn arm.'

'And you enjoyed that, Lieutenant?'

She met Fitzhugh's eyes straight on. 'No, sir, I didn't. But I enjoyed staying alive.'

'Slime,' Eve muttered as she climbed into her vehicle.

'He won't get Salvatori off.' Peabody settled in and, to take the edge off the furnace heat trapped inside, fiddled with the temperature control unit. 'The evidence is too clear cut. And you didn't let him shake you.'

'Yes, I did.' Eve scooped a hand through her hair, then headed into late-afternoon midtown traffic. The streets were choked enough to make her grit her teeth, but overhead, the sky was crisscrossed with airbuses, tourist vans, and midday commuters. 'We limp along, getting pricks like Salvatori off the street, and men like Fitzhugh make fortunes slipping them back out.' She jerked a shoulder. 'Sometimes it pisses me off.'

'Whoever slips them back out, we still limp along and slap them back in again.'

With a half laugh, Eve glanced at her companion. 'You're an optimist, Peabody. I wonder how long that'll last. I'm going to make a detour before we log back on,' she said, changing direction on impulse. 'I want to get the air of that courtroom out of my lungs.'

'Lieutenant? You didn't need me in court today. Why was I there?'

'If you're going after that detective shield, Peabody, you need to see what you're up against. It's not just killers and thieves and chemi-heads. It's the lawyers.'

It didn't surprise her to find the streets clogged and parking nonexistent. Philosophically, Eve nosed into an illegal zone, flipped the on-duty light on.

As she stepped out of the car, she gave a hustler on a glide-board a mild stare. He grinned, winked cheekily, then zoomed away toward more conducive surroundings.

'This area's loaded with hustlers and dealers and off-license hookers,' Eve said conversationally. 'That's why I love it.' She opened the door to the Down and Dirty Club, stepped inside to air thick with the sour smells of cheap liquor and bad food.

Privacy rooms lining one wall were open, airing out the musky stink of stale sex.

It was a joint – one that enjoyed being seamy and just skirted the edge of health and decency laws. A holographic band had the stage and was playing listlessly for the smattering of disinterested customers.

Mavis Freestone was in an isolation booth in the back, her hair a purple fountain, two scraps of glowing silver cloth strategically draped over her small, sassy body. The way her mouth was moving, her hips swiveling, Eve was certain she was rehearsing one of her more interesting vocals.

Eve stepped up to the glass, waiting until Mavis's rolling eyes circled around and landed on her. Mavis's mouth, the same searing purple as her hair, rounded into a huge circle of delight. She did a fast boogie, then shoved the door open. An ear-shattering blast of screaming guitars burst out of the booth with her.

Mavis launched herself into Eve's arms, and though she was shouting, Eve caught only every other word over the thundering music.

'What?' Laughing, Eve slammed the door shut, shook the echo out of her head. 'Christ, Mavis, what was that?'

'My new number. It's going to knock them unconscious.'

'I believe it.'

'You're back.' Mavis gave Eve two smacking and unavoidable kisses. 'Let's sit down. Let's have a drink. Tell me every detail. Leave nothing out. Hey, Peabody. Man, aren't you steaming in that uniform?'

She dragged Eve to a sticky table, punched up the menu. 'What do you want? It's on me. Crack pays me pretty solid for the couple gigs a week I do here. He's going to be dredged that he missed you. Oh, I'm so glad to see you. You look terrific. You look happy. Doesn't she look terrific, Peabody? Sex is so, like, therapeutic, right?'

Eve laughed again, knowing she'd come just for this. Mindless entertainment. 'Just a couple of fizz waters, Mavis. We're on duty.'

'Oh, like somebody in here's going to report you. Unbutton that uniform some, Peabody. I'm getting hot just looking at you. How was Paris? How was the island? How was the resort? Did he fuck your brains out everywhere?'

'Beautiful, wonderful, interesting, and yeah, he did. How's Leonardo?'

Mavis's eyes went dreamy. She smiled and poked a silver-tipped nail onto the menu board. 'He's terrific. Cohabitating's better than I thought it would be. He designed this costume for me.'

Eve studied the thin silver straps that almost covered Mavis's tidy apple breasts. 'Is that what you call it?'

'I've got this new number, see. Oh, I've got so much to tell you.' She snagged the fizz water when it plopped through the slot. 'I don't know where to start. There's this guy, this music engineer. I'm working with him. We're doing a disc, Eve – full treatment. He's sure he can peddle it. He's great, Jess Barrow. He was blazing a couple years back with his own stuff. Maybe you heard of him.'

'No.' Eve knew that, for a woman who'd lived on the streets

a large portion of her life, Mavis remained stunningly naive about certain matters. 'How much are you paying him?'

'It's not like that.' Mavis's lips moved into a pout. 'I've got to dish up the recording fee, sure. That's the way it works; and if we hit, he takes sixty percent for the first three years. After that we renegotiate.'

'I've heard of him,' Peabody commented. She'd unfastened her collar button – a tribute to her fondness for Mavis. 'He had a couple of major hits a couple years ago, and he was hooked up with Cassandra.' At Eve's arched brow, she shrugged. 'The singer, you know.'

'You a music lover, Peabody? You never fail to amaze me.'

'I like to listen to tunes,' Peabody muttered into her bubbly water. 'Like anyone.'

'Well, the Cassandra connection's dumped,' Mavis said cheerfully. 'He's been looking for a new vocalist. And that's me.'

Eve wondered what else he might be looking for. 'What does Leonardo think?'

'He thinks it's mag. You've got to come to the studio, Eve, catch us in action. Jess is a certified genius.'

She intended to catch them in action. The list of people Eve loved was very short. And Mavis was on it.

She waited until she was back in the car with Peabody, heading to Cop Central. 'Run a make on Jess Barrow, Peabody.'

Without surprise, Peabody took out her diary, plugged in the order. 'Mavis isn't going to like that.'

'She doesn't have to know, does she.'

Eve veered around a glide-cart offering frozen fruit on a stick, then swung onto Tenth where automated jackhammers were tearing up the street again. Overhead, an ad blimp hawked a shoppers' special at Bloomingdale's. Preseason sale on winter coats in the men's, women's, and unisex department, twenty percent off. Such a deal.

38

She spotted the man in the trench coat shambling toward a trio of girls and sighed.

'Shit. There's Clevis.'

'Clevis?'

'This is his turf,' Eve said simply as she pulled into a loading zone. 'I used to do this drag when I was in uniform. He's been around for years. Come on, Peabody, let's spare the little children.'

She stepped onto the sidewalk, skirting a pair of men arguing over baseball. From the smell of them, she judged they'd been standing in the heat arguing for much too long. She shouted once, but the jackhammers swallowed her voice. Resigned, she picked up her pace and intercepted Clevis before he reached the unsuspecting, pink-cheeked girls.

'Hey, Clevis.'

He blinked at her through the pale lenses of sunscreens. His hair was sandy blond and curly around a face as innocent as a cherub's. He was eighty, if he was a day. 'Dallas. Hey, Dallas. I haven't seen you in a big blue moon.' He flashed big white teeth as he sized up Peabody. 'Who's this?'

'Peabody, this is Clevis. Clevis, you aren't going to bother those little girls, are you?'

'No, shit, uh-uh. I wasn't going to bother them.' He wiggled his brows. 'I was just going to show 'em, is all.'

'You don't want to do that, Clevis. You ought to get inside, out of this heat.'

'I like it hot.' He wheezed out a chuckle. 'There they go,' he said with a sigh, as the trio of girls ran laughing across the street. 'Guess I won't be able to show 'em today. I'll show you.'

'Clevis, don't—' Then Eve huffed out a breath. He'd already pulled his trench coat apart. Under it, he was naked but for a bright blue bow tied celebrationally around his withered cock. 'Very nice, Clevis. That's a good color for you. Matches your

39

eyes.' She put a companionable hand on his shoulder. 'Let's take a ride, okay?'

'Okeedokee. Do you like blue, Peabody?'

Peabody nodded solemnly as she opened the back door of the unit, helped him inside. 'Blue's my favorite color.' She shut the door of the vehicle, met Eve's laughing eyes. 'Welcome back, Lieutenant.'

'It's good to be back, Peabody. All in all, it's good to be back.'

It was also good to be home. Eve drove through the high, iron gates that guarded the towering fortress. It was less of a shock now, to glide along the curving drive through those well-tended lawns and flowering trees toward the elegant stone and glass house where she now lived.

The contrast of where she worked and where she lived no longer seemed quite so jarring. It was quiet here – the kind of quiet in a massive city only the very rich could afford. She could hear birdsong, see the sky, smell the sweet aroma of freshly shorn grass. Minutes away, only minutes, was the teeming, noisy, sweating mass of New York.

Here, she supposed, was sanctuary. As much for Roarke as for herself.

Two lost souls. He'd once called them that. She wondered if they'd stopped being lost when they'd found each other.

She left her car at the front entrance, knowing its battered body and tasteless shape would offend Summerset, Roarke's poker-backed butler. It was a simple matter to switch it to automatic, send it around the house and into the slot reserved for her unit in the garage, but she enjoyed her petty needling when it came to Summerset.

She opened the door and found him standing in the grand foyer with a sniff in his nose and a sneer on his lips.

'Lieutenant, your vehicle is unsightly.'

'Hey, it's city property.' She reached down to pick up the

fat, odd-eyed cat who'd come to greet her. 'You don't want it there, move it yourself.'

She heard a trill of laughter float down the hall, lifted a brow. 'Company?'

'Indeed.' With his disapproving eye, Summerset scanned her wilted shirt and slacks, skimmed over the weapon harness still strapped to her side. 'I suggest you bathe and change before meeting your guests.'

'I suggest you kiss my ass,' she said cheerfully and strolled by him.

In the main salon, filled with treasures Roarke had collected from around the known universe, an elegant, intimate party was happening. Glossy canapés sat elegantly on silver trays, pale gold wine filled sparkling crystal. Roarke was a dark angel in what he would have seen as casual attire. The black silk shirt open at the collar, the perfectly draped black trousers cinched with a belt gleaming silver at the buckle suited him perfectly, made him look exactly as he was: rich, gorgeous, dangerous.

Only one couple joined him in the spacious room. The man was as bright as Roarke was dark. Long golden hair flowed over the shoulders of a snug blue jacket. The face was square and handsome with lips just slightly too thin, but the contrast of his dark brown eyes kept the observer from noticing.

The woman was stunning. A sweep of deep red hair the color of rich wine was scooped up into curls that tumbled flirtatiously down the nape of her neck. Her eyes were green, sharp as a cat's, and over them were shapely brows as black as ink. She had skin like alabaster creamed over high cheek-bones and a sensually generous mouth.

Her body matched it and was currently poured into a clinging column of emerald that left strong shoulders bare and dipped between her staggering breasts to the waist.

'Roarke.' She let out that fluid laugh again, slid one slim white hand into Roarke's mane of hair and kissed him silkily. 'I have missed you dreadfully.'

41

Eve thought about the weapon strapped to her side and how, on even its lowest setting, it would send the bombshell redhead into a jittery dance. *Just a passing thought*, Eve assured herself, and set Galahad the cat down before she squeezed through the layers of fat and cracked one of his ribs.

'You didn't miss him that time,' Eve said casually as she stepped inside. Roarke, damn him, glanced over and grinned at her.

We'll just have to wipe that smug look off your face, pal, she thought. *Real soon.*

'Eve, we didn't hear you come in.'

'Obviously.' She snagged an unidentifiable canapé from the tray and stuffed it into her mouth.

'I don't believe you've met our guests. Reeanna Ott, William Shaffer, my wife, Eve Dallas.'

'Watch yourself, Ree, she's armed.' With a chuckle, William crossed over to extend a hand. He moved in a lope, like a thin horse going out to pasture. 'A pleasure to meet you, Eve. A genuine pleasure. Ree and I were so disappointed we were unable to attend your wedding.'

'Devastated.' Reeanna smiled at Eve, her green eyes sparkling. 'William and I were desperate to meet, face to face, the woman who brought Roarke to his knees.'

'He's still standing.' Eve flicked Roarke a glance as he handed her a glass of wine. 'For now.'

'Ree and William were in the lab on Tarus Three, working on some projects for me. They've just gotten back on planet for some well deserved R and R.'

'Oh?' Like she gave a rat's skinny ass.

'The on-the-board project's been a particular pleasure,' William said. 'Within a year, two at most, Roarke Industries will introduce new technology that will revolutionize the entertainment and amusement world.'

'Entertainment and amusement.' Eve smiled thinly. 'Well, that's earth shattering.'

42

'Actually, it has the potential to be just that.' Reeanna sipped her wine and sized Eve up: attractive, irritated, competent. Tough. 'There are potential medical breakthroughs as well.'

'That's Ree's end.' William lifted his glass to her with easy, intimate affection in his eyes. 'She's the med expert. I'm just a fun guy.'

'I'm sure, after putting in a long day, Eve doesn't want to hear us talk shop. Scientists,' Reeanna said with an apologetic smile. 'We're so tedious. You're just back from Olympus.' Silk whispered as Reeanna shifted that staggering body. 'William and I were part of the team that designed the amusement and medical centers there. Did you have time to tour them?'

'Briefly.' She was being rude, Eve reminded herself. She would have to become accustomed to coming home and finding elegant company, to seeing gorgeous women drool over her husband. 'Very impressive, even at midconstruction stage. The medical facility will be more so when it's staffed. Was the hologram room in the main hotel yours?' Eve asked William.

'Guilty,' he said with a sparkle. 'I love to play. Do you?'

'Eve considers it work. As it happens, we had an incident while we were there,' Roarke put in. 'A suicide. One of the autotronic techs. Mathias?'

William's brow furrowed. 'Mathias . . . young, red hair, freckles?'

'Yes.'

'Good God.' He shuddered, drank deeply. 'Suicide? Are you sure it wasn't an accident? My recollection is of an enthusiastic young man with big ideas. Not one who'd take his own life.'

'That's what he did,' Eve said shortly. 'He hanged himself.'

'How horrible.' Pale now, Reeanna sat on the arm of a couch. 'Did I know him, William?'

'I don't think so. You might have seen him at one of the clubs while we were there, but I don't remember him as much of a socializer.'

43

'I'm terribly sorry, in any case,' Reeanna said. 'And how awful for you to deal with such a tragedy on your honeymoon. Let's not dwell on it.' Galahad leaped onto the couch, skimmed his head under Reeanna's elegant hand. 'I'd so much rather hear about the wedding we missed.'

'Stay for dinner.' Roarke gave Eve's arm an apologetic squeeze. 'We'll bore you to tears with it.'

'I wish we could.' William offered Reeanna's shoulder the same smooth stroke as she gave the cat's head. 'We're due at the theater. We're already late.'

'You're right, as always.' With obvious regret, Reeanna rose. 'I hope you'll give us a rain check. We'll be on planet for the next month or two, and I'd so love the opportunity to get to know you, Eve. Roarke and I go back . . . a long way.'

'You're welcome any time. And I'll see you both in the office tomorrow, for a full report.'

'Bright and early.' Reeanna set her glass aside. 'Perhaps we can have lunch someday soon, Eve. Just females.' Her eyes twinkled with such easy humor that Eve felt foolish. 'We can compare notes on Roarke.'

The invitation was too friendly to give offense. Eve found herself smiling. 'That should be interesting.' She walked them to the door with Roarke, waved them off. 'Just how many notes,' she said as she stepped back, 'would there be to compare?'

'It was a long time ago.' He snagged her by the waist for a delayed welcome-home kiss. 'Years. Eons.'

'She probably bought that body.'

'I'd have to term it an excellent investment.'

Eve lifted her chin to eye him sourly. 'Is there any beautiful woman who hasn't bounced on your bed?'

Roarke cocked his head, narrowed his eyes in consideration. 'No.' He laughed when she took a swing at him. 'You didn't mean that, or you'd have hit me.' Then he grunted when her fist plowed into his gut. He rubbed it, grateful she'd pulled the punch. 'I should have quit while I was ahead.'

'Let that be a lesson to you, lover boy.' But Eve let him sweep her off her feet and over his shoulder.

'Hungry?' he asked her.

'Starving.'

'Me, too.' He started up the stairs. 'Let's eat in bed.'

Chapter Four

Eve awoke with the cat stretched over her chest and the bedside 'link beeping. Dawn was just breaking. The light through the sky window was thin and gray from the storm rolling in with morning. With her eyes half closed, she reached out to answer.

'Block video,' she ordered, clearing sleep from her voice. 'Dallas.'

'Dispatch, Dallas, Lieutenant Eve. Suspicious death, Five oh oh two Madison Avenue, Unit Thirty-eight hundred. See resident Foxx, Arthur. Code four.'

'Dispatch, received. Contact Peabody, Officer Delia, to assist. My authorization.'

'Confirmed. Transmission terminated.'

'Code four?' Roarke had shifted the cat and was sitting up in bed, lazily stroking Galahad into feline ecstasy.

'It means I have time for a shower and coffee.' Eve didn't spot a robe handy, so she walked toward the bathroom naked. 'There's a uniform on the scene,' she called out. She stepped into the shower unit, rubbing her gritty eyes. 'Full power all jets, one hundred two degrees.'

'You'll boil.'

'I like to boil.' She let out an enormous sigh of pleasure as pulsing jets of steamy water battered her from all sides. Tapping a glass block, she dispensed a palm full of dark green liquid soap. By the time she stepped out of the shower, she was awake.

Her brow lifted as she saw Roarke standing in the doorway, holding a cup of coffee. 'For me?'

'Part of the service.'

'Thanks.' She took the cup into the drying tube, sipping while warm air swirled around her. 'What were you doing, watching me shower?'

'I like to watch you. Something about long, lean women when they're wet and naked.' He stepped into the shower himself and called for sixty-eight degrees.

It made Eve shiver. She couldn't understand why a man with all the luxuries in the world at his fingertips would actually choose cold showers. She opened the drying tube and combed her fingers through her unstyled cap of hair. She used some of the face glop that Mavis was always pushing at her, brushed her teeth.

'You don't have to get up because I am.'

'I'm up,' Roarke said simply and chose a heated towel rather than the drying tube. 'Do you have time for breakfast?'

Eve watched his reflection in the mirror: gleaming hair, gleaming skin. 'I'll catch something later.'

He hooked the towel around his waist, shook back his dripping mane of hair, cocked his head. 'Yeah?'

'I guess I like looking at you, too,' she muttered and went into the bedroom to dress for death.

Street traffic was light. Airbuses rumbled overhead through the sizzling rain, carting night shift workers home, dragging day shifters to work. Billboards were quiet and the ubiquitous glida grills and carts with their offerings of food and drink were already setting up for the day. Smoke billowed through the vents in streets and sidewalks from the underground world of transportation and retail. The air steamed.

Eve headed across town, making good time.

The section of Madison where a body waited for her was pocked with exclusive boutiques and silvery spears of buildings fashioned to house those who could afford to shop there. The skywalks were glassed in to separate the clientele from the elements and from the noise that would begin to boom within an hour or two.

Eve passed a taxi with a lone passenger. The elegant blonde wore a glittery jacket, a sparkling rainbow of color in the dingy light. *Licensed companion*, Eve mused, *heading home after an all-nighter*. The wealthy could afford to buy fancy sex along with their fancy clothes.

Eve swung into an underground garage at the scene, flashed her badge for the security post. It scanned it, scanned her, then the light blinked from red to green and flashed the number of the empty space assigned to her.

It was, of course, at the far end of the facility from the elevator. *Cops*, she thought with resignation as she booted it, *aren't given optimum spaces*.

Eve recited the number of the unit into the speaker box and was whisked up.

There had been a time, not so long before, when she would have been impressed with the sumptuous foyer on the thirty-eighth floor, with its pool of scarlet hibiscus and bronze statuary. That was before she'd entered Roarke's world. She scanned the small, tinkling fountains flanking the entrance and realized that it was highly possible that her husband owned the building.

She spotted the uniform guarding the door of 3800, flipped up her badge.

'Lieutenant.' The cop shifted subtly to attention, sucking in her stomach. 'My partner's inside with the deceased's housemate. Mr Foxx, on discovering his companion's body, called for an ambulance. We responded in addition, as per procedure. The ambulance is on hold, sir, until you clear the scene.'

'Is it secured?'

'It is now.' Her gaze flicked toward the door. 'We weren't able to get much out of Foxx, sir. He's a bit hysterical. I can't be sure what he might have disturbed – other than the body.'

'He moved the body?'

'No, sir. That is, it's still in the tub, but he attempted to, ah, revive the deceased. Had to be in shock to attempt it. There's enough blood in there to swim in. Slashed wrists,' she explained. 'From a visual confirmation, he'd been dead at least an hour before his housemate discovered the body.'

Eve took a firmer grip on her field kit. 'Has the ME been notified?'

'On the way, sir.'

'Fine. Clear Officer Peabody in when she arrives, and continue to stand. Open it,' she added and waited for the uniform to slide her master key in the slot. The door slid open into the wall. Eve immediately heard the hard, ragged sobs of terrible grief.

'He's been like that since we arrived,' the uniform murmured. 'Hope you can tranq him soon.'

Saying nothing, Eve walked in, letting the door slide shut and lock at her back. The entranceway was elaborate in black and white marble. Spiraling columns were draped in some sort of flowering vine, and overhead, a black glass chandelier dripped in five ornate tiers.

Through the portico was a living area that followed the theme. Black leather sofas, white floors, ebony wood tables, white lamps. Drapes striped in black and white were drawn shut, but lights showered from the ceiling, spotlighted up from the floor.

An amusement screen was switched off but hadn't been slipped back into its recess. Glossy white stairs angled up to a second floor, which was ringed with white banisters, atrium style. Lush green ferns hung in enameled pots from the lofted ceiling.

Money might drip, she mused, but death had no respect for it. It was a club without a class system.

The sounds of grief echoed and drew her into a small den lined with antique books and cushy with deep chairs the color of good burgundy.

Sunk into one was a man. His handsome face was pale gold and ravaged from tears. His hair was gold as well, the glint of new coin, and was tufted in spikes from his hands. He wore a white silk robe that was spotted and smeared with drying blood. His feet were bare, and his hands were studded with rings that sparkled as his fingers trembled. There was a tattoo of a black swan on his left ankle.

The uniform who was sitting miserably beside the man glanced over at Eve, started to speak.

Eve shook her head quickly, keeping her badge in plain sight. She gestured toward the ceiling, cocking her head in question.

He nodded, jerked his thumb up, then shook his head.

Eve slipped back out. She wanted to see the body, view the scene before she dealt with the witness.

There were several rooms off the second floor. Still, it was simple enough to find her way. She simply followed the trail of blood. She stepped into a bedroom. Here the scheme was soft greens and blues, so that it felt like floating underwater. The bed was an oblong of blue satin sheets, mountained with pillows.

There was statuary here as well, of the classic nude variety. Drawers were built into the walls, giving it an uncluttered – and to Eve – an unlived-in appearance. The ocean blue carpet was soft as a cloud and spotted with blood.

She followed the trail into the master bath. Death didn't shock her, but it appalled her, and she knew it always would: the waste of it, the violence and cruelty of it. But she lived with it too much to be shocked, even by this.

Blood had spurted, showered, streamed on gleaming tiles

of ivory and seafoam green. It had fountained over glass, pooled over the mirrored floor from the gaping wound in the wrist of the hand that hung limply over the lip of a huge clear-sided tub.

The water inside was a dark, nasty pink, and the metallic smell of blood hung in the air. Music was playing, something with strings perhaps a harp. Fat white candles had been lighted and still burned at both the foot and the head of the long oval tub.

The body that lay in that cloudy pink water had its head resting on a gilt-edged bath pillow, its gaze lifted and fixed on the feathery tails of a fern that hung from the mirrored ceiling. He was smiling, as if he'd been desperately amused to watch himself die.

It didn't shock her, but she sighed as she coated her hands and feet with clear seal, engaged her recorder, and carried her kit inside to stand over the body.

Eve had recognized him. Naked, bled almost dry, and smiling up at his own reflection was the renowned defense attorney S. T. Fitzhugh.

'Salvatori's going to be very disappointed in you, Counselor,' she murmured as she got to work.

Eve had taken a sample of the bloody bathwater, done her initial scan to estimate time of death, bagged the deceased's hands, and recorded the scene when Peabody appeared, slightly out of breath at the doorway.

'I'm sorry, sir. I had some trouble getting uptown.

'It's all right.' She passed Peabody the ivory-handled buck knife she'd secured in clear plastic. 'Looks like he did it with this. It's an antique, I'd guess. Collector's item. We'll run it for prints.'

Peabody tucked the knife in her evidence kit, then narrowed her eyes. 'Lieutenant, isn't that—'

'Yeah, it's Fitzhugh.'

'Why would he kill himself?'

51

'We haven't determined that he did. Never make assumptions, Officer,' she said mildly. 'First rule. Call in the sweepers, Peabody, and let's get the scene tagged. We can release the body to the ME. I'm done with it for now.' Eve stepped back with blood smearing her sealed hands. 'I want you to take a prelim from the two uniforms who responded while I talk to Foxx.'

Eve glanced back at the body, shook her head. 'That's just the way he'd grin at you in court when he figured he'd tripped you up. The son of a bitch.' Still studying the body, she used the cleaner from her kit to remove the blood, tucked the soiled wipe into a bag as well. 'Tell the ME I want toxicology ASAP.'

She left Peabody and followed the blood trail back downstairs.

Foxx was down to choking, whimpering sobs now. The uniform looked ridiculously relieved when Eve reappeared. 'Wait for the ME and my adjutant outside, Officer. Give Officer Peabody your report. I'll speak with Mr Foxx now.'

'Yes, sir.' With almost unseemly delight, he fled the room.

'Mr Foxx, I'm Lieutenant Dallas. I'm sorry for your loss.' Eve located the button that released the drapes, pushed it to let watery light into the room. 'You need to talk to me. You need to tell me what happened here.'

'He's dead.' Foxx's voice was faintly musical, accented. Lovely. 'Fitz is dead. I don't know how that can be. I don't know how I can go on.'

Everyone goes on, Eve thought. *There's little choice*. She sat and put her recorder on the table in plain sight. 'Mr Foxx, it would help us both if you talked to me now. I'm going to give you the standard caution. It's just a matter of procedure.'

She recited the revised Miranda while his sobs trickled off, he lifted his head, and aimed swollen, red-rimmed golden eyes at her.

'Do you think I killed him? Do you think I could hurt him?'

52

'Mr Foxx—'

'I loved him. We've been together for twelve years. He was my life.'

You still have your life, she thought. *You just don't know it yet.* 'Then you'll want to help me do my job. Tell me what happened.'

'He—he's been having trouble sleeping lately. Doesn't like to take tranqs. He can usually read, listen to music, spend an hour with VR or one of his games, whatever, to relax. This case he's working on worried him.'

'The Salvatori case.'

'Yes, I believe, yes.' Foxx wiped at his eyes with a damp and bloodied sleeve. 'We didn't discuss his cases in any depth. There was privilege, and I'm not a lawyer. I'm a nutritionist. That's how we met. Fitz came to me twelve years ago for help with his diet. We became friends, we became lovers, then we simply became.'

She would need to know all of that, but for the moment, she wanted to see the events leading up to that last bath. 'He's been having trouble sleeping,' she prompted.

'Yes. He's often plagued with insomnia. He gives so much to his clients. They prey on his mind. I'm accustomed to him getting up in the middle of the night and going into another room to program a game or doze in front of the view screen. Sometimes he'd take a warm bath.' Foxx's already ravaged face blanched. 'Oh God.'

The tears started again, flowing hotly down his cheeks. Eve took a quick look around and spotted a small serving droid in the corner of the room. 'Bring Mr Foxx some water,' she ordered, and the little droid scooted away to comply.

'Is that what happened?' she continued. 'Did he get up in the middle of the night?'

'I don't even remember.' Foxx lifted his hands, let them fall. 'I sleep soundly, never have a bit of trouble. We'd gone

53

to bed just before midnight, watched some of the late news, had a brandy. I woke early. I tend to.'

'What time was that?'

'Perhaps five, five fifteen. We both like early starts, and it's my habit to program the morning meal personally. I saw that Fitz wasn't in bed, assumed he'd had a bad night and that I'd find him downstairs or in one of the spare bedrooms. Then I went into the bath, and I saw him. Oh God. Oh God, Fitz. All the blood. It was like a nightmare.'

His hand pressed against his mouth, all glittering rings and trembles. 'I ran over, I beat on his chest, tried to revive him. I suppose I went a little mad. He was dead. I could see he was dead; still, I tried to pull him out of the water, but he's a very big man, and I was shaking. Sick.' He dropped his hand from mouth to stomach, pressed. 'I called for an ambulance.'

She'd lose him if she couldn't manage to rein him in. Tranquing him wasn't an option until she had the facts. 'I know this is difficult for you, Mr Foxx. I'm sorry we have to do this now, but it's easier, believe me, if we can.'

'I'm all right.' He reached for the glass of water atop the droid. 'I want to get it over.'

'Can you tell me his frame of mind last night? You said he was worried about a case.'

'Worried, yes, but not depressed. There was a cop he couldn't shake on the stand, and it irritated him.' He took a gulp of water, then another.

Eve decided it was best not to mention she was the cop who had irritated him.

'And there were a couple of other cases pending that he was plotting out the defense for. His mind was often too busy for sleep, you see.'

'Did he receive any calls, make any calls?'

'Certainly, both. He often brought work home with him. Last night he spent a couple of hours in his office upstairs.

He arrived home about five thirty, worked until nearly eight. We had dinner.'

'Did he mention anything that was troubling him besides the Salvatori case?'

'His weight.' Foxx smiled a little. 'Fitz hated to put on an extra pound. We discussed him increasing his exercise program, perhaps having some body adjustment work done when he had the time. We watched a comedy on screen in the living room, then went to bed, as I told you.'

'Did you argue?'

'Argue?'

'You have bruises on your arm, Mr Foxx. Did you and Mr Fitzhugh fight last night?'

'No.' He paled even more, and his eyes glittered with the threat of another bout of weeping. 'We never fought physically. Certainly we argued from time to time. People do. I – I suppose I might have gotten the bruises on the tub when I was – when I tried to—'

'Did Mr Fitzhugh have a relationship with anyone else other than yourself?'

Now those swollen eyes went cool. 'If you mean did he have outside lovers, he did not. We were committed to each other.'

'Who owns this unit?'

Foxx's face went rigid, and his voice was cold. 'It was put in our joint names ten years ago. It belonged to Fitz.'

And now it belongs to you, Eve thought. 'I would assume Mr Fitzhugh was a wealthy man. Do you know who inherits?'

'Other than charitable bequests, I would inherit. Do you think I would kill him for money?' There was disgust in his tone now, rather than horror. 'What right do you have to come into my home at such a time and ask me such horrible questions?'

'I need to know the answers, Mr Foxx. If I don't ask them here, I'll have to ask them at the station house. I believe this is more comfortable for you. Did Mr Fitzhugh collect knives?'

'No.' Foxx blinked, then went pasty. 'I do. I have a large collection of antique blades. Registered,' he added quickly. 'They're duly registered.'

'Do you have an ivory-handled knife, straight blade, about six inches long in your collection?'

'Yes, it's nineteenth century, from England.' His breath began to hitch. 'Is that what he used? He used one of my knives to—? I didn't see. I only saw him. Did he use one of my knives?'

'I've taken a knife into evidence, Mr Foxx. We'll run tests. I'll give you a receipt for it.'

'I don't want it. I don't want to see it.' He buried his face in his hands. 'Fitz. How could he have used one of my knives?'

He fell to weeping again. Eve heard the voices and hums from the next room and knew the sweepers had arrived. 'Mr Foxx.' She rose. 'I'm going to have one of the officers bring you some clothes. I'm going to ask that you stay here for a little while longer. Is there someone I can call for you?'

'No. No one. Nothing.'

'I don't like it, Peabody,' Eve muttered as they rode down to her car. 'Fitzhugh gets up in the middle of an ordinary night, gets an antique knife, runs himself a bath. He lights the candles, puts on the music, then carves up his wrists. For no particular reason. Here's a man at the height of his career with a shit load of money, plush digs, clients beating down his door, and he just decides, "What the hell, I think I'll die"?'

'I don't understand suicide. I guess I don't have the person-ality for big highs and lows.'

Eve understood it. She'd even considered it briefly during her stint in state-run homes – and before that, in the dark time before that, when death had seemed a release from hell.

That was why she couldn't accept it for Fitzhugh.

'There's no motivation here, at least none that shows yet.

But we have a lover who collected knives, who was covered with blood, and who will inherit a sizable fortune.'

'You're thinking maybe Foxx killed him.' Peabody mulled it over when they reached garage level. 'Fitzhugh's nearly twice his size. He wouldn't have gone without a fight, and there wasn't any sign of struggle.'

'Signs can be erased,' Eve muttered. 'He had bruises. And if Fitzhugh was drugged or chemically impaired, he wouldn't have put up too much of a struggle. We'll see the tox report.'

'Why do you want it to be a homicide?'

'I don't. I just want it to make sense, and the self-termination doesn't fit. Maybe Fitzhugh couldn't sleep; maybe he got up. Someone was using the relaxation room. Or it was made to seem so.'

'I've never seen anything like that,' Peabody mused, thinking back. 'All those toys in one place. That big chair with all the controls, the wall screen, the autobar, the VR station, the mood tube. Ever use a mood tube, Lieutenant?'

'Roarke's got one. I don't like it. I'd rather have my moods come and go naturally than program them.' Eve spotted the figure sitting on the hood of her car and hissed, 'Like now, for example. I can feel my mood shifting. I think I'm about to be pissed off.'

'Well, Dallas and Peabody, together again.' Nadine Furst, top on-air reporter for Channel 75, slid gracefully from the car. 'How was the honeymoon?'

'Private,' Eve snapped.

'Hey, I thought we were pals.' Nadine winked at Peabody.

'You didn't waste any time putting our little get-together on the air, pal.'

'Dallas.' Nadine spread her pretty hands. 'You bag a killer and close a very public and intense case at your own bachelor party celebration, to which I was invited, it's news. The public not only has the right to know, they eat it up with a spoon. Ratings rocketed. Now look at this, you're barely back and right in the middle of something else big. What's the deal with Fitzhugh?'

'He's a dead man. I've got work to do, Nadine.'

'Come on, Eve.' Nadine plucked at Eve's sleeve. 'After all we've been through together? Give me a nibble.'

'Fitzhugh's clients had better start looking for another lawyer. That's all I've got to give you.'

'Come on. Accident, homicide, what?'

'We're investigating,' Eve said shortly and coded open her locks.

'Peabody?' But Peabody just grinned and shrugged her shoulders. 'You know, Dallas, it's common knowledge that you and the dearly departed weren't fans of each other. The top sound bite after court yesterday was him referring to you as a violent cop who used her badge as a blunt instrument.'

'It's a shame he won't be able to give you and your associates such catchy quotes anymore.'

As Eve slammed the car door, Nadine leaned doggedly in the window. 'So you give me one.'

'S. T. Fitzhugh is dead. Police are investigating. Back off.' Eve started the engine, torpedoed out of the slot so that Nadine had to dance back to save her toes. At Peabody's chuckle, Eve slid a stony glance in her direction. 'Something funny?'

'I like her.' Peabody couldn't resist looking back, and she noted that Nadine was grinning. 'So do you.'

Eve smothered a chuckle. 'There's no accounting for taste,' she said and drove out into the rainy morning.

It had gone perfectly. Absolutely perfectly. It was an exciting, powerful feeling to know that you had the controls. The reports coming from various news agencies were all duly logged and recorded. Such matters required careful organization and were added to the small but satisfactorily growing pile of data discs.

It was such fun, and that was a surprise. Fun had certainly not been the prime motivator of the operation. But it was a delightful side effect.

Who would succumb next?

At the flick of a switch, Eve's face flashed onto a monitor, all pertinent data split-screened beside her. A fascinating woman. Birthplace and parents unknown. The abused child discovered hiding in an alley in Dallas, Texas, body battered, mind blanked. A woman who couldn't remember the early years of her own life. The years that formed the soul. Years when she had been beaten and raped and tormented.

What did that sort of life do to the mind? To the heart? To the person?

It had made the girl a social worker and had made Eve Dallas into a woman who had become a cop. The cop with the reputation for digging deep, and who had come into some notoriety the previous winter during the investigation of a sensitive and ugly case.

That was when she had met Roarke.

The computer hummed, sliced Roarke's face onto the screen. Such an intriguing couple. His background was no prettier than the cop's had been. But he'd chosen, at least initially, the other side of the law to make his mark. And his fortune.

Now they were a set. A set that could be destroyed on a whim.

But not yet. Not for some little time yet.

After all, the game had just begun.

Chapter Five

'I just don't buy it,' Eve muttered as she called up data on Fitzhugh. She studied his bold, striking face as it flashed onto her monitor, shook her head. 'I just don't buy it,' she repeated.

She scanned his date and place of birth, saw that he'd been born in Philadelphia during the last decade of the previous century. He'd been married to a Milicent Barrows from 2033 to 2036. Divorced, no children.

He'd moved to New York the same year as his divorce, established his criminal law practice, and as far as she could see, had never looked back.

'Annual income,' she requested.

Subject Fitzhugh, annual income for last tax year. Two million, seven hundred USD.

'Bloodsucker,' she murmured. 'Computer, list and detail any arrests.'

Searching. No police record on file.

'Okay, so he's clean. How about this? List all civil suits filed against subject.'

She got a hit on that, a short list of names, and she ordered a hard copy. She requested a list of cases Fitzhugh had lost over the last ten years, noted the names that mirrored the suits filed against him. It made her sigh. It was typical litigation of the era. Your lawyer doesn't get you off, you sue the lawyer. It gave another jab to her hopeful theory of blackmail.

'Okay, so maybe we're going about this the wrong way. New subject, Foxx, Arthur, residence Five oh oh two Madison Avenue, New York.'

Searching.

The computer blipped and whined, causing Eve to slap the unit with the heel of her hand to jog it back. She didn't bother to curse budget cuts.

Foxx appeared on screen, wavering a bit until Eve gave the computer another smack. More attractive, she noted, when he smiled. He was fifteen years younger than Fitzhugh, had been born in East Washington, the son of two career military personnel, had lived in various points of the globe until he had settled in New York in 2042 and joined the Nutrition for Life organization as a consultant.

His annual income just tipped into the six figures. The record showed no marriages but the same-sex license he shared with Fitzhugh.

'List and detail any arrests.'

The machine grumbled as if it were tired of answering questions, but the list popped. One disorderly conduct, two assaults, and one disturbing the peace.

'Well, now we're getting somewhere. Both subjects, list and detail any psychiatric consults.'

There was nothing on Fitzhugh, but she got another hit on Foxx. With a grunt, she ordered a hard copy, then glanced up as Peabody entered.

'Forensics? Toxicology?'

'Forensics isn't in, but we've got tox.' Peabody handed Eve

61

a disc. 'Low level alcohol, identified as Parisian brandy, 2045. Not nearly enough to debilitate. No other drug traces.'

'Shit.' She'd been hopeful. 'I might have something here. Our friend Foxx spent a lot of his childhood on the therapist's couch. He checked himself into the Delroy Institute just two years ago for a month. And he's done time. Piss away time, but time nonetheless. Ninety days lockup for assault. And he had to wear a probie bracelet for six months. Our boy has some violent tendencies.'

Peabody frowned at the data. 'Military family. They tend to be resistant to homosexuality still. I bet they tried to head shrink him into hetero.'

'Maybe. But he's got a history of mental heath problems and a criminal record. Let's see what the uniforms turned up when they knocked on doors in Fitzhugh's building. And we'll talk to Fitzhugh's associates in his firm.'

'You're not buying suicide.'

'I knew him. He was arrogant, pompous, smug, vain.' Eve shook her head. 'Vain, arrogant men don't choose to be found naked in the bathtub, swimming in their own blood.'

'He was a brilliant man.' Leanore Bastwick sat in her custom-made leather chair in the glass-walled corner office of Fitzhugh, Bastwick, and Stern. Her desk was a glass pool, unsmudged and sparkling. *It suited*, Eve thought, *her icy and stunning blond beauty*. 'He was a generous friend,' Leanore added and folded her perfectly manicured hands on the edge of the desk. 'We're in shock here, Lieutenant.'

It was hard to see shock on the polished surface of it all. New York's steel forest rose up glittering behind Leanore's back, lending the lofty illusion that she was reigning over the city. Pale rose and soft gray added elegant muted color to an office that was as meticulously decorated as the woman herself.

'Do you know of any reason why Fitzhugh would have taken his own life?'

'Absolutely none.' Leanore kept her hands very still, her eyes level. 'He loved life. His life, his work. He enjoyed every minute of every day as much as anyone I've ever met. I have no idea why he would choose to end it.'

'When was the last time you saw or spoke with him?'

She hesitated. Eve could almost see wheels working smoothly behind those heavily lashed eyes. 'Actually, I saw him briefly last night. I dropped a file off for him, discussed a case. That discussion is, of course, privileged.' Her slicked lips curved. 'But I will say he was his usual enthusiastic self, and he was very much looking forward to dueling with you in court.'

'Dueling?'

'That's how Fitz referred to cross-examination of expert and police witnesses.' A smile flickered over her face. 'It was a match, in his mind, of wits and nerve. A professional game for an innate game player. I don't know of anything he enjoyed so much as being in court.'

'What time did you drop off the file last night?'

'I'd say about ten. Yes, I think it was around ten. I'd worked late here and slipped by on my way home.'

'Was that usual, Ms. Bastwick, you slipping by to see him on your way home?'

'Not unusual. We were, after all, professional associates, and our cases sometimes overlapped.'

'That's all you were? Professional partners?'

'Do you assume, Lieutenant, that because a man and woman are physically attractive and on friendly terms that they can't work together without sexual tension?'

'I don't assume anything. How long did you stay – discussing your case?'

'Twenty minutes, a half hour. I didn't time it. He was fine when I left, I'll tell you that.'

'There was nothing he was particularly concerned about?'

'He had some concerns about the Salvatori matter – and

63

others, as well. Nothing out of the ordinary. He was a confident man.'

'And outside of work. On a personal level?'

'A private man.'

'But you know Arthur Foxx.'

'Of course. In this firm we take care to know and socialize at least lightly with the spouses of partners and associates. Arthur and Fitz were devoted to each other.'

'No . . . spats?'

Leanore cocked a brow. 'I wouldn't know.'

Sure you would, Eve thought. 'You and Mr Fitzhugh were partners, you had a close professional and apparently a close personal relationship. He must have discussed his homelife with you from time to time.'

'He and Arthur were very happy.' Leanore's first sign of irritation showed in the gentle tapping of a coral-toned nail against the edge of glass. 'Happy couples occasionally have arguments. I imagine you argue with your husband from time to time.'

'My husband hasn't recently found me dead in the bath-tub,' Eve said evenly. 'What did Foxx and Fitzhugh argue about?'

Leanore let out an annoyed huff of breath. She rose, punched in a code on her AutoChef, took out a steaming cup of coffee. None was offered to Eve. 'Arthur had periodic bouts of depression. He is not the most self-confident of men. He tended to be jealous, which exasperated Fitz.' Her brows knit. 'You're probably aware that Fitz was matried before. His bisexuality was somewhat of a problem for Arthur, and when he was depressed, he tended to worry about all the men and women Fitz came into contact with in the course of his work. They rarely argued, but when they did, it was generally about Arthur's jealousy.'

'Did he have reason to be jealous?'

'As far as I know, Fitz was completely faithful. It's not always an easy choice, Lieutenant, being in the spotlight as he was, and given his lifestyle. Even today, there are some who are – let's say – uncomfortable with less-than-traditional sexual preferences. But Fitz gave Arthur no reason to be anything less than content.'

'Yet he was. Thank you,' Eve said as she rose. 'You've been very helpful.'

'Lieutenant,' Leanore began as Eve and the silent Peabody started for the door. 'If I thought for one instant that Arthur Foxx had anything to do with—' She stopped, sucked in a breath. 'No, it's simply impossible to believe.'

'Less possible than believing Fitzhugh slashed his own wrists and let himself bleed to death?' Eve waited a beat, then left the office.

Peabody waited until they'd stepped out onto the skywalk that ribboned the building. 'I don't know whether you were planting seeds or digging for worms.'

'Both.' Eve looked through the glass of the tube. She could see Roarke's office building, shooting tall and polished ebony among the other spears. At least he had no connection with this case. She didn't have to worry about uncovering something he'd done or someone he'd known too well. 'She knew both the victim and the suspect. And Foxx didn't mention her slipping by to discuss work last night.'

'So you've bumped Foxx from witness to suspect?'

Eve watched a man in a tailored robe squawk bad temperedly into a palm 'link as he glided by. 'Until we prove conclusively it was suicide, Foxx is the prime – hell, the only – suspect. He had the means. It was his knife. He had the opportunity. They were alone in the apartment. He had the motive. Money. Now we know he has a history of depression, a record of violence, and a jealous streak.'

'Can I ask you something?' Peabody waited for Eve's nod. 'You didn't care for Fitzhugh on a professional or a personal level.'

'I hated his fucking guts. So what?' Eve stepped off the

skywalk and onto the street level where she'd been lucky enough to find a parking spot. She spied a glida grill, smoking soy dogs and potato rings, and made a beeline through the heavy pedestrian traffic. 'You think I've got to like the corpse? Give me a couple of dogs and a scoop of potatoes. Two tubes of Pepsi.'

'Diet for me,' Peabody interrupted and rolled her eyes over Eve's long, lean form. 'Some of us have to worry about weight.'

'Diet dog, Diet Pep.' The woman running the cart had a dingy CZ stud in the center of her top lip and a tattoo of the subway system on her chest. The A line veered off and disappeared under the loose gauze covering her breasts. 'Reg Dog, Reg Pep, hot potatoes. Cash or credit?'

Eve shoved the limp cardboard holding the food at Peabody and dug for her tokens. 'What's the damage?'

The woman poked a grimy purple-tipped finger at her console, sent it beeping. 'Twenty-five.'

'Shit. You blink and dogs go up.' Eve poured credits into the woman's outstretched hand, grabbed a couple of wafer-thin napkins.

She worked her way back, plopped down on the bench circling the fountain in front of the law building. The panhandler beside her looked hopeful. Eve tapped her badge; he grinned, tapped the beggar's license hung around his neck.

Resigned, she dug out a five credit chip, passed it over. 'Find someplace else to hustle,' she ordered him, 'or I'll run that license and see if it's up to date.'

He said something uncomplimentary about her line of work, but he pocketed the credit and moved on, giving room to Peabody.

'Leanore doesn't like Arthur Foxx.'

Peabody swallowed gamely. Diet dogs were invariably grainy. 'She doesn't?'

'A high-class lawyer doesn't give that many answers unless

she wants to. She fed us that Foxx was jealous, that they argued.' Eve held out the scoop of greasy potatoes. After a brief internal struggle, Peabody dug in. 'She wanted us to have that data.'

'Still isn't much. There's nothing in Fitzhugh's records that implicates Foxx. His diary, his appointment book, his 'link logs. None of the data I scanned points the finger. Then again, none of it indicates a suicidal bent, either '

Contemplatively, Eve sucked on her tube of Pepsi, watched New York lumber by with all its noise and sweat. 'We'll have to talk to Foxx again. I've got court again this afternoon. I want you to go back to Cop Central, get the door-to-door reports, nag the ME for the final autopsy. I don't know what the hang-up is there, but I want the results by end of shift. I should be out of court by three. We'll do another walk-through of Fitzhugh's apartment and see why he omitted Bastwick's little visit.'

Peabody juggled food and duly programmed the duties into her day log. 'What I asked before – about you not liking Fitzhugh. I just wondered if it was harder to push all the buttons when you had bad feelings about the subject.'

'Cops don't have personal feelings.' Then she sighed. 'Bullshit. You put those feelings aside and push the buttons. That's the job. And if I happen to think a man like Fitzhugh deserved to end up bathing in his own blood, it doesn't mean I won't do what's necessary to find out how he got there.'

Peabody nodded. 'A lot of other cops would just file it. Self-termination. End of transmission.'

'I'm not other cops, and neither are you, Peabody.' She glanced over, mildly interested at the explosive crash as two taxis collided. Pedestrian and street traffic barely hitched as smoke billowed, Duraglass pinged, and two furious drivers popped like corks out of their ruined vehicles.

Eve nibbled away at her lunch as the two men pushed, shoved, and shouted imaginative obscenities. She imagined they were obscenities, anyway, since no English was exchanged.

She looked up but didn't spot one of the hovering traffic copters. With a thin smile, she balled up the card-board, rolled up the empty tube, passed them to Peabody.

'Dump these in the recycler, will you, then come back and give me a hand breaking up those two idiots.'

'Sir, one of them just pulled out a bat. Should I call for backup?'

'Nope.' Eve rubbed her hands together in anticipation as she rose. 'I can handle it.'

Eve's shoulder was still smarting when she walked out of court a couple of hours later. She imagined the cab drivers would have been released by now, which wasn't going to happen to the child killer Eve had just testified against, she thought with satisfaction. She'd be in high security lockup for the next fifty years minimum. There was some satisfaction in that.

Eve rolled her bruised shoulder. The cabbie really hadn't been swinging at her, she thought. He'd been trying to crack his opponent's head open, and she'd just gotten in the way. Still, it wasn't going to hurt her feelings that both of them would have their licenses suspended for three months.

She climbed into her car and, favoring her shoulder, put the vehicle on auto to Cop Central. Overhead, a tourist tram blatted out the standard spiel about the scales of justice.

Well, she mused, *sometimes they balanced. If only for a short time*. Her 'link beeped.

'Dallas.'

'Dr Morris.' The medical examiner had heavy-lidded hawk eyes in a vivid shade of green, a squared-off chin that was generously stubbled, and a slicked-back mane of charcoal hair. Eve liked him. Though she was often frustrated by his lack of stellar speed, she appreciated his thoroughness.

'Have you finished the report on Fitzhugh?'

'I have a problem.'

'I don't need a problem, I need the report. Can you transmit it to my office 'link? I'm on my way there.'

'No, Lieutenant, you're on your way here. I have something I need to show you.'

'I don't have time to come by the morgue.'

'Make time,' he suggested and ended the transmission.

Eve ground her teeth once. Scientists were so damned frustrating, she thought as she redirected her unit.

From the outside, the Lower Manhattan City Morgue resembled one of the beehive-structured office buildings that surrounded it. It blended, that had been the point of the redesign. Nobody liked to think of death, to have it spoil their appetite as they scooted out of work at lunchtime to grab a bite at a corner deli. Images of bodies tagged and bagged on refrigerated slabs tended to put you off your pasta salad.

Eve remembered the first time she'd stepped through the black steel doors in the rear of the building. She'd been a rookie in uniform shoulder to shoulder with two dozen other rookies in uniforms. Unlike several of her comrades, she'd seen death up close and personal before, but she'd never seen it displayed, dissected, analyzed.

There was a gallery above one of the autopsy labs and there students, rookies, and journalists or novelists with the proper credentials could witness firsthand the intricate workings of forensic pathology.

Individual monitors in each seat offered close-up views to those with the stomach for it.

Most of them didn't come back for a return trip. Many who left were carried out.

Eve had walked out on her own steam, and she'd been back countless times since, but she never looked forward to the visits.

Her target this time wasn't what was referred to as The Theater, but Lab C, where Morris conducted most of his work.

Eve passed down the white tiled corridor with its pea green floors. She could smell death there. No matter what was used to eradicate it, the sulky stink of it slid through cracks, around doorways, and it tainted the air with the grinning reminder of mortality.

Medical science had eradicated plagues, a host of diseases and conditions, extending life expectancy to an average of one hundred fifty years. Cosmetic technology had insured that a human being could live attractively for his century and a half.

You could die without wrinkles, without age spots, without aches and pains and disintegrating bones. But you were still going to die sooner or later.

For many who came here, that day was sooner.

She stopped in front of the door at Lab C, held her badge up to the security camera, and gave her name and ID number to the speaker. Her palm print was analyzed and cleared. The door slid open.

It was a small room, windowless and depressing, lined with equipment, beeping with computers. Some of the tools ranged neat as a surgeon's tray on the counters were barbaric enough to make the weak shudder. Saws, lasers, the glinting blades of scalpels, hoses.

In the center of the room was a table with gutters on the side to catch fluids and run them into sterilized, airtight containers for further analysis. On the table was Fitzhugh, his naked body bearing the scars of the recent insult of a standard Y cut.

Morris was sitting on a rolling stool in front of a monitor, face pushed close to the screen. He wore a white lab coat that fluttered to the floor. It was one of his few affectations, the coat that flapped and swirled like a highwayman's cape whenever he walked down the corridors. His slicked-back hair was snugged into a long ponytail.

Eve knew, since he'd called her in directly rather than passing her off to one of his techs, that it was something unusual.

70

'Dr Morris?'

'Hmm. Lieutenant,' he began without turning around. 'Never seen anything like it. Not in thirty years of exploring the dead.' He swung around with a flutter of his lab coat. Beneath it he wore stovepipe pants and a T-shirt in loud, clashing colors. 'You're looking well, Lieutenant.'

He gave her one of his quick, charming smiles, and her lips curved up in response. 'You're looking pretty good, yourself. You lost the beard.'

He reached up, rubbed a hand over his stubbly chin. He'd sported a precise goatee until recently. 'Didn't suit me. But Christ, I hate to shave. How was the honeymoon?'

Automatically, she tucked her hands in her pockets. 'It was good. I've got a pretty full plate right now, Morris. What do you have to show me you couldn't show me on screen?'

'Some things take personal attention.' He rode his stool over to the autopsy table until he pulled up with a slight squeal of wheels at Fitzhugh's head. 'What do you see?'

She glanced down. 'A dead guy.'

Morris nodded, as if pleased. 'What we would call a normal, everyday dead guy who expired due to excessive blood loss, possibly self-inflicted.'

'Possibly?' She leaped on the word.

'From the surface, suicide is the logical conclusion. There were no drugs in his system, very little alcohol, he shows no offensive nor defensive wounds or bruising, the blood settlement was consistent with his position in the tub, he did not drown, the angle of the wrist wounds . . .'

He bumped closer, picked up one of Fitzhugh's limp, beautifully manicured hands where on the wrist the carved wounds resembled some intricate, ancient language. 'They are also very consistent with self-infliction: a right-handed man, reclining slightly.' He demonstrated, holding an imaginary blade. 'Very quick, very precise slashes to the wrist, severing the artery.'

71

Though she'd already studied the wounds herself, and photographs of them, she stepped closer, looked again. 'Why couldn't someone have come up from behind him, leaned over, slashed down at that same angle?'

'It's not beyond the realm of possibility, but if that were the case, I'd expect to see some defensive wounds. If someone snuck into your bath and sliced your wrist, you'd be inclined to become annoyed, quarrelsome.' He beamed a smile. 'I don't think you'd just settle back in the tub and bleed to death.'

'So you're going with self-termination.'

'Not so fast. I was prepared to.' He tugged on his bottom lip, let it snap back into place. 'I ran the standard brain analysis required with any self-termination or suspected self-termination. That's the puzzle here. The real puzzle.'

He scooted his stool over to his workstation, gestured over his shoulder for her to follow. 'This is his brain,' he said, tapping a finger on the organ floating in clear liquid and attached to wire thin cables that fed into the mainframe of his computer. 'Abby Normal.'

'I beg your pardon.'

Morris chuckled, shook his head. 'Obviously you don't make time to watch enough classic videos. That's from a takeoff on the Frankenstein myth. What I'm saying is, this brain is abnormal.'

'He had brain damage?'

'Damage – well, it seems an extreme word for what I've found. Here, on the screen.' He swiveled around, tapped some keys. A close-up view of Fitzhugh's brain flashed on. 'Again, on the surface, completely as expected. But we show the cross section.' He tapped again, and the brain was sliced neatly in half. 'So much went on in this small mass,' Morris murmured. 'Thoughts, ideas, music, desires, poetry, anger, hate. People speak of the heart, Lieutenant, but it's the brain that holds all the magic and mystery of the human species. It elevates us, separates us, defines us as individuals.

And the secrets of it – well, it's doubtful we'll ever know them all. See here.'

Eve leaned closer, trying to see what he indicated with the tap of a finger on the screen. 'It looks like a brain to me. Unattractive but necessary.'

'Not to worry, I nearly missed it myself. For this imaging,' he went on while the monitor whirled with color and shapes, 'the tissue appears in blues, pale to dark, the bone white. Blood vessels are red. As you can see, there arc no clots or tumors that would indicate neurological disorders in the making. Enhance quadrant B, sections thirty-five to forty, thirty percent.'

The screen jumped and a section of the image enlarged. Losing patience, Eve started to shrug, then leaned in. 'What is that? It looks like . . . What? A smudge?'

'It does, doesn't it?' He beamed again, staring at the screen where a faint shadow no bigger than a flyspeck marred the brain. 'Almost like a fingerprint, a child's oily finger. But when you enhance again' – he did so with a few brief commands, popping the image closer – 'it's more of a tiny burn.'

'How would you get a burn inside your brain?'

'Exactly.' Obviously fascinated, Morris swiveled toward the brain in question. 'I've never seen anything like that tiny pinprick mark. It wasn't caused by a hemorrhage, a small stroke, or an aneurism. I've run all the standard brain imaging programs and can find no known neurological cause for it.'

'But it's there.'

'Indeed, it is. It could be nothing, no more than a faint abnormality that caused the occasional vague headache or dizziness. It certainly wouldn't be fatal. But it is curious. I've sent for all of Fitzhugh's medical records to see if there were any tests run or any data on this burn.'

'Could it cause depression, anxiety?'

'I don't know. It flaws the left frontal lobe of the right cerebral hemisphere. Current medical opinion is that certain aspects, such as personality, are localized in this specific

73

cerebral area. So it does appear in the section of the brain that we now believe receives and deploys suggestions and ideas.'

He moved his shoulders. 'However, I can't document that this flaw contributed to death. The fact is, Dallas, at the moment, I'm baffled but fascinated. I won't be releasing your case until I find some answers.'

A burn in the brain, Eve mused as she uncoded the locks on Fitzhugh's condo. She'd come alone, wanting the emptiness, the silence, to give her own brain time to work. Until she had cleared the scene, Foxx would have other living quarters.

She retraced her steps upstairs, studied the grisly bath again.

A burn in the brain, she thought again. Drugs seemed the most logical answer. If they hadn't showed on tox, it could be it was a new type of drug, one that had yet to be registered.

She walked into the relaxation room. There was nothing there but the expensive toys of a wealthy man who enjoyed his leisure time.

Couldn't sleep, she mused. *Came in to relax, had a brandy. Stretched out in the chair, watched some screen.* Her lips pursed as she picked up the VR goggles beside the chair. *Took a quick trip. Didn't want to use the chamber for it, just kicked back.*

Curious, she slipped on the goggles, ordered the last scene played. She was popped into a swaying white boat on a cool green river. Birds soared overhead, a fish bulleted up, flashed silver, and dove again. On the banks of the river were wildflowers and tall, shielding trees. She felt herself floating, let her hand dip into the water to trail a quiet wake. It was nearly sunset, and the sky was going pink and purple in the west. She could hear the low hum of bees, the cheerful chirp of crickets. The boat rocked like a cradle.

Stifling a yawn, she pulled the goggles off again. A harmless, sedative scene, she decided and set the goggles down.

Nothing that would have induced a sudden urge to slash one's wrists. But the water might have prompted the urge for a hot bath, so he'd taken one. And if Foxx had crept in, had been quiet enough, quick enough, he could have done it.

It was all she had, Eve decided, and took out her communicator to order a second interview with Arthur Foxx.

Chapter Six

Eve studied the reports on the knock-on-doors from uniforms. Most of them were what she'd expected. Fitzhugh
and Foxx were quiet, kept to themselves, yet friendly with
their neighbors in the building. But she latched on to the
statement of the droid on doorman duty that placed Foxx
at leaving the building at twenty-two thirty and returning at
twenty-three hundred hours.

'He didn't mention he went out, did he, Peabody? Not a
word about a little jaunt in the evening on his own.'

'No, he didn't mention it.'

'Have we got the security discs logged yet from the lobby
and elevator cameras?'

'I loaded them in. They're under Fitzhugh ten-fifty-one on
your unit.'

'Let's take a look.' Eve booted her machine, leaned back
in her chair.

Peabody scanned the monitor over her shoulder and
resisted mentioning that both of them were now officially
off duty. It was exciting, after all, working side by side
with the top homicide detective at Cop Central. Dallas
would sneer at that, Peabody thought, but it was true.
She'd been following the career of Eve Dallas for years,
and there was no one she admired or wished more to
emulate.

The biggest shock of Peabody's life was that somehow, over

the course of a few short months, they had come to be friends as well.

'Stop.' Eve sat up straight as the transmission froze. She studied the classy blonde entering the building at twenty-two fifteen. 'Well, well, there's our Leanore, slipping by.'

'She had the time fairly close. Ten fifteen.'

'Yeah, she's on the mark.' Eve ran her tongue around her teeth. 'What do you think, Peabody? Business or pleasure?'

'Well, she's dressed for business.' Peabody cocked her head and allowed a faint trail of envy to curl up her spine at Leanore's spiffy three-piece suit. 'She's carrying a briefcase.'

'A briefcase – and a bottle of wine. Enhance quadrant D, thirty to thirty-five. An expensive bottle of wine,' Eve murmured when the screen popped and displayed the label clearly. 'Roarke's got some of that little number in the wine cellar. I think it goes for about two hundred.'

'A bottle? Wow.'

'A glass,' Eve corrected, amused when Peabody goggled. 'Something doesn't fit. Resume normal size and speed, shift to elevator camera. Hmm. Yeah, yeah, she's primping,' Eve murmured, watching as Leanore took a gold compact out of her embossed briefcase, powdered her nose, freshened her lipstick as the elevator climbed. 'And lookie there, just flipped open the top three buttons of her blouse.'

'Getting ready for a man,' Peabody said, and shrugged when Eve slanted a look at her. 'I'd guess.'

'I'd guess, too.' Together, they watched Leanore stride down the foyer on the thirty-eighth floor and buzz herself into Fitzhugh's apartment. Eve increased the time delay until Foxx strode out fifteen minutes later. 'Doesn't look happy, does he?'

'No.' Peabody narrowed her eyes. 'I'd say he looks ticked off.' She lifted her brows when Foxx kicked bad temperedly at the elevator door. 'Very ticked off.'

They waited for the drama to resume. Leanore left twenty-two minutes later, color high on her cheeks, eyes glittering.

She jabbed a finger at the elevator, hitched her briefcase on her shoulder. A short time after, Foxx returned carrying a small parcel.

'She didn't stay twenty or thirty minutes, but more than forty-five. What went on inside that apartment that night?' Eve wondered. 'And just what did Foxx bring back with him? Contact the law offices. I want Leanore in here for questioning. I've got Foxx at nine-thirty. Get her in here at the same time. We'll team play them.'

'You want me to interrogate?'

Eve disengaged her machine, rolled her shoulders. 'It's a good place to start. We'll meet here at eight-thirty. No, come by my home office at eight. That'll give us more time.' She glanced at her 'link as it beeped, considered ignoring it, then gave in.

'Dallas.'

'Hey!' Mavis's bright face filled the screen. 'I was hoping I'd catch you before you left. How's it going?'

'Well enough. I'm just about to log out. What's up?'

'Good timing. Great timing. Mag. Listen, I'm at Jess's studio. We're going to do a session. Leonardo's here. We're going to make it a party, so come on by.'

'Hey, listen, Mavis, I've put in a full day. I just want to—'

'Come on.' There were nerves as well as enthusiasm. 'We're going to get food in, and Jess's got the most rocking brew here. It'll debrain you in seconds. He thinks if we can lay something decent down tonight, we could run with it. I'd really like you around. You know, moral support shit. Can't you just stop by for a while?'

'I guess I could.' *Damn it. No backbone.* 'I'll let Roarke know I'll be late. But I can't stay.'

'Hey, I gave Roarke a buzz already.'

'You – what?'

'I 'linked him just a bit ago. Hey, you know, Dallas, I've never been by that meg-cool office of his. He had like the

UN or something in there, all these off country guys. Wild. Anyway, they put me through to the inner sanctum because I was a pal of yours, and I talked to him. So,' Mavis chirped on over Eve's heaved sigh, 'I told him what was up and coming, and he said he'd stop around after the meeting or summit or whatever he was into.'

'Looks like it's all settled.' Eve watched her fantasy involving a whirlpool, a glass of wine, and a fat slab of steak go up in smoke.

'Too tops. Hey, is that Peabody? Hey, Peabody, you come, too. We'll party. See you soon, right?'

'Mavis.' Eve caught her seconds before she disengaged. 'Where the hell are you?'

'Oh, didn't I say? The studio's at Eight Avenue B, street level. Just beat on the door. Somebody'll let you in. Gotta go,' she shouted as something that might have been music boomed. 'They're tuning up. Catch ya.'

Eve blew out a breath, scooped her hair out of her eyes, and glanced over her shoulder. 'Well, Peabody, want to go to a recording session, get your ears fried, eat bad food, and get drunk on bad brew?'

Peabody didn't have to think twice. 'As a matter of fact, Lieutenant, I'd love to.'

It took a lot of banging on a gray steel door that looked as though it had been on the wrong end of a battering ram somewhere along the line. The rain from that morning had turned into steam that smelled unpleasantly of street oil and the recycling units that never seemed to be in full repair in that part of town.

With more resignation than energy, Eve watched two chemi-heads make deals under the dirty light of a street-lamp. Neither of them so much as blinked at Peabody's uniform. Eve turned when one of the powder junkies took a hit less than five feet away.

'Damn it, that's just too arrogant. Bust him.'

Resigned Peabody headed over. The chemi-head focused, swore and, swallowing the paper his powder had been cupped in, swung around to run. He skidded on the wet pavement and banged face first into the lamppost. By the time Peabody reached him, he was flat on his back and bleeding, profusely from the nose.

'He's out cold,' she called to Eve.

'Idiot. Call it in. Get a cruiser over here to haul him into the tank. You want the collar?'

Peabody considered, then shook her head. 'Not worth it. The beat cop can take it.' She pulled out her communicator, gave the location as she walked back to Eve. 'The dealer's still across the street,' she commented. 'He's got air blades, but I could try to chase him down.'

'I sense a lack of enthusiasm.' Eve narrowed her eyes, scanned the dealer hulking across the street, air blades steaming. 'Hey, asshole,' she called out. 'You see this uniform here?' She jerked a thumb at Peabody. 'Take your business someplace else, or I'll tell her to bump her weapon up to level three and watch you piss your pants.'

'Cunt,' he shouted back and whizzed off on his blades.

'You've got a real way with community relations, Dallas.'

'Yeah, it's a gift.' Eve turned back, prepared to beat on the door again, and found herself facing a female of massive proportions. She was easily six five, with shoulders wide as a highway. They rose out of a sleeveless leather vest and rippled with muscles and tattoos. Beneath, she wore a unisuit, snug as skin and the color of a healing bruise. She sported a copper nose ring and close-cropped hair fashioned into tight, glossy black curls.

'Fucking drug pushers,' she said in a voice like a cannon boom. 'Stink up the neighborhood. You Mavis's cop?'

'That's right, and I brought my cop with me.'

The woman sized Peabody up out of milky blue eyes. 'Solid. Mavis says you're right. I'm Big Mary.'

Eve angled her head. 'Yes, you are.'

It took about ten seconds, then Big Mary's moon-sized face creased in a knife-edged grin. 'Come on in. Jess is just heating up.' By way of welcome, she took Eve's arm and lifted her up and into the short hallway. 'Come on, Dallas's cop.'

'Peabody.' With a cautious glance, Peabody kept warily out of Big Mary's reach.

'Pea body. Yeah, you ain't much bigger than a pea.' Roaring at her own joke, Big Mary carted Eve into a padded elevator, waited for the door to close. They were cocooned together, tight as fish in a pan as Mary directed the unit to take them up one level. 'Jess, he says to take you up to control. You got money?'

It was hard to maintain dignity of any kind when Eve's nose was pressed in Mary's armpit. 'What for?'

'We got food coming. You gotta plunk in your share for the eats.'

'All right. Is Roarke here yet?'

'Ain't seen no Roarke. Mavis says you can't miss him 'cause he is fine and prime.'

The padded door opened, and Eve let out the breath she'd been holding. Even as she sucked in air, her ears were assaulted. Mavis's high, wild voice was screeching to the accompaniment of blistering noise.

'She's got a groove going.'

Only deep affection for Mavis prevented Eve from leaping back into the soundproofing. 'Apparently.'

'I'll get your drinks. Jess, he brought the brew.'

Mary hulked off, leaving Eve and Peabody in a glass-walled control booth that curved in a semicircle a half level above a studio where Mavis was singing her heart and lungs out. With a grin, Eve moved closer to the glass, the better to see.

Mavis had scooped up her hair so that it spewed in a purple fountain out of a multicolored band. She was wearing modified overalls, the black leather straps running up the center of her bare breasts. The rest of the material was a shimmering kaleidoscope that started at the midriff and ended barely south of the crotch. She danced to the beat on a fashionable pair of slides that left the feet bare and propped them onto four-inch stilts.

Eve had no doubt that Mavis's lover had designed the costume for her. She spotted Leonardo in a corner of the studio, glowing like a sunbeam at Mavis and wearing a body-skimming jumpsuit that made him look like an elegant grizzly.

'What a pair,' she murmured and hooked her thumbs in the back pockets of her battered jeans. She turned her head to speak to Peabody, but noted her companion's attention was riveted to the left, and the look on Peabody's face, Eve noted with some curiosity, managed to combine shock, admiration, and lust.

Following Peabody's distracted gaze, Eve had her first view of Jess Barrow. He was beautiful. A painting in motion with a long, shining mane of hair the color of polished oak. His eyes were nearly silver, thickly lashed, intensely focused, as he worked the controls of an elaborate console. His complexion was flawless, tanned to bronze, set off by rounded cheekbones and a strong chin. His mouth was full and firm, and his hands, as they flew over the controls, were as finely sculptured as marble.

'Roll up your tongue, Peabody,' Eve suggested, 'before you step on it.'

'God. Holy God. He's better in person. Don't you just want to bite him?'

'Not particularly, but you go ahead.'

Catching herself, Peabody flushed to the roots of her hair. She shifted on her sturdy legs. This was, she reminded herself, her superior. 'I admire his talent.'

'Peabody, you're admiring his chest. It's a pretty good one, so I can't hold it against you.'

'I wish he would,' she murmured, then cleared her throat

82

as Big Mary stomped back with two dark brown bottles. 'Jess gets this brew from his family down South. It's fine.'

Since it was also unmarked and unlabeled, Eve prepared to sacrifice a few layers of stomach lining. She was pleasantly surprised when the liquid slid mellowly down her throat. 'It is fine. Thanks.'

'You add to the kitty, you can have more. I'm supposed to go down to wait for Roarke. I hear he's got money to roll in. How come you're not wearing some flash, you linked up with a rich man?'

Eve decided not to mention the baby-fist-sized diamond resting between her breasts under her shirt. 'My underwear's solid gold. It chafes some, but it makes me feel secure.'

After another brief processing delay, Mary hooted with laughter, slapped Eve on the back hard enough to bop her head into the glass, then headed off in her rock-breaking stride.

'We ought to sign her up,' Eve muttered. 'She wouldn't need a weapon or body armor.'

The music built to an ear-scorching crescendo, then cut off as if severed with a knife. Below, Mavis let out a squeal and launched herself into Leonardo's open arms.

'That was a nice take, sugar.' Jess's voice flowed out like top cream and drifted lazily with a Southern drawl. 'You take ten and rest that golden throat for me.'

Mavis's idea of resting her throat was to let out another scream, then wave desperately at Eve. 'Dallas, you're here. Wasn't that mag? I'm coming up, don't go anywhere.' She scrambled through a door on her trendy stilts.

'So this is Dallas.' Jess pushed away from his console. His body was trim and showed off to advantage in jeans as battered as Eve's and a simple cotton shirt that would retail for a beat cop's monthly paycheck. He wore a diamond stud in his ear that glinted as he crossed the booth and a braided gold chain around his wrist that slid fluidly as he held out one of those beautiful hands. 'Mavis is brimming over with stories about her cop.'

'Mavis brims over habitually. It's part of her charm.'

'That it is. I'm Jess, and I'm delighted to meet you at last.' With his hand still cupped over Eve's, he turned that slow, heart-thudding smile onto Peabody. 'And it seems we have two cops for the price of one.'

'I – I'm a huge fan,' Peabody managed and fought against the nervous stutter. 'I have all of your discs, audio and video. I've seen you in concert.'

'Music buffs are always welcome.' He released Eve's hand to take hers. 'Why don't I show you my favorite toy?' he suggested, leading her toward the console. Before Eve could follow, Mavis burst in.

'What did you think? Did you like it? I wrote it. Jess orchestrated it, but I wrote it. He thinks it could hit.'

'I'm really proud of you. You sounded great.' Eve returned Mavis's enthusiastic embrace and grinned at Leonardo over her shoulder. 'How does it feel to be hooked up with a rising music legend?'

'She's wonderful.' He leaned in to give Eve a one-armed squeeze. 'You look terrific. I noticed on some news clips that you wore a number of my designs. I'm grateful.'

'I'm grateful,' Eve said and meant it. Leonardo was a talented and emerging genius of clothing design. 'I didn't look like Roarke's rag-picking cousin.'

'You always look like yourself,' Leonardo corrected, but he narrowed his eyes and flipped his fingers through her untidy hair. 'You need some work here. If you don't have it styled every few weeks, it loses shape.'

'I was going to trim it up some, I just—'

'No, no.' He shook his head solemnly, but his eyes twinkled at her. 'The days of you hacking at it yourself are over. You call Trina, have her do you.'

'We'll have to drag her again.' Mavis grinned at everything.

'She'll keep making excuses and start clipping at it with kitchen shears when it gets in her eyes.' She giggled when Leonardo shuddered. 'We'll get Roarke to hound her.'

'I'd be delighted to.' He stepped out of the elevator, walked straight to Eve and, framing her face in his hands, kissed her. 'What am I hounding you about?'

'Nothing. Have a drink.' She passed him her bottle.

Instead of drinking, he kissed Mavis in greeting. 'I appreciate the invitation. This is quite a setup.'

'Isn't it mag? The sound system's ace of the line, and Jess works all kinds of magic with the console. He's got like six million instruments programmed in. He can play them all, too. He can do anything. The night he came into the D and D changed my life. It was like a miracle.'

'Mavis, you're the miracle.' Smoothly, Jess led Peabody back toward the group. She was flushed and glassy-eyed. Eve could see the pulse in her throat pounding to its own rhythm.

'Down, girl,' she muttered, but Peabody only rolled her eyes.

'You met Dallas and Peabody, right? And this is Roarke.' Mavis bounced on her stilts. 'My closest friends.'

'It's a genuine pleasure.' Jess offered one of his finely boned hands to Roarke. 'I admire your success in the business world and your taste in women.'

'Thank you. I tend to be careful with both.' Roarke scanned the area, inclined his head. 'Your studio's impressive.'

'I love showing it off. It's been in the planning stages for some time. Mavis is actually the first artist to use it, other than myself. Mary's going to order food. Why don't I show you my prize creation before I put Mavis back to work?'

He led the way back to the console, sat at it like a captain at the helm. 'The instruments are programmed in, of course. I can call up any number of combinations and vary pitch and speed. It's accessed for voice command, but I rarely use that. Distracts me from the music.'

He slid controls and had a simple backbeat playing. 'Recorded vocals.' He tapped his fingers over buttons and Mavis's voice punched out, surprisingly gritty and rich. A monitor displayed the sounds with washing of colors and shapes. 'I use that for computer analysis. Musicologists' – he flashed a charming, self-deprecating smile – 'we can't help ourselves. But that's another story.'

'She sounds good,' Eve commented, pleased.

'And she'll sound better. Overdubbing.' Mavis's voice split, layered over itself in close harmony. 'Layers and fill.' Jess's hands danced over the controls, drawing out guitars, brass, the jingle of a tambourine, the searing wail of a sax. 'Cool it down.' Everything slowed, mellowed. 'Heat it up.' Went into double time, blasted.

'That's all very basic, as is having her duet with recording artists of the past. You'll have to hear her version of "Hard Day's Night" with the Beatles. I can also code in any sound.' With a smile flirting around his mouth, he spun a dial, and skimmed his fingers over the keys. Eve's voice whispered out.

'Down, girl.' The words melded into Mavis's vocal, repeating, echoing, drifting.

'How did you do that?' Eve demanded.

'I'm miked,' he explained, 'and hooked into the console. Now that I have your voice on program, I can have your voice replace Mavis's.' He skimmed the controls again, and Eve winced when she heard herself singing.

'Don't do that,' she ordered, and laughing, Jess switched it back.

'Sorry, I can't resist playing. Want to hear yourself croon, Peabody?'

'No.' Then she gnawed her lip. 'Well, maybe.'

'Let's see, something smoky, understated, and classic.' He

worked for a moment, then sat back. Peabody's eyes rounded when she heard herself quietly torching through 'I've Got You Under My Skin.'

'Is that one of your songs?' she asked. 'I don't recognize it.'

Jess chuckled. 'No, it's before my time. You've got a strong voice, Officer Peabody. Good breath control. Want to quit your day job and join the party?'

She flushed and shook her head. Jess cut out the vocals, tuned the console to a bluesy instrumental. 'I worked with an engineer who designed some autotronics for Disney-Universe. It took nearly three years to complete this.' He patted the console like a well-loved child. 'Now that I have the prototype and a working unit, I'm hoping to manufacture more. She works on remote, too. I can be anywhere and link up, run the board. I got specs on a smaller, portable unit, and I've been working on a mood enhancer.'

He seemed to catch himself, shook his head. 'I get carried away. My agent's starting to complain that I'm spending more time working on electronics than recording.'

'Food's here!' Big Mary bellowed.

'Well, then.' Jess smiled, scanned his audience. 'Let's dig in. You've got to keep your energy level up, Mavis.'

'I'm starving.' She grabbed Leonardo's hand and headed for the door. Below, Mary was carting bags and boxes into the studio.

'Go help yourselves,' Jess told them. 'I've got a little fiddling to do. I'll be right along.'

'What do you think?' Eve murmured to Roarke as they headed down, trailed by Peabody.

'I think he's looking for an investor.'

Eve sighed, nodded. 'Yeah, that was my take. I'm sorry.'

'It's not a problem. He's got an interesting product.'

'I had Peabody run a make on him. Nothing's come up. But I don't like to think of him using you – or Mavis.'

'That's yet to be seen.' He turned her into his arms as they stepped into the studio, ran his hands over her hips. 'I missed you. I miss spending large quantities of time with you.'

She felt the heat kindle between her thighs, hotter, lustier than the moment called for. Her breasts tingled with it. 'I missed you, too. Why don't we figure out how to cut the evening short, go home, and fuck like rabbits?'

He was hard as iron. As he leaned down to nip at her ear, he found himself struggling not to tug at her clothes. 'Good thought. Christ, I want you.'

The hell with where they were, Roarke thought and dragged her head back by the hair to plunder her mouth.

At the console, at the controls, Jess watched them and smiled. Another few minutes, he mused, and they could very well be on the floor, mindlessly mating. Better not. With deft fingers, he skimmed buttons, changed the program. More than satisfied, he rose and started downstairs.

Two hours later, driving home through the dark streets that ran with colors from flashing billboards, Eve pushed her cruiser past the limits of the law. Need was a low, throbbing beat between her thighs, an itch desperate to be scratched.

'You're breaking the law, Lieutenant,' Roarke said mildly. He was rock hard again, like a teenager cruising on hormones.

The woman who prided herself on never abusing her badge muttered, 'Bending it.'

Roarke reached over, cupped her breast. 'Bend it more.'

'Oh Jesus.' She could already imagine what he'd feel like inside her, so she punched the accelerator and shot like a bullet down Park.

A glide-cart operator flipped up her middle finger as Eve screamed around a curb and headed east. Cursing lightly, Eve switched on her duty light, popped up the red and blue globe, and had it flashing.

'I can't believe I'm doing this. I never do this.'

Roarke slid his hand down to her thigh. 'Do you know what I'm going to do to you?'

She gave a hoarse laugh, swallowed hard. 'Don't tell me, for God's sake. I'll kill us.'

Her hands were glued to the wheel and trembling, her body vibrating like a string already plucked. Her breath was already hitching. Clouds slipped past the moon and freed its light.

'Hit the remote for the gate,' she panted. 'Hit the remote. I'm not slowing down.'

He coded it quickly. The iron gate eased majestically open, and she burst through with inches to spare. 'Excellent job. Stop the car.'

'Just a minute, just a minute.' She rocketed up the drive, flying past the gorgeous trees and musical fountains.

'Stop the car,' he demanded again and pressed his hand to her crotch.

She came instantly, violently, barely managing to keep from steering into an oak. Gasping for air, she pulled the vehicle to a stop, fishtailing and ending in a drunken diagonal across the drive.

She flew at him.

They tore at clothes, fighting to find each other in the narrow confines of the car. She bit his shoulder, yanked his trousers open. He was cursing, she was laughing, when he dragged her out of the car. They fell on the grass in a tangle of limbs and twisted clothing.

'Hurry up, hurry up.' It was all she could manage through the unbearable pressure. His mouth was on her breast through her torn shirt, teeth scraping. She pulled at his trousers, dug her fingers into his hips.

His breathing was fast, rough, the raw need clawing through him as urgently as her nails clawed at his back. He could feel his blood roaring, a tidal wave through his veins. His hands bruised her as he rocked her legs back, drove deep inside her.

She screamed, a wild, savage sound of pleasure, her nails raking his back, her teeth fixing on his shoulder. She could feel him pulsing inside her, filling her with each desperate thrust. The punch of the orgasm was painful and did nothing to lessen the monstrous need.

She was wet, hot, her muscles vising over him like teeth with each pump of hips. He couldn't stop, couldn't think, and plunged again and again like a stud covering a mare in heat. He couldn't see her through the red haze that clouded his vision, he could only feel her, racing with him, pistoning her hips. Her voice buzzed in his ears, all whimpers and moans and gasps.

Each sound beat in his blood like a primal chant.

It shattered without warning, beyond his control. His body simply peaked like an engine on maximum power, battered into hers, then erupted. The hot wave of release swamped him, swallowed him, drowned him. It was the only time since he'd first touched her that he didn't know if she had followed him over the edge.

He collapsed, rolled weakly away to try to find air for his overtaxed lungs. In the glowing moonlight, they sprawled on the grass, sweaty, half-dressed, shuddering, like the lone survivors of a particularly vicious war.

With a groan, she rolled over on her stomach, let the grass cool her burning cheeks. 'Christ, what was that?'

'Under other circumstances, I'd call it sex. But . . .' He managed to open his eyes. 'I don't have a word for it.'

'Did I bite you?'

A few aches were making themselves known as his body recovered. He twisted his head, glanced at his shoulder, and saw the imprint of her teeth. 'Someone did. I think it was probably you.'

He watched a star fall, shooting silver from sky to earth. It had been much like that, he thought, like plunging helplessly to oblivion. 'Are you okay?'

'I don't know. I have to think about it.' Her head was still spinning. 'We're on the lawn,' she said slowly. 'Our clothes are torn. I'm pretty sure I have the imprint of your fingers dented into my butt.'

'I did my best,' he murmured.

She snickered first, then chuckled, then broke into fits of giddy, hiccupping laughter. 'Jesus, Roarke, Jesus Christ, look at us.'

'In a minute. I think I'm still partially blind.' But he was grinning as he shifted. She was still shaking with laughter. Her hair stuck up at odd angles, her eyes were glassy, and there were grass stains as well as bruises on her pretty ass. 'You don't look much like a cop, Lieutenant.'

She rolled to sit up as he had, angled her head. 'You don't look much like a rich guy, Roarke.' She tugged on his sleeve – it was all that was left of his shirt. 'But it's an interesting look. How are you going to explain that to Summerset?'

'I'll simply tell him my wife is an animal.'

She snorted. 'He's already decided that for himself.' Blowing out a breath, she looked toward the house. Lights glimmered on the lower level to welcome them home. 'How are we going to get into the house?'

'Well . . .' He found what was left of her shirt, tied it around her breasts, and made her giggle helplessly. They managed to tug on ruined slacks, then sat looking at each other. 'I can't carry you to the car,' he told her. 'I was hoping you'd carry me.'

'We have to get up first.'

'Okay.'

Neither of them moved. The laughter started again, continued as they grabbed onto each other like drunks and staggered to their feet. 'Leave the car,' he decided.

'Uh-huh.' They limped off, weaving. 'Clothes? Shoes?'

'Leave them, too.'

'Good plan.'

Snickering like children breaking curfew, they stumbled

91

up the steps, shushing each other as they fell through the door.

'Roarke!' Shocked tones, rushing feet.

'I knew it,' Eve muttered dourly. 'I just knew it.'

Summerset rushed out of the shadows, his normally set face alive with shock and worry. He saw tattered clothes, bruised skin, wild eyes. 'Was there an accident?'

Roarke straightened up, kept his arm around Eve's shoulders as much for balance as support. 'No. It was on purpose. Go to bed, Summerset.'

Eve glanced over her shoulder as she and Roarke helped each other up the stairs. Summerset stood at the base, gaping. The picture pleased her so much, she snickered all the way to the bedroom.

They fell into bed, exactly as they were, and slept like babies.

Chapter Seven

At shortly before eight the next morning, a bit sore and fuzzy-brained, Eve sat at her desk in her home office. She considered it more of a sanctuary than an office, really, the apartment Roarke had built for her in his home. Its design was similar to the apartment where she had lived when she'd met him, which she'd been reluctant to give up.

He'd provided it so that she could have her own space, her own things. Even after all the time she'd lived there, she rarely slept in their bed when he was away. Instead, she curled into the relaxation chair and dozed.

The nightmares came less often now, but crept back at odd moments.

She could work here when it was convenient, lock the doors if she wanted privacy. And as it had a fully operational kitchen, she often chose her AutoChef over Summerset when she was alone in the house.

With the sun streaming through the view wall at her back, she reviewed her caseload, juggled legwork. She knew she didn't have the luxury of focusing exclusively on the Fitzhugh case, particularly since it was earmarked a probable suicide. If she didn't turn up hard evidence in the next day or two, she'd have no choice but to lower its priority.

At eight sharp there was a brisk knock on the door.

'Come on in, Peabody.'

'I'll never get used to this place,' Peabody said as she walked inside. 'It's like something out of an old video.'

'You should get Summerset to take you on a tour,' Eve said absently. 'I'm pretty sure there are rooms I've never seen. There's coffee.' Eve gestured toward the kitchen alcove and continued to frown at her logbook.

Peabody wandered off, scanning the entertainment units lining the wall, wondering what it would be like to be able to afford any amusement available: music, art, video, holograms, VR, meditation chambers, games. Play a set of tennis with the latest Wimbledon champ, dance with a hologram of Fred Astaire, or take a virtual trip to the pleasure palaces on Regis III.

Daydreaming a bit, she turned into the kitchen. The AutoChef was already programmed for coffee, so she ordered two, carried the steaming mugs back into the office. She waited patiently while Eve continued to mutter.

Peabody sipped her coffee. 'God. Oh God. It's real.' Blinking in shock, she cupped both hands reverently around the mug. 'This coffee is real.'

'Yeah, you get spoiled. I can hardly stomach the slop down at Cop Central anymore.' Eve glanced up, caught Peabody's dazed expression, and grinned. It hadn't been so long before that she'd had a similar reaction to Roarke's coffee. And to Roarke. 'Pretty great, huh?'

'I've never had real coffee before.' As if sipping liquid gold – and with the depletion of the rain forests and plantations it was equally dear – Peabody drank slowly. 'It's amazing.'

'You've got a half hour to OD on it while we work out the day's strategy.'

'I can have more?' Peabody closed her eyes and just inhaled the scent. 'You're a god, Dallas.'

With a snort, Eve reached for her beeping 'link. 'Dallas,' she began, then her face lit with a grin. 'Feeney.'

'How's married life, kid?'

'It's tolerable. Pretty early in the day for you electronic detectives, isn't it?'

'Got a hot one working. A scramble at the chief's office. Some joker hacked into his mainframe and nearly fried the whole system.'

'They got in?' Her eyes widened in surprise. She wasn't sure even Feeney, with his magic touch, could break the security on the Chief of Police and Security's system.

'Looks that way. Tangled shit all to hell and back. I'm unknotting it,' he said cheerfully. 'Thought I'd check in, see what's what since I haven't heard from you.'

'I hit the ground running.'

'You don't know any other speed. You primary on Fitzhugh?'

'That's right. Something I should know?'

'No. Smart money's that he iced himself, and nobody around here's too sorry. That oil slick loved squeezing cops on the stand. Funny though, second big suicide in a month.'

Eve's interest spiked. 'Second?'

'Yeah. Oh, that's right, you were off honeymooning and making cow's eyes.' He wiggled his bushy red eyebrows. 'Senator in East Washington a couple weeks ago. Jumped out the window of the Capitol Building. Politicians and lawyers. They're crazy anyway.'

'Yeah. Could you get me the data on it when you have the chance? Transfer it to my office unit.'

'What, you going to keep a scrapbook?'

'Just interested.' The feeling was back in her gut. 'I'll pick up the tab next time we're in the Eatery.'

'No problem. As soon as I get this system unknotted, I'll feed it to you. Don't be a stranger,' he told her and signed off.

Peabody continued to take miserly sips of coffee. 'You think there's a connection between Fitzhugh and the senator who took the dive?'

'Lawyers and politicians,' Eve murmured. 'And autotronic engineers.'

'What?'

Eve shook her head. 'I don't know. Disengage,' she ordered her unit, then swung her bag over her shoulder. 'Let's go.'

Peabody struggled not to pout about the lack of another cup of coffee. 'Two suicides in two different cities in a month isn't such a weird thing,' she began, lengthening her stride to catch up with Eve.

'Three. There was a kid on Olympus who hanged himself while we were there. Mathias, Drew. I want to see if you can find a connection, anything that ties them together. People, places, habits, education, hobbies.' She rushed down the stairs, gearing up.

'I don't know the politician's name. I didn't pay attention to the reports on the East Washington suicide.' Busily, Peabody tugged out her personal palm computer and began searching for data.

'Mathias was in his early twenties, autotronics engineer. He worked for Roarke. Shit.' She had a bad feeling she was going to be forced to drag Roarke into her work once again. 'If you run into a snag, ask Feeney. He can pop the data handcuffed and drunk, faster than either of us.'

Eve wrenched open the door, scowled when she didn't see her car at the top of the drive. 'Goddamn Summerset. I've told him to leave my car when I park it.'

'I think he did.' Peabody flipped on her sunshades, pointed. 'It's blocking the drive, see?'

'Oh, yeah.' Eve cleared her throat. The car was just as she'd left it, and fluttering in the mild breeze were a few torn articles of clothing. 'Don't ask,' she muttered and started to hoof it down the drive.

'I wasn't going to.' Peabody's voice was smooth as silk. 'Speculation's more interesting.'

'Shut up, Peabody.'

'Shutting up, Lieutenant.' With a smirk, Peabody climbed in the car and swallowed a laugh when Eve swung the vehicle around and cruised down the drive.

Arthur Foxx was sweating. It was subtle, just a faint sheen over his top lip, but Eve found it satisfying. She hadn't been surprised to discovere his chosen representative was an associate of Fitzhugh's, a young cager beaver in a pricey suit with trendy medallions decorating the slim lapels.

'My client is understandably upset.' The lawyer folded his youthful face into somber lines. 'The memorial service for Mr Fitzhugh is scheduled for one P.M. this afternoon. You've chosen an inappropriate time for this interview.'

'Death chooses the time, Mr Ridgeway, and it's usually inappropriate. Interview with Authur Foxx, re Fitzhugh, case number three oh oh nine one-ASD, conducted by Dallas, Lieutenant Eve. Date August 24, 2058, time oh nine thirty-six. Will you state your name for the record?'

'Arthur Foxx.'

'Mr Foxx, you are aware that this interview is being recorded.'

'I am.'

'You have exercised your right to counsel and understand your additional rights and responsibilities?'

'That's correct.'

'Mr Foxx, you gave an earlier statement regarding your activities on the night of Mr Fitzhugh's death. Do you wish to view a replay of that statement?'

'It's not necessary. I told you what happened. I don't know what else you expect me to tell you.'

'To begin, tell me where you were between twenty-two thirty and twenty-three hundred on the night of the incident.'

'I've already told you. We had dinner. We watched a comedy, we went to bed and caught a bit of the late news.'

'You remained at home all evening?'

97

'That's what I've said.'

'Yes, Mr Foxx, that's what you've said, on record. But that's not what you did.'

'Lieutenant, my client is here voluntarily. I see no—'

'Save it,' she suggested. 'You left the building at approximately ten thirty P.M. and returned some thirty minutes later. Where did you go?'

'I—' Foxx tugged at the silver string of his tie. 'I stepped out for a few minutes. I'd forgotten.'

'You'd forgotten.'

'My mind was confused. I was in shock.' His tie made wispy sounds as his fingers worked over it. 'I didn't remember something as unimportant as taking a quick walk.'

'But you remember now? Where did you go?'

'Just for a walk. Around the block a few times.'

'You returned with a parcel. What was in it?'

She saw the moment he realized the security cameras had nailed him. His gaze shifted past her and the fingers on his tie became busier. 'I stopped into a 24/7, picked up a few things. Veggie-Smokes. I have the urge for one occasionally.'

'It's a simple matter to check with the 24/7 and determine exactly what you purchased.'

'Some tranqs,' he spit out. 'I wanted to tranq out for the night. I wanted a smoke. There's no law against it.'

'No, but there is a law against giving false statements in a police investigation.'

'Lieutenant Dallas.' The lawyer's voice was still smooth but a bit frayed around the edges with annoyance. It gave Eve the clue that Foxx had been no more forthcoming with his representative than he had with the police. 'The fact that Mr Foxx left the premises for a short time is hardly germane to your investigation. And discovering a loved one's body is a more than reasonable excuse for neglecting to remember a minor detail.'

'One minor detail, maybe. You didn't mention, Mr Foxx,

that you and Mr Fitzhugh had a visitor on the evening of his death.'

'Leanore is hardly a visitor,' Foxx said stiffly. 'She is – was Fitz's partner. I believe they had some business to discuss, which is another reason I went for a walk. I wanted to give them a few moments of privacy to discuss the case.' He took a shallow breath. 'I generally found that more convenient for everyone.'

'I see. So now your statement is that you left the apartment in order to provide your spouse and his partner with privacy. Why didn't you mention Ms Bastwick's visit in your earlier statement?'

'I didn't think of it.'

'You didn't think of it. You stated that you ate dinner, watched a comedy, and went to bed, but you neglected to add in these other events. What other events have you neglected to tell me, Mr Foxx?'

'I have nothing more to say.'

'Why were you angry when you left the building, Mr Foxx? Did it annoy you to have a beautiful woman, a woman with whom Mr. Fitzhugh works closely, drop by your home so late in the evening?'

'Lieutenant, you have no right to imply—'

She barely spared the lawyer a glance. 'I'm not implying, Counselor, I'm asking, in a very straightforward manner, if Mr Foxx was angry and jealous when he stormed out of his building.'

'I did not storm, I walked.' Foxx fisted a hand on the table. 'And I had absolutely no reason to be angry or jealous of Leanore. However often she chose to throw herself at Fitz, he was completely disinterested in her on that level.'

'Ms Bastwick threw herself at Mr Fitzhugh?' Eve lifted her brows. 'That must have ticked you off, Arthur. Knowing that your spouse had no sexual preference between women or men, knowing they were together hours every day during the work week, having her come by, flaunt herself in front of him in your own home. No wonder you were angry. I'd have wanted to deck her.'

'He thought it was amusing,' Foxx blurted out. 'He was actually flattered to have someone so much younger and so attractive playing for him. He laughed when I complained about her.'

'He laughed at you?' Eve knew how to play the game. Sympathy dripped in her voice. 'That must have infuriated you. It did, didn't it? It ate at you, didn't it, Arthur, imagining them together, him touching her, and laughing at you.'

'I could have murdered her.' Foxx exploded with it, batting away his lawyer's restraining hands as fury spurted color into his face. 'She thought she could lure him away from me, make him want her. She didn't give a damn that we were married, that we were committed to each other. All she wanted to do was win. Fucking lawyer.'

'You don't care much for lawyers, do you?'

His breath was shuddering. He caught it, let it shudder out until it was even again. 'No, as a rule, I don't. I didn't think of Fitz as a lawyer. I thought of him as my spouse. And if I'd been disposed to committing murder that night or any other, Lieutenant, I would have murdered Leanore.'

He unfisted his hands, folded them together. 'Now, I have nothing more to say.'

Gauging it to be enough for the time being, Eve terminated the interview, rose. 'We'll be talking again, Mr Foxx.'

'I'd like to know when you're going to release Fitz's body,' he said, getting stiffly to his feet. 'I've decided not to postpone the service today, though it feels unseemly to go on with it with his body still being held.'

'That's the decision of the medical examiner. His tests are still incomplete.'

'Isn't it enough that he's dead?' Foxx's voice trembled. 'Isn't it enough that he killed himself without you dragging

100

it out, pulling out the small and sordid personal details of our lives?'

'No.' She walked to the door, released the code. 'No, it's not.' She hesitated, decided to take a stab in the dark. 'I imagine Mr Fitzhugh was very shocked and very upset by the recent suicide of Senator Pearly.'

Foxx only jerked his head in a formal nod. 'He was shocked, certainly, though they barely knew each other.' Then a muscle jerked in his cheek. 'If you're implying that Fitz took his own life because he was influenced by Pearly, it's ridiculous. They had no more than a slight acquaintance. They rarely communicated.'

'I see. Thank you for your time.' She ushered them out, glanced down the corridor to the adjoining interview room. Leanore should certainly be inside by now, waiting.

Taking her time, Eve strolled down the corridor to a vending unit, contemplated her choices, jingled loose credits in her pocket. She settled on a Chewy Bar and a half tube of Pepsi. The unit delivered the goods, droned out the standard request to recycle, and offered the consumer a mild warning on sugar intake.

'Mind your own business,' Eve suggested. Leaning back against the wall, she lingered over her snack, dumped the trash into the recycle chute, then walked leisurely down the hall.

She'd estimated the twenty-minute wait would steam Leanore. She was right on target.

The woman was pacing like a cat, elegant legs eating up the worn flooring with quick steps. The minute Eve opened the door, she whirled.

'Lieutenant Dallas, my time is extremely valuable, even if yours is not.'

'Depends on how you look at it,' Eve said easily. 'I don't get to log in billable hours at two K a pop.'

Peabody cleared her throat. 'For the record, Lieutenant Eve Dallas has entered Interview Room C to conduct the remainder of the proceedings. The subject has been informed of all rights and has chosen self-representation during this interview. All data has been logged in record.'

'Fine.' Eve sat, indicated the chair across from her. 'Whenever you've finished prowling, Ms Bastwick, we can get started.'

'I was ready to begin this procedure at the appropriate time.' Leanore sat, crossed her satiny legs. 'With you, Lieutenant, not your subordinate.'

'Hear that, Peabody, you're my subordinate.'

'Duly recorded, sir,' Peabody said dryly.

'Though I consider it insulting and unnecessary.' Leanore brushed at the cuffs of her trim black suit. 'I'm attending Fitz's memorial in a few hours.'

'You wouldn't be here, being unnecessarily insulted, if you hadn't lied in your previous statement.'

Leanore's eyes went glacial. 'I assume you can substantiate that accusation, Lieutenant.'

'You stated for the record that you had gone to the deceased's residence last evening on a professional matter. That you remained, discussing a case, for twenty to thirty minutes.'

'More or less,' Leanore said, her voice frosty around the edges.

'Tell me, Ms Bastwick, do you always take a bottle of vintage wine to a business meeting and groom yourself for said meeting in the elevator like a prom queen?'

'There's no law against good grooming, Lieutenant Dallas.' Her gaze flicked dismissively over Eve's untidy hair down to her battered boots. 'You might try it yourself.'

'Aw, now you've hurt my feelings. You polished yourself up, flicked open the top three buttons of your blouse, and brought along a bottle of wine. Sounds like seduction time to me, Leanore.' Eve shifted closer, nearly winked. 'Come on, we're all girls. We know the drill.'

Leanore took her time, studied a minute chip in her manicure. She remained icy. Unlike Foxx, the woman didn't break a sweat. 'I dropped by that evening to consult with Fitz on a professional matter. We had a brief meeting, and I left.'

'You were alone with him during that time.'

'That's right. Arthur got into one of his snits and went out.'

'One of his snits?'

'It was typical of him.' There was a sneer in her voice now, light and disdainful. 'He was outrageously jealous of me, certain I was trying to lure Fitz away from him.'

'And were you?'

A slow, feline smile curved Leanore's lips. 'Really, Lieutenant, if I'd put any effort into it, don't you think I would have succeeded?'

'I'd say you put effort into it. And not succeeding would have really burned you.'

Leanore lifted a shoulder. 'I'll admit I was giving it some consideration. Fitz was wasting himself on Arthur. Fitz and I had a great deal in common, and I found him very attractive. I was very fond of him.'

'Did you act on your attraction and your fondness that evening?'

'You could say I made it clear that I was open to a more intimate relationship with him. He wasn't immediately receptive, but it was only a matter of time.' She moved her shoulders, a quick, confident movement. 'Arthur would have known that.' Her eyes went cold again. 'And that's why I believe he killed Fitz.'

'Quite a piece of work, isn't she?' Eve muttered when the interview was completed. 'Doesn't see anything wrong with trying to lure a man into adultery, break apart a longstanding relationship. More, she's convinced there isn't a man in the world who could resist her.' She sighed heavily. 'Bitch.'

103

'Are you going to charge her?' Peabody wondered.

'For being a bitch?' With a small smile, Eve shook her head. 'I could try to nail her on the false statement, and she and her legal pals would brush it off like lint. Not worth the time. We can't place her at the scene at time of death or hang any kind of motive on her. And I can't see that self-absorbed bimbo sneaking up on a two hundred fifty pound man and slashing his wrists. She wouldn't have wanted to get all that blood on her nifty suit.'

'So you're back to Foxx?'

'He was jealous, he was pissed, he inherits all the toys.' Eve rose, paced to the door and back. 'And we've got nothing.' She pressed her fingers to her eyes. 'I've got to go with what he said when he lost it during interview. He'd have killed Leanore, not Fitzhugh. I'm going to review the data on the two previous suicides.'

'I haven't got much yet,' Peabody began as she followed Eve out of the interview room. 'There wasn't time.'

'There's time now. And Feeney's probably come through. Get me what you've got, then get me more,' Eve demanded and swung into her office. 'Engage,' she ordered the computer as she plopped down in front of it. 'Play new communications.'

Roarke's face swam onto the screen. 'I assume you're out fighting crime. I'm on my way to London, a little glitch that requires personal attention. I don't imagine it will take long. I should be back by eight, which will give us plenty of time to fly out to New Los Angeles for the premiere.'

'Shit, I forgot.'

On screen, his image smiled. 'I'm sure you've conveniently forgotten the engagement, so consider this a gentle reminder. Take care of yourself, Lieutenant.'

Flying to California to spend the evening rubbing elbows with puffed-up video types, eating the glossy little vegetables people out there considered food, tolerating reporters sticking recorders in her face and asking lame questions was not her idea of an entertaining evening.

The second communication was from Commander Whitney, ordering her to prepare a statement for the media on several ongoing cases. *Hot damn*, she thought sourly. *More headlines.*

Then the data from Feeney flashed on screen. Eve rolled her shoulders, hunkered down, and got to work.

At two, she walked into the Village Bistro. Her shirt was sticking to her back as the temperature control on her unit had once again died an unnatural death. The air inside the tony restaurant was ocean breeze cool. Soft, loving zephyrs flitted through, teasing the feathery palms, which grew in huge, white china pots. Glass tables were arranged on two levels, cleverly situated near a small, black water lagoon or in front of a wide-view screen of a white sand beach. Servers wore short uniforms in tropical hues and threaded their way through the tables with offerings of colorful drinks and artistically arranged dishes.

The maître d' was a droid dressed in a flowing white jumpsuit and programmed with a snooty French accent. He took one look at Eve's worn jeans and limp shirt and wrinkled his prominent nose.

'Madam, I am afraid we have no tables available. You would perhaps prefer the delicatessen on the next block north.'

'Yeah, I would.' Because his attitude annoyed her, she stuck her badge in his face. 'But I'm eating here. I don't give a shit if that puts your chips in a twist, pal. Where's Dr Mira's table?'

'Put that away,' he hissed, looking everywhere at once and fluttering his hands. 'Do you wish my customers to lose their appetites?'

'They'll really lose them if I take my weapon out, which is what I'll do if you don't show me Dr Mira's table and see that I've got a glass of iced fizzy water in the next twenty seconds. Got that program?'

His lips clamped together and he nodded. Stiff-backed, he led the way up a swing of faux stone steps to the second level, and then onto an alcove fashioned to resemble an ocean terrace.

'Eve.' Mira rose immediately from her pretty table and took both of Eve's hands. 'You look wonderful.' To Eve's faint surprise, Mira kissed her cheek. 'Rested. Happy.'

'I guess I am.' After a brief hesitation, Eve leaned forward and touched her lips to Mira's cheek in turn.

The droid had already snapped to a server. 'Dr Mira's companion wishes a fizzy water.'

'Iced,' Eve added, curling her lip at the maître d'.

'Thank you, Armand.' Mira's soft blue eyes twinkled. 'We'll order shortly.'

Eve took another quick scan of the restaurant, the diners in their summer pastels and pricey cottons. She shifted on her padded chair. 'We could have met in your office.'

'I wanted to take you to lunch. This is one of my favorite spots.'

'The droid's an asshole.'

'Well, perhaps Armand is a bit overprogrammed, but the food is wonderful. You should try the Clams Maurice. You won't regret it.' She settled back when Eve's water was served. 'Tell me, how was your honeymoon?'

Eve gulped down half the water and felt human again. 'Tell me how long I can expect people to ask me that question?'

Mira laughed. She was a pretty woman with soft sable hair swept back from a quietly attractive face. She wore one of her habitually elegant suits, this one in pale yellow. She appeared polished and tidy. She was one of the leading behavioral psychiatrists in the country, and was often consulted by the police about the most vicious crimes.

Though Eve was unaware of it, Mira's feelings toward her were strong and deeply maternal.

'It embarrasses you.'

'Well, you know. Honeymoon. Sex. Personal.' Eve rolled her eyes. 'Stupid. I guess I'm just not used it. To being married. To Roarke. To the whole business.'

'You love each other and make each other happy. There's no need to get used to it, only to enjoy it. You're sleeping well?'

'Mostly.' And because Mira knew her deepest and darkest secrets, Eve dropped her guard. 'I still have nightmares, but not as often. The memories come and go. None of it's as bad now that I've dealt with it.'

'Have you dealt with it?'

'My father raped me, abused me, beat me,' Eve said flatly. 'I killed him. I was eight years old. I survived. Whoever I was before I was found in that alley doesn't matter now. I'm Eve Dallas. I'm a good cop. I've made myself.'

'Good.' *There would be more*, Mira thought. Traumas such as the one Eve had lived through cast echoes that never completely faded. 'You still put the cop first.'

'I am a cop first.'

'Yes.' Mira smiled a little. 'I suppose you always will be. Why don't we order, then you can tell me why you called.'

Chapter Eight

Eve chose Mira's recommendation of clams, then treated herself to some of the real yeast bread set in a silver basket on the table. As she ate, she gave Mira a profile of Fitzhugh and the details of his death.

'You'd like me to tell you if he was capable of taking his own life. Disposed to it, emotionally, psychologically.'

Eve cocked a brow. 'That's the plan.'

'Unfortunately, I can't do that. I can tell you that everyone is capable of it, given the right circumstances and emotional state.'

'I don't believe that,' Eve said so firmly, so decisively, that Mira smiled.

'You're a strong woman, Eve. Now. You've made yourself strong, rational, tough-minded. You're a survivor. But you remember despair. Helplessness. Hopelessness.'

Eve did; too well, too clearly. She shifted in her chair. 'Fitzhugh wasn't a helpless man.'

'The surface can hide a great deal of turmoil.' Dr Mira held up a hand before Eve could interrupt again. 'But I agree with you. Given your profile of him, his background, his lifestyle, I wouldn't tag him as a likely candidate for suicide – certainly not one of such an abrupt and impulsive nature.'

'It was abrupt,' Eve agreed. 'I dealt with him in court right before this happened. He was as smug and arrogant and full of his own sense of importance as ever.'

'I'm sure that's true. I can only say that some of us – many of us – confronted with some crisis, some personal upheaval of the heart or mind, choose to end it rather than live through it or change it. You and I can't know what Fitzhugh might have found himself confronted with on the night of his death.'

'That isn't a hell of a lot of help,' Eve muttered. 'Okay, let me give you two more.' Briskly, with a cop's dispassion, she related the other suicides. 'Pattern?'

'What did they have in common?' Mira tossed back. 'The lawyer, the politician, and the tech.'

'A blip in the brain. Maybe.' Tapping her fingers on the cloth, Eve frowned. 'I've got some chains to pull to get all the data, but it could be the motive. The reason behind it all might be physiological rather than psychological. If there's a connection, I've got to find it.'

'You're veering out of my field, but if you find data linking the three cases, I'd be happy to do a workup.'

Eve smiled. 'I was counting on it. I don't have a lot of time. The Fitzhugh case can't stay a priority for much longer. If I can't nail something down soon and use it to convince the commander to keep the file open, I'll have to move on. But for now—'

'Eve?' Reeanna slipped up to the table, looking stunning in an ankle-skimming robe of bleeding rainbow colors. 'Well, how nice. I was lunching with an associate and thought I recognized you.'

'Reeanna.' Eve worked up a smile. She didn't mind looking like a street hawker next to the glamorous redhead, but she did mind having her consult lunch interrupted. 'Dr Mira, Reeanna Ott.'

'Dr Ott.' Gracious, Mira offered a hand. 'I've heard of your work and admired it.'

'Thank you, and I'll say the same. It's an honor to meet one of the top psychiatrists in the country. I've scanned a number of your papers and found them fascinating.'

'You flatter me. Won't you sit down, join us for some dessert?'

'I'd love to.' Reeanna flicked a questioning glance at Eve. 'If I'm not interrupting official business.'

'We seem to be finished with that part of the program.' Eve looked up at the waiter summoned by a discreet flick of Mira's finger. 'Just coffee. House brand. Black.'

'I'll have the same,' Mira said. 'And a dish of the Blueberry Trifle. I'm weak.'

'So am I.' Reeanna beamed at the waiter as though he would personally prepare her selection. 'A double latte, and a slice of Chocolate Sin. I'm so tired of processed food,' she confided to Mira. 'I intend to gorge myself while I'm in New York.'

'And how long will you be in town?'

'It depends a great deal on Roarke' – she smiled at Eve – 'and how long he finds it useful to have me here. I have a feeling he'll be shipping both William and me off to Olympus within a few weeks.'

'The Olympus Resort's quite an undertaking,' Mira commented. 'All the blips I've seen on the news and entertainment channels have been fascinating.'

'He'd like to have it up and fully operational by next spring.' Reeanna ran her hand up and down the trio of gold links she wore around her neck. 'We'll see. Roarke usually gets what he wants. Wouldn't you agree, Eve?'

'He didn't get where he is by taking no for an answer.'

'No, indeed. You were just on the resort. Did he give you a tour of the Autotronics Arcade?'

'Briefly.' Eve's lips quirked a little. 'We had . . . a lot of ground to cover in a short time.'

Reeanna's smile was slow and sly. 'I imagine you did. But I hope you tried a few of the programs that are in place. William's so proud of those games. And you did mention you'd seen the hologram room in the Presidential Suite of the hotel.'

'I did. Made use of it several times. Very impressive.'

'Most of that's William's doing – the design – but I will take partial credit. We plan to utilize that new system to enhance the treatment of addicts and certain psychoses.' She shifted as their coffee and dessert was served. 'That might be of interest to you, Dr Mira.'

'It certainly would. It sounds fascinating.'

'It is Wickedly expensive right now, but we hope to refine and bring the cost down. But for Olympus, Roarke wanted the best – and he's getting it. Such as the Lisa droid.'

'Yeah.' Eve remembered the stunning female droid with the sultry voice. 'I've seen her.'

'She'll be in PR and customer service. A very superior model that took months to perfect. Her intelligence chips are unmatched by anything on the market. She'll have decision making and personality capabilities well beyond the current available units. William and I—' She broke off, chuckled at herself. 'Listen to me. I just can't get away from work.'

'It's fascinating.' Mira dipped delicately into her trifle. 'Your study of brain patterns and their genetic thrust on personality, and their application to electronics is compelling, even to a dug-in-at-the-roots psychiatrist such as myself.' She hesitated, glanced at Eve. 'As a matter of fact, your expertise might lend a new angle on a particular case Eve and I were discussing.'

'Oh?' Reeanna forked up some chocolate and all but hummed over it.

'Hypothetical.' Mira spread her hands, well aware of the official ban of layman consults.

'Naturally.'

Eve drummed her fingers on the table again. She preferred Mira's take, but weighing the options, decided to expand.

'Apparent self-termination. No known motive, no known predisposition, no chemical inducement, no family history. Behavioral patterns up to point of termination normal. No substantiated signs of depression or personality fluctuations. Subject is a sixty-two-year-old male, professional, high-end education, successful, financially solvent, bisexual, with long-term same-sex marriage.'

'Physical disabilities?'

'None. Clean health card.'

Reeanna's eyes narrowed in concentration, either over the profile or the dessert she was slowly spooning into her mouth. 'Any psychological defects, treatment?'

'No.'

'Interesting. I'd love to see the brain wave pattern. Available?'

'Currently classified.'

'Hmm.' Reeanna sipped her latte contemplatively. 'Without any known physical or psychiatric abnormalities, no chemical addictions or usage, I'd lean toward a brain blip. Possible tumor. Yet I assume none showed up in autopsy?'

Eve thought of the pinprick, but shook her head. 'Not a tumor, no.'

'There are cases of predisposition that slide through genetic scanning and evaluation. The brain is a complicated organ and still baffles even the most elaborate technology. If I could see his family history . . . Well, to take a wild guess, I'd say your man had a genetic time bomb that went undetected through normal analysis. He'd reached the point in his life where the fuse ran short.'

Eve cocked a brow. 'So he just blew?'

'In a manner of speaking.' Reeanna leaned forward. 'We're all coded in, Eve, in the womb. What we are, who we are. Not just the color of our eyes, our build, our skin tones, but our personalities, our tastes, our intellect, and our emotional scale. The genetic code is stamped on us at the moment of conception. It can be altered to a certain extent, but the basis of what we are remains. Nothing can change it.'

'We are what we're born?' Eve thought of a filthy room, a

blinking red light, and a young girl curled into a corner with a bloody knife.

'Precisely.' Reeanna's smile beamed out.

'You don't take into account environment, free will, the basic human drive to better oneself?' Mira objected. 'To consider us merely physical creatures without heart, soul, and a range of choices to be made over a lifetime lowers us to the level of animals.'

'And so we are,' Reeanna said with a sweep of her fork. 'I understand your viewpoint as a therapist, Dr Mira, but mine, as a physiologist, runs down a different lane, so to speak. The decisions we make throughout our life, what we do, how we live, and what we become were printed on our brains while we swam in the womb. Your subject, Eve, was fated to take his life at that time, in that place, and in the manner he chose. Circumstances might have altered it, but the results would have been the same, eventually. It was, in essence, his destiny.'

Destiny? Eve thought. Had it been hers to be raped and abused by her own father? To become less than human, to fight her way through that abyss?

Mira shook her head slowly. 'I can't agree. A child born in poverty on the edge of Budapest, taken from the mother at birth and raised in privilege, with love and care in Paris, would reflect that upbringing, that education. The emotional nest,' she insisted, 'and the basic human drive to better oneself can't be discounted.'

'I agree, to a point,' Reeanna qualified. 'But the stamp of the genetic code – that which predisposes us to achievement, failure, good or evil, if you will – overrides all else. Even with the most loving and nurturing of backgrounds, monsters breed; and in the toilets of the universe, goodness, even greatness survives. We are what we are – the rest is window dressing.'

'If I subscribe to your theory,' Eve said slowly, 'the subject in question was fated to take his life. No circumstances, no twists or turns of environment would have prevented it.'

'Precisely. The predisposition was there, lurking. Likely an event set it off, but it may have been a minor thing, something easily passed off in another brain pattern. Research still under way at the Bowers Institute has compiled strong evidence of genetic brain patterns and their unassailable influence on behavior. I can get you discs on the subject, if you like.'

'I'll leave the head studies to you and Dr Mira.' Eve shoved her coffee aside. 'I've got to get back to Cop Central. I appreciate the time, Dr Mira,' she said as she rose. 'And the theories, Reeanna.'

'I'd love to discuss them further. Any time.' Reeanna lifted a hand and shook Eve's warmly. 'Do give my best to Roarke.'

'I will.' Eve shifted slightly on her feet when Mira rose to kiss her cheek. 'I'll be in touch.'

'I hope you will, and not just when you've a case to discuss. Tell Mavis hello for me when you see her.'

'Sure.' Hitching her bag on her shoulder, Eve swung her way out, pausing briefly to sneer at the maître d'.

'A fascinating woman.' Reeanna slid her tongue in one long, slow lick over the back of her spoon. 'Controlled, a little angry underneath, straight focused, and unused and vaguely uncomfortable with casual displays of affection.' She laughed lightly at Mira's lifted brow. 'Sorry, professional pitfall. It drives William mad. I didn't mean any offense.'

'I'm sure you didn't.' Mira's lips curved, and her eyes warmed with understanding. 'I often find myself doing the same. And you're right, Eve is a very fascinating woman. Quite self-made, which, I'm afraid, might unbalance your genetic printing theory.'

'Really?' Obviously intrigued, Reeanna leaned forward. 'You know her well?'

'As well as possible. Eve is a . . . contained individual.'

'You're very fond of her,' Reeanna commented with a nod. 'I hope you won't take it the wrong way if I say she wasn't at all what I expected when I learned Roarke was to marry. That

114

he was to marry at all was a surprise, but I imagined his spouse as a woman of polish and sophistication. A homicide detective who wears her shoulder harness as another woman might an heirloom necklace wasn't my conception of Roarke's choice. Yet they look right together, suited. One might even say,' she added with a smile, 'destined.'

'That I can agree with.'

'Now, tell me, Dr Mira, what is your opinion of DNA harvesting?'

'Oh, well now . . .' Happily, Mira settled down for a lively busman's holiday.

At her desk unit, Eve juggled the data she'd compiled on Fitzhugh, Mathias, and Pearly. She could find no link, no common ground. The only real correlation between the three was the fact that none of them had exhibited any suicidal tendencies before the fact.

'Probability the subject cases are related?' Eve demanded.

Working Probability five point two percent

'In other words, zip.' Eve blew out a breath, scowling automatically when an airbus rumbled by, rattling her stingy window. 'Probability of homicide in the matter of Fitzhugh using currently known data.'

With currently known data, probability of homicide is eight point three percent.

'Give it up, Dallas,' she told herself in a mutter. 'Let it go.'

Deliberately, she swiveled in her chair, watching the air traffic clog the sky outside her window. Predestination. Fate. Genetic imprint. If she were to believe in any of that, what was the point of her job – or her life, for that matter? If there was no choice, no changing, why struggle to save lives or stand for the dead when the struggle failed?

If it was all physiologically coded, had she simply followed the pattern by coming to New York, fighting her way out of the dark to make something decent out of herself? And had it been a smear on that code that had blocked out those early years of her life, that continued to shadow bits and pieces of it even now?

And could that code kick in, at any given moment, and make her a reflection of the monster who had been her father?

She knew nothing of her other blood kin. Her mother was a blank. If she had siblings, aunts, uncles, or grandparents, they were all lost in that dark void in her memory. She had no one to base her genetic code on but the man who had beaten and raped her throughout childhood until in terror and pain she had struck back.

And killed.

Blood on her hands at eight years of age. Is that why she'd become a cop? Was she constantly trying to wash away that blood with rules and law and what some still called justice?

'Sir? Dallas?' Peabody laid a hand on Eve's shoulder and jumped when Eve jolted. 'Sorry. Are you all right?'

'No.' Eve pressed her fingers to her eyes. The discussion over dessert had troubled her more than she'd realized. 'Just a headache.'

'I've got some departmental-issue painkillers.'

'No.' Eve was afraid of drugs, even officially sanctioned doses. 'It'll back off. I'm running out of ideas on the Fitzhugh case. Feeney fed me all known data on the kid on Olympus. I can't find any correlation between him and Fitzhugh or the senator. I've got nothing but piddly shit to hang on Leanore and Arthur. I can request truth detection, but I won't get it. I'm not going to be able to keep it open more than another twenty-four hours.'

116

'You still think they're connected?'

'I want them to be connected, and that's a different thing. I haven't exactly given you an impressive lift on with your first assignment as my permanent aide.'

'Being your permanent aide is the best thing that ever happened to me.' Peabody flushed a little. 'I'd be grateful if we got stuck shoveling through inactives for the next six months. You'd still be training me.'

Eve leaned back in her chair. 'You're easily satisfied, Peabody.'

Peabody shifted her gaze until her eyes met Eve's. 'No, sir, I'm not. When I don't get the best, I get real cranky.'

Eve laughed, dragged a hand through her hair. 'You sucking up, Officer?'

'No, sir. If I was sucking up, I'd make some personal observation, such as marriage obviously agrees with you, Lieutenant. You've never looked lovelier.' Peabody smiled a little when Eve snorted. 'That's how you'd know I was sucking up.'

'So noted.' Eve considered a moment, then cocked her head. 'Didn't you tell me your family are Free-Agers?'

Peabody didn't roll her eyes, but she wanted to. 'Yes, sir.'

'Cops don't usually spring from Free-Agers. Artists, farmers, the occasional scientist, lots of craft workers.'

'I didn't like weaving mats.'

'Can you?'

'If held at laser point.'

'So, what? Your family pissed you off and you decided to break the mold, go into a field dramatically removed from pacifism?'

'No, sir.' Puzzled at the line of questioning, Peabody shrugged. 'My family's great. We're still pretty tight. They're not going to understand what I do or want to do, but they never tried to block me. I just wanted to be a cop, the same way my brother wanted to be a carpenter and my sister a farmer. One of the strongest tenets of Free-Ageism is self-expression.'

'But you don't fit the genetic code,' Eve muttered and drummed her fingers on her desk. 'You don't fit. Heredity and environment, gene patterns – they all should have influenced you differently.'

'The bad guys wished I had been,' Peabody said soberly. 'But I'm here, keeping our city safe.'

'If you get an urge to weave a mat—'

'You'll be the first to know.'

Eve's unit beeped twice, signaling incoming data. 'Additional autopsy report on the kid.' Eve gestured for Peabody to come closer. 'List any abnormal brain pattern,' she ordered.

Microscopic abnormality, right cerebral hemisphere, frontal lobe, left quadrant. Unexplained. Further research and testing under way.

'Well, well, I think we just caught a break. Display visual of frontal lobe and abnormality.' The cross section of the brain popped on screen. 'There.' A quick surge of excitement churned in her belly as Eve tapped the screen. 'That shadow – pinprick. See it?'

'Barely.' Peabody leaned closer until she was all but cheek to cheek with Eve. 'Looks like a flaw on the display.'

'No, a flaw in the brain. Increase quadrant six, twenty percent.'

The picture shifted, and the section with the shadow filled the screen. 'More of a burn than a hole, isn't it?' Eve said half to herself. 'Hardly there, but what kind of damage, what kind of influence would it have on behavior, personality, decision making?'

'I pretty well dumped my required Abnormal Physiology at the Academy.' Peabody moved her sturdy shoulders. 'I did better in Psych, better yet in Tactics. This is over my head.'

118

'Mine, too,' Eve admitted. 'But it's a link, our first one. Computer, cross section of brain abnormality, Fitzhugh, file one two eight seven one. Split screen with current display.'

The screen jittered, went to fuzzy gray. Eve swore, smacked it with the heel of her hand, and bumped out a shaky image blurred across the center.

'Son of a bitch. Son of a bitch. This cheap shit we have to use around here. It's a wonder we can close a case on jaywalking. Download all data, you bastard, on disc.'

'Maybe if you sent this unit into Maintenance,' Peabody suggested and received a snarl.

'It was supposed to be overhauled while I was away. The fuckers in Maintenance have their fingers up their butts. I'm going to run this through one of Roarke's units.' She caught Peabody's lifted brow and tapped her foot as she waited for the wheezy machine to download. 'You got a problem with that, Officer?'

'No, sir.' Peabody tucked her tongue in her cheek and decided against mentioning the series of codes Eve was about to break. 'No problem here.'

'Fine. Get to work on the red tape and get me the brain scan of the senator for comparison.'

Peabody's smug little smile fell away. 'You want me to bump heads with East Washington?'

'Your head's hard enough to handle it.' Eve ejected the disc and pocketed it. 'Call me when you get it. The minute you get it.'

'Yes, sir. If we get a link there, we're going to need an expert analyst.'

'Yeah.' Eve thought of Reeanna. 'I might just have one. Get moving, Peabody.'

'Moving, Lieutenant.'

Chapter Nine

Eve wasn't one for breaking rules, yet she found herself standing outside the locked door of Roarke's private room. It was disconcerting to realize that after a decade of going by the book, she could find it so easy to circumvent procedure.

Do the ends justify the means? she wondered. *And are the means really so out of line?* Maybe the equipment in the room beyond was unregistered and undetectable to Compuguard and therefore illegal, but it was also top of the line. The pathetic electronics budgeted to the Police and Security Department had been antiquated nearly before it was installed, and Homicide's slice of the budget pie was stingy and stale.

She tapped her fingers on her pocket where the disc rested and shifted her feet. *The hell with it,* she decided. She could be a law-abiding cop and walk away or she could be a smart one.

She placed her hand on the security screen. 'Dallas, Lieutenant Eve.'

The locks disengaged with a quiet snick and opened into Roarke's huge data center. The long curve of windows, which were shielded against sun and flybys, kept the room in shadows. She ordered lights, secured the door, and walked over to face the wide, U-shaped console.

Roarke had programmed her palm and voice print into the system months before, but she'd never used the equipment alone. Even now that they were married, she felt like an intruder.

She made herself sit, snugged the chair into the console. 'Unit one, engage.' She heard the silky hum of high-level equipment responding and nearly sighed. Her disc slid in smoothly, and within seconds had been decoded and read by the civilian unit. 'And so much for our elaborate security at NYPSD,' she muttered. 'Wall screen on full. Display data, Fitzhugh File H-one two eight seven one. Split screen with Mathias File S-three oh nine one two.'

Data flowed like water onto the huge wall screen facing the console. In her admiration, Eve forgot to feel guilty. She leaned forward, scanning birth dates, credit ratings, purchasing habits, political affiliations.

'Strangers,' she said to herself. 'You couldn't have had less in common.' Then her lips pursed as she noted correlations on a section of purchasing habits. 'Well, you both liked games. Lots of on-line time, lots of entertainment and interactive programs.' Then she sighed. 'Along with about seventy percent of the population. Computer, split screen display, brain scan both loaded files.'

With an almost seamless segue, Eve was studying the images. 'Increase and highlight unexplained abnormalities.'

The same, she mused, eyes narrowed. Here the two men were the same, like brothers, twins in the womb. The burn shadow was precisely the same size and shape, in precisely the same location.

'Computer, analyze abnormality and identify.'

Working ... Incomplete data ... Searching medical files. Please wait for analysis.

'That's what they all say.' She pushed away from the console to pace while the computer juggled its brain. When the door opened, she spun around on her heel and very nearly flushed when Roarke walked in.

'Hello, Lieutenant.'

'Hi.' She dipped her hands in her pockets. 'I – ah – had some trouble with my unit at Cop Central. I needed this analysis, so I . . . I can put a hold on it if you need the room.'

'No need for that.' Her obvious discomfort amused him. He strolled to her, leaned down, and kissed her lightly. 'And no need for you to fumble through an explanation as to why you're using the equipment. Digging for secrets?'

'No. Not the way you mean.' The fact that he was grinning at her increased the embarrassment level. 'I needed something a little more competent than the tin cans we have at Cop Central, and I figured you'd be gone for a couple more hours.'

'I got an early transport back. Need some help with this?'

'No. I don't know. Maybe. Stop grinning at me.'

'Was I?' His grin only widened as he slid his arms around her and tucked his hands in the back pockets of her jeans. 'How was your lunch with Dr Mira?'

She scowled. 'Do you know everything?'

'I try. Actually, I had a quick meeting with William, and he mentioned that Reeanna had run into you and the doctor. Business or pleasure?'

'Both, I guess.' Her brows lifted as his hands got busy on her butt. 'I'm on duty, Roarke. Your hands are currently rubbing the ass of a working cop.'

'That only makes it more exciting.' He shifted to nibble her neck. 'Want to break a few laws?'

'I already am.' But she turned her head instinctively to give him better access.

'Then what are a few more?' he murmured and slid his hand out of her pocket and around her body to cup her breast. 'I love the feel of you.' His mouth was trailing along her jawline toward her mouth when the computer beeped.

Analysis complete. Display or audio?

'Display,' Eve ordered and wiggled free.

'Damn,' Roarke sighed. 'I was so close.'

'What the hell is this?' Hands fisted on her hips, Eve scanned the display on the view screen. 'It's gibberish. Fucking gibberish.'

Resigned, Roarke sat on the edge of the console and studied the display himself. 'It's technical; medical terms, primarily. A bit out of my realm. A burn, electronic in origin. Does that make sense?'

'I don't know.' Thoughtfully, she tugged on her ear. 'Does it make sense for a couple of dead guys to have an electric burn hole in the frontal lobe of their brains?'

'Some fumbling with the equipment during autopsy?' Roarke suggested.

'No.' Slowly, she shook her head. 'Not on two of them, examined by different MEs in different morgues. And they're not surface flaws. They're inside the brain. Microscopic pin-pricks.'

'What's the relationship between the two men?'

'None. Absolutely none.' She hesitated, then shrugged. He was already involved in a peripheral manner, why not drag him into the center? 'One of the men is yours,' she told him. 'The autotronics engineer from the Olympus Resort.'

'Mathias?' Roarke pushed off the console, his half-amused, half-intrigued expression going dark. 'Why are you investigating a suicide on Olympus?'

'I'm not officially. It's a hunch, that's all. The other brain your fancy equipment's analyzing is Fitzhugh's. And if Peabody can untangle the red tape, I'll plug in Senator Pearly's.'

'And you expect to find this microscopic burn in the senator's brain?'

'You're a quick study, Roarke. I've always admired that about you.'

'Why?'

123

'Because it's annoying to have to explain everything step by step.'

His eyes narrowed. 'Eve.'

'All right.' She held up her hands, let them fall. 'Fitzhugh just didn't strike me as the type to do himself. I couldn't close the case until I'd explored all the options. I've been running out of options. I might have put it to bed anyway, but I kept thinking about that kid hanging himself.'

She began to pace restlessly. 'No predisposition there, either. No obvious motive, no known enemies. He just has himself a snack and makes a noose. Then I heard about the senator. That makes three suicides without logical explanations. Now, for people like Fitzhugh and the senator, with their kind of financial base, there's counseling at the snap of a finger. Or in cases of terminal illness – physical or emotional – voluntary self-termination facilities. But they took themselves out in bloody and painful ways. Doesn't fit.'

Roarke nodded. 'Go on.'

'And the ME on Fitzhugh came up with this unexplained abnormality. I wanted to see if, on the off chance, the kid had anything like it.' She gestured to the screen. 'He does. Now I need to know what put it there.'

Roarke shifted his eyes back to the screen. 'Genetic flaw?'

'Possibly, but the computer says unlikely. At least it's never come across anything like it before – through heredity, mutation, or outside causes.' She moved behind the console, scrolled the screen. 'See there, in the projection of possible mental affects? Behavioral alterations. Pattern unknown. A lot of help that is.'

She rubbed her eyes, thought it through. 'But that says to me that the subject could, and likely would, behave out of pattern. Suicide would be out of pattern for these two men.'

'True enough,' Roarke agreed. Leaning back against the console, he crossed his legs at the ankles. 'But so would dancing naked in church or kicking elderly matrons off a skywalk. Why did they both choose self-termination?'

'That's the question, isn't it? But this gives me enough, once I figure out how to spin it to Whitney, to keep both cases open. Download data to disc, print hard copy,' she ordered, then turned to Roarke. 'I've got a few minutes now.'

His brow quirked, a habitual gesture she secretly adored. 'Do you?'

'Which laws did you have in mind to break?'

'Several, actually.' He glanced at his watch as she stepped forward to unbutton his elegant linen shirt. 'We have a premiere in California tonight.'

Her fingers stopped, her face fell. 'Tonight.'

'But I think we have time for a few misdemeanors first.' With a laugh, he scooped her off her feet and laid her back on the console.

Eve was tugging on a floor-length, siren-red sheath and complaining bitterly about the impossibility of wearing so much as a scrap of underwear under the clinging material when her communicator beeped. Naked to the waist, with the flimsy bodice hanging to her knees, she pounced.

'Peabody?'

'Sir.' Several expressions passed over Peabody's face before it went carefully blank. 'That's a lovely dress, Lieutenant. Are you premiering a new style?'

Baffled, Eve looked down, then rolled her eyes. 'Shit. You've seen my tits before.' But she set the communicator down and struggled the bodice into place.

'And may I say, sir, they're quite lovely.'

'Sucking up, Peabody?'

'You bet.'

Eve stifled a chuckle and sat on the edge of the sofa in the dressing room. 'Report?'

'Yes, sir. I . . . ah . . .'

Noting that Peabody's eyes had shifted and glazed over, Eve glanced over her shoulder. Roarke had just walked into the room, damp from his shower, tiny beads of water glistening on his bare chest, a white towel barely hitched at his hips.

'Stay out of view, will you, Roarke, before my aide goes brain dead.'

He looked toward the communicator screen, grinned. 'Peabody, hello.'

'Hi.' Even over the unit, her swallow was audible. 'Nice to see you – I mean, how are you?'

'Very well, and you?'

'What?'

'Roarke.' Eve heaved a sigh. 'Give Peabody a break, will you, or I'll have to block video.'

'You don't have to do that, Lieutenant.' Voice rusty, Peabody deflated as Roarke slipped out of view. 'Jesus,' she said under her breath and grinned foolishly at Eve.

'Settle your hormones, Peabody, and report.'

'Settling, sir.' She cleared her throat. 'I've untangled most of the bureaucratic tape, Lieutenant. Just a couple more snags. At this juncture, we should have the requested data by oh nine hundred. But we have to go to East Washington to view it.'

'I was afraid of that. All right, Peabody. We'll catch the shuttle at oh eight hundred.'

'Don't be foolish,' Roarke said from behind her while he critically studied the lines of the dinner jacket he held. 'Take my transport.'

'It's police business.'

'No reason to squeeze yourselves into a tuna can. Traveling in comfort doesn't make it less official. In any case, I've some business I can see to in East Washington myself. I'll take you.' He leaned over Eve's shoulder, smiled at Peabody. 'I'll have a car sent for you. Seventy forty-five? Is that convenient?'

'Sure.' She wasn't even disappointed that he was now wearing a shirt. 'Great.'

126

'Listen, Roarke—'

'Sorry, Peabody.' He cut Eve off smoothly. 'We're running a bit late here. See you in the morning.' Reaching over, he manually disengaged the communicator.

'You know, it really pisses me off when you do that kind of thing.'

'I know,' Roarke said equably. 'That's why it's irresistible.'

'I've spent half my life on one sort of transport or another since I met you,' Eve grumbled as she settled into her seat in Roarke's private Jet Star.

'Still cranky,' he observed, and signaled the flight attendant. 'My wife needs another dose of coffee, and I'll join her.'

'Right away, sir.' She slipped into the galley with silent efficiency.

'You really get a bang out of saying that, don't you? My wife.'

'I do, yes.' Roarke tipped her face up with a fingertip and kissed the shallow dent in her chin. 'You didn't sleep enough,' he murmured, rubbing his thumb under her eye. 'You so rarely turn off that busy brain of yours.' He flicked a glance up at the flight attendant as she set steaming coffee on the table in front of them. 'Thank you, Karen. We'll take off as soon as Officer Peabody arrives.'

'I'll inform the pilot, sir. Enjoy your flight.'

'You don't really have to go to East Washington, do you?'

'I could have handled it from New York.' He shrugged, lifted his coffee. 'Personal attention always has more impact. And I have the added benefit of watching you work.'

'I don't want you involved in this.'

'You never do.' He lifted her cup, handed it to her with an easy smile. 'However, Lieutenant, I'm involved with you, and therefore you can't shut me out.'

'You mean you won't be shut out.'

'Precisely. Ah, here's the redoubtable Peabody now.'

She came aboard pressed and polished, but spoiling the effect with her jaw hanging open as she swiveled her head right and left in an attempt to see everything at once.

The cabin was as plush and sumptuous as a five-star hotel, with deep, cushy seats and gleaming tables, the glint of crystal holding flowers so fresh they gleamed with dew.

'Stop gaping, Peabody, you look like a trout.'

'Nearly finished, Lieutenant.'

'Don't mind her, Peabody, she woke up surly.' Roarke rose, disconcerting Peabody until she realized he was offering her a seat. 'Would you care for coffee?'

'Well, ah, sure. Thanks.'

'I'll fetch it and leave you two to discuss your work.'

'Dallas, this is . . . ultra.'

'It's just Roarke,' Eve muttered into her coffee.

'Yeah, like I said. Ultra.'

Eve glanced up as he came in with more coffee. *Dark and gorgeous and just a bit wicked*, she thought. *Yeah*, she supposed, *ultra was the word all right*. 'Well, strap in, Peabody, and enjoy the ride.'

The takeoff was smooth, and the trip was short, providing Peabody with just enough time to fill Eve in on the details. They were to report to the office of the Chief of Security for Government Employees. All data would be viewed in house, and nothing could be transferred or transported.

'Fucking politics,' Eve complained as they jumped into a cab. 'Who are they protecting, for Christ's sake? The man's dead.'

'Standard CYA procedure. And there are always plenty of asses to cover in East Washington.'

'Fat asses.' Eve eyed Peabody consideringly. 'Been to East Washington before?'

'Once, when I was a kid.' Peabody moved her shoulders.

'With my family. The Free-Agers staged a silent protest against artificial insemination of cattle.'

Eve didn't bother to muffle a snort. 'You're full of surprises, Peabody. Since you haven't been here in a while, you may want to take in the scenery. Check out the memorials.' She gestured as they whizzed by the Lincoln Memorial and its throng of tourists and street hawkers.

'I've seen plenty of videos,' Peabody began, but Eve lifted her brows.

'Check out the scenery, Peabody. Consider it an order.'

'Sir.' With what on another face might have been considered a pout, Peabody turned her head.

Eve nipped a card recorder out of her bag and tucked it under her shirt. She doubted security was so tight it would involve X rays or a strip search And if it did, she'd simply claim she always carried her spare on her person. Eve flipped a glance at the driver, but the droid had her eyes bland and on the road.

'Not a bad town for sightseeing,' Eve commented as they veered onto the vehicle bypass of the White House where the old mansion could just be seen through reinforced gates and steel bunkers.

Peabody swivcled her head, looked dead into Eve's eyes. 'You can trust me, Lieutenant. I thought you knew that.'

'It's not a matter of trust.' Because she heard the hurt in Peabody's voice, Eve spoke gently. 'It's a matter of not being willing to put anyone's ass but my own in a sling.'

'If we're partners—'

'We're not partners.' Eve inclined her head, and there was authority in her tone now. 'Yet. You're my aide, and you're in training. As your superior, I decide how far your butt sticks out in the wind.'

'Yes, sir,' Peabody said stiffly and made Eve sigh.

'Don't get your briefs in a twist, Peabody. There'll come a time when I'll let you take your lumps with the commander. And believe me, he's got a hell of a punch.'

The cab pulled over to the curb outside the gates of the Security Building. Eve shoved credits through the safety slot, climbed out, and approached the view screen. She placed her palm on the plate, slipped her badge into the identification slot, and waited for Peabody to mirror the procedure.

'Dallas, Lieutenant Eve, and aide, appointment with Chief Dudley.'

'One moment for verification. Authorization confirmed. Please place all weapons in holding bin. Warning. It is a federal offense to bring any weapons into the facility. Any individual entering with a weapon in his or her possession will be detained.'

Eve slipped her police issue out of her holster, then, with some regret, bent down to take her clinch piece out of her boot. At Peabody's bland look, she shrugged. 'I started carrying a spare after my experience with Casto. A clinch piece might have saved me some grief.'

'Yeah.' Peabody dumped her standard-issue stunner in the bin. 'I wish you'd blasted the son of a bitch.'

Eve opened her mouth, closed it again. Peabody had been careful not to mention the Illegals detective who'd charmed her, bedded her, and used her while he'd killed for profit.

'Look,' Eve said after a moment. 'I'm sorry about the way things went down there. If you want to vent about it sometime—'

'I'm not much of a venter.' Peabody cleared her throat. 'Thanks, anyway.'

'Well, he'll be stretching those long legs of his in lockup into the next century.'

Peabody's mouth curved grimly. 'There is that.'

'You are cleared to enter. Please step through the gate, proceed to the autotram on the green line for transport to second level clearing.'

'Jesus, you'd think we were going to see the president instead of some suit-and-tie cop.' Eve walked through the

130

gate that efficiently shut and bolted behind them. She and Peabody settled down on the stiff plastic seats of the tram. With a mechanical hum, it sped them through bunkers and into a steel-walled passageway that angled down until they were ordered to step out into an anteroom filled with harsh, artificial light and walls of view screens.

'Lieutenant Dallas, Officer.' The man who approached wore the smoke gray uniform of Government Security with the rank of corporal. His blond hair was buzz cut so close his pale white scalp peeked through. His thin face was equally pale, the skin tone of a man who spent his time indoors and underground.

His uniform shirt bulged under hefty mountains of biceps.

'Leave your bags with me, please. No electronic or recording devices are permitted beyond this point. You are under surveillance and will remain so until you leave the facility. Understood?'

'Understood, Corporal.' Eve handed him her bag, then Peabody's, and pocketed the receipts he gave her. 'Some place you've got here.'

'We're proud of it. This way, Lieutenant.'

After depositing the bags in a bomb-safe lockup, he led them to an elevator, programmed it for Section Three, Level A. The doors closed without a sound; the car ran with barely a trace of movement. Eve wanted to ask how much the taxpayers had paid for the luxury, but decided the corporal wouldn't appreciate the irony.

She was certain of it when they were deposited in a wide lobby decorated with foam scoop chairs and potted trees. The carpet was thick and undoubtedly wired for motion detection. The console at which three clerks busily worked was equipped with a full range of computers, monitors, and communications systems. The piped-in music was beyond soothing and edging toward mind dulling.

The clerks weren't droids, but they were so stiff and polished, so radically conservative in dress, that she thought

131

they'd have been better off as automatons. Mavis, she thought with deep affection, would have been appalled at the lack of style.

'Reconfirmation of palm prints, please,' the corporal requested, and obediently, Eve and Peabody laid their right hands flat on the plate. 'Sergeant Hobbs will escort you from here.'

The sergeant, tucked neatly into her uniform, stepped from behind the console. She opened another reinforced door and led the way down a silent corridor.

At the last checkpoint, there was a final screen for weapons, then they were key-coded into the chief's office.

Here was a sweeping view of the city. Eve supposed, after one glance at Dudley, that he considered it his city. His desk was as wide as a lake, and one wall flashed with screens spot-checking various areas of the building and grounds. On another were photos and holograms of Dudley with heads of state, royalty, ambassadors. His communications center rivaled the control room at NASA Two.

But the man himself cast the rest in shadow.

He was enormous, easily six seven and a beefy two seventy. His wide, rawboned face was weathered and tanned, with his brilliantly white hair cropped short. On hands as big as Virginia hams, he wore two rings. One was the symbol of military rank; the other was a thick gold wedding band.

He stood poker straight and studied Eve out of eyes the color and texture of onyx. For Peabody, he never spared a glance.

'Lieutenant, you're inquiring into the death of Senator Pearly.'

So much for amenities, Eve thought and answered in kind. 'That's affirmative, Chief Dudley. I'm investigating the possibility that the senator's death is connected to another case on which I am primary. Your cooperation in this matter is duly noted and appreciated.'

'I find the possibility of a connection slim to none. However,

132

after reviewing your record with NYPSD, I found no objection to allowing you to view the senator's file.'

'Even a slim possibility bears investigating, Chief Dudley.'

'I agree, and I admire thoroughness.'

'Then, might I ask if you knew the senator personally?'

'I did, and though I did not agree with his politics, I considered him a dedicated public servant and a man with a strong moral base.'

'One who would take his own life?'

Dudley's eyes flickered for a moment. 'No, Lieutenant, I would say not. Which is why you're here. The senator has left behind a family. In the area of family, the senator and I were in harmony. Therefore, his apparent suicide does not fit the man.'

Dudley touched a control on his desk, inclined his head to the view wall. 'On screen one, his personal file. On screen two, his financial records. Screen three, his political file. You'll have one hour to review data. This office will be under electronic surveillance. Simply request Sergeant Hobbs when you've completed your hour.'

Eve's opinion of Dudley was a little hum in her throat as he left the office. 'He's making it easy for us. If he didn't particularly like Pearly, I'd say he respected him. Okay, Peabody, let's get to work.'

She scanned the screens as her cop's eyes had already scanned the room. She was nearly certain she'd spotted all the security cameras and recorders, and taking a chance on a very uncomfortable detention, shifted so that her body was partially blocked by Peabody's.

She pulled the diamond Roarke had given her from under her shirt, ran it idly along its chain, and with her free hand slid the small recorder out, kept it pressed just at her throat as she aimed it at the screens.

'A clean life,' she said aloud. 'No criminal record whatsoever. Parents married, still living, still based in Carmel. His father did military time, ranked colonel, served during the Urban Wars. Mother an MT with time off as professional parent. That's a pretty solid upbringing.'

Peabody kept her eyes on the screen and off the recorder. 'Solid education, too. Graduate of Princeton, with postgrad work at the World Learning Center on Space Station Freedom. That was right at its conception, and only the top students could get in. Married at thirty, just before his first run for office. Adjusted Population advocate. Requisite one child, male.'

She shifted her gaze to another screen. 'His politics are dead center Liberal Party. Butted heads with your old friend DeBlass over the appeal of the Gun Ban and the Morality Bill DeBlass was pushing.'

'I have a feeling I would have liked the senator.' Eve turned slightly. 'Scroll personal data to medical history.'

The screen flipped, and the technical terms made her eyes want to cross. She'd have them translated later, she thought, if she managed to get out of the facility with the recorder.

'Looked like a healthy specimen. Physical and mental records show no abnormality. Tonsils treated in childhood, a broken tibia in his twenties as a result of a sport injury. Sight correction, standard, in middle forties. A permanent sterilization procedure during the same period.'

'This is interesting.' Peabody continued to scan the political screen. 'He was endorsing a bill that would require all legal representatives and technicians to be rescreened every five years, at their own expense. That wouldn't sit too well with the legal community.'

'Or with Fitzhugh,' Eve murmured. 'Looks like he was after the electronic empire, too. Tougher testing requirements for new devices, new licensing laws. That wouldn't have made him Mister Popularity, either. Autopsy report,' she demanded, then narrowed her eyes when it flashed on screen.

She skimmed through the jargon, shook her head. 'Boy, was he a mess when they scraped him up. Didn't leave them a hell of a lot to work with. Brain scan and dissection. Nothing,' she said after a moment. 'No report here of an abnormality or flaw.'

'Display,' she demanded, and stepped closer to the screen to study the visual herself. 'Cross section. Side view, enhance. What do you see, Peabody?'

'Unattractive gray matter, too damaged for transplant.'

'Enhance right hemisphere, frontal lobe. Jesus, what a fucking mess he made out of himself. You just can't see. Can't be sure.' She stared until her eyes burned. Was that a shadow, or was it simply part of the trauma caused when a human skull smashed brutally into concrete?

'I don't know, Peabody.' She had all she needed, and she slid the recorder under her shirt again. 'But I do know that there's no motive or predisposition for self-destruct in this data. And that makes three. Let's get the hell out of this place,' she decided. 'It gives me the creeps.'

'I'm with you all the way on that one.'

They got tubes of Pepsi and what passed for a hash sandwich at a glide-cart on the corner of Pennsylvania Avenue and Security Row. Eve was just about to hail a transport back to the airport when a sleek black limo glided to the curb. The rear window slid down, and Roarke smiled out at them.

'Would you ladies like a lift?'

'Wow,' was all Peabody could manage as she scanned the car from bumper to bumper. It was a gleaming antique, a luxury from another era, and as romantic and tempting as sin.

'Don't encourage him, Peabody.' When Eve started to climb in, Roarke took her hand and tumbled her into his lap. 'Hey.' Mortified, she jabbed with her elbow.

'I love to fluster her when she's on duty,' Roarke said, wrestling Eve back onto his lap. 'And how was your day, Peabody?'

135

Peabody grinned, delighted to see her lieutenant flushed and cursing. 'It just got better. If this thing has a privacy screen, I can leave you two alone.'

'I said not to encourage him, didn't I?' This time her elbow had better aim, and Eve managed to slide off onto the seat. 'Idiot,' she muttered at Roarke.

'She dotes on me so.' He sighed, settled back. 'It's almost smothering. If you've finished your police business, can I offer you a tour of the city?'

'No,' Eve said before Peabody could open her mouth. 'Straight back to New York. No detours.'

'She's a real party animal, too,' Peabody said soberly, then neatly folded her hands and watched the city stream by.

Chapter Ten

Before Eve left for home, she perfected a detailed report on the similarities in the alleged suicides and why her suspicions that the senator's death was due to the same as yet unknown causes. She transferred her findings to the commander's unit, with a flag to his home 'link.

Unless his wife was hosting one of her ubiquitous dinner parties, she knew Whitney would review the report before morning. With that hope, she took the sky glide from homicide to the Electronic Detective Division.

She found Feeney at his desk, his stubby fingers holding delicate tools, microglasses turning his eyes to saucers as he stripped down a miniboard.

'You doing repair and maintenance these days?' She eased a hip on the edge of his desk, careful not to jar his rhythm. She'd expected no more than the grunt she received in response and waited while he transferred a sliver of something onto a clear dish.

'Somebody's having fun and games,' he muttered. 'Managed to get a virus of some kind right into the chief's unit. Memory's been boosted, the GCC compromised.'

She glanced at the silver sliver and imagined that was the GCC. Computers weren't her forte. 'Got a line on it?'

'Not yet.' With tiny tweezers, he lifted the sliver, studied it through his glasses. 'But I will. I found the virus, dosed it, that's first priority. This poor little bastard's dead, though. When I autopsy it, we'll see.'

She had to smile. It was so like Feeney to think of his components and chips in human terms. He replaced the sliver, sealed the dish, then tugged off his glasses.

His eyes shrank, blinked, refocused. And there he was, Dallas thought, rumpled, wrinkled, and baggy, just as she liked him best. He'd made her a cop, giving her the kind of in-the-field training she could never have learned through discs or VR. And though he'd transferred from Homicide to captain in EDD, she continued to depend on him.

'So,' she began. 'Did you miss me?'

'Were you gone?' He grinned at her, reached a hand into a bowl for some candied almonds. 'Did you like your fancy honeymoon?'

'Yeah, I did.' She took a nut herself. It had been a long time since lunch. 'Even with a body at the end of it. I appreciate the data you dug up for me.'

'No problem. A lot of fuss for self-terminations.'

'Maybe.' His office was larger than hers, due to his rank and his love of space. His boasted a view screen which, as usual, was tuned to a classic film channel. Just now Indiana Jones was being lowered into a pit of asps. 'It's got a few interesting aspects, though.'

'Want to share?'

'That's why I'm here.' She'd copied the data she'd taken from the senator's file and took the disc from her pocket. 'I've got a brain dissection on here, but the picture's a little rough. Can you clean it up, boost it some?'

'Can bears shit in the reforested park?' He took the disc, swiveled to his unit, and loaded it. Moments later, he was scowling over the image. 'Pitiful imaging. What did you do, use a portable to record off screen?'

'It would be better if we didn't get into that.'

He turned his head, studied her with that same scowl. 'You teetering on a line, Dallas?'

'My balance is good.'

138

'Let's hope so.' Preferring to work manually, he slid out a keyboard. His workingman's fingers danced over keys and controls like a master harpist's over strings. He jerked a shoulder when she leaned close. 'Don't crowd me, kid.'

'I need to see.'

Under his expertise the picture was clearing, contrasts sharpening. She struggled for patience as he fine tuned, diddled, humming to himself as he worked. Behind her all hell was breaking loose between Harrison Ford and the snakes.

'That's about the best we can do on this unit. You want more, I have to take it into master.' He flicked a glance up at her. 'You gotta log on for master. Technically.'

She knew he'd bypass regulations for her and risk an interview with IAD. 'Let's go with this for now. You see that, Feeney?' She tapped a finger against the screen just under the tiny shadow.

'I see a hell of a lot of trauma. This brain must have been bashed good and proper.'

'But this.' She could just make it out. 'I've seen this before. On two other scans.'

'I'm no neurologist, but I'd guess it's not supposed to be there.'

'No.' She straightened. 'It's not supposed to be there.'

She got home late and was met by Summerset at the door. 'There are two . . . gentlemen to see you, Lieutenant.'

With a quick jolt, she thought of the data she'd commandeered. 'Are they wearing uniforms?'

Summerset's pursed mouth pruned further. 'Hardly. I've put them in the front parlor. They insisted on waiting, though you had not indicated when you would arrive, and Roarke is detained at the office.'

'Okay, I'll handle it.' She wanted a huge plate of anything edible, a hot bath, and some thinking time. Instead, she wound her way down to the parlor and found Leonardo and

139

Jess Barrow. Relief came first, then annoyance. Summerset, the creep, knew Leonardo and could have told her who was waiting to see her.

'Dallas.' Leonardo's moon-sized face creased into a grin when he spotted her. He swept across the room, a giant in a magenta skin suit overbloused with emerald gauze. No wonder Mavis adored him. He caught Eve up in a bone crushing hug, then narrowed his eyes. 'You haven't dealt with your hair yet. I'll call Trina myself.'

'Oh. Well.' Intimidated, Eve raked her fingers through her short, messy cap of hair. 'I don't really have time right now to—'

'You have to make time for personal appearance. Not only are you an important public figure in your own right, but you're Roarke's wife.'

She was a cop, damn it. Suspects and victims didn't give a rat's ass about her hairdo. 'Right. As soon as—'

'You're neglecting your treatments,' he accused her, simply rolling over her excuses like a big smooth boulder down a bumpy slope. 'Your eyes are strained and your brows need shaping.'

'Yeah, but—'

'Trina will be in touch to set up a session. Now then.' He propelled her across the room, all but dumped her into a chair. 'Relax,' he ordered. 'Put your feet up. You've had a long day. Can I get you anything?'

'No, really. I'm—'

'Some wine.' Inspired, he beamed, gave her shoulder a quick rub. 'I'll see to it. And don't worry. Jess and I won't keep you long.'

'No use arguing with a born nurturer,' Jess commented as Leonardo moved off to order the wine for Eve. 'Nice to see you, Lieutenant.'

'Aren't you going to tell me I've lost weight, or gained it, or need a facial?' But she blew out a breath and leaned back. It

140

did feel incredibly good to sit in a chair that wasn't designed to torture the ass. 'Okay, let's have it. Something must be up for you to tolerate Summerset insulting you until I got home.'

'Actually, he just looked appalled and closed us in here. I do think he's going to run a room scan after we're gone to be sure we didn't lift any of the knickknacks.' Jess sat down, cross-legged, on the cushion at her feet. His silver eyes were smiling, his voice smooth as Davarian cream. 'Great knickknacks, by the way.'

'We like them. If you'd wanted the tour, you should have said so before Leonardo set me down. I'm going to stay here awhile.'

'Looking at you will do just fine. I hope you don't mind me saying you're the most attractive cop I've ever . . . rubbed shoulders with.'

'Have we rubbed shoulders, Jess?' Her brows lifted, disappearing under her bangs. 'I hadn't noticed.'

He chuckled, patted her knee with one of his beautiful hands. 'I would love that tour, sometime or other. But right now we have a favor to ask.'

'Got a traffic blot you need fixing?'

His lovely face beamed. 'Well, now that you mention it—'

Leonardo carried the crystal glass filled with pale gold wine across the room himself. 'Don't tease her, Jess.'

Eve accepted the glass, glanced up at Leonardo. 'He's not teasing me, he's flirting with me. He likes to live dangerously.'

Jess let out an appealingly musical laugh. 'Caught. Happily married women are the safest to flirt with.' He spread his hands as she sipped, considered him 'No harm, no foul.' He picked up her hand, ran a fingertip along the intricate carving on her wedding ring.

'The last man who messed with me is doing life in lockup,' Eve said casually. 'That's after I beat the crap out of him.'

'Oops.' Chuckling, Jess released her hand. 'Maybe I'd better let Leonardo ask for the favor.'

'It's for Mavis,' Leonardo said, and his eyes became warm and liquid as he spoke her name. 'Jess thinks the demo disc is ready. Music and entertainment is a tough field, you know. Crowded, competitive, and Mavis has her heart set on making it. After what happened with Pandora—' He shuddered delicately. 'Well, after what happened before, and Mavis being arrested, fired from the Blue Squirrel, going through all of that . . . It's been rough on her.'

'I know.' The guilt set in again, for her part in it. 'It's behind her now.'

'Thanks to you.' Though Eve shook her head, Leonardo insisted. 'You believed her, you worked for her, you saved her. Now I'm going to ask you for something else because I know you love her as much as I do.'

Eve's eyes narrowed. 'You're boxing me in very neatly, aren't you?'

He didn't bother to suppress the smile. 'I hope so.'

'It's my idea,' Jess interrupted. 'Leonardo had to be nudged some to approach you with it. He didn't want to take advantage of your friendship or your position.'

'My position as a cop?'

'No.' Jess smiled, reading her reaction perfectly. 'As Roarke's wife.' *Oh, she didn't care for that*, he thought, amused. This was a woman who wanted to stand firm, on her own. 'Your husband has a great deal of influence, Dallas.'

'I know what Roarke has.' It wasn't precisely true. She didn't have a clue as to the full extent of his holdings and operations. She didn't want to. 'What do you want from him?'

'Just a party,' Leonardo said quickly.

'A what?'

'A party for Mavis.'

'A splashy one,' Jess put in, grinning. 'A busting one.'

'An event.' Leonardo shot Jess a warning look. 'A stage, so to speak, where Mavis can mingle with people, perform. I haven't mentioned the idea to her in case you objected. But we thought if Roarke could invite . . .' There was obvious embarrassment now as she only stared at him. 'Well, he knows so many people.'

'People who buy performance discs, go to clubs, look for entertainment.' Not embarrassed in the least, Jess smiled winningly. 'Maybe we should get you some more wine.'

Instead, she set the barely touched glass aside. 'You want him to give a party.' Wary of a trap, she scanned both faces. 'That's it?'

'More or less.' Hope sprang in Leonardo's chest. 'We'd like to run the demo during it, have Mavis give a live performance as well, I know it's an expense. I'm more than willing to pay—'

'It won't be the money that concerns him.' Eve considered, tapped her fingers on the arm of the chair. 'I'll talk to him about it and get back to you. I guess you want it soon.'

'As soon as possible.'

'I'll get back to you,' she repeated, then rose.

'Thank you, Dallas.' Leonardo bent in several places to kiss her cheek. 'We'll get out of your way.'

'She's going to be a huge hit,' Jess predicted. 'She just needs a liftoff.' He took a disc out of his pocket. 'This is a copy of the demo,' he told her. *A specially doctored copy*, he thought, *just for the lieutenant*. 'Give it a try. See what we've come up with.'

She smiled at it, thinking of Mavis. 'I will.'

Upstairs, alone, Eve programmed the AutoChef and came up with a steaming plate of pasta and what was certainly fresh sauce from garden-grown tomatoes and herbs. It never ceased to amaze her what Roarke had access to. She wolfed it down while she ran a bath. As an afterthought, she tossed in some of the foaming salts he'd bought her in Paris.

She thought they smelled like her honeymoon: rich and romantic. She sank into a tub the size of a small lake and sighed greedily. *Blank the mind before thinking*, she decided and popped open the control panel in the wall. She'd already loaded the demo in the bedroom unit and switched it to play on the recessed screen in the bathroom.

She settled back into hot, frothy water, a second glass of vintage wine in her hand, and shook her head. What the hell was she doing here? Eve Dallas, a cop who'd come up the hard way; a nameless kid found in an alley, abandoned and abused, with a murder on her hands blocked from her memory.

Even a year before, that memory had been patchy and her life had been one of work, survival, and more work. Standing for the dead was her business, and she was good at her job. That had been enough. She'd made it enough.

Until Roarke. The glitter of the ring on her finger continued to puzzle her.

He loved her. He wanted her. He, the competent, successful, and enigmatic Roarke, even needed her. That was the biggest puzzle of all. And maybe, since she couldn't seem to solve it, she would eventually learn to simply accept it.

She brought the wine to her lips, sank a little lower into the water, and hit the remote.

Instantly, color and sound exploded into the room. In defense, she lowered the volume before her eardrums burst. Then Mavis swirled across the screen, as exotic as a sprite, potent as straight whiskey. Her voice was a screech, but it was appealing, nonetheless, and it suited her as well as the music Jess had designed to showcase the vocals.

It was hot, ruthless, and raw. Very much Mavis. But as Eve soaked it in, she realized that the sound and the show had more polish. Oh, there had always been flash and sparkle when it came to Mavis's work, but now there was a thin sheen of gloss she had lacked before.

Production values, she supposed. *Orchestration. And someone who has the eye to recognize a rough diamond and the talent and willingness to help buff it up.*

Eve's opinion of Jess took a step up. Maybe he'd looked like a cocky boy showing off on his complicated console, but he obviously knew how to make it work. More, he understood Mavis, Eve realized. He appreciated her for what she was and what she wanted to do, and he'd found a way for her to do it well.

Eve chuckled to herself and lifted her glass in toast to her friend. It looked like they were going to have a party at that.

In his studio downtown, Jess reviewed the demo. He sincerely hoped that Eve was watching the disc. If she did, her mind would be open. Wide open to dreams. He wished he knew what they would be, where they would take her. Then he could see what she would see. He could document. Relive. But his research hadn't yet allowed him to find the path into the dreams. *One day*, he thought, *one day*.

Eve's dreams took her back into the dark, into the dread. They were jumbled, then shockingly clear, then scattered again like leaves in the wind. It was terrifying. She dreamed of Roarke, and that was soothing. Watching an explosive sunset with him in Mexico, making reckless love in the dark, bubbling water of a lagoon. Hearing his voice in her ear when he was inside her, urging her to let go. Just let go.

Then it was her father, holding her down, and she was a child, helpless, hurting, frightened.

Please don't.

The smell of him was there, candy over liquor. Too sweet, too strong. She was gagging on it and weeping, and his hand was over her mouth to stifle her screams when he raped her.

145

Our personalities are programmed at conception. Reeanna's voice floated in, cool and sure. *We are what we are made. Our choices are already set at birth.*

And she was a child, in a terrible room, a cold room that smelled of garbage and urine and death. And there was blood on her hands.

Someone was holding her, pinning her arms, and she fought like a wild thing, like a terrified, desperate child would fight.

'Don't. Don't. Don't.'

'Ssh, Eve, it's a dream.' Roarke gathered her closer, rocked, while the clammy sweat on her skin soaked into his shirt and broke his heart. 'You're safe.'

'I killed you. You're dead. *Stay dead.*'

'Wake up now.'

He pressed his lips to her temple, struggling to find the right way to soothe her. If he'd had the power, he would have gone back in time and cheerfully murdered what haunted her.

'Wake up, darling. It's Roarke. No one's going to hurt you. He's gone,' he murmured when she stopped fighting him and began to shudder. 'He's never coming back.'

'I'm all right.' It humiliated her, always, to be caught in the grip of a nightmare. 'I'm okay now.'

'I'm not.' He continued to hold her, stroking until her tremors eased. 'It was a bad one.'

She kept her eyes shut, tried to concentrate on the scent of him: clean and male. 'Remind me not to go to bed after gorging on spiced spaghetti.' She realized he was fully dressed and the bedroom lights were on low. 'You haven't been to bed.'

'I just got in.' He eased her back to study her face and brushed a drying tear from her cheek. 'You're still pale.' It tore at him, and his voice was edgy. 'Why the hell won't you take a soother at least?'

'I don't like them.' As usual, the nightmare had left her with the dull throb of a headache. Knowing he would see it if he looked too closely, she shifted away. 'I haven't had one in a while. Weeks really.' Calmer now, she rubbed her tired eyes. 'That one was all jumbled up. Strange. Maybe it was the wine.'

'And maybe it's stress. You will work until you collapse.'

She angled her head, glanced at the watch on his wrist. 'And who's just coming in from the office at two A.M.?' She smiled, wanting to erase the worry from his eyes. 'Buy any small planets lately?'

'No, just a few minor satellites.' He rose, stripped off his shirt, then lifted a brow when he caught the considering look she gave his bare chest. 'You're too tired.'

'I don't have to be. You could do all the work.'

Laughing, he sat to take off his shoes. 'Thank you very much, but why don't we wait until you have the energy to participate?'

'Christ, that's so married.' But she slid down in the bed, exhausted. The headache was just on the edge of her brain, cannily waiting to strike. When he slipped into bed beside her, she rested her tender head on his shoulder. 'I'm glad you're home.'

'So am I.' He brushed his lips over her hair. 'You'll sleep now.'

'Yeah.' It soothed her to feel the rhythm of his heart under the palm of her hand. She only felt slightly ashamed of needing it there, needing him there. 'Do you think we're programmed at conception?'

'What?'

'I wonder.' She was drifting into that twilight sleep already, and her voice was thick and slow. 'Is it just the luck of the draw, the gene pool, what slips in with egg and sperm? Is that it? What does that make us, Roarke, you and me?'

'Survivors,' he said, but he knew she was asleep. 'We survived.'

He lay awake a long time, listening to her breathe, watching the stars. When he was certain she slept without scars, he let himself follow.

She was awakened at seven by a communiqué from Commander Whitney's office. She'd been expecting the summons. She had two hours to prep for the face-to-face report.

It didn't surprise her that Roarke was already up, dressed, and sipping coffee while he scanned the stock reports on his monitor. She grunted at him, her usual morning greeting, and took coffee into the shower with her.

He was on the 'link when she came back. His broker, she imagined from the bits and pieces of conversation she caught. She snagged a muffin, intending to stuff it into her mouth as she dressed, but Roarke grabbed her hand, pulled her down on the sofa.

'I'll get back to you by noon,' he told his broker, then ended transmission. 'What's your hurry?' he asked Eve.

'I've got to meet Whitney in an hour and a half and convince him there's a link between three unrelated victims, talk him into letting me pursue the matter, and to accept data I accessed illegally. Then I'm due in court, again, to testify so that a lowlife pimp, who ran an unlicensed stable of minors and beat one of them to death with his hands, goes into a cage and stays there.'

He kissed her lightly. 'Just another day at the office. Have some strawberries.'

She had a weakness for them and plucked one out of the bowl. 'We don't have any – you know – *thing* scheduled for tonight, do we?'

'No. What did you have in mind?'

'I was thinking we could just hang.' She moved her shoulders. 'Unless I'm in Interview being kicked because of breaching government security.'

'You should have let me do it for you.' He grinned at her. 'A little time, and I could have accessed the data from here.'

148

She closed her eyes. 'Don't tell me that. I really don't want to know that.'

'What do you say to watching some old videos, eating popcorn, and necking on the sofa?'

'I say, thank you, God.'

'It's a date then.' He topped off their coffee. 'Maybe we'll even manage to have dinner together. This case – or these cases – are troubling you.'

'I can't get a hook, a focal point. There's no why, there's no how. Other than Fitzhugh's spouse and his associate, no one's been even one step out of line. And they're both just idiots.' She moved her shoulders. 'It's not homicide when it's self-termination, but it feels like homicide.' She huffed out a disgusted breath. 'And if that's all I've got to convince Whitney, I'm going to be dragging my ass out of his office after he stomps it.'

'You trust your instincts. He strikes me as a man who's smart enough to trust them as well.'

'We'll soon see.'

'If they arrest you, darling, I'll wait for you.'

'Ha ha.'

'Summerset said you had visitors last night,' Roarke added as she rose to go to the closet.

'Oh, shit, I forgot.' Dumping the robe on the floor, she pawed naked through her clothes. It was a process Roarke never failed to enjoy. She found a shirt of plain blue cotton, shrugged it on. 'I had a couple of guys over for a quick orgy after work.'

'Did you take pictures?'

She chuckled and found some jeans, remembered court, and switched to tailored slacks. 'It was Leonardo and Jess. They're looking for a favor. From you.'

Roarke watched as Eve started to pull on the slacks, remembered underwear, and yanked open a drawer. 'Oh-oh. Will it hurt?'

'I don't think so. And actually, I'm kind of for it. They were thinking you could throw a party for Mavis here. Let her perform. The demo disc is done. I watched it myself last night and it's really good. It would give her a chance to, like, premiere it before they start hawking it.'

'All right. We could probably do it in a week or two. I'll check my schedule.'

Half dressed, she turned to him. 'Just like that?'

'Why not? It's not a problem.'

She pouted a little. 'I figured I'd have to persuade you.'

Anticipation lit wickedly in his eyes. 'Would you like to?'

She fastened her slacks, kept her face bland. 'Well, I really appreciate it. And since you're being so accommodating, I guess this is a good time to hit you with part two.'

Idly, he poured more coffee, flicked a glance at the monitor as the off planet agriculture reports began to scroll. He'd recently bought a minifarm on Space Station Delta.

'What's part two?'

'Well, Jess has worked out this one number. He ran it by me last night.' She looked at Roarke, making it up as she went along. 'It's a duet, really impressive. And we thought, if for the party – the live portion of the performance – you could do it with Mavis.'

He blinked, lost all interest in crops. 'Do what with Mavis?'

'Perform it. Actually it was my idea,' she continued, nearly losing it when he paled. 'You've got a nice voice. In the shower, anyway. The Irish comes out. I mentioned it, and Jess thought it was fabulous.'

He managed to shut his mouth, but it wasn't easy. Slowly he reached over to disengage the monitor. 'Eve—'

'Really, it would be great. Leonardo has a terrific design for your costume.'

'For my—' Thoroughly shaken, Roarke got to his feet. 'You want me to wear a costume and sing a duet with Mavis? In public?'

'It would mean so much to her. Just think of the press we could get.'

'Press.' Now he blanched. 'Christ Jesus, Eve.'

'It's really a sexy number.' Testing them both, she walked over, began to toy with the buttons of his shirt as she looked hopefully up into his eyes. 'It could put her right over the top.'

'Eve, I'm fond of her, really I am. I just don't think—'

'You're so important.' She trailed her finger down the center of his chest. 'So influential. And so . . . gorgeous.'

It was just a little too thick. He narrowed his eyes, caught the laughter in hers. 'You're putting me on.'

Her laughter burst out. 'You bought it. Oh, you should have seen your face.' She pressed a hand to her belly, yelping when he yanked her ear. 'I would have talked you into it.'

'I don't think so.' Not at all sure of himself, he turned away, started to reach for his coffee again.

'I could have. You'd have done it if I'd played it right.' All but doubled over with laughter, she threw her arms around him, hugged herself to his back. 'Oh, I love you.'

He went very still as emotion delivered a hard, bruising punch to his heart. Shaken, he turned, gripped her arms.

'What?' The laughter died out of her face. He looked stunned, and his eyes were dark and fierce. 'What is it?'

'You never say it.' Swamped, he dragged her close and buried his face in her hair. 'You never say it,' he repeated.

She could do nothing but hold on, rocked by the emotions pulsing from him. *Where had this come from?* she wondered. *Where had he hidden it?* 'Yes, I do. Sure I do.'

'Not like that.' He hadn't known how much he'd needed to hear her say it, just like that. 'Not without prompting. Without thinking about it first.'

She opened her mouth to deny it, then closed it again. It was true, and it was foolish, cowardly. 'I'm sorry. It's hard

151

for me. I do love you,' she said quietly. 'Sometimes it scares me because you're the first. And the only.'

He held her there until he was sure he could speak, then eased her back, looked into her eyes. 'You've changed my life. Become my life.' He touched his lips to hers, let the kiss deepen slowly, silkily. 'I need you.'

She linked her arms around his neck, pressed close. 'Show me. Now.'

Chapter Eleven

Eve started off to work humming. Her body felt soft and strong, her mind rested. She took it as an omen when her vehicle purred to life on the first attempt, and the temperature control hung at a pleasant seventy-two degrees.

She felt ready to face her commander and convince him she had a case to pursue.

Then she got to Fifth and Forty-seventh and hit the jam. Street traffic was stopped, air traffic was circling like vultures, and no one was paying any heed to the noise pollution laws. The horns, shouts, curses, catcalls screamed out and echoed. The minute she stopped, her temperature control gleefully pumped up to ninety-five.

Eve slammed out of her car and joined the melee.

The glide-cart hawkers were taking advantage of the moment, slipping and sliding through the pack and doing a monster business on frozen fruit sticks and coffee. She didn't bother to flash her badge and remind any of them they weren't allowed the vend off the curbs. Instead, she snagged a vendor, bought a tube of Pepsi, and asked what the hell was going on.

'Free-Agers.' Eyes shifting for more customers, he slid her credits into his safe slot. 'Protest on conspicuous consumption. Hundreds of 'em, stretched across Fifth like a pretty ribbon. Singing. Want a wheat muffin to go with that? Fresh.'

'No.'

'Gonna be here awhile,' he warned and stepped onto his cart to glide through standing traffic.

'Son of a bitch.' Eve scanned the scene. She was blocked in on all sides by furious commuters. Her ears were ringing and heat was pumping out of her car like a furnace.

She slammed back in, beat on the control panel with her fist, and managed to knock the temperature down to a brisk sixty. Overhead, a tourist blimp trundled by, full of gawkers.

With no faith whatsoever in her vehicle, Eve rammed it into vertical lift and hit her official warning siren. The siren wheezed on, no match for the cacophony of noise, but she managed a shaky lift. Her wheels missed the roof of the car in front of her by at least an inch as her vehicle coughed and choked its way into the air.

'Next stop, recycling heap. I swear it,' she muttered and she punched at her communicator. 'Peabody, what the fuck is going on here?'

'Sir.' Peabody popped on screen, eyes bland, mouth sober. 'I believe you've encountered the jam incited by the protest on Fifth.'

'That wasn't scheduled. I know damn well it wasn't on the boards for this morning. They can't have a permit.'

'Free-Agers don't believe in permits, sir.' She cleared her throat when Eve snarled. 'I believe if you head west, you'll have better luck on Seventh. Traffic is heavy there, but it's moving. If you check your dash monitor—'

'Yeah, like that's going to work in this piece of shit. Call Maintenance and tell them they're meat. Then contact the commander, explain that I may be a few minutes late for the meeting.' As she spoke, she wrestled with the car, which tended to dip and cause both pedestrians and other drivers to stare up in terror. 'If I don't fall on someone, I should be there in twenty minutes.'

She avoided, barely, the edge of a billboard hologram touting the delights of private air travel. She and the Jet

154

Star headed in opposite directions with varying degrees of success. She nicked the curb as she set down on Seventh and couldn't blame the suit and tie pumping up his air skates for flipping her the bird.

But she'd missed him, hadn't she?

She was just indulging in a sigh of relief when her communicator shrilled.

'Any unit, any unit. Twelve seventeen, roof of Tattler Building, Seventh and Forty-second. Respond immediately. Unidentified female, considered armed.'

Twelve seventeen, Eve thought. Self-termination threat. What the hell was this? 'Dispatch, Dallas, Lieutenant Eve, responding. ETA five minutes.'

She beat her siren into life and hit vertical again.

The Tattler Building, home of the nation's most popular tabloid, was shiny and new. The buildings on its former site had been razed in the thirties for the urban beautification program, which was a euphemism for the decay of infrastructure and construction that had plagued New York during the period.

It speared up in silvery steel, bullet-shaped, and was ringed by circling skywalks and glides with a fresh-air restaurant spilling out from its base.

Eve double parked, grabbed her field kit, and pushed her way through the crowd gathered on the sidewalk. She flipped her badge at the security guard and watched relief drown his face.

'Thank Christ. She's up there, holding everybody off with antimugging spray. Got Bill dead in the eyes when he tried to grab her.'

'Who is she?' Eve demanded as he hustled his way toward the interior elevator banks.

'Cerise Devane. She owns the fucking place.'

'Devane?' Eve knew her vaguely. Cerise Devane, CEO of Tattler Enterprises, was one of the privileged and influential people who sauntered in Roarke's circles. 'Cerise Devane is on the roof threatening to jump? What is this, some sort of insane publicity stunt to bump up their circulation?'

'Looks real to me.' He puffed out his cheeks. 'She's buck ass naked, too. That's all I know,' the guard claimed as the elevator shot upward. 'Her assistant made the call. Frank Rabbit. You can get more out of him – if he's conscious by now. Guy keeled right over when she went out on the ledge. That's what I heard.'

'You call for psych?'

'Somebody did. We got the company shrink up there now, and a specialist in self-termination is on the way. Fire department, too, and air rescue. Everything's backed up. Bad traffic jam on Fifth.'

'Tell me about it.'

The doors opened onto the roof, and Eve stepped out into a brisk, cooling wind that hadn't been able to find its way through the towering walls of buildings to the valley of the streets. She took a quick scan.

Cerise's office was built onto the roof, or more accurately, into it. Slanted walls of treated glass formed a peak and would afford the CEO a three hundred sixty degree view of the city and people she loved to dish up in her paper.

Through the glass, Eve could see the artwork, decor, and equipment designed for a top-flight office. And on the U-shaped lounging sofa, a man was stretched out with a compress on his forehead.

'If that's Rabbit, tell him to pull himself together and get out here to fill me in. And get anyone who isn't essential off this roof. Clear that crowd off the streets. If she goes off, we don't need her squashing bystanders.'

'I just don't have the man power,' the guard began.

'Get Rabbit out here,' she repeated and called Cop Central. 'Peabody, I've got a situation.'

'I heard. What do you need?'

'Get down here, send a crowd dispersal unit to move those

people off the street. Bring me all available data on Cerise Devane. See if Feeney can put a freeze on her 'links – home, personal, and portable – for the last twenty-four hours. Make it snappy.'

'Done,' Peabody responded and broke transmission.

She turned as the guard all but carried a young man across to her. Rabbit's company tie was loose, his stylishly shaped hair was mussed and matted. His hands, neatly manicured, shook

'Tell me exactly what happened,' she snapped. 'Make it fast, and make it clear. You can fall apart when I'm finished with you.'

'She just – just walked out of the office.' His voice hitched and dipped and he sagged weakly against the supporting arm of the guard. 'She looked so happy. She was almost dancing. She – she'd taken off her clothes. She'd taken them off.'

Eve cocked a brow. At the moment, Rabbit seemed more shocked by his boss's sudden whim for exhibitionism than the possibility of her death. 'What led up to it?'

'I don't know. I swear, I have no idea. She'd wanted me to come in early, about eight. She was upset over one of the lawsuits. We're always getting sued. She was smoking and gulping coffee and pacing. Then she sent me out to light a fire under Legal and said she was going to take a few minutes to relax and level out.'

He stopped, covered his face with his hands. 'Fifteen minutes later she walked out, smiling and – and nude. I was so stunned, I just sat there. Just sat there.' His teeth began to chatter. 'I've never even seen her without her shoes.'

'Being naked's not her big problem now,' Eve pointed out. 'Did she speak to you, say anything?'

'I, well, I was so stunned, you see. I said something, something like, 'Ms Devane, what are you doing? Is something wrong?' And she just laughed. She said it was perfect. She had it all figured out now, and everything was wonderful. She was going to sit out on the ledge awhile before she jumped.

I thought she was joking, and I was nervous so I laughed a little.'

His eyes were stricken. 'I laughed, and then I saw her go to the edge of the roof. Jesus. She just popped over the side. I thought she'd jumped, and I ran out and over. There she was, sitting on the ledge, swinging her legs and humming. I asked her please to come back up before she lost her balance. She just laughed, spritzed a little of the spray at me, and told me she'd just found her balance and to go away like a good boy.'

'She get any calls, make any?'

'No.' He wiped his mouth. 'Any transmissions would have gone through my unit. She's going to jump, I tell you. She leaned over while I was watching, nearly went over then. And she said what a nice trip it was going to be. She's going to jump.'

'We'll see about that. Stay available.' Eve turned away. The company shrink was easy enough to spot. He was dressed in a knee-length white smock and black pipestem pants. His comforting gray hair was twisted into a neat queue, and he was leaning over the edge of the roof, his posture transmitting anxiety.

Even as Eve started toward him, she swore. She heard the whirl of flybys, then cursed the media again as she spotted the first air van. Channel 75, naturally, she mused. Nadine Furst was always first out of the gate.

The shrink straightened, smoothed down his smock for the cameras. Eve decided she was going to detest him. 'Doctor?' She held up her badge and noticed the undisguised excitement in his eyes. All Eve could think was, a company the size and strength of Tattler could afford better.

'Lieutenant, I believe I'm making some progress with the subject.'

'She's still on the ledge, isn't she?' Eve pointed out and brushed past him to lean over. 'Cerise?'

'More company?'

Sleek and pretty, skin the color of blushing rose petals, her well-toned legs swinging merrily, Cerise looked up. Her hair was jet black, its carefully groomed waves blowing in the breeze. She had a foxy, intelligent face and sharp green eyes. Just now, those eyes were soft and dreamy.

'Why, it's Eve, isn't it? Eve Dallas, the new bride. Lovely wedding, by the way. Really the social event of the year. We moved thousands of units with our coverage.'

'Good for you.'

'You know, I had research and data search busting butt to try to get the honeymoon itinerary. I don't think anybody but Roarke could have managed a full media blackout.' She wagged her finger playfully, and her perky breasts swayed. 'You could have shared, just a little. The public's dying to know.'

She giggled at that, shifted, and nearly overbalanced. 'We're all dying to know. Whoops. Not yet. Too much fun, don't want to rush it.' Straightening, she waved at the air vans. 'Usually I hate the damn visual media. Can't think why, just now. I love everybody!' She shouted the last, tossing her arms wide.

'That's nice, Cerise. Why don't you come back up for a minute. I'll give you some data on the honeymoon. Exclusive.'

Cerise smiled slyly. 'Uh-uh-uh.' The refusal was playful again, almost a giggle. 'Why don't you come down and join me? You can go with me. I'm telling you, it's the ultimate.'

'Now, Ms Devane,' the shrink began, 'all of us have moments of despair. I understand. I'm with you. I hear your sorrow.'

'Oh stuff it.' Cerise brushed him back with a gesture. 'I'm talking to Eve. Come on down, sweetie. But not too close.' She shook the spray and giggled. 'Come on and join the party.'

'Lieutenant, I don't recommend that you—'

'Shut up and go wait for my aide,' Eve told him as she swung a leg over the steel safety wall, lowered herself over the edge.

The wind didn't seem quite so pleasant when she was dangling seventy stories over the street, nudged on a steel ledge barely two feet wide. Here it buffeted and swirled, aided by the backwash from the air vans. It plucked at the clothes and slapped the skin. She ordered her heart to stop jumping and pressed her back to the building.

'Isn't it beautiful,' Cerise sighed. 'I'd love to have some wine now, wouldn't you? No, a big flute of champagne. Roarke's Reserve forty-seven would go down smooth right now.'

'I think we've got a case at home. Let's go open one.'

Cerise laughed, turned her head, and smiled hugely. And it was the smile, Eve realized as her heart lurched again, she'd seen on the face of a young man hanging from a homemade noose. 'I'm already drunk on happiness.'

'If you're happy, why are you sitting naked on a ledge considering taking the last leap?'

'That's what makes me happy. I don't know why you don't understand.' Cerise lifted her face to the sky, closed her eyes. Eve risked shifting a few inches closer. 'I don't know why everyone doesn't understand. It's so beautiful. It's so thrilling. It's everything.'

'Cerise, you go off this ledge, it's nothing. It's over.'

'No, no, no.' She opened her eyes again, and they were glazed. 'It's just the beginning, don't you see? Oh, we're all so blind.'

'Whatever's wrong can be fixed. I know.' Carefully, Eve laid a hand on Cerise's. She didn't grip, didn't want to risk it. 'Surviving's what counts. You can change things, make things better, but you have to survive to do it.'

'Do you know how much work that is? And what's the point when there's so much pleasure just waiting. I feel so good. Don't.' Chuckling, Cerise aimed the spray at Eve's face. 'Don't spoil it now. I'm having such a nice time.'

'You have people who are worried about you. You have

family, Cerise, who love you.' Eve strained to remember. Was there a child, a spouse, parents? 'If you do this, you'll hurt them.'

'Only until they understand. The time's coming when everyone will understand. It's going to be better then. Beautiful then.' She looked dreamily into Eve's eyes, that beaming and terrifying smile on her lips. 'Come with me.' She grabbed Eve's hand, clutched. 'It's going to be wonderful. You only have to let go.'

Sweat snaked a line down Eve's back. The woman's grip was like a vise, and a struggle for freedom could doom them both. She forced herself not to resist, to ignore the twisting wind and the hum of the air vans documenting every movement. 'I don't want to die, Cerise,' she said calmly. 'And neither do you. Self-termination is for cowards.'

'No, it's for explorers. But suit yourself.' Cerise patted Eve's hand, released it, and gave a long, trilling laugh to the wind. 'Oh God, I'm so happy,' she said and, throwing her arms wide, leaned forward into space.

Instinctively, Eve grabbed. She nearly lost her perch as her fingertips brushed the trim line of Cerise's hip. She banged onto her side, fought the roll forward as wind and space pulled at her. Gravity worked fast, mercilessly. Eve stared down into that wildly smiling face until it was only a blur.

'Jesus God. Oh, Jesus God.' Dizzy with reaction, she pushed herself up, leaned her head back, shut her eyes. Screams and shouts rained on her, and the air displaced by the media van coming in for a close-up struck her cheeks.

'Lieutenant. Dallas.'

The voice was like a bee buzzing in her ears, and Eve simply shook her head.

On the roof, Peabody stared down and fought against the nausea rising into her throat. All she could see now was that Eve was pressed on the ledge, white as a sheet, and one careful move would send her after the woman she'd tried

161

to save. Taking a deep breath, Peabody trained her voice to sharp, professional tones.

'Lieutenant Dallas, you're needed here. I require your recorder for a full report.'

'I hear you,' Eve said wearily. Keeping her eyes straight ahead, she reached behind to grip the edge of the roof. As a hand locked over hers, she got to her feet. Turning her back to the fall, she looked dead into Peabody's eyes, read the fear. 'The last time I thought about jumping, I was eight.' Though her legs shook a bit, she swung back onto the roof. 'I won't go that way.'

'Jesus, Dallas.' Forgetting herself for a moment, Peabody gave Eve a hard hug. 'You scared the hell out of me. I thought she was going to pull you off.'

'So did I. She didn't. Get a grip here, Peabody. The press is having a field day.'

'Sorry.' Peabody pulled back, coloring a bit. 'Sorry.'

'No problem.' Eve looked over to where the shrink was standing at the edge, one hand to his heart in a pose for the busy cameras. 'Asshole,' she muttered. She dug her hands into her pockets. She needed a minute, just another minute, to settle. 'I couldn't stop her, Peabody. I couldn't find the right button to push.'

'Sometimes there isn't one.'

'There was one that switched her onto this.' Eve said quietly. 'There had to be one to switch her off.'

'I'm sorry, Dallas. You knew her.'

'Not really. Just one of the people who walk past a corner of your life.' She pushed it away, had to push it away. Death, however it came, always left responsibilities. 'Let's see what we can do here. Did you tag Feeney?'

'Affirmative. He locked on her 'links from EDD and said he would head over personally. I downloaded data on the subject, didn't take time to scan it.'

They walked toward the office. Through the glass, Rabbit

162

could be seen sitting with his head between his knees. 'Do me a favor, Peabody. Pass that limp rag off to a uniform for a formal statement. I don't want to deal with him right now. I want her office secured. Let's see if we can figure out what the hell she was doing that set her off.'

Peabody marched in, had Rabbit up and out with a uniform in seconds. With wicked efficiency, she cleared the room, sealed the outer doors. 'It's all ours, sir.'

'Haven't I told you not to call me sir?'

'Yes, sir,' Peabody said with a smile she hoped would lift the heavy mood.

'There's a smart-ass lurking under that uniform.' Eve blew out a breath. 'Recorder on, Peabody.'

'Already on.'

'Okay, here she is. She's in early, pissed off. Rabbit says she was hyped about some litigation. Get data on that.' As she spoke, Eve wandered the room, absorbing details. Sculptures, mostly mythological figures in bronze. Very stylized. Deep blue carpet to match the sky, the desk in rose tones with a mirror gloss. Office equipment sleek and modern and tinted that same flowery shade. A huge copper urn exploded with exotic blooms, and Eve noticed a pair of potted trees.

She crossed to the computer, took her master pass out of her field kit, and called for the last use report.

Last use, 8: 10 a.m., call for file number 3732-L Legal, Custler v Tattler Enterprises.

'That'd be the lawsuit she was pissed about,' Eve concluded. 'Jibes with Rabbit's earlier statement.' She glanced down at a marble ashtray loaded with a half dozen cigarette butts. Using tweezers, she picked one up, examined it. 'Caribbean tobacco. Web filter. Pricey. Bag these.'

'You think they might be laced with something?'

'She was laced with something. Her eyes were wrong.' She

163

wouldn't forget them, Eve knew, for a long, long time. 'We can hope there's enough left of her for a tox report. Take a sample of those coffee dregs, too.'

But Eve didn't think they would find what she was looking for in the tobacco or the coffee. There had been no chemical trace in any of the other suicides.

'Her eyes were wrong,' Eve repeated. 'And her smile. I've seen that smile before, Peabody. A couple of times now.'

As she tucked the evidence bags away, Peabody glanced up. 'You think this is connected with the others?'

'I think Cerise Devane was a successful, ambitious woman. And we'll go through procedure, but I'm willing to lay odds we won't find a motive for self-termination. She sends Rabbit out,' Eve continued, pacing the office. Annoyed by the constant hum, she glanced up, scowled at the air van still hovering. 'See if you can find the privacy shields. I'm tired of those jerks.'

'A pleasure.' Peabody hunted up the control panel. 'I thought I saw Nadine Furst in one of them. The way she was leaning out, it was a good thing she was wearing a harness. She might have ended up as the lead on her own newscast.'

'At least she'll get it right,' Eve said half to herself and nodded when the privacy shields slid into place and closed off the glass. 'Good. Lights,' she ordered, and brought the brightness back up. 'She wanted to relax, level herself off for the rest of the day.'

Eve poked into a cold box, found soft drinks, fruit, wine. One of the wine bottles had been opened and air sealed, but there was no glass to indicate Cerise had started drinking early. And it wasn't a couple of belts that had put that look in her eyes, Eve mused.

In the adjoining bath, complete with whirlpool, personal sauna, and mood enhancer tube, she found a cupboard filled with soothers and tranqs and legalized lifters. 'A big believer in chemical assistance, our Cerise,' she commented. 'Take them in for testing.'

164

'Jesus, she's got her own pharmacy. The mood tube's set on concentration mode, and the last use was yesterday morning. She didn't take a spin this morning.'

'So what does she do to relax?' Eve stepped into an adjoining room, which was a small sitting room, she noted, complete with full entertainment unit, sleep chair, serving droid.

A lovely, sage-green suit was neatly folded on a small table. Matching shoes stood on the floor under it. Jewelry – a heavy linked gold chain, complicated twists of earrings, a slim bracelet watch-recorder – had been slipped tidily in a glass bowl.

'She undressed in here. Why? What was the point?'

'Some people relax better without the confines of clothes,' Peabody said, then flushed when Eve cast a considering glance over her shoulder. 'I've heard.'

'Yeah. Maybe. But it doesn't suit her. She was a real put-together woman. Her assistant told me he'd never even seen her without shoes, and suddenly she's a closet nudist. I don't think so.'

Her gaze landed on the VR goggles on the arm of the sleep chair. 'Maybe she took a trip after all,' Eve murmured. 'She's frazzled, wants to smooth the edges. So she comes in here, stretches out, programs something, and takes a little ride.'

Eve sat, picked up the goggles. *VR goggles*, she mused. Fitzhugh and Mathias had taken trips before death as well. 'I'm going to see where she went and when. Ah, if I appear to have any suicidal urges after I'm done – or decide I can relax better without the confines of my clothes – you're ordered to knock me cold.'

'Without hesitation, sir.'

Eve cocked a brow. 'But you're not expected to enjoy it.'

'I'll hate every minute of it,' Peabody promised, and folded her hands.

With a weak laugh, Eve slipped the goggles on. 'Display

165

log,' she ordered. 'Bull's-eye. She went VR at 8:17 this morning.'

'Dallas, if that's the case, maybe you shouldn't do this. We can take it in and test it under controlled conditions.'

'You're my control, Peabody. If I look too happy to live shortly, zap me. Replay last run program,' Eve ordered and settled back. 'Jesus.' She hissed it out as two young studs walked toward her. Dressed only in strips of glossy black leather studded with silver, they were oiled, muscled, and fully aroused.

Her environment was now a white room, mostly bed, and there was satin under her naked body, gauze draped overhead to filter the candlelight from a soaring chandelier of glittery crystal.

Music, something low and pagan, throbbed on the air. She was draped over a mountain of feather pillows, and as she started to shift, the first young god straddled her.

'Hey, listen, pal—'

'For your pleasure only, mistress,' he crooned and rubbed her breasts with scented oil.

This is a bad idea, she thought as little involuntary shivers of pleasure centered in her gut. Oil was slicked over her stomach, her thighs, down her legs to her toes.

She could understand how the current situation could make a woman strip and smile, but not how it could drive her to suicide.

Stick it out, she ordered herself and turned her mind to something else. She thought of the report she needed to give her commander. Of unexplained shadows on the brain.

Teeth closed delicately over her nipple, a tongue slid wetly over the captured point. She arched in reaction, but the hand she shot out in protest slipped off a taut, oil-slicked shoulder.

Then the second stud knelt between her legs and went to work on her with his mouth.

166

She came before she could stop herself, a small pop of release. Panting, she ripped the goggles off and found Peabody gaping at her.

'It wasn't a walk on a quiet beach,' Eve managed.

'I could see that. What was it, exactly?'

'A couple of mostly naked guys and a big satin bed.' Eve blew out a breath, set the goggles down. 'Who'd have thought she relaxed with sex fantasies?'

'Ah, Lieutenant. Sir. As your aide, I believe it's my responsibility to test that unit. For evidence control.'

Eve tucked her tongue in her cheek. 'Peabody, I couldn't let you take that kind of risk.'

'I'm a cop, sir. Risk is my life.'

Eve rose, held out the goggles as Peabody's eyes lit. 'Bag it, Officer.'

Deflated, Peabody dumped the goggles into a seal. 'Hell. Were they good looking?'

'Peabody, they were gods.' She stepped back into the office proper, gave it one more scan. 'I'm going to order in sweepers, but I don't think they'll find anything. I'll take the disc you downloaded into Central, contact next of kin – though the media will already have this all over the fucking airwaves.'

She hitched up her field kit. 'I don't feel at all suicidal.'

'I'm relieved to hear it, Lieutenant.'

Still, Eve frowned at the goggles. 'How long was I riding that, five minutes?'

'Nearly twenty.' Peabody gave a sour smile. 'Time flies when you're having sex.'

'I wasn't having sex.' Guilt had her worrying her wedding ring. 'Exactly. If there'd been something in that program, I should have felt it, so that looks like a dead end. Have it analyzed anyway.'

'Will do.'

'You wait for Feeney. Maybe he'll find something interesting on her 'link logs. I'm going to go grovel to the commander.

When you finish here, deliver the bags to the lab, then report to my office.' Eve started for the door, tossed a look over her shoulder. 'And Peabody, no playing with the evidence.'

'Spoilsport,' she muttered when Eve was out of earshot.

Chapter Twelve

Commander Whitney sat behind his massive, well-organized desk and listened. He appreciated the fact that his lieutenant delivered a clean and concise report, and he admired that she could omit certain details without a flicker.

A good cop had to stand cool under fire. Eve Dallas, he was pleased to know, was ice.

'You had the autopsy data on Fitzhugh analyzed outside the department.'

'Yes, sir.' She didn't blink. 'The analysis required more sophisticated equipment than NYPSD currently has access to.'

'And you had access to this more sophisticated equipment.'

'I was able to gain access.'

'And run the analysis?' he asked, quirking a brow. 'Computer science is not your strong suit, Dallas.'

She looked him dead in the eye. 'I've been working on improving my skills in that area, Commander.'

He doubted that, sincerely. 'Subsequently, you gained entry to the files at the Government Security Center, and there, confidential reports fell into your hands.'

'That's correct. I don't wish to reveal my source.'

'Your source?' he repeated. 'Are you telling me you have a weasel at GSC?'

'There are weasels everywhere,' Eve said coolly.

'That might fly,' he murmured. 'Or you might find yourself facing a subcommittee back in East Washington.'

Eve's stomach shimmied, but her voice stayed steady. 'I'm prepared for that.'

'You'd better be.' Whitney sat back, steepled his hands, tapped his fingertips against his chin. 'The case on the Olympus Resort. You also accessed data there. That's quite a bit out of your jurisdiction, Lieutenant.'

'I was on scene during that incident, and I reported my findings to interspace authorities.'

'Who then took over the disposition of the matter,' Whitney added.

'I'm authorized to request data when an outside case relates to one of mine, Commander.'

'That's yet to be substantiated.'

'The data's necessary for me to substantiate the connection.'

'That would hold, Dallas, if there was a homicide.'

'I believe there are four of them, including Cerise Devane.'

'Dallas, I've just viewed the recording of that incident. I saw a cop and a jumper on a ledge, the cop attempting to talk the subject in, and the subject choosing the leap. She was not pushed, she was not coerced, she was not threatened in any way.'

'It's my professional opinion that she was coerced.'

'How?'

'I don't know.' And for the first time, frustration leaked through. 'But I'm sure, dead sure, that if they had enough of her brain to scrape up off the street for analysis, they'd find that same burn on the frontal lobe. I know it, Commander. I just don't know how it's getting there.' She waited a beat. 'Or being put there.'

His eyes flickered. 'Are you theorizing that someone is influencing certain individuals to self-termination through some sort of brain implant?'

170

'I can't find any genetic link among the subjects. No social group, education sphere, or religious affiliation. They didn't grow up in the same town, they didn't drink the same water, attend the same health clubs or centers. But they all had the same flaw in the brain. That's beyond coincidence, Commander. It was caused, and if by being caused it coerced those people to end their lives, then it's murder. And it's mine.'

'You're walking a thin wire, Dallas,' Whitney said after a moment. 'The dead have families, and the families want this put away. Your continued investigation extends the grieving process.'

'I'm sorry for that.'

'It's also raising questions from The Tower,' he added, referring to the Chief of Police and Security.

'I'm willing to present my report to Chief Tibble, if directed.' But she hoped she wouldn't be. 'I'll stand on my record, Commander. I'm not a rookie playing terrier with a dead case.'

'Even experienced cops overfocus, make mistakes.'

'Then let me make them.' She shook her head before he could speak. 'I was on that ledge today, Commander. I looked at her face, into her eyes when she went off. And I know.'

He folded his hands on the edge of the desk. Administration was always a struggle in compromise. He had other cases, and he needed her on them. The budget was thin, and there was never enough time or man power. 'I can give you a week, no more. If you don't have the right answers by then, you close the files.'

She drew a breath. 'And the chief?'

'I'll speak with him personally. Get me something, Dallas, or be prepared to move on.'

'Thank you, sir.'

'Dismissed,' he said, then added when she reached the door. 'Oh, and Dallas, if you're going to go outside the official sphere for . . . research, watch your step. And give my best to your husband.'

She colored slightly. He'd pinned her source, and they both knew it. She mumbled something and escaped. Dodged that stun stream, she thought and dragged a hand through her hair. Then, with an oath, she dashed toward the nearest down glide. She was going to be late for court.

She was approaching the end of her shift when she made it back to her office and found Peabody settled at the desk, a cup of coffee in her hand.

Eve leaned against the doorjamb. 'Comfortable, Officer?'

Peabody jerked, sloshed a little coffee, cleared her throat. 'I didn't know your ETA.'

'Apparently. Something wrong with your unit?'

'Ah, no. No, sir. I thought it more efficient to enter the new data directly into yours.'

'That's a good story, Peabody, you stick with it.' Eve walked to her AutoChef and programmed coffee for herself. It was Roarke's blend rather than the poison served in the bull pen area, which explained Peabody cozying up at her superior's desk.

'What new data?'

'Captain Feeney pulled all communications on Devane's 'links. Doesn't appear to be anything that relates, but it's all here. We have her personal datebook with all appointments and the most current data from her last health exam.'

'She have any problems there?'

'Not a one. She was a tobacco addict, registered, and took regular anticancer injections. She had no sign of disease: physical, emotional, or mental. Tended toward stress and overwork, which was counteracted with soothers and tranqs. She was cohabitating, happily, by all reports. Her partner is currently off planet. You have the name of next of kin, her son from a previous partnership.'

172

'Yeah, I contacted him. He's based at the Tattler offices in New L.A. He's coming in.' Eve angled her head. 'Comfortable, Peabody?'

'Yes, sir. Oh, sorry.' She got up quickly from behind the desk and resettled in the ratty chair beside it. 'Your meeting with the commander?'

'We've got a week,' Eve said briskly as she sat. 'Let's make the most of it. ME's report on Devane?'

'Not yet available.'

Eve turned to her 'link. 'Let's see if we can give him a little shove.'

By the time she got home, she was staggering. She'd missed dinner, which she thought was just as well since she'd ended the day at the morgue viewing what was left of Cerise Devane.

Even the stomach of a veteran cop could turn.

And she would get nothing there, nothing at all. She doubted even Roarke's equipment could reconstruct enough of Devane to be of any help.

She walked in, nearly tripped over the cat who was stretched at the threshold, and drummed up the energy to bend down and lift him. He studied her, annoyance gleaming in his bicolored eyes.

'You wouldn't get kicked, pal, if you draped your fat ass somewhere else.'

'Lieutenant.'

She shifted the cat, looked over at Summerset who, as usual, had appeared out of nowhere. 'Yeah, I'm late,' she snapped. 'Give me a demerit.'

He didn't add his normal withering remark. He had seen the clips on the news channel, and he had watched her on the ledge. He had seen her face. 'You'll want dinner.'

'No, I don't.' She wanted bed and headed for the stairs.

'Lieutenant.' He waited for her bad-tempered oath, waited

until she'd turned her head to scowl at him. 'A woman who steps out on a ledge is either very brave or very stupid.'

The scowl turned into a sneer. 'I don't have to ask what category you put me in.'

'No, you don't.' He watched her climb up and thought her courage was terrifying.

The bedroom was empty. She told herself she'd run a house scan for Roarke's location in just a minute, then fell facedown on the bed. Galahad wiggled out of the crook of her arm and climbed onto her butt to circle and knead his way to comfort.

Roarke found her there minutes later, sprawled out in exhaustion, a sausage-shaped cat guarding her flank.

He simply studied her for a while. He, too, had seen the news clips. They had paralyzed him, dried the saliva in his mouth, and turned his bowels to water. He knew how often she faced death – others' and her own – and told himself he accepted it.

But that morning he had watched, helpless, while she'd teetered on the brink. He'd looked into her eyes, seen the grit and the fear. And he had suffered.

Now she was here, home, a woman with more bone and muscle than curves, with hair that badly needed tending and boots worn out at the heels.

He walked over, sat on the edge of the bed, and laid a hand over the one curled loosely on the spread.

'I'm just getting my second wind,' she murmured.

'I can see that. We'll go dancing in a minute.'

She managed a chuckle. 'Can you move that boulder off my butt?'

Obligingly, Roarke picked up Galahad, smoothed the ruffled fur. 'You've had quite a day; Lieutenant. The media's been full of you.'

She rolled over but kept her eyes shut a minute longer. 'I'm glad I missed it. You know about Cerise then.'

'Yes, I had Channel 75 on while I was preparing for my first meeting this morning. I caught it all live.'

She heard the strain in his voice and opened her eyes. 'Sorry.'

'You'll say you were doing your job.' He set the cat aside and brushed the hair back from Eve's cheek. 'But it was above and beyond, Eve. She could have taken you with her.'

'I wasn't ready to go.' She cupped a hand over the one he held to her cheek. 'I had a flash when I was up there. Memory flash of when I was a kid, standing at the window of some filthy flop he'd booked us into. I thought about jumping then, just getting it the hell over with. I wasn't ready to go. I'm still not.'

Galahad climbed out of Roarke's lap and stretched his bulk over Eve's belly. It made Roarke smile. 'Looks like we both intend to keep you here for a while. What have you eaten today?'

She pursed her lips. 'Is this a quiz?'

'Nothing to speak of,' he decided.

'Food's not high on my list right now. I've just come from the morgue. Contact with concrete after seventy-story flights does unattractive things to flesh and bone.'

'I don't imagine there was enough to scan for comparison with the others.'

Despite the grisly image, she grinned, sat up, and gave him a quick, loud kiss. 'You're cued up, Roarke. That's one of the things I like best about you.'

'I thought it was my body.'

'That's right up on the list,' she told him as he rose and went over to the recessed AutoChef. 'No, there isn't going to be enough, but there has to be a connection. You see it, don't you?'

He waited until the protein drink he'd ordered came through. 'Cerise was an intelligent, sensible, and driven woman. She was often selfish, continually vain, and could be an enormous

175

pain in the ass.' He came back to the bed, held out the glass. 'She wasn't the type to jump off the roof of her own building – and let the visual media scoop her own organization.'

'I'll add that to my data.' She frowned at the creamy, mint-colored drink in her hand. 'What is this?'

'Nutrition. Drink it.' He tipped it up to her lips. 'All.'

She took the first sip out of self-defense, decided it wasn't altogether hideous, and gulped it down. 'There. Feel better now?'

'Yes. Did Whitney give you room to pursue?'

'I've got a week. And he knows I've been using your . . . facilities. He's pretending he doesn't.' She set the glass aside, started to stretch back out, then remembered. 'We were supposed to watch videos, eat popcorn, and neck.'

'You stood me up.' He tugged on her hair. 'I'll have to divorce you.'

'God, you're strict.' Suddenly nervous, she rubbed her hands together. 'While you're in that mode, I guess I'd better come clean.'

'Oh, were you out necking with someone else?'

'Not exactly.'

'I beg your pardon?'

'You want a drink? We've got some wine up here, don't we?' She started to get off the bed, but she wasn't at all surprised to have his hand snake out and grip her arm.

'Clarify.'

'I'm going to. I just think it might go down better with some wine. Okay?' She tried a smile but knew it fell far short of charming when he met it with a long, steely stare. His grip loosened enough for her to scoot up and hurry over to the bedroom cold box. She took her time pouring it, and kept her distance as she began.

'Peabody and I were doing the first sweep of Devane's office and quarters. She has a relaxation room.'

'I'm aware of that.'

176

'Sure you are.' She took a sip first to fortify her for confession before she crossed back. 'Anyway, I noticed she had VR goggles on the arm of her sleep chair. Mathias had been on VR before he hanged himself. Fitzhugh liked to use VR. It's a slim link, but I figured it was better than no link.'

'Over ninety percent of the population of this country has at least one VR per household,' Roarke pointed out, eyes still narrowed on her face.

'Yeah, but you have to start somewhere. This is a brain flaw, VR links to the brain as well as the senses. It occurred to me that if there was a defect, intentional or accidental, in the goggles, it might have caused the suicidal urge.'

He nodded slowly. 'All right. I follow that.'

'So I tried her set.'

'Wait.' He held up a hand. 'You suspected the goggles were a contributor to her death, so you merrily put them on yourself. Are you out of your mind?'

'Peabody was there as control, with orders to stun me if necessary.'

'Well then.' Disgusted, he flung up a hand. 'That's just fine. That's perfectly reasonable then. She'd knock you unconscious before you jumped off the roof.'

'There you are.' She sat down beside him, handed him his glass. 'I checked the last use log. She'd gone VR minutes before she walked out and onto that ledge. I was sure I was going to find something in whatever program she'd been on.' She paused to scratch the back of her neck. 'You know, I figured it would be some relaxation program. Maybe a meditation run, your standard sea cruise, or a country meadow.'

'I take it it wasn't.'

'No, it wasn't. It was, ah, a fantasy run. You know, a sexual fantasy.'

Intrigued now, he folded his legs under him, cocked his head. His mouth remained sober, his Irish blue eyes bland.

177

'Was it really?' He took a casual sip of wine before setting the glass aside. 'And consisted of?'

'Well, there were these guys.'

'Plural?'

'Just two.' She could feel the heat rising up to her throat and detested it. 'It was an official investigation.'

'Were you naked?'

'Jesus, Roarke.'

'I believe it's a perfectly reasonable question.'

'Maybe for a minute, okay? It was the program, and I had to test the program, and it wasn't my fault these guys were all over me – and I aborted it before, well almost before . . .'

She stumbled to a guilty halt and saw with shock that he was grinning at her. 'You think it's funny?' Bunching her fist, she punched him in the shoulder. 'I've been feeling like slime all day, and you think it's funny.'

'Before what?' he asked, nipping the glass out of her hand before she could upend it over his head. He set it down beside his own. 'You aborted the program almost before what, precisely?'

Her eyes went to slits. 'They were great. I'm getting a copy of the program for my personal use. I won't need you anymore, because I've got a couple of love slaves.'

'Wanna bet?' He pushed her back on the bed, wrestled with her, and managed to get her shirt over her head.

'Cut it out. I don't want you. My love slaves keep me satisfied.' She flipped him, nearly had him pinned when his mouth closed over her breast, and his hand slid neatly down to cup her over the thin wool snug at her crotch.

Heat speared through her like lightning.

'Damn it.' She gasped out a breath. 'I'm just pretending to enjoy this.'

'Okay.'

He tugged the slacks over her hips, then skimmed his fingertips over her. She was already wet, luring him in. His

178

teeth closed over her nipple, tugged, just as he nudged her to peak.

It wasn't a gentle pop this time. The orgasm came in one hard, fast wave that swamped her, drowned her, then tossed her helplessly over the next crest.

She moaned out his name. It was always his name. But when she reached for him, he cuffed her wrists, drew her arms over her head. 'No.' His own breathing was uneven and thick as he stared down at her. 'Just take it. Take me.'

He slipped inside her slowly, inch by inch, watching her eyes go blind and dark as he moved. Clamping down on the urge to ravish, to answer the sudden wild pistoning of her hips, he let her drive herself over the next edge.

And when she was limp and her breathing in tatters, he shifted to long, steady strokes. 'Take more,' he murmured, swallowing her groans, holding her captive, hands, mouth, loins. 'And more.'

Her system was overloaded, scrambled like her pulse. Her body was under siege, her sex so sensitized the wild pleasure was akin to pain. And still he moved slowly, lazily. 'I can't,' she managed, and her head whipsawed even as her hips arched for more. 'It's too much.'

'Let go, Eve.' He was holding onto control by his fingernails. 'Once more.'

He didn't let himself fall until she did.

Her head was still spinning when she managed to push herself up on her elbows. Amazingly, they were both still half dressed and on top of the spread. From the corner of the bed, Galahad sat watching her with feline disgust. Or maybe it was envy.

Roarke had rolled over on his back and had what could only be interpreted as a smug smile on his lips.

'I guess that flexed your testosterone.'

His smile spread wider. She jabbed a finger into his ribs.

'If that was to punish me, you missed the target.'

179

Now he opened his eyes and they were filled with warm amusement. 'Darling Eve, did you really think I'd consider your little adventure some sort of virtual adultery?'

She pouted a little. However ridiculous it was, she was miffed that he wasn't at all jealous. 'Maybe.'

With a long sigh, he sat up, set his hands on her shoulders. 'You can indulge in fantasy professionally or personally. I'm not your keeper.'

'It doesn't bother you?'

'Not in the least.' He gave her a friendly kiss, then caught her chin firmly in his hand. 'Try it in the flesh, even once, and I'll have to kill you.'

Her pupils widened, and foolishly her heart gave a pleased little leap. 'Oh, well, that's fair.'

'That's fact,' he said simply. 'Now that we have that straightened out, you should get some sleep.'

'I'm not tired anymore.' She tugged her slacks back over her hips and made him sigh again.

'I suppose that means you want to work.'

'If I could use your system, just for a couple of hours, I could get a jump on my legwork tomorrow.'

Resigned, he pulled on his own slacks. 'Let's go then.'

'Thanks.' She tucked her hand in his companionably as they walked toward the private elevator. 'Roarke, you wouldn't really kill me, would you?'

'Oh yes, I would.' Smiling easily, he nudged her into the car. 'But, given our relationship, I would trouble to do so quickly, and with as little pain as possible.'

She shot him a glance. 'Then I'll have to say same goes.'

'Naturally. East wing, third level,' he ordered, and gave her hand a companionable squeeze. 'I wouldn't have it any other way.'

Chapter Thirteen

For the next few days, Eve beat her head against the wall of every dead end. When she needed a change of pace to clear her mind, she beat Peabody's head against the wall. She hounded Feeney to eke out whatever free time he could to find her something. Anything.

She gritted her teeth when other cases landed on her desk, and she worked overtime.

When the lab boys dragged their feet, she hopped on their backs and rode them mercilessly. It got to the point that the lab began to dodge her communications. To combat that, she hauled Peabody down to the lab for a little face-to-face persuasion.

'Don't try to sell me that SOS about backup, Dickie.'

Dickie Berenski, privately known as Dickhead, looked pained. As chief lab tech, he should have been able to delegate a half dozen drones to ward off a personal confrontation with an irate detective, but every one of them had deserted him.

Heads would roll, he thought, and sighed. 'What do you mean SOS?'

'Same old shit, Dickie. It's always SOS with you.'

He scowled but decided to make the acronym his own. 'Listen, Dallas, I got you the breakdown on all the over the counters, didn't I? Flagged them personally as a favor.'

'Favor, my ass, I bribed you with box seats for the Arena Ball play-offs.'

His face went prim. 'I assumed that was a gift.'

'And I'm not bribing you again.' She jabbed a finger into his puny chest. 'What's the deal with the VR goggles? Why haven't I got your report?'

'Because I haven't found anything to report. It's a hot program, Dallas—' His eyebrows did a little suggestive dance. 'But it was clean. No defects. So are all the other options on that unit – clean and up to code. Better than,' he added, his voice whining faintly. 'We should have so good. I had Sheila take the whole unit apart and put it back together. Damn fine equipment, top of the line – higher than top. The technology's off the scale. But that's to be expected. It's a Roarke product.'

'It's a—' She broke off, struggling not to show her surprise or distress at this new tidbit of information. 'Which plant manufactures it?'

'Hell, Sheila's got that data. Off planet, I'm pretty sure. Cheaper labor. And that baby was right off the ship. Hasn't been on the open market more than a month.'

Her stomach had clutched and tightened further. 'But it's not defective?'

'Nope. It's a real honey. I've already put in for one of my own.' He wiggled his brows hopefully. 'Of course, you could probably get me a unit at cost.'

'You get me the report, now, every single detail, and release the unit to me, and I'll think about it.'

'It's Sheila's flex day,' he whined, his mouth stretching down in a search for pity. 'She'll have the report finished up and on your desk by noon tomorrow.'

'Now, Dickie.' A good cop knew her quarry's weaknesses. 'And I'll see about making you a gift of your own unit.'

'Well, in that case . . . hang for ten.' Cheery now, he hurried over to a computer bank tucked in one of the cubbyholes in the lab's beehive.

'Dallas, one of those units probably goes for two thousand,

base.' Peabody stared after Dickie in disgust. 'You overbribed him.'

'I want that report.' Eve imagined that Roarke had a case of the units somewhere for promotional giveaways. Giveaways, she thought with a sick roll in her stomach, to politicians, employees, prominent citizens. 'I'm down to three days. And nothing. I won't be able to waltz Whitney toward an extension.' She looked back over as Dickie pushed out of the cubicle.

'Sheila had it almost nailed down.' He offered a sealed disc and a hard copy. 'Look at this. This is a compu-graft of the VR pattern for the last program. Sheila's highlighted a couple of blips.'

'What do you mean, blips?' Eve snatched the page and studied what appeared to be a series of lightning bolts and swirls.

'Can't say for certain. Probably the subliminal relaxation, or in this case, substimulation option. Some of the newer units are offering several extended subliminal packages. You can see these shadow the program, slide in every few seconds.'

'Suggestions?' She felt her energy surge. 'You mean the program was fitted with subliminal suggestions to the user?'

'Common enough practice. It's been used for habit breaking, sexual enhancement, mind expanding, and so on for decades. My old man quit tobacco on subliminals fifty years ago.'

'What about planting urges . . . such as self-termination?'

'Look, subs give you little nudges toward hunger, consumer goods, or aid in habit breaking. That kind of direct suggestion?' He tugged at his lip, shook his head. 'You'd have to go deeper, and I'd say it would take a long series of sessions to make the suggestion stick on a normal brain. Survival instinct's too strong.'

He shook his head again, convinced. 'We played those programs over and over.'

Particularly the sexual fantasy sequences, Eve thought.

'Ran them on test subjects, into the droid for analysis. We got nobody jumping off the roof. In fact, we got no unusual reaction from anyone or out of the droid. It's just a top flight, that's it.'

'I want a full analysis on the subliminal shadows.'

He'd already anticipated that. 'I need to keep the unit then. Sheila's started on it, as you can see, but it takes time. You've got to run the program, back out the overt VR, expunge the subliminals. Then it takes compu time to test, analyze, and report. A good subliminal, and I guarantee this one's an ace, is subtle. Chasing down its pattern isn't like reading a truth analysis.'

'How much time?'

'Two days, a day and a half if we get lucky.'

'Get lucky,' she suggested and passed the hard copy to Peabody.

Eve tried not to worry about the fact that the VR was one of Roarke's toys, or what the consequences could be if it was indeed found to be part of the coercion. Subliminal shadows. That could be the connection she'd been searching for. The next step was to tag the VR units that had been in Fitzhugh's, Mathias's, and Pearly's possession at time of death.

With Peabody keeping pace, she hustled down the side-walk. Her vehicle was – still – in Maintenance. Eve didn't think it worth the incredible headache of requisitioning a sub for a three-block hike.

'Autumn's coming.'

'Huh?'

Curious that Eve seemed oblivious to the freshening in the air, the balmy scent on the eastward breeze, Peabody paused to take a deep breath. 'You can smell it.'

'What are you doing?' Eve demanded. 'Are you crazy? Suck in enough of New York and you'll have to spend a day in detox.'

184

'You get past the transport fumes and the body odor and it's wonderful. They might just pass that new fresh air bill this election.'

Eve spared her aide a glance. 'Your Free-Ager's showing, Peabody.'

'Nothing wrong with environmental concerns. If it wasn't for the tree huggers, we'd all be wearing filter masks and sunshades year round.' Peabody looked longingly at a people glide but matched her pace to Eve's long-legged stride. 'Not to put a damper on things, Lieutenant, but you're going to have to do a major tap dance to access those VR units. SOP would be for them to have been returned to the deceaseds' estates by this time.'

'I'll get them – and I want this kept quiet, on a need-to-know basis only – until I sort it out.'

'Understood.' She waited a moment. 'I'd imagine Roarke has so many tentacles out there it would be impossible to know who's doing exactly what at any given time.'

'It's a conflict of interest and we both know it. I'm putting your ass on the line with this.'

'Sorry to disagree, sir, but I'm in charge of my own ass. It's only on the line if I put it there.'

'So noted and appreciated.'

'Then you can also note that I'm a big fan of Arena Ball as well, sir.'

Eve stopped, took a long look, then laughed. 'One ticket or two?'

'Two. I could get lucky.'

They exchanged grins just as a shrill siren split the air. 'Oh hell, oh shit, five minutes either way and we'd have slipped by this.'

Eve drew her weapon and spun on her heel. The alarm pealed from the credit exchange center directly in front of her. 'What fool hits a CEC two blocks from Cop Central? Clear the street, Peabody,' she ordered, 'then cover the back exit.'

The first order was almost unnecessary as pedestrians were already scattering, trampling each other over glides and skywalks in a rush for cover. Eve whipped out her communicator, gave the standard order for backup before she dived through the automatic doors.

The lobby was a mass of confusion. Her only advantage was that the wave of people were rushing out as she rushed in, and they offered some cover. Like most CECs, the lobby area was small, windowless, banked with high counters for personal privacy. Only one of the personal service counters was manned by a human, the other three by droids who had gone into automatic shutdown once the panic button had been pushed.

The lone human was a female, probably midtwenties, with closely cropped black hair, a tidy, conservative white jumpsuit, and an expression of utter terror on her face as she was held through the security port by the throat.

The man who gripped her was busy squeezing off her air and waving what was certainly a homemade explosive with his free hand.

'I'll kill her. I'll fucking stuff it down her throat.'

The threat didn't worry Eve nearly as much as the calm, deliberate manner in which it was delivered. She discounted chemicals and a professional status. From the appearance of his threadbare jeans and shirt, the tired, unshaven face, she concluded she had one of the city's desperately poor on her hands.

'She hasn't done anything to you.' With the first mad rush already out the door, Eve approached slowly. 'She's not responsible. Why don't you let her go?'

'Everyone's done something to me. Everyone's part of the system.' He yanked, pulling the hapless clerk a little farther through the security port. She was wedged now to the shoulders and turning faintly blue. 'Keep back,' he said quietly. 'I've got nothing to lose and nowhere to go.'

'You're choking her. Snuff her and you've got no shield. Ease up a little. What's your name?'

'Names don't count for shit.' But he did loosen his grip enough to have the young clerk wheeze in a desperate breath. 'Money's what matters. I walk out with a bag of credits, nobody gets hurt. Hell, they'll just make more.'

'It doesn't work that way.' Cautious, Eve took another three steps, keeping her eyes on his. 'You know you're not going to get out of here. By now the street's blocked, the security units are deployed. Jesus, pal, the area's lousy with cops any time of the day or night. You could've picked better than this.'

Out of the corner of her eye, she saw Peabody slide through the rear access and take up her position. Neither of them could risk firing while he had the clerk and the explosive in his hands.

'If you drop that thing, even sweat too much, it could blow. Then everybody dies here.'

'Then we'll all die here. It doesn't matter anymore.'

'Let the clerk go. She's a civilian. She's just trying to make a living.'

'So was I.'

She saw it in his eyes just an instant too late. The utter despair. In a blink he tossed the hand-held boomer high and right. Eve's life flashed obscenely before her eyes as she sprinted forward and made the dive. She missed by a fingertip.

Even as she braced for the insult of the blast, the crudely made ball rolled into a corner, bobbled, then settled quietly.

'Dud.' The would-be thief let out a weak laugh. 'Doesn't it just figure?' Then, as Eve popped to her feet, he charged.

She didn't have time to aim, much less fire her weapon. He hit her like a battering ram, driving her back hard into one of the self-service counters. The explosion came now, inside her head as her hip slammed painfully into the edge. Sheer luck had her holding onto her weapon as stars burst in her head.

She hoped the crack she heard was the cheap laminate giving and not bone.

He had her gripped in a pathetically loverlike embrace that was surprisingly effective. It blocked her weapon and pinned against the counter, so she was forced to shift her body weight rather than pivot.

They hit the floor, and this time she was unlucky enough to land first so that his thin, panic-fueled body dropped heavily on hers. Her elbow cracked on the tile, her knee jarred and twisted viciously. With more enthusiasm than finesse, she rammed the side of her weapon against his temple.

The move proved to be as effective as a stun. His eyes rolled up white before she shoved him aside and got to her knees.

Panting, fighting back the nausea that was a result of taking some bony part of his body in the stomach, she blew the hair out of her eyes. Peabody was also on her knees, the boomer in one hand, her weapon in the other.

'I couldn't get a clear shot. I went for the boomer first, thought you could take him.'

'Fine, that's just dandy.' She hurt everywhere, and now her pulse began to hammer at the sight of her aide clutching a bomb. 'Don't move.'

'Not moving. Barely breathing.'

'I'll call the goddamn bomb disposal unit. Get a safe box in here now.'

'I was just about—' Peabody broke off, went pale as death. 'Oh hell, Dallas. It's heating up.'

'Dump it. Dump it now! Take cover.' Swiping out one handed, Eve dragged the unconscious man with her behind the counter, draped herself over him, then locked her arms over the back of her head.

The explosion blasted the air, fumed out a fist of heat and had God knew what raining down on her. The auto fire control system whirled into action, spewing sprays of icy water, shrilling out a new alarm, warning employees and customers to vacate the building in a calm and orderly manner.

She sent up a quick thanks to whoever was listening that she felt no bright pain, and that all her body parts appeared to be attached.

Coughing against the thick wash of smoke, she crawled out from behind what was left of the counter. 'Peabody. Christ.' She hacked, wiped her stinging eyes, and kept crawling over the wet, now filthy floor. Something hot burned the heel of her hand, made her swear again. 'Come on, Peabody. Where the hell are you?'

'Here.' The answer was weak, followed by a fit of throaty coughing. 'I'm okay. I think.'

They met on hands and knees through the curtain of smoke and water and eyed each other's blackened faces. Casually, Eve reached out and rapped Peabody several times on the side of the head. 'Your hair was on fire,' she said mildly.

'Oh. Thanks. How's the asshole?'

'Still unconscious.' Eve sat back on her heels and took a quick self-inventory. She didn't see any blood, which was no small relief. Most of her clothes were still there, which hardly mattered since they were ruined. 'You know, Peabody, I think Roarke owns this building.'

'Then he's probably going to be pissed. Smoke and water damage is a bitch.'

'You're telling me. Let's call it a goddamn day. The credit cops can handle this. I'm giving a party tonight.'

'Yeah.' Mouth twisted, Peabody tugged on the torn sleeve of her uniform. 'I'm looking forward to it.' Then she swayed, squinted. 'Dallas, how many pairs of eyes did you have when we came in here?'

'One. Just one.'

'Shit. Now you've got two. I think one of us has a problem.' With this, Peabody pitched forward into Eve's arms.

There wasn't time to clean up. After she'd hauled Peabody

out of the wreckage and dumped her on the medical techni-cians, she had a report to relay to the officer in charge of the security team, then she fed the same data to the bomb disposal unit. Between reports she harassed the MTs about Peabody's condition and blocked their attempts to treat her to an injury scan.

Roarke was already dressed for the evening when she rushed in the door. He cut off his conversation with Tokyo on his palm link, shifted away from the team of florists currently arranging pink and white hibiscus in the foyer.

'What the hell happened to you?'

'Don't ask.' She raced past him and hit the stairs at a dead run.

She was out of what was left of her shirt by the time he came into the bedroom, closed the door. 'I will ask.'

'The bomb wasn't a dud after all.' Unwilling to sit down and smear whatever was on her slacks onto the furniture, she balanced on one foot and fought off a boot.

Roarke took a deep breath. 'The bomb?'

'Well, a homemade boomer. Very unreliable.' She pried off the second boot, then began to peel off her torn and blackened slacks. 'Guy hits a CEC two blocks from Cop Central. Idiot.' She dumped the tatters on the floor, swung around to head to the bath, only to come up short when Roarke took her arm.

'Name of God.' He turned her to get a closer look at the purpling bruise that spread over her hip. It was bigger than his spread hand. Her right knee was raw and there were more bruises blooming on her arms and shoulders. 'You're a mess, Eve.'

'You should see the other guy. Well, at least he'll get three square and a roof for a few years, courtesy of the state. I've got to get cleaned up.'

He didn't release her, only shifted his gaze to hers. 'I don't suppose you bothered to let the MTs work on you.'

'Those butchers?' She smiled. 'I'm fine, just sore. I can get a quick treatment tomorrow.'

'You'll be lucky if you can walk by tomorrow. Come on.'

'Roarke—' But she winced and hobbled, and he pulled her into the bath.

'Sit. Be quiet.'

'We don't have time for this.' She sat, rolled her eyes. 'It's going to take me a couple hours to get the stink and soot off. Christ, those boomers smell.' She turned her head to sniff at her shoulder and grimaced. 'Sulfur.' Then she eyed him warily. 'What's that?'

He approached with a thick pad soaked in something pink. 'The best we can do at the moment. Stop wiggling.' He laid the pad over her injured knee, holding it in place and ignoring her curses.

'That stings. Christ, are you crazy?'

'I'm beginning to think so.' With his free hand, he caught her chin, carefully examined her blackened face. 'At the risk of repeating myself, you're a mess. Hold that pad in place.' He squeezed lightly on her chin. 'I mean it.'

'Okay, okay.' She huffed out a breath and kept the pad over her knee as he walked back to a wall cabinet. The sting was easing. She didn't want to admit that the ripe ache in her knee was backing off. 'What's in this stuff?'

'This and that. It'll ease the swelling and numb the injury for a few hours.' He came back with a small tube of liquid. 'Drink it.'

'Uh-uh, no drugs.'

Very calmly, he laid a hand on her shoulder. 'Eve, if you're not in pain at the moment, it's due to adrenaline. You're going to hurt, and hurt big time, very shortly. I know what it feels like to be bruised and battered all over. Now drink it.'

'I'll be fine. I don't want—' She gasped when he pinched her nose, drew her head back, and poured the liquid down

191

her throat. 'Bastard,' she managed, choking and batting at him.

'That's a good girl. Now, into the shower.' He walked to the glass-enclosed tube and ordered the spray at half force and a soothing eighty-six degrees.

'I'll get you for that. I don't know how, I don't know when, but I'll do it.' She limped into the shower, still muttering. 'Son of a bitch pours drugs down my throat. Treats me like a goddamn imbecile.' The moan of relief came involuntarily as the soft water slid over her abused body.

He watched her, smiling as she braced both hands against the wall and ducked her head under the spray. 'You'll want to wear something loose and floor length. Try the blue ankle sweep Leonardo designed for you.'

'Oh, go to hell. I can dress myself. Why don't you stop staring at me and go order some of your minions around?'

'Darling, they're our minions now.'

She bit off a chuckle and rapped her hand against the shower panel to access the 'link recessed there. 'Brightmore Health Center,' she ordered. 'Fifth floor admissions.' She waited for the connection and managed to soap up her hair one-handed. 'This is Lieutenant Eve Dallas. You have my aide, Officer Delia Peabody. I want status.' She listened to the standard line for approximately five seconds before she cut off the charge nurse. 'Then find out, and find out now. I want her full status, and believe me, you don't want me coming down there to get it.'

It took her an hour, a relatively painless hour, she was forced to admit. Whatever Roarke had made her drink didn't leave her with that helpless, floaty feeling she detested. Instead, she felt alert and only slightly giddy.

It might have been the drug that made her admit, at least to herself, that he'd been right about the dress. It slid weightlessly over her skin, concealing the bruises stylishly with its high neck, long, tapering sleeves, and draping skirt. She added the diamond he'd given her as a symbolic apology for swearing at him – even though he'd deserved it.

With less resentment than usual, she fussed with her face, struggled with her hair. The result, she decided as she gave herself a study in the triple mirrors in the closet, wasn't half bad. She supposed she looked as close to elegant as she was ever going to get.

When she walked onto the roof terrace where the performance session of the party was to take place, Roarke's quick smile agreed with her. 'There she is,' he murmured and walked over to take both of her hands, bringing them to his lips.

'I don't think I'm talking to you.'

'All right.' He lowered his head and, mindful of bruises, kissed her lightly. 'Feel better?'

'Maybe.' She sighed and didn't bother to tug her hands away. 'I guess I'll have to tolerate you, since you're doing all this for Mavis.'

'We're doing it for Mavis.'

'I haven't done anything.'

'You married me,' he pointed out. 'How's Peabody? I heard you calling the health center from the shower.'

'Mild concussion, bumps, and bruises. She was a little shocky, but she's stabilized. She went after the boomer.' Remembering that moment, Eve blew out a slow breath. 'It started to heat up right in her hand. No way I could get to her.' She closed her eyes, shook her head. 'Scared the hell out of me. I thought I'd find pieces of her everywhere.'

'She's tough and smart, and she's learning from the best.'

Eve opened her eyes, narrowed them. 'Flattery isn't going to make me forgive you for drugging me.'

'I'll find something else that will.'

She surprised him by reaching up, framing his face with her hands. 'We're going to talk about that, ace.'

'Anytime. Lieutenant.'

But she didn't smile. Her eyes only went more intense. 'There's another thing we have to talk about. It's serious.'

'I can see that.' Concerned, he glanced around at the bustling caterers, the wait staff already lined up for their final briefing. 'Summerset can handle the last of this. We can use the library.'

'It's bad timing, I know, but it can't be helped.' She took his hand, an instinctive gesture of support, as they headed out of the room and down the wide corridor toward the library.

Inside, he closed the door, ordered lights, then poured drinks. Mineral water for Eve. 'You'll have to forgo alcohol for a few hours,' he told her. 'The painkiller doesn't mix well with it.'

'I think I can restrain myself.'

'Tell me.'

'Okay.' She set the glass aside without drinking, pushed both hands through her hair. 'You've got a new VR unit on the market.'

'I do.' He sat on the arm of a leather sofa, took out a cigarette, and lighted it. 'It hit a month, six weeks ago, depending on region. We've improved a number of the options and programs.'

'With subliminals.'

He blew out smoke thoughtfully. It wasn't difficult to read her, he thought, when you understood her. She was worried, stressed, and the soothing power of the drug couldn't overtake her in that area. 'Naturally. Several of the option packages include a variety of subliminals. They're very popular.' Still watching her, he nodded. 'I take it Cerise had one of the new units and was using it before she jumped.'

'Yeah. The lab hasn't yet been able to identify the subliminal. May turn out to be nothing, but—'

'You don't think so,' he finished.

'Something triggered her. Something triggered all of them. I'm working on confiscating the VR units owned by the other

subjects. If it turns out they all owned that new model . . .
the investigation's going to circle around your company.
On you.'

'I had a sudden urge to encourage self-termination?'

'I know you had nothing to do with it,' she said quickly and
fiercely. 'I'm going to do everything I can to keep you out of
it. I want—'

'Eve,' he interrupted quietly, shifted to crush out his cigarette, 'you don't have to explain yourself to me.' He reached in
his pocket, took out his memo card, and tapped in a code. 'The
R and D on that model was done in two locations. In Chicago
and on Travis II. Manufacturing was handled by one of my
subsidiaries, again on Travis II. The distribution and shipping,
on and off planet, by Fleet. The packaging through Trillium,
marketing by Top Drawer here in New York. I can have all
the data sent to your office unit, if that's most convenient.'

'I'm sorry.'

'Stop.' He tucked the card away and rose. 'There are literally
hundreds, perhaps thousands of employees in these companies.
I can certainly get you a list, for whatever good that would do.'
Then he paused, reached down, and rubbed a thumb over the
diamond she wore. 'You should know I personally worked on
and approved the design, initialed the schematics. The unit's
been in development for more than a year, and I spot-checked
every stage at one time or another through that period. My
hands are all over it.'

She'd been sure of that, afraid of that. 'It could come to
nothing. Dickhead claims my theory of subliminal coercion
to self-termination is over the edge of unlikely into the
impossible.'

Roarke smiled a little. 'How can one trust a man called
Dickhead? Eve, you used the unit yourself.'

'Yeah, which also put a big wrench in my pet theory. All
I got out of it was an orgasm.' She couldn't quite bring off
a smile herself. 'I want to be wrong, Roarke. I want to be

195

wrong and close these cases as voluntary self-terminations. But if I'm not—'

'We'll deal with it. First thing tomorrow, I'll look into it myself.' She started to shake her head, but he took her hand. 'Eve, I know the drill; you don't. I know my people, at least the department heads in each stage. You and I have worked together before.'

'I don't like it.'

'That's a pity.' He toyed with the diamond between her breasts again. 'I believe I do.'

Chapter Fourteen

'Roarke sure knows how to dish a party.' Mavis stuffed a dev-iled quail egg in her mouth and chattered over it. 'Everybody, and I mean everybody's here. Did you see Roger Keene? He's like top hound at Be There Records. And Lilah Monroe? She's tearing them up with her new audience participation show on Broadway. Maybe Leonardo can charm her into using him for new costume design. And there's—'

'Take a breath, Mavis,' Eve advised as her friend babbled and continually pushed canapés into her mouth. 'Adjust the speed.'

'I'm so nervous.' With her hands momentarily free, Mavis pressed them to her stomach – bare but for an artistic rendering of a ripe, red orchid. 'I can't level, you know? When I'm this hyped I've just gotta eat and talk. And eat and talk.'

'And throw up if you don't slow down,' Eve warned. She scanned the room and had to admit that Mavis was right. Roarke knew how to dish up a party.

The room glittered, and so did the people. Even the food seemed to be glossy and polished, almost too ornamental to eat, though you couldn't prove that by Mavis. Since the weather had cooperated, the roof was open, inviting in the fresh breeze and showers of starlight. One wall was filled with a view screen, and Mavis whirled and pranced over it, her music sizzling out into the room.

Roarke had been canny enough to keep the volume muted.

'I'm never going to be able to pay you back for this.'

'Come on, Mavis.'

'No, I mean it.' After sending Leonardo a beaming smile and an exaggerated air kiss, she turned back to Eve. 'You and me, Dallas, we go back awhile. Hell, if you hadn't busted me, I'd probably still be picking pockets and running the grift.'

Eve chose an interesting-looking blot on a cracker for herself. 'That's digging deep, Mavis.'

'Maybe, but it doesn't change the facts. I did a lot to straighten myself out and change direction. I'm kind of proud of it.'

Remaking ourselves, Eve thought. *It could happen. It did happen.* She glanced over to where Reeanna and William were chatting with Mira and her spouse. 'You should be. I'm proud of you.'

'But what I'm talking about is this. I want to get it out – okay? – before I get up there and try to blow the diamonds off the ears of this group.' Mavis cleared her throat and promptly forgot the little speech she'd prepared. 'Hell with it. I know you, and I really love you. Like really love you, Dallas.'

'Christ, Mavis, don't start getting me all weepy. Roarke's already drugged me.'

Unashamed, Mavis swiped her hand under her nose.

'You'd have done this for me – if you knew how.' When Eve blinked and frowned, Mavis found her sentiment turning to amusement. 'Shit, Dallas, you wouldn't have the first clue how to order up anything more complicated than soy dogs and veggie hash. Roarke's hands are all over this bash.'

'*My hands are all over it.*' Roarke's words echoed in Eve's mind and made her shudder. 'Yeah, they are.'

'You asked him to do it, and he did it for you.'

Determined to let nothing shadow the evening, Eve shook off the dread. She shook her head. 'He did it for you, Mavis.'

Slowly, Mavis's lips curved and her eyes got misty again.

198

'Yeah, I guess he did. You've got a fucking prince, Dallas. A fucking prince. I've got to go throw up now. Be right back.'

'Sure.' With a half laugh, Eve grabbed some fizzy water from a passing tray and headed for Roarke. 'Excuse me, one minute,' she said and tugged him away from a group of people. 'You're a fucking prince,' she told him.

'Why thank you. I think.' He slid an arm around her waist, gently, put his other hand over hers that held the stem of her glass. He surprised her by moving her into a very smooth dance. 'You have to use your imagination with Mavis's . . . style,' he decided. 'But this one could almost be considered romantic.'

Eve lifted a brow and turned in to Mavis's voice rising over clashing brass. 'Yeah, it's a real old-fashioned, sentimental tune. I'm a lousy dancer.'

'You wouldn't be if you didn't try to lead. I decided since you weren't going to sit down and rest that battered body of yours, you could lean on me a while.' He smiled down at her. 'You're starting to limp again, just a bit. But you do look almost relaxed.'

'The knee's a little stiff,' Eve admitted. 'But I am pretty relaxed. I guess it was listening to Mavis babble. She's throwing up now.'

'Lovely.'

'It's just nerves. Thanks.' She went with impulse and gave him one of her rare public kisses.

'You're welcome. For?'

'For making sure we're not eating soy dogs and veggie hash.'

'My pleasure.' He drew her closer, keeping his arms easy. 'Believe me, it's my pleasure. Well, Peabody wears basic black and a mild concussion well,' he noted.

'What?' Jerking back, Eve followed his gaze and spotted her aide just coming through the wide double doors and snagging a flute off a tray. 'She should be flat on her back,' Eve muttered

199

and pulled away from Roarke. 'Excuse me while I go put her there.'

She stalked across the room, eyes narrowing as Peabody tried out a toothy smile. 'Some party, Lieutenant. Thanks for the invite.'

'What the hell are you doing out of bed?'

'It's just a bump on the head, and all they were doing was poking at me. I wasn't going to let a little thing like an explosion keep me from doing a party at Roarke's.'

'Are you on meds?'

'Just a couple of regulation pain blockers, and—' Her face fell when Eve snatched the champagne out of her hand. 'I was just going to hold it. Really.'

'Hold this,' Eve suggested and shoved her water into Peabody's hand. 'I ought to cart your butt right back to the health center.'

'You didn't go,' Peabody muttered, then lifted her chin. 'And I'm off duty. On personal time. You can't order me back.'

However much she sympathized and admired determination, Eve held firm. 'No liquor,' she snapped out. 'No dancing.'

'But—'

'I hauled you out of that building today, and I can haul you out of here. By the way, Peabody,' Eve added. 'You could lose a few pounds.'

'So my mother's always telling me.' Peabody huffed out a breath. 'No liquor, no dancing. Now, if you've finished with the restrictions, I'm going to go talk to somebody who doesn't know me.'

'Fine. Oh, Peabody?'

Peabody turned, scowling. 'Yes, sir?'

'You did good today. I won't have to think twice about going through the door with you.'

As Eve walked away, Peabody gaped after her. It had been

200

simply, even casually said, but it was the finest professional compliment she'd ever been given.

Socializing wasn't Eve's favorite pastime, but she did her best. She even resigned herself to dancing when she couldn't slide her way out of it. So she found herself being steered – it was the way she thought about dancing – around the floor by Jess.

'Your pal William?' Jess began.

'More Roarke's pal. I don't know him well.'

'Anyhow, he had some interesting input on designing an interactive to go with this disc. Bring the audience into the music – into Mavis.'

Brow lifted, Eve glanced back to the screen. Mavis was swiveling her barely covered hips and shrieking about burning up in the fire of love while red and gold flames spurted around her.

'You actually think people would want to go in there?'

He chuckled, let his voice cruise deeper south. 'Sugar, they'll trample each other to get in. And pay big for the chance.'

'And if they do,' she said, turning back to him, 'you get a nice fat percentage.'

'That's standard on development deals like this. Check with your man. He'll tell you.'

'Mavis made her choice.' She softened, noting that several guests were absorbed in the screen show. 'I'd say she made a good one.'

'We both did. I think we've got a hit,' he told her. 'And when we give them a taste of the show live and in the flesh – well, if the roof wasn't already off, we'd blow it off.'

'You're not nervous?' She looked at him: confident eyes, cocky mouth. 'No, you're not nervous.'

'I've been playing for my supper for too many years. It's a job.' He smiled at her, walked his fingers casually up her

201

back. 'You don't get nervous tracking killers. Revved, right? Psyched, but not nervous.'

'Depends.' She thought of what she was tracking now, and her stomach fluttered.

'No, you're steel. I could see that the first time I looked at you. You don't give, you don't back off. You don't flinch. It makes your brain, well your makeup, so to speak, a fascination. What drives Eve Dallas? Justice, revenge, duty, morality? I'd say it's a very unique combination of all of those, fueled by a conflict of confidence and self-doubt. You've got a strong sense of what's right, and you're constantly questioning who you are.'

She wasn't sure she liked the turn of the conversation. 'What are you, a musician or a shrink?'

'Creative people study other people; and music is a science as much as an art, an emotion as much as a science.' His silvery eyes stayed on hers as he guided her smoothly around other couples. 'When I design a series of notes, I want it to affect people. I have to understand, even study human nature if I'm to get the right reaction. How will this make them behave, make them think, make them feel?'

Eve spared an absent smile as William and Reeanna danced by, absorbed in each other. 'I thought it was for enter-tainment.'

'That's the surface. Just the surface.' His eyes were excited, gleaming with it as he spoke. 'Any music hack can run a theme through a computer and come out with a competent tune. The music business has gotten more and more ordinary and predictable because of technology.'

Brows lifted, Eve glanced toward the screen, and Mavis. 'I'd have to say I don't hear anything ordinary or predict-able here.'

'Exactly. I've put in time studying how tones, notes, and rhythms affect people, and I know what buttons to push. Mavis is a treasure. She's so open, so malleable.' He smiled when

202

Eve's eyes hardened. 'I meant that as a compliment, not that she's weak. But she's a risk taker, a woman who's willing to strip herself down and become a vessel for the message.'

'The message is?'

'Depends on the mind of the audience. The hopes and dreams. I wonder about your dreams, Dallas.'

So do I, she thought, but she met his gaze blandly. 'I'd rather stick with reality. Dreams are deceptive.'

'No, no, they're revealing. The mind, and the unconscious mind in particular, is a canvas. We paint on it constantly. Art and music can add such colors, such style. Medical science has understood that for decades and uses it to treat and study certain conditions, both psychological and physiological.'

She angled her head. *Was there another message here?* 'You sound more like a scientist than a musician now.'

'I've blended. One day, you'll be able to pick a song personally designed for your own brain waves. The mood enhancement capabilities will be endless and intimate. That's the key. Intimacy.'

She sensed he was making a pitch and stopped dancing. 'I wouldn't think it would be cost effective. And research into technology designed to analyze and coordinate with individual brain waves is illegal. For good reason. It's dangerous.'

'Not at all,' he disagreed. 'It's liberating. New processes, any sort of real progress usually starts out as illegal. As for the cost, it would be high initially, then come down as the design was adjusted for mass production. What's a brain but a computer, after all? You have a computer analyze a computer. What could be simpler?'

He glanced over at the screen. 'That's the intro for the last number. I've got to check my equipment before my cue.' He leaned in, kissed her cheek lightly. 'Wish us luck.'

'Yeah, luck,' she murmured, but her stomach was knotted.

What was a brain but a computer? Computers analyzing computers. Individualized programs designed for personal brain wave patterns. If it was possible, would it be possible to add suggestive programs linked directly with the user's brain? She shook her head. Roarke would never have approved it. He wouldn't have taken such a foolish risk. But she made her way through the crowd to him, laid a hand on his arm.

'I need to ask you a question,' she said quietly. 'Have any of your companies been doing under-the-table research on designing VR for personal brain wave patterns?'

'That's illegal, Lieutenant.'

'Roarke.'

'No. There was a time when I would have ventured into any number of not essentially legal areas in business. That wouldn't have been one of them. And no,' he added, anticipating her. 'That VR model is universally, not individually designed. Only the programs can be personalized by the user. What you're talking about is cost prohibitive, logistically tangled, and simply too damn much trouble.'

'Okay, that's what I figured.' Her muscles relaxed. 'But can it be done?'

He paused a moment, then lifted his shoulder. 'I have no idea. You'd have to have the individual's cooperation or access to a brain scan. That also involves personal approval and consent. And then . . . I have no idea,' he repeated.

'If I can get Feeney alone—' She swiveled her head, trying to find the electronics detective in the whirling crowd.

'Take the evening off, Lieutenant.' Roarke slipped an arm around her. 'Mavis is about to get her spotlight.'

'Okay.' She forced herself to push the worry to the back of her mind as Jess settled at his console and gave an introductory riff. *Tomorrow*, she promised herself and led the applause as Mavis spun onto the floor.

Then the worry was gone, melted away by the blast of Mavis's energy and her own wild pleasure as lights, music, and showmanship combined in a dizzy kaleidoscope.

'She's good, isn't she?' She was unaware she'd gripped

Roarke's arm like a mother with a child in the school play. 'Different, weird, but good.'

'She's all of that.' The clashing edge of notes, sound effects, and vocals would never be his music of choice, but he found himself grinning. 'She's caught the crowd. You can relax.'

'I'm relaxed.'

He laughed and hugged her closer. 'If you were wearing buttons, you'd pop them.' He didn't mind the fact that he had to put his mouth on her ear for her to hear him. And since he was there, anyway, he added an inventive suggestion for after the party.

'What?' She went hot all over. 'I believe that particular act is illegal in this state. I'll check my code book and get back to you. Cut it out.' She hunched up her shoulder in reaction as his teeth and tongue got busy on her earlobe.

'I want you.' Lust prickled over his skin like a rash, instant, itchy, immediate. 'Right now.'

'You can't be serious,' she began, but she found he was, fiercely, when his mouth closed over hers in a wild and urgent kiss. Blood thudded her pulse to vibrant life and the muscles in her thighs went limp. 'Get ahold of yourself.' She managed to ease back a half inch and was breathless, shocked, and very near blushing. Not everyone's attention was focused on Mavis. 'We're in the middle of an event here. A public one.'

'Then let's leave.' He was hard as rock, painfully ready. There was a wolf inside him, poised to lunge. 'There are a lot of private rooms in this house.'

She would have laughed if she hadn't felt the need vibrating from him. 'Get a grip, Roarke. This is Mavis's big moment. We're not running off into a closet like a couple of randy teenagers.'

'Yes, we are.' Half blind, he pulled her through the crowd and out of it while she babbled in stunned protest.

'This is nuts. What are you, a pleasure droid? You can damn well hold yourself in check for a couple of hours.'

'The hell with it.' He yanked open the closest door and shoved her inside what was indeed a closet. 'Now, goddamn it.' Her back rapped up against the wall, and before she could so much as gasp, he pulled up her skirts and drove himself into her.

She was dry, unprepared, shocked. *Ravaged*, was all she could think as she bit down on her lip to keep from crying out. He was rough, careless, and sent the bruises singing as he rammed her, over and over, into the wall. Even as she shoved at him, he pounded into her, his hands hiking up her hips, digging in and ripping a startled cry of pain from her throat.

She could have stopped him, her training was thorough. But training had dissolved into sheer feminine distress. She couldn't see his face, wasn't sure she'd recognize it if she could.

'Roarke.' It was shock, bone deep, that quavered in her voice. 'You're hurting me.'

He muttered something, a language she didn't understand and had never heard, so she stopped struggling, gripped his shoulders, and shut her eyes to what was happening to both of them.

Still he plowed into her, hands digging into her hips to keep her open for him, his breath whistling in her ear. He took her brutally, and with none of the finesse or control that was such an innate part of him.

He couldn't stop. Even as part of his brain stepped back, appalled at what he was doing, he simply couldn't stop. The need was like a cancer eating at him and he had to sate it to survive. There was a voice somewhere in his head, greedy and gasping. *Harder. Faster. More.* It drove him, pushed him, until with one final vicious thrust, he emptied.

She held on. It was that or slide to the floor. He was shuddering like a man with a fever and she didn't know whether to soothe him or belt him.

'Goddamn it, Roarke.' But when he pressed a hand to the

wall to keep balance as he swayed, she lost any sense of insult in worry.

'Hey, what is it? How much have you had to drink, anyway? Come on, lean on me.'

'No.' With the violent need met, his mind cleared. And remorse was a hot weight in his belly. He shook off the dizziness and eased himself back. 'Good God, Eve. Good God. I'm sorry. I'm so sorry.'

'Okay. It's okay.' He was sheet white. She'd never seen him look even remotely ill and was terrified. 'I should get Summerset, somebody. You've got to lie down.'

'Stop it.' He very carefully nudged away her stroking hands and stepped back until they were no longer touching. How could she bear to have him touch her? 'For Christ's sake. I raped you. I just raped you.'

'No.' She said it firmly, hoping the tone of her voice would be as effective as a slap. 'You did not. I know what rape is. What you did wasn't rape, even if it was a little overenthusiastic.'

'I hurt you.' When she reached out, he held up his hands to stop her. 'Goddamn it, Eve, you're bruised from head to foot, and I shoved you against the wall in some fucking closet and used you. Used you like a—'

'Okay.' She stepped forward, but he shook his head. 'Don't back away from me, Roarke. That's what will hurt. Don't do that.'

'I need a minute.' He rubbed his hands over his face. He still felt light-headed and queasy, and worse, slightly out of himself. 'Christ, I need a drink.'

'Which brings me back to my question. How much have you had?'

'Not enough. I'm not drunk, Eve.' He dropped his hands and looked around. *A closet*, was all he could think. *For God's pity, a closet.* 'I don't know what happened, what came over me. I'm sorry.'

'I can see that.' But she still couldn't see the whole picture. 'You kept saying something. Weird. Like *liomsa*.'

His eyes darkened. 'It's Gaelic. *Mine* it means. I haven't used Gaelic in . . . not since I was a boy. My father used it often when he was . . . on a drunk.'

He hesitated, then he reached out to graze his fingertips over her cheek. 'I was so rough with you. So careless.'

'I'm not one of your crystal vases, Roarke. I can take it.'

'Not like that.' He thought of the whimpers and protests of the alley whores that had come through the thin walls and haunted him when his father had bedded them. 'Never like that. I never thought of you. I didn't care, and there's no excuse.'

She didn't want him humble. It unnerved her. 'Well, you're too busy beating yourself up for me to bother, so let's go back.'

He touched her arm before she could open the door. 'Eve, I don't know what happened. Literally. One minute we were standing there, listening to Mavis, and the next . . . it was overpowering, vicious. Like my life depended on having you. Not just sex, but survival. I couldn't control it. That's not excusing what—'

'Wait.' She leaned back against the door a moment, struggled to separate woman from cop, wife from detective. 'You're not exaggerating?'

'No. It was like a fist around my throat.' He managed a very weak smile. 'Well, perhaps that's the wrong portion of the anatomy. There's nothing I can say or do to—'

'Eject the guilt a minute, will you, and think.' Her eyes were cold now, hard as agate. 'A sudden and irresistible urge – more a compulsion. One you, a very controlled man, couldn't control? You just pounded yourself into me with all the finesse of a sweaty celibate breaking fast with a rented sex droid.'

He winced at that, felt the tear of guilt. 'I'm all too aware of that.'

'And it's not your style, Roarke. You've got moves, I can't keep up with all of them, but they're all slick, practiced. You may get rough, but never mean. And as one who's made love with you in about every way that's anatomically possible, I can certify that you're never selfish.'

'Well.' He wasn't quite certain how to react. 'You humble me.'

'It wasn't you,' she murmured.

'I beg to differ.'

'It wasn't what you've made yourself into,' she corrected. 'And that's what counts. You snapped off. Something inside you snapped off. Or on. That son of a bitch.' Her breath shuddered out as she met Roarke's eyes, and in them she saw the dawning of understanding. 'That son of a bitch has something. He was telling me while we were dancing. He was fucking bragging, and I didn't get it. But he just had to give a little demonstration. And that's what's going to hang him.'

This time Roarke's grip on her arm was firm. 'You're talking about Jess Barrow. About brain scans and suggestions. Mind control.'

'Music should affect how people behave, how they think. How they feel. He said that to me minutes before the performance began. Cocky bastard.'

Roarke remembered the shock in her eyes when he'd thrown her against the wall and driven himself into her like a battering ram. 'If you're right,' his voice was cool now, too cool, 'I want a moment alone with him.'

'It's police business,' she began, but he stepped slightly closer, and his eyes were cold and determined.

'You'll give me a moment alone with him, or I'll find a way to take it. Either way, I'll have it.'

'All right.' She laid a hand over his, not to ease his grip but in solidarity. 'All right, but you'll wait your turn. I have to be sure.'

'I'll wait,' he agreed. But the man would pay, Roarke

209

promised himself, for wedging even one instant of fear and distrust into their relationship.

'I'll let the performance wind up first,' she decided. 'I'll interview him, unofficially, in my office downstairs, with Peabody as control. Don't make a move on him, Roarke. I mean that.'

He opened the door, let her slip out. 'I said I'd wait.'

The music was still going strong, and it hit them with a high, gritty pitch yards before they reached the doorway. But she had only to step in and through the crowd before Jess's eyes shifted from his controls and met hers.

His smile was quick, cocky, amused.

And she was sure.

'Find Peabody and ask her to go down to my office and set up for a prelim interview.' She stepped in front of Roarke, willed his gaze to move to hers. 'Please. We're not talking about just a personal insult here. We're talking about murder. Let me do my job.'

Roarke turned without a word. The moment she lost him in the crowd, she worked her way through to Summerset. 'I want you to watch Roarke.'

'I beg your pardon?'

'Listen to me.' Her fingers dug through his neat jacket and into bone. 'It's important. He could be in trouble. I don't want you to let him out of your sight until at least an hour after the performance. If anything happens to him, I'll fry your ass. Understood?'

Not in the least, but he did understand her urgency. 'Very well.' He spoke with dignity, crossed the room with grace, but his nerves were shattered.

Confident that Summerset would watch Roarke like a mother hawk, she wound her way through the audience again until she stood on the front edge of the group. She applauded with the rest, schooled herself to flash a supportive smile as Mavis wound up for the encore. And when the next round of applause rang out, she slipped toward Jess and skirted the controls.

'Quite a triumph,' she murmured.

'I told you, she's a treasure.' There was a wicked gleam in his eyes as he smiled up at her. 'You and Roarke missed a couple of numbers.'

'Some personal business,' she said levelly. 'I really need to talk to you, Jess. About your music.'

'Glad to. Nothing I like better.'

'Now, if you don't mind. Let's go someplace a little more private.'

'Sure.' He shut down his console, locked on the code. 'It's your party.'

'Damn right it is,' she murmured, and led the way.

Chapter Fifteen

She chose the elevator, wanting to move quickly and privately. She programmed it for the short vertical glide, then the horizontal shift from wing to wing.

'I've got to tell you, you and Roarke have a fantastic place here. Just ultra mag.'

'Oh, it'll do until we find something bigger.' She said it dryly and refused to let his laughter grate on her nerves. 'Tell me, Jess, did you decide to work with Mavis, seriously, before or after you knew the connection with Roarke?'

'I told you, Mavis is one in a million. Only had to see her a couple of times, doing a short gig down at the Down and Dirty to know we'd meld well.' The grin flashed. Charming. A choirboy holding a frog under his robe. 'It sure didn't hurt a thing that she had a contact like Roarke on her side. But she had to have the goods.'

'But you knew about the connection before.'

He moved a shoulder. 'I'd heard about it. That's why I went down to see her. That kind of club isn't my usual venue. But she flashed for me. If I can move her into some hot gigs, then if Roarke, or someone of his ilk, let's say, is interested in investing in a coming act, it smooths everybody.'

'You're smooth, Jess.' She stepped out of the car when the doors slid open. 'Real smooth.'

'Like I said, I've been shaking gigs since I was a kid. I think I got it down.' He looked around the corridor as she led the way.

Old art, the real thing, he noted, pricey wood, carpet some craftsman had worn his fingers weaving a century before.

This was money, he thought. The kind that built empires.

At the doorway of her office, she turned. 'I don't know how much he's got,' she said, reading him perfectly. 'And I don't really care.'

The smile still in place, he lifted a brow, lowered his gaze to the fat tear shaped diamond lying against the bodice of soft midnight silk. 'But you ain't wearing paste and rags, sugar.'

'I have, and I might again. And Jess?' She flicked off the coded lock. 'Don't call me sugar.'

Eve glided in, nodded to a puzzled but attentive Peabody. 'Have a seat,' she told Jess and moved directly to her desk.

'Nice milieu. Well, hi, sweetie.' He couldn't for the life of him remember her name, but he beamed at Peabody as if they were old, dear friends. 'Did you catch the act?'

'Most of it.'

He dropped into a chair. 'So, what do you think?'

'I thought it was great. You and Mavis really put on a show.' She risked a smile, not at all sure what Eve wanted from her. 'I'm ready to buy the first disc.'

'That's what I like to hear. Can a guy get a drink in here?' he asked Eve. 'I like to stay dry before a performance, and I'm more than ready to get wet.'

'No problem. What would you like?'

'That champagne looked good.'

'Peabody, there should be a bottle in the kitchen. Pour our guest here a glass of wine, will you? And why don't you get us some coffee?'

She leaned back and considered. Technically, she should record from this point, but she wanted a lead-in before she went on log. 'Someone like you, who designs music and the atmosphere surrounding it, has to be as much technician as artist, right? That's what you were explaining to me before the performance.'

213

'That's the way the business shakes down now, has for a lot of years.' He flicked one of his beautiful hands, braceleted with gold. 'I'm lucky I've got an aptitude for both and an interest. The days of plucking out a tune on the piano or playing a riff on a guitar have gone the way of fossil fuel. Almost extinct.'

'Where'd you get your tech training? I'd have to say it's way above run of the mill.'

He shot a fresh smile as Peabody came back with the drinks. He was comfortable, relaxed, and assumed he was in the middle of a kind of job interview. 'On the job, mostly, a lot of late-night hacking. But I did a stretch of home ed with MIT.'

She already knew some of the data from Peabody's make, but she wanted to lull him. 'Impressive. You've made a name for yourself both in performance and design. Isn't that right, Peabody?'

'Yeah. I've got all your discs, and I'm looking forward to something new. It's been a while.'

'I heard that somewhere.' Eve picked up the ball Peabody was unaware she'd tossed. 'Have a dry spell, Jess?'

'Not at all. I wanted to take my time perfecting the new equipment, putting together just the right elements. When I hit with the new stuff, it's going to be something no one's ever seen or heard before.'

'And Mavis is like a springboard.'

'In a manner of speaking. She was a lucky break. She'll showcase some of the material that wasn't right for me, and I've individualized some pieces to match her. I figure on doing some of my own sessions in a few months.'

'After everything's in place.'

He toasted her, sipped. 'Exactly.'

'You ever design soundtracks for VR?'

'Now and again. It's not a bad gig, if the program's interesting.'

'And I bet you know how to lay down subliminals.'

He paused, then sipped again. 'Subliminals? That's straight tech.'

'But you're a damn good tech, aren't you, Jess? Good enough to know computers in and out. And brains. A brain's just a computer, isn't it? Isn't that what you told me?'

'Sure.' His focus was all for Eve so that he didn't notice that Peabody had come to attention.

'And you're into mood enhancements, which lead to mood shifts. Behavioral and emotional patterns. Brain wave patterns.' She took a recorder out of her desk, placed it in plain sight. 'Let's talk about that.'

'What the hell is this?' He set down his glass, scooted to the edge of his seat. 'What's the deal?'

'The deal is, I'm going to advise you of your rights, then we're going to have a chat. Officer Peabody, engage backup recording and log on, please.'

'I didn't agree to a fucking interview.' He got to his feet. Eve got to hers.

'That's all right. We can make it obligatory, and take you to Cop Central. There might be a wait. I haven't booked an interview room. But you won't mind spending a few hours in lockup.'

Slowly, he sat again. 'You turn cop fast, Dallas.'

'No, I don't. I stay cop. Always. Dallas, Lieutenant Eve,' she began for the recorder, and fed in time and place before reciting the revised Miranda. 'Do you understand your rights and options, Jess?'

'Yeah, I get it. But I don't know what the hell this is about.'

'I'm going to make that very clear for you. You are being questioned in the matters of the unresolved deaths of Drew Mathias, S. T. Fitzhugh, Senator George Pearly, and Cerise Devane.'

'Who?' He looked convincingly baffled. 'Devane? Isn't that the woman who jumped off the Tattler Building? What am I supposed to have to do with suicide? I didn't even know her.'

215

'You were unaware that Cerise Devane was CEO and majority stockholder of Tattler Enterprises?'

'No, I guess I knew who she was, but—'

'I imagine you found yourself in *The Tattler* from time to time during your career.'

'Sure, they're always digging for dirt. They've tossed some my way. It's just part of the business.' Fear had backed off and left him mildly irritated. 'Look, the lady jumped. I was downtown, in session, when she took the leap. I've got witnesses. Mavis for one.'

'I know you weren't there, Jess. I was. At least I know you weren't there in the flesh.'

His sculpted mouth curled into a sneer. 'What am I, a goddamn ghost?'

'Do you know or have you ever had contact with an autotronics tech by the name of Drew Mathias?'

'Never heard of him.'

'Mathias also did a pass through MIT.'

'So have thousands. I opted for in-home. I never even set foot on campus.'

'And never had any contact with other students?'

'Sure I did. Over the 'link, E-mail, laser fax, whatever.' He shrugged his shoulders, drummed his fingers over the top of the hand-tooled boot he'd cocked on his knee. 'I don't remember any autotronics tech by that name.'

She decided to change tacks. 'How much work have you done on individualized subliminals?'

'I don't know what you're talking about.'

'You don't understand the term?'

'I know what it means.' This time his shrug was jerky. 'And as far as I know, it's never been done, so I don't know what you're asking me.'

Eve took a chance. She looked over at her aide. 'Do you know what I'm asking him, Peabody?'

'I think it's clear enough, Lieutenant.' She was struggling

through the mud of confusion. 'You'd like to know how much work the interview subject has done on individualized subliminals. Perhaps the interview subject should be reminded that it is not currently illegal to research or have an interest in this area. Only development and implementation are against current state, federal, and international laws.'

'Very good, Peabody. Does that help clear things up for you, Jess?'

The byplay had given him enough time to settle. 'Sure, I'm interested in the area. Lots of people are.'

'It's a little out of your field, isn't it? You're just a musician, not a licensed scientist.'

It was exactly the right button. His sat up in his chair, his eyes flashing once. 'I'm fully certified in Musicology. Music isn't just a bunch of notes strung together, sweetheart. It's life. It's memory. Songs trigger specific and often predictable emotional reactions. Music's an expression of emotion, desires.'

'And here I thought it was just a nice way to pass the time.'

'Entertainment is only a slice of the pie. The Celts went to war with bagpipes. They were as much a weapon to them as a broadax. Warring natives in Africa psyched themselves up with drums. Slaves survived on their spirituals, and men have been seducing women to music for centuries. Music plays the mind.'

'Which brings us back to the question. When did you decide to take it a step further and tie in to individual brain patterns? Did you just stumble across it, sort of blind luck, while you were noodling out a tune?'

He gave a short laugh. 'You really think what I do is just a slide, don't you? Just sit down, punch in some notes, and go. It's work. It's hard, demanding work.'

'And you're damned proud of your work, aren't you? Come on, Jess, you wanted to tell me earlier.' Eve rose, came around

217

the desk to sit on the front edge. 'You've been dying to tell me. To tell someone. What good is it, what satisfaction is there in creating something so amazing, then having to keep it to yourself?'

He picked up his glass again, ran his fingers down the long, slim stem. 'This isn't exactly the way I'd pictured this.' He took a sip, considered the consequences – and the rewards. 'Mavis says you can be flexible. It's not just code books and procedure with you.'

'Oh, I can be flexible, Jess.' When it's warranted. 'Talk to me.'

'Well, let's just say that if – hypothetically – I had worked out a technique for individualized subs, mood enhancements on a personal brain pattern, it could be big. People like Roarke and you, with your contacts and financial base, your influence, let's say, could work around a few antiquated laws and make a big pile. Revolutionize the personal entertainment and enhancement industry while you were at it.'

'Is this a business offer?'

'Hypothetically,' he said and gestured with his glass. 'Roarke industries has the R and D, the facilities, the man power, and the credits to take something like this and run with it. And a smart cop, seems to me, could find a way to bend the law, just enough, to make it go down smooth.'

'Gosh, Lieutenant,' Peabody said with a smile that didn't touch her eyes. 'Sounds like you and Roarke are the perfect couple. Hypothetically.'

'And Mavis as the conduit,' Eve murmured.

'Hey, Mavis is chilled. She got what she wanted. After tonight, she's going to cruise.'

'And you figure that evens out using her to get to Roarke.'

He moved a shoulder again. 'Backs gotta be scratched, honey. I gave hers a real full treatment.' The wicked amusement flashed into his eyes again. 'Did you enjoy the informal demonstration of my hypothetical system?'

Not certain even her training could keep the fury off her face, she turned, slipped back behind the desk. 'Demonstration?'

'The night you and Roarke came by the studio to watch the session. Seemed to me you two were pretty eager to leave, to be alone.' His smile sharpened at the corners. 'A little honeymoon revisited?'

She kept her hands behind the desk a moment until she could unclutch her fists. She glanced over toward the door of Roarke's connecting office, and saw with a jolt that the monitoring light blinked green over it.

He was watching, she realized. That was not only illegal, but dangerous under the circumstances. She flicked her eyes back to Jess. She couldn't afford to break rhythm. 'It seems you're unusually interested in my sex life.'

'I told you, you fascinate me, Dallas. You've got a mind. It's fucking steel, with all these dark spaces burned into it I wonder what would happen if you opened those spaces. And sex is a master key.' He leaned forward, eyes locked on hers. 'What do you dream, Dallas?'

She remembered the dreams, the sick horror of them, the night she'd watched the disc of Mavis. The disc he'd given her. Her hands trembled once before she could control them. 'You son of a bitch.' She rose slowly, planted her hands on the desk. 'You like giving demonstrations, asshole? Is that what Mathias was to you? A demonstration?'

'I told you, I don't know who that is.'

'Maybe you needed an autotron tech to perfect your system. Then you tried it out on him. You had his brain waves, so you programmed them in. Did you program in him tying his own noose and slipping it around his neck, or did you leave the method up to him?'

'You just veered way out of orbit.'

'And Pearly? What's the connection there? Political statement? Were you looking ahead? You're a real visionary. He'd

219

have tossed his weight against legalizing your new toy. Why not use it on him?'

'Hold it. Hold it.' He got to his feet. 'You're talking about murder. Christ, you're trying to wrap me up with murder.'

'Then Fitzhugh. Did you need a couple more demonstrations, Jess? Or did you just get a taste for it? Powerful, isn't it, being able to kill without getting your hands bloody?'

'I never killed anyone. You can't wrap this on me.'

'Devane was a bonus, with the media right there. You got to watch. I bet you really love to watch, don't you, Jess? I bet you got hot watching. Like you got hot thinking about where you'd push Roarke tonight with your goddamn toy.'

'That's what's rocking you, isn't it?' Furious, he leaned on the desk. His smile wasn't charming now, but feral. 'You want to sting me because I wired into your man. You should be thanking me. I bet the two of you fucked like wild minks.'

Her hand was in a fist, her fist slamming into his jaw before her brain registered the act. He went down like a stone, face first, arms splayed, and sent her 'link flying.

'Goddamn it.' Breath hitching, she uncurled her fist, clutched it again. 'Goddamn it.'

Peabody's voice came cool and calm through the buzzing in her ears. 'Let the backup record show that subject physically threatened the lieutenant during questioning. As a result, subject lost his balance and struck his head on the desk. He appears to be momentarily stunned.'

While Eve could do no more than stare at her, Peabody rose, stepped over, and dragged Jess up by the collar of his shirt. She held him there a moment, as if considering his condition. His knees sagged, his eyes rolled back white.

'That's affirmative,' she stated, then dumped him into a chair. 'Lieutenant Dallas, I believe your recorder has been damaged.' With a brush of her hand, Peabody tipped Eve's coffee onto the unit, effectively frying its chips. 'Mine is in working order and will be sufficient for reporting this interview. Are you injured?'

'No.' Eve shut her eyes, snapped her control back into place. 'No, I'm fine. Thank you. The interview breaks at oh one thirty-three. Subject Jess Barrow will be transported to the Brightmore Health Center for examination and treatment, and there be detained until nine hundred hours, when this interview will continue at Cop Central. Officer Peabody, please arrange for transport. Subject is to be held for questioning, charges pending.'

'Yes, sir.' Peabody glanced over as the door to Roarke's office slid open. It only took one look at his face to realize that there might be trouble. 'Lieutenant,' she began, careful to keep the recorder turned away. 'I'm getting interference on my communicator, and your 'link may have been damaged when the subject knocked it to the floor. Permission to use another room to send for the MTs.'

'Go ahead,' Eve said and sighed as she watched Roarke come in and Peabody stride out. 'You had no business monitoring this interview,' she began.

'I beg to differ. I had every business.' He glanced down at the chair as Jess moaned and shifted. 'He's coming around. I'd like my moment with him now.'

'Listen, Roarke—'

He cut her off with one swift, ice-edged stare. 'Now, Eve. Leave us alone.'

That was the trouble between them, she decided. Both of them were so used to giving orders that neither of them took orders well. But she remembered the stricken look in his eyes when he'd backed away from her. They had both been used, she thought, but Roarke had been victimized.

'You've got five minutes. That's it. And I'm going to warn you right now. The record shows he's relatively undamaged. If there are marks on him, it's going to swing back on me and compromise my case against him.'

His lips twitched in a bare flicker of a smile as he took her arm and led her to the door. 'Lieutenant, give me some credit. I'm a civilized man.' He shut the door in her face, locked it.

And, he thought, he knew how to cause great discomfort to the human body without leaving so much as a dent.

He walked over, hauled Jess out of the chair, and shook him until his eyes blinked into focus. 'Awake now, are you?' Roarke said softly. 'And aware?'

Sweat pooled cold at the base of Jess's spine. He was looking into the face of murder, and he knew it. 'I want a lawyer.'

'You're not dealing with the cops now. You're dealing with me. At least for the next five minutes. And you have no rights or privileges here.'

Jess swallowed, struggled for a show of cool. 'You can't lay a hand on me. If you do, it'll slap right back on your wife.'

Roarke's lips curved and struck a fresh fist of terror in Jess's gut. 'I'm going to show you just how mistaken you are in that.'

His eyes never left Jess's face as he reached down, grabbed onto his penis, and twisted. It was some satisfaction to see every drop of blood drain out of the man's face and watch his mouth work like a guppy's as it gasped for air. With his thumb, he pressed gently on Jess's windpipe and cut off even that thin passage of air until the silver eyes bulged.

'Hell, isn't it, to be led around by the cock?' He gave one last jerk of the wrist before letting Jess collapse into the chair and curl up like a shrimp.

'Now, let's talk,' he said pleasantly enough. 'About private matters.'

Out in the corridor, Eve paced up and down, glancing every few seconds at the thick door. She knew very well if Roarke had implemented the soundproofing, Jess could be shrieking his lungs out and she wouldn't hear.

If he killed him . . . Good God if he killed him, how was

222

she going to handle it? She stopped, appalled, and pressed a hand to her stomach. How could she even consider it? She was duty bound to protect the bastard. There were rules. Whatever her personal feelings, there were rules.

She marched to the door, coded in, and hissed out a breath as her code was denied. 'Son of a bitch. Goddamn it, Roarke.' He knew her too well. With little hope, she raced down the corridor, into his office, and tried the connecting door.

Entrance denied.

She streaked to the monitor, cued up the security camera for her office, and found he'd locked her out of that as well.

'God almighty, he is killing him.' She rushed the door again, beat on it uselessly with her fist. Moments later, like magic, the locks slicked back, and the door slid quietly open. She went through at a dead run and saw Roarke calmly sitting at her desk, smoking.

Her heart pounded as she looked down at Jess. He was pale as death, his pupils the size of pinpricks, but he was breathing. In fact, he was wheezing out air like a faulty temperature control.

'He's unmarked.' Roarke picked up the brandy he'd poured himself. 'And I believe he's begun to see the error of his ways.'

Eve leaned down, peered closely into Jess's eyes, and watched him cringe back into the chair like a kicked dog. The sound he made was barely human. 'What the hell did you do to him?'

He doubted Eve or the NYPSD would approve of the tricks he'd picked up in his more shadowy travels. 'Much less than he deserved.'

She straightened and now took a long, hard look at Roarke. He looked like a man about to entertain late night guests or chair an important business meeting. His suit was unwrinkled, his hair unmussed, his hands perfectly steady. But his eyes, she noted, were just on the down side of wild.

'Christ, you're scary.'

Carefully, he set his brandy down. 'I'll never hurt you again.'

'Roarke.' She pushed back the urge to go to him, close her arms around him. It wasn't what the moment called for, she decided. Or what he wanted. 'This can't be personal.'

'Yes.' He drew in smoke, blew it out slowly. 'It can. And is.'

'Lieutenant.' Peabody stepped in, her face bland. 'The MTs are here. With your permission, I'll accompany the suspect to the health center.'

'I'll go.'

'Sir.' Peabody slid a glance toward Roarke. He'd yet to take his eyes off Eve, she noted. And those eyes looked more than a little dangerous. 'If you'll excuse me, I believe you have more pressing matters here. I can handle this. You still have a number of guests in the house, including the press. I'm sure you'd prefer this matter remain quiet until its disposition.'

'All right. I'll contact Central from here, make the necessary arrangements. Prepare for second phase interview tomorrow, nine hundred hours.'

'I'm looking forward to it.' Peabody glanced over at Jess, lifted a brow. 'He must have hit his head pretty hard. Still looks dazed, skin's clammy.' She offered Roarke a wide smile. 'I know just how that feels.'

Roarke laughed, feeling more of the tension drain away. 'No, Peabody. In this case, I don't believe you do.'

He got up, walked to her and, framing her square face with his elegant hands, kissed her. 'You're beautiful,' he murmured before turning to Eve. 'I'll see to the rest of our guests. Take your time.'

As he walked out, Peabody touched her fingertips to her lips. Pleasure had radiated down to her toes and out through the reinforced tips of her boots. 'Oh wow. I'm beautiful, Dallas.'

'I owe you, Peabody.'

'I think I just got paid.' She stepped back to the door. 'Here come the MTs. We'll get our boy out of here. Tell Mavis she was absolutely ultra.'

'Mavis.' Eve pressed her fingers to her eyes. How was she going to tell Mavis?

'If I were you, Dallas, I'd give her tonight to glow. You can tell her about this later. She'll be fine. In here,' she called, gesturing. 'We got us what looks like a mild concussion.'

Chapter Sixteen

Getting a warrant for search and seizure at two in the morning was a tricky business. She lacked the straightforward data to cop an automatic clearance and needed a judge. Judges tended to be cranky about calls in the middle of the night. And trying to explain why she needed clearance for a sweep and scan of a music console currently on her own premises was a dicey job.

This being the case, Eve tolerated the clipped, angry lecture from her judge of choice.

'I understand that, Your Honor. But this can't wait until a decent hour in the morning. I have a strong suspicion that the console in question is linked to the deaths of four people. Its designer and operator is currently being detained, and I cannot expect his immediate cooperation.'

'You're telling me music kills, Lieutenant?' The judge snorted. 'I could have told you that. The crap they're pumping out these days could murder an elephant. In my day, we had *music*. Springsteen, Live, Cult Killers. That was music.'

'Yes, sir.' She rolled her eyes. She'd had to pick a classic music buff. 'I really need that warrant, Your Honor. Captain Feeney is available to begin the initial scan. The operator had admitted to using the console illegally, on the record. I need more to tie it to the cases in question.'

'You ask me, those music consoles should be banned and burned. This is piddly shit here, Lieutenant.'

'Not if the evidence bears out my belief that this console and its operator are linked to the death of Senator Pearly and others.'

There was a pause, a wheeze. 'That's a big leap. No pun intended.'

'Yes, sir. I need the warrant to bridge the gap.'

'I'll send it through, but you better have something, Lieutenant. And it better be solid.'

'Thank you. Sorry to have disturbed—' The 'link clicked in her ear, forcefully. 'Your sleep,' she finished, then picked up her communicator and tagged Feeney.

'Hey, Dallas.' His face was flushed with fun, wide with a grin. 'Where ya been, kid? Party's just breaking up. You missed Mavis doing a set with a hologram of the Rolling Stones. You know how I feel about Jagger.'

'Yeah, he's like a father to you. Don't take off, Feeney. I've got a job for you.'

'Job? It's two A.M., and my wife's feeling, you know—' He winked sloppily. 'Interested.'

'Sorry, put the glands on hold. Roarke will arrange to have your wife taken home. I'll be up in ten. Take a dose of Sober-Up if you need it. It could be a long night.'

'Sober-Up?' His face fell into its usual morose lines. 'I've been working all night to get drunk. What's this about?'

'Ten minutes,' she repeated and cut him off.

She took the time to change out of the party dress, and discovered bruises she hadn't been aware of throbbing fresh. She took a quick moment to slap a coat of numbing cream where she could reach and winced her way into a shirt and trousers.

Still, she was true to her word and walked onto the roof terrace ten minutes later.

Roarke had been at work here, she noted, and had cleared out lingering guests. If there were any stragglers, he was dealing with them elsewhere, giving her a clear stage.

Feeney sat alone on a chair beside a decimated buffet spread, glumly eating pâté. 'You sure know how to put me out of a party mood, Dallas. The wife was so dazzled to get a limo ride home, she forgot she was going to jump me. And Mavis was looking all over for you. I think she was a little hurt you didn't hang around to congratulate her.'

'I'll make it up to her.' Her porta-link hummed, signaling an incoming transmission. She read the display, hit print out. 'Here's our warrant.'

'Warrant?' He reached for a truffle and popped it in his mouth. 'For what?'

Eve shifted, gestured toward the console. 'For that. Ready to work your magic?'

Feeney swallowed the truffle, looked toward the console. The light some would have called love gleamed in his eyes. 'You want me to play with that? Hot damn.'

He was up, almost bounding toward the equipment and running reverent hands over it. She heard him mumbling something about TX-42, high velocity sound trips, and mirror merging capabilities. 'The warrant clears me to override his lock off code?'

'It does. Feeney, it's serious.'

'You're telling me.' He lifted his hands, rubbing fingertips together like an old-world safe cracker about to hit the big time. 'This baby is one serious mother. The design's inspired, the payload's off the scale. It's—'

'Very likely responsible for four deaths,' Eve interrupted. She walked over to join him. 'Let me bring you up to date.'

Within twenty minutes, using the portable kit out of his car, Feeney was at work. Eve couldn't understand what he was muttering about, and he didn't take it kindly when she leaned over his shoulder.

That gave her time to pace, then to call in for a report on Jess's status. She had just finished ordering Peabody to turn duty over to a uniform guard and go home to get some sleep when Roarke came in.

'I gave your regrets to our guests,' he told her and helped himself to another brandy. 'I explained that you'd been called to duty suddenly. I had much sympathy on living with a cop.'

'I tried to tell you it was a bad deal.'

He only smiled, but the smile didn't quite reach his eyes. 'It placated Mavis. She's hoping you'll get in touch tomorrow.'

'I will. I'll need to explain things. Did she ask about Barrow?'

'I told her he was . . . indisposed. Rather abruptly.' He didn't touch her. He wanted to, but he wasn't quite ready. 'You're hurting, Eve. I can see it.'

'You pinch my nose again, and I'll flatten you. Feeney and I have a lot of work here, and I have to be sharp. I'm not fragile, Roarke.' The message was in her eyes, asking him to put it aside. 'Get used to it.'

'Not yet.' He put down his brandy, slipped his hands into his pockets. 'I could help there,' he said, inclining his head toward Feeney.

'It's police business. You're not authorized to touch that unit.'

When he only shifted his eyes back to hers with some of the old humor in them, she let out a huge sigh. 'It's up to Feeney,' she snapped. 'He outranks me, and if he wants your fingers in his pie, it's his deal. I don't want to know about it. I've got reports to put together.'

She started out, irritation in every body line. 'Eve.' When she stopped and scowled over her shoulder at him, he shook his head. 'Nothing.' He lifted his shoulders, feeling helpless. 'Nothing,' he said again.

'Put it to bed, goddamn it. You're pissing me off.' She stalked out, nearly making him smile.

'I love you, too,' he murmured, then wandered toward Feeney. 'What have we here?'

'Brings tears to my eyes, I swear it. It's beautiful, brilliant. I tell you the guy's a genius. Certified. Come here and take a look at this image board. Just look at it.'

Roarke slipped off his jacket, hunkered down, and went to work.

She never went to bed. For once, Eve buried her prejudice and took her sanctioned dose of uppers. The Alert All cleared the drag of fatigue and most of the cobwebs from her brain. She used the shower off her office, broke down and wrapped an ice bandage over her sore knee, and told herself she'd deal with the bruises later.

It was six A.M. when she went back to the roof terrace. The console had been methodically taken apart. Wires, boards, chips, discs, drives, panels were arranged over the gleaming floor in what she could only assume were organized piles.

In his elegant silk shirt and tailored slacks, Roarke sat cross-legged among them, diligently entering data in a logbook. He'd tied his hair back, she noted, to keep it from falling over his face. And that face was intense, focused, the dark blue eyes ridiculously alert for the hour.

'I've got that,' he muttered to Feeney. 'Running the components now. I've seen something like this before. Something close. It's calibrating.' He held the logbook out and under the kick panel of the console. 'Have a look.'

A hand shot out, grabbed the logbook. 'Yeah, this could do it. It could fucking do it. Suck my dick.'

'Irishmen have such a way with words.'

At Eve's dry tone, Feeney's head popped up. His hair stuck straight up, as if he'd shocked himself while fiddling with the electronics. His eyes were bright and wild. 'Hey, Dallas. I think we just nailed it.'

230

'What took you so long?'

'What a kidder.' Feeney's head disappeared again.

Eve exchanged a long, sober study with Roarke. 'Good morning, Lieutenant.'

'You're not here,' she said as she walked past him. 'I don't see you here. What have you got, Feeney?'

'Got a lot of options on this baby,' he began, and popped up again to settle in the molded chair of the console. 'Lotsa doodads, and they are impressive. But the one we had to dig deep to find, under layers of some pretty hunky security, is the honey.'

He ran his hands over the console again, stroking fingers over the smooth surface that now topped empty guts. 'The designer would have made a hell of an E-detective. Most of the guys under me can't do what he can. Creativity, see.' He wagged a finger at her. 'It's not just formulas and boards. Creativity turns the corner into an open field. This guy's walked that field. He fucking owns it. And this is what he'd call his crowning glory.'

He offered the logbook, knowing she'd scowl over the codes and components. 'So?'

'It took some art to get down to that. He had it locked under his private pass, his voice pattern, his palm print. Some layers of fail safe, too. Nearly blew ourselves up about an hour ago, right, Roarke?'

Roarke rose and tucked his hands in his pockets. 'I never doubted you for an instant, Captain.'

'Like hell.' In tune with his man, Feeney grinned. 'If you weren't saying your prayers, boyo, I was saying mine. Still, I can't think of many others I'd be pleased to be blown to hell with.'

'The feeling's nearly mutual.'

'If you two have finished your little male bonding dance, would you care to explain what the hell I'm supposed to be looking at here?'

231

'It's a scanner. The most intricate I've seen outside of Testing.'

'Testing?'

It was a procedure every cop dreaded, and one every cop faced whenever they were forced to set their weapon on maximum for termination.

'Even though every member of NYPSD's brain pattern is on record, a scan's taken during Testing. Search for damage, flaws, any abnormalities that might have contributed to the use of maximum force. That scan's compared with the last taken, then the subject is taken on a couple of VR rides that use the data downloaded from the scan. Nasty business.'

Feeney had only faced it once and hoped never to go through the process again.

'And he's managed to duplicate or simulate that process?' Eve asked.

'I'd say he's improved on it on a couple of levels.' Feeney gestured toward the stack of discs. 'That's a lot of brain wave patterns. Shouldn't be too difficult to compare them with the victims' and identify.'

Her pattern would be on one, she thought. Her mind, on disc. 'Tidy,' she said half to herself.

'Brilliant, really. And potentially deadly. Our boy's got some spiffy twists on mood sets. They're all tied into musical patterns, you know, notes and chords. He picks the tune, see, then enhances what you'd call the tone of it, to pump along the target's reaction, their state of mind say, their unconscious impulses.'

'So he uses it to get into their head, deep. The subconscious.'

'Got a lot of medical technology I'm not real familiar with, but I'd say that's about it. Heavy into sexual urges,' Feeney added. 'That's our boy's specialty. I've got a little more breakdown to do, but I'd say he could program the brain pattern, set the mood enhance, and give the target mind a nice hefty push.'

232

'Off a ledge?' she demanded.

'That's tricky, Dallas. Where I'm at here is enhancement, suggestive shit. Sure, if somebody was leaning toward the ledge, thinking about going over, this might give them that last nudge. But to coerce a mind to act in a manner completely adverse, completely out of character, I'd have to back off on that for now.'

'They jumped, choked, and bled to death,' she reminded him impatiently. 'Maybe we've all got suicidal urges buried in the subconscious. And this just brings them to the surface.'

'You need Mira for that, not me. I'll keep digging.' He smiled hopefully. 'After breakfast?'

She forced down impatience. 'After breakfast. I appreciate the long night, Feeney, and the quick work. But I needed the best.'

'And you got it. The guy you decided to link yourself up with isn't half bad, either, as a tech. I'd make a decent E-man out of him if he'd give up the drudgery of his lifestyle.'

'My first offer of the day.' Roarke smiled. 'You know where the kitchen is, Feeney. You're welcome to the AutoChef, or you can ask Summerset to arrange for the meal of your choice.'

'Around here, that means real eggs.' He stretched kinks out, popped joints. 'You want me to tell him breakfast for three?'

'You get started,' Roarke suggested. 'We'll be down shortly.' He waited until Feeney had sauntered out, whistling at the thought of eggs Benedict and blueberry pancakes. 'You haven't much time, I know.'

'I have enough, if you have something to say.'

'I do.' It was rare for him to feel awkward. He'd almost forgotten the sensation until it swamped him. 'What Feeney just pointed out to you, about his opinion on the capabilities here. The fact that it's unlikely for the subject to be influenced to act out of character, to do something abhorrent.'

233

She saw immediately where he was going and wanted to curse. 'Roarke—'

'I'll finish this. I've been the man who took you last night. I've lived in that skin, and it hasn't been so long ago that I've forgotten him. I turned him into something else because I wanted to. And I could. Money helped, and a certain need for . . . polish. But he's still there. He's still part of me. I was reminded of that rather violently last night.'

'Do you want me to hate you for it, to blame you for it?'

'No, I want you to understand it, and me. I came from the kind of man who hurt you last night.'

'So did I.'

That stopped him, had emotion swimming back into his eyes. 'Christ, Eve.'

'And it scares me. It wakes me up in the middle of the night, the wondering just what's inside me. I live with it every single day. I knew where you came from when I took you on, and I don't care. I know you've done things, broken laws, lived outside them. But I'm here.'

She huffed out a breath, shifted her feet. 'I love you, okay? That's it. Now, I'm hungry, and I've got a full day ahead of me, so I'm going down before Feeney cleans us out of eggs.'

He stepped in front of her before she could storm out. 'One more minute.' He framed her face with his hands, lowered his mouth to hers, and turned her scowl into a sigh with a kiss so tender it made her throat ache and her toes curl.

'Well,' she managed when he eased back. 'That's better, I guess.'

'Much better.' He linked his fingers with hers. And because he had used it when he'd hurt her, he balanced that out by using it now. '*A ghra.*'

'Huh?' A line appeared between her brows. 'Is that Gaelic again?'

'Yes.' He brought their joined fingers to his lips. 'Love. My love.'

'It's got a nice ring.'

'It does, yes.' He sighed a little. It had been a long time since he'd let himself hear the music of it.

'It shouldn't make you sad,' she murmured.

'It doesn't. Just thoughtful.' He gave her hand a friendly squeeze. 'I'd love to buy you breakfast, Lieutenant.'

'Talked me into it.' Comfortable, she tightened her grip. 'We got any crepes?'

The trouble with chemicals, Eve thought as she set up for the next interview with Jess Barrow, was that no matter how safe, mild, and helpful they claimed to be, they always made her feel false. She knew she wasn't naturally alert, that underneath that surging, induced energy, her body was a mass of desperate fatigue.

She kept imagining her system wearing a huge clown's mask of enthusiasm over a gray, exhausted face.

'Back in the saddle, Peabody?' Eve asked as her aide walked into the white-walled, uncluttered room.

'Yes, sir. I briefed myself via your reports, dropped by your office on the way here. You have a message from the commander on hold, and two from Nadine Furst. I think she smells a story.'

'She'll have to wait. I'll relay to the commander during our first break here. Know anything about baseball, Peabody?'

'I played short for two years at the Academy. Golden Glove.'

'Well, warm up. When I toss you a ball, you field it, zing it back. We're going Tinker to Evers to Chance here, with Feeney coming in before the end of the inning.'

Peabody's eyes lit. 'Hey, didn't know you were a historian.'

'I have many hidden facets. Just field the ball, Peabody. I want to dust this son of a bitch at the plate. You've read the report, you know the drill.' She signaled for the suspect to be brought in. 'Let's cook him. If he lawyers up, we'll have to juggle. But I'm banking on him being too arrogant to go that route initially.'

'Mostly, I like cocky men. I guess I'll have to make an exception here.'

'And he's got such a pretty face,' Eve added, then moved aside as a uniform delivered her man. 'How's it going, Jess? Feeling better today?'

He'd had time to regroup and time to stew. 'I could hang you on undue force. But I'm going to let it pass because before this is done, you'll be the top joke of your idiot department.'

'Yep, he's feeling better. Have a seat.' She stepped to the small table, engaged the recording unit. 'Dallas, Lieutenant Eve, with Peabody, Officer Delia, as aide. The time is oh nine hundred, September 8, 2058. Interview subject Barrow, Jess, file number S-one nine three oh five. Would you please state your name for the record?'

'Jess Barrow. You got that much right.'

'I have, during our previous interview, given you your rights and options under the law, is that correct?'

'You gave me the drill, sure.' For all the good it had done him, he thought, and shifted carefully in his seat. His cock ached like a rotted tooth.

'And you understand those rights and options as stated?'

'I got them then; I get them now.'

'Do you wish, at this time, to make use of your right to an attorney or representative?'

'I don't need anybody but myself.'

'All right then.' Eve sat, linked her fingers, smiled. 'Let's get started. In your previous statement, you admitted to the design and use of equipment built for tampering with personal brain patterns and behavior.'

'I didn't admit to shit.'

She kept smiling. 'That's a matter of interpretation. Do you now deny that during a social gathering at my home last

236

evening, you utilized a program you have designed to make certain suggestions, subliminally, to the subject Roarke?'

'Hey, if your husband took you off and tossed your skirts over your head, it's your business.'

Her smile never faltered. 'It certainly is.' She needed to hang him here, on this one point, to hang him on the rest. 'Peabody, perhaps Jess is unaware of the penalty for giving false statement to a police official during Interview.'

'That penalty,' Peabody said smoothly, 'carries a maximum term of five years in full lockup. Shall I replay the pertinent data from the initial interview, Lieutenant? The subject's memory might be faulty due to the injury received while assaulting an officer.'

'Assault, my ass.' He snarled at Peabody. 'You think you can double-team me this way? She struck me without provocation, then let that bastard she married come in and . . .'

He trailed off, remembering the warning Roarke had issued in a soft, silky voice directly in his ear. While the pain, almost sweet in its intensity, had radiated through his system.

'You wish to make an official complaint?' Eve asked.

'No.' Even now, a light line of sweat beaded on his upper lip and made Eve wonder just what Roarke had done to him. 'I was upset last night. Things got out of hand.' He took a steadying breath. 'Listen, I'm a musician. I take a lot of pride in my work, in the art of it. I like to think what I do influences people, touches them. My pride in that might have given you the wrong impression as to the scope of my work. Basically, I don't know what all the fuss is about.'

He smiled again, with a good deal of his usual charm, and spread his handsome hands. 'Those people you talked about last night. I don't know them. I've heard of some of them, sure, but I didn't know them personally or have anything to do with their decision to self-terminate. I'm against it, myself. In my opinion, life's too short as it is. This is all a misunderstanding, and I'm willing to forget it.'

Eve leaned back in her chair, sent a look toward her aide. 'Peabody, he's willing to forget it.'

'That's generous of him, Lieutenant, and not surprising, under the circumstances. A stretch for breaking the statute on personal privacy through electronics is stringent. And, of course, there's the added charge of designing and implementing equipment designed for individual subliminals. Right there, with the multiple counts, you're looking at a ten-year minimum in the cages.'

'You can't begin to prove any of it. Any of it. You've got no case here.'

'I'm giving you a chance to roll over here, Jess. They go easier on you when you roll. And as to the civil case that my husband and I are entitled to bring against you, I will state here, for the record, that I will waive that right, contingent on your admission of guilt on the criminal charges – if that admission comes in the next thirty seconds. Think about it.'

'I don't have to think about anything, because you've got nothing.' He leaned forward. 'You're not the only one with people behind you. What do you think will happen to your big, bad career if I go to the press with this?'

She said nothing, just watched him, then glanced at the time count on the recorder. 'Offer is rescinded.' Eve nodded at the monitoring camera. 'Peabody, please uncode the door for Captain Feeney.'

When Feeney walked in, he was beaming. He set a disc and file on the table and stuck out his hand to Jess. 'I've got to tell you, your work's the best I've ever seen. It's a real pleasure to meet you.'

'Thanks.' Jess shifted to audience mode, shook hands warmly. 'I love my work.'

'Oh, it shows.' Feeney sat down, made himself comfortable. 'I haven't enjoyed anything for years as much as I did taking that console apart.'

Another time, another place, it might have been comic, the

way Jess's face underwent the transformation from obliging star to blank shock to ripe fury. 'You fucked with my equipment? Took it apart? You had no right laying a hand on it! You're meat! You're dead! You're destroyed!'

'Let the record show the subject is overwrought,' Peabody recited blandly. 'His threats against the person of Captain Feeney are accepted as emotional rather than literal.'

'Well, the first time, anyway,' Feeney said cheerfully. 'You want to watch your step there, friend. Put too much of that on record, and we tend to get pissy. Now.' He leaned forward on his elbows. 'Let's talk shop. You had some great security, admirable. Took me a while to bypass. But then, I've been in the game as long as you've been breathing. Designing that personal brain scanner was some accomplishment. So compact, so delicate to the touch. I gauged its range at two yards. Now, that's damn good for that small and portable a unit.'

'You didn't get into my equipment.' Jess's voice wavered. 'You're bluffing. You couldn't get down to the core.'

'Well, the three fail safes were tricky,' Feeney admitted. 'I spent nearly an hour on the second one, but the last was really just padding. I guess you never figured you'd need anything at that level.'

'Did you run the discs, Feeney?' Eve asked him.

'Started on them. You're on there, Dallas. We don't have Roarke's on file. Civilian, you know. But I found yours and Peabody's.'

Peabody blinked. 'Mine?'

'I'm running comparison checks on the names you requested, Dallas.' He smiled broadly at Jess again. 'You've been busy, collecting specimens. That's a fine storage option you designed, terrific data compression capabilities. It's going to break my heart to destroy that equipment.'

'You can't!' It was sincere pain and distress now. His eyes swam with it. 'I've put everything I've got into that. Not just money, but time and thought and energy. Three years of my life, almost straight through without a break. I stepped back from my career to design it. Do you have any idea what I can accomplish with it?'

Eve picked up the ball. 'Why don't you tell us, Jess? In your own words. We'd love to hear it.'

Chapter Seventeen

Jess Barrow started slowly, in fits and starts, speaking of his experiments and research, his fascination with the influence of outside stimuli on the human brain; the senses, and the enhancement of the senses through technology.

'What we can do for pleasure, for punishment – we haven't even tapped the surface. That's what I wanted to do,' he explained. 'Tap the surface and go under it. Dreams, Dallas. Needs, fears, fantasies. All my life, music's been what's moved me to . . . everything: hunger, passion, misery, joy. How much more intense would all that be if you could just get inside, really use the mind to exploit and explore?'

'So you worked on it,' she prompted. 'Devoted yourself to it.'

'Three years. More really, but three solid on the design, experimentation, perfecting. Every penny I had went into it. I've got next to nothing left now. That's why I needed backing. Why I needed you.'

'And Mavis was your link to me, and from me to Roarke.'

'Look.' He lifted his hands, rubbed them over his face, dropped them onto the table. 'I like Mavis, and she's got a real spark. Yeah, I'd have used her if she was bland as a droid, but she's not. I didn't do her any harm. If anything, I gave her a boost up. Her ego level was ditch low when we hooked up. Oh, she was masking it pretty good, but she'd lost confidence in herself from what happened before. I gave her confidence a jolt.'

'How?'

He hesitated, decided he'd take a bigger fall by evading. 'Okay, I gave her some subliminal nudges in the right direction. She should be grateful,' he insisted. 'And I worked with her, straight stuff, getting her shined up without taking away her natural edge. You heard her yourself. She's better than she ever was.'

'You experimented on her,' Eve said, and wanted to hang him for that alone, 'without her knowledge or consent.'

'It wasn't like she was some droid rat. Christ, I'd perfected the system.' He jabbed a finger at Feeney. 'You know it's prime.'

'It's beautiful,' Feeney agreed. 'Doesn't make it legal.'

'Shit, genetic engineering was illegal, in vitro work, prostitution. What did that get us? We've come a long way, but we're still in the dark ages, man. This is a benefit, this is a way to push the mind forward into dreams and make what we dream real.'

'Not all of us want our dreams to be reality. What gives you the right to make that choice for someone else?'

'Okay.' He held up a hand. 'Maybe I got over-enthusiastic a few times. You get caught up. But all I did with you was expand on what was there. So I enhanced the lust bars that night in the studio. What did it hurt? Another time I gave your memory a little push, jiggled a few locks. I wanted to be able to prove what could be done, so when the time was right, I could approach you and Roarke with a business proposition. And last night . . .'

He trailed off, knowing he'd miscalculated badly there. 'Okay, last night I went too far, the tone was too dark. I got carried away with it. Performing before a real audience again, it's like a drug. It hypes you. Maybe I punched the power a little hard on him. An honest mistake.' He tried that

242

smile again. 'Look, I've used it on myself, dozens of times. There's no harm, nothing permanent. Just temporary mood enhancement.'

'And you pick the mood?'

'That's part of it. With standard equipment, you don't have as much control, not nearly the depth of field. With what I've developed, you can turn it on and off like a light. Sexual need or satisfaction, euphoria, melancholy, energy, relaxation. Name it, you got it.'

'A death wish?'

'No.' He shook his head quickly. 'I don't play those games.'

'But it's all a game to you, isn't it? You push the buttons, and the people dance. You're the electronic god.'

'You're missing the big picture,' he insisted. 'Do you know what people would pay for this kind of capability? You can feel anything you want.'

Eve opened the file Feeney had brought in. She tossed photos out, faceup. 'What did they feel, Jess?' She pushed the morgue shots of four deaths at him. 'What was the last thing you made them feel so that they killed themselves with smiles on their faces?'

He went white as death itself, eyes glazing before he managed to shut them. 'No. No way. No.' Doubling over, he retched out his health center breakfast.

'Let the record show the suspect is momentarily indisposed,' Peabody said dryly. 'Should I call for maintenance and a health aide, Lieutenant?'

'Christ, yes,' Eve muttered as Jess continued to heave. 'We'll break this interview at oh ten fifteen. Dallas, Lieutenant Eve, record off.'

'Great brain, weak stomach.' Feeney went to the dispenser in the corner and poured a cup of water. 'Here, boy, see if you can choke some of this down.'

Jess's eyes watered. His stomach muscles were raw. Water

sloshed in the cup so that Feeney had to guide it to his mouth. 'You can't hang that on me,' he managed. 'You can't.'

'We'll see about that.' Eve stepped aside so that the incoming aide could cart him off to the infirmary. 'I need some air,' she muttered and walked out.

'Hold on, Dallas.' Feeney hurried after her, leaving Peabody to direct maintenance and gather up the file. 'We need to talk.'

'My office is closer.' She swore lightly as her knee throbbed. The ice bandage was wearing off and needed to be replaced. Her hip was murderous.

'Took a beating with that CEC hit yesterday, didn't you?' Feeney clucked sympathetically as she hobbled. 'Been looked over yet?'

'Later. I've been pressed for time. Let's give the creep an hour to get his stomach back in place, then hit him again. He hasn't cried lawyer yet, but it's coming. Won't matter a damn once we match those brain patterns to the victims.'

'That's the problem. Sit down,' he advised when they stepped into her office. 'Take a load off that leg.'

'It's the knee, and sitting's making it stiffen up. What's the problem?' she asked and headed for the coffee.

'Nothing matches.' He studied her mournfully when she turned. 'Not one match in the whole lot. Plenty as yet unidentified, but I've got the prints on all victims, no autopsy scan on Devane, but I got the one from her last physical. There's no match, Dallas.'

So she did sit, heavily. There was no need to ask if he was sure. Feeney was as thorough as a domestic droid searching for dust in corners. 'Okay, he's got them someplace else. Did we get the warrant for his studio and quarters?'

'A team's going through it right now. I haven't gotten a report.'

'He could have a lock box, some safe hole.' She shut her eyes. 'Shit, Feeney, why would he keep them when he was done with them? He's probably destroyed them. He's arrogant, but he's not stupid. They'd hang him and he'd know it.'

'The possibility's high there. Then again, he could have kept them as souvenirs. It never fails to surprise me what people keep. That guy last year that cut up his wife? Kept her eyes, remember. In a damn music box.'

'Yeah, I remember.' *Where had this headache come from?* she wondered and rubbed uselessly at her temples to erase it. 'So, maybe we'll get lucky. If we don't, we've got plenty now. And a good shot of breaking him.'

'Here's the thing, Dallas.' He sat on the edge of her desk, reached into his pocket for his bag of candied almonds. 'It doesn't feel right.'

'What do you mean, it doesn't feel right? We've got him cold.'

'We've got him cold, all right. But not on murder.' Thoughtfully, Feeney chewed a coated nut. 'I can't resolve myself to it. The guy who designed that equipment is brilliant, twisted some sure, self-absorbed. The guy we just shook down is all of those things, and you can add childish. It is a game to him, one he wants to make a big profit on. But murder . . .'

'You're just in love with his console.'

'That I am,' he admitted without shame. 'He's weak, Dallas, and not just his stomach. How's he going to make himself rich by killing people off?'

She arched a brow. 'I guess you've never heard of murder for hire.'

'That boy doesn't have the guts for it, or the steel.' He ate another nut. 'And where's the motive? Did he pick those people out of a hat? And there's this. What he's got requires proximity to tap the subconscious. You can't place him at any of the scenes.'

'He said something about remote capabilities.'

'Yeah, it had a fine one, but it wouldn't command this option. Not that I can figure.'

245

She sat back, deflated. 'You're not making my day here, Feeney.'

'Just food for thought. If he's got a hand in it, he's got help. Or a more personal, portable unit.'

'Could it be adjusted into VR goggles?'

The idea intrigued him, made his hangdog eyes gleam. 'Can't say for sure. It'll take some time to work that out.'

'I hope you've got the time. He's all I've got, Feeney. If I can't crack him, he's going to walk on the murders. Tucking him away for ten to twenty on what we've got doesn't do it for me.' She huffed out a breath. 'He'll go for a psych evaluation. He'll go for anything he thinks will buy him a shot. Maybe Mira can pin him.'

'Send him over after the break,' Feeney suggested. 'Let her take him for a few hours, and do yourself a favor. Go home and get some sleep. You run on empty long enough, you drop.'

'Maybe I will. I'll set it up, deal with Whitney. A couple hours off might clear my head. I must be missing something.'

For once, Summerset wasn't hovering. Eve snuck in the house like a thief, limped her way upstairs. She left a trail of clothes on her way to the bed, and she sighed greedily when she fell on it.

Ten minutes later, she was on her back, staring at the ceiling. The aches were bad enough, she thought grumpily. But the stimulator she'd taken hours before hadn't worn off. It was passing, leaving her light-headed with fatigue, while her system still bubbled like a brew.

Sleep was not going to happen.

She found herself picking apart the pieces of the case, putting them back together. Each time the puzzle formed differently until it was a blurred jumble of facts and theories.

At this rate, she wouldn't be close to coherent when she met with Mira.

She considered indulging in a long, hot bath in lieu of sleep.

Then, inspired, she popped up and grabbed a robe. She took the elevator, with the purpose of avoiding Summerset, and stepped up on the lower level into the garden path of the solarium. A session in the lagoon pool, she decided, was just the ticket.

She dumped the robe, padded naked to the dark water walled in genuine stone and framed with fragrant blooms. When she dipped a toe, she found it blissfully warm. She sat on the first step and set the control panel for jets and bubbles. As the water began to churn, she started to program music. With a quick grimace, she decided she wasn't in the mood for tunes.

She simply floated at first, grateful there was no one around to hear her whimpering as the pulsing water worked on her aches. She let herself breathe. Floral perfume. She let herself drift. Simple pleasures.

The conflict of fatigue and stimulation balanced out into relaxation. Drugs, she decided, were highly overrated. Water worked wonders. Turning over lazily, she began to swim, slowly at first while her muscles warmed and limbered. Then she put some kick into it, hoping to work off the excess of the stimulant and revive herself with natural exercise.

When the timer clicked and the water calmed, she continued with long, steady strokes, skimmed down to the glossy black bottom until she felt like an embryo in the womb, then broke the surface with a loud, satisfied groan.

'You swim like a fish.'

Instinct had Eve reaching for her side arm only to encounter her own naked ribs. Quickly, she blinked the water out of her eyes and focused on Reeanna.

'It's a cliché.' She walked to the edge of the pool. 'But accurate.' She set her shoes aside, sat, and slid her legs into the water. 'Do you mind?'

'Help yourself.' Eve didn't consider herself fanatically modest, but she dipped a little lower. She hated being caught naked. 'Were you looking for Roarke?'

'No, actually, I've just left him. He and William are still at it upstairs in his office. I was just leaving for a salon appointment.' She tugged at her gorgeous, glossy red curls. 'I've got to do something about this mop. Summerset mentioned you were down here, so I thought I'd just drop in on you.'

Summerset. Even smiled grimly. He'd spotted her after all. 'I had a couple of hours personal time. Thought I'd take advantage of it.'

'And what a lovely spot to take it. Roarke's got such amazing class, doesn't he?'

'Yeah, you could say so.'

'I really just wanted to stop for a moment to tell you how much I enjoyed last evening. I barely got to speak to you – such a crowd. And then you were called away.'

'Cops are lousy socializers,' Eve commented and wondered how to get out and to her robe without feeling like an idiot.

Reeanna reached down, cupped water, and let it pour out of her hand. 'I hope it wasn't anything . . . dreadful.'

'Nobody died, if that's what you mean.' Then Eve made herself smile. She *was* lousy at socializing, and she told herself to make a better effort. 'Actually, I got a break in the case I've been working on. We took a suspect into custody.'

'That's good.' Reeanna tilted her head, her eyes intrigued. 'Would that be the suicide matter we discussed before?'

'I'm not really free to say one way or the other at this time.'

Reeanna smiled. 'Cop talk. Well, one way or the other, I've been giving it quite a bit of thought. Your case, or whatever you'd call it, would make a fascinating paper. I've been so busy with tech, I haven't done any writing in some time. I hope, when you resolve the matter and it's public record, I can discuss it with you in some detail.'

'I can probably do that. If and when.' She bent a little. The woman was an expert, after all, and could be of some help. 'As it happens, the suspect is being evaluated by Dr Mira right about now. Do you ever do behavioral and personality evaluations?'

'I have, certainly. From a different angle than Mira. You'd have to say we're two sides of one coin. Our final diagnosis would often be the same, but we'd use a different process and a different viewpoint.'

'I might need two viewpoints before this one's over,' Eve mused, measuring Reeanna. 'You don't happen to have security clearance, do you?'

'As it happens, I do.' She continued to swing her legs lazily, but her eyes were alert, interested. 'Level Four, Class B.'

'That just skims by. If it comes up, how would you feel about working for the city as a temporary consultant? I can guarantee long hours, lousy conditions, and low pay.'

'Who could resist that kind of offer?' Reeanna laughed, tossed back her hair. 'Actually, I'd love the opportunity for some hands on again. Too long in labs, working with machines. William adores that, you know, but I need people.'

'I might just give you a call.' Deciding it was more foolish to huddle in the water than to climb casually out, Eve stood.

'You know where to reach me – Dear God, Eve, what happened to you?' Instantly, Reeanna was swinging her legs back, rising. 'You're black and blue.'

'Hazards of the job.' She managed to snag one of the body towels stacked near the edge and started to wind it around her when Reeanna tugged it away.

'Let me have a look at you. You haven't been treated.' Her fingers probed at Eve's hip.

'Hey, do you mind?'

'I certainly do.' Impatient, Reeanna lifted her eyes. 'Oh, be still. Not only am I female and have personal knowledge of the female body, but I've got a medical degree. What have you done for that knee? It's looks nasty.'

'Ice bandage. It's better.'

'Then I'd hate to have seen it when it wasn't. Why haven't you been to a health center, or at least an MT stop?'

'Because I hate them. And I haven't had time.'

'Well, you've got time now. I want you to lie down on that massage table. I'll get my emergency kit out of the car and deal with this.'

'Look, I appreciate it.' She had to raise her voice as Reeanna was already striding away. 'But they're just bruises.'

'You'll be lucky if you didn't chip a bone in that hip.' With this dark promise, Reeanna stepped into the elevator, and the doors snapped shut.

'Oh, thanks, I feel heaps better now.' Resigned, Eve toweled off, put on her robe, then reluctantly went to the padded table beneath an arbor of wildly blooming wisteria. She'd no more than settled when Reeanna was back, stalking over the tiles with a neat leather case in her hand.

The woman could move, Eve mused. 'I thought you had a salon date.'

'I called, switched times. Lie back, we'll deal with that knee first.'

'You charge extra for house calls?'

Reeanna smiled a little as she opened her case. Eve took one glance inside, turned her head away. Christ but she hated medicine.

'This one's free. We can consider it practice. I haven't worked on a human in nearly two years.'

'That inspires confidence.' Eve closed her eyes as Reeanna took out a miniscanner and examined her knee. 'Why haven't you?'

'Hmm. Well, it's not broken, so that's something. Badly wrenched and inflamed. Why?' She dug into her case again. 'Roarke's part of the reason. He made William and me an offer impossible to refuse. The money was seductive, and Roarke knows which buttons to push.'

Eve hissed as something stingingly cold was pressed to her knee. 'You're telling me.'

'He was aware I had a long, personal interest in behavioral patterns and effects of stimulation. The opportunity to create new technology, working with virtually unlimited funds, was too tempting to miss. Vanity couldn't resist the chance to be a part of something new, and with Roarke behind it, undoubtedly successful.'

Closing her eyes had been a mistake, Eve realized. She was starting to float. The throbbing in her hip slowed. She felt Reeanna's gentle fingers smoothing something cool and slick over it. Her shoulder received the same treatment. The absence of pain was like a tranq and tugged her deeper.

'He never seems to miss.'

'No. Not since I've known him.'

'I've got a meeting in a couple hours,' Eve said thickly.

'Rest first.' Reeanna removed the poultice from Eve's knee and was pleased to see the swelling had already gone down. 'I'm going to put another deep healing poultice on this, then an ice bandage to finish it off. It's still likely to be a bit stiff after prolonged use. I'd advise you to baby it for the next couple of days.'

'Sure. Baby it.'

'Did you get all this last night, rounding up your suspect?'

'No, before. He didn't give me any trouble. Little bastard.' Her brows knit, digging a line between them. 'Can't nail him though. Just can't nail it down.'

'I'm sure you will.' Reeanna's voice was soothing as she continued the treatment. 'You're thorough and involved. I saw you on one of the news channels. Going out on the ledge with Cerise Devane. Risking your life.'

'Lost her.'

'Yes, I know.' Efficiently, Reeanna coated the treated bruises with numbing cream. 'It was horrible. Visually shocking. More so for you, I'd imagine. You'd have seen her face, her eyes, up close, as she went off.'

'She was smiling.'

'Yes, I could see that.'

'She wanted to die.'

'Did she?'

'She said it was beautiful. The ultimate experience.'

Satisfied she'd done all she could, Reeanna picked up another towel, spread it over Eve. 'There are some who believe that. Death as the ultimate human experience. No matter how advanced medicine and technology, none of us escape it. Since we're destined for it in any case, why not see it as a goal rather than an obstacle?'

'It's meant to be fought. Every bloody inch of the way.'

'Not everyone has the energy or the need to fight. Some go gently.' She picked up Eve's limp hand, automatically checking the pulse. 'Some go resistantly. But all go.'

'Somebody sent her. That makes it murder. That makes it mine.'

Reeanna tucked Eve's arm under the towel. 'Yes, I suppose it does. Get some sleep. I'll tell Summerset to wake you in time to make your meeting.'

'Thanks. Really.'

'It's nothing.' She touched Eve's shoulder. 'Between friends.'

She studied Eve a moment longer, then glanced at her diamond-studded watch. She was going to have to push to make her rescheduled salon date, but there was just one minor detail to see to yet.

She repacked her kit, left a tube of numbing cream on the table for Eve, and hurried out.

Chapter Eighteen

Eve paced the soft, pretty carpet in Dr Mira's office, hands jammed in her pockets, head lowered like a bull preparing for the charge.

'I don't get it. How can his profile not fit? I've got him cold on the lesser charges. The little prick's been playing with people's brains, reveling in it.'

'It isn't a matter of fitting, Eve. It's a matter of probabilities.'

Patient, calm, Mira sat in her comfy, body-molding chair and sipped jasmine tea. She needed it, she mused. The air was foaming with Eve's frustration and energy.

'You have his confession and the evidence that he has been experimenting with individualized brain pattern influence. And I quite agree he has a lot to answer for. But as to coercion to self-termination, I can't, in any decisive manner, corroborate your suspicions through my evaluation.'

'Well, that's just great.' She spun on her heel. Reeanna's treatment and the hour's nap had restored her. If anything, her color was high, her eyes overbright. 'Without your corroboration, Whitney's not going to buy the package, which means the PA won't buy it.'

'I can't adjust my report to suit you, Eve.'

'Who's asking you to?' Eve threw up her hands, then dug them into her pockets. 'What doesn't fit, for Christ's sake? The man's got a God complex any idiot before vision reconstruction surgery could spot.'

'I agree that his personality pattern leans toward an excess of ego and his temperament has a high caliber of the artiste under siege.' Mira sighed. 'I wish you'd sit down. You're making me tired.'

Eve dropped into a chair, scowled. 'There, I'm sitting. Explain.'

Mira had to smile. The sheer drive and unrelenting focus was admirable. 'Do you know, Eve, I can never understand why impatience is so attractive on you. And how, with such a high volume of it, you still manage to be thorough in your work.'

'I'm not here for analysis, Doctor.'

'I know. I only wish I could convince you to agree to regular sessions. But that's another subject, for another time. You have my report, but to summarize my findings, the subject is egocentric, self-congratulatory, and one who habitually rationalizes his antisocial behavior as art. He's also brilliant.'

Dr Mira signed a little, shook her head. 'A truly fine mind. He was nearly off the scale in the standard Trislow and Secour tests.'

'Good for him,' Eve muttered. 'Let's put his brain on disc and give *him* a few suggestions.'

'Your reaction is understandable,' Mira said mildly. 'Human nature is resistant to any sort of mind control. Addicts rationalize by deluding themselves that they're in control.' She rolled her shoulders. 'In any case, the subject has an admirable, even astonishing skill for visualization and logic. He's also fully aware, and smug if you will, about those skills. Under the surface charm, he is – to use your unscientific term – a prick. But I cannot, in good conscience, label him a murderer.'

'I'm not worried about your conscience.' Eve set her teeth. 'He's able to design and operate equipment that is capable of influencing behavior in targeted individuals. I have four dead bodies whose minds I believe – no, I know – were influenced to self-termination.'

'And logically, there should be a connection.' Mira sat back, reached over, and programmed tea for Eve. 'But you don't have a sociopath in holding, Eve.' She passed Eve a fragrant, steaming cup they both knew she didn't want. 'As there is, of yet, no clear motive for these deaths, and if they were indeed coerced, it's my considered opinion that it's a sociopath who is responsible.'

'So what separates him?'

'He likes people,' Mira said simply, 'and wants, quite desperately, to be liked and admired by them. Manipulative, yes, but he believes he's created a great boon to humankind. One he'll make a profit on, certainly.'

'So, maybe he just got carried away.' *Isn't that what he called his use of Roarke the night before?* Eve though. *He'd just gotten carried away.* 'And maybe he isn't as much in control of his equipment as he thinks.'

'That's possible. From another angle, Jess enjoys his work; he needs to be a party to the results of it. His ego requires that he see, experience at least a part of what he's caused.'

He wasn't in the damn closet with us, Eve thought, but was afraid she understood Mira's meaning: the way Jess had looked for her, at her when they'd come back to the party, the way he'd smiled. 'This isn't what I want to hear.'

'I know that. Listen to me.' Mira set her cup aside. 'This man is a child, an emotionally stunted savant. His vision and his music are more real to him, certainly more important than people, but he doesn't discount people. Overall, I simply find no evidence that he would risk his freedom and his freedom of expression to kill.'

Eve sipped tea out of reflex rather than desire. 'If he had a partner?' she speculated, thinking of Feeney's theory.

'It's possible. He wouldn't be a man who would happily share his accomplishments. Still, he had a great need for both adulation and financial success. It might be possible, if he found himself in need of assistance on some level of his design, he entered into a partnership.'

'Then why didn't he roll over?' Eve shook her head. 'He's a coward; he'd have rolled. No way he'd take the heat for this alone.' She sipped again, letting her thoughts play out. 'What if he were genetically imprinted toward sociopathic behavior? He's intelligent, canny enough to mask it, but it's simply part of his makeup.'

'Branded at conception?' Mira nearly sniffed. 'I don't subscribe to that school. Upbringing, environment, education, choices both moral and immoral form us into what we are. We are not born monsters or saints.'

'But there are experts in the field who believe we are.' And she had one, Eve mused, at her disposal.

Mira read her easily enough and couldn't prevent the prick to her pride. 'If you wish to consult with Dr Ott on this matter, it's your privilege. I'm sure she'd be thrilled.'

Eve wasn't sure whether to wince or smile. Mira very rarely sounded testy. 'That wasn't meant as an insult to your skills, Doctor. I need a hammer here; you can't provide it.'

'Let me tell you what I think about the branding at birth issue, Lieutenant. It's a cop-out, plain and simple. It's a crutch. I couldn't help setting fire to that building and burning hundreds of people alive. I was born an arsonist. I couldn't stop myself from battering that old woman to death for her handful of credits. My mother was a thief.'

It quite simply infuriated her to think of that ploy being used to blot out responsibility – and on the other side to scar those who were defenseless against the monsters who bore them.

'It excuses us from humanity,' she continued, 'from morality, from right and wrong. We can say we were marked in the womb and never had a chance.' She angled her head. 'You of all people should know better.'

'This isn't about me.' Eve set her cup down with a snap. 'It isn't about where I came from or what I made myself. It's about four people, that I'm aware of, who weren't given a choice. And someone has to answer for that.'

'One thing,' Mira added as Eve rose. 'Are you focused on this man because of personal insults to you and those you love, or because of the dead you represent?'

'Maybe it's both,' Eve admitted after a moment.

She didn't contact Reeanna, not yet. She wanted a little time to let it stew in her mind. And she was delayed by finding Nadine Furst in her office.

'How'd you get past desk security?' Eve demanded.

'Oh, I have my ways.' Nadine swung her leg, beamed a friendly smile. 'And most of the cops around here know you and I have a history.'

'What do you want?'

'I wouldn't say no to a cup of coffee.'

Grudgingly, Eve turned to the AutoChef, pumped up two cups. 'Make it fast, Nadine. Crime is rampant in our city.'

'And that keeps us both in business. What did you get called out on last night, Dallas?'

'Excuse me?'

'Come on. I was at the party. Mavis was terrific, by the way. First you and Roarke take off.' She sipped delicately. 'It didn't take a sharp reporter like me to get an inkling of what that was about.' She wiggled her brows, chuckling when Eve simply stared. 'But your sex life isn't news – at least on my beat.'

'We were running out of shrimp patties. We ran down to the kitchen and made some up. It would have been so embarrassing.'

'Yeah, yeah.' Nadine waved that away and concentrated on her coffee. Even in the upper echelons of Channel 75 they rarely had access to such potent brew. 'Then I notice, being the keen observer that I am, that you sweep Jess Barrow off and out at the end of the set. Never came back. Either of you.'

'We're having a mad, illicit affair,' Eve said dryly. 'You may want to turn that over to the gossip desk.'

'And I'm boinking a one-armed sex droid.'

'You always were an explorer.'

'Actually, there was this unit once . . . but I digress. Roarke, in his usual charming fashion, manages to move the lingering guests along, herds the hangers-on into the recreation center – great hologram deck, by the way – and gives your regrets. Duty calls?' Nadine angled her head. 'Funny. Nothing shows on my cop scanner that would have pulled our ace homicide detective out at that time of night.'

'Not everything goes out on the scanner, Nadine. And I'm just a soldier. I go when and where I'm told.'

'Sell it to someone else. I know how tight you are with Mavis. Nothing but top level would have pulled you away at her big moment.' She leaned forward. 'Where's Jess Barrow, Dallas? And what the hell has he done?'

'I don't have anything to give you, Nadine.'

'Come on, Dallas, you know me. I'll hold it down until I get the go-ahead. Who'd he kill?'

'Switch the channel,' Eve advised, then pulled out her communicator when it beeped. 'Display only, no audio.'

Quickly, she scanned the transmission from Peabody, manually requested a meeting, including Feeney, in twenty minutes. She set the communicator on the desk, turned back to the AutoChef to see if there were any soy chips available. She needed something to sop up the caffeine.

'I've got work, Nadine,' Eve continued, when she discovered she had nothing but an irradiated egg sandwich in stock. 'And nothing to bump up your ratings.'

'You're holding out on me. I know you've got Jess in custody. I've got sources in Holding.'

Annoyed, Eve turned back. Holding was innately ripe with leaks. 'I can't help you.'

'Are you charging him?'

'The charges are not for broadcast at this time.'

'Damn it, Dallas.'

'I'm on the edge here,' Eve snapped. 'And it could go either way. Don't push me. If and when I'm free to speak to the media on the matter, you'll be the first. You'll have to be satisfied with that.'

'You mean I have to be satisfied with nothing.' Nadine rose. 'You're got something big, or you wouldn't be so snotty about it. I'm only asking for a—'

She broke off as Mavis burst in. 'Jesus, Dallas, Jesus. How could you arrest Jess? What are you doing?'

'Mavis, damn it.' She could visualize Nadine's reporter's ears growing longer and sharper. 'Sit,' she demanded, stabbing a finger at a chair, then at Nadine. 'You, out.'

'Have a heart, Dallas.' Nadine attached herself to Mavis. 'Can't you see how upset she is? Let me get you some coffee, Mavis.'

'I said out, and I mean it.' At her wit's end, Eve rubbed her hands over her face. 'Take off, Nadine, or I'll put you on the blackout list.'

As a threat, it had punch. The blackout list meant there wouldn't be a cop in the homicide division who'd give Nadine the right time, much less a story lead. 'Okay, fine. But I'm not dropping this.' There were other ways to dig, she thought, and other tools to dig with. She snatched up her bag, gave Eve one last bitter look, then flounced out.

'How could you?' Mavis demanded. 'Dallas, how could you do this?'

To insure some level of privacy, Eve shut the door. Her headache had come full circle and was now gleefully throbbing behind her eyes. 'Mavis, this is my job here.'

'Your job?' Her eyes were laser blue today, and redrimmed from weeping. It was touching the way they matched the cobalt streaks in her scarlet hair. 'What about my career? I finally get the break I've been waiting for, working for, and you toss my partner into a cage. And for what?' Her voice hitched. 'Because he came on to you and pissed Roarke off.'

'What?' Her mouth fell open, worked silently before she could get her tongue around words. 'Where the hell did you get that?'

'I just got off the 'link with Jess. He's devastated. I can't believe you'd play this way, Dallas.' Her eyes began to leak again. 'I know Roarke's premiere with you, but we've got history.'

At that moment, with Mavis noisily weeping into her hands, Eve could have cheerfully strangled Jess Barrow. 'Yeah, we've got history, and you should know I don't play that way. I don't toss someone in a cage because I find them a personal annoyance. Would you sit down?'

'I don't need to sit.' She wailed it, made Eve wince as the sound acted as the dull point of an edgy knife on her brain.

'Well, I do.' She dropped into a chair. How much could she safely tell a civilian without crossing the line? And how far over the line was she willing to go? She looked at Mavis again, sighed. As far as it took. 'Jess is the prime suspect in four deaths.'

'What? What bend did you go around since last night? Jess wouldn't—'

'Be quiet,' Eve snapped. 'I haven't got him solid on that yet, but I'm working on it. I do, however, have him on other charges. Serious charges. Now, if you'd stop blubbering and sit the hell down, I'll tell you what I can.'

'You didn't even stay and watch my whole act.' Mavis managed to fall into a chair, but she didn't manage to stop blubbering.

'Oh, Mavis, I'm sorry.' Eve dragged a hand through her hair. She was lousy with weepers. 'I couldn't – there was nothing I could do. Mavis, Jess is into mind control.'

'Huh?' It was such a wild statement coming from the most grounded person she knew that Mavis stopped crying long enough to sniffle and gape. 'Huh?'

'He's developed a program that accesses brain wave patterns

and influences behavior. And he's used it on me, on Roarke, and on you.'

'On me? No, he didn't. Get genuine here, Dallas, this is too Frankenstein. Jess isn't a mad scientist. He's a musician.'

'He's an engineer, a musicologist, and a prick.' Eve took a deep breath, then related as much as she felt was necessary. As she spoke, Mavis's tears dried up, hardening her eyes. Her bottom lip quivered once, then thinned.

'He used me to get to you, to get to Roarke. I was just a spring. Then once I'd bounced him to you, he fucked with your mind.'

'This is not your fault. Stop it,' Eve ordered when Mavis's eyes started to shimmer again. 'I mean it. I'm tired, I'm pressed, and my head is about to explode. I don't need this soggy routine from you right now. It's not your fault. You were used, and so was I. He was hoping for Roarke's backing on his project. It doesn't make me less of a cop or you less of a performer. You're good, and you got better. He knew you could, and that's why he used you. He's too damn arrogant about his talent to have linked himself up with a dud. He wanted somebody who could shine. And you did.'

Mavis swiped a hand under her nose. 'Really?'

It was that one word delivered with such shaky hope that made Eve realize how far Mavis's ego had sunk. 'Yeah, really. You were great, Mavis. That's solid.'

'Okay.' She wiped at her eyes. 'I guess my feelings got hurt when you didn't hang for the act. Leonardo said I was being silly. You wouldn't have split if you hadn't had to split.' She took a long breath that lifted her thin shoulders, then dropped them again. 'Then Jess, when he called, he laid all this stuff on me. I shouldn't have bought into it.'

'It doesn't matter. We'll smooth out the rest later. I'm pressed here, Mavis. I don't have much time to wrap this up.'

'You think he killed people?'

'I have to find out.' She looked over at the knock on her door. Peabody stepped in, hesitated.

'Sorry, Lieutenant. Should I wait outside?'

'No, I'm going.' Mavis sniffled, rose, sent Eve a watery smile. 'Sorry about the flood and everything.'

'We'll mop it up. I'll talk to you when I can. Don't worry about this.'

Mavis nodded, and her lowered lashes concealed the quick flare in her eyes. She intended to do more than worry.

'Everything all right here, Lieutenant?' Peabody asked when Mavis left them alone.

'Actually, Peabody, everything's fucked.' Eve sat, tried to drill holes in her temples with her fingers to release the pressure. 'Mira doesn't think our boy has the personality profile for murder. I've insulted her because I'm going for another consultant. Nadine Furst is sniffing too close to the center, and I've just broken Mavis's heart and shattered her ego.

Peabody waited a beat. 'Well, other than that, how are things?'

'Cute.' But it did prod a reluctant smile. 'Damn, give me a nice clear murder any day over this physiological crap.'

'Those were the good old days, all right.' Peabody shifted to make room as Feeney stepped in. 'Well, the gang's all here.'

'Let's get to work. Status?' Eve asked Feeney.

'Sweepers found more discs at the suspect's studio. So far, no matches on victims. He kept a log of his work.' Uncomfortable, Feeney shifted. Jess had been very explicit in his speculations on results, including the sexual nudge he'd given Eve and Roarke. 'He names names, times, ah, suggestions. There's no mention of any of the four dead. I've been through his communications system. No transmissions to or from any of the victims.'

'Well, that's dandy.'

Feeney shifted his feet again, and his color fluctuated into a blush. 'I've sealed the work log for your eyes only.'

Her brows knit. 'Why?'

'He, ah, talks about you a lot. On a personal level.' He focused his eyes an inch over Eve's head. 'Again, he's very explicit in his speculations.'

'Yeah, he made it clear he was overly interested in my head.'

'He isn't just interested in that part of your anatomy.' Feeney puffed out his cheeks, blew the air out. 'He considered it would be an entertaining experiments to attempt to ah . . .'

'What?'

'Influence your behavior toward him . . . in a sexual manner.'

Eve let out a snort. It wasn't just the words, but Feeney's stiffly formal delivery. 'He figured he could use his toy to get me into the sack? Great. We can lay another charge on him. Intent to sexually molest.'

'Did he say anything about me?' Peabody wanted to know and received a glare from Eve.

'That's sick, Officer.'

'Just wondering.'

'We're adding to his cage time,' Eve continued, 'but we're not pinning him on the big one. And Mira's profile is going to work against us.'

'Lieutenant.' Peabody sucked in her breath and took the chance. 'Have you considered that she's right? That's he's not responsible?'

'Yeah, I have. And that scares the hell out of me. If she's right, there's someone else out there with a brain toy, and we're not even close. So we all better hope we've got our man safely locked away.'

'Speaking of our man,' Feeney broke in. 'You better know he's lawyered himself.'

'I figured he would. Anybody we know?'

'Leanore Bastwick.'

'Well, hell. Small world.'

'She wants to make points off of you, Dallas.' Feeney took out his bag of nuts, offered them to Peabody. 'She's raring to go. Wants to set up a media conference. Word is she took him on pro bono, just for the shot at you, and the media coverage this will get once it hits.'

'She can take her shot. We can block the press conference for twenty-four hours. We'd better solidify before then.'

'I pulled a thread loose,' Peabody told her. 'It might unravel more with some tugging. Mathias did indeed attend MIT for two semesters. Unfortunately, his term there was three years after Jess did his at-home degree, but Jess used his alumni status to access data from their files. He also taught an E-class elective on musicology, which the university uploaded into their library curriculum. Mathias took the course during his last semester.'

Eve felt a quick power surge. 'That's something to tug on. Good work. It connects, finally. And maybe we've been looking in the wrong place. Pearly was the first known victim. What if he's the one who was connected with the others? It could be as simple as their common interest in electronic games.'

'We looked there already.'

'So look again,' she told Peabody. 'And look deeper. Not all the clubs and loops are above ground. If Mathias was used to help develop the system, he might have bragged about it. Those hobby hackers use all kinds of compunames. Can you find his?'

'Eventually,' Feeney agreed.

'You can contact Jack Carter. He was his roommate on Olympus. Maybe he can give you a boost on them. Peabody, contact Devane's son, see what you can shake out of him on this angle. I'll work on the Fitzhugh angle.' She glanced at her watch. 'I'll make a stop first. Maybe I can cut through some of the layers.'

*

She felt she was back to square one, looking for the connection. There had to be one, and she was going to have to involve Roarke to find it. She called him from her car 'link.

'Well, hello, Lieutenant. How was your nap?'

'Too short and too long ago. How long are you going to be in midtown?'

'Another few hours at any rate. Why?'

'I'm coming by. Now. Can you squeeze me in?'

He smiled. 'Always.'

'It's business,' she said, and cut him off before she could smile back. Daring her auto-drive, she programmed destination, then used her 'link again. 'Nadine.'

Nadine angled her head, shot Eve a cold look. 'Lieutenant.'

'Nine A.M., my office.'

'Should I bring a lawyer?'

'Bring your recorder. I'll give you a jump on tomorrow's press conference re Jess Barrow.'

'What press conference?' The image and voice quality sharpened as Nadine went immediately to private, dragging headphones over her hair. 'There's nothing on schedule.'

'There will be. You want that jump, and you want the official report from the primary, be there at nine.'

'What's the catch?'

'Senator Pearly. Get me everything. Not the official data, the quiet stuff. His hobbies, playgrounds. His underground connections.'

'Pearly was clean as a church choir.'

'You don't have to be dirty to play underground, you just have to be curious.'

'And what makes you think I can get private data on a government official?'

'Because you're you, Nadine. Feed the data to my home unit, and I'll see you at nine hundred hours. You'll beat the pack by two hours easy. Think of those ratings.'

'I'm thinking. Deal,' she snapped and signed off.

When Eve was able to glide smoothly into the parking facility at Roarke's midtown office, she began to think more kindly toward vehicle maintenance. Her VIP space was waiting, locking its security shield the moment she shut down.

The elevator accepted her palm print and zoomed her up to the top floor in a quiet, dignified ride.

She'd never get used to it.

Roarke's personal assistant beamed at her, welcomed her home, welcomed her in, and escorted her through the plush outer offices, down the streamlined corridor, and into the elegant efficiency of Roarke's private office.

But he wasn't alone.

'Sorry.' She struggled not to frown at Reeanna and William. 'I'm interrupting.'

'Not at all.' Roarke walked over, kissed her lightly. 'We're just finishing up.'

'Your husband's quite the slave driver.' William held out a hand to shake Eve's warmly. 'If you hadn't come along, Reeanna and I would have to do without our dinner.'

'That's William.' Reeanna laughed. 'He's either thinking of electronics or his stomach.'

'Or you. Can you join us?' he asked Eve. 'I thought we'd try the French place on the skyline level.'

'Cops never eat.' Eve tried to adjust herself to the easy social tone. 'But thanks.'

'You need regular fuel to help the healing process.' Reeanna narrowed her eyes for a quick, professional survey. 'Any pain?'

'Not much. I appreciate the personal service. And I wonder if I could speak to you for a few minutes on an official matter – if you have time after your meal.'

'Of course.' Curiosity flitted over her face. 'Could I ask what it's about?'

'The possibility of doing a consult on a case I'm working on. If you're agreeable, I'd need to do it tomorrow, early.'

266

'A consult on an actual human being? I'm there.'

'Reeanna's weary of machines,' William put in. 'She's been making noises for weeks about going back into private practice.'

'VR, holograms, autotronics.' She rolled her beautiful eyes. 'I long for flesh and blood. Roarke has us set up on the thirty-second level, west wing. I should be able to nudge William through a meal in an hour. Just meet me there.'

'Thanks.'

'Oh, and Roarke,' Reeanna continued as she and William started toward the door. 'We'd love to have that personal take on the new unit as soon as you can manage it.'

'And she calls me a slave driver. Tonight, before I leave.'

'Wonderful. Later, Eve.'

'Food, Reeanna. I'm dreaming of coquille St Jacques.' William was laughing as he pulled her out of the door.

'I didn't mean to break up your meeting,' Eve began.

'You didn't. And you've given me a breather before I have to dig into a mountain of status reports. I've had all the data on that VR unit you're concerned about transmitted. I've skimmed the surface, but I've found nothing out of line so far.'

'That's something.' She'd rest easier once she could eliminate that angle.

'William would be able to spot any problem quicker,' he added. 'But as he and Ree were in on the development, I didn't think you'd care to pass it by him.'

'No. Let's keep it close.'

'Reeanna was concerned about you. So am I.'

'She gave me a going-over. She's good.'

'Yes, she is.' Still, he tipped Eve's face back with a fingertip. 'You've got a headache.'

'What's the point of illegal brain scans when you can already see into my head?' She closed her hand over his wrist before he could drop his arm. 'I can't see into yours. It's annoying.'

'I know.' His lips curved as he pressed them to her brow. 'I love you. Ridiculously.'

'I didn't come here for this,' she murmured when his arms wound around her.

'Take a minute anyway. I need it.' He could feel the outline of the diamond around her neck, one she had worn first reluctantly, and now habitually. 'That'll do it.' He eased her back, pleased that she'd held on another moment. She so rarely held on. 'What's on your mind, Lieutenant?'

'Peabody dug up a thin connection between Barrow and Mathias. I want to see if I can tighten it. How much trouble would it be to access underground transmissions, using MIT's on-line services as a starting point?'

His eyes lighted. 'I love a challenge.' He moved around the desk, engaged his unit, then slid open a hidden panel under it, flicked a switch manually.

'What's that?' Her teeth went on edge. 'Is that a block system? Did you just tune out Compuguard?'

'That would be illegal, wouldn't it?' he said cheerfully. He reached over his shoulder to pat her hand. 'Don't ask the question, Lieutenant, if you don't want to hear the answer. Now, what time period are you interested in, particularly?'

Scowling, she dug out her log, read off the dates of Mathias's attendance at MIT. 'I'm looking for Mathias specifically. I don't know what line names he used yet. Feeney's getting them.'

'Oh, I think I can find them for you. Why don't you see about ordering us a meal? No reason to go hungry.'

'Coquille St Jacques?' she said dryly.

'Steak. Rare.' He slid out a keyboard and began to work manually.

Chapter Nineteen

Eve ate standing up, breathing down Roarke's neck. When he'd had enough of that, he simply reached around and pinched her.

'Back off.'

'I'm just trying to see.' But she backed off. 'You've been at it a half hour.'

He imagined, with the equipment available at Cop Central, even Feeney would have taken twice as long to get to that same point. 'Darling Eve,' he said, then sighed when she only frowned at him. 'There are layers here, Lieutenant. Layers over layers. That's why they call it underground. I've located two of the coded names our young, doomed autotronics ace used. There'll be more. Still, it takes some doing to unscramble transmissions.'

He turned the machine on auto so he could enjoy his own dinner.

'It's all just games, isn't it?' Eve shifted so she could see the screen run with figures and odd symbols as it worked. 'Just grown-up kids playing games. Secret societies. Hell, they're just high-tech clubhouses.'

'More or less. Most of us enjoy diversions, Eve. Games, fantasies, the anonymity of a computer mask so we can pretend we're someone else for a time.'

Games, she thought again. Maybe it all boiled down to games, and she just hadn't looked closely enough at the rules and players. 'What's wrong with being who you are?'

'It's not enough for everyone. And this sort of thing attracts the lonely and the egocentric.'

'And fanatics.'

'Certainly. E-services, particularly underground ones, provide the fanatic with an open forum.' He cocked a brow, cut neatly into his steak. 'They also provide a service – educational for that matter – informative, intellectual. And can be perfectly harmless entertainment. They're legal,' he reminded her. 'Even the underground ones aren't closely regulated. And that stems mainly from the fact that it's nearly impossible to do so. And cost prohibitive.'

'EDD keeps a line on them.'

'To some extent. Look here.' He swung back, tapped out a few keys, and had a display sliding onto one of the wall screens. 'See that? It's nothing more than a somewhat amusing diatribe about a new version of Camelot. A multiuser role playing program, hologram optional,' he explained. 'Everyone wants to be king. And there.' He gestured to another screen. 'A very straightforward advertisement for a partner in Erotica, a sexual fantasy VR program, dual remote controls mandatory.' He grinned at her knitted brow. 'One of my companies manufactures it. It's quite popular.'

'I bet.' She didn't ask if he'd tried it out himself. Some data she didn't need. 'I don't get it. You can rent a licensed companion, probably cheaper than the cost of that program. You get sex in the flesh. Why do you need this?'

'Fantasy, darling. Having control or abdicating it. And you can run the program over and over, with nearly unlimited variations. It's mood again, and mind. All fantasies are mood and mind.'

'Even the fatal ones,' she said slowly. 'Isn't that what this is all about? Having control. Ultimate control over someone else's mood and mind. They don't even know they're playing the game. That's the big kick. You'd need a huge ego and no conscience. Mira says Jess doesn't fit.'

270

'Ah. That's a problem, isn't it?'

She flicked a look down at him. 'You don't sound surprised.'

'He's what, in my alley days in Dublin, we would have called a fug – cross between a fuck and a pug. Lots of mouth and no balls. I never met a fug who could draw blood without whining.'

She cleaned the steak off her plate and set it aside. 'It seems to me that killing in this manner is bloodless. Cowardly. Fuglike.'

He grinned at that. 'Well put, but fugs don't kill, they just talk.'

She hated that she was beginning to agree and had muscled her way down what looked like a dead end with Jess Barrow. 'I've got to have more. How much longer do you figure?'

'Until I'm through. You can keep yourself occupied with the data on the VR unit.'

'I'll come back to it. I'm going to go down to Reeanna's office. I can just leave her a memo about Jess if she's not back from dinner.'

'Fine.' He didn't try to dissuade her. She had to move, he knew. To take some action. 'Will you come back up when you're done, or will I meet you at home?'

'I don't know.' He looked perfect there, she thought, sitting in his snazzy office, manipulating controls. Maybe everyone wanted to be king, she mused, but Roarke was content being Roarke.

His gaze shifted to hers, held. 'Yes, Lieutenant?'

'You're exactly what you want to be. That's a pretty good deal.'

'Most of the time. And so are you what you want to be.'

'Most of the time,' she murmured. 'I'll check in with Feeney and Peabody after I meet with Reeanna. See if anything's come loose. Thanks for dinner – and the computime.'

271

'You can pay me back.' He took her hand, rose. 'I want, very much, to make love with you tonight.'

'You don't have to ask.' Flustered, she moved her shoulders. 'We got married and everything.'

'Let's say asking is part of the fantasy.' He moved in, just a little; touched his lips to hers, just a whisper. 'Let me woo you tonight, darling Eve. Let me surprise you. Let me . . . seduce you.' He laid a hand on her heart, felt the hard, thick beat of it. 'There,' he murmured. 'I've already started.'

Her knees were quivering. 'Thanks. That's just what I need to keep my mind focused on my work.'

'Two hours.' This time he lingered over the kiss. 'Then let's take something for ourselves.'

'I'll try.' She stepped back while she was sure she still could, walked quickly toward the door. Then she turned back, just looked at him. 'Two hours,' she told him. 'Then you can finish what you started.'

She heard him laugh as she closed the door and hurried toward the elevator. 'Thirty-nine, west,' she ordered, then found herself smiling.

Yes, they'd take something for themselves, she decided. Something Jess and his nasty little toy had tried to steal from them.

Then she stopped, and her smile faded. *Was that the problem here?* she wondered. Was she so focused on that – on a kind of personal retribution – that she was missing something bigger? Or smaller?

If Mira was right, and Roarke with his fug theory was on the mark, then she was off. It was time, she admitted, to pull back a bit. Refocus.

It was a tech crime, she mused. *But tech crimes still require the human element: motive, emotion, greed, hate, jealousy, and power*. Which of those – or which combination of those – was at the core of this? She could see both greed and a hunger for power in Jess. But would he kill for them?

Steely minded, she replayed his reaction to the morgue shots in her mind. Would a man who had caused that to happen, had directed it to happen, react with such violent distress when faced with the results?

Not impossible, she decided. But it didn't fit her image of the hand on the button.

He enjoyed seeing the results of his work, she remembered. He liked to snicker over them and note them down in his log. Did he have another log, one the sweepers missed? She'd have to take a trip through his studio herself.

Deep in thought, she stepped out on thirty-nine, scanned the shielded glass walls of a lab. It was quiet here, security in full swing as indicated by the cameras in full view, the warning red beep of motion detectors. If there were any drones still at work, they were behind closed doors.

She placed her palm on a plate, received verification, answered the request for voice print by giving her name, then requested the location of Reeanna's office.

You are cleared for top level, Dallas, Lieutenant Eve. Proceed left through breezeway, then right at termination. Dr Ott's office is five meters beyond this point. It will not be necessary to repeat this procedure to gain entry. You are cleared.

She wondered if Roarke or Reeanna had cleared her through and followed the directions. The breezeway impressed her, offering a full view of the city on all sides. She could look between her own feet and see the life bustling on the street below. The music piped in was energetic, and made her think sourly of some musicologist's idea of fueling drones with enthusiasm for their work. *Wasn't that just one more kind of mind control?*

She passed a door bearing an imprint that identified it as William's. A game master, she thought. It might be helpful to get his input, pick his brain, jiggle a few hypotheses out of him. She knocked, watched his recorder light beep red for locked.

I'm sorry, William Shaffer is not currently in his office. Please leave your name and any message. He will respond as soon as possible.

'It's Dallas. Look, William, if you've got a couple minutes when you finish dinner, I've got something I'd like to run by you. I'm going to drop by Reeanna's office now. I'll leave a memo if she's not there. I'll be in the building or at home later if you've got time to talk to me.'

As she turned away, she glanced at her watch. How long did it take to eat, for God's sake? You picked up food, put it in your mouth, chewed, and swallowed.

She found Reeanna's office, knocked. She hesitated for less than five seconds when the recorder light beeped green, then slid the door open. If Reeanna didn't want her inside, she'd have kept it locked, Eve decided, and indulged herself in a thorough study.

It looked like Reeanna, she decided. Polished to a bright sheen, underlying sexual tones in the slashes of fiery red in the laser art against cool white walls.

The desk faced the window to provide Reeanna with a constant view of the busy sky traffic.

The sitting area was plush with a deeply cushioned body-form lounger that still held the imprint of its last occupant. Reeanna's curves were impressive, even in silhouette. The clear Plasticide table was hard as stone and was intricately carved with diamond patterns that caught and refracted the light from an arched-neck lamp with a rose-toned shade.

Eve picked up the VR goggles laid on it, saw they were indeed Roarke's latest model, and set them down again. They still made her uncomfortable.

Turning away, she studied the workstation across the room.

274

Nothing soft or feminine about that area, she noted. It was all business. Slick white counter, muscle flexing equipment even now hard at work. She heard the low hum of a computer on auto, frowned at the symbols flickering on the monitor. They looked similar to what she'd tried to decipher from Roarke's screen.

But then, computer codes all looked the same to her.

Curious, she walked over to the desk, but nothing interesting had been left out to examine. A silver pen, a pair of pretty gold earrings, a hologram of William wearing a flight suit and grinning youthfully. A short printout, again in that baffling computer code.

Eve sat on the edge of the desk. She didn't want to fit her wiry build into the imprint left by Reeanna's. Pulling out her communicator, she tagged Peabody.

'Anything?'

'Devane's son is willing to cooperate. He's aware of the interest she had in games, particularly role playing. It wasn't an interest he shared, but he claims he knows one of her usual partners. He dated her for a short time. I've got her name. She lives right here in New York. I have the data. Should I transmit?'

'I think you can handle an interview solo. Arrange a meet, bring her in only if she refuses to cooperate. Report back.'

'Yes, sir.' Peabody's voice remained sober, but her eyes lighted with the assignment. 'I'm on my way.'

Satisfied, Eve tried for Feeney, hit his frequency occupied recording. She had to settle for leaving a request for contact.

The door opened. Reeanna stopped her rush inside when she spotted Eve at her desk. 'Oh, Eve. I didn't expect you quite yet.'

'Time's part of my problem.'

'I see.' She smiled, let the door shut. 'I suppose Roarke cleared you in.'

'I guess he did. Problem?'

'No, no.' Reeanna waved her hand. 'I'm distracted, I suppose. William went on endlessly about some glitches he's concerned about. I left him brooding over his crème brûlée.' She flicked a glance toward her humming computer. 'The work never stops around here. R and D's a twenty-four/seven proposition.' She smiled. 'Like police work, I imagine. Well, I didn't take time for brandy. Would you like some?'

'No, thanks. On duty.'

'Coffee then.' Reeanna moved over to a counter, requested a snifter of brandy, a cup of black coffee. 'You'll have to excuse my lack of focus. We're a little behind schedule today. Roarke needed data on the new VR model, and he wanted it from conception to implementation.'

'That was yours. I didn't realize that until he mentioned it just now.'

'Oh, William's mostly. Though I had a small part. Now.' She handed Eve the coffee, then took her brandy around the desk to sit. 'What can I do for you?'

'I'm hoping you'll agree to that consult. The subject is currently in custody, now lawyered, but I don't think we'll be blocked there. I need a profile, angling from your particular area of expertise.'

'Genetic branding.' Reeanna tapped her fingers. 'Interesting. What are the charges?'

'I'm not free to discuss that until I have your agreement and clear the session with my commander. Once that's done, I'd like the testing scheduled for seven hundred.'

'Seven A.M.?' Reeanna winced. 'Ouch. And here I'm a night owl rather than a lark. You want me up and running at that hour, give me some incentive.' She smiled a little. 'I can assume you've already had Mira test your subject – and the results weren't to your liking.'

'Second opinions aren't unusual.' It was a defensive answer. She felt defensive. And, Eve realized, she felt guilty.

276

'No, but Dr Mira's reports are sterling, and they're very rarely questioned. You want him badly.'

'I want the truth badly. To find it, I have to separate theory and lies and deceptions.' She pushed off the desk. 'Look, I thought you were interested in doing this sort of thing.'

'I am, very. But I like to know what I'm dealing with. I'd need the subject's brain scan.'

'I've got it. In evidence.'

'Really?' Her eyes gleamed, catlike. 'It's also important to have all available data on his biological parents. Are they known?'

'We accessed that data for Dr Mira's test. It'll be available to you.'

Reeanna leaned back, swirling her brandy. 'It must be murder.' Her lips twitched at Eve's expression. 'After all, that's your field. The study of the taking of lives.'

'You could put it that way.'

'How do you put it?'

'The investigation of the takers.'

'Yes, yes, but in order to do so, you study the dead – and death itself. How it happened, what caused it, what transpired in those last moments between the taker and the victim. Fascinating. What kind of personality is required to study death routinely, day after day, year after year, as a vocation? Does it scar you, Eve, or harden you?'

'It pisses you off,' she said shortly. 'And I don't have time to philosophize.'

'Sorry, bad habit.' Reeanna let out a sigh. 'William tells me I analyze everything to death.' She smiled. 'Not that it's a crime – that sort of murder. And I am interested in assisting you. Call your commander,' she invited. 'I'll wait and see if clearance is forthcoming. Then we can go over details.'

'I appreciate it.' Eve removed her communicator, turned away, and requested display only. It took longer and was, she felt, less effective. The coding through of information and request. How could you add your instincts, your determination to a display?

But she did her best and waited.

What the hell are you trying to do, Dallas, override Mira?

I want another opinion, Commander. It's well within procedure. I'm pursuing all angles. If I'm unable to convince the PA to charge Jess with coercion to self-terminate, I don't want the lesser charges to slide. I need verification of intent to harm.

It was pushing it, and she knew it. Eve waited with a knotted stomach while Whitney mulled over his decision.

Just give me the opening, she thought. *He needs his ears pinned back. He needs to pay.*

You're cleared to proceed on my authorization, Lieutenant. This better not be a waste of budget. We both know Mira's report will weigh heavily.

Understood and appreciated. Dr Ott's report will give Barrow's lawyer a headache, if nothing else. I'm currently working on detailing connection between suspect and victims. Results will be available by nine hundred hours.

Be damn sure of it. My butt is now swinging with yours. Whitney out.

Eve let out a long, quiet breath. She'd bought a little more time, and that was all, she admitted to herself, she was after. With time, she could dig deeper. If Roarke and Feeney couldn't pull out data, there was no one, off or on planet, who could.

Jess would pay, but murder would go unavenged. She closed her eyes a moment. And that was where she stood. Avenging the dead.

She opened her eyes again, wanting to align herself before she relayed the details to Reeanna.

That's when she saw it, in black and white there on the computer monitor.

Mathias, Drew logged as AutoPhile. Mathias, Drew logged as Banger. Mathias, Drew logged as HoloDick.

Her heartbeat jerked, but her hand was steady as a rock as she switched her communicator from off to open, signaling to Peabody and Feeney on code one. Backup required. Respond immediately to transmission source.

She pocketed the card, turned. 'The commander okayed the consult. Reluctantly. I'm going to need results, Reeanna.'

'You'll get them.' Reeanna sipped her brandy, then shifted her gaze to the sleek little unit on her desk. 'Your heart rate just spiked, Eve, and your adrenaline level rose dramatically.' She angled her head. 'Oh dear,' she murmured, and lifted her sparkling hand. It held an official NYPSD stunner. 'That's a problem.'

Several floors above, Roarke scanned the new data on Mathias, hummed over it. *Now we're getting somewhere*, he thought. He switched back to auto and tuned in to the data on the new VR unit. Wasn't it odd, he thought, and interesting, that some of the components on Jess Barrow's magic console so closely mirrored the components of his new unit?

Then he swore softly when his interoffice 'link buzzed.

'I don't want interruptions.'

'I'm sorry, sir. There's a Mavis Freestone here. She claims you'll see her.'

He switched the second computer to auto, blocked both audio and video. 'Let her in, Caro. And you can log out for the day. I won't need you anymore.'

'Thank you. I'll bring her back directly.'

Roarke frowned to himself, idly picked up the VR unit Reeanna had left him to try out. A few adjustments, he mused. Improved for the next release. It was loaded with subliminal options, and could explain the coincidence of similarity. Still, he didn't care for it. He began to consider a possible leak in his R and D division.

He wondered just what William had come up with as alterations for the second manufacturing run and tucked a disc into his alternate unit. It wouldn't hurt to run the data while he saw just what Mavis had on her mind.

His machine beeped acceptance, began to upload as his door opened. Mavis whirled in like a freak storm.

'It's my fault, all my fault, and I don't know what to do.'

Roarke came around the desk, took Mavis's hands, and sent an understanding look at his baffled assistant. 'Go on home. I'll deal with this. Oh, and leave the security open for my wife, please. Sit down, Mavis.' He steered her to a chair. 'Take a breath.' Reading her accurately, he patted her head. 'And don't cry. What's all your fault?'

'Jess. He used me to get to you. Dallas said it wasn't my fault, but I've thought about it, and it is.' She gave one long, heroic sniffle. 'I've got this.' She held up a disc.

'And this is?'

'I don't know. Maybe evidence. You take it.'

'Okay.' He nipped the disc out of her hand as she waved wildly. 'Why haven't you given it to Eve?'

'I would – I was going to. I thought she was here. I don't think I'm supposed to have it. I didn't even tell Leonardo about it. I'm a terrible person,' she finished.

Hysterical women had come his way before. Roarke slipped the disc into his pocket, walked over, and ordered a tall soother of the milder variety. 'Here, drink this. What sort of evidence do you think this is, Mavis?'

'I dunno. You don't hate me, do you?'

'Darling, I adore you. Drink it down.'

'Really?' She gulped obediently. 'I really like you, Roarke, and not just because you're rolling in credits or anything. It's good that you are, 'cause poor sucks, right?'

'It does indeed.'

'But either way, you make her so happy. She doesn't even know how happy because she's never been. You know?'

'Yes. Three slow quiet breaths now. Ready? One.'

'Okay.' She took them, very seriously, her eyes on his. 'You're good at this. Calming people down. I bet she doesn't let you do it for her much.'

'No, she doesn't. Or she doesn't know it when I do.' He smiled. 'We know her, don't we, Mavis?'

'We love her. I'm so sorry.' Tears came, but they were soothing and soft. 'I figured it out after I ran the disc I gave you. At least I figured out some of it. It's a copy of the lay down from my video. I ran it off on the sly. I wanted it for posterity, you know? But there's a memo after it.'

She looked down at her hands. 'This is the first time I played it, the first time I heard it all. He gave a copy to Dallas, but he made notes after this version, about . . .' She broke off, lifted suddenly dry eyes. 'I want you to hurt him for this. I want you to hurt him really bad. Play it, from where I've cued it.'

Roarke said nothing, but he rose and slid the disc into his entertainment unit. The screen filled with light, with music, then the volume and intensity lowered as a background for Jess's voice.

'I'm not sure what the results will be. One day I'll find the key to tapping in at the source. For now, I can only specualte. The suggestion is to the memory. The reenactment of trauma. Something's at the core of those shadows on Dallas's mind. Something fascinating. What will she dream tonight after playing the disc? How long will it be before I can seduce her to share it all with me? What secrets does she hide? It's such fun to wonder. I'm just waiting for the chance to tap into Roarke's darker side. Oh, he has one, so close to the surface you can almost see it. Thinking of them together, with just the animal in control, gives me such a rush. I can't think of two more fascinating subjects for this project. God bless Mavis

281

for opening the door. Within six months I'll know these two so well, anticipate their reactions so clearly, I'll be able to lead them right where I want them. Then there's no limit. Fame, fortune, adulation. I'll be the goddamn father of virtual pleasure.'

Roarke remained silent as the disc ran out. He didn't remove it, certain his fingers would crush it like powder.

'I've already hurt him,' he said at length. 'But not enough. Not nearly enough.' He turned to Mavis. She'd risen and stood, small as a fairy, her slip-shouldered dress of pink gauze somehow valiant. 'You aren't responsible for this,' Roarke told her.

'Maybe that's true. I have to work that out. But I know he wouldn't have gotten that close to her, or you, without me. Will that help keep him in a cage?'

'I think he'll hear the lock turn and wait a long time before he hears it open again. You'll leave it with me?'

'Yeah. I'll get out of your hair now.'

'You're always welcome here.'

Her mouth quirked. 'If it wasn't for Dallas, you'd have run like hell in the opposite direction the first time you saw me.'

He came to her, kissed her firmly on that crooked mouth. 'That would have been my mistake – and my loss. I'll call a car for you.'

'You don't have to—'

'A car will be waiting for you at the front entrance.'

She rubbed a hand under her nose. 'One of those mag limos?'

'Absolutely.'

He walked her to the door, closed it thoughtfully behind her. The disc would be enough, he hoped, to drive another nail in Jess. But it still didn't point to murder. He went back, ordered both of his machines to display on screen.

Sitting behind his desk, he picked up the VR goggles and studied the data.

*

Eve lowered her gaze to the stunner. From her angle, she couldn't be sure which setting was clicked. A sudden move, she knew, could result in anything from mild discomfort and partial paralysis to death.

'It's illegal for a civilian to own or operate that weapon,' she said coolly.

'I don't believe that's particularly relevant, under the circumstances. Take yours out, Eve, slowly, and by the fingertips. Then set it on the desk. I don't want to hurt you,' Reeanna added when Eve made no move to obey. 'I never have. Not really. But I'll do whatever's necessary.'

Keeping her eyes on Reeanna's, Eve reached slowly for her side arm.

'And don't think about trying to use it. I don't have this on max, but it is on a very high setting. You won't have use of your extremities for days, and though the possible brain damage isn't necessarily permanent, it is very inconvenient.'

Eve knew very well what the stunner could do, and she took out her weapon carefully, laid it on the corner of the desk. 'You'll have to kill me, Reeanna. But you'll have to do it face to face, in person. It won't be like the others.'

'I'm going to try to avoid that. A short, painless, even enjoyable session on VR, and we can adjust your memory and direct your target. You're well aimed at Jess, Eve. Why don't we just keep it that way?'

'Why did you kill those four people, Reeanna?'

'They killed themselves, Eve. You were right there when Cerise Devane jumped off that building. One has to believe what one sees with one's own eyes.' She sighed. 'Or most do. You're not most, are you?'

'Why did you kill them?'

'I merely encouraged them to end their lives in a certain manner at a certain time. And why?' Reeanna shrugged her lovely shoulders. 'Why, because I could.'

She smiled beautifully and gave her bell tinkle of a laugh.

Chapter Twenty

It wouldn't take long, Eve calculated, for Peabody or Feeney to home in on her signal. She just needed time. And she had a feeling Reeanna would provide it. Some egos, like some people, fed on regular admiration. Reeanna fit on both levels.

'Did you work with Jess?'

'That amateur.' Reeanna tossed her hair at the idea. 'He's a piano player. Not that he doesn't have a certain talent for basic engineering, but he lacks vision – and guts,' she added with a slow, feline smile. 'Women are so much more courageous and more vicious than men, all in all. Don't you agree?'

'No. I think courage and viciousness have no gender.'

'Well.' Disappointed, Reeanna pursed her lips briefly. 'In any case, I corresponded with him briefly a couple of years ago. We exchanged ideas, theories. The anonymity of underground E-services are handy. I enjoyed his pontificating and was able to flatter him into sharing some of his technical progress. But I was well ahead of him. Frankly, I never thought he'd get as far as he apparently has. Simple mood expanding, I imagine, with some direct suggestion.' She cocked her head. 'Close enough?'

'You went farther.'

'Oh, leagues. Why don't you sit down, Eve? We'd both be more comfortable.'

'I'm comfortable on my feet.'

'As you like. But a few steps back, if you don't mind.' She

284

gestured with the stunner. 'I wouldn't want you to try for your weapon. I'd have to use this, and I'd hate to lose such a good audience.'

Eve took a step back. She thought of Roarke, several floors above. He wouldn't come down to seek her out. At least she didn't have that concern. If anything, he'd call down if he locked onto something. So he was safe, and she could stall.

'You're a medical doctor,' Eve pointed out. 'A psychiatrist. You've spent years studying to help the human condition. Why take lives, Reeanna, when you're trained to save them?'

'Branded at conception perhaps.' She smiled. 'Oh, you don't like that theory. You'd have used it to push your case, but you don't like it. You don't know where you came from, or from what.' She saw Eve's eyes flicker and nodded, pleased. 'I've studied all available data on Eve Dallas as soon as I learned Roarke was involved with you. I'm very attached to Roarke, once toyed with the idea of making our all-too-brief liaison into something more permanent.'

'He dumped you?'

The smile froze as the insult hit target. 'That's beneath you, such a petty female hit. No, he didn't. We simply drifted in opposite directions. I had intended to drift back, let's say, eventually. So I was intrigued when he took such an avid interest in a cop, of all things. Not his usual taste, certainly not his usual style. But you are . . . interesting. More so after I accessed data on you.'

She made herself comfortable on the arm of the relaxation chair. The weapon stayed aimed and steady. 'The young, abused child found in a Dallas alley. Broken, battered, confused. No memory of how she'd gotten there, who'd beat her, raped her, abandoned her. A blank. I found that fascinating. No past, no parents, no hint of what made her. I'm going to enjoy studying you.'

'You won't get your hands in my head.'

'Oh, but I will. You'll even suggest it yourself, once you

take a trip or two on the unit I've made just for you. I really hate that I'm going to have to see to it that you forget everything we discuss here. You have such a keen mind, such a strong energy. But it will give us a chance to work together. As fond as I am of William, he's so . . . short-sighted.'

'How involved is he?'

'He has no idea. The first test I ran on the doctored unit was on William. Quite a success, and it made things so much easier. I could direct him to adjust each unit I wanted. He's quicker, more adept electronically than I. He actually helped me refine the design and personalize the one I sent to Senator Pearly.'

'Why?'

'Another test. He was very vocal about the misuse of subliminals. He enjoyed games, as I'm sure you've discovered, but he continually pushed for regulations. Censorship, if you ask me. He stuck his nose into pornography, consenting adult dual controls, commercial advertising and its use of suggestion, all manner of things. I thought of him as my sacrificial lamb.'

'How did you gain access to his brain pattern?'

'William. He's very clever. It took him several weeks of intense work, but he managed to hack through security.' She angled her head, enjoying the moment. 'At the top level of NYPSD as well. He injected a virus there. Just to keep your EDD men occupied.'

'And that's where you accessed my pattern.'

'Indeed it is. He has a soft heart, my William, it would pain him horribly to know he had a vital part in coercion.'

'But you used him, you made him part of it. And it doesn't pain you at all.'

'No, it doesn't. William made it all possible. And if not him, there would have been another.'

'He loves you. You can see it.'

'Oh please.' It made her laugh. 'He's a puppy. All men are when it comes to an attractive female form. They simply sit up and beg. That's amusing, occasionally irritating, and always useful.' Intrigued, she touched her tongue to her top lip. 'Don't tell me you haven't used your basic female advantage on Roarke.'

'We don't use each other.'

'You're missing a simple advantage.' But Reeanna flicked it away. 'The esteemed Dr Mira would label me a sociopath with violent tendencies and a driving need for control. A pathological liar with an unhealthy, even dangerous fascination with death.'

Eve waited a beat. 'And would you agree with that analysis, Dr Ott?'

'Yes, indeed. My mother self-terminated when I was six. My father never got over it. He turned me over to my grandparents and wandered off to heal. I don't believe he ever did. But I saw my mother's face after she'd taken the lethal handful of pills. She looked quite beautiful and very happy. So why shouldn't death, taken, be an enjoyable experience.'

'Try it,' Eve suggested, 'and see.' Then she smiled. 'I'll help you.'

'One day, perhaps. After I've completed my study.'

'We're laboratory rats then; not toys, not games, but experiments. Droids for dissecting.'

'Yes. Young Drew. I regretted that because he was young and had potential. I'd consulted with him, rashly I see now, when William and I were working on the Olympus Resort. He fell in love with me. So young. I was flattered, and William's very tolerant of outside distractions.'

'He just knew too much, so you sent him a modified unit and told him to hang himself.'

'Basically. It wouldn't have been necessary, but he didn't want to let the relationship die. It meant he had to, before he lost that glaze infatuation puts over a man's eyes, and looked too closely.'

'You stripped your victims,' Eve added. 'The final humiliation?'

'No.' Reeanna appeared shocked and insulted by the idea. 'Not at all. Basic symbolism. We're born naked, and naked we die. We complete the circle. Drew died happy. They all did. No suffering, no pain at all. Joy, in fact. I'm not a monster, Eve. I'm a scientist.'

'No, you're a monster, Reeanna. And these days, society puts their monsters in a cage and keeps them there. You won't be happy in a cage.'

'It won't happen. Jess will pay. You'll fight to put him there after my report tomorrow. And if you can't make the coercion charges stick, you'll always believe he was responsible. And when there are others, I'll be very select, very careful, and I'll see to it that each subject self-terminates well out of your range. You won't be bothered by it again.'

'You arranged for two in my range.' A sickness churned in her stomach. 'To get my attention.'

'In part. I did want to watch you at work. Watch you closely, step by step. Just to see if you were as good as reported. You detested Fitzhugh, and I thought why not do my new friend Eve a little favor? He was a pompous ass, an irritant to society, and a very poor game player. I wanted his death to be bloody. He perferred blood games, you know. I never met him in person, but matched with him in cyberspace now and again. A poor loser.'

'He had family,' Eve managed. 'Like Pearly, Mathias, and Cerise Devane.'

'Oh, life goes on.' She waved a dismissing hand. 'All will adjust. That's human nature. And as for Cerise, she was no more maternal than an alley cat. It was all ambition with her. She bored me senseless. The most entertainment she ever provided was dying on camera. What a smile. They all smiled. That was my little joke – and my gift to them. The final suggestion. Die, it's so beautiful, it's amusing, and so joyful.

Die and experience the pleasure. They died experiencing the pleasure.'

'They died with a frozen smile and a burn on the brain.'

Reeanna's brows drew together. 'What do you mean, a burn?'

Where the hell was her backup? How much longer could she stall? 'You didn't know about that? Your little experiment has a slight defect, Reeanna. It burns a hole in the frontal lobe, leaves what we could call a shadow. Or a fingerprint. Your fingerprint.'

'That's nothing.' But she worried her lip as she considered it. 'The intensity of the subliminal could cause that, I suppose. It has to get in, firmly, to bypass the instinctive resistance, the knee-jerk survival instinct. We'll have to work on that, see what can be adjusted.' Annoyance shadowed her eyes. 'William will have to do better. I don't like flaws.'

'Your experiment's full of them. You have to control William to continue. How many times have you used the system on him, Reeanna? Would continued use expand that burn? I wonder what kind of damage it could cause.'

'It can be fixed.' She tapped the fingers of her free hand on her thigh, distracted. 'He'll fix it. I'll do a new scan on him, study the flaw – if he has one. Repair it.'

'Oh, he'll have one.' Eve stepped closer, judging the distance, the risk. 'They all had one. And if you can't repair William's, you'll probably have to terminate him. You couldn't risk that flaw becoming larger, causing uncontrolled behavior. Could you?'

'No. No. I'll look into this immediately. Tonight.'

'It may already be too late.'

Reeanna's eyes snapped back. 'Adjustments can be made. Will be made. I haven't come this far, accomplished this much, to accept any sort of failure.'

'And yet to succeed fully, you'll have to control me, and I won't make it easy.'

'I already have your brain pattern,' Reeanna reminded her. 'I've already implemented your program. It's going to be very easy.'

'I'll surprise you,' Eve promised. 'And Roarke. You can't manufacture without him, and he'll find out. Do you expect to control him as well?'

'That will be a particular pleasure. I did have to adjust the time schedule. I'd hoped to enjoy him first. A little trip, you might say, down memory lane. Roarke's so creative in bed. We haven't taken time to compare those notes, but I'm sure you'll agree.'

It put Eve's teeth on edge, but she spoke coolly. 'Using your toy for sexual gratification, Dr Ott? How unscientific.'

'And what fun. I'm not the master William is, but I do enjoy a good, creative game.'

'And that's how you met all your victims.'

'So far. Through the loops and the underground. Games can be relaxing and entertaining. And both William and I agreed that processing input from players would help us develop more creative options for the new VR.' She fluffed at her hair. 'Not that anyone had in mind what I was creating.'

Her gaze shifted to the monitor, frowned over the data being transmitted from Roarke's office. He was processing the VR specs now, she noted. 'But you've already got Roarke digging. Not just on young Drew, but on the unit itself. I wasn't happy about that, but there are always ways around inconveniences.' Her smile tilted up at the corners. 'Roarke isn't as necessary as you believe. Who do you suppose will own all of this if something happened to him?'

She laughed again, pure delight, as Eve stared blankly.

'Why, you will, darling. It will all be yours, in your control, and therefore mine. Don't worry, I won't let you stay a widow long. We'll find someone for you. I'll choose him personally.'

Terror froze her blood, iced her muscles, closed frigidly around her heart. 'You made a unit for him.'

290

'Just completed this afternoon. I wonder if he's tested it yet?
Roarke is so efficient, and so personally interested in all of his
holdings.'

She shot a stream at Eve's feet, anticipating her. 'Don't. I'll
just stun you, and this will take longer.'

'I'll kill you with my own hands.' Eve forced air in and out
of her lungs, ordered herself to think. 'I swear it.'

In his office, Roarke frowned over the data he'd converted.
Missing something, he thought. *What am I missing?*

He rubbed the strain out of his eyes, sat back. He needed a
break, he decided. Clear the mind, rest the eyes. Picking up
the VR unit on his desk, he turned it over in his hands.

'You won't chance it. If you do, and I stun you, you'll never
get to him in time. There's always the hope you can stop
it, save him.' Her smile spread again, derisively. 'You see,
I understand you, Eve, perfectly.'

'Do you?' Eve asked, and instead of lunging forward, leaped
back. 'Lights out,' she shouted, snatching for her weapon as
the room pitched into darkness. She felt the slight sting as
Reeanna's aim wavered, skimmed her shoulder.

Then she was down, blocked by the desk, and gritting her
teeth against the pain. She'd rolled fast, but not well, and had
come down hard on her bad knee.

'I'm better at this than you,' Eve said calmly. But the fingers
in her right hand tingled and shook, forcing her to switch
the weapon to her left. 'You're the amateur here. Ditch the
weapon, and I might not kill you.'

'Kill me?' Reeanna's voice was a hiss. 'You've got too
much cop programmed into you. Maximum force only when
all other methods fail.'

Near the door, Eve told herself, holding her breath, training
her ears. To the right of it. 'There's no one here but you and
me. Who's to know?'

'Too much conscience. Don't forget, I know you. I've been in your head. You wouldn't be able to live with it.'

Moving closer to the door. That's it, keep going. Just a little more. Try to get out, you bitch, and I'll drop you like a piece of spoiled meat.

'Maybe you're right. Maybe I'll just cripple you.' Weapon gripped, Eve bellied around the desk.

The door opened, but instead of Reeanna rushing out, William started in. 'Reeanna, what are you doing in the dark?'

Even as Eve leaped to her feet, Reeanna's finger twitched on the weapon, sending William's nervous system jittering.

'Oh, William, for God's sake.' It was disgust rather than distress. As he started to topple, Reeanna ducked under him and threw herself at Eve. Her nails scraped viciously across Eve's breasts as both women crashed to the floor.

She knew where to aim. She'd tended every bump and bruise on Eve's body and now battered at them, twisted, jabbed. A knee rammed against that tender hip, a balled fist slammed into the wrenched knee.

Blind with pain, Eve shot out an elbow, heard the satisfactory crunch of cartilage as it connected with Reeanna's nose. Reeanna screamed, a high, female sound, and dug in with her teeth.

'Bitch.' Sinking to the same level, Eve grabbed a handful of hair and yanked. Then, slightly ashamed of the lapse, she jammed her weapon under Reeanna's chin. 'Breathe too hard, and I'll put you out. Lights on.'

She was panting, bloody, her body singing with pain. She hoped there would be satisfaction later at seeing her opponent's beautiful face bruised, smeared with blood that continued to stream out of her broken nose. But for now there was too much fear.

'I'm putting you out anyway.'

'No, you won't.' Reeanna's voice was steely calm, and her

lips curved into a wide, brilliant smile. 'I will,' she said, and twisted the wrist of the weapon hand Eve pinned until the point rested against the side of her neck. 'I hate cages.' And smiling, she fired.

'Jesus, Jesus Christ.' She scrambled up while Reeanna's body still shuddered, shoved William over, snatched out his pocket 'link. He was breathing, but she didn't much give a damn.

She started to run.

'Answer me, you answer me!' she shouted at the 'link as she fumbled it on. 'Roarke,' she ordered, 'main office. Answer me, goddamn it.' Then she bit back a scream as the transmission refused to go through.

Line currently in use. Please wait or retry momentarily.

'Bypass, you son of a bitch. How do you bypass with this thing?' She increased her pace to a limping gallop, not even aware she was weeping.

Footsteps pounded toward her in the breezeway, but she didn't even pause.

'Dallas, holy God.'

'Back there.' She raced past Feeney, barely heard his frantic questions through the roaring sea of terror in her head. 'Back there. Peabody, with me. Hurry.'

She hit the elevator, pounded on the call control. 'Hurry, hurry.'

'Dallas, what's happened?' Peabody touched her shoulder, was jerked off. 'You're bleeding. Lieutenant, what's the status?'

'Roarke, oh God, oh God, please.' Tears were streaming, scalding her, blinding her. Panic sweat flooded out of her pores, soaking her skin. 'She's killing him. She's going to kill him.'

In reaction, Peabody pulled her weapon as they rushed

through the opening doors of the elevator. 'Top floor, east wing,' Eve shouted. 'Now, now, now!' She all but threw the 'link at Peabody. 'Get this fucker to bypass.'

'It's damaged. It's been dropped or something. Who's got Roarke?'

'Reeanna. She's dead. Dead as Moses, but she's killing him.' She couldn't breathe, couldn't. Her lungs wouldn't hold air. 'We'll stop him. Whatever she told him to do to himself, we'll stop him.' She turned wild eyes on Peabody. 'She's not taking him.'

'We'll stop him.' Peabody was through the doors with her before they fully opened.

Eve was still faster, even injured, she gained speed through terror. She wrenched at the door, cursed security, and slammed her hand down on the palm plate.

She all but ran over him as he stepped to the threshold.

'Roarke.' She burrowed into him, would have climbed inside him if she could. 'Oh God. You're all right. You're alive.'

'What's happened to you?' He tightened his grip on her as she shuddered.

But she was jerking back, grabbing his face in her hands, staring into his eyes. 'Look at me. Did you use it? Did you test the VR unit?'

'No. Eve—'

'Peabody, drop if he moves wrong. Call the MTs. We're taking him in for a brain scan.'

'The hell you are, but go ahead and call them, Peabody. She's going to the health center this time, if I have to knock her unconscious.'

Eve stepped back, fighting for breath as she carefully measured him. She couldn't feel her legs, wondered why she could still stand upright. 'You didn't use it.'

'I said I didn't.' He pushed a hand through his hair. 'It's aimed at me this time, is it? I should have seen it.' He turned away, glanced over his shoulder as Eve lifted her weapon. 'Oh, put that damn thing down. I'm not suicidal. I'm pissed. She slipped it right by me. It just started to click five minutes ago. Mindoc. Mind doctor,' he elaborated. 'That's the name she used in her game playing. She's still using it, still playing. Mathias had dozens of transmissions to her in the year before he died. And I took a close look at the data report on the unit. The one they just gave me, and the stats from the files. They hadn't buried those deeply enough.'

'She knew you'd find it. That's why she—' Eve broke off, sucked in air that she could hear whistle eerily in her swimming head. 'That's why she personalized a unit for you.'

'I might have gotten around to testing it if I hadn't been interrupted.' He thought of Mavis, nearly smiled. 'I doubt Ree put much effort into altering data. She knew I trusted her and William.'

'It wasn't William – not voluntarily.'

He only nodded, looked at her ruined shirt, the bright red splashes. 'Did she bloody you?'

'It's mostly hers.' She hoped. 'She didn't want to be taken in.' Eve blew out a breath. 'She's dead, Roarke. Self-terminated. I couldn't stop her, Maybe I didn't want to. She told me – the unit, your unit.' Her breath was wheezing again, hitching, skipping. 'I thought – I didn't think I'd be in time. I couldn't make the 'link work, and I couldn't get here.'

She didn't hear Peabody close the door to give her privacy. She didn't care about privacy. She only continued to stare, blind now, and shudder. 'I couldn't,' she said again. 'I stalled her, all that time I was stalling her, building my case, and you could have been—'

'Eve.' He came to her, gathered her close. 'I'm not. And you did get here. I won't leave you.' He pressed his lips to her hair when she buried her face against his shoulder. 'It's over now.'

She knew she'd replay that endless run, the panic and

the helpless grief, a thousand times in her dreams. 'It's not. There'll be a full investigation, not just of Reeanna, but of your company, the people who worked with her on the project.'

'I can stand it.' He tipped her head back. 'The company's clean. I promise. I won't cause you any official embarrassment, Lieutenant, by being arrested.'

She took the handkerchief he pressed into her hand, blew her nose. 'Be hell for my career, being married to a con.'

'Be easy on that account. Why did she do it?'

'Because she could. That's what she said. She enjoyed the power, the control.' Briskly, she rubbed her cheeks dry with the heels of her hands, hands that were nearly steady now. 'She had big plans for me.' The shudder was hard but brief. 'Kind of a pet, I imagine. Like William. Her little trained dog. And with you dead, she figured I'd inherit all your goodies. You're not going to do that to me, are you?'

'What, die?'

'Leave me all this stuff.'

He laughed, kissed her. 'Only you would be annoyed by that.' He brushed her hair back from her face. 'She had a unit for you.'

'Yeah, we didn't get around to testing it out. Feeney's down there now. I'd better let him know what happened.'

'We'll have to go down. She disengaged the 'link, which is why I was on my way to you when you jumped me. I was worried when I couldn't get through.'

'It's tough.' She touched his face. 'Caring.'

'I can live with it. You'll want to go into the station, I imagine, to clean this up tonight.'

'It's procedure. I've got a corpse – and four deaths to close.'

'I'll take you, after you've been to the health center.'

'I'm not going to the health center.'

'Yes, you are.'

Peabody rapped on the door, opened it. 'Excuse me, the MTs are here. They need to be cleared through security.'

'I'll take care of it. Have them meet us in Dr Ott's office, would you, Peabody? They can examine Eve there before I take her in for full treatment.'

'I said I'm not going in for a treatment.'

'I heard you.' He pressed a control on his desk. 'Clear the medics through, please. Peabody, are you carrying restraints?'

'They're standard issue.'

'I wonder if you might loan them to me so I can restrain your lieutenant until I deliver her to the nearest medical facility.'

'Just try it, pal, and see who needs a doctor.'

Peabody gnawed manfully on the inside of her cheek. A smirk at the moment wouldn't please her lieutenant. 'I sympathize with your problem, Roarke, but am unable to comply. I need the job.'

'Never mind, Peabody.' He scooped an arm around Eve's waist, taking her weight as she limped toward the door. 'I'm sure I can find a substitute.'

'I've got a report to file, work to finish. I've got a dead body to transport.' Eve scowled at him as he called for the elevator. 'I don't have time for an exam.'

'I heard you,' he repeated and simply picked her up bodily and carried her into the elevator. 'Peabody, tell those MTs to come armed. She's liable to make a run for it.'

'Put me down, you idiot. I'm not going.' She was laughing as the doors closed on them.

Ceremony in Death

There are more things in heaven and earth, Horatio,
Than are dreamt of in your philosophy.

—Shakespeare

We may not pay Satan reverence, for that would be
indiscreet, but we can at least respect his talents.

—Mark Twain

Chapter One

Death surrounded her. She faced it daily, dreamed of it nightly. Lived with it always. She knew its sounds, its scents, even its texture. She could look it in its dark and clever eye without a flinch. Death was a tricky foe, she knew. One flinch, one blink, and it could shift, it could change. It could win.

Ten years as a cop hadn't hardened her toward it. A decade on the force hadn't made her accept it. When she looked death in the eye, it was with the cold steel of the warrior.

Eve Dallas looked at death now. And she looked at one of her own.

Frank Wojinski had been a good cop, solid. Some would have said plodding. He'd been affable, she remembered. A man who hadn't complained about the bilge disguised as food at the NYPSD Eatery, or the eye-searing paperwork the job generated. Or, Eve thought, about the fact that he'd been sixty-two and had never made it past the rank of detective sergeant.

He'd been on the pudgy side and had let his hair gray and thin naturally. It was a rare thing in 2058 for a man to bypass body sculpting and enhancements. Now, in his clear-sided view casket with its single spray of mournful lilies, he resembled a peacefully sleeping monk from an earlier time.

He'd been born in an earlier time, Eve mused, coming into the world at the end of one millennium and living his life in the next. He'd been through the Urban Wars, but hadn't talked of them as so many of the older cops did. Frank hadn't been one for war stories, she recalled. He was more likely to pass around the latest snapshot or hologram of his children and grandchildren.

He liked to tell bad jokes, talk sports, and had a weakness for soydogs with spiced pickle relish.

A family man, she thought, one who left behind great grief. Indeed, she could think of no one who had known Frank Wojinski who hadn't loved him.

He had died with half his life still ahead of him, died alone, when the heart everyone had thought so huge and so strong had just stopped.

'Goddamn it.'

Eve turned, laid a hand on the arm of the man who stepped up beside her. 'I'm sorry, Feeney.'

He shook his head, his droopy camel's eyes filled with misery. With one hand he raked through his wiry red hair. 'On the job would have been easier. I could handle line of duty. But to just stop. To just check out in his easy chair watching arena ball on the screen. It's not right, Dallas. A man's not supposed to stop living at his age.'

'I know.' Not knowing what else to do, Eve draped an arm over his shoulder and steered him away.

'He trained me. Looked after me when I was a rookie. Never let me down.' Pain radiated through him and glinted dully in his eyes, wavered in his voice. 'Frank never let anyone down in his life.'

'I know,' she said again, because there was nothing else that could be said. She was accustomed to Feeney being tough and strong. The delicacy of his grief worried her.

She led him through the mourners. The viewing room was packed with cops as well as family. And where there were cops and death, there was coffee. Or what passed for it at such places. She poured a cup, handed it to him.

'I can't get around it. I can't get a hold of it.' He let out a long, uneven breath. He was a sturdy, compact man who wore his grief as openly as he wore his rumpled coat. 'I haven't talked to Sally yet. My wife's with her. I just can't do it.'

'It's all right. I haven't talked to her, either.' Since she had nothing to do with her hands, Eve poured a cup for herself that she didn't intend to drink. 'Everybody's shook up by this. I didn't know he had a heart problem.'

'Nobody did,' Feeney said quietly. 'Nobody knew.'

She kept a hand on his shoulder as she scanned the over-crowded, overwarm room. When a fellow officer went down in the line of duty, cops could be angry, they could be focused, fix their target. But when death snuck in and crooked a capricious finger, there was no one to blame. And no one to punish.

It was helplessness she felt in the room and that she felt in herself. You couldn't raise your weapon to fate, or your fist.

The funeral director, spiffy in his traditional black suit and as waxy-faced as one of his own clients, worked the room with patting hands and sober eyes. Eve thought she'd rather have a corpse sit up and grin at her than listen to his platitudes.

'Why don't we go talk to the family together?'

It was hard for him, but Feeney nodded, set the untouched coffee aside. 'He liked you, Dallas. "That kid's got balls of steel and a mind to match," he used to tell me. He always said if he was ever jammed, you'd be the one he'd want guarding his back.'

It surprised and pleased her, and it simultaneously added to her sorrow. 'I didn't realize he thought of me that way.'

Feeney looked at her. She had an interesting face, not one he'd have called a heart-stopper, but it usually made a man look twice with its angles and sharp bones, the shallow dent in the chin. She had cop's eyes, intense and measuring, and he often forgot they were a dark golden brown. Her hair was the same shade, cut short and badly in need of some shaping. She was tall and lean and tough-bodied.

He remembered it had been less than a month since he had come across her, battered and bloodied. But her weapon had been firm in her hand.

'He thought of you that way. So do I.' While she blinked at him, Feeney squared his hunched shoulders. 'Let's talk to Sally and the kids.'

They slipped through the crowd jammed together in a room oppressed with dark simulated wood, heavy red draperies, and the funereal smell of too many flowers crammed into too small a space.

Eve wondered why viewings of the dead were always accompanied by flowers and draping sheets of red. What ancient ceremony did it spring from, and why did the human race continue to cling to it?

She was certain that when her time came, she wouldn't choose to be laid out for study by her loved ones and associates in an overheated room where the pervasive scent of flowers was reminiscent of rot.

Then she saw Sally, supported by her children and her children's children, and realized such rites were for the living. The dead were beyond caring.

'Ryan.' Sally held out her hands – small, almost fairy-like hands – and lifted her cheek to Feeney's. She held there a moment, her eyes closed, her face pale and quiet.

She was a slim, soft-spoken woman who Eve had always thought of as delicate. Yet a cop's spouse who had survived the stress of the job for more than forty years had to have steel. Against her plain black dress she wore her husband's twenty-five-year NYPSD ring on a chain.

Another rite, Eve thought. *Another symbol.*

'I'm so glad you're here,' Sally murmured.

'I'll miss him. We'll all miss him.' Feeney patted her back awkwardly before drawing away. Grief was in his throat, choking him. Swallowing it only lodged it cold and heavy in his gut. 'You know if there's anything . . .'

'I know.' Her lips curved slightly, and she gave his hand a quick and comforting squeeze before turning to Eve. 'I appreciate you coming, Dallas.'

'He was a good man. A solid cop.'

'Yes, he was.' Recognizing it as high tribute, Sally managed a smile. 'He was proud to serve and protect. Commander Whitney and his wife are here, and Chief Tibble. And so many others.' Her gaze drifted blindly around the room. 'So many. He mattered, Frank mattered.'

'Of course he did, Sally.' Feeney shifted from foot to foot. 'You, ah, know about the Survivor's Fund.'

She smiled again, patted his hand. 'We're fine there. Don't worry. Dallas, I don't think you really know my family. Lieutenant Dallas, my daughter Brenda.'

Short, with rounded curves, Eve noted as they clasped hands. *Dark hair and eyes, a bit heavy in the chin. Took after her father.*

'My son Curtis.'

Slim, small boned, soft hands, eyes that were dry but dazed with grief.

'My grandchildren.'

There were five of them, the youngest a boy of about eight with a pug nose dashed with freckles. He eyed Eve consideringly. 'How come you've got your zapper on?'

Flustered, Eve tugged her jacket over her side arm. 'I came straight from Cop Central. I didn't have time to go home and change.'

'Pete.' Curtis shot Eve an apologetic wince. 'Don't bother the lieutenant.'

'If people concentrated more on their personal and spiritual powers, weapons would be unnecessary. I'm Alice.'

A slim blonde in black stepped forward. She'd have been a stunner in any case, Eve mused, but having sprung from such basic stock, she was dazzling. Her eyes were a soft, dreamy blue, her mouth full and lush and unpainted. She wore her hair loose so that it rained straight and glossy over the shoulders of her flowing black dress. A thin silver chain fell to her waist. At the end of it was a black stone ringed in silver.

'Alice, you're such a zip head.'

She flicked a cool glance over her shoulder toward a boy of about sixteen. But her hands kept fluttering back to the black stone, like elegant birds guarding a nest.

'My brother Jamie,' she said in a silky voice. 'He still thinks name-calling deserves a reaction. My grandfather spoke of you, Lieutenant Dallas.'

'I'm flattered.'

'Your husband isn't with you tonight?'

Eve arched a brow. *Not just grief*, she deduced, *but nerves*. It was easy enough to recognize. Signals as well, but they weren't clear. *The girl was after something*, she mused. *But what?*

'No, he's not.' She shifted her gaze back to Sally. 'He sends his sympathies, Mrs Wojinski. He's off planet.'

'It must take a great deal of concentration and energy,' Alice interrupted, 'to maintain a relationship with a man like Roarke while pursuing a demanding, difficult, even dangerous career. My grandfather used to say that once you had a grip on an investigation, you never let go. Would you say that's accurate, Lieutenant?'

'If you let go, you lose. I don't like to lose.' She held Alice's odd gaze for a moment, then on impulse crouched down and whispered to Pete. 'When I was a rookie, I saw your grandfather zap a guy at ten yards. He was the best.' She was rewarded with a quick grin before she straightened. 'He won't be forgotten, Mrs Wojinski,' she said, offering her hand. 'And he mattered very much to all of us.'

She started to step back, but Alice laid a hand on her arm, leaned close. The hand, Eve noted, trembled slightly. 'It was interesting meeting you, Lieutenant. Thank you for coming.'

Eve inclined her head and slipped back into the crowd.

Casually, she reached a hand into the pocket of her jacket and fingered the thin slip of paper Alice had pushed inside.

It took her another thirty minutes to get away. She waited until she was outside and in her vehicle before she took the note out and read it.

Meet me tomorrow, midnight. Aquarian Club.
TELL NO ONE. Your life is now at risk.

In lieu of a signature, there was a symbol, a dark line running in an expanding circle to form a sort of maze. Nearly as intrigued as she was annoyed, Eve stuffed the note back in her pocket and started home.

Because she was a cop, she saw the figure draped in black, hardly more than a shadow in the shadows. And because she was a cop, she knew he was watching her.

Whenever Roarke was away, Eve preferred to pretend the house was empty. Both she and Summerset, who served as Roarke's chief of staff, did their best to ignore the other's presence. The house was huge, a labyrinth of rooms, which made it a simple matter to avoid one another.

She stepped into the wide foyer, tossed her scarred leather jacket over the carved newel post because she knew it would make Summerset grind his teeth. He detested having anything mar the elegance of the house. Particularly her.

She took the stairs, but rather than go to the master bedroom, she veered off to her office suite.

If Roarke had to spend another night off planet as expected, she preferred to spend hers in her relaxation chair rather than their bed.

She often dreamed badly when she dreamed alone.

Between the late paperwork and the viewing, she hadn't had time for a meal. Eve ordered up a sandwich – real Virginia ham on rye – and coffee that jumped with genuine caffeine.

309

When the AutoChef delivered, she inhaled the scents slowly, greedily. She took the first bite with her eyes closed to better enjoy the miracle.

There were definite advantages to being married to a man who could afford real meat instead of its by-products and simulations.

To satisfy her curiosity, she went to her desk and engaged her computer. She swallowed ham, chased it with coffee. 'All available data on subject Alice, surname unknown. Mother Brenda, née Wojinski, maternal grandparents Frank and Sally Wojinski.'

Working . . .

Eve drummed her fingers, took out the note and reread it while she polished off the quick meal.

Subject Alice Lingstrom. DOB June 10, 2040. First child and only daughter of Jan Lingstrom and Brenda Wojinski, divorced, Residence, 486 West Eighth Street, Apartment 4B, New York City. Sibling, James Lingstrom, DOB March 22, 2042. Education, high school graduate, valedictorian. Two semesters of college: Harvard. Major, anthropology. Minor, mythology. Third semester deferred. Currently employed as clerk, Spirit Quest, 228 West Tenth Street, New York City. Marital status, single.

Eve ran her tongue around her teeth. 'Criminal record?'

No criminal record.

'Sounds fairly normal,' Eve murmured. 'Data on Spirit Quest.'

Spirit Quest. Wiccan shop and consultation center, owned by Isis Paige and Charles Forte. Three years in Tenth Street location.

Annual gross income one hundred twenty-five thousand dollars. Licensed priestess, herbalist, and registered hypnotherapist on site.

'Wicca?' Eve leaned back with a snort. 'Witch stuff? Jesus. What kind of scam is this?'

Wicca, recognized as both a religion and a craft, is an ancient, nature-based faith which—

'Stop.' Eve blew out a breath. She wasn't looking for a definition of witchcraft, but an explanation as to why a steady-as-a-rock cop ended up with a granddaughter who believed in casting spells and magic crystals.

And why that granddaughter wanted a secret meeting.

The best way to find out, she decided, was to show up at the Aquarian Club in a bit over twenty-four hours. She left the note on the desk. It would be easy to dismiss it, she thought, if it hadn't been written by a relative of a man she'd respected.

And if she hadn't seen that figure in the shadows. A figure she was sure hadn't wanted to be seen.

She walked to the adjoining bath and began to strip. It was too bad she couldn't take Mavis with her for the meet. Eve had a feeling the Aquarian Club would be right up her friend's alley. Eve kicked her jeans aside, leaned over to stretch out the kinks of a long day. And wondered what she would do with the long night ahead.

She had nothing hot to work on. Her last homicide had been so open and shut that she and her aide had put it to bed in under eight hours. Maybe she'd spend a couple hours glazing out watching some screen. Or she could pick a weapon out of Roarke's gun room and go down and run a hologram program to burn off excess energy until she could sleep.

She'd never tried one of his auto-assault rifles. It might be interesting to experience how a cop took out an enemy during the early days of the Urban Wars.

She stepped into the shower. 'Full jets, on pulse,' she ordered. 'Ninety-eight degrees.'

She wished she had a murder to sink her teeth into. Something that would focus her mind and drain her system. And damn it, that was pathetic. She was lonely, she realized. Desperate for a distraction, and he'd only been gone three days.

They both had their own lives, didn't they? They'd lived them before they met and continued to live them after. The demands of both their businesses absorbed much time and attention. Their relationship worked – and that continued to surprise her – because they were both independent people.

Christ, she missed him outrageously. Disgusted with herself, she ducked her head under the spray and let it pound on her brain.

When hands slipped around her waist, then slid up to cup her breasts, she barely jolted. But her heart leaped. She knew his touch, the feel of those long, slim fingers, the texture of those wide palms. She tipped her head back, inviting a mouth to the curve of her shoulder.

'Mmm. Summerset. You wild man.'

Teeth nipped into flesh and made her chuckle. Thumbs brushed over her soapy nipples and made her moan.

'I'm not going to fire him.' Roarke trailed a hand down the center of her body.

'It was worth a shot. You're back . . .' His fingers dipped expertly inside her, slick and slippery, so that she arched, moaned, and came simultaneously. 'Early,' she finished on an explosive breath. 'God.'

'I'd say I was just on time.' He spun her around, and while she was shuddering and blinking water out of her eyes, he covered her mouth in a long, ravenous kiss.

He'd thought about her on the interminable flight home. Thought about this, just this: touching and tasting and hearing that quick catch in her breath as he did. And here she was, naked and wet and already quivering for him.

He braced her in the corner, gripped her hips, and slowly lifted her off her feet. 'Miss me?'

Her heart was thundering. He was inches away from driving into her, filling her, destroying her. 'Not really.'

'Well, in that case . . ' He kissed her lightly on the chin. 'I'll just let you finish your shower in peace.'

In a flash, she wrapped her legs around his waist, took a firm hold of his wet mane of hair. 'Try it, pal, and you're a dead man.'

'In the interest of self-preservation then.' To torture them both, he slipped into her slowly, watched her eyes go opaque. He closed his mouth over hers again so that her shallow breaths shuddered through him.

The ride was slow and slippery, and more tender than either had expected. Climax came on a long, quiet sigh. Her lips curved against his. 'Welcome home.'

She could see him now, those stunning blue eyes, the face that was both saint and sinner, the mouth of a doomed poet. His hair was streaming with water, black and sleek, just touching broad shoulders roped with subtle and surprisingly tough muscle.

Looking at him after these brief, periodic absences always made something unexpected lurch through her. She doubted she would ever get used to the fact that he not only wanted her but loved her.

She was smiling still as she combed her fingers through his thick, black hair. 'Everything okay with the Olympus Resort?'

'Adjustments, some delays. Nothing that can't be dealt with.' The elaborate space station resort and pleasure center would open on schedule, because he wouldn't accept any less.

He ordered the jets off, then took a towel to wrap around

her when she would have used the drying tube. 'I began to understand why you stay in here while I'm away. I couldn't sleep in the Presidential Suite.' He took another towel, rubbed it over her hair. 'It was too lonely without you.'

She leaned against him a moment, just to feel the familiar lines of his body against hers. 'We're getting so damn sappy.'

'I don't mind. We Irish are very sentimental.'

It made her smirk as he turned to get robes. He might have had the music of Ireland in his voice, but she seriously doubted if any of his business friends or foes would consider Roarke a sentimental man.

'No fresh bruises,' he observed, helping her into her robe before she could do it for herself. 'I take that to mean you've had a quiet few days.'

'Mostly. We had a john get a bit overenthusiastic with a licensed companion. Choked her to death during sex.' She belted the robe, scratched fingers through her hair to scatter more water. 'He got spooked and ran.' She moved her shoulders as she stepped into the office. 'But he lawyered up and turned himself in a few hours later. PA took it down to manslaughter. I let Peabody handle the interview and booking.'

'Hmm.' Roarke went to a recessed cabinet for wine, poured them both a glass. 'It's been quiet then.'

'Yeah. I had that viewing tonight.'

His brow furrowed, then cleared. 'Ah, yes, you told me. I'm sorry I couldn't make it home in time to go with you.'

'Feeney's taking it really hard. It would be easier if Frank had gone down in the line of duty.'

This time Roarke's brow quirked. 'You'd prefer that your associate had been killed rather than, say, go gently into that good night?'

'I'd just understand it better, that's all.' She frowned into her wine. She didn't think it wise to tell Roarke she'd prefer a fast and violent death herself. 'There is something odd, though. I met Frank's family. The oldest granddaughter's on the weird side.'

'How?'

'The way she talked, and the data I accessed on her after I got home.'

Intrigued, he lifted his wine to sip. 'You ran a make on her?'

'Just a quick check. Because she passed me this.' Eve walked to the desk, picked up the note.

Roarke scanned it, considered. 'Earth labyrinth.'

'What?'

'The symbol here. It's Celtic.'

Shaking her head, Eve eased closer to look again. 'You know the strangest things.'

'Not so strange. I spring from the Celts, after all. The ancient labyrinth symbol is magical and sacred.'

'Well, it fits. She's into witchcraft or something. Got herself the start of a top-flight education. Harvard. But she drops out to work in some West Village shop that sells crystals and magic herbs.'

Roarke traced the symbol with a fingertip. He'd seen it before, and others like it. During his childhood, the cults in Dublin had run the range between vicious gangs and pious pacifists. All, of course, had used religion as the excuse to kill. Or be killed.

'You have no idea why she wants to meet you?'

'None. I'd say she figures she read my aura or something. Mavis ran a mystic grift before I busted her for pinching wallets. She told me people will pay most anything if you tell them what they want to hear. More, if you tell them what they don't want to hear.'

'Which is why cons and legitimate businesses are very much the same.' He smiled at her. 'I take it you're going, anyway.'

315

'Sure, I'll follow through.'

Naturally she would. Roarke glanced at the note again, then set it aside. 'I'm going with you.'

'She wants—'

'It's a pity what she wants.' He sipped his wine, a man accustomed to getting precisely what he wanted. One way or another. 'I'll stay out of your way, but I'm going. The Aquarian Club is basically harmless, but there are always unsavory elements that leak through.'

'Unsavory elements are my life,' she said soberly, then cocked her head. 'You don't, like, own the Aquarian, do you?'

'No.' He smiled. 'Would you like to?'

She laughed and took his hand. 'Come on. Let's drink this in bed.'

Relaxed by sex and wine, she fell peacefully asleep, draped around Roarke. That's why she was baffled to find herself suddenly and fully awake only two hours later. It hadn't been one of her nightmares. There was no terror, no pain, no cold, clammy sweat.

Yet she had snapped awake, and her heart wasn't quite steady. She lay still, staring up through the wide sky window over the bed, listening to Roarke's quiet, steady breathing beside her.

She shifted, glanced down at the foot of the bed, and nearly yelped when eyes glowed out of the dark. Then she registered the weight over her ankles. *Galahad*, she thought and rolled her eyes. The cat had come in and jumped onto the bed. That's what had awakened her, she told herself. That's all it was.

She settled again, turned onto her side, and felt Roarke's arm slide around her in sleep. On a sigh, she closed her eyes, snuggled companionably against him.

Just the cat, she thought sleepily.

But she would have sworn she'd heard chanting.

316

Chapter Two

By the time Eve was elbow deep in paperwork the next morning, the odd wakefulness in the night was forgotten. New York seemed to be content to bask in the balmy days of early autumn and behave itself. It seemed like a good time to take a few hours and organize her office.

Or rather to delegate Peabody to organize it.

'How can your files be this skewed?' Peabody demanded. Her earnest, square face expressed deep remorse and disappointment.

'I know where everything is,' Eve told her. 'I want you to put everything where I'll still know where it is, but where it also makes sense for it to be. Too tough an assignment, Officer?'

'I can handle it.' Peabody rolled her eyes behind Eve's back. 'Sir.'

'Fine. And don't roll your eyes at me. If things are a bit skewed, as you put it, it's because I've had a busy year. As we're in the last quarter of this one and I'm training you, it falls to me to dump this on you.' Eve turned and smiled thinly. 'With the hope, Peabody, that you will one day have an underling to dump shit assignments on.'

'Your faith in me is touching, Dallas. Chokes me up.' She hissed at the computer. 'Or maybe it's the fact that you've got yellow sheets in here from five years ago that's choking me. These should have been downloaded to the main and cleared out of your unit after twenty-four months.'

317

'So download and clear now.' Eve's smile widened as the machine hacked, then droned out a warning of system failure. 'And good luck.'

'Technology can be our friend. And like any friendship, it requires regular maintenance and understanding.'

'I understand it fine.' Eve stepped over, pounded her fist twice on the drive. The unit hiccupped back into running mode. 'See?'

'You have a real smooth touch, Lieutenant. That's why the guys in Maintenance shoot air darts at your picture.'

'Still? Christ, they hold a grudge.' With a shrug, Eve sat on the corner of the desk. 'What do you know about witchcraft?'

'If you want to cast a spell on your machine here, Dallas, it's a little out of my field.' Teeth clenched, she juggled and compressed files.

'You're a Free-Ager.'

'Lapsed. Come on, come on, you can do it,' she muttered at the computer. 'Besides,' she added. 'Free-Agers aren't Wiccans. They're both earth religions, and both are based on natural orders, but . . . son of a bitch, where'd it go?'

'What? Where did what go?'

'Nothing.' Shoulders hunched, Peabody guarded the monitor. 'Nothing. Don't worry, I'm on it. You probably didn't need those files, anyway.'

'Is that a joke, Peabody?'

'You bet. Ha ha.' A line of sweat dribbled down her back as she attacked the keys. 'There. There it is. No problem, no problem at all. And off it goes into the main. Neat and tidy.' She let out an enormous sigh. 'Could I maybe have some coffee? Just to keep alert.'

Eve shifted her gaze to the screen, saw nothing that looked ominous. Saying nothing, she rose and ordered coffee from the AutoChef.

'Why do you want to know about Wicca? You thinking

of converting?' At Eve's bland look, Peabody tried a smile. 'Another joke.'

'You're full of them today. Just curious.'

'Well, there's some overlap on basic tenets between Wiccans and Free-Agers. A search for balance and harmony, the celebration of the seasons that goes back to ancient times, the strict code of nonviolence.'

'Nonviolence?' Eve narrowed her eyes. 'What about curses, casting spells, and sacrifices? Naked virgins on the altar and black roosters getting their heads chopped off?'

'Fiction depicts witches that way. You know, 'Double, double, toil and trouble.' Shakespeare. *Macbeth*.'

Eve snorted. '"I'll get you, my pretty, and your little dog, too"' The Wicked Witch of the West. Classic vid channel.

'Good one,' Peabody admitted. 'But both examples feed into the most basic of misconceptions. Witches aren't ugly, evil crones mixing up cauldrons of goop or hunting down young girls and their friendly, talking scarecrows. Wiccans like to be naked, but they don't hurt anything or anyone. Strictly white magic.'

'As opposed to?'

'Black magic.'

Eve studied her aide. 'You don't believe in that stuff? Magic and spells?'

'Nope.' Revived with coffee, Peabody turned back to the computer. 'I know some of the basics because I have a cousin who shifted to Wicca. He's into it big time. Joined a coven in Cincinnati.'

'You've got a cousin in a coven in Cincinnati.' Laughing, Eve set her own coffee aside. 'Peabody, you never cease to amaze me.'

'One day I'll tell you about my granny and her five lovers.'

'Five lovers isn't abnormal for a woman's lifetime.'

'Not in her lifetime; last month. All at the same time.'

Peabody glanced up, deadpan. 'She's ninety-eight. I hope to take after her.'

Eve swallowed her next chuckle as her tele-link beeped. 'Dallas.' She watched Commander Whitney's face swim on-screen. 'Yes, Commander.'

'I'd like to speak with you, Lieutenant, in my office. As soon as possible.'

'Yes, sir. Five minutes.' Eve disengaged, shot a hopeful glance at Peabody. 'Maybe we've got something going. Keep working on those files. I'll contact you if we're heading out.'

She started out, stuck her head back in. 'Don't eat my candy bar.'

'Damn,' Peabody said under her breath. 'She never misses.'

Whitney had spent most of his life behind a badge and a large part of his professional life in command. He made it his business to know his cops, to judge their strengths and weaknesses. And he knew how to utilize both.

He was a big man with workingman hands and dark, keen eyes that some considered cold. His temperament, on the surface, was almost terrifyingly even. And like most smooth surfaces, it coated something dangerous brewing beneath.

Eve respected him, occasionally liked him, and always admired him.

He was at his desk when she stepped into his office, lines of concentration puckering his brow as he read over some hard copy. He didn't glance up, merely gestured toward a chair. She sat, watched an air tram rumble by his window, baffled as always by the number of passengers with binoks and spy glasses.

What did they expect to see behind the windows where cops worked? she wondered. *Suspects being tortured, weapons discharged, victims bleeding and weeping? And why would the fantasy of such misery entertain them?*

'I saw you at the viewing last night.'

Eve shifted her thoughts and attention to her commander. 'I imagine most every cop in Central made an appearance.'

'Frank was well-liked.'

'Yes, he was.'

'You never worked with him?'

'He gave me some pointers when I was a rookie, helped out on legwork a couple of times, but no, I never worked with him directly.'

Whitney nodded, kept his eyes on hers. 'He was partnered with Feeney, before your time. You were partnered with Feeney after Frank shifted from the streets to a desk,'

She began to get an uncomfortable feeling in the gut. *Something here*, she thought. *Something's off.* 'Yes, sir. This has hit Feeney pretty hard.'

'I'm aware of that, Dallas. Which is why Captain Feeney isn't here this morning.' Whitney propped his elbows on his desk, linked his fingers, folded his fingers over. 'We have a possible situation, Lieutenant. A delicate situation.'

'Regarding DS Wojinski?'

'The information I'm going to relay to you is confidential. Your aide can be apprised per your discretion, but no one else on the force. No one in the media. I am asking you, ordering you,' he corrected, 'to essentially work alone, on this matter.'

The discomfort in her stomach spread into little licks of fear as she thought of Feeney. 'Understood.'

'There is some question regarding the circumstances of DS Wojinski's death.'

'Question, Commander?'

'You'll require some background data.' He laid his folded hands on the edge of the desk. 'It has come to my attention that DS Wojinski was either pursuing an investigation of his own off the clock or involved with illegals.'

'Drugs? Frank? Nobody was cleaner than Frank.'

Whitney didn't so much as blink. 'On September twenty-second of this year DS Wojinski was spotted by an undercover

321

illegals detective allegedly conducting business in a suspected chemical distribution center. The Athame is a private club, religious in theme, which offers its members group and individual ritual services and is licensed for private sexual functions. The Illegals Division has had it under investigation for nearly two years. Frank was seen making a buy.'

When Eve said nothing, Whitney drew a long breath. 'This situation was subsequently reported to me. I questioned Frank, and he was not forthcoming.' Whitney hesitated, then followed through. 'Frankly, Dallas, the fact that he would neither confirm nor deny, refused to explain or discuss, seemed very out of character. And it worried me. I ordered him to submit to a physical, including a drug scan, advised him to take a week's leave. He agreed to both. The scan was, at that point, clear. Due to his record and my personal knowledge and opinion of him, I did not mark the incident in his file, but sealed it.'

He rose then, turned to his window. 'Perhaps that was a mistake. It's possible if I had pursued the matter at that point, he would still be alive, and we wouldn't be having this discussion.'

'You trusted your judgment and your man.'

Whitney turned back. His eyes were dark; they were intense but not cold, Eve thought. They felt. 'Yes, I did. And now I have more data. The standard autopsy on DS Wojinski detected traces of digitalis and Zeus.'

'Zeus.' Now Eve rose. 'Frank was not a user, Commander. Putting aside who and what he was, a chemical as powerful as Zeus shows. You see it in the eyes, in the personality shift. If he'd been using Zeus, every cop in his division would have known it. The drug scan would have picked it up. There has to be a mistake.'

She dug her hands into her pockets, willed herself not to pace. 'Yeah, there are cops who use, and there are cops who figure their badges shield them from the law. But not Frank. No way was he dirty.'

322

'But the traces were there, Lieutenant. As well as traces of other chemicals, identified as designer clones. The combination of those chemicals resulted in cardiac arrest and death.'

'You suspect he OD'd, or self-terminated?' She shook her head. 'That's wrong.'

'I repeat, the traces were there.'

'Then there had to be a reason. Digitalis?' She frowned. 'That's heart medicine, isn't it? You said he'd had a physical a couple of weeks ago. Why didn't it show he had heart trouble?'

Whitney's gaze remained level. 'Frank's closest friend on the force is the top E-detective in the city.'

'Feeney?' Eve took two strides forward before she could stop herself. 'You think Feeney covered for him, doctored his records? Damn it, Commander.'

'It's a possibility I can't ignore,' Whitney said evenly. 'Nor can you. Friendship can and does shadow judgment. I am trusting that your friendship with Feeney will not, in this case, shadow yours.'

He walked to the desk again, his position of authority. 'These allegations and suspicions must be investigated and resolved.'

The hot licks in her stomach had grown and were burning like acid. 'You want me to investigate fellow officers. One of which is dead, leaving a grieving family behind. The other of which was my trainer and is my friend.' She put her hands on the desk. 'Is your friend.'

He'd expected the anger, accepted it. Just as he expected she would do the job. He wouldn't accept less. 'Would you prefer I gave this to someone who didn't care?' His brow lifted on the question. 'I want this done quietly, with each piece of evidence and all investigative records sealed for my eyes only. It may be necessary for you to speak with DS Wojinski's family at some point. I trust you will

323

do so discreetly and tactfully. There is no need to add to their grief.'

'And if I turn something up that smears a lifetime of public service?'

'That will be for me to deal with.'

She straightened. 'It's a hell of a thing you're asking me to do.'

'Ordering you to do,' Whitney corrected. 'That should make it easier, Lieutenant. On you.' He handed her two sealed discs. 'View these on your home unit. Any and all transmissions on this matter are to be sent from your home unit to my home unit. Nothing is to go through Cop Central until I tell you differently. Dismissed.'

She turned on her heel, walked to the door. There she paused but didn't look back. 'I won't roll over on Feeney. Damned if I will.'

Whitney watched her stride out, then closed his eyes. She would do what needed to be done, he knew. He only hoped it wasn't more than she could live with.

Her temper was bubbling by the time she got back to her own office. Peabody sat in front of the monitor, smirking.

'Just about got it knocked. Your unit's a real whiner, Dallas, but I've been slapping it into shape.'

'Disengage,' Eve snapped and grabbed up her jacket and bag. 'Get your gear, Peabody.'

'We've got a case?' Revving up, Peabody jumped out of the chair and hustled after Eve. 'What kind of case? Where are we going?' She broke into a trot to keep up. 'Dallas? Lieutenant?'

Eve slapped the control on the elevator, and the single furious look she shot at Peabody was enough to stifle any further questions. Eve stepped into the elevator, shuffled into position with several noisy cops, and stood in stony silence.

'Hey, Dallas, how's the newlywed? Why don't you get your rich husband to buy the Eatery and stock some real food.'

She flicked a steely glare over her shoulder, stared into a face of a grinning cop. 'Bite me, Carter.'

'Hey, I gave that a shot three years ago, and you nearly broke all my teeth. Holding out for a civilian,' he said when laughter erupted.

'Holding out for somebody who isn't the major asshole of Robbery,' someone else put in.

'Better than being the minor one, Forenski. Hey, Peabody,' Carter continued. 'Want me to bite you?'

'Is your dental plan up to date?'

'I'll check on that and get back to you.' With a wink, Carter and several others piled out.

'Carter puts the moves on anything female,' Peabody said conversationally, worried that Eve continued to stare straight ahead. 'Too bad he's an asshole.' No response. 'Ah, Forenski's kind of cute,' Peabody continued. 'He doesn't have a steady personal partner, does he?'

'I don't poke into the private lives of fellow officers,' Eve snapped back, and strode out onto the garage level.

'You don't mind poking into mine,' Peabody said under her breath. She waited while Eve uncoded her car locks, then climbed into the passenger seat. 'Am I to log in destination, sir, or is it a surprise?' Then she blinked when Eve simply laid her head against the wheel. 'Hey, are you all right? What's going on, Dallas?'

'Log in home office.' Eve drew a breath, straightened. 'I'll fill you in on the way. All information you're given and all records on the ensuing investigation are to be coded and sealed.' Eve maneuvered out of the garage and onto the street. 'All said information and records are confidential. You are to report only to me or the commander.'

'Yes, sir.' Peabody swallowed the obstruction that had lodged in her throat. 'It's internal, isn't it? It's one of us.'

'Yeah. Goddamn it. It's one of us.'

*

Her home unit didn't have the eccentricities of her official computer. Roarke had seen to that. The data scrolled smoothly on-screen.

'Detective Marion Burns. She's been undercover at The Athame for eight months, working as a bartender.' Eve pursed her lips. 'Burns. I don't know her.'

'I do, slightly.' Peabody scooted her chair a bit closer to Eve's. 'I met her when I was . . . you know, during the Casto thing. She struck me as a solid, eyes-on-the-job sort. If memory serves, she's third generation cop. Her mother's still on the job. Captain, I think, in Bunko. Her grandfather went out line of duty during the Urban Wars. I don't know why she'd have fingered DS Wojinski.'

'Maybe she reported what she saw, or maybe it's something else. We'll have to find out. Her report to Whitney's pretty cut and dried. At one hundred thirty hours, September 22, 2058, she observed DS Wojinski seated at a private booth with known chemical dealer Selina Cross. Wojinski exchanged credits for a small package, which appeared to contain an illegal substance. The conversation and exchange lasted fifteen minutes, at which time Cross moved to another booth. Wojinski remained in the club another ten minutes, then left. Detective Burns tailed the subject for two blocks at which time he engaged a public transport.'

'So she never saw him use.'

'No. And she never saw him return to the club that night or on any subsequent night during her watch. Burns goes top of our list for questioning.'

'Yes, sir. Dallas, since Wojinski and Feeney were tight, wouldn't it follow that Wojinski would have confided in him? Or failing that, that Feeney would have noticed . . . something.'

'I don't know.' Eve rubbed her eyes. 'The Athame. What the hell's an athame?'

'I don't know.' Peabody pulled out her palm PC and

requested the data. 'Athame, ceremonial knife, a ritual tool normally fashioned of steel. Traditionally the athame is not used for cutting, but for casting or banishing circles in earth religions.'

Peabody glanced up at Eve. 'Witchcraft,' she continued. 'That's quite a coincidence.'

'I don't think so.' She took the note from Alice out of her desk drawer, passed it to Peabody. 'Frank's granddaughter slipped this to me at the viewing. Turns out she works at some shop called Spirit Quest. Do you know it?'

'I know what it is.' Troubled now, Peabody set the note down. 'Wiccans are peaceful, Dallas. And they use herbs, not chemicals. No true Wiccan's going to buy, sell, or use Zeus.'

'How about digitalis?' Eve cocked her head. 'That's kind of an herb, isn't it?'

'It's distilled from foxglove. It's been used medicinally for centuries.'

'It's what, like a stimulant?'

'I don't know that much about healing, but yeah, I'd think.'

'So's Zeus. I wonder what kind of effect you'd get combining the two. Bad mix, wrong dosage, whatever, I wouldn't be surprised if you'd get heart failure.'

'You think Wojinski self-terminated?'

'The commander suspects it, and I've got questions,' Eve said impatiently. 'I don't have answers. But I'm going to get them.' She picked up the note. 'We'll start tonight, with Alice. I want you there at eleven, in civilian clothes. Try to look like a Free-Ager, Peabody, not a cop.'

Peabody winced. 'I've got this dress my mother made for my last birthday. But I'll get really pissed off if you laugh.'

'I'll try to control myself. For now, let's see what we can dig up on this Selina Cross and The Athame Club.'

Five minutes later, Eve was smiling grimly at her machine. 'Interesting. Our Selina's been around. Spent some time in a cage. Just look at this yellow sheet, Peabody. Soliciting sex without a license, '43, '44. Assault charge also in '44, subsequently dropped. Ran into Bunko in '47, running a medium scam. What the hell do people want to talk to the dead for, anyway? Suspected of animal mutilations, '49. Not enough evidence for arrest. Manufacturing and distribution of illegals. That's what tagged her and put her away from '50 to '51. All small-time shit, though. But here in '55, she was brought in and questioned in connection with the ritual slaying of a minor. Her alibi held.'

'Illegals has had her under observation since she was sprung in '51,' Peabody added.

'But they haven't brought her in.'

'Like you said, she's small-time. They must be looking for a bigger fish.'

'That would be my take. We'll see what Marion has to say. Look here, it says Selina Cross owns The Athame Club, free and clear.' Eve pursed her lips. 'Now, where would a small-time dealer get the credit power to buy and run a club? She's a front. I wonder if Illegals knows for who. Let's take a look at her. Computer, display image of subject, Cross, Selina.'

'Whew.' Peabody gave a little shudder as the image floated on-screen. 'Spooky.'

'Not a face you'd forget,' Eve murmured.

It was sharp and narrow, the lips full and vibrant red, the eyes black as onyx. There was beauty there, in the balance of features, the white, smooth skin, but it was cold. And as Peabody had observed, spooky. Her hair was as dark as her eyes, parted perfectly in the center, and it hung straight. There was a small tattoo over her left eyebrow.

'What's that symbol?' Eve wondered. 'Zoom and enhance segment twenty to twenty-two, thirty percent.'

'A pentagram.' Peabody's voice quivered, causing Eve to glance over curiously. 'Inverted. She's not Wiccan, Dallas.' Peabody cleared her throat. 'She's a Satanist.'

*

328

Eve didn't believe in such things – the white or the black of it. But she was prepared to believe others did. And more inclined to believe that some used that misguided faith to exploit.

'Be careful what you discount, Eve.'

Distracted, she glanced over. Roarke had insisted on driving. She couldn't complain as any one of his vehicles beat the hell out of hers.

'What do you mean?'

'I mean, when certain beliefs and traditions survive for centuries, there's a reason for it.'

'Sure there is, human beings are, and always have been, gullible. And there are, and always have been, individuals who know how to exploit that gullibility. I'm going to find out if someone exploited Frank's.'

She had told Roarke everything, and had justified it professionally by telling herself since she couldn't tap Feeney for his computer expertise, she could, and would, tap Roarke for his.

'You're a good cop and a sensible woman. Often, you're too good a cop and too sensible a woman.' He stopped for traffic, turned to her. 'I'm asking you to be particularly careful when delving into an area such as this.'

His face was in shadows, and his voice much too serious. 'You mean witches and devil worshipers? Come on, Roarke, we're into the second millennium here. Satanists, for Christ's sake!' She pushed her hair back from her face. 'What the hell do they think they'd do with him if he existed and they managed to get his attention?'

'That's the problem, isn't it?' Roarke said quietly and turned west toward the Aquarian Club.

'Devils exist.' Eve frowned as he slid his vehicle up to a second-level spot on the street. 'And they're flesh and blood, they walk on two legs. You and I have seen plenty of them.'

She got out, took the ramp down to street level. It was

breezy, and the freshening wind had cleared the smells and smoke away. Overhead, the sky was a thick black, unrelieved by moon or stars. Crisscrossing beams from sluggish air traffic flickered, chased by the muffled grumble of engines.

Here on the street was an arty, up-market part of town where even the glida grill on the corner was spotless, and its menu ran to fresh hybrid fruit rather than smoked soy-dogs. Most of the street vendors had closed up for the night, but during the day, they would unfold their carts and discretely hawk offerings of handmade jewelry, hooked rugs and tapestries, herbal baths, and teas.

Panhandlers in this area would likely be polite, their licenses clearly displayed. And they would probably spend their daily earnings on a meal rather than a chemical high.

The crime rate was low, the rents murderous, and the median age of its residents and merchants carelessly young.

She would have hated to live there.

'We're early,' she murmured, scanning the street as a matter of habit. Then her mouth curved into a smirk. 'Look at that, will you? The Psychic Deli. I guess you go in, order the veggie hash, and they claim they knew you were going to do that. Pasta salad and palm readings. They're open.' On impulse, she turned to Roarke. She wanted something that would turn her sour mood. 'You game?'

'You want your palm read?'

'What the hell.' She grabbed his hand. 'It'll put me in the groove for investigating Satanic chemi-dealers. Maybe they'll cut us a deal and do yours for half price.'

'No.'

'You never know unless you ask.'

'I'm not having mine read.'

'Coward,' she muttered and tugged him through the door.

'I prefer the word *careful*.'

She had to admit, it smelled wonderful. There was none of the usual overlay of onion and heavy sauces. Instead, there was a light fragrance of spice and flowers that meshed perfectly with the airy music.

Small white tables and chairs were arranged at a nice distance from the display counter where bowls and plates of colorful food were presented behind sparkling glass. Two customers sat together over bowls of clear soup. Both of them sported flowing white robes, jeweled sandals, and shaved heads.

Behind the counter was a man with silver rings on every finger. He wore a wide-sleeved shirt in quiet blue. His blonde hair was neatly braided and twined with silver cord. He smiled in welcome.

'Blessed be. Do you wish food for the body or for the soul?'

'I thought you were supposed to know.' Eve grinned at him. 'How about a reading?'

'Palm, Tarot, runes, or aura?'

'Palm.' Enjoying herself, Eve stuck her hand out.

'Cassandra is our palmist. If you'd take a comfortable seat, she'll be happy to help you. Sister,' he added as she started to turn, 'your auras are very strong, vibrant. You are well-matched.' With this, he picked up a wooden stick with a rounded edge and ran it gently over the rim of a white frosted bowl.

Even as the vibration sang, a woman stepped through the beaded curtain separating a back room. She wore a silver tunic with a silver bracelet coiled above her elbow. Eve noted that she was very young, barely twenty, and like the man, her hair was blonde and coiled into a braid.

'Welcome.' Her voice held a hint of Ireland. 'Please be comfortable. Would you both like a reading?'

'No, just me.' Eve took a seat at a far table. 'What's it run?'

'The reading is free. We request a donation, only.' She sat gracefully, smiled at Roarke. 'Your generosity will be appreciated. Madam, the hand you were born with.'

'I came with both of them.'

'The left, please.' She cupped her fingers under Eve's offered hand, barely touching at first. 'Strength and courage. Your fate was not set. A trauma, a break in the lifeline. Very young. You were only a child. Such pain, such sadness.' She lifted her gaze, clear gray. 'You were, and are, without blame.'

She tightened her grip when Eve instinctively drew back. 'It's not necessary to remember all, until you're ready. Sorrow and self-doubt, passions blocked. A solitary woman who chose to focus on one goal. A great need for justice. Disciplined, self-motivated . . . troubled. Your heart was broken, more than broken. Mauled. So you guarded what was left. It's a capable hand. One to trust.'

She took Eve's right hand firmly, but barely looked at it. Those clear gray eyes stayed on Eve's face. 'You carry much of what was inside you. It will not be quiet, it will not rest. But you've found your place. Authority suits you, as does the responsibility that marches with it. You're stubborn, often single-focused, but your heart is greatly healed. You love.'

She flicked a glance at Roarke again, and her mouth softened when she looked back at Eve. 'It surprises you, the depth of this. It unnerves you, and you are not easily unnerved.' Her thumb skimmed over the top of Eve's palm. 'Your heart runs deep. It is . . . choosy. It is careful, but when it's given, it's complete. You carry identification. A badge.' She smiled slowly. 'Yes, you made the right choice. Perhaps the only one you could have made. You've killed. More than once. There was no alternative for you, yet this weighs heavy on your mind and heart. In this, you find it difficult to separate the intellect from the emotion. You'll kill again.'

The gray eyes went glassy, and the light grip tightened. 'It's dark. The forces are dark here. Evil. Lives already lost, and others yet to lose. Pain and fear. Body and soul. You must protect yourself and those you love.'

She turned to Roarke, snagging his hand and speaking rapidly in Gaelic. Her face had gone very white, and her breath hitched.

'That's enough.' Shaken, Eve snatched her hand back. 'Hell of a show.' Irritated that her palm tingled, she rubbed it hard against the knee of her slacks. 'You've got a good eye, Cassandra, is it? And an impressive spiel.' She dug into her pocket, took out fifty in credits and laid them on the table.

'Wait.' Cassandra opened a small, embroidered pouch at her waist, plucked out a smooth stone in pale green. 'A gift. A token.' She pushed it into Eve's hand. 'Carry it with you.'

'Why?'

'Why not? Please come again. Blessed be.'

Eve caught one last glance at her pale face before Cassandra hurried into the back room with a musical jingle of beads.

'Well, so much for "You're taking a long ocean voyage,"' Eve muttered as she headed for the door. 'What did she say to you?'

'Her dialect was a bit thick. I'd say she's from the west counties.' He stepped outside, oddly relieved to draw in the night air. 'The gist was that if I loved you as much as she believed, I would stay close. That you're in danger of losing your life, perhaps your soul, and you need me to survive it.'

'What a crock.' She glanced down at the stone in her hand.

'Keep it.' Roarke closed her fingers over it. 'Couldn't hurt.'

With a shrug, Eve pushed it into her pocket. 'I think I'm going to steer clear of psychics.'

'An excellent idea,' Roarke said with feeling as he walked with her across the street and into the Aquarian Club.

Chapter Three

It was quite a place, Eve mused, and certainly quieter than any club she'd been in before. Both conversation and music were muted, and both had an elegant little lilt. Tables were packed together as was the norm, but they were arranged to provide circular traffic patterns that reminded Eve of the symbol at the base of Alice's note.

Ringing the walls were mirrors fashioned into the shapes of stars and moons. Each held a burning candle, a white pillar, that reflected light and flame. Between each mirror were plaques of symbols and figures she didn't recognize. The small dance floor was circular as well, as was the bar where patrons sat on stools that depicted signs of the zodiac. It took her a moment to place the woman seated on the twin-faces of Gemini.

'Jesus, that's Peabody.'

Roarke shifted his gaze, focused on the woman in a long, sweeping dress in swirling hues of blue and green. Three long strands of beads sparkled to her waist, and earrings of varicolored metals jingled beneath the fringes of her straight, cropped hair.

'Well, well,' he said and smiled slowly, 'our sturdy Peabody makes quite a picture.'

'She sure . . . blends,' Eve decided. 'I have to meet with Alice alone. Why don't you go over and talk to Peabody?'

'A pleasure. Lieutenant . . .' He took a long look at her

worn jeans, battered leather jacket, and unadorned ears. 'You don't blend.'

'Is that a dig?'

'No.' He flicked a finger over the dent in her chin. 'An observation.' He strolled over, slid onto the stool beside Peabody. 'Now, let's see, what would be the standard line? What's a nice witch like you doing in a place like this?'

Peabody slid him a sidelong look, grimaced. 'I feel like an idiot in this getup.'

'You look lovely.'

She snorted. 'Not exactly my style.'

'You know the fascinating thing about women, Peabody?' He reached out, tapped a finger against her dangling earrings to send them dancing. 'You have so many styles. What are you drinking?'

Ridiculously flattered, she struggled not to flush. 'A Saggitarius. That's my sign. The drink's supposed to be metabolically and spiritually designed for my personality.' She sipped from the clear chalice. 'Actually, it's not bad. What's your, you know, birth sign?'

'I have no idea. I believe I was born the first week of October.'

Believe; Peabody mused. *How odd not to know*. 'Well, that would make you Libran.'

'Well then, let's be metabolically and spiritually correct.' He turned to order drinks, watched Eve sitting at a table. 'What sign would you attribute to your lieutenant?'

'She's a tough one to pin down.'

'Indeed she is,' Roarke murmured.

From her table on the outer circle, Eve watched everything. There was no band or holographic image of one. Instead, the music seem to come from nowhere and everywhere. Windy flutes and plucked strings, a soothing female voice that sang with impossible sweetness in a language Eve didn't recognize.

She saw couples in earnest conversations, others laughing quietly. No one flicked an eyelash when a woman in a sheer white sheath rose to dance alone. Eve ordered water and was amused when it was served in a goblet of simulated silver.

She tuned in to the conversation at the table behind her and was further amused to hear the group's sober discussion on their experiences with astral projection.

At a table in the next ring, two women talked about their former lives as temple dancers in Atlantis. She wondered why former lives were always more exotic than the one being lived. The only shot a person had, in her opinion.

Harmless weirdos, Eve thought, but caught herself rubbing her still tingling palm on her jeans.

She saw Alice the minute the girl walked in. *Agitated*, Eve thought. *Nervous hands, tensed shoulders, jittery eyes*. She waited until Alice scanned the room, spotted her, then she inclined her head in acknowledgment. With a last backward glance at the door, Alice hurried over.

'You came. I was afraid you wouldn't.' Quickly, she dipped into her pocket and drew out a smooth black stone on a silver chain. 'Put this on. Please,' she insisted when Eve only studied it. 'It's obsidian. It's been consecrated. It'll block evil.'

'I'm all for that.' Eve slipped the chain around her neck. 'Better?'

'This is the safest place I know. The cleanest.' Still darting glances around the room, Alice sat. 'I used to come here all the time.' She gripped the amulet she wore in both hands as a server glided to the table. 'A Golden Sun, please.' She took a deep breath as she looked back at Eve. 'I need courage. I've tried to meditate all day, but I'm blocked. I'm afraid.'

'What are you afraid of, Alice?'

'That those who killed my grandfather will kill me next.'

'Who killed your grandfather?'

'Evil killed him. Killing is what evil does best. You won't believe what I tell you. You're too grounded in what can be

336

seen only with the eyes.' She accepted the drink from the server, closed her eyes a moment as if in prayer, then slowly lifted the cup to her lips. 'But you won't ignore it, either. You're too much a cop. I don't want to die,' Alice said and set her cup down.

That, Eve thought, was the first sensible statement she'd heard. The fear was genuine enough, she decided, and unmasked tonight. At the viewing, Alice had been careful to slick on a layer of composure and calm.

For her family, Eve realized.

'Who are you afraid of, and why?'

'I have to explain. All of it. I have to purge before I can atone. My grandfather respected you, so I come to you in his memory. I wasn't born a witch.'

'Weren't you?' Eve said dryly.

'Some are, and some, like me, are simply drawn to the craft. I became interested in Wicca through my studies, and the more I learned, the more I felt a need to belong. I was drawn to the rituals, the search for balance, the joy, and the positive ethics. I didn't share my interest with my family. They wouldn't have understood.'

She dipped her head and her hair flowed down like a curtain. 'I enjoyed the secrecy of that and was still young enough to find the experience of going skyclad at an outdoor celebration slightly wicked. My family . . .' She lifted her head again. 'They're conservative, and a part of me simply wanted to do something daring.'

'A small rebellion?'

'Yes, that's true. If I had left it at that,' Alice murmured, 'if I had truly accepted my initiation into the craft, and what it meant, everything would be different now. I was weak, and my intellect too ambitious.' She picked up her drink again, wet her dry throat. 'I wanted to know. To compare and analyze, rather like a thesis, the contrasts of white and black magic. How could I fully appreciate the

337

one without fully understanding its antithesis? That was my rationale.'

'Sounds logical.'

'False logic,' Alice insisted. 'I was deluding myself. The ego and the intellect were so arrogant. I would study the black arts on a purely scholarly level. I'd talk to those who had chosen the other path and discover what had turned them away from the light. It would be exciting.' She smiled tremulously. 'I thought it would be exciting, and for a short time, it was.'

A child, Eve thought, *in the body of a stunning woman. Bright and curious, but a child, nonetheless.* It was pitifully easy to tug information from the young. 'Is that how you met Selina Cross?'

Paling, Alice made a quick forking gesture with her fore-finger and pinky. 'How do you know of her?'

'I did some research. I didn't walk in here blind, Alice. As a cop's granddaughter, you shouldn't have expected me to.'

'Be afraid of her.' Alice compressed her lips. 'Be afraid of her.'

'She's a second-rate grifter and chemi-dealer.'

'No, she's much more.' Alice gripped her amulet again. 'Believe that, Lieutenant. I've seen. I know. She'll want you. You'll challenge her.'

'Do you believe she had something to do with Frank's death?'

'I know she did.' Tears swam into her eyes, deepening the soft blue. One huge and lovely drop spilled over and slid down her white cheek. 'Because of me.'

Eve leaned closer to comfort, and to block the tearful face from any onlookers. 'Tell me about it, about her.'

'I met her nearly a year ago. On the sabbat of Samhain. All Hallow's Eve. More research, I told myself. I didn't realize how deeply I'd already been drawn in, how utterly seduced I was by the power, the pure selfish greed of the other side. I hadn't performed any of the rituals, not then.

338

I was still observing. Then I met her, and the one they call Alban.'

'Alban?'

'He, serves her.' Alice lifted a hand, laid her fingers against her mouth. 'That night still isn't clear in my mind. I realize now they cast a spell over me. I let them lead me into the circle, strip off my robes. I heard the bells ring, and the chant to the dark prince. I watched the sacrifice of the goat. And I shared in the blood.'

Her head drooped again as shame whirled inside her. 'I shared in it, drank of it, and enjoyed. I was the altar that night. I was tied to the stone. I don't know how or by whom, but I wasn't afraid. I was aroused.'

Her voice dropped to a whisper. The music changed, slid from strings to drums and bells, cheerfully sexual. Alice never lifted her gaze.

'Each member of the coven touched me, rubbed oils and blood over me. The chanting was inside me, and the fire was so hot. Then Selina laid over me. She . . . did things. I'd never had any sexual experience. Then while she slid up my body, Alban straddled me. She watched me. His hands were on her breasts and he was inside me. And she watched my face. I wanted to close my eyes, but I couldn't. I couldn't. I couldn't stop looking into her eyes. It was like she was the one – the one inside me.'

Her tears plopped on the table now. Even though Eve had shifted to sheild her from most of the room, and Alice's voice was barely more than a whisper, several heads were turning curiously.

'You were drugged, Alice. And exploited. You have nothing to be ashamed of.'

Her eyes lifted briefly and threatened to break Eve's heart. 'Then why am I so ashamed? I was a virgin, and there was pain, but even that was arousing. Unbearably. And the pleasure that came with it was huge, monstrous. They used me, and I begged

339

to be used again. And was, by the entire coven. By sunrise I was lost, enslaved. I woke in bed, between them. Alban and Selina. I'd already become their apprentice. And their toy.'

Tears were running down her cheeks as she drank again. 'Sexually, there was nothing I would not allow them, or one of their choosing, to do to me. I embraced the dark. And I became careless in my arrogance. Someone told my grandfather. He would never give me a name, but I know it was a Wiccan. He confronted me, and I laughed at him. I warned him to stay out of my affairs. I thought he had.'

Saying nothing, Eve slid her water across the table. Gratefully, Alice picked it up, drained it. 'A few months ago, I discovered Selina and Alban were performing private rituals. I'd come down from college a day early. I went to their house, and I heard the ceremonial chant. I opened the door of the ritual room. They were there, together, performing a sacrifice.' Her hands shook. 'Not a goat this time, but a child. A young boy.'

Eve's hand closed tight over Alice's wrist. 'You saw them murder a child?'

'Murder is too tame a word for what they did.' The tears dried up in horror. 'Don't ask me to tell you. Don't ask me that.'

She would have to, Eve knew, but it could wait. 'Tell me what you can.'

'I saw . . . Selina, the ritual knife. The blood, the screams. I swear you could see the screams like black smears on the air. It was too late to stop it.'

She looked at Eve again, those swimming eyes begging to be believed in this one thing. 'I was too late to do anything for the boy, even if I'd had the power or the courage to try.'

'You were alone, shocked,' Eve said carefully. 'The woman was armed, the boy was dead. You couldn't have helped him.'

For one long moment, Alice stared at her, then covered her

face with her hands. 'I try to believe that. Try so hard. Living with it is destroying me. I ran away. I just ran.'

'You can't change it.' Eve kept her hand on Alice's wrist, but her grip gentled. She had once seen a child mutilated, had been too late. Seconds too late. She hadn't run, she had killed. But the child was just as dead, either way. 'You can't go back and change it. You have to live with what is.'

'I know. Isis tells me that.' Alice took a shuddering breath, lowered her hands. 'They were engrossed in their work and never saw me. Or I pray they never saw me. I didn't go to my grandfather or the police. I was terrified, sick. I don't know how much time went by, but I went to Isis, the high priestess who had initiated me into Wicca. She took me in; even after all I'd done, she took me in.'

'You didn't tell Frank what you'd seen?'

Alice winced at the bite in Eve's voice. 'Not then. I spent time in reflection and purification. Isis performed several cleansing rites and auric healings. Isis and I felt it best that I stay in seclusion for a while, concentrate on finding the light, and atonement.'

Eve's eyes were hot and hard as she leaned closer. 'Alice, you saw a child murdered and told no one but your neighborhood witch?'

'I know how it sounds.' Her lip quivered before she caught it between her teeth and steadied it. 'The child's physical being was beyond help. I could do nothing for him but pray for the safe passage of his soul to the next plane. I was afraid to tell Grandpa. Afraid of what he might do and what Selina would do to him. When I did go to him last month, I told him everything. Now he's dead, and I know she's responsible.'

'How do you know?'

'I saw her.'

'Wait.' Eyes narrowed, Eve held up a hand. 'You saw her kill him?'

'No, I saw her outside my window. I looked out the night

341

he died, and she was standing below, looking up. Looking up at me. The call came from my mother to tell me Grandpa was dead. And Selina smiled. She smiled and she beckoned to me.' Alice buried her face in her hands again. 'She sent her forces against him. Used her power to stop his heart. Because of me. Now the raven comes every night to my window and watches me with her eyes.'

Christ, Eve thought, where were they going with this? 'A bird?'

Alice laid her trembling hands on the table. 'She's a shape-shifter. She takes what form she wills. I've protected myself as best I can, but my faith may not be strong enough. They're pulling at me, calling to me.'

'Alice.' While sympathy remained, Eve found her patience waning. 'Selina Cross might have had a part in your grand-father's death. If we find that he didn't die of natural causes, it wasn't some spell; it was calculated, simple murder. If so, there'll be evidence, and a trial, and she'll be dealt with.'

'You can't find smoke.' Alice shook her head. 'You won't find evidence in a curse.'

Enough was enough. 'At this point, you're a witness to a crime. Potentially the only witness, and if you're afraid, I can arrange a safe house for you.' Her voice was flat and brisk, all cop. 'I need you to give me a description of the child so that I can check missing persons. With your formal statement, I can get a warrant to search the room where you allegedly witnessed the murder. I need you to give me details, straight details. Times, places, names. I can help you.'

'You don't understand,' Alice said, shaking her head slowly. 'You don't believe me.'

'I believe you're an intelligent and curious woman who got in over her head with some very nasty people. And I believe you're confused and upset. I have someone you can talk to who can help you sort things out.'

'Someone?' Alice's eyes went cold and her voice hard. 'A

psychiatrist? You think I'm imagining things, making them up.' Her body trembled as she surged to her feet. 'It's not my mind that's in danger, it's my life. My life, Lieutenant Dallas, and my soul. If you find yourself in battle with Selina, you'll believe. And may the goddess help you.'

She whirled and ran out, leaving Eve cursing.

'That seemed remarkably unsuccessful,' Roarke commented as he came up behind her.

'The girl's whacked out, but she's terrified.' Eve heaved a long breath and rose. 'Let's get the hell out of here.' She signaled Peabody, then headed for the door.

Outside, a thin fog crept along the ground, stealthily, like twining gray snakes. Rain, thin and chilly, was just beginning to slick the street.

'There she is,' Eve murmured when she caught sight of Alice rushing around the corner. 'Headed south. Peabody, tail her, make sure she gets home safe.'

'Got her,' Peabody headed off at a half trot.

'That kid's a mess, Roarke. They've fucked with her in every way possible.' Disgusted, she dug her hands into her pockets. 'I probably could've handled it better, but I don't see how it would help to encourage her delusions. Spells and curses and shape shifters. Jesus.'

'Darling Eve.' He kissed her brow. 'My own practical cop.'

'The way she tells it, she was practically the bride of Satan.' Grumbling, Eve started for the car, turned on her heel, and paced back. 'I'll tell you how it went, Roarke. She wanted to play, wanted to dabble in the occult, and she ran into real bad news. She's a naive, pretty girl, and it doesn't take a crystal ball to see it. So she went to one of their meetings, or whatever the hell you call them, and they drugged her. Then they gang-raped her. Bastards. She's drugged and in shock and vulnerable to suggestions, and it's easy for a couple of professional cons to convince her she's part of their cult. Pull a couple of magic tricks out of their hat and fascinate her. Use sex to keep her in line.'

'She got to you,' Roarke murmured and touched her hair, brushing away the wet.

'Maybe she did. Damn it, did you look at her? She's well-named. Looks like that kid in the fairy story. Probably believes in talking rabbits, too.' Then she sighed, struggled to put her emotions back into place. 'But we're not in a fairy story here. She claims she walked in on a ritual murder. A little boy, she said. I've got to get her in to Mira. A shrink will be able to sort out the fact from fiction. But I believe that murder was fact, and if they killed one child, they've killed more. People like them prey on the helpless.'

'I know.' He reached out to rub the tenstion in her shoulders. 'Close to home?'

'No. It's not like what happened to me. Or you.' But there were enough echoes to unnerve her. 'We're still here, aren't we?' She laid a hand on his but frowned into the shadows. 'Why didn't Frank make a log of what she'd told him? Why the hell did he go solo on this?'

'Maybe he did make a log. A private one.'

She blinked, stared at him. 'God, how could I be so slow!' She clapped her hands on either side of his face and kissed him hard. 'You're brilliant.'

'Yes, I know.' He jerked her back as a figure darted out of the shadows and over the ramp. 'Black cat,' he said, simultaneously uneasy and amused at himself. 'Bad luck.'

'Yeah, right.' She started up the ramp, cocked her head as the cat sat at the side of Roarke's car, watching her out of bright and glittering green eyes. 'You don't look hungry, ace. Too sleek and glossy for an alley cat. Too perfect,' she realized. 'Must be a droid.' Still, she crouched, reached out to stroke. The cat hissed, arched, and swiped. Eve would have found her palm laid open if she hadn't been quick enough to dodge. 'Well, that's friendly.'

'You should know better than to offer your hand to strange animals – or droids.' But he stepped in front of Eve to uncode the car and kept his eyes on the gleaming green of the cat's. When Eve was in the car, he spoke softly. The cat's fur bristled, its tail switched, then it leaped nimbly from the ramp to the street, and it was swallowed by the fog.

Roarke couldn't have said why he'd given the order to go in Gaelic. It had simply come out that way. He was still pondering it when he slid in beside Eve.

'Listen, Roarke, I can't tap Feeney for any E-work on this. At least not until the commander loosens up. I may have to go to the family for access to Frank's personal records, but if I do that, I'll have to tell them something.'

'And you'd rather not.'

'Not yet, in any case. So how do you feel about using your . . . skills to access Frank's personal unit and logs?'

His mood lifted as he started the car, guiding it down to street level. 'That depends, Lieutenant. Do I get a badge?'

Her lips twitched into a smirk. 'No. But you get to have sex with a cop.'

'Do I get to pick the cop?' He only smiled when she punched his arm. 'I'd pick you. Probably. And I suppose you want me to begin my unofficial consultation tonight.'

'That's the idea.'

'All right, but I want sex first.' He tucked his tongue in his cheek as she chuckled. 'How long do you think Peabody's going to be busy? Just joking,' he said quickly, but shifted into autodrive just in case Eve got violent. 'She did look quite appealing tonight though.'

Laughing, he caught her fist in his hand, then snuck the other one up to her breast. 'Listen, pal, you're in deep enough without trying that. Engaging in any sexual act in a moving vehicle is in violation of inner city codes.'

'Arrest me,' he suggested and nipped her bottom lip.

'I might. When I'm done with you.' She wiggled free and

shoved him back. 'And just for that smart-ass remark about my aide, no sex until after the consult.'

He disengaged auto, then slid her a slow, smiling glance. 'Wanna bet?'

She met that arrogant glance narrow-eyed. 'Fifty credits, even odds.'

'Done.' And he whistled his way through the iron gates that led home.

Chapter Four

'Pay up.'

Eve rolled over, rubbed her bare butt, and wondered if she'd have rug burns. Still vibrating from the last orgasm, she closed her eyes again. 'Huh?'

'Fifty credits.' He leaned over, gently kissed the tip of her breast. 'You lost, Lieutenant.'

Her eyes blinked open and stared into his gorgeous and very satisfied face. They were sprawled on the rug of his private room, and their clothes, as best she could recall, were scattered everywhere. Starting at the stairway where he'd trapped her against the wall and had started to . . . win the bet.

'I'm naked,' she pointed out. 'I don't generally keep credits up my—'

'I'm happy to take your IOU.' He rose, all graceful, gleaming muscles, and took a memo card from his console. 'Here you are.' Handed it to her.

She stared down at it, knowing dignity was as lost as the fifty credits. 'You're really enjoying this.'

'Oh, more than you can possibly imagine.'

Scowling at him, she engaged the memo. 'I owe you, Roarke, fifty credits, Dallas, Lieutenant Eve.' She shoved the memo at him. 'Satisfied.'

'In every possible way.' He thought, sentimentally, that he would tuck the memo away with the little gray suit button he'd kept from their very first meeting. 'I love you, Dallas, Lieutenant Eve, in every possible way.'

She couldn't help it. She went soft all over. It was the way he said it, the way he looked at her that had rapid pulses beating under melting skin. 'Oh, no, you don't. That kind of thing's how you took me for fifty.' She scrambled up before he could distract her again. 'Where the hell are my pants?'

'I haven't the faintest idea.' He walked to a section of the wall, touched a mechanism. When the panel slid open, he drew out a robe. It was silk and thin and made her eyes narrow again.

He was always buying her things like that, and they always seemed to find their way to various parts of the house. Conveniently.

'That's not working attire.'

'We can do this naked, but you'd certainly lose another fifty.' When she snatched the robe out of his hand, he turned and took out another for himself. 'This could take some time. We'll want coffee.'

As she went to the AutoChef to get coffee, Roarke moved behind the console. The equipment here was first flight, and unregistered. CompuGuard couldn't track it nor block him from hacking into any system. Still, even with those advantages, finding a personal log that may or may not have existed was like separating individual grains of sand from a bucketful.

'Engage,' he ordered. 'More likely his home unit, wouldn't you think?'

'Anything on his unit at Cop Central would have been transferred, and official units record all logging. If he wanted to keep something to himself, he'd have used a private system.'

'Do you have his home address? Never mind,' he said before Eve could speak. 'I'll get it. Data, Wojinski, Frank . . . what was his rank?'

'Detective Sergeant, attached to Records.'

'Data on screen one, please.'

As it began to scroll, Roarke reached for the coffee Eve held out to him, then waved his fingers when his 'link beeped. 'Get that, would you?'

It was the careless order of a man used to giving them. Automatically, she bristled, then just as quickly bumped aside the annoyance. She supposed the situation called for her to act as assistant.

'Roarke's residence. Peabody?'

'You didn't answer your communicator.'

'No, I . . .' God knew where it was, she thought. 'What's up?'

'It's bad. Dallas, it's bad.' Though her voice was steady, her face was dead white, and her eyes too dark. 'Alice is dead. I couldn't stop it. I couldn't get to her. She just—'

'Where are you?'

'On Tenth Street, between Broad and Seventh. I called the MTS, but there was nothing—'

'Are you in jeopardy?'

'No, no. I just couldn't stop her. I just watched while—'

'Secure the scene, Officer. Relay to Dispatch. I'm on my way. Call backup as required, and stand. Understood?'

'Yes, sir. Yes.'

'Dallas out. Oh, Christ,' she murmured when she disengaged.

'I'll take you.' He was already up, his hand on her shoulder.

'No, this is my job.' And she prayed it wasn't her doing. 'I'd appreciate it if you'd stay here and get whatever data you can.'

'All right. Eve.' He took both of her shoulders now, firmly, before she could turn away. 'Look at me. This was not your fault.'

She did look at him, and there was grief in her eyes. 'I hope to God it wasn't.'

*

There wasn't a crowd. Eve could be grateful for that. It was after two in the morning, and only a few gawkers huddled together behind the barricade. She saw a Rapid Cab tipped drunkenly on the curb and a man sitting beside it, his head in his hands, as an MT spoke with him.

On the rain-slicked street, lit dimly by the glow of a security light with fog billowing like clouds, was Alice. Her body sprawled there, faceup, her arms and legs flung out as if in wild welcome. Blood, her own, had soaked through the filmy material of her dress and turned it to dark, doomed red.

Peabody stood by her, assisting a uniform in the erecting of a privacy screen.

'Officer Peabody.' Eve said it softly, waited for Peabody to turn, straighten her shoulders, and cross to her. 'Your report?'

'I followed the subject to her residence, as per your orders, Lieutenant. I watched her enter the building, and subsequently observed the light go on in the second window from the east, third floor. On my own initiative, I decided to keep watch for a period of fifteen minutes, to insure the subject remained inside. She did not.'

Peabody trailed off, and her gaze shifted to the body. Eve sidestepped, blocked the view. 'Look at me when you report, Officer.'

'Yes, sir.' Peabody snapped back. 'Subject exited building approximately ten minutes later. She appeared agitated, continually looked over her shoulder as she walked west at a rapid pace. She appeared to be crying. I maintained the standard distance. That's why I couldn't stop her.' Peabody had to suck in air. 'I maintained the standard distance.'

'Stop it.' Eve snapped it out, gave Peabody a quick shake. 'Complete your report.'

Peabody's eyes went flat and cold as they met Eve's. 'Yes, sir. The subject stopped suddenly, took several steps in retreat. She spoke. I was too far away to discern what she said, but it was my impression that she was speaking to someone.'

She played it back through her mind, every step, leaning on her training like a crutch. 'I closed the distance somewhat, in the event the subject was in jeopardy. I observed no one on the street other than the subject herself. The fog may have been a factor, but there was no one on the sidewalk or the street that I could see.'

'She stood there, talking to no one?' Eve asked.

'That's how it appeared, Lieutenant. She became increasingly agitated. She begged to be left alone. Her words were, "Haven't you done enough, haven't you taken enough? Why won't you leave me in peace."'

Peabody stared back at the sidewalk, saw it all again. Heard it as well. That hitch of desperation and despair in Alice's voice. 'I thought I heard a response, but can't be definite. The subject was speaking too loudly and too rapidly for me to make a clear statement on that. I decided to move closer, to make myself known.'

A muscle in her jaw jumped as she continued to stare over Eve's shoulder. 'At this time, a Rapid Cab, traveling east, approached. The subject turned and ran into the street, directly into the path of the oncoming vehicle. The driver attempted to stop and evade, but was unable to do so and struck the subject head-on.'

She paused just long enough to take another breath. 'Road conditions were fair to poor, and played a minor factor. Even with optimum conditions, it would be my opinion the driver would have been unable to avoid the collision.'

'Understood. Continue.'

'I reached the body within seconds, and though I observed that she was already dead, I called for the medical technicians, then attempted to contact you via your communicator. When this was unsuccessful, I utilized the portalink in my bag and reached you at home to report the situation. Following your orders, I relayed to Dispatch and requested a uniform, then secured the scene.'

It was hell to be too late, Eve knew, and no amount of sympathy could ease that bitter guilt. So she offered none. 'Very well, Officer. That's the driver?'

Peabody continued to stare straight ahead, and her voice was hollow. 'Yes, Lieutenant.'

'Arrange for his vehicle to be taken in for analysis, then consult with the MTs and find out if he's in shape to give a statement.'

'Yes, sir.' Peabody clutched her hand into a fist at her side. She kept her voice low, but it vibrated with emotion. 'You had a drink with her barely an hour ago. And it doesn't mean a damn to you.'

Eve took the hit and waited until Peabody turned away before she walked back to Alice. 'Yes, it does,' she murmured. 'And that's the problem.'

Opening her field kit, she crouched down to do her job.

It wasn't homicide. Technically, Eve should have turned the matter over to Traffic after Peabody's report and the ensuing statement from the weeping cabbie. But she watched Alice's body being loaded into the morgue wagon and knew she had no intention of doing so.

She took a last look at the scene. The rain had nearly stopped and wouldn't wash away the blood. The few gawkers who had gathered were already breaking up and moving along, tearing the last thin curtains of fog as they shuffled home.

Across at the curb, a city tow unit was already hitching up the damaged cab for transferral to the police compound.

Accidents, some would say, happened all too often. And so, Eve thought, did murder. All too often.

'You've had a long night, Peabody. You're off duty.'

'I would prefer to stay on, Lieutenant, and see this through.'

'You won't help her or me unless you can see it through objectively.'

'I can do my job, sir. My feelings are my own business.'

Eve hitched up her field kit, took a long look at her aide. 'Yes, they are. Just don't let them get in my way.' She took her recorder out of her kit, held it out to Peabody. 'On record, Officer. We'll examine the subject's residence.'

'Do you intend to notify the next of kin? Sir?'

'When we're done here.'

They headed east, back to Alice's building. She hadn't gotten far, Eve thought, barely a block. What had driven her back out? And what had driven her into the path of the cab?

The building was a pretty, restored brownstone of three stories. The entrance doors sported beveled glass with an etched design of peacocks. The security camera was in full repair, and the locks coded for palm prints. Eve disarmed them with a master code and entered a small, well-scrubbed foyer with faux marble floors. The elevator had a mirrored bronze sheen and ran with silent efficiency.

Alice, she thought, had had taste and the financial resources to indulge it. There were three apartments on the third floor, and again Eve used her master to gain entrance.

'Dallas, Lieutenant Eve, and aide, Peabody, Officer D., entering residence of deceased for standard examination. Lights,' she ordered, then frowned when the room remained dark.

Peabody reached around the door, flicked a switch. 'She must have preferred manual to voice-activated.'

The room was cluttered and colorful. Pretty scarves and throws were draped over chairs, tables. Tapestries depicting attractive naked people and mythological animals romped over the walls. Candles were everywhere, on tables, on shelves, on the floor, as were bowls of colored stones, of herbs, of dried flower petals. Chunks and wands of crystal, sparkling clean, crowded every flat surface.

A mood screen was engaged and showed a wide field of meadow grass and wildflowers blowing gently in the breeze. Its audio played the song of birds and zephyrs.

'She liked pretty things,' Eve observed. 'And lots of them.' Moving over, she glanced at the controls of the mood screen and nodded as they corroborated her thought. 'She flipped this on as soon as she walked in. Wanted to mellow out, I'd say.'

Leaving Peabody to follow, she walked into the adjoining room. The bedroom was small, cozy, and again cluttered. The spread on the narrow bed was embroidered with stars and moons. A glass mobile, dancing with fairies, hung above it and even now clinked musically in the breeze through the open window.

'This would have been the window, the light you saw come on.'

'Yes, sir.'

'So she flipped on the screen, then came straight into the bedroom. Probably wanted to change, get out of the damp dress. But she didn't.' Eve stepped on to a small area rug with the face of a smiling sun. 'It's cluttered, but tidy in its way. No sign of disturbance or struggle.'

'Struggle?'

'You said she was agitated, crying when she came back out. The country meadow program didn't mellow her, or didn't have enough time to.'

'She didn't bother to shut it down again.'

'No,' Eve agreed. 'She didn't. There's the possibility someone was here when she got home. Someone who upset or frightened her. We'll check the security logs.' She opened what she assumed was a closet, and let out a hum. 'Well, look at this. She'd turned it into a room of some kind. Not a lot of clutter here. Get this on record.'

Peabody stepped up, scanned the recorder over a small, white-walled room. The floor was wood with a white pentagram

354

painted on it. A ring of white candles were arranged in careful symmetry around the edge. A small table held a clear crystal ball, a bowl, a mirror, and a dark-handled knife with a short, blunted blade.

Eve sniffed the air, but caught no hint of smoke or candle wax. 'What do you figure she did in here?'

'I'd say it was kind of ritual room, for meditation, or casting spells.'

'Jesus.' With a shake of her head, Eve stepped back. 'We'll leave that for now and check out her 'link. If no one was here to scare her back out, maybe she got a call that did. She came into the bedroom first,' Eve murmured, wandering back to the small bedside 'link. 'Maybe she intended to go in there and play witch after she'd changed and calmed down. She wasn't carrying anything when she went back out. She didn't come in here to get something and go out again. She was upset, she came home.'

Eve engaged the 'link, requested a replay of the last call transmitted or received. And the room filled with low, rhythmic chanting.

'What the hell is that?'

'I don't know.' Uneasy, Peabody stepped closer.

'Replay,' Eve demanded.

Hear the names. Hear the names and fear them. Loki, Beelzebub, Baphomet. I am annihilation. I am revenge. In nomine Dei nostri Santanas Luciferi excelsi. Vengeance for you who strayed from the law. Hear the names and fear.

'Stop.' Eve gave a quick, involuntary shudder. 'Beelzebub, that's devil shit, isn't it? The bastards were playing with her, tormenting her. And she was already on the edge. No wonder she ran out of here. Where were you, you son of a bitch, where were you? Location of last transmission. Display.' Her mouth thinned as she read the data. 'Tenth and Seventh, right down the goddamn street. Probably a public 'link. Fuckers. She was heading right for them.'

'There wasn't anyone there.' But Peabody was watching Eve's face now, and the fury that fired in her eyes. 'Even with the fog, the rain, I would have seen someone if they'd been laying for her. There wasn't anything there but a cat.'

Eve's heart took a bad jump. 'A what?'

'Just a cat. I caught a glimpse of a cat, but there was no one on the street.'

'A cat.' Eve walked to the window. Suddenly, she felt the need for a good gulp of air. There, on the sill, she saw the long, black feather. 'And a bird,' she murmured. She took out tweezers, held the feather up to the light. 'We've still got the occasional crow in New York. A crow's the same thing as a raven, isn't it?'

'More or less. I think.'

'Bag it,' Eve ordered. 'I want it analyzed.' She rubbed her fingers over her eyes as if to push away fatigue. 'Next of kin would be Brenda Wojinski, mother. Run that for an address.'

'Yes, sir.' Peabody took out her PPC, then simply held it while shame washed over her. 'Lieutenant, I'd like to apologize for my earlier comment and my behavior.'

Eve took the disc from the 'link, sealed it herself. 'I don't recall any comment, Peabody, or any unsatisfactory behavior.' She gave Peabody a level look. 'While the recorder is still engaged, do another scan of the apartment.'

Understanding, Peabody inclined her head. 'I'm aware the recorder is still engaged, Lieutenant. I want this on the record. I was insubordinate and out of line both professionally and personally.'

Damn stiff-necked idiot, Eve though and bit back an oath. 'There was no insubordination in my opinion or in my recollection, Officer.'

'Dallas.' Peabody loosed a sigh. 'I damn well was. I was shaky and having a hard time dealing with the situation. It's one thing to see a body after it's done, and another to see a

356

woman get tossed ten feet in the air and land on the pavement. She was under my watch.'

'I was rough on you.'

'Yes, sir, you were. And you needed to be. I thought that because you were able to maintain, you were able to do your job, it meant you didn't care. I was wrong, and I'm sorry.'

'Acknowledged. Now, put this on record, Peabody. You followed orders, you followed procedure. You were not at fault for what happened tonight. You could not have prevented it. Now, put it aside so we can find out why she's dead.'

Eve thought that a cop's daughter knew when another cop knocked on the door at five in the morning, it was with news of the worst kind. She saw, the minute Brenda recognized her, that she was right.

'Oh God. Oh God. Mama?'

'No, it's not your mother, Ms Wojinski.' There was only one way, Eve knew, and that was fast. 'It's Alice. May we come in?'

'Alice?' She blinked glazed eyes, propped a hand on the door for balance. 'Alice?'

'I think we should go inside.' As gently as possible, Eve took her arm, stepped through the door. 'Let's go in and sit down.'

'Alice?' she said again. Grief cracked the glaze over her eyes. Tears poured through. 'Oh no, not my Alice. Not my baby.'

Brenda swayed, would have slid to the floor, but Eve tightened her grip and headed quickly for the nearest seat. 'I'm sorry. I'm so sorry for your loss, Ms Wojinski. There was an accident early this morning, and Alice was killed.'

'An accident? No, you've made a mistake. It was someone else. It wasn't Alice.' She clutched at Eve, flooded eyes pleading. 'You can't be sure it was my Alice.'

'It was. I'm sorry.'

She collapsed then, burying her face in her hands, pressing her hands to her knees so her body was balled in a defensive shield.

'I could make her some tea,' Peabody murmured.

'Yeah, go.' It was the part of the job that made Eve feel the most helpless, the most inadequate. There was no solution for fresh grief. 'Is there someone I can call for you? Do you want me to contact your mother? Your brother?'

'Mama. Oh God, Alice. How will we bear it?'

There was no answer for that, Eve thought. Yet they would. Life demanded it. 'I can give you a soother, or contact your doctor, if you'd prefer.'

'Mom?'

As Brenda continued to rock, Eve looked over. The boy stood in the doorway, blinking sleepy, confused eyes. His hair was tousled from sleep and he wore grubby sweatpants with holes at the knees.

Alice's brother, Eve remembered. She'd forgotten.

Then he focused on Eve, his eyes suddenly alert, and much too adult. 'What's wrong?' he demanded. 'What's happened?'

What the hell was his name? Eve struggled to remember, then decided it didn't matter at the moment. She rose. He was a tall boy, she realized, with sleep creases in his cheeks and a body already braced to take the worst. 'There's been an accident. I'm sorry but—'

'It's Alice.' His chin quivered, but his eyes stayed steady on hers. 'She's dead.'

'Yes, I'm sorry.'

He continued to stare at her as Peabody came in with a cup of tea, set it awkwardly on the table. 'What kind of accident?'

'She was hit by a car early this morning.'

'Hit and run?'

'No.' Eve watched him carefully, considering. 'She stepped

358

into the path of a cab. The driver was unable to stop. We're in the process of analyzing his vehicle and the scene, but there was a witness who corroborates the driver's statement. I don't believe he was at fault. He didn't attempt to flee the scene, and his driving record is clean.'

The boy simply nodded, dry-eyed, while his mother's weeping filled the room. 'I'll take care of her. It'd be best if you left us alone now.'

'All right. If you have any questions, you can reach me at Cop Central. I'm Lieutenant Dallas.'

'I know who you are. Leave us alone now,' he repeated and went to sit by his mother.

'The kid knows something,' Eve stated as they stepped outside.

'That would be my take. Maybe Alice felt more comfortable talking to him than other members of the family. They were pretty close in age. Brothers and sisters squabble, but they confide in each other.'

'I wouldn't know.' She started her car, pined for coffee. 'Where the hell do you live, Peabody?'

'Why?'

'I'll drop you at home. You can catch some sleep, report to Central at eleven.'

'Is that what you're going to do, catch some sleep?'

'Yeah.' That was probably a lie, but it served her purposes. 'Which way?'

'I live on Houston.'

Eve winced only a little. 'Well, if it's going to be inconvenient, it might as well be way inconvenient.' She headed south. 'Houston? Peabody, you bohemian.'

'It was my cousin's place. When she decided to move to Colorado and weave rugs, I took it over. Rent control.'

'A likely story. You probably spend all your free time hanging at poetry bars and performance art clubs.'

'Actually, I prefer the mating lounges. Better food.'

359

'You'd probably get more sex if you didn't think about it so much.'

'No, I tried that, too.' She yawned, abruptly and hugely. 'Sorry.'

'You're entitled. When you report in, check on the status of the autopsy. I want to be sure there's nothing weird in the tox report. And make sure to change out of that silly dress.'

Peabody shifted on her seat. 'It's not that silly. A couple guys at the Aquarian seemed to like it. So did Roarke.'

'Yeah, he mentioned it.'

Jaw dropped, Peabody swiveled her head. 'He did? Really?' *Foolishness*, Eve thought, *helped soothe*. 'He said something about you looking appealing. So I hit him. Just in case.'

'Appealing. Jesus.' Peabody patted her heart. 'I'm going to have to dig through some of the other stuff my mother's made for me. Appealing.' She sighed. 'Roarke doesn't have any brothers, cousins, uncles, does he?'

'As far as I know, Peabody, he's one of a kind.'

She found him dozing. Not in bed, but on the sofa in the sitting area of the master suite. The moment she stepped into the room, his eyes opened.

'You've had a long, rough one, Lieutenant.' He reached out a hand. 'Come here.'

'I'm going to grab a shower, some coffee. I've got some calls to make.'

He'd tagged onto the police scanner and knew exactly what she'd been dealing with. 'Come here,' he repeated, and closed his hand over hers when she reluctantly obliged. 'Are the calls going to make any difference if you make them an hour from now?'

'No, but—'

So he tugged until she tumbled onto the sofa with him. Because her struggle was only halfhearted, he managed to snuggle her down beside him quickly. And wrapping an arm around her, he kissed her hair. 'Sleep a little,' he said quietly. 'There's no need to exhaust yourself.'

'She was so young, Roarke.'

'I know. Close it off, just for a little while.'

'The data? Frank's log. Did you find anything?'

'We'll talk about it after you sleep.'

'An hour. Just an hour.' Linking her fingers with his, she let herself go under.

Chapter Five

Sleep helped. So did the hot shower and the food Roarke ordered up. Eve shoveled eggs into her mouth as she studied the data he'd unearthed on-screen.

'More like a diary than an investigative log,' she decided. 'Lots of personal comments, and obviously he was worried about Alice. *"I'm not sure how deeply they've influenced her mind, or hurt her heart."* He was thinking like a grandfather, not like a cop. You got this off his home unit?'

'Yes. He had it coded and passkeyed. I suspect he didn't want his wife stumbling across it.'

'If he had it coded, how did you access?'

Roarke took a cigarette from a carved box, studied it. 'You don't really want me to explain that, do you? Lieutenant?'

'No.' Eve forked up more eggs. 'Guess not. Still, his personal thoughts and worries aren't going to be a lot of help. I need to know what he found out, and how far his private investigation went before he died.'

'There's more.' Roarke scrolled over dates. 'There, he talks about tailing Selina Cross, and lists some of her . . . associates.'

'But there's nothing there. He suspects she's dealing illegals. He believes she's holding unacceptable ceremonies in her club and perhaps her home. He observes suspicious characters coming and going, but he bases it all on emotion. No facts. Frank had been off the streets too long.' Eve set her plate aside and rose. 'If he didn't want to involve cops, why the hell didn't he at least hire a PI to handle the legwork? What's this?'

Frowning, she stepped closer to the screen.

I think she made me. Can't be sure, but it's almost as though she's leading me along now. I'm going to have to make a move soon. Alice is terrified, begging me to stay away from Cross, and from her. The poor kid spends too much time with that Isis character. Isis may be a harmless weirdo, but she can't be a good influence on Alice. I've told Sally I'm working late. Tonight, I'm going in. Cross spends Thursday nights at the club. The apartment should be empty. If I can get inside and find anything, anything at all to prove Alice saw a child murdered, I can report to Whitney anonymously. She's going to pay for what she and her filthy lover did to my little girl. One way or the other, she's going to pay.

'Christ, nighttime breaking and entering, illegal search and seizure.' Frustrated, Eve dragged both hands through her hair. 'What the hell was he thinking? He had to know that anything he found would get tossed out in court. He'd never nail them this way.'

'I have a feeling he wasn't worried about court, Eve. He wanted justice.'

'And now he's dead, isn't he? And so's Alice. Where's the rest?'

Roarke scrolled to the last entry.

Security's too tight on the building, couldn't get through it. I've been off the streets too damn long. I may have to tag someone to help me on this after all. I'm going to see that witch pays if it's the last thing I do.

'That's all on this – that entry was logged on the night before he died. There may be more, under a different code.'

So, he hadn't made her pay, Eve thought. *And he hadn't had time to get help. Not enough time*, she thought again with twin surges of relief and sorrow. The entries went a long way toward clearing both Frank and Feeney.

'But you don't think so. You don't think there's anything else.'

'No, I don't. There's the timing, of course. And he wasn't that clever with electronics,' Roarke explained. 'It was child's play to find this. Still, we'll look. It'll take some time to break through if there's anything there. And it'll have to be later. I have several meetings this morning.'

She turned to him. Odd, she realized, she'd forgotten for a moment he wasn't working with her. His business and the direction of it was in a much different sphere from hers. 'So many billions, so little time.'

'How true. But I should be able to fiddle a bit more this evening.'

She knew he hadn't so much as glanced at the stock reports or taken the morning calls that never failed to come in daily. 'I'm taking up a lot of your time.'

'You are, indeed.' He came around the console, leaned back against it. 'And the payment will be your time, Lieutenant. A day or two away when we can both manage it.' Then his smile faded. He took her hand, ran his thumb over the carving on her wedding ring. 'Eve, I don't like to interfere with your work, but I'll ask you to be particularly careful in this matter.'

'A good cop's always careful.'

'No,' Roarke said, looking into her eyes, 'she's not. She's courageous, she's smart, she's driven, but she's not always careful.'

'Don't worry, I've dealt with worse than Selina Cross.' She kissed him lightly. 'I've got to go in, check on some reports. I'll try to let you know if I'm going to be late.'

'Do that,' he murmured, and watched her go.

She was wrong, he mused. He doubted very much if she'd

ever dealt with worse than Selina Cross. And he had no intention of letting her deal with it alone. Moving to the 'link, Roarke called his assistant and arranged to have all his off-planet and out-of-town trips for the next month canceled.

He intended to stay very close to home. And his wife.

'No drugs,' Eve stated as she looked over the toxicology report on Alice. 'No alcohol. She wasn't under the influence. But you heard her talking to someone who wasn't there, and she runs out into the path of an oncoming cab. She's worked herself up into a state of terror, then was triggered by the chanting on the phone. They knew how to get to her, how to manipulate her.'

'It's not illegal to chant over a 'link.'

'No.' Eve considered. 'But is it illegal to threaten to harm over a public transmitter.'

'That's reaching,' Peabody returned. 'And it's only a misdemeanor.'

'It's a start. If we manage to tie the transmission to Selina Cross, we can hassle her. In any case, I think it's time we met. How about a little trip to Hell, Peabody?'

'I've been dying to go.'

'Who isn't?' But before she could rise, Feeney burst into her office. His eyes were shadowed, his face unshaven.

'Why are you primary on Alice's case? A traffic accident. Why the hell is a homicide lieutenant handling a traffic fatality?'

'Feeney—'

'She was my goddaughter. You didn't even call me. I heard it on the goddamn news.'

'I'm sorry. I didn't know. Sit down, Feeney.'

He jerked away when she touched his arm. 'I don't need to sit down. I want answers, Dallas. I want some fucking answers.'

'Peabody,' Eve murmured, and waited until her aide had

gone out and closed the door. 'I am sorry, Feeney, I didn't know you were her godfather. I spoke to her mother and her brother, and simply assumed they would let the rest of the family know.'

'Brenda's under sedation,' Feeney tossed out. 'What the hell do you expect? She lost her father and her daughter within days of each other. Jamie's only sixteen. By the time he called a doctor and saw to his mother, got a hold of Sally, I'd already heard it on-screen. Jesus, Jesus, she was just a kid.'

He turned away, pulled at his hair. 'I used to give her piggyback rides, sneak her candy.'

This was what it was like to lose someone you loved, she thought. And was grateful she loved so few. 'Please sit down, Feeney. You shouldn't have come in today.'

'I said I don't need to sit down.' His voice leveled as he turned back to study her. 'I want an answer, Dallas. Why are you on Alice's accident?'

She couldn't afford to hesitate, couldn't afford not to lie. 'Peabody was a witness,' she began, grateful she could give him that much. 'She was on a free evening, and she'd been to a club. She saw the accident. It shook her, Feeney, and she called me. It was knee-jerk, I guess. I couldn't be sure what had happened, so I told her to relay to Dispatch, to secure the scene, and I responded. Since I had, and I had all the data, I notified next of kin. I figured it would be easier on the family if I handled it.' She moved her shoulders, bitterly ashamed at using old friends. 'I thought it was the least I could do, for Frank.'

He never took his eyes off her face. 'Is that all of it?'

'What else is there? Listen, I just got the tox report. She wasn't using, Feeney. She wasn't drunk. Maybe she was still upset about Frank, or something else. I don't know. Could be she didn't even see the damn cab. It was a lousy night, fog, rain.'

'The bastard was speeding, wasn't he?'

366

'No.' She couldn't give him anyone to blame, couldn't offer even that prickly comfort. 'He was within the limit. His record's clean, and so was the on-site drug and alcohol. Feeney, she bolted out in front of him, and there was nothing he could do. I want you to understand that. I talked with the driver myself, and I investigated the scene. It wasn't his fault. It wasn't anyone's.'

It had to be someone's, he thought. He couldn't lose two people back to back for no reason. 'I want to talk to Peabody.'

'Give her a little time, will you?' Layers of guilt added onto the burden she already carried. 'It really wrecked her. I'd really like to keep her focused on something else until she settles with it.'

He drew a deep breath, shuddered it out. Beneath his tearing grief was gratitude that someone he trusted would care for his godchild. 'You'll close it then, personally? And give me all the data?'

'I'll close it, Feeney. I promise you.'

He nodded, rubbed his hands over his face. 'Okay. I'm sorry I jumped you.'

'It's all right. It doesn't matter.' She hesitated, then put her hand on his arm, squeezed lightly. 'Go home, Feeney. You don't want to be here today.'

'I guess I will.' He put a hand on the door. 'She was a sweetheart, Dallas,' he said quietly. 'My God, I don't want to go to another funeral.'

When he left, Eve sank into her chair. Misery and guilt and anger twisted around her throat like barbs. She rose again, grabbed her bag. She was, she told herself, in the perfect mood to meet Selina Cross.

'How do you want to play it?' Peabody asked as they pulled up in front of an elegant old building downtown.

'Straight. I want her to know Alice talked to me, and that I

367

suspect her of harassment, dealing, and conspiracy to murder. If she's got any brains, she'll know I don't have anything solid. But I'll give her something to think about.'

Eve stepped out of the car, ran her gaze over the building with its carved glass windows and grinning gargoyles. 'She lives here, she's not hurting financially. We're going to have to find out just where she gets her money. I want everything on record, Peabody, and keep your eyes open. I want your impressions.'

'I'll give you one right now.' Peabody clamped her recorder onto her uniform jacket, but kept her eyes on the topmost window of the building, a wide, round glass intricately carved. 'That's another inverted pentagram. Satanic symbol. And those gargoyles don't look friendly.' She smiled wanly. 'You ask me, they look hungry.'

'Impressions, Peabody. Try to keep the fantasies down to a minimum.' Eve approached the security screen.

'Please state your name and your business.'

'Lieutenant Eve Dallas and aide, NYPSD.' She held up her badge to be scanned. 'To see Selina Cross.'

'Are you expected?'

'Oh, I don't think she'll be surprised.'

'One moment.'

While she waited, Eve studied the street. There was plenty of pedestrian and vehicular traffic, she noted. But most of those who walked used the other side of the street, and many of those eyed her and the building warily.

Oddly, there wasn't a single glida grill or street hawker in sight.

'You are cleared to enter, Lieutenant. Please proceed to elevator one. It is already programmed.'

'Fine.' Eve looked up, caught the shadow of movement behind the topmost glass. 'Look official, Peabody,' she murmured as they approached the heavily grilled front doors. 'We're under observation.'

The grills slid back, locks snicked open. The light on a recessed security panel blinked from red to green. 'A lot of hardware for an apartment building,' Peabody commented, and ignoring the fluttering in her stomach, stepped in behind Eve.

Like a viewing parlor, the lobby area was heavily into red. A two-headed serpent slithered over the bloodred carpet, the gold threads of its eyes glinted as it watched a black-robed figure slice a curved knife over the throat of a white goat.

'Lovely art.' Eve lifted a brow as Peabody carefully picked her way around the snake. 'Wool doesn't bite.'

'You can't be too careful.' She glanced back as they stepped to the elevator. 'I really hate snakes. My brother used to catch them out in the woods and chase me with them. Always had a phobia.'

The ride up was smooth and fast, but it gave Eve enough time to detect yet another security camera in the small, black-mirrored car.

The doors opened into a spacious foyer with floors of black marble. Twin red velvet settees flanked an archway and boasted carved arms of snarling wolves. A floral arrangement speared out of a pot shaped like a boar's head.

'Wolfbane,' Peabody said quietly, 'belladonna, foxglove, skullcap, peyote.' She shrugged at Eve's considering look. 'My mother's an amateur botanist. I can tell you that's not your usual flower arrangement.'

'But the usual is so tedious, isn't it?'

They got their first face-to-face look at Selina Cross exactly as she wanted to be seen. Flanked by the archway in a snug black dress that brushed the floor, her feet bare with the toenails painted a violent red, she posed. And smiled.

Her skin was vampire white, the slash of red over her full lips glossy as fresh blood. Her eyes glittered green and feline in a narrow, undoubtedly witchlike face that wasn't beautiful, but was eerily compelling. Her hair fell, black against black, from that rigid center part, to her waist.

369

The hand she gestured with held rings on every finger and her thumb. A silver chain was attached to each and twisted into an intricate mesh over the back of her hand.

'Lieutenant Dallas and Officer Peabody, isn't it? What interesting visitors on such a dull day. Will you come in . . . to my parlor?'

'Are you alone, Ms Cross? It would simplify this if we could speak with Mr Alban as well.'

'Oh, what a shame.' She turned, silks whispering, and slipped through the arch. 'Alban's busy this morning. Sit down.' She gestured again, encompassing a generous room crowded with furniture. Every seat boasted the heads or claws or beaks of some predator. 'Can I offer you something?'

'We'll skip the refreshments.' Considering it apt, Eve chose a chair with the arms of a hound.

'Not even coffee? That is your drink, isn't it?' Then she shrugged, slicked a fingertip over the pentagram above her eyebrow. 'But suit yourself.' With that same studied skill, she lowered to a curved settee that stood on cloven feet and draped her long arms over the back. 'Now, what can I do for you?'

'Alice Lingstrom was killed early this morning.'

'Yes, I know.' She continued to smile pleasantly, as though discussing the nice run of weather. 'I could tell you I witnessed the . . . accident through my scrying mirror, but I doubt you'd believe that. Of course, I'm not one to disdain technology and often watch the news and other forms of entertainment on-screen. The information's been public for hours.'

'You knew her.'

'Of course; she was a pupil of mine for a time. A dissatisfactory one as it turned out. Alice complained to you about my tutelage.' It wasn't formed as a question, but she waited, as if for an answer.

'If you mean she reported to me that she was drugged, sexually abused, and was a witness to an atrocity, then yes, she complained.'

370

'Drugs, sex, and atrocities.' Selina let out a low, purring laugh. 'What an imagination our little Alice had. A shame she couldn't use it to broaden her vision. How is your imagination, Lieutenant Dallas?' She flicked the hand gloved with mesh. In the small marble fireplace, flames burst to life.

Peabody jolted, didn't manage to muffle a yelp, but neither woman acknowledged her. They continued to stare, unblinking at each other.

'Or may I call you Eve?'

'No. You can call me Lieutenant Dallas. It's a little warm for a fire, don't you think? And a bit early in the day for parlor tricks.'

'I like it warm. You have excellent nerves, Lieutenant.'

'I also have low tolerance for grifters and dealers and child killers.'

'Am I all of that?' Selina tapped her sharp red nails on the back of the settee, her only outward sign of annoyance in Eve's lack of response. 'Prove it.'

'I will. Where were you last night between the hours of one and three A.M.?'

'I was here, in my ritual room, with Alban and a young initiate we call Lobar. We were engaged in a private sexual ceremony from midnight until nearly dawn. Lobar is young and . . . enthusiastic.'

'I'll want to talk to them both.'

'You can contact Lobar any evening between eight and eleven at our club. As for Alban, I don't keep his schedule, but he is generally here or at the club most nights. Unless you believe in magic, Lieutenant, you're wasting your time. I could hardly have been here, fucking two very entertaining men, and out luring poor Alice to her death.'

'Is that what you consider yourself, a magician?' Eve glanced toward the still burning fire with a mild sneer. 'That's nothing more than trickery and distraction of the eye. You can be licensed to juggle on the streets for two thousand credits a year.'

Selina's muscles quivered as she sat forward. Her eyes were burning now, as the fire did. 'I am a high priestess of the dark lord. Our numbers are legion, and I have powers that would make you weep.'

'I don't cry easily, Ms Cross.' *Ah, a temper*, Eve thought with satisfaction. *And easily ruffled pride*. 'You're not dealing with an impressionable eighteen-year-old girl now, or her frightened grandfather. Which one of your legion called Alice last night and played a tape of chanting threats?'

'I have no idea what you're talking about. And you're beginning to bore me.'

'The black feather on the windowsill was a nice touch. Or simulated feather, I should say, but she wouldn't have known that. Are you into droid pets, Ms Cross?'

Idly, Selina lifted a hand, skimmed it through then down her hair. 'I don't care for . . . pets at all.'

'No? No cats and ravens?'

'How predictable that would be.'

'Alice believed you were a shape-shifter,' Eve said and watched as Selina smiled. 'Care to give us a demonstration of that little talent?'

Selina's nails began to tap again. Eve's tone was as insulting as a backhanded slap. 'I'm not here to entertain you. Or to be mocked by your small mind.'

'Is that what you call it? Were you entertaining Alice with cats and birds and threatening chants over her 'link? How could she feel safe in her own home? Was she such a threat to you?'

'She was nothing to me but an unfortunate failure.'

'You were seen selling illegals to Frank Wojinski.'

The abrupt switch had Selina blinking. When her lips curved now, the smile didn't reach her eyes. 'If that were true, we wouldn't be having this discussion here in my home, but in

Interview. I'm an herbalist, again licensed, and I often sell or trade perfectly legal substances.'

'Do you grow your herbs here?'

'As a matter of fact, I do, and distill my potions and medications.'

'I'd like to see them. Why don't you show me your work area?'

'You'll need a warrant for that, and we both know you haven't cause for one.'

'You're right. I guess that's why Frank didn't bother with a warrant.' Eve rose slowly, spoke softly. 'You knew he was onto you, but did you suspect he might get in here, inside? You didn't see that in your magic ball, did you?' Eve said when Selina's breath shortened and thickened. 'What would you think if I told you he was in your house, and he documented what he saw, and what he found.'

'You have nothing. Nothing.' Selina sprang to her feet. 'He was an aging man with slow wits and bad reflexes. I made him for a cop the first time he tried to tail me. He was never in my home. He told you nothing when he was alive, and he can't tell you anything now.'

'No? Don't you believe in talking to the dead, Ms Cross? I make my living at it.'

'And do you think I don't recognize smoke and mirrors, Lieutenant?' Her spectacular breasts strained against the material of her dress as she struggled to even her breathing. 'Alice was a foolish girl who believed she could flirt with dark forces, then run back to her pathetic white magic and tidy little family. She paid the price for her ignorance and her cowardice. But not at my hand. I have nothing more to say to you.'

'That'll do for now. Peabody?' She started toward the archway. 'Your fire's going out, Ms Cross,' she said mildly. 'Pretty soon you're going to have nothing but a mess of ashes.'

Selina stood where she was, shaking with rage. When the

door closed and security engaged, she balled her hands into fists and screamed with temper.

A panel on the wall slid open. The man who stepped out was tall and golden. His chest gleamed and rippled with muscle. The tattoo over his heart was of a horned goat. He wore only an open black robe carelessly belted at the waist with silver cord.

'Alban.' Selina ran to him, threw her arms around him.

'There, my love.' His voice was deep, soothing. On the hand that stroked her hair was a large silver ring carved with an inverted pentagram. 'You mustn't unbalance your chakras.'

'Fuck my chakras.' She was weeping now, wildly, pounding on him like a child in a blind tantrum. 'I hate her. I hate her. She has to be punished.'

With a sigh, he let her go to storm the room, cursing, smashing crockery. He knew the temper would pass more quickly if he stood back and let it purge.

'I want her dead, Alban. Dead. I want her to suffer agonies, to scream for mercy, to bleed and writhe and bleed. She insulted me. She challenged me. She all but laughed in my face.'

'She doesn't believe, Selina. She has no vision.'

Exhausted as always after a fit of temper, she collapsed on the settee. 'Cops. I've hated them all my life.'

'I know.' He picked up a tall, slim bottle, poured her some thick, cloudy liquid. 'We'll have to be careful with her. She's very high-profile.' He passed her a chalice. 'But we'll think of something, won't we?'

'Of course we will.' She smiled again, sipped slowly at the brew. 'Something very special. The master would want something . . . inventive in her case.' Now she laughed, full-throated, head thrown back. The police had been the bane of her existence – until she'd discovered a higher power. 'We'll make a believer out of her, won't we, Alban?'

'She'll believe.'

She drank deeply now, felt the lovely haze coat her tangled emotions. And let the chalice drop. 'Come here, and take me.' Eyes glittering, she slid down. 'Force me.'

And when he covered her body with his, she turned her head, bared her teeth, and dug them into his shoulder to draw blood.

'Hurt me,' she demanded.

'With pleasure.' he replied.

And when they lay apart, their violent passion sated, he lay quiet beside her. She would revive now, he knew. She would cool and she would calm, and she would think.

'We should preform a ceremony tonight. Call together the entire coven for a Black Mass. We need power, Alban. She isn't weak, and she wants to destroy us.'

'She won't.' With affection now, he stroked her cheek. 'She can't. After all, she's only a cop with no past and a limited future. But you're right, of course, we'll call the coven. We'll perform the rite. And, I think, we'll provide Lieutenant Dallas with a distraction – or two. She won't have the time or inclination to worry overmuch about little Alice for long.'

Fresh arousal rippled through her, a dark wave that flooded into her eyes. 'Who dies?'

'My love.' He lifted her, speared her, sighed when her muscles clamped viciously around him. 'You have only to choose.'

'You really pissed her off.' Peabody struggled to ignore the light sweat of fear that dried on her skin as Eve drove away from the building.

'That was the idea. Now that I know control isn't her strong point, I'll be sure to piss her off again. She's all ego,' Eve decided. 'Imagine, thinking we'd fall for a second-rate trick like the fire.'

'Yeah.' Peabody managed a sickly smile. 'Imagine.'

Eve tucked her tongue in her cheek and decided against

ragging on her aide. 'Since we're into witches, let's swing by and check out this Isis at Spirit Quest.' She slid her eyes right. Well, maybe she'd rag just a little. 'You can probably buy a talisman or some herbs,' she said solemnly. 'You know, to ward off evil.'

Peabody shifted in her seat. Feeling foolish wasn't nearly as bad as worrying about being cursed. 'Don't think I won't.'

'After we deal with Isis, we can grab a pizza sub – with plenty of garlic.'

'Garlic's for vampires.'

'Oh. We can have Roarke get us a couple of his antique guns. With silver bullets.'

'Werewolves, Dallas.' Amused at both of them now, Peabody rolled her eyes. 'A lot of good you're going to do if we have to defend ourselves against witchcraft.'

'What does it to witches, then?'

'I don't know,' Peabody admitted. 'But I'm damn sure going to find out.'

Chapter Six

Shopping wasn't something Eve considered one of the small pleasures in life. She wasn't a browser, a window shopper, or a electronic catalogue surfer. She avoided, whenever possible, the shops and boutiques in, above, and below Manhattan. She shuddered at the very thought of a trip to one of the sky malls.

She imagined her outward resistance to the consumption of merchandise was the primary reason Isis pegged her as a cop the minute she stepped into Spirit Quest.

As stores went, Eve considered it tolerable. She wasn't interested in the crystals and cards, the statues and candles, even though they were attractively displayed. The background music was soft, more of a murmur than a tune, and the light was allowed to play over the edges of raw crystals and polished stones in pretty rainbows.

The place smelled, she thought, not offensively of forest.

If witches were what she was dealing with, Eve decided, Isis and Selina couldn't have been more dramatically opposed in appearance. Selina had been pale and slim and feline. Isis was an exotic amazon of a female with gypsy curls of flaming red, round black eyes, and cheekbones that could have carved wood. Her skin was the soft gold of a mixed-race heritage, her features bold and broad. Eve measured her at just over six feet and a well-packed and curvy one-seventy.

She wore a loose, flowing robe of blinding white with a belt studded with rough stones. Her right arm was wound with gold coils from elbow to shoulder, and her large hands winked and flashed with as many as a dozen rings.

'Welcome.' The voice suited her, oddly accented and throaty. Her lips curved, but it was a smile of grieving rather than pleasure. 'Alice's cop.'

Eve lifted a brow as she took out her shield. She figured she looked like a cop. And, since Roarke, her face had been in the media relentlessly. 'Dallas. You'd be Isis, then?'

'I would. You'll wish to talk. Excuse me.' She walked to the door. Graceful, Eve observed, the way an athlete is graceful. She turned an old-fashioned hand-lettered sign to Closed, pulled the shade over the glass of the door, and flicked a thumb latch.

When she turned back, her eyes were intense, her mouth grim. 'You bring dark shadows into my light. She clings – such a stench.' At Eve's narrowed look, she inclined her head. 'Selina. One moment.'

She went to a wide shelf and began to light candles and cones of incense. 'To purify and shield, to protect and defend. You have shadows of your own, Dallas.' She smiled briefly at Peabody. 'And not just your aide.'

'I'm here to talk about Alice.'

'Yes, I know. And you're impatient with what you see as my foolish window dressing. I don't mind. Every religion should be open to questions and change. Will you sit?'

She gestured to a corner where two chairs flanked a round table etched with symbols. Again, she smiled at Peabody. 'I can get another chair from the back for you.'

'No problem. I'll stand.' She couldn't help it; her gaze traveled the room, lingering now and then wistfully on some pretty bauble.

'Please feel free to browse.'

'We're not here to shop.' Eve took a seat, shot Peabody a withering glance. 'When did you last see or speak with Alice?'

'On the night she died.'

378

'At what time?'

'I believe it was about two A.M. She was already dead,' Isis added, folding her large, beautiful hands.

'You saw her after she was dead.'

'Her spirit came to me. You find this foolish; I understand. But I can only tell you what is, and was. I was asleep, and I awoke. She was there, beside the bed. I knew we'd lost her. She feels she's failed. Herself, her family, me. Her spirit is restless and full of grief.'

'Her body's dead, Isis. That's my concern.'

'Yes.' Isis picked up a smooth, rose-colored stone from the table, worried it in her hand. 'Even for me, with my beliefs, it's difficult to accept her death. So young, so bright.' The huge, dark eyes swam. 'I loved her very much, as you would a younger sister. But it wasn't meant for me to save her in this life. Her spirit will return, be reborn. I know we'll meet again.'

'Fine. Let's concentrate on this life. And this death.'

Isis blinked back the tears and managed a quick, genuine smile. 'How tedious you must find all of this. You have such a logical mind. I want to help you, Dallas, for Alice. For myself, perhaps for yourself as well. I recognize you.'

'I gathered that.'

'No, from another time. Another place. Another plane.' She spread her hands. 'I last saw Alice alive on the day of her grandfather's memorial service. She blamed herself, was determined to make an atonement. She'd strayed for a time, been misled, but she had a strong and bright heart. Her family was dear to her. And she was afraid, desperately afraid of what Selina would do to her – body and soul.'

'You know Selina Cross?'

'Yes. We've met.'

'In this life?' Eve asked dryly, and made Isis smile again.

'In this life, and others. She's no threat to me, but she is dangerous. She seduces the weak, the confused, and those who prefer her way.'

'Her claims to be a witch—'

'She is no witch.' Isis drew her shoulders back, lifted her head. 'We who embrace the craft do so in the light and live by an unbreakable code. *And it harm none*. She used what pitiful power she has to call on the dark, to exploit its violence, its ugliness. We know what evil is, Dallas. We've both seen it. Whatever form it takes doesn't change its basic nature.'

'We can agree on that. Why would she harm Alice?'

'Because she could. Because she would enjoy it. There's no question that she's responsible for this death. You won't find it easy to prove it. You won't give up.' Isis kept her eyes on Eve's, looking long, looking deep. 'Selina will be surprised and infuriated by your tenacity, your strength. Death offends you, and the death of the young cuts small slices from your heart. You remember too well, but not all. You weren't born Eve Dallas, but you've become her, and she you. When you stand by the dead, stand for the dead, nothing moves you aside. His death was necessary for your life.'

'Stop,' Eve ordered.

'Why should it haunt you?' Isis's breathing was slow and thick, her eyes dark and clear. 'The choice was made correctly. Innocence was lost, but strength took its place. For some, it must be so. You'll need all before this cycle passes. A wolf, a boar, and a silver blade. Fire, smoke, and death. Trust the wolf, slay the boar, and live.'

Abruptly, she blinked. Her eyes clouded as she lifted a hand to press fingers to her temple. 'I'm sorry. I didn't intend—' She let out a quiet moan, squeezed her eyes shut. 'Headache. Vicious. Excuse me one minute.' She got shakily to her feet and hurried into the back.

'Jesus. Dallas, this is getting way too weird. Do you know what she was talking about?'

'His death was necessary for your life.' Her father, Eve thought, fighting off a shudder. A cold room, a dark night, and blood on the knife clutched in a desperate child's hand.

'No, it's just jibberish.' Her palms were damp, infuriating her. 'These people figure they have to pull out some magic tricks to keep us interested.'

'I studied at the Kijinsky Institute in Prague,' Isis said as she stepped back into the room. 'And was studied.' She set a small cup aside, managed a smile as the headache eased. 'My psychic abilities are documented – for those who need documentation. But I apologize, Dallas. I didn't intend to drift in that manner. It's very rare for it to happen without my consciously controlling it.'

She came back to sit as she spoke, spread the skirts of her robe gracefully. 'It would be sheer hell to be privy to thoughts and memories without some power to control and block. I don't like to pry into personal thoughts. And it hurts,' she added, gently rubbing her temple again. 'I want to help you do what Alice wanted, so she can rest. I want, for personal and selfish reasons, to see Selina pay the proper price for what she's responsible for. I'll do whatever I can, whatever you'll allow me to do, to help you.'

Trust didn't come easily for Eve, and she would check very thoroughly into Isis's background. But for now, she'd use her. 'Tell me what you know about Selina Cross.'

'I know she's a woman without conscience or morals. I would think your term would be *sociopath*, but I find that too simple and too clean for what she is. I prefer the more direct term of *evil*. She's a clever woman with a skill for reading weaknesses. As for her power, what she can read or see or do, I can't say.'

'What about Alban?'

'About him I know next to nothing. She keeps him close. I assume he's her lover and she finds him useful or she would have – dispatched him by now.'

'This club of hers?'

Isis smiled thinly. 'I don't frequent such . . . establishments.'

'But you know of it?'

'One hears rumors, gossip.' She lifted her broad shoulders.

'Dark ceremonies, Black Masses, the drinking of blood, human sacrifice. Rape, murder, infanticide, the calling up of demons.' Then she sighed. 'But then, you might hear such talk about Wiccans from those who have no understanding of the craft and who see black draped crones and eye of newt when they think of witches.'

'Alice claimed to have seen a child murdered.'

'Yes, and I believe she did. She couldn't have invented such a thing. She was in shock and ill when she came to me.' Isis pressed her lips together, shuddered out a breath. 'I did what I could for her.'

'Such as encouraging her to report the incident to the police?'

'That was for her to decide.' Isis lifted her chin again, met the iced anger in Eve's eyes. 'I was more concerned with her emotional and spiritual survival. The child was already lost; I had hoped to save Alice from the same fate.' Her eyes dropped now, and dampened. 'And I regret, bitterly, that I didn't act differently. And that, in the end, I failed her. Perhaps it was pride.' She looked at Eve again. 'You'd understand the power and the deception of personal pride. I thought I could handle it, that I was wise enough, strong enough. I was wrong. So, Dallas, to atone, I'll do anything you ask, avail you of all knowledge and any power the goddess grants me.'

'Information will do.' Eve angled her head. 'Selina treated us to a little demonstration of what she'd call power. It impressed Peabody.'

'It caught me off guard,' Peabody muttered, studying Isis warily. She didn't think she was up for another demonstration. To Peabody's surprise, and Eve's, Isis threw back her magnificent head and laughed. It was like hearing silver buoys clang in pearly fog.

'Should I call up the wind?' With one hand pressed to her breast, she chuckled. 'Summon the dead, strike the cold fire? Really, Dallas, you believe in none of that, so it would be a waste of my time and energy. But perhaps you'd be interested

382

in observing one of our gatherings. We have one at the end of next week. I can arrange it.'

'I'll think about it.'

'You smirk,' Isis said lightly, 'yet the pledge you wear on your finger carries the ancient symbol of protection.'

'What?'

'Your wedding ring, Dallas.' With that quiet smile, Isis lifted Eve's left hand. 'It's carved with an old Celtic design for protection.'

Baffled, Eve studied the pretty etching in the slim gold ring. 'It's just a design.'

'It's a very specific and powerful one, to give the wearer protection from harm.' Amused, she raised her brows. 'I see you didn't know. Is it so surprising, really? Your husband has the blood of the Celts, and you lead a very precarious life. Roarke loves you very much, and you wear the symbol of it.'

'I prefer facts to superstitions,' Eve said and rose.

'As you should,' Isis agreed. 'But you will be welcome at the next gathering, should you choose to attend. Roarke will also be welcome.' She smiled at Peabody. 'And your aide. Will you accept a gift?'

'It's against the rules.'

'And rules are to be respected.' Rising, Isis moved behind a display counter, took out a small, clear bowl with a wide lip. 'Then perhaps you will buy this. I have, after all, lost potential business by closing to speak to you. Twenty dollars.'

'Fair enough.' Eve dug into her pocket for credits. 'What is it?'

'We'll call it a worry bowl. In this you place all your pain, your sorrow, your worries. Set it aside and sleep without shadows.'

'Such a deal.' Eve set the credits on the counter and waited for Isis to wrap the bowl in protective paper.

Eve got home early, a rarity. She thought she could dive into work in the quiet of her home office. She could get past

Summerset easily enough, she mused as she pulled up at the end of the drive. The butler would simply sniff and ignore her. She'd have a couple of hours clear to run data on Isis and to contact Dr Mira's office and make an appointment with the psychiatrist. It would, Eve decided, be interesting to get Mira's take on personalities such as Selina Cross and Isis.

Eve got no farther than the front door when her plans disintegrated.

Music pounded, blasting out of the front parlor like compact nuclear explosions. Staggering against the waves, Eve slapped her hands over her ears and shouted.

She didn't have to be told it was Mavis. No one else in her sphere would play clashing, discordant notes at that decibel. When she reached the doorway, the volume was still revved high. Her shouted demands reached neither the remote nor the single occupant of the room.

Alone, decked out in a micro robe of searing magenta that echoed the spiral curls shooting out of her head, Mavis Freestone lounged on the couch, doing the impossible. She slept like a baby.

'Jesus Christ.' Since vocal commands were useless, Eve risked her eardrums and dropped her hands to fumble with the recessed control unit. 'Off, off, off!' She shouted stabbing buttons. The noise shut down in midblast and made her moan.

Mavis's eyes popped open. 'Hey, how's it going?'

'What?' Eve shook her head to try to dispel the high-pitched ringing. 'What?'

'That was a new group I picked up this morning. Mayhem. Pretty decent.'

'What?'

With a chuckle, Mavis unfolded her neat little body and bounced to a cabinet. 'Looks like you could use a drink, Dallas. I must have zoned. Up pretty late the last few nights. Wanted to talk to you – about stuff.'

384

'Your mouth is moving,' Eve observed. 'Are you talking to me?'

'It wasn't that loud. Have a drink. Summerset said it would be all right if I hung for awhile. Didn't know when you'd check in.'

For reasons that eluded Eve, the stiff-necked butler appeared to have a major crush on Mavis. 'He's probably in his cage, composing odes to your legs.'

'Hey, it's nothing sexual. He just likes me. So.' Mavis clunked her glass against Eve's. 'Roarke's not around, right?'

'With that music blasting?' Eve snorted, sipped. 'Figure it out.'

'Well, that's good, because I wanted to roll it out with you.' But she sat, twisted the glass in her hands, and said nothing.

'What's the problem? You and Leonardo have a fight or something?'

'No, no. You can't really fight with Leonardo. He's too sweet. He's in Milan for a few days. Some fashion deal.'

'Why didn't you go with him?' Eve sat, rested her booted feet on the priceless coffee table, crossed her ankles.

'I've got the gig at the Down and Dirty. I wouldn't let Crack down after he bailed me.'

'Hmm.' Eve rolled her shoulders and began to relax. Mavis's career as a performer – it was difficult to use the term *singer* when defining Mavis's talents – was moving along. There had been some serious roadblocks, but they'd been overcome. 'I didn't figure you'd work there much longer. Not with a recording contract.'

'Yeah, well, that's the thing. The contract. You know, after finding out Jess was using me – and you and Roarke – for his mind games, I didn't figure the demo I'd cut with him would go anywhere.'

'It was good, Mavis; flashy, unique. That's why it got picked up.'

'Is it?' She rose again, a tiny woman with wild hair. 'I found out today that Roarke owns the recording company that offered the contract.' Gulping her drink, she paced away. 'I know we go back a ways, Dallas, a long ways, and I appreciate you putting Roarke up to it, but I don't feel right about it. I wanted to thank you.' She turned then, her silver eyes tragic and bleak. 'And tell you that I'm going to turn it down.'

Eve pursed her lips. 'Mavis, I don't know what the hell you're talking about. Are you telling me that Roarke, the guy who lives here, is producing your disc?'

'It's his company. Eclectic. It produces everything from classical to brain drain. It's *the* company. Totally mag, which was why I was so wired up about the deal.'

Eclectic, Eve mused. *The company*. It sounded just like him. 'I don't know anything about it. I didn't ask him to do anything, Mavis.'

She blinked, lowered slowly to the arm of a chair. 'You didn't? Solid?'

'I didn't ask,' Eve repeated, 'and he didn't tell me.' Which was also just like him. 'I'd have to say that if his company is offering you a contract, it's because Roarke, or whoever he's put in charge of that stuff, figures you're worth it.'

Mavis took slow breaths. She'd worked herself up to the selfless sacrifice, unwilling to take advantage of friendship. Now she teetered. 'Maybe he arranged it, like a favor.'

Eve cocked a brow. 'Roarke's business is business. I'd say he figures you're going to make him richer. And if he did do it as a favor, which I doubt, then you'll just have to prove to him that you're worth it. Won't you, Mavis?'

'Yeah.' She let out a long breath. 'I'm going to kick ass, you wait and see.' Her smile beamed out. 'Maybe you could come by the D and D tonight. I've got some new material, and Roarke could get another close-up of his latest investment.'

'Have to pass tonight. I've got work. I've got to check out The Athame.'

Mavis grimaced. 'What the hell are you going there for? Nasty place.'

'You know it?'

'Only by rep, and the rep's down below bad news.'

'Someone I've got to talk to there, connected with a case I'm working on.' She considered. There was no one she knew more likely to have a line on the unusual. 'Know any witches, Mavis?'

'Yeah, sort of. A couple of servers down at the Blue Squirrel were into it. Brushed a few way back when I was on the grift.'

'You believe in that stuff? Chanting and spells and palm reading?'

Mavis cocked her head and looked thoughtful. 'It's major bullshit.'

'You never fail to surprise me,' Eve decided. 'I figured you'd be into it.'

'I ran a con once. Spirit guide. I was Ariel, reincarnation of a fairy queen. You'd be amazed how many straights paid up for me to contact their dead relatives or tell them their future.'

To demonstrate, she let her head fall back. Her eyes fluttered, her mouth went slack. Slowly, her arms lifted, palms turned up. 'I feel a presence, strong, seeking, sorrowful.' Her voice had deepened, attained a faint accent. 'There are dark forces working against you. They hide from you, wait to do harm. Beware.'

She dropped her arms and grinned. 'So, you tell the mark you need to have trust in order to offer protection from the dark forces. All they have to do is put say, a thousand cash – cash is all that works – in an envelope. Seal it. You make sure you tell them to seal it with this special wax you're going to sell them. Then you're going to do this cool chant over it, and bury the envelope in a secret place under the dark of the moon. After the moon's cycled, you'll dig up the envelope and give it back. The dark forces will have been vanquished.'

'That's it? People just hand over the money?'

'Well, you string it out a little longer, do some research so you can hit them with names and events and shit. But basically, yeah. People want to believe.'

'Why?'

'Because life can really suck.'

Yes, Eve thought when she was alone agian, she supposed it could. Hers certainly had for long stretches of time. Now she was living in a mansion with a man who, for some reason, loved her. She didn't always understand her life or the man who now shared it, but she was adjusting. So well, in fact, that she decided not to go bury herself in work, but to go outside, into the golden autumn evening and take an hour for herself.

She was used to streets and sidewalks, crowded skyglides, jammed people movers. The sheer space Roarke could command always astonished her. His grounds were like a well-tended park, quiet and lush, with the foliage of rich man's trees in the dazzling flame of fall. The scents were of spicy flowers, the faintly smoky fragrance of October in the country.

Overhead, the sky was nearly empty of traffic, and even that was a dignified hum. No rumbling airbuses or lumbering tourist blimps over Roarke's land.

And the world she knew, and that knew her, was beyond the gates and over the walls, in the seamy dark.

Here she could forget that for a short time. Forget New York existed with its death and its anger – and its perpetually appealing arrogance. She needed the quiet and the air. As she walked over thick, green grass, she worried the ring with its odd symbols on her finger.

On the north side of the house was an arbor of thin, somehow fluid iron. The vines twisting and tumbling over it were smothered with flowers wildly red. She had married him there, in an old, traditional ceremony where vows were exchanged and promises made. A ceremony, she thought now. A rite that included music, flowers, witnesses, words that were repeated time after time, place after place, century through century.

And so, she thought, other ceremonies were preserved and repeated and believed to hold power. Back to Cain and Abel, she mused. One had planted crops, the other tended a flock. And both had offered sacrifice. One had been accepted, the other dismissed. Thus, she imagined, some would say good and evil were born. Because each needed the balance and challenge of the other.

So it continued. Science and logic disproved, but the rites continued, incense and chanting, offerings and the drinking of wine that symbolized blood.

And the sacrifice of the innocent.

Annoyed with herself, she rubbed her hands over her face. Philosophizing was foolish and useless. Murder had been done by human force. And it was human force that would dispense justice. That was, after all, the ultimate balance of good and evil.

She sat on the ground under the arbor of bloodred blossoms and drew in the burning scent of evening.

'This isn't usual for you.' Roarke came up quietly behind her – so quietly, her heart gave a quick trip before he settled on the grass beside her. 'Communing with nature?'

'Maybe I spent too much time inside today.' She had to smile when he handed her one of the red flowers. She twirled it in her fingers, watched it spin before she looked over at him.

He was relaxed, his dark hair skimming his shoulders, as he leaned back on his elbows, legs stretched out, feet crossed at the ankles. She imagined his pricey and beautiful suit would pick up grass stains that would horrify Summerset. He smelled male, and expensive. Lust curled comfortably in her stomach.

'Successful day?' she asked.

'We'll have bread on the table another day or two.'

She flicked her fingers at the ends of his hair. 'It's not the money, is it? It's the making it.'

'Oh, it's the money.' His eyes laughed at her. 'And the

389

making it.' In a quick move she told herself she should have seen coming, he reached up, cupped the back of her neck, and overbalanced her onto him and into a hot kiss.

'Hold on.'

She didn't squirm quickly enough and ended up under him.

'I am.'

His mouth fastened greedily on her throat and sent little licks of heat straight down her body to her toes.

'I want to talk to you.'

'Okay, you talk while I get you out of these clothes. Still wearing your weapon,' he observed as he hit the release for the harness. 'Thinking of zapping some wildlife?'

'That's against city ordinance. Roarke.' She caught his wrist as his hand closed sneakily over her breast. 'I want to talk to you.'

'I want to make love with you. Let's see who wins.'

It should have infuriated her, the fact that he already had her shirt open and her breasts aching. Then his mouth closed over that sensitive flesh and had her eyes all but crossing in pleasure. Still, it wouldn't do to let him win too easily.

She let her body go limp, moaned, and combed her fingers through his hair, ran them over his shoulders. 'Your jacket,' she murmured and tugged at it. When he shifted to shrug free, she had him.

It was a basic tenet of hand-to-hand. Never lower your guard. She scissored, shoved, and pinned him with a knee to the crotch and an elbow to the throat.

'You're tricky.' He calculated he could dislodge the elbow, but the knee . . . There were some things a man didn't care to risk. He kept his eyes on hers and slowly, carefully skimmed his fingertips up her bare torso, circled her breast. 'I admire that in a woman.'

'You're easy.' His thumb brushed lightly over her nipple, quickening her breath. 'I admire that in a man.'

'Well, you've got me now.' He unsnapped her waistband, teased her stomach muscles to quiver. 'Be kind.'

She grinned, levered her elbow away to brace her hands on either side of his head. 'I don't think so.' Lowering her head, she caught his mouth with hers.

She heard his breath suck in, felt his arms come around her, fingers digging in. His groan thundered through her pulse.

'Your knee,' he managed.

'Hmm?' Lust was full-blown now and raging. She shifted lips and teeth to his throat.

'Your knee, darling.' She moved to attack his ear and nearly unmanned him. 'It's very effective.'

'Oh, sorry.' Snorting, she lowered her knee, lowered her body, and let him roll her over. 'Forgot.'

'A likely story. You may have caused permanent damage.'

'Aw.' With a wicked grin, she tugged open his trousers. 'I bet we can make it all better.'

His eyes went dark when she stroked him, stayed open and on hers when their lips met again. This kiss, surprisingly tender, twined that terrifyingly strong emotion with the easy lust.

The lower edges of the sky were as wildly red as the blossoms arching over them. The shadows were long and soft. She could hear birdsong and the whisper of air through the dying leaves. The touch of his hands on her was like a miracle, chasing away all the ugliness and pain of the world she walked in.

She didn't even know she needed to be soothed, he thought as he stroked, and he soothed, so that arousal was slow and warm and liquid. Perhaps neither had he, until they held like this, touched like this. The romance of the air, the light, the gradual surrender of a strong woman was gloriously seductive.

He eased into her, watching her face as the first orgasm rolled through her, feeling her body clench, shudder, go pliant as his fueled it and filled it.

She kept her eyes open, as fascinated by the intensity of

his stare as the silvery ripples of sensation that pumped through her. She matched his pace, silky and smooth even as her breath tore. And when she saw those dark Celtic eyes cloud, go opaque, she framed his face with her hands, pulled his mouth to hers to savor his long, long groan of release.

When his body was ranged weightily over hers; his face buried in her hair, she wrapped her arms companionably around him. 'I let you seduce me.'

'Uh-huh.'

'I didn't want to hurt your feelings.'

'Thank you. You tolerated it all so stoically, too.'

'It's the training. Cops have to be stoic.'

He reached out, ran a hand over the grass, and plucked up her shield. 'Your badge, Lieutenant.'

She snickered, slapped him on the ass. 'Get off me. You weigh a ton.'

'Keep sweet-talking me, and God knows what could happen.' Lazily, he rolled aside, noted that the sky had gone from cloudy blue to pearl gray. 'I'm starving. You distracted me and now it's well past dinnertime.'

'It's going to be a little more past.' She sat up and began to tug on her clothes. 'You had your sex, pal. Now it's my turn. We have to talk.'

'We could talk over dinner.' He sighed when she sent him a steely stare. 'Or we could talk here. Problem?' he asked and skimmed his thumb over the dent in her chin.

'Let's just say I have some questions.'

'I might have the answers. What are they?'

'To begin with—' She broke off, blew out a breath. He was sitting there, mostly naked, looking very much like a sleek, well-satisfied cat. 'Put some clothes on, will you? You're going to distract *me*.' She tossed his shirt at him when he only grinned. 'Mavis was waiting for me when I got home.'

'Oh.' He shook out his shirt, noted its deplorable condition, but slipped it on. 'Why didn't she stay?'

'She's got a gig at the Down and Dirty. Roarke, why didn't you tell me you own Eclectic?'

'It's not a secret.' He hitched into his slacks, then handed her her weapon harness. 'I own a number of things.'

'You know what I'm talking about.' She would be patient here, Eve told herself, because it was a delicate area for everyone. 'Eclectic's offered Mavis a contract.'

'Yes, I know.'

'I know you know,' she snapped, slapping away his hand as he attempted to smooth down her hair. 'Damn it, Roarke, you could have told me. I'd have been prepared when she asked me about it.'

'Asked you what? It's a standard contract. She'll certainly want an agent or representative to look it over, but—'

'Did you do it for me?' she interrupted, and her eyes were focused on his face.

'Did I do what for you?'

Now her teeth went on edge. 'Offer Mavis the recording contract.'

He folded his hands, cocked his head. 'You're not planning on giving up law enforcement to be a theatrical agent, are you?'

'No, of course not. I—'

'Well then, it has nothing to do with you.'

'You're not going to sit there and tell me you like Mavis's music.'

'Music is a term I'm not sure applies to Mavis's talents.'

'There.' She jabbed a finger into his chest.

'That talent, however, is – I believe – commercial. Eclectic's purpose is to produce and distribute commercial recording artists.'

She sat back, tapped her finger on her knee. 'So it's a business thing. Straight business.'

'Naturally. I take business very seriously.'

'You could be snowing me,' she said after a moment. 'You're good enough.'

'Yes, I am.' Pleased that he was one of the very few who could snow her, he smiled at her. 'Either way, the deal's done. Is that all?'

'No.' She hissed out a breath, then leaned forward and kissed him. 'Thanks, either way.'

'You're welcome.'

'Next, I have to hit The Athame tonight, check a guy out.' She saw the flicker in his eyes, the tensing of his jaw. 'I'd like you to go with me.' She had to bite her tongue to keep from snickering when he narrowed those eyes at her.

'Just like that? It's police business, but you're not going to make an issue out of it?'

'No, first because I think you might be helpful, and second because it saves time. We'd argue about it, and you'd just go, anyway. This way, I ask you to come and you go, understanding I'm in charge.'

'Clever of you.' He took her hand and drew her to her feet. 'Agreed. But after dinner. I missed lunch.'

'One more thing. Why did you have a Celtic symbol of protection carved into my wedding ring?'

He felt the jolt of surprise, covered it smoothly. 'Excuse me?'

'No, you weren't quick enough that time.' It pleased her that she'd spotted that minute and masterfully covered awareness. 'You know exactly what I'm talking about. One of our friendly neighborhood witches tagged it today.'

'I see.' *Caught*, he realized, and he stalled by lifting her hand to examine the ring. 'It's an appealing design.'

'Don't bullshit me, Roarke. I'm a professional.' She stepped in until their eyes were level again. 'You buy into it, don't you? You actually buy all this hocus-pocus.'

'It's not a matter of that.' He fumbled and knew it when she furrowed her brow.

394

'You're embarrassed.' Her brow cleared in surprise and amusement. 'You're never embarrassed. By anything. This is weird. And kind of sweet.'

'I'm not embarrassed.' *Mortified*, he decided, *but not embarrassed*. 'I'm simply . . . not entirely comfortable explaining myself. I love you,' he said and stilled her muffled chuckle. 'You risk your life, a life that's essential to me, just by being who you are. This . . .' He brushed his thumb over her wedding band. 'Is a small and very personal shield.'

'That's lovely, Roarke. Really. But you don't really believe all that magic nonsense.'

His gaze lifted, and as twilight turned to night, his eyes glinted in the dark. Like a wolf's, she thought.

And it was a wolf, she remembered, she was to trust.

'Your world is relatively small, Eve. You couldn't call it sheltered, but it's limited. You haven't seen a giant's dance, or felt the power of the ancient stones. You haven't run your hand over the Ogham carving in the trunk of a tree petrified by time or heard the sounds that whisper through the mist that coats sacred ground.'

Baffled, she shook her head. 'It's, what, an Irish thing?'

'If you like, though it's certainly not limited to a single race or culture. You are grounded.' He ran his hands up her arms to her shoulders. 'Almost brutal in your focus and your honesty. And I've lived, let's say, a flexible life. I need you, and I'll use whatever comes to hand to keep you safe.' He lifted the ring to his lips. 'Let's just call it covering the bases.'

'Okay.' This was a new aspect of him it would take time to explore. 'But you don't have, like, a secret room where you dance around naked and chant?'

He tucked his tongue in his cheek. 'I did, but I turned it into a den. More versatile.'

'Good thinking. Okay, let's eat.'

'Thank God.' He took her hand and tugged her toward the house.

Chapter Seven

The Athame slicked a high-gloss sheen over depravity, like the baby-kissing smile on a corrupt politician. One scan convinced Eve she'd have preferred to spend an evening in a low-level dive, smelling stale liquor and staler sweat.

Dives didn't bother with disguises.

Revolving balconies of smoky glass and chrome trim ringed the main level in two tiers so that those who preferred a loftier view could circle slowly and check out the action. The central bar speared out in five points, and each was crowded with patrons perched on high stools fashioned to resemble optimistically exaggerated body parts.

A couple of women decked out in micro skirts sat spread-legged on a pair of bulging, flesh-toned cocks and laughed uproariously. A skinheaded bar surfer checked them out by prying his hand down their snug blouses.

All the walls were mirrored, and they pulsed with cloudy red lights. Some of the tables flanking the dance floor were tubed for privacy, some were smoked so that silhouettes of couples in various states of fornication wavered against the glass to entertain the crowd, and all were coated with a shiny black lacquer that made them resemble small, dark pools.

On a raised platform, the band pumped out harsh and clever rock. Eve wondered what Mavis would think of their wildly painted faces, tattooed chests, and black leather cod-pieces studded with silver spikes. She decided her friend would probably have dubbed them mag.

'Do we sit?' Roarke murmured in her ear, 'or case the joint?'

'We go up,' she decided. 'For the overview. What's that smell?'

He stepped onto the auto-stairs with her. 'Cannabis, incense. Sweat.'

She shook her head. There was something under that mix, something metallic. 'Blood. Fresh blood.'

He'd caught it as well. That broody underlayer. 'In a place like this, they put it in the air vents for mood enhancement.'

'Charming.'

They stepped off onto the second level. Here, rather than tables and chairs, there were floor pillows and thick rugs where patrons could lounge as they sipped their brew of choice. Those on the prowl leaned on the ornate chrome rail, scoping, Eve imagined, for a likely partner to lure into one of the privacy rooms.

There were a dozen such rooms on this level, all with heavy black doors bearing chrome plaques with such names as Perdition, Leviathan, and – more direct, in Eve's opinion – Hell and Damnation.

She could too easily imagine the personality type who would find such invitations seductive.

As she watched, a man whose eyes were glazed with liquor began to slurp his way up his companion's legs. His hand snuck under her crotch-skimming skirt as she giggled. Technically, she could have busted them both for engaging in a sexual act in public.

'What would be the point?' Roarke commented, reading her perfectly. His voice was mild. Anyone taking a casual glance would have seen a man faintly bored with the ambiance. But he was braced to attack or defend, whichever became necessary.

'You've got more interesting things to do than toss a horny couple from Queens in lockup.'

That wasn't really the point, Eve thought as the man tugged apart the self-stick fly on his baggy blue trousers. 'How do you know they're from Queens?'

Before he could answer, a young, attractive man with a flowing mane of blond hair and bare, gleaming shoulders, hunkered down beside the busy couple. Whatever he said had the woman giggling again then grabbing him into a sloppy kiss.

'Why don't you come, too?' she demanded in an unmistakable accent. 'We could have ourselves a manage and twas.'

Eve lifted a brow at the borough massacre of the French term, and at the easy skill with which the bouncer disengaged himself and led the staggering couple off.

'Queens,' Roarke said, smug. 'Definitely. And that was smoothly done.' He inclined his head as the couple was taken through a narrow door. 'They'd add the price of the privacy room to the tab, and no harm done.' There was a scream of female laughter as the bouncer came back out and secured the door. 'Everyone's happy.'

'Queens might not be in the morning. The cost of a privacy room in a place like this has to hurt. Then again . . .' She scanned the crowd. Ages varied from the very young – many of whom she was sure had gained entrance with forged ID – to the very mature. But from the wardrobe and jewelry, the tone of faces and bodies that slyly hinted at salon enhancements, the clientele was solidly upper middle-class.

'Money doesn't look to be a problem here. I've spotted at least five high-credit licensed companions.'

'My count was more like ten.'

She quirked a brow. 'Twelve bouncers with low-grade palm zappers.'

'On that count, we agree.' He slipped an arm around her waist and walked to the rail. Below, the dance floor was packed, bodies rubbing suggestively against bodies. Wild laughter bounced off the mirrored walls and shot upward.

The band was into their performance mode. The two female vocalists were being bound to dangling silver chains with leather straps. The music pounded, heavy on the drums. The dancers surged forward, closing in, as eager as a mob at a lynching. Audience participation was realized as a man was brought forward and accepted the invitation to strip the women out of their flimsy robes. Beneath, they were naked but for glittery stars over nipples and pubes.

The crowd began to chant and howl as he coated them with thick oil, and they writhed and screamed and begged for mercy.

'That's skirting the line,' Eve muttered.

'Performance art.' Roarke watched the man scourge the first vocalist with a velvet cat 'o nine tails. 'Still within the law.'

'A simulation of debasement encourages the real thing.' She set her teeth as a band member began to lightly slap the second vocalist as their voices soared in fervent duet. 'We're supposed to be beyond this kind of female exploitation. But we're not. We never are. What are they looking for?'

'Thrills. Of the cheaper and meaner variety.' His hand soothed the base of her back. She knew what it was to be bound, to be abused. There was nothing artful and nothing entertaining about it. 'There's no need to watch this, Eve.'

'What makes them do it?' she wondered. 'What makes a woman let herself be used that way, in simulation or in reality? Why doesn't she kick his balls into his throat?'

'She's not you.' He kissed her on the brow and firmly turned her away.

The railing was thick with people, now straining to see the show.

As they took a quick tour of the top floor, a woman in a sheer black gown glided up to them. 'Welcome to The Master's Level. Do you have a reservation?'

Enough was enough, Eve thought. She flipped out her badge. 'I'm not interested in what you're selling here.'

'Fine food and wine,' the hostess said after only a quick hitch at the sight of police identification. 'You'll find we're completely within code here, Lieutenant. However, if you wish to speak with the owner—'

'I've already done that. I want to see Lobar. Where do I find him?'

'He doesn't work this level.' With the subtlety and discretion that would have made the poshest maître d' proud, the hostess steered Eve back toward the stairs. 'If you will go to the main level, you will be met, and a table provided. I'll contact Lobar and send him to you.'

'Fine.' Eve studied her, saw an attractive woman in her mid-twenties. 'Why do you do this?' she asked and glanced at one of the screens where a woman screamed and struggled as she was strapped to a raised slab of marble. 'How can you do this?'

The hostess merely glanced down at Eve's badge, then smiled sweetly. 'How can you do that?' she countered and drifted away.

'I'm letting it get to me,' Eve admitted as they headed down to the main level. 'I know better.'

The band continued to play, the music a frenzy now. But the performance aspect had switched to a huge view screen that filled the wall behind the stage. It took Eve only a glance to see why. The club wasn't licensed for live sex acts, but such minor inconveniences were transcended by video.

The female vocalists were still bound, still singing their hearts out without missing a beat. But they were behind the stage now, on camera, along with the man from the audience and a second man who wore nothing but an ornate mask of a boar's head.

'Pigs,' was all Eve had to say, then looked into gleaming red eyes.

'Your table is this way.' The young man smiled, revealing

gleaming teeth with incisors sharpened to vicious fangs. He turned. His hair streamed down his naked back, black, tipped with red like flames. He opened the rounded door on a privacy tube, stepped in ahead of them.

'I'm Lobar.' He grinned again. 'I've been expecting you.'

He might have been pretty without the affectation of vampire fangs and demon eyes. As it was, Eve thought he looked like an overgrown child dressed up for Halloween. If he was of legal age, she deduced it couldn't have been by much. His chest was thin and hairless, his arms slim as a girl's. But she didn't think it was the red tint of his eyes that took away his innocence. It was the look in them.

'Sit down, Lobar.'

'Sure.' He dropped into a chair. 'I'll have a drink. You're buying,' he told Eve. 'You want my time during work hours, you gotta pay.' He punched out a selection on the electronic menu, adjusted his chair so that he could see the view screen. 'Great show tonight.'

Eve glanced over.

'The script could use work,' she said dryly. 'You got ID, Lobar?'

He peeled his lips back from his fangs, lifted his hands, palm out. 'Not on me. Unless you think I got secret pockets in my skin.'

'What's your legal name?'

His smile disappeared, and his eyes were suddenly the sulky eyes of a child. 'It's Lobar. That's who I am. I don't have to answer your questions, you know. I'm cooperating.'

'You're a real sterling citizen.' Eve waited while his drink slid out of the serving slot. Another show; she mused, as the heavy glass chalice smoked with some murky gray brew. 'Alice Lingstrom. What do you know about her?'

'Not much, except she was a dumb bitch.' He sipped the drink. 'She hung around for awhile, then went crying off. It was fine with me. The master doesn't need any weaklings.'

'The master.'

He sipped again, smiled. 'Satan,' he said, relishing it.

'You believe in Satan?'

'Sure.' He leaned forward, slid his hand with its long, black-painted nails toward Eve. 'And he believes in you.'

'Careful,' Roarke murmured. 'You're too young and stupid to loose a hand.'

Lobar snorted, but he slid his hand back again. 'Your watchdog?' he said to Eve. 'Your rich watchdog. We know who you are,' he added, fixing his red eyes on Roarke. 'Big fucking deal. You don't have any power here. And neither does your cop bitch.'

'I'm not his cop bitch,' Eve said mildly, shooting a warning glance at Roarke. 'I'm my own cop bitch. And as to power . . .' She leaned back. 'Well, I've got the power to take you down to Cop Central and slap you into Interview.' She smiled, letting her gaze run over the naked chest and gleaming nipple rings. 'The guys would just love to get a load of you. Cute, isn't he, Roarke?'

'In an apprentice demon sort of fashion. You must have a very . . . interesting dentist.' As it was a privacy booth, he took out a cigarette, lighted it.

'I could use one of those,' Lobar said.

'Could you?' With a shrug, Roarke slid another cigarette onto the table. When Lobar picked it up, looked at him expectantly, Roarke grinned. 'Sorry, you want a light? I assumed you'd shoot flame out of your fingertips.'

'I don't do tricks for straights.' Lobar leaned forward, sucking on the filter as Roarke flicked his lighter at the tip. 'Look, you want to know about Alice, and I can't help you. She wasn't my type. Too inhibited, and always asking questions. Sure I banged her a couple of times, but those were like community fucks, you know? Nothing personal.'

'And on the night she was killed?'

He blew out smoke, sucked more in. He hadn't had real

402

tobacco before, and the expensive drug made him light-headed and relaxed. 'Never saw her. I was busy. I had a private ceremony with Selina and Alban. Sexual rites. After, we fucked around most of the night.'

He took another deep drag, holding it in as he would a toke from a prime joint, then exhaling lustily through his nostrils. 'Selina likes double bangers, and when she's done, she likes to watch and get herself off. Was dawn, easy, before she'd had enough.'

'And the three of you were together the entire night. No one left, even for a few minutes.'

He moved his bony shoulders. 'That's the thing about three people. No waiting.' He lowered his gaze suggestively to her breasts. 'Want to try it?'

'You don't want to solicit a cop, Lobar. And I like men. Not skinny boys in silly costumes. Who called Alice and played the recording. The chant?'

He was sulky again, his ego pricked. If she'd come alone, he thought, he'd have shown her a few things. A bitch was a bitch as far as he was concerned, badge or no badge. 'I don't know what you're talking about. Alice was nothing. Nobody gave a shit about her.'

'Her grandfather did.'

'Heard he was dead, too.' The red eyes gleamed. 'Old fart. Desk cop, button pusher. Means nothing to me.'

'Enough to know he was a cop,' Eve put in. 'A cop who rode a desk. How'd you know that, Lobar?'

Realizing his mistake, he crushed out what was left of the cigarette in quick, vicious little jabs. 'Somebody must've mentioned it.' He exposed his fangs in a wide grin. 'Probably Alice did, while I was banging her.'

'Doesn't say much for your performance rating, does it, if she was talking about her grandfather when you were . . . banging her.'

'I heard it somewhere, all right?' He grabbed his drink,

403

gulped deeply. 'What's the big fucking deal where? He was old, anyway.'

'Did you ever see him? In here?'

'I see a lot of people in here. I don't remember any old cop.' He waved a hand. 'Place rocks like this most every night. How the hell do I know who comes in? Selina hired me to keep the occasional asshole in line, not to remember faces.'

'Selina's got quite the enterprise going here. Is she still dealing? She deal for you?'

His eyes went sly. 'I get power from my beliefs. I don't need illegals.'

'Have you ever participated in human sacrifice? Ever slice up a child for your master, Lobar?'

He polished off his drink. 'That's an outsider's hallucination. People like you like to make Satanists out to be monsters.'

'People like us,' Roarke murmured, skimming his gaze over Lobar from the fire-tipped hair to the nipple rings. 'Yes, obviously we're biased when anyone can see you're simply . . . devout.'

'Look, it's a religion, and we've got freedom of religion in this country. You want to push your God down our throats? Well, we reject him. We reject him and all his weak-kneed creeds. And we'll rule in Hell.'

He shoved back from the table and stood. 'I've got nothing more to say.'

'All right.' Eve spoke quietly, looking up into his eyes. 'But you think about this, Lobar. People are dead. Somebody's going to be next. It might just be you.'

His lips trembled, then firmed. 'It might just be you,' he shot back and slammed out of the booth.

'What an attractive young man,' Roarke commented. 'I do believe he'll be a delightful addition to Hell.'

'That may be where he's going.' After a quick glance around, Eve nudged the empty glass into her bag. 'I want to find out where he came from. I can run his prints at home.'

'Fine.' He rose, took her arm. 'But I want a shower first. This place leaves something nasty coated on the skin.'

'I can't argue with that.'

'Robert Allen Mathias,' Eve stated, reading data off her monitor. 'Turned eighteen six months ago. Born in Kansas City, Kansas, son of Jonathan and Elaine Mathias, both of whom are Baptist deacons.'

'A PK.' Roarke put in. 'Preacher's kid. Some can rebel in extreme manners. Looks like little Bobby has.'

'History of problems,' Eve continued. 'I got his juvie file here. Petty theft, break in, truancy, assault. Ran way from home four times before he hit thirteen. At fifteen, after a joy ride that landed him a grand theft auto, his parents had him termed legally incorrigible. Did a year at a state school, which ended with him being kicked to a state institution after an attempted rape on a teacher.'

'Bobby's a sweetheart,' Roarke murmured. 'I knew there was a reason I wanted to jab his little red eyes out. They kept latching onto your breasts.'

'Yeah.' Unconsciously, Eve rubbed a hand over them as if to erase something vile. 'Psych profile's pretty much what you'd expect. Sociopathic tendencies, lack of control, violent mood swings. Subject harbors deep, unresolved resentment toward parents and authority figures, particularly female. Displays both fear and resentment toward females. Intelligence rating, high, violence quotient, high. Subject displays complete lack of conscience and an abnormal interest in the occult.'

'Then what is he doing out on the street? Why isn't he in treatment?'

'Because it's the law. You have to kick him when he turns eighteen. Until you nail him as an adult, he's clear.' Eve puffed out her cheeks, blew out the air. 'He's a dangerous little bastard, but there's not much I can do about him. He corroborates Selina's statement for the night of Alice's death.'

405

'He'd have been instructed to,' Roarke pointed out.

'Still sticks – unless I can break it.' She pushed back. 'I've got his current address. I can check it out, knock on doors. See if his neighbors can give me something on him. If I can get him in on something, lay on some pressure, I think little Bobby would break.'

'Otherwise?'

'Otherwise, we keep digging.' She rubbed her eyes.

'We'll deal with him. Sooner or later, he'll revert to type – bust somebody's face, assault some woman, kick the wrong ass. Then we'll lock him in a cage.'

'Your job is miserable.'

'Most of the time,' she agreed, then looked over her shoulder. 'Are you tired?'

'Depends.' He glanced at the screen where Lobar's data scrolled. He had an image of her diving deeper, spending the quiet hours of night wading through the muck. He didn't bother to sigh. 'What do you need?'

'You.' She could feel her color rise as he lifted a curious brow. 'I know it's late, and it's been a long day. I guess I was thinking of it kind of like the shower. Something to wash away the grime.' Embarrassed, she turned back, stared hard at the screen. 'Stupid.'

It was always hard for her to ask, he mused. For anything. 'Not the most romantic proposal I've ever had.' He laid his hands on her shoulders, massaged gently. 'But far from stupid. Disengage,' he ordered and the screen went dark. He turned her chair around, drew her to her feet. 'Come to bed.'

'Roarke.' She put her arms around him, held tight. She couldn't explain how or why the images she'd seen that night had left something inside her shaky. With him, she didn't have to. 'I love you.'

Smiling a little, she lifted her head and looked into his eyes. 'It's getting easier to say. I think I'm starting to like it.'

406

With a short laugh, he pressed a kiss to her chin. 'Come to bed,' he repeated, 'and say it again.'

The rite was ancient, its purpose dark. Cloaked and masked, the coven gathered in the private chamber. The scent of blood was fresh and strong. The flames spearing above black candles flickered to send shadows slithering over the walls like spiders hunting prey.

Selina chose to be the altar and lay naked, a candle burning between her thighs, a bowl of sacrificial blood nestled between her generous breasts.

She smiled as she glanced toward the silver bowl over-flowing with the cash and credits the membership had paid for the privilege to belong. Their wealth was now her wealth. The master had saved her from a scrabbling life on the streets and brought her here, into power and into comfort.

She had gladly traded her soul for them.

Tonight there would be more. Tonight there would be death, and the power that came from the rending of flesh, the spilling of blood. They would not remember, she thought. She had added drugs to the blood-laced wine. With the right drugs, in the right dosage, they would do and say and be what the master wanted.

Only she and Alban would know that the master had demanded sacrifice for his protection, and the demand had been happily met.

The coven circled her, their faces hooded, their bodies swaying, as the drug, the smoke, the chanting hypnotized them. At her head stood Alban, with the boar's mask and the athame.

'We worship the one,' he said in his clear and beautiful voice.

And the coven answered. 'Satan is the one.'

'What is his, is ours.'

'Ave, Satan.'

As Alban lifted the bowl, his eyes met Selina's. He took up a sword, thrust it at the four points of the compass. The princes of hell were called, the list long and exotic. Voices were a hum. Fire crackled in a blackened pot set on a marble slab.

She began to moan.

'Destroy our enemies.'

Yes, she thought. *Destroy.*

'Bring sickness and pain on those who would harm us.'

Great pain. Unbearable pain.

When Alban laid a hand on her flesh, she began to scream. 'We take what we wish, in your name. Death to the weak. Fortune to the strong.'

He stepped back, and though it was his right to take the altar first, he gestured to Lobar. 'Reward to the loyal. Take her,' he commanded. 'Give her pain as well as pleasure.'

Lobar hesitated a moment. The sacrifice should have come first. The blood sacrifice. The goat should have been brought out and slaughtered. But he looked at Selina, and his drug-clouded brain shut off. There was woman. Bitch. She watched him with cold, taunting eyes.

He would show her, he thought. He would show her he was a man. It wouldn't be like the last time when she had used and humiliated him.

This time, he would be in charge.

He cast aside his robe and stepped forward.

Chapter Eight

The steady beep of an alarm had Eve rolling over and cursing. 'It can't be time to get up. We just went to bed.'

'It's not. That's security.'

'What?' Now she sat up quickly. '*Our* security?'

Roarke was already out of bed, already pulling on slacks, and answered with a grunt. Instinctively Eve reached for her weapon first, clothes second. 'Someone's trying to break in?'

'Apparently someone has.' His voice was very calm. As the lights were still off, she could see only his silhouette in the scattered light of the moon through the sky window. And joining that silhouette was the unmistakable outline of a gun in his hand.

'Where the hell did you get that? I thought they were all locked up. Goddamn it, Roarke, that's illegal. Put it away.'

Coolly, he plugged a round in the chamber of the antique and banned-for-use Glock nine millimeter. 'No.'

'Damn it, damn it.' She snatched up her communicator, shoved it in the back pocket of her jeans out of habit. 'You can't use that thing. I'll check it out – that's my job. You call Dispatch, report a possible intruder.'

'No,' he said again and started for the door. She was on him in two steps.

'If someone's on the grounds or in the house, and if you shoot him with that, I'm going to have to arrest you.'

'Fine.'

'Roarke.' She grabbed at him as he reached for the door. 'There's procedure for something like this, and reasons for that procedure. Call it in.'

His home, he thought. Their home. His woman, and the fact that she was a cop didn't mean a damn at the moment. 'And won't you feel foolish, Lieutenant, if it's a mechanical malfunction?'

'Nothing of yours ever malfunctions,' she muttered and made him smile despite the circumstances.

'Why, thank you.' He opened the door, and there was Summerset.

'It appears someone is on the grounds.'

'Where's the breech?'

'Section fifteen, southwest quadrant.'

'Run a full video scan, employ full house security when we're out. Eve and I will check the grounds.' Absently, he ran a hand down her back. 'A good thing I live with a cop.'

She looked down at the gun in his hand. Attempting to disarm him would likely prove unsuccessful. And it would take too much time. 'We're going to talk about this,' she said between her teeth. 'I mean it.'

'Of course you do.'

They went side by side down the stairs, through the now silent house. 'They haven't gotten in,' he said as he paused by a door leading onto a wide patio. 'The alarm for a breech of the house is different. But they're over the wall.'

'Which means they could be anywhere.'

The moon was waxing toward full, but the clouds were thick and shadowed its light. Eve scanned the dark, the sheltering trees, the huge ornamental bushes. All provided excellent cover for observation. Or ambush. She heard nothing but the air teasing leaves going brittle with age.

'We'll have to separate. For Christ's sake don't use that weapon unless your life's threatened. Most B and E men aren't armed.'

410

And most B and E men, they both knew, didn't attempt to ply their trade on a man like Roarke. 'Be careful,' he said quietly and slipped like smoke into the shadows.

He was good, Eve assured herself. She could trust him to handle himself and the situation. Using the dim and shifting moonlight as a guide, she headed west, then began to circle.

The quiet was almost eerie. She could barely hear her own footsteps on the thick grass. Behind her, the house stood in darkness, a formidable structure of old stone and glass, guarded, she thought, by a skinny snob of a butler.

Her lips curled. She'd love to see an unsuspecting burglar come up against Summerset.

When she reached the wall, she scanned for any breech. It was eight feet high, three feet thick, and wired to deliver a discouraging electric shock to anything over twenty pounds. Security cameras and lights were set every twelve feet. She whispered out an oath when she noted the narrow beams were blinking red rather than green.

Disengaged. Son of a bitch. Weapon drawn and ready, she circled to the south.

Roarke did his own circuit in silence, using the trees. He'd bought this property eight years before, had had it remodeled and rehabbed to his specifications. He'd supervised the design and implementation of the security system personally. It was in a very real sense his first home, the place he'd chosen to settle after too many years of wandering. Beneath the icy control, as he slipped from shadow to shadow, was a bubbling, grinding fury that his home had been invaded.

The night was cool, clear, quiet as a tomb. He wondered if he was up against a very ballsy thief. It could be as simple as that. Or it could be something, someone much more dangerous. A pro hired by a business competitor. An enemy – and he hadn't fought his way to where he was without making them. Particularly since many of his interests had been on the dark side of the law.

411

Or the target could be Eve. She, too, had made enemies. Dangerous enemies. He glanced over his shoulder, hesitated. Then told himself not to second-guess his wife. He knew of no one better equipped to take care of herself.

But it was that hesitation, that instinctive need to protect that turned his luck. As he paused in the shadows, he caught the faint sound of movement. Roarke took a firmer grip on the gun, stepped back, stepped to the side. And waited.

The figure was moving slowly, in a crouch. As the distance between them melted away, Roarke could hear the puff of nervous breathing. Though he couldn't make out features, he judged male, perhaps five-ten, and on the lean side. He could see no weapon, and thinking of the difficulty Eve might have explaining why her husband had held off an intruder with a banned handgun, tucked the Glock into the back of his slacks.

He braced, looking forward to a little hand-to-hand, then lunged when the figure slunk by. Roarke had an arm around a throat, a fist clenched and raised in anticipation of quiet, perhaps petty revenge, when he realized it wasn't a man, but a boy.

'Hey, you son of a bitch, let go. I'll kill you.'

A very rude and very frightened boy, Roarke decided. The struggle was short and all one-sided. It took seconds only for Roarke to pin the boy against the trunk of a tree. 'How the hell did you get inside?' Roarke demanded.

The kid's breath was coming in whistles, and his face was pale as a ghost. Roarke could hear the audible click in his throat as he swallowed. 'You're Roarke.' He stopped struggling and tried to smirk. 'You've got pretty good security.'

'I like to think so.' *Not a thief*, Roarke decided, *but ballsy, certainly*. 'How did you get past it?'

'I—' He broke off, eyes going huge as they shot over Roarke's shoulder. 'Behind you!'

With a smoothness the boy would later appreciate, Roarke

pivoted, keeping his grip unbreakable. 'We have our intruder, Lieutenant.'

'So I see.' She lowered her weapon, ordered her heart to slow to normal. 'Jesus, Roarke, it's just a kid. It's—' She stopped, narrowed her eyes. 'I know this kid.'

'Then perhaps you'd introduce us.'

'It's Jamie, right? Jamie Lingstrom. Alice's brother.'

'Good eye, Lieutenant. Now, you want to tell him to stop choking me?'

'I don't think so.' She holstered her weapon, stepped up. 'What the hell are you doing, breaking into private property in the middle of the night? You're a cop's grandson, for Christ's sake. You want to end up in juvie?'

'I'm not your big problem right now, Lieutenant Dallas.' He made a valiant attempt to sound tough, but his voice wavered. 'You've got a dead body outside the wall. Really dead,' he added and began to shake.

'Did you kill someone, Jamie?' Roarke asked mildly.

'No, man. No way. He was there when I came by.' Terrified his stomach would revolt and humiliate him, Jamie swallowed hard again. 'I'll show you.'

If it was a trick, Eve considered it a fine one. She couldn't take a chance. 'All right. Let's go. And if you try to run, pal, I'll zap you.'

'Wouldn't make any sense to run, would it, when I went to all this trouble to get in? This way.' His legs were rubber, and he sincerely hoped neither of them noticed that his knees kept knocking together.

'I'd like to know how you got in,' Roarke said as they headed for the main gate. 'How you bypassed security.'

'I fool around with electronics. A hobby. You've got a really high-grade system. The best.'

'So I thought.'

'I guess I didn't disengage all the alarms.' Jamie turned his head, tried another weak smile. 'You knew I was here.'

'You got in,' Roarke repeated. 'How?'

'This.' Jamie pulled a small palm-sized unit out of his pocket. 'It's a jammer I've been working on for a couple of years. It'll read most systems,' he began, frowning when Roarke plucked it out of his hand. 'When you engage this,' he continued, leaning over to point, 'it'll scan the chips, run a cloning program. Then it's just a matter of backing out the program step by step. Takes some time, but it's pretty efficient.'

Roarke stared at the mechanism. It was no bigger than one of the E-games one of his companies manufactured. Indeed, the casing looked distressingly familiar. 'You adapted a game unit into a jammer. Yourself. One that read and cloned and breached my security.'

'Well, most of it.' Jamie's eyes clouded in annoyance. 'I must have missed something, one of the backups maybe. Your system must be ultra mag. I'd like to see it.'

'Not in this lifetime,' Roarke muttered and shoved the unit into his pocket.

When they reached the gates, he disengaged and opened them manually, sliding a narrow look at Jamie as the boy craned over his shoulder to see.

'Way impressive,' Jamie commented. 'I didn't figure I could get through this way. That's why I had to come over the wall. Needed a ladder.'

Roarke simply closed his eyes. 'A ladder,' he said to no one in particular. 'He climbed up a ladder. Lovely. And the cameras?'

'Oh, I blanked them from across the street. The unit's got a range of ten yards.'

'Lieutenant.' Roarke snagged Jamie by the collar. 'I want him punished.'

'Later. Now, where's this body you're supposed to have seen?'

The cocky smile fell away from his face. 'To the left,' he told her, paling again.

414

'Keep a hold of him, Roarke. Stay here.'

'I've got him,' Roarke replied, but he'd be damned if he'd stay back. He tugged Jamie through the gate, met Eve's annoyed stare blandly. 'Our home, our problem.'

She said something nasty under her breath and turned left. She didn't have to go far. It wasn't hidden, it wasn't subtle.

The body was naked and strapped to a wooden form in the shape of a star. No, she realized. A pentagram. Inverted so that the head with its dead doll eyes and gaping throat hung over the bloody sidewalk. The arms were outstretched, the legs parted in a wide vee. The center of his chest was a mass of black blood and gore, the hole hacked out of it bigger than a man's fist.

She doubted the ME would find a heart inside when he opened the body for autopsy.

She heard the choked sound behind her and turned to see Roarke shift his grip on Jamie and step over to shield the boy from the view.

'Lobar,' was all he said.

'Yeah.' She stepped closer. Whoever had taken his heart had also plunged a knife through a sheet of paper and through his groin.

DEVIL WORSHIPPER
BABY KILLER
BURN IN HELL

'Take the boy inside, will you, Roarke?' She glanced at the collapsible ladder tilted against the wall. 'And get rid of that. Pass the kid off to Summerset for now. I can't leave the scene.' She turned, her face blank and impassive. Her cop face. 'Will you bring me my field kit?'

'Yes. Come on, Jamie.'

'I know who he is.' Tears swam in Jamie's eyes and were viciously blinked away. 'He's one of the bastards who killed my sister. I hope he rots.'

Because his voice had broken at the end, Roarke slipped an arm around his shoulder. 'He will. Come inside. Let the Lieutenant do her job.' Roarke sent Eve one last look before hefting the ladder and leading Jamie back through the gates.

With her gaze still fixed on the body, Eve pulled out her communicator. 'Dispatch, Dallas, Lieutenant Eve.'

'Dispatch, acknowledged.'

'Reporting homicide, requesting assistance.' She gave the necessary data, then replaced her communicator. Turning, she stared across the wide, quiet street into the dark, shifting shadows of the great park. In the east the sky was stripping off the first layers of night, and the stars, such as they were, were blinking out.

Murder had come into her life before and would again. But someone would pay for bringing it into her home.

She turned as Roarke approached not only with her field kit but her battered leather jacket. 'It gets chilly this close to dawn,' he said and handed it to her.

'Thanks. Jamie all right?'

'He and Summerset are eyeing each other with mutual dislike and distrust.'

'I knew I liked that kid. You can go inside and referee,' she told him as she took out Seal-It and clear-coated her hands, her boots. 'I've called it in.'

'I'm staying.'

Since she'd already figured he would, she didn't argue. 'Then make yourself useful and record the scene.' She took her recorder out of the kit, passed it to him, then covered his hand with hers. 'I'm sorry.'

'You're too smart to be sorry for something that isn't your responsibility. He wasn't killed here, was he?'

'No.' Confident that Roarke could function as her aide until Peabody arrived, Eve approached the body again. 'Not nearly enough blood. He'd have gushed from the jugular. That was likely the cause of death. We'll find the other wounds are

416

postmortem. In any case, there'd be splatters all over hell and back. We'd be wading in it. Record on?'

'Yes.'

'Victim identified as Robert Mathias, aka Lobar. White male, eighteen years of age. Preliminary visual exam indicates death was caused by a sharp-bladed instrument that severed the throat.' Shutting off everything but training, she took out a pencil light, examined the chest wound. 'Additional insults include a wound in the chest, probably inflicted by the same weapon. The victim's heart has been removed. The organ is not on scene. I need close-ups here,' she said to Roarke.

She took instruments out of her kit to calibrate. 'The throat wound is six and a quarter inches across, approximately two inches deep.' Quickly, competently, she measured and recorded the other wounds. 'A knife, black-handled with carving, was left in the body in the groin area to anchor what appears to be a computer-generated note on treated paper.'

She heard the shrill sound of sirens coming closer. 'Uniforms,' she told Roarke. 'They'll secure the scene. Not much traffic out this way at this time of night.'

'Fortunately.'

'The body has been strapped by leather strips to a wooden structure, pentagram shape. The small amount of blood and blood patterns indicate victim was killed and mutilated elsewhere and transported to scene. Perimeter security to be scanned. Possibility of breech onto private property beyond security gate and wall. Body discovered at approximately four-thirty A.M. by Lieutenant Eve Dallas and Roarke, residents.'

She turned and walked over as the first black-and-white screeched up to the curb. 'I want a privacy screen employed. Now. Block off the street in a twenty-foot perimeter. I don't want gawkers here. I don't want the fucking media. Got it?'

'Sir.' The two uniforms hustled out of the car and to the trunk. They wrestled out the privacy screen.

'I'm going to be awhile,' she told Roarke. Taking the

417

recorder from him, she passed it to another uniform. 'You should go inside, keep an eye on the kid.' Wearily, she watched the cruiser cops erect the screen. 'He should call his mother or something. But I don't want him to leave until I talk to him again.'

'I'll take care of it. I'll cancel my appointments for the day. I'll be available.'

'That would be best.' She started to touch him, wanted to badly, then realized her sealed hands were smeared with blood and dropped them again. 'It would help if you kept him occupied, kept his mind off of it for now. Goddamn it, Roarke, this bites.'

'A ritual killing,' he murmured, and understanding, laid a hand on her cheek. 'But which side did it?'

'I guess I'm going to be spending a lot of time interviewing witches.' She huffed out a breath, then frowned when she saw Peabody striding double-time down the street. 'Where the hell's your vehicle, Officer?'

Her uniform might have been pressed to within an inch of its life, but her face was flushed and her breathing short. 'I don't have a vehicle, Lieutenant. I use city transpo. The closest public stop is four blocks from here.' She slanted a look at Roarke as though it was his personal responsibility. 'Rich people don't use public transportation.'

'Well, requisition a damn vehicle,' Eve ordered. 'We'll be in as soon as we're done out here,' she told Roarke, then turned away. 'Body's behind the screen. Get the recorder from the uniform, I don't trust his eye, and his hands are shaking. I want measurements on the blood pool and stills of the wounds, all angles. Seal up. I don't think the sweepers are going to find much here, but I don't want anything compromised. I'll do the prelim for time of death. The ME's on the way.'

Roarke watched her march off, flip through the screen, and figured she was finished with him.

Inside the house, he found Jamie, guarded by a visibly irritated

418

Summerset. 'You will not be allowed free range of this house,' Summerset snapped out. 'You will touch nothing. If you break one piece of crockery, soil one centimeter of fabric, I will resort to violence.'

Jamie continued to pace, continued to paw the statuary in the small – and as Summerset thought of it lesser – parlor. 'Well, now I'm shaking. You really put the fear of God in me, old man.'

'Your manners continue to disintegrate,' Roarke commented as he stepped into the room. 'Someone should have taught you to show some respect for your elders.'

'Yeah, well, someone should have taught your guard dog to be polite to guests.'

'Guests don't tamper with security systems, climb over walls, and skulk around private property. You are not a guest.'

Jamie deflated. It was tough to stand up under those cool blue eyes. 'I wanted to see the Lieutenant. I didn't want anyone to know.'

'Next time, try using the 'link,' Roarke suggested. 'It's all right, Summerset, I'll deal with this.'

'As you wish.' Summerset shot Jamie one last withering look, then stalked, stiff-backed, out of the room.

'Where'd you find Count Boredom?' Jamie asked and slumped into a chair. 'The morgue?'

Roarke sat on the arm of a sofa, took out a cigarette. 'Summerset can eat runts like you for breakfast,' he said mildly and flicked on his lighter. 'I've seen him.'

'Right.' Still Jamie sent a cautious look toward the doorway. Nothing in this house was what he'd expected, so he wouldn't underestimate the butler. 'Speaking of breakfast, you got anything to eat around here? It's been like hours since I had anything.'

Roarke blew out smoke. 'You want me to feed you now?'

'Well, you know. We got to hang anyway. Might as well eat.'

Cheeky little bastard, Roarke thought, not without admiration. Only youth, he supposed, could have an appetite after seeing what was outside the wall. 'And what did you have in mind? Crêpes, an omelette, perhaps a few bowls of sugar-soaked cereal?'

'I was thinking more of pizza, maybe a burger.' He fixed on a winning smile. 'My mom's a real nutrition fanatic. We only get health shit at home.'

'It's five in the morning, and you want pizza?'

'Pizza goes down smooth anytime.'

'You may be right.' And he thought he could use something, himself, after all. 'Let's go then.'

'It's like a museum in here,' Jamie said as he followed Roarke into the hall with its luminous paintings and gleaming antiques. 'I mean, in a good way. You must be rolling in it.'

'I must be.'

'People say you just touch something and the credits fly out.'

'Do they?'

'Yeah, and you didn't make all of it exactly on the upside, you know? But being hooked up with a cop like Dallas, you'd have to be straight.'

'One would think,' Roarke murmured and swung through a door into a huge kitchen.

'Wow. Ultimate. You got people who, like, cook things – by hand and stuff?'

'It's been known to happen.' Roarke watched the boy prowl, toy with controls on the compu-range, the subzero refrigerator. 'It's not going to happen this morning.' He walked to a large AutoChef. 'What is it then, pizza or burger?'

Jamie grinned. 'Both? I could probably drink a gallon of Pepsi.'

'We'll start with a tube.' Roarke programmed the AutoChef, then went to the refrigerator himself. 'Sit down, Jamie.'

'Frigid.' But he kept his eye on Roarke as he slid onto the padded bench of a breakfast nook.

After a short debate, Roarke punched in for two tubes, slipped them out of the door slot when they slid down. 'You'll want to contact your mother,' he said. 'You can use the 'link there.'

'No.' Jamie put his hands under the table, rubbed them on his jeans. 'She's zoned. She can't handle it. Alice. She's tranqued out. We – the viewing's tonight.'

'I see.' And because he did, Roarke let it drop. He handed the drink to Jamie, then took a large bubbling pizza from the AutoChef. He set it, then the burger that followed, on the table.

'Rocking A.' With the appetite of the young, Jamie grabbed the burger and bit in. 'Man! Man, it's meat,' he said with his mouth full. 'It's meat.'

It took a master not to let his mouth twitch. 'You'd prefer soy?' Roarke asked politely. 'Veggie?'

'No way.' Jamie wiped his mouth with the back of his hand, grinned. 'Really decent. Thanks.'

Roarke got two plates and a slicer. He went to work on the pizza. 'I suppose breaking and entering stimulates the appetite.'

'I'm always hungry.' Without shame, Jamie transferred the first slice to his plate. 'Mom says it's growing pains, but I just like to eat. She's real worried about junk intake, so I've got to sneak real food in. You know how moms are.'

'No, actually, I don't. I'll take your word.' And because he'd never been quite as young as Jamie, or quite as innocent, he took a slice for himself and prepared to enjoy watching the boy devour the rest.

'Parents are okay.' Jamie shrugged, alternating between the pizza and the burger. 'I don't see my father – not in a few years.

He's got a life over in Europe, the Morningside Community outside London.'

'Structured, programmed residential,' Roarke put in. 'Very tidy.'

'Yeah, and very boring. Even the grass is programmed. He digs on it, though, him and his foxy new wife – his third already.' He jerked a shoulder, sucked on the Pepsi. 'He isn't much on the father game. It bothered Alice a lot. Me, I can take it or leave it.'

No, Roarke thought, he didn't think so. Wounds were there. Odd what deep and permanent injury a parent could cause a child. 'Your mother hasn't married again?'

'Nah. She's not into it. She was bummed pretty bad when he took off. I was six. I'm sixteen now, and she still thinks I'm a kid. I had to nag for weeks to get her to let me go for my vehicle license. She's okay really. She's just . . .' He trailed off, stared down at his plate as if he wondered how food had gotten there. 'She doesn't deserve this. She does the best she can. She doesn't deserve this. She loved Grandpa. They were really tight. And now Alice. Alice was really weird, but she . . .'

'She was your sister,' Roarke said quietly. 'You loved her.'

'It shouldn't have happened to her.' He lifted his gaze slowly, met Roarke's with a kind of terrifying fury. 'When I find them, the one who hurt her, I'm going to kill them.'

'You want to be careful what you say, Jamie.' Eve stepped in. Her eyes were shadowed, her face pale with fatigue. Though she'd been careful, there were a few smears of blood on her jeans. 'And you want to put away any thoughts of revenge and leave investigation to the cops.'

'They killed my sister.'

'It hasn't been determined that your sister was a victim of homicide.' Eve headed to the AutoChef, programmed coffee. 'And you're in enough trouble,' she added before he could speak, 'without hassling me.'

'Be smart,' Roarke said when Jamie opened his mouth again. 'Be quiet.'

Peabody stood in the humming silence. She studied the boy, felt a little tug. She had a brother his age. With this in mind, she slapped on a smile. 'Pizza for breakfast,' she said with determined cheer. 'Got more?'

'Help yourself,' Roarke invited and patted the bench beside him in invitation. 'Jamie, this is Officer Peabody.'

'My grandfather knew you.' Jamie studied her with cautious, appraising eyes.

'Did he?' Peabody picked up a slice. 'I don't think I ever met him. I knew about him, though. Everybody at Central was sorry when he died.'

'He knew about you. He told me Dallas was molding you.'

'Peabody's a cop,' Eve broke in, 'not a lump of clay.' Annoyed, she picked up the last slice of pizza, bit in. 'This is cold.'

'It's great cold.' Peabody winked at Jamie. 'Nothing better than cold pizza for breakfast.'

'Eat while you can.' Respecting her own advice, Eve took another bite. 'It's going to be a long day.' She pinned Jamie with a glance. 'Starting now. Until you have a guardian or representative present, I can't record your statement or officially question you. Do you understand?'

'I'm not an idiot. And I'm not a child. I can—'

'You can be quiet,' Eve interrupted. 'With or without representation, I can toss you into juvenile lockup for trespassing. If Roarke chooses to press charges—'

'Eve, really—'

'You be quiet, too.' She rounded on him, all frustration and fatigue. 'This isn't a game, it's murder. And the media is already outside, sniffing blood. You're not going to be able to step outside your own house without having them jump you.'

'Do you think that disturbs me?'

'It disturbs me. It damn well disturbs the hell out of me. My job doesn't come here. It doesn't come here.' She stopped herself, turned away.

This, she realized abruptly, was what ate at her insides, chewed at her control. There was blood on her home, and she had brought it there.

Steadier, she turned back. 'That's all beside the point for now. You have some explaining to do,' she said to Jamie. 'Do you want to do it here or down at Central after I contact your mother?'

He didn't speak for a moment, just watched her as if measuring. It was, she realized, the same look that had been in his eyes when she had told him his sister was dead. It was very adult, very controlled.

'I know who the dead guy is. His name is Lobar, and he's one of the bastards who killed my sister. I saw him.'

Chapter Nine

Jamie's eyes were fierce, furious. Eve kept hers on his as she laid her palms on the table and leaned forward. 'Are you telling me that you saw Lobar kill your sister?'

Jamie's mouth worked as if he was chewing the words, and the words were bitter. 'No. But I know. I know he was one of them. I saw him with her. I saw all of them.' His chin wobbled and his voice cracked, reminding her he was only sixteen. But his eyes stayed ageless. 'I got in one night. In that apartment downtown.'

'What apartment?'

'Spooky Selina and Asshole Alban.' He shrugged a shoulder, but the movement was more nervous than cocky. 'I watched one of their devil shows.' His hand wasn't quite steady as he picked up his drink and sucked down the last of the Pepsi.

'They let you observe a ceremony?'

'They didn't *let* me do anything. They didn't know I was there. You could say I let myself in.' He glanced at Roarke. 'Their security isn't nearly as jazzy as yours.'

'There's good news.'

'You've been a busy boy, Jamie,' Eve said evenly. 'Planning on cat burglary as a career?'

'No.' He didn't smile. 'I'm going to be a cop. Like you.'

Eve blew out a breath, scrubbed her hands over her face, and sat. 'Cops who make a habit of illegal entry end up on the wrong side of a cage.'

'They had my sister.'

'Were they holding her against her will?'

'They messed with her mind. That's the same thing.'

Touchy area, Eve mused. She couldn't go back and stop the kid from breaking into private property. His grandfather had been a solid cop, she remembered, and had tried to do the same. The boy had simply succeeded.

'I'm going to do you a favor because I liked your grandfather. We're going to keep this off the record. As far as the record goes, you were never there. Never inside that place. You got that?'

'Sure.' He jerked a shoulder. 'Whatever.'

'Tell me what you saw. Don't exaggerate, don't speculate.'

Jamie's lips curved a little. 'Grandpa always said that.'

'That's right. You want to be a cop, give me a report.'

'Okay. Cool. Alice was in Weird City, right? She'd been cutting classes, making noises about dropping out. Mom was really wrecked over it. She thought it was a guy, but I knew it wasn't. Not that she was talking to me. She'd stopped talking to me.'

He broke off then, his eyes dark and miserable. Then he shook his head, sighed once, and continued. 'But I knew her. Alice would get all moony over a guy, dreamy-eyed and spastic. But with this, she was different. I figured she'd started experimenting. Illegals. I know my mom had talked to my grandfather, and he'd talked to Alice, but nobody was getting anywhere. So I figured I'd check it out. I followed her a couple times. I thought it would be good practice. Surveillance. She never tagged me. None of them did. A lot of people don't see kids, or if they do, they think they're harmless idiots.'

Eve kept her eyes hard on his face. 'I don't think you're harmless, Jamie.'

His lips twisted in a smirk. He recognized that Eve's statement wasn't exactly flattering. 'So I tailed her to that club. The Athame. First time I had to wait outside. I wasn't

426

prepped for it. She went in about ten, came out about twelve, with the ghoul patrol.'

He smirked again when Eve lifted a brow. 'Okay, subject exited premises in the company of three individuals, two male, one female. You already got their descriptions, so I'll say they were later identified by investigator as Selina Cross, Alban, and Lobar. They proceeded east, on foot, then entered multiunit housing structure owned by Selina Cross. Investigator observed light go on in top window. After weighing the options, investigator decided to enter building. Security was bypassed with minimal to average effort. Can I have another Pepsi?'

Saying nothing, Roarke took the empty tube, slipped it into the recycling slot, and fetched the boy another.

'It was really quiet inside,' Jamie continued as he broke the seal. 'Like dead. Dark. I had a minilight, but I didn't use it. I got upstairs, bypassed the palm plate and the cameras. The locks weren't that tricky. I figure they didn't think anybody'd have the nerve to come that far without an invite, you know? I got inside and the place was empty. I couldn't figure it. I'd seen them go in, I'd seen the light, but the place was empty. So I poked around. They've got some screwy stuff in there. And it smelled . . . off. Sorta like the incense and junk in a Free-Agers' shop, but different. Just off. I was in one of the bedrooms. There's this wild statue in there. This guy with a pig head and a man's body with a really monster cock at full alert.'

He stopped, flushed a little as he remembered he was talking to females as well as cops. 'Sorry.'

'I've seen cocks at full alert before,' Eve said mildly. 'Go on.'

'Okay. So I was just sort of looking at it, and this guy comes in. I thought, *Shit, I'm busted*, but he didn't see me. He got something out of a drawer, turned around, and walked out. Never even looked my way.' Jamie shook his head, sipped deeply, as he reexperienced the bowel-liquefying fear. 'I got to the doorway just as he was going through the wall. Secret panel,' he explained

427

with a quick grin. 'I thought they were only in old videos. I gave it a couple of minutes and went in after him.'

At this, Eve simply pressed her hands to her face, digging her fingers into the knots. 'You went in after him.'

'Yeah, my luck was holding pretty good. There's this stairway, narrow. I think it was stone. I could hear music. Not really music, more like voices, sort of humming. And that off smell was stronger. The stairway turns and there's this room. About half the size of this one, with mirrored walls. Lots of candles and more horny statues. It's smoky. Something's in the smoke, because it makes me light-headed. I try to be careful not to breathe too much in.'

He stared down at the drink in his hand. This part was hard, he realized. Harder than he'd thought it would be. 'There's this raised platform, all this carving. Some sort of words, I think, but I can't make it out. Alice is lying on it. She's naked. The three of them are standing over her saying something. Singing it, I guess, but I can't understand them. They're doing things to her, to each other.'

He had to swallow again. His face was bone white with high, red blotches on the cheeks. 'They've got like sex toys and she's . . . letting them. Both of them. And she lets them, she lets them do her while that Cross bitch watches. Alice just lets them . . .'

Without realizing it, Eve reached out, took his hand, let him grip her fingers hard enough to rub bone.

'I couldn't stay there. I was sick, seeing that, and the smoke, the sounds. I had to get out.' His eyes were wet now as he looked up. 'She wouldn't have let them do that if they hadn't messed with her mind. She wasn't a slut. She wasn't.'

'I know. Did you tell anyone?'

'I couldn't.' He swiped the back of one hand over his face. 'It would've killed my mom. I wanted to hit Alice with it, hit her hard with it. I was so pissed off. But I couldn't. I was embarrassed I'd seen her like that, I guess. My sister.'

'It's all right.'

'I went back to the club a couple nights later and got in.'

'They let you inside?'

'I got fake ID. Places like that, they don't care if you look twelve if you got ID that says different. Security's tighter there. They've got scanners, electronic and human, every damn where. I spotted Alice with that Lobar creep. They went upstairs, all the way up to the fancy level. I couldn't get in, but I got close enough to see they'd disappeared again. So I figure there must be a room up there, too. Like the one in the apartment. I was working out a way to get in after hours, then Alice ditched them. She moved in with that Isis character for awhile, got her own place and that job. And she didn't go to the club anymore, or back to the apartment.'

He let out a sigh. 'I thought she'd straightened herself out, that it had gotten through what creeps they were. She talked to me a little.'

'Did she tell you about the people she'd been involved with?'

'Not really. She just said she'd made a mistake, a terrible one. That she was like, atoning, cleansing, that zip brain stuff of hers. I knew she was scared, but she talked to my grandfather, so I figured things would be mellow again. Did they kill him, too?'

'There's no evidence of that. I'm not going to discuss it with you,' she added when he lifted his haunted eyes to hers. 'And you're not to discuss this with anyone. You're not to go near that club or that apartment again. If you do and I find out – and I will find out – I'll slap a security bracelet on you and you won't be able to burp without a scanner picking it up.'

'It's my family.'

'Yes, it is. And if you want to be a cop, you'd better learn that if you can't be objective, you can't do the job.'

'My grandfather wouldn't have been objective,' Jamie said quietly. 'And now he's dead.'

She had no answer for that, so she rose. 'Now the problem is getting you out of here and keeping your involvement out of the media. They'll be watching the gate.'

'There's always an alternative,' Roarke commented. 'I'll arrange it.'

She had no doubt he could, and nodded. 'I've got to change, get down to Central. Peabody.' She flicked a meaningful look in Jamie's direction. 'Stand by.'

'Yes, sir.'

'She means guard dog me,' Jamie muttered as Eve and Roarke left the kitchen.

'Yeah.' But Peabody flashed a companionable smile. 'Want another Pepsi?'

'I guess.'

She got up to play with the delivery slot on the fridge, helped herself to a cup of Roarke's magnificent coffee. 'So how long have you wanted to be a cop?'

'For as long as I remember.'

'Me, too.' She settled down to talk shop.

'I'll take him out by air,' Roarke told her as he and Eve cleaned up and changed in the bedroom.

'By air?'

'I've been meaning to take the minichopper out for a spin, anyway.'

'This area isn't zoned for personal choppers.'

Wisely, he disguised a laugh with a cough. 'Say that again when you're wearing your badge.'

She muttered to herself and pulled on a clean shirt. 'Take him home, will you? I appreciate it. The kid's lucky to be alive.'

'He's resourceful, bright, focused.' Roarke smiled as he picked up the jammer, admired it. 'Now, if I'd had one of these at his age . . . ah, the possibilities.'

'You do well enough with your magic fingers.'

'True.' He tucked the jammer in his pocket. He was going to

have one of his engineers analyze and very possibly reproduce it. 'I'm afraid youth today doesn't appreciate the satisfaction of hands on. If young Jamie changes his mind about law enforcement, I think I could find a nice slot for him in my little world.'

'Don't even mention it. You'll corrupt him.'

Roarke picked up his slim gold wrist unit, fastened it on. 'You did very well with him. Firm without being cold. A nice, authoritative, yet maternal style.'

She blinked. 'Huh?'

'You're good with children.' He grinned as she paled. 'I'd wondered.'

'Get a grip. A good strong grip,' she advised and strapped on her weapon harness. 'I'm going to hit Central first, file my report, feed Whitney the data that's not going into it. Officially, Jamie's name isn't going to be linked with this. I'm sure, if necessary, the two of you can work out a plausible story for his mother.'

'Child's play,' Roarke said with tongue in cheek.

'Hmm. From my prelim, Lobar was killed at oh three thirty. That would be about an hour after we left the club. Hard to tell how long he'd been propped outside the gate, but at a guess, no more than fifteen minutes or so before Jamie happened on him. It's not likely that whoever left Lobar hanging, let's say, stuck around. But if they did, and spotted Jamie, he could be a target. I want the kid under surveillance, and until Whitney uncuffs me, I can't use a cop.'

'Would you like me to put one of my trusted employees on him?'

'No, but that's what I'm going to ask you to do.' She turned to the mirror, raked fingers through her hair in lieu of a comb. 'I'm bringing this home, too many angles of it. I'm sorry.'

He walked to her, turned her around, caught her face in his hands. 'You can't separate what you do from who you are. I don't expect or want you to. What touches you, touches me. That's what I expect and what I want.'

'The last case that touched me almost killed you.' She wrapped her hands around his wrist, squeezed. 'I need you too much. It's your own fault.'

'Exactly.' He bent down, kissed her. 'That's what I want as well. Go to work, Lieutenant.'

'I'm going.' She strode to the door, paused, glanced back. 'I don't want to hear from Traffic that my husband was hotdogging the skyways in his minichopper.'

'You won't. I bribe too well.'

It made her laugh as she headed back down to fetch Peabody and face the first media onslaught.

She'd no more than strapped into her vehicle when she heard the throaty purr of an expensive engine. Wincing only a little, she glanced east and saw the sleek little copter with its tinted one-way glass cabin and whirling silver blades rise, circle playfully – and illegally – before bulleting off.

'Wow! What a machine. Is that Roarke's? Have you been up?' Peabody craned her head to try to get a last look. 'That is one rapid mother.'

'Shut up, Peabody.'

'I've never been up in a personal.' With a wistful sigh, Peabody settled. 'Makes the units Traffic use look like dog meat.'

'You used to be intimidated when I told you to shut up.'

'Those were the good old days.' Grinning, Peabody crossed her ankles. 'You handled the kid really well, Lieutenant.'

Eve rolled her eyes. 'I know how to interview a cooperative witness, Peabody.'

'Not everybody can handle a teenager. They're brutal, and fragile. That one's seen more than anyone should.'

'I know.' So had she by that age, Eve remembered. Perhaps that's why she'd understood. 'Prepare yourself, Peabody. The sharks are circling.'

Peabody grimaced at the pack of reporters crowded outside the gate. There were minicams, recorders, and hungry looks. 'Gee, I hope they get my best side.'

'Tough when you're sitting on it.'

'Thanks. I've been working out.' Automatically, Peabody wiped off the grin and assumed a blank, professional expression. 'I don't see Nadine,' she murmured.

'She's around.' Eve hit the remote for the gates. 'Furst wouldn't miss this one.' She timed it, opening the gates seconds before the nose of the car would have brushed iron. Reporters streamed forward, engulfing the car, aiming their cameras, shouting their questions. One or two were ballsy or stupid enough to step onto private property. Eve took note, switched the volume on her outside speakers to blast.

'The investigation is ongoing,' she announced. 'There will be an official statement at noon. Any media representative who trespasses on this property will not only be prosecuted but will be blocked from all data.'

She all but slammed the gates on scrambling feet. 'Where the hell are the uniforms I left on duty?'

'Probably eaten alive by now.' Peabody stared through the reporter who plastered himself against her side of the windshield. 'This one's kind of cute, Lieutenant. Try not to damage his face.'

'His choice.' She kept driving. Someone bounced off her fender and cursed. There was a slight bump, and a very loud scream.

'That's ten points for the foot,' Peabody commented, secretly thrilled. 'See if you can swipe that one there. The woman with the yard of legs in the green suit. That'll get you five more.'

The reporter clinging to the windshield slid off as Eve juggled the wheel. 'Missed her. Well, can't win them all.'

'Peabody.' Eve shook her head, hit the accelerator, and headed downtown. 'Sometimes I worry about you.'

She wanted to see Whitney first, but wasn't surprised to find Nadine waiting in ambush at the first-level interior glide at Central.

433

'Busy night, Dallas.'

'That's right, and I'm still busy. There'll be a press release by noon.'

'You can give me something now.' Nadine elbowed her way onto the glide. She wasn't a big woman, but she was a sneaky one. You didn't get to be one of the top on-air reporters in the city without some quick moves. 'Just a nibble, Dallas. Something I can take to the public for my ten o'clock bumper.'

'Dead guy,' Eve said shortly, 'identification withheld until next of kin are notified.'

'So you know who he was. Got any leads on who opened his throat?'

'My professional opinion would be someone with a sharp implement,' Eve said dryly.

'Um-hmm.' Nadine's eyes narrowed. 'There's a rumor rolling around that there was a message left at the scene. And that it was a ritual killing.'

Goddamn leaks. 'I can't comment on that.'

'Wait a minute.' At the top of the glide, Nadine took Eve's arm. 'You want me to hold something, you know I'll hold it. Give me something, and let me work.'

Trusting the media was a dicey business, but she'd trusted Nadine before. To their mutual benefit. As a research tool, Eve knew Nadine was a finely honed instrument. 'If it was a ritual killing, which is not substantiated and not for broadcast, my next step would be to gather all pertinent data on established cults and their members – registered and otherwise – in the city.'

'There are all kinds of cults, Dallas.'

'Then you'd better get busy.' She shook her arm free before dropping one more crumb. 'Funny, cult must be the root word for occult. Or maybe it's just a coincidence.'

'Maybe it is.' Nadine swung to the downward glide. 'I'll let you know.'

'That was tidy,' Peabody decided.

'Let's hope it stays that way. I'm for Whitney. I want you

434

to find out the names of every uniform that was on scene this morning. I want to have a talk about internal security with every one of them.'

'Ouch.'

'Damn right,' Eve muttered and stalked to the elevator.

Whitney didn't make her wait. She noted as she took her seat in his office that he didn't appear to have slept any more than she the night before.

'Internal Affairs is beefing on the Wojinski matter. They're pushing for an official investigation.'

'You can't hold them off.'

'Not past end of shift today.'

'My report should help.' She took a disc out of her bag. 'There is absolutely no evidence that DS Wojinsky was using illegals. There's every indication that he was running his own sting on Selina Cross. His reasons were personal, Commander, but even IAD should understand them. I have Alice's statement, recorded, and fully transcribed in the report. In my opinion, she had been drugged, and her . . . naïveté exploited. She was used sexually. She became involved with the cult established by Selina Cross and Alban. And when she broke with them, she was threatened, and she was frightened. Eventually, she went to Frank.'

'Why did she break loose?'

'She claims she witnessed the ritual slaying of a child.'

'What?' His knuckles went white as he surged up from his desk. 'She witnessed a murder, reported this to Frank, and he didn't file?'

'She waited some time before telling him, Commander. There was no evidence to support her allegations. I can't substantiate them now. But I can say that Alice believed she saw the killing. And she was terrified for her life. She also felt she was responsible for the death of her grandfather. She believed, strongly, that he had been murdered because

435

of his private investigation of Selina Cross. Her claim was that Selina Cross has expert knowledge of chemicals and essentially poisoned Frank.'

'We don't have enough to prove foul play.'

'Not yet. Alice was certain she would be next, and she died the same night she gave her statement to me. She also claimed Cross was a shape-shifter.'

'Excuse me?'

'She believed that Cross could take other forms. A raven, for one.'

'She thought Cross could become a crow and fly? Jesus, Dallas, the boys in IAD are going to love that one.'

'It doesn't have to be real for her to have believed it. She was a terrified young girl, tormented by these people. I found a black feather on her windowsill the night she died – a simulated feather, and there was a threatening message on her 'link. They were tormenting her, Commander. There's no mistake there. What Frank did, he did to try to protect his family. Maybe he went about it wrong, but he was a good cop. He died a good cop. IAD isn't going to change that.'

'We'll make sure they don't.' He locked the disc away. 'For now, this stays here.'

'Feeney—'

'Not at this time, Lieutenant.'

Damn if she'd be brushed off like a fly, she thought, and set her jaw. 'Commander, my investigation to this point discloses absolutely no connection between DS Wojinski's private investigation and Captain Feeney. I can find no evidence that Feeney tampered with any records for Frank.'

'Do you actually believe Feeney would leave evidence, Dallas?'

She kept her eyes level. 'I'd know if he was involved. He's grieving for both his friend and his goddaughter, and he doesn't know anything other than the official line on either. He doesn't know, Commander, and he has a right to.'

It was going to cost them, Whitney knew. All of them. But it couldn't be helped. 'I can't take his personal rights into consideration, Lieutenant. Believe me, IAD won't. All data here is on need-to-know only. It's a rough spot. You'll have to handle it.'

It ate a hole in her gut, but she nodded. 'I'll handle it.'

'What connection is this to the body left outside your home this morning?'

Left with no choice, she fell back on training and delivered data. 'Robert Mathias, known as Lobar, white male, eighteen years. My report on cause of death is the throat wound, but the body was also mutilated. The victim was a member of Cross's cult. I also interviewed him last night at his place of employment. A club called The Athame, owned by Selina Cross.'

'People you talk to are ending up dead very quickly, Dallas.'

'He was Cross's alibi for the night Alice was killed. Hers and Alban's. He corroborated this during questioning.' She opened her bag. 'He wasn't killed at the scene, and he was left there in a manner designed to indicate a ritual killing.' She placed one of the death stills on Whitney's desk.

'The murder weapon was likely the knife he's got stuck in his groin. It's an athame – a ritual knife. Supposedly, Wiccans dull the blade and use it only for symbolism.' She took out another shot, a close-up of the note. 'The message appears to indicate the murder was done by an enemy of the Church of Satan.'

'Church of Satan,' Whitney muttered. The death photo didn't sicken him, it tired him. He'd seen far too many. 'The ultimate oxymoron. Someone took a dislike to the practices and took him out.'

'The scene was set that way. It's possible, and I've got a couple of lines I can tug on that angle.'

He looked up from the photo. 'You're thinking Cross had a hand in this. She'd execute her own alibi.'

'She'd execute her own progeny if she had any. I think she's smart,' Eve continued. 'And I think she's crazy. I'll be consulting with Mira on that end. But I also think she'd get a real bang out of doing this, out of rubbing it in my face. She didn't need him anymore. I had his statement.'

Whitney nodded, pushed the photos back to her. 'Talk to her again. And this Alban.'

'Yes, sir.' She put the photos away. 'There's more. It's . . . delicate.'

'What?'

'I've deleted any reference to this from the official report. Slightly altered the timing. For the record, Roarke and I were awakened by the security alarm, which was tripped when the body was placed against the perimeter wall. Off the record, we didn't discover the body initially. Jamie Lingstrom did.'

'Jesus,' Whitney said after a long minute. He pressed his fingers over his eyes. 'How?'

Eve cleared her throat and gave a quick and concise report of everything that took place after the alarm. She concluded with what Jamie had told her at the breakfast table.

'I don't know how much of that you want to feed to IAD. Jamie's statement corroborates Alice's contention that Frank was trying to trap Cross.'

'I'll filter out what I can.' He continued to rub his eyes. 'First his granddaughter, now his grandson.'

'I think I shook him enough to keep him in line.'

'Dallas, teenagers are remarkably hard to shake. I've been there.'

'I do want him to have some protection, as well as sur-veillance. Using my own judgment, I'm arranging for this privately.'

Whitney lifted a brow. 'You mean Roarke's arranging it?'

Eve folded her hands. 'The boy will be watched.'

'We'll leave it at that.' He leaned back. 'A homemade, hand-held jammer, you said? One the kid jerry-rigged that managed to bypass the outer layers of the security on that fortress you live in?'

'So it would seem.'

'Where is it? You didn't give it back to him.'

'I'm not an idiot,' she said as if she'd been slapped on the wrist. 'Roarke has it.' And as she completed the sentence, and the thought, her training slipped enough for her to wince.

'Roarke has it.' Despite the situation, Whitney threw back his head and laughed. 'Oh that's rich. You gave the wolf the key to the henhouse.' He caught her narrow-eyed scowl and muffled the next chuckle. 'Just trying for a little levity, Lieutenant.'

'Yes, sir. Ha ha. I'll get it back.'

'No offense, Dallas, but if you're taking bets, I've got a hundred I'll put on Roarke. In any case, unofficially, the department appreciates his assistance and cooperation.'

'You'll excuse me if I don't relay that. It'll only go to his head.' Recognizing dismissal, she rose. 'Commander, Frank was clean. IAD is going to confirm that. Whether his death was of natural causes or induced is going to be more difficult to establish. I could use Captain Feeney.'

'You know you don't need Feeney on this, Dallas, not in an investigative sense. I appreciate your feelings, but this stays here until further notice. You might find yourself sitting in this chair one day,' he said and watched her brow furrow in surprise. 'Difficult decisions sit here with you. And giving unpleasant orders is every bit as frustrating as taking them. Keep me posted.'

'Yes, sir.' She walked out, knowing that she didn't want his chair, his rank, or his responsibilities.

Chapter Ten

Her first duty was to inform Lobar's next of kin. Once it was done, Eve spent a few moments pondering family. They hadn't cared. The woman's face on-screen had stayed blank, as if Eve had informed her of the death of a stranger rather than a son she had birthed and raised. She had thanked Eve politely, asked no questions, agreed that the remains be sent home when released.

They would, she'd said, give him a decent, Christian burial.

She imagined they would have done the same for a family pet.

What calcified the feelings to that extent? she wondered. *If there had been feelings to begin with. What made one mother grieve so pitifully, as Alice's mother was, and another take the news of her child's death without a single tear?*

What had her own mother felt on her birth? Had she been happy, or simply relieved to have the nine-month intruder finally evicted from her body?

She had no memory of a mother, not even some shadowy female form in her life. Only of her father, of the man who had dragged her from place to place, kept her in locked rooms. Who had raped her. And the memories of him, after so many years of denial, were much too clear.

Perhaps some people were fated to survive without family, she thought. *Or simply to survive them.*

Because her thoughts were dark, it was with mixed feelings she called Dr Mira's office for a consultation. After she'd managed to intimidate Mira's assistant into squeezing her in the next day, she grabbed her bag, beeped Peabody, and headed out.

She didn't miss Peabody's wary expression as they pulled up in front of Selina's apartment, but she ignored it. It was starting to rain, a nasty, surprisingly cold drip out of suddenly leaden skies. The wind was up, whistling down the long canyon of street and biting where it struck exposed flesh.

On the opposite sidewalk, a man rushed east, huddled under a black umbrella. He turned quickly into a shop with a grinning skull and the words The Arcane painted on the door.

'Perfect day to pay a visit to Satan's handmaid.' Peabody strained for false cheer and surreptitiously fingered a bit of Saint-John's-wort she'd stuck in her pocket. Her mother's advice for protection against black magic. The stalwart Peabody had discovered she believed in witches after all.

They went through the same routine with security, only the wait was longer and more unpleasant as the rain began to stream down in earnest. Nasty forks of lightning jabbed at the sky, their tines bright bloodred at the edges.

Eve glanced up, then back at her aide. Her smile was hard and cold. 'Yeah, perfect.'

They trailed water into the lobby, into the elevator, and into the foyer of Selina Cross's apartment.

And it was Alban who greeted them. 'Lieutenant Dallas.' He offered a beautifully sculptured hand graced with a single ring of thick brushed silver. 'I'm Alban, Selina's companion. I'm afraid she's meditating at the moment. I hesitate to disturb her.'

'Let her meditate. You'll do for now.'

'Well then, come in and sit down. Please.' His manner was sophisticated, faintly formal, and at odds with the barechested black leather unisuit he wore. 'Can I get you something? Some tea perhaps to ward off the chill. Such an interesting change in the weather.'

'Nothing.' Eve thought she'd have preferred a quick hit of Zeus to anything brewed in that place.

The gloom suited it, she decided. *The dank light, the wicked hiss of rain and wind on the windows. Then there was Alban, with his pretty poet's face and warrior god body. A perfect fallen angel.*

'I'd like your whereabouts for last night between the hours of three hundred and five hundred hours.'

'Three and five A.M.?' He blinked as if translating the military time. 'Last night – or this morning, rather. Why, here. I think we got back from the club a bit before two. We haven't been out yet today.'

'We?'

'Selina and myself. We had a coven meeting, which concluded around three. We cut it a little short as Selina wasn't feeling herself. Normally, we might entertain afterwards, or continue with a smaller, more private rite.'

'But you didn't do so last night.'

'No. As I said, Selina wasn't feeling well, so we went to bed early. Early for us,' he explained with a smile. 'We're night people.'

'Who attended the coven meeting?'

His smile shifted into a serious, almost studious expression. 'Lieutenant, religion is a private matter. And still in this day and age, one such as ours is persecuted. Our membership prefers discretion.'

'One of your membership was indiscreetly murdered last night.'

'No.' He rose, slowly, keeping his hand braced on the arm of his chair as if unsteady. 'I knew it was something horrible. She was so disturbed.' He took a deep breath as if preparing both mind and body. 'Who?'

'Lobar.' Selina said the name as she stepped through a narrow archway. She was deathly pale, her cat's eyes shadowed. She wore her black hair loose today, with a wide dip over generous breasts. 'It was Lobar,' she repeated. 'I saw it just now, in the smoke. Alban.' She pressed a hand to her head, swayed.

442

'Quite a show,' Eve murmured as Alban rushed across the room to catch her, to hold her against him. 'You saw it in the smoke.' Eve cocked her head. 'That's handy. Maybe I should take a look at the smoke myself, see who cut his throat.'

'There's nothing in the smoke for you but your own ignorance.' Leaning on Alban, Selina walked slowly to the sofa. She sat with a rustle of her robes, lifted a hand to Alban's. 'I'm all right.'

'My love.' He brought her hand to his lips. 'I'll get you a soother.'

'Yes, yes, thank you.'

She bowed her head while he went quietly out. Oh, it was hard to keep a cat grin off her face, to stop the glorious images from playing back in her brain of the rite, the sacrifice, the blood.

And only she and Alban knew of the excitement, the power of that moment when Lobar had been offered to the master.

Only she fully understood the thrill of making that sacrifice with her own hand. She shuddered once with dark pleasure, stirred by the memory. The way Lobar's eyes had met hers, the way the athame had fit cold in her hand. Then the hot fountain of blood when she'd used it.

Imagining the shock, the fury Eve must have felt when she'd found Lobar so carefully positioned at the entrance to her own sanctuary, Selina nearly snickered. She pressed her fingers to her lips a moment, as if holding back a sob.

Alban was a genius, she thought, for truly only a genius would have created such beautiful irony.

'Visions can be a blessing or a curse.' She continued in a voice strained with weariness. 'I prefer to think of them as blessings, even when they cause me sorrow. Lobar is a heavy loss.'

'Laying it thick, aren't you?'

Selina's head shot up, and her eyes glimmered with something more of hate than grief. 'Don't mock my feelings, Dallas. Do you think power such as mine means I don't have them? I feel, I experience. I bleed,' she added and, with a lightning movement, raked one of her long, lethal nails over her own palm. Blood welled dark and red.

'A demonstration wasn't necessary,' Eve said easily. 'I know you bleed. Lobar certainly did.'

'His throat. Yes, that's what I saw in the smoke.' She reached out for Alban when he came in, carrying a shallow silver bowl. 'But there was more. Something else.' She took the bowl, tipped it up to her lips. 'Mutilation. Oh, how they despise us.'

'They?'

'The weak and the white.'

She took a black swatch of cloth from the pocket of her robe, passed it to Alban. He lifted her injured hand, raised it to his lips. With quick efficiency, he bound up her wounded palm. Selina never spared him a glance.

'Those who view our master with hate,' she continued. 'And more, those who practice the magic of the foolish.'

'So, in your opinion, this was a religious murder?'

'Of course; I have no doubt.' She finished the soother, set the bowl aside. 'Do you?'

'Quite a number of them; but then, I have to investigate the old-fashioned way. I can't call up the devil and ask for a consult. Lobar was here last night.'

'Yes, until nearly three. He would have taken the mark soon.' Selina sighed, idly running her red-tipped nails up and down Alban's arm. 'One of his last acts was to join his body with mine.'

'You had sex with him last night.'

'Yes. Sex is an important part of our rituals. I chose him last night.' She shuddered again because the choice had been hers. And the deed. 'Something must have told me.'

'A bird maybe. A big black bird.' Lifting a brow, Eve studied Alban. 'So, it's no problem with you to watch while other men have sex with your . . . companion. Most men are a little territorial. They might harbor unhealthy resentments.'

444

'We don't believe in monogamy. We find it limiting and foolish. Sex is pleasure, and we don't put restrictions on our pleasures. Consensual sex in a private home or licensed club isn't against your laws, Lieutenant.' He smiled. 'I'm sure you engage in it yourself.'

'You like to watch, Alban?'

His brows lifted. 'Is that an invitation?' At Selina's quick chuckle, he shifted and took her hand. 'There, you're feeling better now.'

'Grief passes, doesn't it, Selina?'

'It must,' she agreed, nodding at Eve. 'Life is to be lived. You'll look for who did this, and perhaps you'll find them. But the punishment of our master is greater and more terrible than any you could invent.'

'Your master isn't my concern. Murder is. Since you have an interest in the deceased, maybe you'll let me take a look around.'

'Get a warrant, and you're welcome.' The tranq had clouded her eyes, but her voice was strong enough when she stood. 'You're more a fool than I originally thought if you believe I had anything to do with this. He was one of ours. He was loyal. It is against the law to harm a loyal member of the cult.'

'And he talked to me last night in a privacy booth. Did the smoke tell you what he told me, Selina?'

Her eyes shifted, darkened. 'You'll have to find other waters to fish in, Dallas. I'm tired, Alban. Show them out.' She glided away, back through the arch.

'There's nothing we can do for you, Lieutenant. Selina needs to rest.' He glanced toward the arch, worry in his eyes. 'I need to tend her.'

'Got you trained, does she?' With light disdain coating her voice, Eve rose. 'Do you do tricks, too?'

Sadly, he shook his head. 'My devotion to Selina is personal. She has powers, and the powerful have needs. I meet hers, gratefully.' He walked back into the foyer, opened the door.

'We would like to take Lobar's body when it's possible. We have our death ceremony.'

'So does his family, and they come ahead of you.'

'What do we have on this Alban?' Eve demanded the moment they were outside in the now drenching rain.

'Next to nothing.' Peabody ducked into the car and immediately felt more at ease. She knew it was foolish to hope she never had to go back inside that building, but she hoped in any case. 'No priors, next to no background. If he was born with a name other than Alban, it doesn't pop.'

'There's more. There's always more.'

Not so, Eve thought, drumming her fingers against the wheel. She'd once investigated another suspicious character and had found little to nothing. His only name was Roarke.

'Look again,' she ordered and pulled away from the curb.

'Funny, isn't it?' she continued while Peabody plugged in her data unit. 'There's next to no traffic on this block. Turn the corner . . .' She did so and immediately hit a snarl of nasty and comforting vehicular traffic, bumping bad-temperedly through the rain. People hustled along sidewalks and glides, huddled in doorways. Two glide-cart operators on opposing corners hunched under ratty awnings and scowled at each other.

'People have instincts they're not even aware of.' Still less than comfortable, Peabody glanced back, as if expecting something not quite human might be scrabbling behind them. 'There's a bad feeling around that building.'

'It's brick and glass.'

'Yeah, but places tend to take on the personalities of the people who live in them.'

A car turned the corner ahead, blasting its horn at the sea of pedestrians who streamed across against the go light. Insults were cheerfully hurled both verbally and through equally graphic hand signals. Someone spat.

Steam poured up through the vents from the underground

system in dirty clouds. It tangled thickly with the smoke belching from a ratty and obviously under code glida grill fighting its way through the mass of wet humanity. A level up, the nearest skywalk shuddered to a halt and sent all its passengers into a riot of cursing and complaints.

Overhead, a tourist blimp blasted out a spiel of the advantages and highlights of living in an urban wonderland.

Peabody took a cleansing breath, pleased to be back in the midst of the arrogant and crowded New York she understood. 'Take Roarke's place,' she continued. 'It's grand and elegant and intimidating, but it's also sexy and mysterious.' She was too busy fiddling with the unit to notice the amused look Eve shot her. 'My parents' place? It's all open and warm and a little confused.'

'What about your place, Peabody? What's that?'

'Temporary,' Peabody said definitely. 'Dallas, your car unit isn't cooperating here. I should be able to transfer data to—' She broke off as Eve leaned over, smacked the dash above the car screen. An image popped on, wobbling drunkenly. 'That's some better,' Peabody decided and requested a run on Alban.

Alban – no known alternate name – born 3–22–2020 Omaha, Nebraska.

'Funny,' Eve interrupted, 'he didn't look corn fed.'

ID number, the computer continued with a definite hiccup in its program, 31666-LRT-99. Parents unknown. Marital status, single. No known means of support. No financial data available.

'Interesting. Sounds like he's leeching off Selina. Criminal records, all arrests.'

No criminal record.

'Education?'

Unknown.

'Our boy's wiped, or had somebody wipe records,' Eve told Peabody. 'You don't get to be nearly forty years old without generating more data than this. He's got connections somewhere.'

She needed Feeney, she thought grumpily. Feeney could tickle the computer and trick additional data. Instead, she was going to have to go to Roarke and add another layer to his involvement.

'Well, shit.' She pulled up in front of Spirit Quest, frowned at the Closed sign on the door. 'Run up for a look-see, Peabody. Maybe she's inside.'

'Got an umbrella or a rain shield?'

Eve arched a brow. 'Are you trying to be funny?'

Peabody only sighed, then pushed out of the car. She plodded and splashed through the rain, peered into windows. Shivering a little, she turned back, shook her soaking head, then groaned when Eve jerked a thumb toward the apartment over the shop. Resigned, Peabody trudged around the side, climbed a set of rickety metal stairs. Moments later, she was back, streaming water.

'No answer,' she told Eve. 'Minimal security. Unless you count the swatch of Saint-John's-wort over the entrance.'

'She has a swatch of warts? That's disgusting.'

'Not warts.' Despite her wet uniform and dripping hair, Peabody indulged in a good laugh. 'It's a plant. Saint-John's-wort.' Amused enough, she dug into her pocket for her sprig. 'Like this. It's for protection. Guards against evil.'

'You carry plants in your pocket, Officer?'

'I do now.' Peabody pushed it back in her pocket. 'Want some?'

'No, thanks, I prefer trusting my weapon to guard against evil.'

'I consider this my clutch piece.'

'Whatever works for you.' Eve scanned the area. 'Let's try that café place across the street. Maybe they know why she's closed in the middle of a business morning.'

'Maybe they've got decent coffee,' Peabody said and sneezed twice, hard. 'If I catch a cold, I'll kill myself. It takes me weeks to throw one of those suckers off.'

'Maybe you need a plant to cart around that wards off common germs.' Leaving it at that, Eve hopped out of the car, coded the locks, and jogged across the street into Coffee Ole.

The stab at a Mexican theme wasn't bad, she decided. Bright colors – heavy on orange – gave it a sunny appearance even on a filthy day. It might have fallen far short of Roarke's gorgeous villa on the west coast of Mexico, but it had a certain tacky charm with its plastic flowers and papier-mâché bulls. Bright mariachi music piped through the speakers.

Either the rain or the ambiance had brought in a crowd. But as Eve scanned the room, she noted that the people packed around tables weren't wolfing down plates of enchiladas. Most were huddled over single stingy cups of what smelled remotely like overboiled soy coffee.

'Baseball's closing in on the league titles, isn't it, Peabody?'

Peabody sneezed again. 'Baseball? I guess. Arena ball's my game.'

'Uh-huh. Seems to me there a pennant race going on. Pivotal game today. I imagine lots of money's going to change hands.'

Peabody's head was starting to feel stuffy – a very bad sign – but it was still clear enough for her to latch on. 'You figure this is a front, an illegal betting parlor.'

449

'Just a hunch. We may be able to use it.' She sidled up to the counter, tagged a harassed-looking man. Short of stature, dark of complexion, weary of eye.

'Eat in or carry out?'

'Neither,' she began, then relented as she heard Peabody sniffle. 'One coffee, for her. And a couple of answers.'

'I've got coffee.' He swiveled around to plug thick dark brew into a cup barely bigger than a thimble. 'I got no answers.'

'Maybe you should hear the questions.'

'Lady, I got a full house here. I serve coffee. I got no time for conversation.' He dumped the cup on the counter and would have backed away, but Eve snagged his wrist. 'What are the house odds on the game today?'

His eyes shifted left and right before settling on her face. But he'd spotted Peabody and her uniform. 'Don't know what you're talking about.'

'You know, if me and my pal here settle in for a few hours, your business is going into the recycler. Personally, I don't give a good damn about your business, any of your business. But I could.' Still holding his wrist, she turned her head and stared hard at two of the men seated at the counter.

It took less than ten seconds for them to decide to drink coffee elsewhere. 'How long do you think it'd take me to clear this place out?'

'What do you want? I make my contribution. I'm covered.'

She let him go. It annoyed her to find out that he had cop protection. Didn't surprise her, just annoyed. 'I'm not going to interfere unless you irritate me. Tell me about the shop across the street. Spirit Quest.'

He snorted, visibly relaxed. She wasn't after him. Feeling cooperative, he refilled Peabody's cup, then picked up a rag and wiped the counter. He ran a clean place. 'The witch? She don't come in here. Don't drink coffee, if you know what I mean.'

450

'She's closed today.'

'Yeah?' He narrowed his eyes to try to see through the window, through the rain. 'Not usually.'

'When did you see her last?'

'Shit.' He scratched the back of his neck. 'Let's see. Seems I saw her yesterday. Closing time? Yeah, yeah, she closes about six, and I was washing the front windows. You gotta keep on the windows in this city. Dirt just jumps right on them.'

'I bet. She closed about six. Then what?'

'Went off with that guy she lives with. Walking. They don't got transpo.'

'You haven't seen her today?'

'Now that you mention it, guess not. She lives up above, you know. Me, I live across town. Keep business and personal life separate, that's my motto.'

'Any of her people ever come over here?'

'Nah. Some of her customers, sure. And some of mine go over there looking for lucky charms. We bump along okay. She ain't no problem for me. Even bought the wife a birthday present over there. Pretty little bracelet, colored stones. Kinda stiff in the price, but women like that glitter shit.'

He tossed the rag aside and ignored the request for coffee from down the counter. 'Look, she in trouble? She's okay in my book. Weird maybe, but ain't no harm in her.'

'What do you know about the girl who used to work there? Young girl, about eighteen. Blonde.'

'The spooky one? Sure, I used to see her come and go. Always looking over her shoulder that one, like somebody was going to jump out and say boo.'

Someone did, Eve thought. 'Thanks. If you see Isis come back today, give me a call.' She slipped a card onto the counter along with credits for the coffee.

'No problem. Wouldn't like to see her get in trouble, though. She's okay for a whacko. Hey.' He lifted a finger as Eve started to turn. 'Speaking of whackos, I saw one a couple of nights ago when I was closing up.'

'What sort of whacko?'

'Just a guy. Well, might have been a woman. Couldn't tell 'cause they was all wrapped up in this black robe, hood and everything. Just standing there on the curb, staring across the street at her place. Just standing and staring. Gave me the creeps. I walked the other way. Twice as far to the bus stop, but I didn't like the feel of it. And you know what? I looked back, and there wasn't no one there. Nothing but a damn cat. Whacko, huh?'

'Yeah,' Eve murmured. 'Whacko.'

'I saw a cat,' Peabody began when they headed back to the car, 'on the street when Alice was killed.'

'There are lots of cats in the city.'

But Eve remembered the one on the ramp. Sleek and black and mean. 'We'll follow up with Isis later. I want to check with the ME before I feed the statement to the media.' She uncoded the car as Peabody sneezed again. 'Maybe he'll have something for that cold.'

Peabody rubbed her hand under her nose. 'I'd just as soon stop by a pharmacy, if you don't mind. I don't want Dr Death treating me until absolutely necessary.'

After she was back in her office and Peabody was off changing into a dry uniform and dosing herself with a small fortune of over-the-counters, Eve studied the autopsy report on Lobar.

She'd had the time of death right in the prelim, and the cause. Then again, she mused, it was tough to miss a mile-wide gash in the throat and a crater in the chest. And, fancy that, there had been traces of a hallucinogen, a stimulant, and a mind hazer – all of the illegals variety – in his bloodstream.

So he'd died sexually fulfilled and zoned. Some, she imagined, would say that wasn't such a bad deal. But then, most of them hadn't had a knife raked over their throats.

She lifted the sealed weapon, studied it. No prints, of course, and none expected. No blood on it but for the victim's. She studied the carved black handle, scanning the symbols and letters that meant nothing to her. It appeared to be old and rare, but she doubted that would help her pin ownership. The blade was under legal limit, required no registration.

Still, she would check antique shops, knife shops, and, she supposed, witch shops. That would only take weeks, she thought in disgust, and was unlikely to lead anywhere.

Since she had twenty minutes before she had to face the media, she turned to her machine and got started. She'd no more than plugged in the description of the weapon when Feeney walked in, shut her door.

'Heard you had a rude awakening this morning.'

'Yeah.' Her stomach clutched, not in memory of what had come into her home, but at knowing she would have to weigh every word with him. 'Not the kind of package I like to receive.'

'You need help on it?' He smiled wanly. 'I'm looking for busywork.'

'I've got it covered for now, but I'll let you know.'

He paced to her narrow window, back to her door. He looked exhausted, she thought. So tired. So sad.

'What's the story? Did you know the guy?'

'Not really.' Oh, Christ, what did she do here? 'I'd talked to him once about a case I was on. Didn't pan out. Could be he knew more than he was telling me. It's going to be hard to say now.' She took a deep breath, hating herself. 'I figure it was someone who wanted to take a swipe at me or Roarke. Most cops can keep their home addresses quiet. I can't.' She shrugged.

'Price you pay for falling for a public figure. You happy?' he said abruptly and turned to study her face.

'Sure.' She wondered if guilt was plastered on her forehead like a neon sign.

453

'Good. Good.' He paced again, jiggling the bag of nuts he habitually carried in his pocket and no longer seemed to have the appetite for. 'It's tough to be on the job and make a decent personal life. Frank did.'

'I know.'

'Alice's viewing is tonight. You going to make it?'

'I don't know, Feeney. I'll try.'

'It rips me, Dallas. It really rips me. My wife's with Brenda now. She's wrecked. Just wrecked. I couldn't handle it anymore so I came in. But I can't focus.'

'Why don't you go back home, Feeney?' She rose, reached out to touch his arm. 'Jus' go home. Maybe you and your wife could go away for a few days. You've got the time coming. Get away from this.'

'Maybe.' His eyes were bleak, heavy with bags. 'But where do you go to get away from what's always there?'

'Listen, Roarke's got this place in Mexico. It's great.' She was fumbling and knew it, desperate to give. 'It's got a monster view, and it's fully equipped. It would be.' She managed a smile. 'It's Roarke's. I'll square it with him. You can go there, take your family.'

'Take the family.' He repeated it slowly, finding the idea was almost soothing. 'Maybe I will. You never seem to make time to be with your family. I'll think about it,' he decided. 'Thanks.'

'It's nothing. It's Roarke. It's just there.' She turned blindly toward her desk. 'I'm sorry, Freeney, I've got to get it together for a media statement.'

'Sure.' He worked up a smile for her. 'I know how much you love that. I'll let you know about using the place.'

'Yeah, do that.' She stared hard at her screen until he went out. She'd followed orders, she reminded herself. She'd done the right thing.

So why did it make her feel like a traitor?

Chapter Eleven

She made the tail end of the viewing, grateful that Roarke had come with her. It was too familiar, the same memorial parlor, the same scents, many of the same people.

'I hate this,' she murmured. 'Sanitized death.'

'It comforts.'

Eve looked over to where Brenda was supported by her mother and her son while tears ran slowly down her cheeks. She had the glazed and delicate look of the heavily medicated.

'Does it?'

'It closes,' he corrected and took her cold hand in his. 'For some.'

'When it's my turn, don't do this. Recycle the parts, burn the rest. Get it done.'

He felt the fist clutch around his heart and gave her hand a hard squeeze. 'Don't.'

'Sorry. I tend to have morbid thoughts in places like this. Well.' Her room scan stopped when she spotted Isis. 'There's my witch.'

Roarke followed her gaze and studied the imposing woman with flame-colored hair and wearing a simple robe of pure white. She stood by the viewing box beside a man a full head shorter than she. He wore a plain, almost conservative suit, also in white. Their fingers were linked.

'The man with her?'

'I don't know him. Might be a member of her sect or whatever. Let's check it out.'

They moved across the room and by tacit agreement, flanked the couple. Eve looked down at Alice first, at the young face, composed now. Death had a way of relaxing the features. After the insult had passed.

'She's not here.' Isis spoke quietly. 'Her spirit still searches for peace. I'd hoped . . . I'd hoped to find her here. I'm sorry I missed you today, Dallas. We were closed in Alice's memory.'

'You weren't at home, either.'

'No, we gathered at another place, for our own ceremony. The man across the street told me you'd been looking for me.' A faint smile wisped around her mouth. 'He was concerned that I had a cop on my trail. He has a good heart, despite a certain imbalance.'

She stepped back to introduce the man beside her. 'This is Chas. My mate.'

Training kept Eve's eyes bland, but she was surprised. He was as ordinary as Isis was spectacular. His hair was a washed-out blond, thin in texture. His body was almost fragile, narrow in the shoulders, short in the leg. His square, unremarkable face was stopped just short of homely by a pair of surprisingly lovely deep gray eyes. When he smiled, it was with a sweetness that demanded a smile in return.

'I'm sorry to meet you under such sad circumstances. Isis told me you were a very strong and purposeful soul. I see she was right, as always.'

She nearly blinked at his voice. It was a deep, creamy baritone any opera singer would have wept for. She caught herself watching his mouth move and imagining a ventriloquist's dummy. It wasn't a voice that should have come out of that body and that face.

'I need to talk to you both as soon as possible.' She glanced around, wished for a discreet way to slip out and conduct an interview. It would have to wait. 'This is Roarke.'

456

'Yes, I know.' Isis offered a hand. 'We've met before.'

'Have we?' His smile was politely curious. 'I can't imagine forgetting meeting a beautiful woman.'

'Another time, another place.' Her eyes stayed on his. 'Another life. You saved mine once.'

'That was wise of me.'

'Yes, it was. And kind. Perhaps someday you'll revisit the county of Cork and see a small stone dance alone in a fallow field . . . and you'll remember.' She slipped the silver cross she wore off her neck, handed it to him. 'You gave me a talisman then. Similar to this Celtic cross. I suppose that's why I wore it tonight. To close a circle.'

The metal was warmer against his hand than it should have been, and it stirred something in cloudy memory he didn't care to explore. 'Thank you.' He slipped it into his pocket.

'One day I may return the favor you did me.' She turned to Eve then. 'I'll speak with you whenever you like. Chas?'

'Of course, whenever it's convenient for you, Lieutenant Dallas. Will you attend our ceremony? We'd very much like to share it with you. Night after next. We have a small place upstate. It's quiet and private and, when the weather cooperates, perfect for outdoor rites. I hope you—'

He broke off, his stunning eyes going dark. His thin body shifting to what Eve recognized immediately as a guard stance. 'He's not one of us,' he said.

She glanced around, spotted a man in a dark suit. His face was cell-block white and framed by a black wedge of hair. The suit was expensive, his skin wan, making him appear both sickly and successful.

He started toward the viewing box, saw the group already there. In one jerky move he turned on his heel and hurried out.

'I'll check it out.'

She was moving quickly when Roarke caught up with her. 'We'll check it out.'

'It would be better if you stayed inside with them.'

'I'm staying with you.'

She only shot him a frustrated look. 'Don't cramp my style.'

'Wouldn't dream of it.'

The retreating man was nearly at a run as he hit the door. Eve only had to touch his arm to have him jolt. 'What? What do you want?' He whirled, pressing the door for release, backing out of it into the rainy night. 'I haven't done anything.'

'No? He sure looks guilty for an innocent man, doesn't he?' She took a firmer grip on his arm to keep him from rabbiting away. 'Maybe you should show me some ID.'

'I don't have to show you anything.'

'It's not necessary,' Roarke said smoothly. He'd gotten a better look now. 'Thomas Wineburg, isn't it? Of Wineburg Financial. You've nabbed yourself a deadly type here, Lieutenant. A banker. Third generation. Or is it fourth?'

'It's fifth,' Wineburg said, struggling to look down his narrow nose at what his family would consider new and not quite decent money. 'And I've done nothing to warrant being accosted by a police officer and a financial rogue.'

'I'm the cop,' Eve decided glancing at Roarke. 'You must be the financial rogue.'

'He's just mad because I don't use his bank.' Roarke flashed a wolfish grin. 'Aren't you, Tommy?'

'I have nothing to say to you.'

'Well, then, you can talk to me. What's the rush?'

'I – I have an appointment I'd forgotten. I'm quite late.'

'Then a couple more minutes won't matter. Are you a friend of the deceased's family?'

'No.'

'Oh, I get it, you just like to while away a rainy evening at a viewing parlor. I've heard that's the coming thing for singles.'

'I – I'd mistook the address.'

458

'I don't think so. What did you come to see? Or who?'

'I—' His eyes widened when Isis and Chas stepped out. 'Stay away from me.'

'I'm sorry, Dallas. We were concerned when you didn't come back.' Isis turned her exotic eyes on Wineburg. 'Your aura is dark and muddy. You dabble without belief. Toy with power beyond your scope. If you don't change your path, you damn yourself.'

'Keep her away from me.' Straining against Eve's grip, Wineburg cringed back.

'She's not hurting you. What do you know about Alice's death, Wineburg?'

'I don't know anything.' His voice went shrill. 'I don't know anything about anything. I mistook the address. I have an appointment. You can't hold me.'

No, she couldn't, but she could scare the hell out of him. 'I could take you down to Central, play with you awhile before your representative managed to get there. Wouldn't that be fun?'

'I haven't done anything.' To Eve's surprise and mild disgust, he began to sob like a baby. 'You have to let me go. I'm not part of this.'

'Part of what?'

'It was just for sex. That's all. Just for sex. I didn't know anybody would die. Blood everywhere. Everywhere. Dear God. I didn't know.'

'Where? What have you seen?'

He continued to sob, and when she started to shift her grip, he rammed his bony elbow hard into her gut, sending her flying violently back into Roarke so that they both hit the pavement.

Later, she could curse herself for letting him catch her off guard with his sniveling. But for now, she scrambled up, struggling to suck in air and gave chase.

Son of a bitch. She could only think it. He'd knocked the

wind out of her and prevented her from swearing aloud or shouting out an order for him to freeze.

She reached for her weapon just as he dove into an underground garage and darted into the forest of vehicles.

'Shit.' She had enough air for that, then snarled at Roarke as he rushed in behind her. 'Get out. Damn it, he's probably not armed, but you're sure as hell not. Call it in if you want to do something.'

'The day I let a pissant banker knock me on my ass and walk away has not come.' He veered off to circle around and left her scowling at him.

The security lights were blinding, but the opportunity for cover was endless. Echoes of running footsteps bounced off the floor and walls and ceiling. Trusting instinct, she moved left.

'Wineburg, you aren't helping yourself. You've got assaulting an officer on you now. You come out without making me dig you out, I might cut you a break.'

Crouched, she swung toward the narrow opening between cars, scanned under, behind, moved on.

'Roarke, hold still a minute, goddamn it, so I can tag location.' The echoes softened a bit, allowing her to strain her ears and venture farther to the left at running speed. He was heading up, she decided, hoping to lose himself on the next level.

She darted up the first ramp, then whirled and braced, weapon aimed, when footsteps pounded behind her. 'I should have known,' was all she said as Roarke passed her. She dug in and continued pursuit. 'He's heading up,' she snapped out. 'He keeps going, he'll corner himself. All the idiot has to do is stop, lay low. It would take a fucking platoon to find him in here.'

'He's scared. When you're scared, you run away.' He glanced at Eve, and felt ridiculously exhilarated as they hit the next ramp. 'Or some do.'

Then the footsteps silenced. Eve threw out an arm to hold

Roarke in place, held her breath as she strained to hear. 'What is that?' she whispered. 'What the hell is that sound?'

'Chanting.'

Her heart jumped. 'Jesus Christ.' She broke into a fresh run just as one long, terrified scream ripped the air. It seemed to go on, endlessly, high and inhuman and horrible. Then it snapped off into silence. She dragged out her communicator without breaking stride. 'Officer needs assistance. Officer needs assistance, parking garage, Forty-ninth and Second. Dallas, Lieutenant Eve in pursuit of . . . Goddamn it.'

'Dispatch, Dallas, Lieutenant Eve, please say again.'

She didn't bother to stare at the body spread in a growing pool of blood on the concrete floor. One glance at the terrified, wide eyes and the carved hilt of a knife plunged into the heart had been enough to determine death.

Wineburg had run the wrong way.

'I need backup, immediately. I've got a homicide. Perpetrator or perpetrators possibly still on premises. Dispatch all available units to this address for blockade and search. I need a field kit and my aide.'

'Received. Units en route. Dispatch out.'

'I've got to look,' she said to Roarke.

'Understood.'

'I don't have my clutch piece or I'd give it to you. I need you to stay here, with the body.'

Roarke looked down at Wineburg and felt a stir of pity. 'He's not going anywhere.'

'I need you to stay here,' she repeated. 'In case they come back this way. Don't be a hero.'

He nodded. 'You, either.'

She took one last glance at the body. 'Fuck,' she said wearily. 'I should have had a better grip on him.'

She moved off slowly, scanning cars and corners, but without much hope.

He'd watched her work before, studied and admired the efficient, concentrated field she created around the dead. Roarke wondered if she fully understood why she did it, or how she could, while examining a lifeless, violently dispatched body with such clear-cut objectivity, see through the pity that haunted her eyes.

He'd never asked her. He doubted he ever would.

He watched her order Peabody to record the scene from a different angle, saw her jerk her thumb at a uniform – obviously a rookie who wasn't holding up well. Sending him off on an errand, Roarke imagined, so he could be sick in private.

Some of them never got used to the blood or the smell of bladder and bowels releasing with death.

The lights were viciously bright, merciless, really. The heart wound had bled profusely. She'd worn heels and a little black suit to the viewing. Of course, she would ruin both now. She was kneeling beside the body, tearing her stockings on the concrete and removing the murder weapon now that the scene had been duly recorded.

She sealed it, bagged it for evidence, but he'd gotten a good look at it. The handle was a deep brown, possibly horn of some sort. Yet there had been no mistaking its similarity to the one left at the last murder. An athame. The knife of ritual.

'Bad business.'

Roarke made a sound of assent as Feeney walked up to him. The man looked uncharacteristically fragile, Roarke observed. Eve was right to be concerned about him.

'You know anything about it? I'm not getting much buzz except that Dallas was talking to him outside, he ran, and ended up dead.'

'That's about it. He seemed nervous about something. Apparently he had reason to be.' It wasn't a place they could go together, Roarke decided and shifted away from it. 'I hope you'll take Eve up on the offer of the house in Mexico.'

462

'I'll talk it over with my wife. I appreciate it.' Then he moved his shoulders. 'I guess she doesn't need me here. I should get home.' But he studied the scene another minute. Behind the fatigue in his eyes lurked the cop. 'Screwy business. Some guy getting stuck in here. Fancy knife took out that stiff left at your place last night, too, right?'

'The other had a black handle. Some sort of metal, I think.'

'Yeah, well . . .' He rocked back on his heels a moment. 'I'd better head home.'

He crossed to Eve, careful to avoid getting too close in his untreated shoes. She looked up, distracted, wiping the blood off her sealed hands with a rag.

And she watched him walk away until he was out of sight.

She rose, raked her not quite clean hands through her hair. 'Bag him,' she ordered, and walked to Roarke. 'I'm going to go in, do the report while it's fresh in my mind.'

'All right.' He took her arm.

'No, you should go home. I'll catch a ride with one of the team.'

'I'll take you.'

'Peabody—'

'Peabody can catch a ride with one of the team.' She needed a few minutes, he knew, to decompress. He touched a button on his wrist unit to signal his driver.

'I feel stupid going into Central in a limo,' she muttered.

'Really? I don't.' He walked her out of the garage, then around to the front of the funeral parlor. The limo streamed up to the curb. 'You can catch your breath,' he suggested as he slid in behind her. 'And I can have a brandy.' He poured one from a crystal decanter, and knowing Eve, programmed her coffee.

'Well, since we're going it this way, you can tell me what you know about Wineburg.'

'One of the irritating rich and pampered.'

She took the hot, rich coffee served in a thin, classy cup of bone china, and gave Roarke – his plush limo, his pricey brandy – a long, cool look. 'You're rich.'

'Yes.' He smiled. 'But pampered? Certainly not.' He swirled his brandy, kept smiling. 'That's what stops me from being irritating.'

'You think so?' The coffee helped, got her circuits running. 'So he was a banker. He ran Wineburg Financial.'

'Hardly. His father's still hale and hearty. This little fish would have been more of a minion. The type given busy-work and a useless title and a big office. He'd gobble up his expense account, shuffle forms, and have his cosmetician in for weekly sessions.'

'Okay, you didn't like him.'

'I didn't know him, actually.' He gave the brandy a lazy swirl and sip. 'Just the type. I don't have any business dealings with Wineburg. In the dawn of my . . . career, I needed some backing for a couple of projects. Legal projects,' he added at Eve's speculative look. 'They wouldn't let me in the door. I wasn't up to their level of client. So I went elsewhere, got the backing, and made a killing. Figuratively speaking. The Wineburg organization took it poorly.'

'So they're a conservative, established, family-run institution.'

'Exactly.'

'It would be embarrassing to have the scion . . . Would he be like the scion?'

'If there's such a thing as a minor scion, I suppose.'

'Okay if he was into Satanism, it probably wouldn't go down well at the company picnic.'

'It would turn the board of directors white with shock – and, family or not, this little Wineburg would have been out on his ass.'

'He didn't look like the type to risk it, but you never know. Sex, he said. Just for the sex. He could have been one of the ones who had at Alice. Then he's guilty or curious and comes by the viewing. The one thing he was, was scared. He saw something, Roarke. He saw someone murdered. I know it. If I'd gotten him in, I'd have pulled it out of him. I could have broken him in ten minutes.'

'Apparently, someone else thought so, too.'

'Someone who was right there. On the spot. Watching him. Watching the viewing.'

'Or watching you,' Roarke finished. 'Which is more likely.'

'I hope they keep watching, because before long, I'm going to turn around and bite them on the throat.' She glanced up as the limo pulled up to the front of Cop Central. Vaguely embarrassed, she peered out, hoping no cops were loitering nearby. She'd be ragged on for days. 'I'll see you at home. Couple hours.'

'I'll wait.'

'Don't be ridiculous. Go home.'

He simply leaned back, ordered the screen to engage and list the latest stock information. 'I'll wait,' he repeated and poured another brandy.

'Hardhead,' she muttered as she got out, then winced when someone called her name.

'Woowee, Dallas, going to slum with us working poor for awhile?'

'Bite me, Carter,' she muttered, and rushed inside before the delighted laughter forced her to break someone's face.

An hour later, she was back, bone weary and sparking mad. 'Carter just had it announced over the main that my carriage awaited anon. What an idiot. I don't know whether to kick his ass or yours.'

'Kick his,' Roarke suggested and draped an arm around her. He'd switched from work to pleasure mode and had an old video on screen.

She caught the scent of expensive tobacco clinging to the

air and wished she could claim it irritated her. But it soothed, along with his arm and the ancient black-and-white video.

'What is this?'

'Bogart and Bacall. First film together. She was nineteen, I think. Here's the line.'

Eve stretched out her legs and listened to Bacall ask Bogie if he knew how to whistle. Her lips twitched. 'Clever.'

'It's a good film. We'll have to watch it all the way through sometime. You're tense, Lieutenant.'

'Maybe.'

'We'll have to fix that.' He shifted, poured a stemmed glass full of straw-colored liquid. 'Drink.'

'What is it?'

'Wine, just wine.'

She sniffed it suspiciously. He wasn't above doctoring it, she knew. 'I was going to work a little when we get home. I need my head clear.'

'You have to shut down sometime. Relax. Your head can be clear in the morning.'

He had a point. She had too much data in her head, and none of it was helping. Four deaths now, and she was no closer. Maybe if she backed off for a few hours, she'd see better.

'Whoever did Wineburg was quick and quiet. And smart, going for the heart. Hit the throat like Lobar, and you get blood all over you. Hit the heart, it's over fast and with minimal mess.'

'Umm-hmm.' He began to knead the back of her neck. It was always a magnet for her stress.

'What were we, thirty, forty seconds behind? Fast, really fast. If Wineburg cracked, there could be another. I've got to get the membership list. There has to be a way.' She sipped at the wine. 'What were you and Feeney talking about?'

'Mexico. Stop worrying.'

'Okay, okay.' She leaned her head back, closed her eyes for what seemed like three seconds. But when she opened them again, they were through the gates and pulling up in front of the house. 'Did I fall asleep?'

'For about five minutes.'

'That was just wine, right?'

'Absolutely. The next part of our program is a hot bath.'

'A bath isn't . . .' She reconsidered as they stepped inside. 'Actually, that sounds pretty good.'

Ten minutes later, while water gushed into the tub and swirled in the power of jets, it began to sound better. But she arched a brow when she saw Roarke begin to undress. 'Who's the bath for, me or you?'

'Us.' He gave her a tap on the butt, nudging her forward.

'That's fine then. It'll give you a chance to tell me all about saving the life of a beautiful woman.'

'Hmm.' He slipped into the frothy water, facing her. 'Oh. I can't be held responsible for actions that took place in a former life.' He passed her another glass of wine he'd had the foresight to pour. 'Now, can I?'

'I don't know. Isn't the theory something like you repeat things, or learn from them, or don't?' She held the glass aloft and dunked herself down, resurfacing with a sigh. 'You figure you were lovers, or what?'

Considering, he trailed a fingertip up and down Eve's leg. 'If she looked then the way she looks now, I'd certainly hope so.'

She gave him a sour smile. 'Yeah, I'd guess you'd go for the big, beautiful, exotic type then and now.' With a shrug, she drank more wine, then toyed with the stem. 'Most people figure you stepped wide of the mark with me.'

'Most people?'

She downed the rest of the wine, set the glass aside. 'Sure, I get the drift when we've got to make time with some of those rich and high-toned business associates of yours. Can't blame them for wondering what came over you. I'm not big, beautiful, or exotic.'

'No, you're not. Slim, lovely, strong. It's a wonder I looked twice.'

She felt ridiculous and flustered. He could do that to her just by the way he looked at her. 'I'm not fishing,' she muttered.

'And it surprises me that you'd give a damn what any of my associates thought of either one of us.'

'I don't.' Damn it, she'd stepped right in it. 'I was just making an observation. The wine's got my tongue running away with me.'

'You annoy me, Eve.' His voice was dangerously cool. A warning she recognized. 'Criticizing my taste.'

'Forget it.' She dunked again, surfaced like a shot when his hands clamped over her waist. 'Hey, what are you doing? Trying to drown me?' She blinked water out of her eyes and saw that his were indeed annoyed. 'Listen—'

'No, you listen. Or better yet.' He crushed his mouth to hers, hot, hungry, hurried. It made the top of her lead lift off and spin. 'We'll just move to the third part of our program a little early,' he said when he let her suck in a gulp of air. 'And I'll show you why I'm precisely on the mark with you, Lieutenant. Precisely. I don't make mistakes.'

She scowled at him even as the blood hummed under her skin. 'That arrogant routine doesn't work for me. I said it was the wine.'

'You won't blame what I can do to you on the wine,' he promised. He tilted his hands so that his thumbs traced the vulnerable fold between thigh and crotch. 'You won't blame it on the wine when I make you scream.'

'I won't scream.' But her head fell back as a moan tore through her lips. 'I can't breathe when you do that.'

'Then don't. Don't breathe.' He lifted her up until her breasts were above water, and his hands busy below. He dipped, caught one dripping point between his teeth. 'I'm going to take you. You're going to let me.'

'I don't want to be taken, unless I take back.' But even as

468

her arms came around him, he ripped her to peak, made her body buck and her arms go limp.

'Not this time.' He was suddenly ravenous for her, just this way, limp and open and mindless.

'How do you do that?' Her voice was weak and slurred.

He nearly chuckled, though the need was growing painful. Saying nothing, he stood, lifted her. Her eyes fluttered open as he carried her out of the bath.

'I want you in bed,' he said. 'I want you wet, inside and out. I want to feel your body tremble when I touch you.' He laid her down, fastened his mouth on her throat. 'And taste you.'

She felt drunk, too loose for control, too pliant for shock, as his hands got busy again. She bucked, she reached for him, but he slipped away, sliding down her damp body, hands fast, mouth urgent. She couldn't keep up. Now her body was tight, a white-knuckled fist, ready to strike. She came abruptly, violently, and didn't hear her own scream.

He took what he wanted. Everything. His blood pounded harder and hotter every time he dragged her over the next edge. Their flesh was wet with sweat now as he drove them both ruthlessly.

When the need to be inside of her was unbearable, he pulled her up, parted her legs until they clamped around his waist. And when her arms were around him as well, clinging, her body trembling hard against his, he gripped her hips and filled her in one deep stroke.

His mouth found her breast, felt the wild, ragged beat of her heart beneath the damp flesh. And when she climaxed again, vising around him like silk-coated iron, he held himself back.

'Look at me.' He arched her back, watching as her body shuddered, her hips moved. Arousal built fresh as he took himself deeper into her. 'Look at me, Eve.' He stroked his hands over her, molding each curve again while he continued to thrust, slow, steady. His breath came in pants. His control vibrated on a thin, fraying wire.

She opened her eyes. They were glazed, heavy, but they watched him. 'You're the one,' he said, and braced himself over her. 'You're the only.'

His mouth swooped down to hers, found it eager and open as he emptied himself into her.

For once, he slept first. She lay in the dark, listening to him breathe, stealing a little of his warmth as her own body cooled. Since he was asleep, she stroked his hair.

'I love you,' she murmured. 'I love you so much, I'm stupid about it.'

With a sigh, she settled down, closed her eyes, and willed her mind to empty.

Beside her, Roarke smiled into the dark.

He never slept first.

Chapter Twelve

In his midtown office high above the city, Roarke dealt with his last meeting of the morning. As originally scheduled, he should be concluding this business in Rotterdam, but he had arranged to take the meeting holographically so as to remain close to home. Close to Eve.

He sat at the head of his gleaming conference table, aware that his image sat at a similar one an ocean away. His assistant sat on his left, feeding him the necessary hard copy for his approval and signature. His translator sat on his right, as backup, should there be any problem with the computer headset's language program.

The board of ScanAir filled the other seats. Or their images did. It had been a very good year for Roarke Enterprises and its subsidiaries. It had not been a good year nor a good several years for ScanAir. Roarke was doing them the favor of buying them out.

From the stony expressions on several holographic faces, they were not entirely grateful.

The company needed to be right-sized, which meant several of the cushier positions would be adjusted in salary and responsibility. Some would be eliminated altogether. He had already hand-picked several men and women who were willing to relocate to Rotterdam and whip the skyline back into shape.

As the computer-generated translation of the contract droned in his ears, he watched the faces, the body language.

Occasionally, he conferred with his translator for subtleties and syntax.

He already knew every phrase, every word of the buyout agreement. He wasn't paying what the board had hoped for. Then again, they had hoped his examination of the company wouldn't turn up some of the more delicate – and well-hidden – financial difficulties.

He couldn't blame them for that. He would have done the same. But his examinations were always thorough and turned up everything.

He signed his name on each copy, added the date, then passed the contracts to his assistant for her to witness and seal. She rose, fed the contacts into a laser fax. Seconds later, the copy was across the ocean and being signed by his counterpart.

'Congratulations on your retirement, Mr Vanderlay,' Roarke said pleasantly when the countersigned and witnessed copies were faxed back to him. 'I hope you'll enjoy it.'

This was acknowledged by a brief nod and a short formal statement. The holograms winked off.

Roarke eased back, amused. 'People aren't always grateful when you give them large quantities of money, are they, Caro?'

'No, sir.' She was tidy, with hair shockingly white and gloriously styled. She rose, taking both the hard copy and the record disc of the transaction for filing. Her trim, rust-colored suit showed off beautifully shaped legs. 'They'll be less grateful when you turn ScanAir into a financial success. Within a year, I'd say.'

'Ten months.' He turned to the translator. 'Thank you, Petrov, your services were invaluable, as always.'

'My pleasure, sir.' He was a droid, created by one of Roarke's science arms. His body was slim, garbed in a well-cut dark suit. His face was attractive, but not distractingly so, and formed to simulate trustworthy middle age. Several of his line were leased by the UN.

472

'Give me an hour, Caro, before the next. I have some personal business to tend to.'

'You have a one o'clock lunch with the department heads of Sky Ways to discuss the absorption of ScanAir, and the publicity strategies.'

'Here, or off site?'

'Here, sir, in the executive dining hall. You approved the menu last week.' She smiled. 'In anticipation.'

'Right. I remember. I'll be there.' He moved through the side door and into his office. Before going to the desk, he engaged locks. It wasn't strictly necessary. Caro would never come in unannounced, but it paid in certain areas to be cautious. The work he intended to do couldn't go on his log. He would have preferred to handle it at home, but he was squeezed for time. And so, he thought, was Eve.

At his desk unit, he engaged the jamming field that would block any scan by CompuGuard. The law frowned on unauthorized hacking, and the penalties were stiff.

'Computer, membership data, Church of Satan, New York City branch, under direction of Selina Cross.'

Working ... That data is protected under religious privacy act. Request denied.

Roarke only smiled. He'd always preferred a challenge. 'Oh well, I think we can change your mind about that.' Prepared to enjoy himself, he slipped off his suit jacket, rolled up his sleeves, and got to work.

Downtown, Eve paced Dr Mira's pretty, designed-to-soothe office. She was never completely relaxed there. She trusted Mira's judgment; she always had. More recently, she had come to trust the doctor on a personal level. As much as it was possible. But it didn't make her relax.

Mira knew more about her than anyone. More, Eve suspected

473

than she knew about herself. Facing someone with that kind of intimate knowledge wasn't relaxing.

But she hadn't come to talk about personal matters, Eve reminded herself. She was here to talk murder.

Mira opened the door and stepped in. Her smile was slow and warm and personal. She always looked so . . . perfect, Eve decided. Never too glossy, never undone, never less than competent. Today, instead of her customary suit, Mira wore a slim, pumpkin-colored dress with a single-button matching coat of the same above-the-knee length. Her shoes were of a slightly darker tone and boasted the skinny heels that Eve always marveled a woman would wear by choice.

Mira offered both hands, a gesture of affection that simultaneously baffled and pleased Eve.

'It's good to see you back in fighting shape, Eve. No problem with the knee?'

'Oh?' With a faint frown Eve glanced down, remembering the injury she'd suffered while closing a recent case. 'No. The MTs did a good job. I'd forgotten about it.'

'A side affect of *your* job.' Mira settled in one of her scoop chairs. 'I'd think it would be a bit like childbirth.'

'Excuse me?'

'The ability to forget the pain, the trauma to both body and mind, and go on to do the same thing again. I've always believed women make good cops and doctors because they're inherently resilient that way. Won't you sit, have some tea, tell me what I can do for you?'

'I appreciate you fitting me in.' Eve sat, shifted restlessly. She always felt inclined to bare her soul once she was settled in this room with this woman. 'It's about a case I'm working on. I can't give you many details. There's an internal block.'

'I see.' Mira programmed tea. 'Tell me what you can.'

'One subject is a young woman, eighteen, very bright, and apparently very impressionable.'

474

'It's an age for explorations.' Mira took out the tea steaming fragrantly in delicate china cups, offered one to Eve.

Eve would drink it, but she wouldn't particularly like it. 'I suppose. The subject has family. Close family. Though the father is out of the picture, there is extended family – grandparents, cousins, that kind of thing. She wasn't – isn't,' Eve corrected, 'alone.'

Mira nodded. *Eve had been alone*, she thought, *brutally alone*.

'The subject had an interest in ancient religions and cultures, was studying same. Over the past year, she developed a certain interest in the occult.'

'Hmm. That's also fairly typical. Youth often explores various creeds and beliefs in order to find and cement their own. The occult, with its mystique and its possibilities is very attractive.'

'She became involved in Satanism.'

'As a dabbler?'

Eve frowned. She'd expected Mira to show some surprise or disapproval. Instead, she was sipping tea with that slight attentive smile playing around her mouth. 'If that means was she toying with it, I'd say she went deeper.'

'Initiated?'

'I'm not sure what that involves.'

'Depending on the sect, there would be slight variations. Broadly, it would entail a waiting period, the taking of vows, a physical mark on the body, generally on or near the genitalia. The initiate would be accepted into the coven with a ceremony. There would be an altar, a human one, probably female, within a circle. The princes of hell would be called while the initiate or initiates knelt. Symbolism would include flame, smoke, the ringing of a bell, graveyard dirt, preferably from an infant. They would be given water or wine mixed with urine to drink, then the high priest or priestess would mark the initiate with a ceremonial knife.'

'An athame.'

'Yes.' Mira smiled, as though pleased with a bright student.

475

'And though it's illegal, if the coven is able, they will then sacrifice a young goat. With some, the blood of the goat is mixed with wine and consumed. Once done, the coven engages in sex. The altar may be used by all or many. It would be considered both a duty and a pleasure.'

'Sounds like you've been there.'

'No, but I was allowed to observe a sabbat ceremony once. It was quite fascinating.'

'You don't actually believe that stuff.' Stunned, Eve set the cup aside. 'Calling up the devil.'

Mira lifted a smoothly arched brow. 'I believe in good and evil, Eve, and I don't by any means discount the likelihood of an ultimate good, or an ultimate evil. In my profession, and yours, we see too much of both to deny it.'

Humans committed evil, Eve thought. *Evil was human.* 'But devil worship?'

'Those who choose to focus their lives – and shall we say souls – on this creed generally do so for its freedom, its structure, and its celebration of selfishness. Others are seduced by the promise of power. And many by the sex.'

'*It was just sex.*' *That's what Wineburg had said, had sobbed*, Eve remembered, *before he died.*

'Your young woman, Eve, was likely drawn in first by the intellect. Satanism is centuries old, and like most pagan religions, predates Christianity. Why does it survive, and in some eras even prosper? It's filled with secrets and sins and sex, its rites are mysterious and elaborate. She would have wondered, and coming from a close and likely sheltered homelife, was at an age ripe for rebellions against the status quo.'

'The ceremony you described was similar to one she described to me. But she had only begun to observe and she was sexually used. She was a virgin, and was, I suspect drugged.'

'I see. There are always sects that diverge from the established rules of law. Some can be dangerous.'

'She had blanks, time losses, and became almost slavishly

476

devoted to two of the members. She backed away from her family and her studies. Until she witnessed the ritual murder of a child.'

'Human sacrifice is an old practice, and a deplorable one.' Mira sipped delicately. 'If drugs were involved, it's highly possible she was made an addict, dependent upon these people. That would explain the blanks. I take it the murder she witnessed shocked her away from the cult and its rituals.'

'She was terrified. She didn't go to her family, didn't report the incident. She ran to a witch.'

'A white witch? A Wiccan?'

Eve compressed her lips. 'She did what I expect would be considered a religious one eighty. Started burning white candles instead of black. And she lived in terror, claimed that one of the membership could turn into a raven.'

'Shape-shifting.' Thoughtfully, Mira rose to program more tea. 'Interesting.'

'She believed they would kill her, had killed someone close to her, though that death is for now officially listed under natural causes. I have no doubt they tormented her, found a way to play on her delusions and fears. I'm thinking some of that came from her own sense of guilt and shame.'

'You could be right. Emotions influence the intellect.'

'Just how much?' Eve demanded. 'Enough for her to see things that weren't there? Enough for her to run from an illusion into the path of an oncoming car and kill herself?'

Mira sat again. 'She's dead then. I'm sorry. Are you quite sure she ran from an illusion?'

'A trained observer was on the scene. There was nothing there. Except,' Eve added with a twist of her lips, 'a black cat.'

'The traditional familiar. That alone might have been enough to push her over the edge. Even if the cat was planted in order to frighten her, you would have a difficult time terming it homicide.'

'They played on her mind, drugged her, possibly used

hypnosis. They tormented her with tricks and 'link transmissions. Then they pushed her over. Damned if that isn't murder. And I will make it stick.'

'Taking religion, particularly religions the masses don't wish to acknowledge, into court won't be easy.'

'I don't care about easy. The people behind this cult are dirty. And I believe they have killed four people in the last two weeks.'

'Four.' Mira paused, set the cup down. 'The body that was left near your home. The details in the media were sketchy. It's connected?'

'Yeah. He was an initiate, and he had his throat slit by an athame. It was left in him, stuck in his groin with a note that condemned Satanism. He was strapped to an inverted pentagram.'

'Mutilation and murder.' Mira pursed her lips. 'If it was Wiccans, it's very much out of character. Very much against their creed.'

'People do things out of character and against their creeds all the time,' Eve said impatiently. 'But at this time, I suspect a member or members of his own cult. Another man was killed last night with an athame. We held it from the morning reports, but it'll be all over the media within a couple of hours. I was on scene, chasing him down. I didn't run fast enough.'

'He was killed quickly, without ritual? With a police officer in pursuit?' Mira shook her head. 'A desperate or arrogant move. If this was committed by the same people, it shows a growing boldness.'

'And maybe a taste for it. Blood becomes addictive. I want to know where the weaknesses are in the kind of personality who runs a cult like this. I've got a female, long yellow sheet involving illegal sex and drug trafficking. Bisexual. She heads up the club, lives well. Her companion is a well-built male who caters to her. She likes to show off,' Eve added, remembering the fire trick. 'She claims to be clairvoyant. She's edgy, with a slippery temper.'

'Pride would likely be the first weakness. If she's in a position of power and authority, she would likely take disrespect badly. Is she clairvoyant?'

'Are you serious?'

'Eve.' Mira sighed lightly. 'Psychic abilities exist, and always have. Studies have established that.'

'Yeah, yeah.' Eve waved a hand in dismissal. 'The Kijinsky Institute, for one. I've got a detailed report on the white witch from there. They claim she's off the charts.'

'And you don't agree with the Kijinsky Institute?'

'Crystal balls and palm reading? You're a scientist.'

'Yes, I am, and as such, I accept that science is fluid. It changes as we learn more about the universe and what inhabits it. Many well-respected scientists believe that we're born with what we can term this sixth sense, or a heightened sense, if you will. Some develop it, some block it. Most of us retain at least some level. We'd call it instinct, hunches, intuition. You rely on that yourself.'

'I rely on evidence, on facts.'

'You have hunches, Eve. And your intuition is a finely crafted tool. And Roarke.' She smiled when Eve's brows drew together. 'A man doesn't rise so high so young without a strong instinct for making the right move at the right time. Magic, if you want to use a more romantic term, exists.'

'You're telling me you believe in mind reading and spell casting?'

'I can intuit what's going through your mind right now.' Mira chuckled, finished her tea. 'Mira, you're thinking, is full of shit.'

Eve's lips curved in a reluctant smile of her own. 'Close enough.'

'Let me say this, since I believe it's part of what you came here for. Witchcraft, black and white, has existed since the dawn of humanity. And where there is power, there is benefit, and there is abuse. That, too, is the nature of humanity. We can't, through all our scientific and technical skill, destroy one without damaging the other. Power requires tending, as do beliefs, so we have our ceremonies and our rituals. We need the structure, the comfort, and yes, the mystery of them.'

'I don't have any problem with ceremonies and rituals, Dr Mira. Unless they cross the line of the law.'

'I would agree. But the law can also be fluid. It changes, adapts.'

'Murder stays murder. Whether it's accomplished with a stone spear or a laser blast.' Her eyes were dark and fierce. 'Or whether it's done with smoke and mirrors. I'll find the perpetrator, and no magic in the world is going to stop me.'

'No.' A small, niggling fear – what might have been called a hunch – knotted in Mira's gut. 'I would agree with that as well. You're not without power, Eve, and you'll match yours against this.' She folded her hands. 'I can provide you with a more detailed analysis on both Satanism and Wicca, if it might help.'

'I like to know what I'm dealing with. I'd appreciate it. Can you give me a profile of a typical member of both cults?'

'There isn't a typical member, any more than there are typical members of the Catholic faith or of Buddhism, but I can generalize certain personality types who are often attracted to the occult. The Wiccan the young woman went to, is she a suspect?'

'She's not the prime, but she's a suspect. Revenge is a strong motive, and if Satanists keep ending up with a ritual knife in vital organs, I won't overlook revenge.' Unable to resist, Eve ran her tongue over her teeth. 'But I suppose she'd be more likely to put a curse on them.'

'Check the nails and hair of your victims, or of any subsequent ones. If a curse is involved, there should be signs of recent snippings.'

'Yeah? I'll do that.' Eve rose. 'I appreciate the help.'

'I'll get you a report by tomorrow.'

'Great.' She started out, paused. 'You seem to know a lot about all of this. Is it the kind of thing you study for psychiatry?'

'To some extent, but I have a more personal interest and studied fairly extensively.' Her lips curved. 'My daughter is Wiccan.'

Eve's jaw dropped. 'Oh.' *What the hell did she say now?* 'Well. I guess that explains it.' Uncomfortable, she dug her hands into her pockets. 'Around here?'

'No, she lives in New Orleans. She finds it less restrictive there. I may be a bit unobjective on the matter, Eve, under the circumstances, but I think you'll find it's a lovely faith, very earthy and generous.'

'Sure.' Eve edged for the door. 'I'm going to observe a meeting tomorrow night.'

'You'll have to let me know what you think. And if you have questions I'm unable to answer, I'm sure my daughter would be happy to speak with you.'

'I'll let you know.' She headed to the elevator, blowing out a long breath. *Mira's daughter was a witch, for Christ's sake,* she thought. *That was a hell of a capper.*

She headed back to Central with the intention of rounding up Peabody, then heading to Wineburg's townhouse. She wanted to get a look at his lifestyle, his logs, and his personal records. She had a feeling a drone like him would have kept some private list of names and places.

The sweepers had already been through, routinely, and had turned up nothing of particular interest. But she could get lucky.

She passed Peabody in the bullpen as she swung through. 'My vehicle, fifteen minutes. I want to check my messages, make a couple of calls.'

'Yes, sir. Lieutenant—'

'Later,' Eve said shortly, hurrying by and missing Peabody's wince.

The reason for it was waiting in her office.

'Feeney?' She tugged her jacket off, tossed it on a chair: 'You decide to head to Mexico? You're going to need to call Roarke for the details. He should be—'

She broke off when Feeney stood up, walked over, and shut her door. It had only taken one look at his face to know.

'You lied to me.' There was a quaver in his voice that came as much from hurt as anger. But his eyes were flat and cold. 'You fucking lied to me. I trusted you. You've been investigating Frank behind my back. Over his own dead body.'

There was no point in denying, less in asking how he'd found out. She'd known he would. 'There was going to be an internal investigation. Whitney wanted me to clear him, and that's what I've done.'

'Internal investigation my ass. Nobody was cleaner than Frank.'

'I know that, Feeney. I was—'

'But you investigated. You went through his records, and you did it around me.'

'That's the way it had to be.'

'Bullshit. I goddamn trained you. You'd still be in uniform if I hadn't put you here. And you back stab me.' He stepped closer, fists clenched at his sides.

She preferred him to use them.

'You've got Alice's file open, suspected homicide. She was my goddaughter, and you don't tell me you think some son of a bitch killed her? You block me out of the investigation, you lie to me. You looked right in my face and lied to me.'

Her stomach had gone to ice. 'Yes.'

'You think she'd been drugged and raped and murdered, and you don't take me in?'

He'd gotten into the records, the reports, she realized. They'd been sealed and coded, but that wouldn't have stopped

482

him if he'd gotten a whiff. And, she decided, he'd gotten one the night before, over Wineburg's body.

'I couldn't,' she said in a flat voice. 'Even if I hadn't been under orders, I couldn't. You were too close. You can't objectively assist on an investigation involving family.'

'What the hell do you know about family?' he exploded and made her jerk.

Yes, she'd have preferred his fists.

'Orders?' he continued, bitterness spewing out and scalding her. 'Fucking orders? Is that your line, Dallas? Is that your reason for treating me like some lame rookie? "Take a vacation, Feeney. Use my rich husband's fancy house in Mexico."' His lips peeled back in a sneer. 'That would have been fine for you, wouldn't it? Get me out of your way, shuffle me off and out from underfoot because I'm useless to you on this one.'

'No. God, Feeney—'

'I've gone through doors with you.' His voice was abruptly quiet, and made her throat burn. 'I trusted you. I'd have put my back up against yours anytime, anyplace. But no more. You're good, Dallas, but you're cold. The hell with you.'

She said nothing when he walked out, leaving her door swinging open. Could say nothing. He'd nailed it, she decided. And he'd nailed her.

'Dallas.' Peabody rushed the door. 'I couldn't—'

Eve cut her off, simply lifting a finger, turning her back. Slowly, with slow even breaths, she pulled her guts back in. Even then, they ached. She could still smell him in the room. That stupid cologne his wife always bought him.

'We're going to do a follow-up sweep of Wineburg's townhouse. Get your gear.'

Peabody opened her mouth, closed it again. Even if she'd known what to say, she didn't imagine it would be welcome. 'Yes, sir.'

Eve turned back. Her eyes were blank, cool, composed. 'Then let's move.'

Chapter Thirteen

She was in a pisser of a mood by the time she got home. She'd turned Wineburg's townhouse inside out, reworking every step already taken by the sweepers. For three hours she and Peabody had searched closets and drawers, run logs, and traced 'link records.

She found two dozen all-but-identical dark suits, shoes so glossy she'd seen her own scowl reflected in the tips, an incredibly boring collection of music discs. Though he'd had a lock box, the contents hadn't been very illuminating. Two thousand in cash, another ten in credits, and an extensive collection of hard-core pornographic videos might have given some insight into the man, but no solid leads toward his killer.

He'd kept no personal diary, and his appointment book listed times and dates and very little about the content of any meeting, personal or professional. His financial records were ordered and precise, as one might expect from a man who dealt with money as an occupation. All expenses and income were carefully logged. Though the large and regular bimonthly withdrawals from credit into cash over the last two-year period of Wineburg's fussy life gave Eve a solid notion just how Selina managed to live so well, the withdrawals were all logged under personal expenses.

The consistency of late-night appointments over the last two years, again bimonthly and always on the same date as the personal cash withdrawal, wasn't enough to establish a solid connection with Selina Cross's cult.

The lady herself was never mentioned.

He'd been divorced, childless, and he'd lived alone.

So she knocked on doors, talked to neighbors. Eve learned Wineburg hadn't been the sociable sort. He'd rarely had visitors, and none of his neighbors had been curious enough or would admit to paying close enough attention to any of those rare visitors to give a description.

She came away with nothing but a raw feeling in the gut and a mounting sense of frustration. She knew, without a doubt, that Wineburg had been part of Cross's cult, that he'd paid heavily, first monetarily and then with his life, for the privilege. But she was no closer to proving it, and her mind wasn't as focused on the business at hand as it should have been.

When she headed home, alone, Feeney's angry face and bitter words played back in her head, and frustration slammed up hard against misery.

She'd more than let him down, she knew. She had betrayed him by doing precisely what he had helped train her to do. She'd followed orders, she'd been a cop. She'd done her job.

But she hadn't been a friend, she thought, as her temples throbbed with stress. She'd weighed her loyalties, and in the end had chosen the job over the heart.

Cold, he'd called her, she remembered and squeezed her eyes shut. And cold she had been.

The cat padded to her the moment Eve stepped in the door, winding around her legs as she stepped into the foyer. She kept walking, cursing lightly when he tripped her. Summerset slipped out of a doorway.

'Roarke has been trying to reach you.'

'Yeah? Well, I've been busy.' She nudged Galahad away impatiently with her foot. 'Is he here?'

'Not as yet. You might reach him at his office.'

'I'll talk to him when he gets home.' She wanted a drink, something strong and mind-misting. Recognizing the danger and the weakness of that crutch, she turned away from the parlor and walked in the opposite direction. 'I'm not here to anybody else. Get it?'

'Certainly,' Summerset said stiffly.

As she strode away, Summerset bent and picked up the cat to stroke – something he never would have done had anyone been around to observe. 'The lieutenant is very unhappy,' Summerset murmured. 'Perhaps we should make a call.'

Galahad purred, stretched his neck in appreciation of Summerset's long, bony fingers. Their mutual affection was their little secret.

It would have surprised Eve, though she wasn't thinking of either of them. She took the stairs, moved through the indoor pool and garden area, and into the gym. Physical exertion, she knew, blocked emotional distress.

Keeping her mind blank, she changed into a black skin suit and high tops. She programmed the full body unit, ordering the machine to take her through a brutal series of reps and resistance exercises, gritting her teeth as the clipped computer voice demanded that she squat, lift, stretch, hold, repeat.

She'd worked up a satisfactory sweat by the time she switched machines for aerobics. The combo-unit took her on a punishing run, up inclines, down them, a race up endless flights of stairs. She'd set it for variety, and found the change of texture on her running surface from simulated asphalt to sand to grass to dirt interesting, but it wasn't doing anything to ease the ache in her belly.

You could run, she thought with dull fury, *but you couldn't hide.*

Her heart was pumping hard, her skin suit soaked with sweat, but her emotions were still fragile as glass. What she needed, Eve decided as she tugged on soft, protective gloves, was to pound on something.

She'd never tried out the sparring droid. It was one of Roarke's newest toys. The unit was a middleweight: six feet,

486

one ninety, and firmly muscled. Good reach, Eve decided with her hands on her hips as she sized him up.

She punched in the code on his storage tube. There was a faint hum as circuits were engaged. The unit opened dark, polite brown eyes. 'You wish a match?'

'Yeah, pal, I wish a match.'

'Boxing, karate – Korean or Japanese – tae kwon do, kung fu, street style. Self-defense programs are also available. Contact is optional.'

'Straight hand-to-hand,' she said, backing up and gesturing. 'Full contact.'

'Timed rounds?'

'Hell, no. We go till one of us is down, pal. And out.' She curled her fingers in a come-ahead gesture.

'Acknowledged.' There was a faint humming from the unit as he self-programmed. 'I outweigh you by approximately seventy pounds. If you prefer, my program includes a handicap—'

She brought her fist up hard and fast, an uppercut to the jaw that snapped his head back. 'There's my handicap. Come on.'

'As you wish.' He crouched as she did and began to circle. 'You did not indicate if you desired vocal additions to the program. Taunting, insults—' He staggered back as her foot whipped up and plowed into his guts. 'Compliments or suitable exclamations of pain are available.'

'Come at me, will you, for Christ's sake?'

He did, with a swiftness and force that had her stumbling back, nearly losing her footing. This, she decided as she pivoted and caught him backhanded, was more like it.

He blocked her next blow, shifted weight, and wrapped his arm around her throat. Eve planted her feet, elbowed, and flipped him over her shoulder. He was up like lightning before she could attempt a pin.

His gloved fist made a solid connection with her solar plexus, pushing a whoosh of air out of her lungs and ringing bright pain straight into her head. Doubled over, she followed through with a head butt, stomped hard on his instep.

When Roarke walked in ten minutes later, he watched his wife fly through the air and go skidding across the mat. Lifting a brow, he leaned back against the door and settled down to watch.

She didn't have time to gain her feet before the droid was on her, so she grabbed one of his ankles, twisted, hauled, and thrusted. Her mind was a blank now, a black blank. Her breath was heaving, and she could taste the metallic flavor of blood inside her mouth.

She went at her opponent like a hail storm, cold and relentless. Each jab, each blow, each kick given or received sang through her body with icy, primitive rage. Her eyes were flat with violence now, her fists merciless as she concentrated on the head, working the droid back, back.

Frowning, Roarke straightened. Her breath was wheezing out now, all but sobbing, yet she didn't stop. When the droid staggered, went down on its knees, she crouched for the kill.

'End program,' Roarke ordered, and caught his wife's rigid arm before she could kick the droid's lolling head. 'You're going to damage the unit,' he said mildly. 'It isn't designed for to the death.'

She bent over, resting her hands on her knees, to catch her breath. Her mind was full of red now, red rage, and she needed to clear it. 'Sorry, I guess I got carried away.' She eyed the droid, who remained slumped on his knees, mouth slack, eyes blank as a doll's. 'I'll run a diagnostic on it.'

'Don't worry about it.' He started to turn her to face him, but she broke away, moved across the room for a towel. 'In the mood for a fight?'

'I guess I wanted to pound something.'

'Should I suit up?' He was smiling a little. Until she lowered the towel. The rage had drained from her face. All that was left in her eyes was misery. 'What is it, Eve? What happened?'

'Nothing. Just a rough day.' She tossed the towel aside,

moved to the cold box unit for a bottle of mineral water. 'So far, Wineburg's house is a bust. Nothing there to help us. Sweepers didn't find anything in the garage, either. Didn't expect them to. I jabbed some at Cross again, and at Alban the Magnificent. Had a consult with Mira. Her daughter's a Wiccan. Can you beat that?'

It wasn't work, he thought, *that put that painful unhappiness in her eyes*. 'What is it?'

'Isn't that enough? It's going to be tough to get an objective consult from Mira when her daughter's into spellcasting. Then there's Peabody. She's caught a damn cold, and her head's so full of snot I have to say everything twice before it gets through.'

She was talking too fast, Eve realized. Words were tumbling out of her mouth and she couldn't seem to stop them. 'A hell of a lot of good she's going to be to me hacking and sneezing all goddamn day. The media picked up on Wineburg, and the fact that you and I were on scene when it went down. My 'link's jammed with fucking reporters. Leaks everywhere. Fucking leaks everywhere. Feeney found out I've been holding back on him.'

Ah, Roarke thought, *there we are*. 'He was hard on you?'

'Why shouldn't he be?' Her voice rose as she whirled and searched for temper to cover the hurt. 'He should've been able to trust me. I lied to him, right to his face.'

'What choice did you have?'

'There's always a choice.' She bit the words off, heaved the half-empty bottle at the wall, where it bounced and spewed out bubbling water. 'There's always a choice,' she repeated. 'I made mine. I knew how he felt about Frank, about Alice, but I blocked him out. I followed orders. I walked the line.'

She could feel the pain rising, straining to spew as the water had spewed out of the bottle. She fought to block it back. 'He was right, everything he said to me. Everything. I could have gone to him on the side.'

'Is that what you were trained to do? Is that what he trained you to do?'

'He made me,' she said fiercely. 'I owe him. I should have told him how it was going down.'

'No.' He stepped to her, took her by the shoulders. 'No, you couldn't.'

'I could have.' She shouted it. 'I should have. I wish to God I had.' And broke. Covered her face with her hands and broke. 'Oh God, what am I going to do?'

Roarke gathered her close. She cried rarely, a last resort, and always when the tears finally came they were vicious. 'He needs time. He's a cop, Eve. Part of him already understands. The rest just needs to catch up.'

'No.' Her hands fisted in his shirt, held on. 'The way he looked at me . . . I've lost him, Roarke. I've lost him. I swear I'd rather lose my badge.'

He waited while the tears stormed out, while her body shook with them. There was such strong emotions in her, he thought, rocking as her hands clenched and unclenched against his back. Emotions she'd spent a lifetime bottling up, so they were only the more potent when they broke free.

'Damn it.' She let out a breath, long and shaky. Her head felt achy, muffled, her throat raw. 'I hate doing that. It doesn't help.'

'More than you think.' He stroked a hand over her hair, then tipped it under her chin to lift her face. 'You need food and a decent night's sleep, so you can do what you need to do.'

'What I need to do?'

'Close the case. Once you have, you can put all this behind you.'

'Yeah.' She pushed her hands over her hot, wet cheeks. 'Close the case. That's the bottom line.' She hissed out a breath. 'That's the goddamn job.'

'That's justice.' He brushed a thumb over the dent in her chin. 'Isn't it?'

She looked up at him, her eyes reddened, swollen, exhausted. 'I don't know anymore.'

She didn't eat, and he didn't press her. There had been grief in his life, and he knew food wasn't the answer. He'd considered browbeating her into taking a sedative. That, he knew, would have been an ugly business. So he was grateful when she went to bed early. He made some excuse about a conference call.

From his office, he watched on the monitor until her restless twists and turns stopped, and she slept. What he had to do would take no more than an hour or two. He doubted she'd surface before then and miss him.

He'd never been to Feeney's. The apartment building was comfortably shabby, well-secured, and unpretentious. Roarke thought it suited the man. Because he didn't want to risk being refused entrance, he bypassed the security buzzer and entrance locks.

That suited him.

He strolled through the tiny lobby, caught the faint scent of a recent insect extermination. Though he approved the intent, he disliked the lingering reminder of it, and made a note to have it dealt with.

After all, he owned the building.

He stepped into an elevator, requested the third floor. He noticed when he stepped out again that the corridor carpet could use replacing. But it was well lit, the tiny beam on the security cameras blinking efficiently. The walls were clean and thick enough to muffle all but a faint hum of life behind closed doors.

A low drift of music, a quick rumble of laughter, a fretful baby's nighttime wail. Life, Roarke thought, and a pleasant one. He rang the bell at Feeney's door and waited.

His eyes stared soberly at the peep screen, continued to stare when Feeney's irritated voice came through the intercom.

'What the hell do you want? You slumming?'

'I don't think this building qualifies as a slum.'

'Anything does, compared to that palace you live in.'

'Do you want to discuss the difference in our living arrangements through the door, or are you going to ask me in?'

'I asked what you want.'

'You know why I'm here.' He quirked a brow, making sure it was just insulting enough. 'You've got guts enough to face me, don't you, Feeney?'

It had, as Roarke had expected, the right effect. The door swung open. Feeney stood, blocking entrance with his compact body braced for war, his rumpled face bright with fury. 'It's none of your fucking business.'

'On the contrary.' Roarke stood where he was, kept his voice even. 'It's very much my fucking business. But I don't believe it's any of your neighbors'.'

Teeth clenched, Feeney stepped back. 'Come in and say what you have to say, then get the hell out.'

'Is your wife at home?' Roarke asked when Feeney slammed the door at his back.

'She's got a girl's thing tonight.' Feeney inclined his head, much like a bull, Roarke thought, preparing to charge. 'You want to take a shot at me, you go ahead. I wouldn't mind pounding that pretty face of yours.'

'Christ Jesus, she's just like you.' Shaking his head, Roarke wandered the living room. Homey, he decided. Not quite tidy. The viewing screen was set on the ball game, the sound muted. The batter swung, the ball flew in total silence. 'What's the score?'

'Yanks are up by one, bottom of the seventh.' He caught himself on the verge of offering Roarke a beer, then stiffened again. 'She told you, didn't she? Filled you in right from the get-go.'

'She wasn't under orders not to. And she thought I could help.'

He could help, Feeney thought and tasted bitterness. *Her rich, fancy husband could help, but not her former trainer, not her former partner. Not the man who had worked side by side with her with pride, and goddamn it, affection, for ten years.* 'Doesn't make you less of a civilian.' His tired eyes went broody. 'You didn't even know Frank.'

'No, I didn't. But Eve did. She cared.'

'We'd been partners, me and Frank. We were friends. Family. She had no business bumping me out of it. That's how I feel, that's what I told her.'

'I'm sure you did.' Roarke turned away from the view screen, looked Feeney dead in the eye. 'And however you told her, it broke her heart.'

'Dented her feelings some.' Feeney walked away, picked up a half-empty bottle of beer. Even through the murky haze of his fury, he'd seen the devastation in her eyes when he'd come down on her. And had willed himself not to give a damn. 'She'll get over it.' He drank deeply, knowing the taste wouldn't overpower the bitterness lodged in his throat. 'She'll do her job. She just won't do it with me anymore.'

'I said you broke her heart. I meant it. How long have you known her, Feeney?' Roarke's voice hardened, demanding attention. 'Ten years, eleven? How many times have you seen her fall apart? I imagine you could count them on the fingers of one hand. Well, I watched her fall apart tonight.' He took a careful breath. Temper wasn't the answer here, not for any of them. 'If you wanted to crush her, you succeeded.'

'I told her how things were, that's all.' Guilt was already seeping in. He slammed down the bottle, determined to chase it away. 'Cops back each other, they trust each other or they've got nothing. She was digging on Frank. She should have come to me.'

'Is that what you'd have told her to do?' Roarke countered. 'Is that the kind of cop you helped her become? It wasn't you in Whitney's office, taking the orders, doing the job,' he went on without giving Feeney time to answer. 'And suffering for it.'

'No.' A fresh wave of bitterness passed through him. 'It wasn't me.' He sat, deliberately turned up the sound, and stared at the ancient battle on the screen.

Stubborn, thick-headed Irish bastard, Roarke thought with twin tugs of sympathy and impatience. 'You did me a favor once,' Roarke began. 'When I was first involved with Eve and I hurt her because I misunderstood a situation. You straightened me out on that, so I'm going to do you a similar favor.'

'I don't want your favors.'

'You'll have it, anyway.' Roarke sat in a chair comfortably sprung. He helped himself to Feeney's nearly empty bottle. 'What do you know about her father?'

'What?' Baffled now, Feeney turned his head and stared. 'What the hell does that have to do with anything?'

'It has everything to do with her. Did you know he beat her, tortured her, raped her repeatedly until she was eight years old?'

A muscle worked in Feeney's jaw as he turned away again, muted the screen. He'd known that she'd been found in an alley at eight, beaten, broken, sexually abused. That was on record, and he never worked with anyone without knowing their official data. But he hadn't known it was her father who'd done it. He'd suspected as much, but he hadn't known. His stomach twisted, his hands clenched.

'I'm sorry for that. She never brought it up.'

'She didn't always remember. Or, more likely, she did and refused to remember. She still has nightmares, flashbacks.'

'You got no business telling me this.'

'She'd likely say the same, but I'm telling you, anyway. She made herself what she is, and you helped. She'd go to the wall for you; you know that.'

'Cops back up cops. That's the job.'

'I'm not talking about the job. She loves you, and she

doesn't love easily. It's difficult for her to feel it, and to show it. Part of her may always be braced for betrayal, for a blow. You've been her father for ten years, Feeney. She didn't deserve to be broken again.'

Roarke stood, and saying nothing more, walked out.

Alone, Feeney raked his hands up over his face, into his wiry red hair, then let them drop on his lap.

It was six fifteen when Eve rolled over, blinked at the light streaming through the windows. Roarke preferred waking to sun. Unless she snuck out of bed or climbed in well after him, she didn't get her shot at pulling the privacy screens.

She felt logy, decided it was too much sleep, and started to slip out of bed.

Roarke's arm swept out and pinned her. 'Not yet.' His voice was husky, his eyes still closed as he tugged her back over.

'I'm awake. I can get an early start.' She wiggled. 'I've been in bed nearly nine hours. I can't sleep anymore.'

He opened one eye – sufficient to note that she did indeed look rested. 'You're a detective,' he pointed out. 'I'll bet if you investigated, you'd uncover the startling fact that there are activities that can be done in bed other than sleep.'

His lips curved as he rolled on top of her. 'Allow me to give you the first clue.'

It shouldn't have surprised her that he was already hard, or that she would be so instantly ready for him. He slid inside her, smooth, slow, deep, and watched the lingering sleep clear from her eyes into awareness.

'I think I've figured it out already.' She lifted her hips, matched his lazy pace.

'You're such a quick study.' He lowered his lips to nuzzle just under her jawline. 'I like this spot,' he murmured. 'And this one.' His hand trailed up her rib cage, cupped her breast.

The arousal was sweet, simple, and made her sigh. 'Let me know when you get to something you don't like.'

She wrapped her arms around him, her legs. He was so solid, so warm, the steady beat of his heart against hers so comforting. Pleasure built in gauzy layers, floating over her mind, stroking through her body.

'Go over for me.' He nibbled her lips, then swept his tongue inside to tangle with hers. To nip, to suck. 'Go over,' he repeated. 'Slow.'

'Well . . .' Her breath was already hitching, catching in her throat. 'Since you ask so nice.'

The climax rolled through her, one long, lingering wave. She felt him follow, caught in the same current, and pressed her cheek to his.

'Was that like a cookie?' she wondered.

'Hmmm?'

'You know, have a cookie. You'll feel better.' She put her hands on either side of his face, lifting it as he laughed. 'Were you making me feel better?'

'I certainly hope so. It worked for me.' He dipped his head to kiss her lightly. 'I wanted you. I always do.'

'It's funny how men can wake up with their brains in their cocks.'

'It makes us what we are.' Still chuckling, he rolled her over him, patted her butt. 'Let's take a shower. I'll give you another cookie.'

Thirty minutes later, she stumbled out of the shower and into the drying tube. He was a quick change artist when it came to mood, she thought dizzily. From lazy to amused to hot, steamy, mind-numbing sex, all in one short morning.

Because her system was still frazzled, she braced a hand against the curve of the tube as warm air blew around her. When he stepped out of the shower, she jabbed out a finger.

'Stay away from me. You grab me again, I'll have to take you down. I mean it. I've got work.'

He hummed a tune and used a towel. 'I like making love to

496

you in the morning. You only wake up fast if you get a call from dispatch or if I seduce you.'

'I'm awake now.' She stepped out, pushed a hand through her hair. Giving herself safe distance, she reached for a robe. 'Go look at the stock reports or something.'

'I intend to. You'll want breakfast,' he added as he left the room. 'I'll order it up.'

She started to tell him she wasn't hungry. She wasn't. But she knew without fuel she wouldn't make it through the day.

When she joined him in the bedroom, he was slipping into a shirt, his gaze focused on the table monitor where he could view the headlines and financial reports. She walked past him to her closet, chose plain gray trousers.

'I'm sorry I lost it last night.'

He lifted his gaze, noted she kept her back to him as she pawed out a shirt. 'You were upset. You had a right to be.'

'Anyway, I appreciate you not making me feel like an idiot.'

'How do you feel now?'

She jerked a shoulder. 'I've got a job to do.' She'd come to that end while she'd tossed her way into sleep. 'I'm going to do it. Maybe . . . Well, maybe if I do it right, Feeney won't hate me so much when it's over.'

'He doesn't hate you, Eve.' When she didn't answer, he let it drop. He'd already programmed their meal in the recessed AutoChef. 'I thought ham and eggs would do the trick this morning.'

He got the coffee first, brought it to the table in the sitting area.

'It'll do the trick any morning.' She pasted on a determined smile, went over to get the food herself. He ordered the viewing screen on Channel 75 while she shoveled in creamy eggs.

She scowled as the on-air reporter, glossy as a china doll at seven thirty in the morning, recited the data on the Wineburg homicide.

'Though Lieutenant Eve Dallas, assigned to the homicide division of NYPSD, was on the scene, only yards away from the murder site, the police have no solid leads. The investigation continues. This is the second stabbing death connected with Lieutenant Dallas in as many days. When asked if the cases are linked, Dallas refused to comment.'

'A ten-year-old kid with a vision defect could see they're linked, for Christ's sake.' She had been eating on automatic, and now shoved the plate aside. 'That Cross bitch is sitting in her hell house, laughing.'

Springing up, she began to pace. Roarke took it as a good sign. If she was angry, she wasn't feeling sorry for herself. He chose some fresh strawberry jam for his croissant.

'I'm going to nail her, I swear to God, I'm going to nail her. For all of them. I need to connect Wineburg to her. If I can do that, I can harass her some more. May not be enough to get me a warrant to toss her place, but I can keep on her ass.'

'Well, then.' Roarke wiped his fingers with a pale blue linen cloth, set it aside. 'I should be able to help you with that.'

As she continued to pace and mutter, he rose, walked to a dresser, took a sealed disc from a drawer. 'Lieutenant?'

'What? I'm thinking.'

'Then I won't interrupt your train of thought with the list of membership from Cross's cult.' With a half smile on his face, he tapped the disk against his palm and waited for her eyes to clear and shoot to him.

'The list? You got the membership roster? How?'

He cocked his head. 'You don't really want to know how, do you?'

'No.' She said it immediately. 'No, I guess I don't. Just tell me he's on it.' She closed her eyes briefly. 'Just tell me Wineburg's on the list.'

'He certainly is.'

Her grin flashed quick and fever bright. 'I love you.'

Roarke handed her the disc. 'I know you do.'

Chapter Fourteen

Feeney wanted to see Whitney first. So he made it early, and he made it personal. They, too, went back together a long way, Feeney thought as he pulled up in front of the neat two-level home in the 'burbs. He'd been here socially over the years. The commander's wife loved to throw parties.

His mood wasn't sociable now as he strode up the pebbled walk toward the quiet house in the wakening neighborhood. A few yards down, a dog was barking in high, monotonous yips. The bark had none of the faintly metallic ring that said droid, but held a vibrancy of flesh and blood. The kind of dog that shit in the yard, Feeney thought with a shake of his head, and scratched at fleas.

Leaves skittered playfully along the street, most of them making beelines for lawns. Lawns that were, in a neighborhood like this, tended like a religion.

Feeney, himself, didn't get 'burb life, where you had to rake and mow and water or hire someone to rake and mow and water. He'd raised his family in the city, used the public parks. Hell, you had to pay for them, anyway. He moved his shoulders restlessly, not quite comfortable with the morning silence.

Anna Whitney answered his knock, and though she couldn't have been expecting company at that hour, she was already decked out in a trim jumpsuit. Her light hair waved stylishly, and her makeup was subtle and perfect. Her lips curved in welcome. Her eyes may have flickered with surprise and curiosity, but she was too much the cop's wife to ask questions.

'Feeney, how nice to see you. Come in, please, have some coffee. Jack's just having his second cup in the kitchen.'

'Sorry to disturb you at home, Anna. I need a few minutes of the commander's time.'

'Of course. And how's Sheila?' she asked as she led the way down the hall toward the kitchen.

'She's fine.'

'She looked just wonderful the last time I saw her. Her new stylist is terrific. Jack, you've got company for coffee.' She breezed into the kitchen, caught the surprise, then the speculation in her husband's eyes. She knew enough to make a quick exit. 'I'll let you two chat. I've got a million things to do this morning. Feeney, you give Sheila my best, now.'

'I will. Thanks.' He waited until the door swung closed, never taking his eyes off Whitney's. 'Goddamn it, Jack.'

'This should be discussed in my office, Feeney.'

'I'm talking to you.' Feeney jabbed a finger. 'To someone I've known twenty-five years. To someone who knew Frank. Why'd you cut me out of this? Why did you order Dallas to lie to me?'

'That was my decision, Feeney. The investigation had to be on a need-to-know basis.'

'And I didn't need to know.'

'No.' Whitney folded his big hands. 'You didn't need to know.'

'Frank and I raised some of our kids together. Alice was my godchild. Frank and I rode as partners for five fucking years. Our wives are like sisters. Who the hell are you to decide I don't need to know he's being investigated?'

'Your commander,' Whitney said shortly and pushed his still steaming coffee aside. 'And the reasons you just stated are the very reasons I made the decision.'

'You pushed me aside. You know damn well my division should have been involved. You needed records.'

'Records were part of the problem,' Whitney said evenly. 'There was no record of a heart defect in his medical files, no record of a connection, personal or professional, between him and a known chemi-dealer.'

'Frank had nothing to do with illegals.'

'No records,' Whitney continued. 'And his closest friend is the best E-detective in the city.'

Feeney's eyes went wide, and his color rose hot. 'You think I wiped records? You had Dallas looking at me?'

'No, I didn't think you wiped records, but it wasn't something I could ignore with IAD breathing down my neck. Who would you have picked to do the work, Feeney?' Whitney demanded with an impatient gesture. 'I knew that Lieutenant Dallas would be thorough and careful and that she'd bust her ass to clear both you and Frank. I knew she had – contacts – that could access those records.'

Deluged by emotion, Feeney turned to stare out of the gleaming window into the backyard with its tidily mowed grass and majestic fall flowers. 'You put her in a bad spot. You ordered her into a lousy position, Jack. Is that what happens when you command? You put your troops' backs to the wall?'

'Yeah, that's what happens.' Whitney ran a hand over his dark, grizzled hair. 'You do what needs to be done, and you live with it. I had IAD drooling. My priority was to clear Frank and shield his family from anymore hardship. Dallas was my best shot. You trained her, Feeney, you know she was my best shot.'

'I trained her,' Feeney agreed, sick inside.

'What would you have done?' Whitney demanded. 'Straight, Feeney. You've got a dead cop who's been tagged buying illegals from a suspected dealer who's under surveillance. There were drugs in his system when he died. Your gut tells you no way, no way he was dirty. And maybe your heart's telling you, too, because you remember when you were both rookies. But IAD's got no gut, and it's got no heart. What would you have done?'

And because he'd had a sleepless night to think on it, to worry the steps, Feeney shook his head. 'I don't know. But I know I don't want your job. Commander.'

'You've got to be crazy to want this job.' Whitney's wide face relaxed slightly. 'Dallas has gone a long way to clearing Frank, and she took you out of it within the first twenty-four hours. She'd hardly had more than a week on this, and she's already cleared a path. With her reports, I've been able to back IAD off. They're not happy about Frank setting up his own sting, but they've eased the pressure.'

'That's good.' Feeney dug his hands into his pockets as he turned back. 'She's good. Christ, Jack, I hit her hard.'

Whitney's brows knit. 'You should have come to me. Going after her was off, Feeney. I gave the orders.'

'I took it personal. I made it personal.' He remembered how she'd looked at him, her face pale, her eyes blank. He'd seen people with that look before – victims, he thought now, who were used to taking a fist in the face. 'I've got to fix it with her.'

'She called in a couple minutes before you showed up. She's doing a follow-through on a new lead. At home.'

Feeney jerked his head in a nod. 'I'd like a couple hours personal time.'

'You've got it.'

'And I want in on this.'

Whitney sat back, considered. 'That'll be up to Dallas. She's primary. If we're opening this up, she chooses her own team.'

'Answer the 'link, will you, Peabody?' Eve continued to scan the data on-screen as her 'link beeped insistently. It was a

502

wonder to her how many names she recognized from the social, political, and professional registers. It was doubtful she'd have recognized quite so many a year before, but connecting with Roarke had broadened her horizons.

'Doctors, lawyers,' she muttered. 'Christ, this guy's been to dinner here. And I think Roarke used to sleep with this woman. This dancer. She's got a hit on Broadway and a mile of leg.'

'It's Nadine,' Peabody announced and wondered if Eve was talking to herself or really wanted to share that particular information. She hacked, sneezed, then added in her now raspy voice. 'Furst.'

'Perfect.' Eve cleared the screen, just in case, and turned to the 'link. 'So, Nadine, what's the story?'

'You're the story, Dallas. Two dead people. It's dangerous to know you.'

'You're still breathing.'

'So far, so good. I thought you might be interested in some data that's come my way. We can do a trade.'

'Show me yours, maybe I'll show you mine.'

'Exclusive one on one, in your home, with you discussing the investigation of both knifings, for the noon broadcast.'

Eve didn't bother to snort. 'One on one reporting the status of my investigation, in my office, for the evening broadcast.'

'The first body was found at your house. I want in.'

'It was found outside on the sidewalk, and you're not getting in.'

Nadine huffed out a breath. The pout was for her own benefit. She knew better than to think it would budge Eve. 'I want the noon.'

Eve checked her watch, calculated, considered. 'I'll clear you into my office. Arrival time eleven forty-five. If I can make it, I'll be there. If not . . .'

'Damn it, we need setup time. Fifteen minutes isn't—'

'It's enough, Nadine, for someone as good as you are. Be sure your data makes this worth my while.'

'Make sure you don't look like a rag picker,' Nadine shot back. 'Do something with your hair, for God's sake.'

Rather than respond, Eve ended transmission. 'What is this obsession people have with my hair and wardrobe?' She raked a bad-tempered hand through the hair in question.

'Mavis told me you're overdue for a style session. Leonardo's bummed about it.'

'You hanging with Mavis?'

'I've gone down to catch her act a couple times.' She blew her nose heartily. Over-the-counters were pure crap, she decided. 'I like watching her.'

'I haven't had time for a style session,' Eve muttered. 'I trimmed it myself a couple days ago.'

'Yeah, I could tell.' At Eve's narrow look, Peabody smiled blandly. 'It looks just lovely, sir.'

'Kiss ass.' Eve switched her screen back on. 'And if you're finished with your critique of my personal appearance, maybe you'd like to run a few of these names.'

'I recognize some of them.' Peabody bent over Eve's shoulder. 'Louis Trivane: big shot celebrity lawyer. Gets the stars out of legal jams. Marianna Bingsley: department store heiress and professional manhunter. Carlo Mancinni, cosmetic enhancement guru – medical doctor – you have to be way rich to have him even consider doing body sculpting on you.'

'I know the names, Peabody. I want background, personal data, financial data, medical data, and arrests. I want to know the names of their spouses and kids and pets. I want to know when and how they connected with Cross and why they decided Satan was a cool guy.'

'It'll take days.' Peabody said it mournfully and reminded Eve painfully of Feeney. 'Even shooting them into the IRCCA.'

Eve said nothing. The International Resource Center on Criminal Activity was one of Feeney's prides and joys.

'If I could tag someone in the E-Division for help, we could cut the time in half. Maybe less.' Peabody jerked a shoulder. 'So, where do you want me to start?'

'We've got a hop on Wineburg, so dig deeper there, and on Lobar – Robert Mathias. Then start at the top and work down. I'll start at the bottom and work up. Look for withdrawls of large amounts at regular intervals. We damn well better have what we need when we meet in the middle.'

She narrowed her eyes, thinking. The financial data on Selina's cult would be protected by the Privacy Act and its status as a registered religion. Still, there was a chance, a slim one, that she'd been cocky enough to make deposits in her personal account.

That was a simple matter to check on. For the other, she would have to decide if the data would hold solid if she was able to access it, and to access it, she needed Roarke.

She'd wait, she decided, a day or two. Once they ascertained how much money the membership list was suspected of feeding into Selina's pockets, she'd reassess.

It would be tough to sell the PA on religious contributions as extortion, but it might be a start.

'With Wineburg's name linked to Cross's cult, I can pull her into Interview. I think we'll make it, say, around eleven thirty.'

'You've got the spot with Nadine at eleven forty-five.'

'Yeah.' Eve's smile spread. 'That'll work.'

'Oh.'

'It's not my fault if some big-nosed reporter finds out I'm questioning Selina Cross, knows I'm primary on two recent homicides, then puts two and two together.'

'And goes on air with it.'

'Might shake up some of these fine, upstanding Satanists. Some people get real chatty when they're shook. Get me that data, and I can shake them harder.'

'I bow to you.'

'Save it until we see if it works. You use this unit. I can

505

use one of Roarke's to make the first pass. Computer, copy disc, print out hard copy.' She glanced up at the movement in the doorway, went very still. 'Abort,' she murmured and braced to take the next hit from Feeney.

'Peabody.' He sent her a quiet look out of sleep-starved eyes. 'I need a moment with your lieutenant.'

'Sir?' Though she rose, Peabody waited for Eve's signal.

'Take a break, Peabody. Get yourself some coffee.'

'Yes, sir.' She headed out, feeling the needles of edgy tension prickling the air.

Eve didn't speak, simply stood. Her body was set, he noted, not to defend, but to absorb the next blow. Her eyes were carefully empty. But her hand that she braced on the desk shook. He stared at it a moment, amazed and ashamed that he'd caused that.

'Your, ah, Summerset said I should just come up.' It was warm in the room, but he didn't remove his rumpled overcoat. Instead, he shoved his hands in the pockets. 'I was off yesterday. Coming down on you was off. You were doing your job.'

He saw her lip tremble, as if she would speak or make some sound. Then she firmed it again and said nothing. She looked, he realized, whipped.

You broke her heart.'

'Her father beat her, tortured her, raped her.'

'You've been her father for ten years.'

How the hell was he supposed to deal with that? And how could he possibly ignore it?

'The things I said – I shouldn't have.' He pulled his hands free to scrub them hard over his face. 'Jesus, Dallas. I'm sorry.'

'Did you mean them?' It was out before she could stop it. She held up a hand, turned away, stared blindly out the window.

'I wanted to mean them. I was pissed.' He crossed to her,

his hands flapping uselessly. 'I got no excuse,' he began. He touched her, then snatched his fingers away from her shoulder when she cringed. 'I got no excuse,' he said again after a steadying breath. 'And you got a right to step back from me. I jumped hard where I shouldn't have jumped.'

'You don't trust me now.' She skimmed the back of her hand over her cheek, ashamed the single tear had gotten past her guard.

'That's bullshit, Dallas. There's nobody I trust more. Look, goddamn it, it takes a laser hit to get me to apologize to my own wife. I'm telling you I'm sorry.' Impatient now, he grabbed her arm, pulled her around. She froze. Her eyes were bright, tears sheening them but not, thank Christ, falling. 'Don't go female on me, Dallas. I can't kick myself in the ass much harder than I already am.'

He jerked up his chin, tapped a finger on it. 'Go ahead. Free shot. We won't say anything about you punching out a superior officer.'

'I don't want to hit you.'

'Goddamn it, I outrank you. I said take your shot.'

A ghost of a smile flitted around her mouth. He looked so fierce, she thought, those drooping camel eyes sparking with temper and frustration. 'Maybe after you shave. That stubble'd skin my knuckles.'

Relief flooded through him at the slight curve of her lips. 'You're going soft. Living the high life with that rich Irish son of a bitch.'

'I beat hell out of a sparring droid last night. One of Roarke's finest.'

'Yeah?' Pride swelled in him, ridiculously.

She tucked her tongue in her cheek. 'I pretended it was you.'

He grinned, took out the bag of candied almonds from his pocket, offered it. 'E-detectives don't have to use their fists. They use their brains.'

507

'You taught me to use both.'

'And to follow orders,' he added, his eyes resting on hers again. 'I'd have been ashamed of you if you'd forgotten that. You did right, Dallas, for Frank, for the department. For me,' he said and watched her eyes swim again. 'Don't do that.' His voice shook with the plea. 'Don't start that shit. That's an order.'

She swiped the back of her hand under her nose. 'I'm not doing anything.'

He waited a moment, just to be sure she wasn't going to lose it and embarrass them both. When her eyes cleared, he nodded in both relief and approval. 'Good.' He jiggled the bag in his hand. 'Now, are you going to let me in?'

She opened her mouth, shut it.

'I've seen Whitney,' he told her. Feeney found he wanted to smile. This was the cop he'd trained. Solid, sturdy, and straight. 'Chewed him out in his own kitchen.'

'Did you?' She lifted her brows. 'I'd like to have seen it.'

'Trouble was, once it was over, I had to agree with him. He'd picked the best cop for the job. I know you've been busting ass to push IAD out of the picture, clear Frank. Me,' he added. 'And I know you've been working on finding out who did him and Alice.' He had to take a breath because it hurt, still hurt. 'I want in, Dallas. I'm going to tell you straight, I need in to clear this out of my gut. Whitney said it was up to you.'

The tension seeped out of her. She could give him this, give both of them this. 'Let's get to work.'

Eve was so pleased to have Selina Cross in Interview, she'd missed anticipating the obvious bonus of having her represented by Louis Trivane. She flashed grins at both of them as she secured the door to Interview Room A.

'Ms Cross, I appreciate your cooperation. Mr Trivane.'

'Eve—'

'Lieutenant Dallas,' she corrected, snapping off the grin. 'We're not socializing here.'

'You know each other.' Selina's eyes went icy, pinned her lawyer.

'Your representative knows my husband on a social level. I'm acquainted with a number of attorneys in the city, Ms Cross. This doesn't affect my or their job performance. We'll go on record.'

Eve engaged the recorder, recited the pertinent data. After reading the revised Miranda, she sat. 'You've exercised your right to an attorney, Ms Cross.'

'I certainly have. I've already been harassed by you twice, Lieutenant Dallas. I prefer that this continued harassment go on record.'

'Me, too.' Eve smiled. 'You were acquainted with Robert Mathias, also known as Lobar.'

'He *was* Lobar,' Selina corrected. 'It was his chosen name.'

'*Was* is the operative word, seeing as he's in a refrigerated unit at the morgue. And so is Thomas Wineburg. Are you acquainted with him?'

'I don't believe I've had the pleasure.'

'Well, that's interesting. He was a member of your cult.'

Selina set her chin, waved away Trivane as he leaned forward to speak to her. 'I can't be expected to recognize the name of every member of my church, Dallas. We are . . .' She spread her hands on the small table. 'Legion.'

'Maybe this will refresh your memory.' Eve opened a file, took a still out, and slid it across the table. Death shots were always ugly.

Selina studied it with a small smile tugging at her mouth. A finger of the hand she wore webbed again today traced the spread of harsh red blood. 'I can't say for certain. We meet in the dark.' Her gaze lifted to Eve. 'It's our way.'

'I can say for certain. Both he and Lobar were yours, and both were murdered with a style of knife used in your rituals.'

'An athame, yes. We are not the only religion who uses such an instrument in ceremony. I feel, after this violence, this persecution of members of my church, the police should be concerned with protecting us rather than pointing fingers. Obviously, there is a person or persons determined to eliminate us.'

'I figured you had your own protection. Doesn't your master look out for his own?'

'Your mockery only shows your ignorance.'

'Having sex with an eighteen-year-old delinquent shows yours. Did you have sex with Wineburg, too?'

'I said I can't be sure I knew him. But if I did, I very likely had sex with him.'

'Selina.' Trivane cut her off, his voice firm. 'You're goading my client, Lieutenant. She's stated she can't positively identify this victim.'

'She knew him. Both of you did. He was a weasel. Do you know what a weasel is in cop-speak, Ms Cross? An informant.' Eve rose, leaned over, bending her body close to Selina's. 'Were you worried about how much he'd told me? Is that why you arranged for him to die? Were you having him followed?' She slanted her gaze toward Trivane briefly. 'Maybe you have all your . . . faithful followed.'

'I see whatever I need to see in the smoke.'

'Yeah, in the smoke. The psychic's version of the Peeping Tom. It was risky for Wineburg to come by the viewing room. Why do you suppose he wanted a look at Alice? Had he been there the night she was drugged, raped? Did you let him have her?'

'Alice was an initiate. A willing one.'

'She was a child, a confused one. You like luring the young, don't you? They're so much more interesting than stubby fools like Wineburg. With their firm bodies, their malleable minds. People like Wineburg and the distinguished counsel here, they're just for the money, and the cachet. But those like Alice, they're so tender. So tasty.'

510

Selina looked up smugly through her thick, dark lashes. 'She was. She enjoyed and was enjoyed. She didn't have to be lured, Dallas. She came to me.'

'Now she's dead. Three deaths. Your members must be getting nervous.' Eve smiled thinly at Trivane. 'I would be.'

'Martyrdom isn't new, Dallas. People have been killed because of their faith for centuries. And still, the faith survives. We'll survive. We'll triumph.'

Eve took out another still, slapped it on the table. 'He didn't.'

It was Lobar, his mutilated body caught it the garish lights of the crime scene. The wound on his throat gaped open like a scream.

It was Trivane who Eve watched. His eyes blinked rapidly, horror flickering through. His skin went pasty, and his chest rose and fell in jerks.

'He didn't survive,' Eve said softly, 'did he, Selina?'

'His death is a symbol. He will not be forgotten.'

'Do you own an athame?'

'I own several, naturally.'

'Like this?' She took out another photo, this one a close-up of the weapon left pinned into Lobar. Blood crusted the blade.

'I have several,' Selina repeated. 'Some similar to this, as one might expect. But I don't recognize this particular one.'

'Hallucinogens were found in Lobar's system. You use drugs during rituals.'

'Herbals, and some chemicals. All legal.'

'Not everything found in Lobar's system was on the legal list.'

'I can't be responsible for the choices other people make.'

'He was with you the night he died. Was he using?'

'He had taken the ritual wine. If he took something otherwise, it was without my knowledge.'

'You have priors as a chemi-dealer.'

'And paid my debt to so-called society. You have nothing on me, Lieutenant.'

'I have three bodies. And they're yours. I've got a dead cop, and he's on you, too. I'm closing in on you, Selina. Step by step.'

'Keep out of my face.'

'Or?'

'Do you know pain, Dallas?' Selina's voice went low and thick. 'Do you know the pain that eats at the stomach like drops of acid spreading? You beg for relief, but none comes. The pain becomes agony, and agony almost pleasure. The pain becomes so intense, so unspeakable that if a knife came to your hand, you would gladly slice through your own guts to cut out the source of it.'

'Would I,' Eve said coolly. 'Would I really?'

'I can offer you that. I can offer you pain.'

Eve smiled, and her smile was slow and humorless. 'That slips into the area of threatening a police officer. And that'll get you some time in a cage until your lawyer finesses you out again.'

'You bitch.' Furious that she'd been trapped so neatly and with so little effort, Selina sprang to her feet. 'You can't hold me for that.'

'Sure, I can. Selina Cross, you're under arrest for verbal threat to physically harm a police officer.'

She was fast, but Eve's reflexes were sharp. She blocked the first blow as Selina flew at her. But the second rapid swipe caught her along the throat with those lethal dark nails. She smelled her own blood and indulged herself by bringing her elbow up to ram Selina's chin.

The dark eyes rolled back, went glassy. 'Looks like we add resisting arrest. You're going to have your hands full for the next couple hours, counselor.'

He hadn't moved, not a muscle. Trivane continued to sit, staring at the photos of the dead. When Feeney opened the

512

door, a uniform behind him, Eve nodded. 'Book her,' she ordered. 'Verbal threat and resisting.'

Selina staggered as Eve passed her to the uniform. But her eyes cleared and fixed on Eve's face with bubbling malice. She began to speak softly, in a chant that rose and fell almost musically. She swiveled her head, looking over her shoulder as the uniform took her out.

Eve dabbed fingers on her throat, disgusted when they came away smeared with blood. 'Did you catch what she was saying there?'

Feeney took out a handkerchief, handed it to her. 'Sounded like Latin, bastardized some. My mother made me learn when I was a kid. Had delusions about me becoming a priest.'

'See if you can make any of it out from the record. We may be able to add to the charges. Shit, this burns. Interview is concluded,' she added and logged the time and date. 'Trivane, you want to talk to me?'

'What?' He looked over, swallowed, shook his head. 'I'll see my client, Lieutenant, as soon as she's booked. These charges won't hold.'

Eve held out her bloody fingers. 'Oh, I think they will. Take a good look, Louis.' She stepped closer, jammed her fingers under his nose. 'It could be yours next time.'

'I'll see my client,' he repeated, and his face was still white as death as he hurried from the room.

'That bitch is loony,' Feeney commented.

'Tell me something I don't know.'

'She hates your ever fucking guts,' he said pleasantly, happy to be in tandem again. 'But you knew that, too. Put the hoodoo on you.'

'Huh?'

'Cursed you.' He winked at her. 'Let me know if you start getting stomach cramps. You're starting to get to her.'

'Not enough,' Eve murmured. 'But my money's on the lawyer. Let's keep a man on him, Feeney. I don't want him ending up dead before he breaks. It was the way he looked at the shot of Lobar. Shock, then something like recognition.' She shook her head. 'Let's not lose him.' She glanced at her watch, hummed with satisfaction. 'Just in time to make my nooner with Nadine.'

'You want to have that neck looked after. Nasty.'

'Later.' She headed out, moving fast. Nadine wouldn't miss the injury. Nor, Eve thought, would the all-seeing eye of the camera.

'What the hell happened to you?' Nadine demanded. She stopped pacing, stopped looking at her watch.

'Little problem in Interview.'

'You cut it close, Dallas, we got two minutes before air. You don't have time to clean up.'

'Fine, we'll go like we are.'

'Get a voice and light level,' Nadine told her camera operator. She took out a mirrored compact, polishing up her face when she sat. 'Looks like female,' she added. 'Long, nasty nails, four separate grooves.'

'Yeah.' Eve patted the already stained handkerchief against the wound. 'Somebody was curious, they could check booking, get the data.'

Nadine's eyes went sharp. 'I imagine someone could,' she purred. 'You didn't do anything with your hair.'

'I cut it.'

'I meant anything constructive. Coming up in thirty. Set, Suzanna?'

The operator made a circle of forefinger and thumb. 'The fresh blood shows up real good. Nice touch.'

'Gee, thanks.' Eve settled back, hooked one booted foot over her knee. 'Let's keep this short, Nadine. I haven't seen yours yet.'

'Here's a preview then. What local white witch is the son of infamous mass murderer David Baines Conroy, who is currently doing five separate life stretches, no parole options, in maximum lockup on Penal Station Omega?'

'Who—'

'In five,' Nadine said sweetly, delighted to have snagged Eve's full attention. 'Four, three . . .' She signaled the last of the countdown with her fingers, below camera level. On cue, she stared into the camera with sober eyes. 'Good afternoon, this is Nadine Furst, leading off the noon hour with an exclusive interview with homicide Lieutenant Eve Dallas in her office at Cop Central . . .'

Eve was prepared for the questions. She knew Nadine's style well, too well to allow herself to be rattled by the information that had been dumped on her seconds before air time. As, she imagined, Nadine had hoped. She answered briefly, carefully, and knew she was bumping up Channel 75's and Nadine's rating points with every on-the-air second.

'The department is proceeding with the belief that the cases are connected as evidence indicates. Though different weapons were left at the scene of each murder, they are of similar style.'

'Can you describe the weapons?'

'I can't comment on that.'

'But they were knives.'

'They were sharp instruments. I'm not at liberty to go into any more detail. Doing so would jeopardize our investigation at this point.'

'The second victim. You were pursuing him at the time of his death. Why?'

She was ready for this, had already decided to exploit the question for her own benefit. 'Thomas Wineburg had indicated he had information which would be useful to my investigation.'

'What information?'

Zip, Eve thought, but kept her eyes level. 'I'm not at liberty to divulge that. I can only say we spoke, and he became agitated and ran. I pursued.'

'And he was killed.'

'That's correct. Running didn't help him.'

Annoyed that her director indicated her time was up through her earpiece, Nadine wound the interview to a close. 'And we're clear. Suzanna?' Nadine simply gestured to the door and sent her operator out. 'Off the record,' she began.

'Nope. Gimme.'

'All right then.' Nadine sat back, crossed her pretty legs. 'Charles Forte took his mother's maiden name legally twelve years ago after his father was convicted of the ritual slayings of five people. It's believed he killed countless others, but it's never been proved. The bodies have never been found.'

'I know the story behind Conroy. I didn't know he had a kid.'

'That was kept locked. Privacy Act. The family was already out of it. The mother had divorced and relocated a few years before Baines was caught. The kid was sixteen when she took him and left. Twenty-one when his father was tried and convicted. My sources claim the son attended court every day.'

Eve thought of the small, unassuming man she'd met at Alice's viewing. Son of a monster. How much of that came through the blood? She thought of her own father, nearly shuddered. 'I appreciate it. If it comes to anything, I'll owe you.'

'Yeah, you will. I've got lots of data on cults in the city. Nothing as dramatic as this, but it may lead somewhere. Meanwhile, if you were in Interview with someone pissed off enough to try to slice your jugular, should I assume you have a suspect?'

Eve studied her nails. She supposed some would have said she was overdue for a manicure. 'I can't comment on that. You know, Nadine, cameras aren't allowed down in Booking.'

'Damn shame. Thanks for the spot, Dallas. I'll be in touch.'

'Do that.' Eve watched her stroll out, had no doubt Nadine was making tracks to Booking. And that Selina Cross was going to have her name broadcast by the end of the noon report.

All in all, she decided, *not a bad morning.*

Wincing, she dragged through her drawers hoping for a first aid kit.

Chapter Fifteen

'I won't make it home.' Eve juggled the call to Roarke while her computer searched for all data on David Baines Conroy. 'Can you swing by here about six? We can drive upstate for the witch party.'

Roarke lifted an elegant brow. 'As long as it's not in your vehicle.' He frowned, gestured. 'Come a little closer to the screen. What now?' he asked.

'What do you mean, "What now"? I'm busy.'

'No, your neck.'

'Oh, that.' She touched her fingers to the still-raw scratches. She'd never found that first aid kit. 'A difference of opinion. I won.'

'Naturally. Put something on it, Lieutenant. I should be able to make it there by six thirty. We can eat on the way.'

'Fine.' *Eat on the way?* 'Wait a minute. Don't bring the limo.'

He only smiled. 'Six thirty.'

'I mean it, Roarke, don't—' She hissed when the screen blanked. 'Damn.' With a sigh, she swiveled back to the computer.

The IRCCA was a fount of data on this one, she thought. she skimmed through, pausing over pertinent facts on David Baines Conroy.

Divorced, one child, male, Charles, born January 22, 2025,

custody awarded to mother, Ellen Forte.

Big surprise, Eve thought. Mass murderers weren't generally given custody of minor children. 'Let's get down to it,' she murmured. 'Charges and convictions.'

Charged and convicted, Murder in the first, torture killing, posthumous rape, and dismemberment of Doreen Harden, mixed race female, age 23. Sentenced to life, maximum facility, no parole option.
Charged and convicted, Murder in the first, rape, torture killing, and dismemberment of Emma Tangent, black female, age 25. Sentenced to life, maximum facility, no parole option.
Charged and convicted, Murder in the first, sodomy, rape, torture killing, and dismemberment of Lowell McBride, white male, age 18. Sentenced to life, maximum facility, no parole option.
Charged and convicted, Murder in the first, rape, torture killing, and dismemberment of Darla Fitz, mixed race female, age 23. Sentenced to life, maximum facility, no parole options.
Charged and convicted, Murder in the first, sodomy, posthumous rape, torture killing, and dismemberment of Martin Savoy, mixed race male, age 20. Sentenced to life, maximum facility, no parole options.
Currently serving term on Penal Station Omega.
Suspected of twelve additional murders, cases open. Insufficient evidence to charge. Primary investigators available on request.

'List primaries,' Eve ordered and watched as names and data scrolled. 'Moved around, did you, Conroy?' she muttered, noting that the detectives in charge were scattered all over the country.

She'd still been a teenager when Conroy had dominated the news. She remembered snatches, weeping family members begging Conroy to tell them where to find the remains of loved ones, grim-faced cops giving statements, and Conroy himself, a quiet face slashed with vicious, dark eyes.

They'd called him evil, she remembered. The Antichrist. That was the term used over and over again to describe him, to try, perhaps, to separate him from the human.

But he'd been human enough to conceive a child. A son. And that son was on her current list of suspects. Maybe, just maybe, she'd been focused too relentlessly on Selina Cross.

The son was drawn to power, she mused. Witchcraft was about power, wasn't it? He'd known at least one of the victims. And two had been killed with a knife. Conroy had been very handy with a knife.

He'd also claimed to have been the instrument of a god, she recalled, scanning data. Yes, there, there in one of his rambling statements. She highlighted. 'Give me audio on this.'

Working ...

'I am a force beyond you,' Conroy's voice crooned out, beautiful diction, almost musical. The son's voice, Eve thought, was equally charismatic. 'I am the instrument of the god of vengeance and pain. What I do in his name is grand. Tremble before me for I will never be vanquished. I am legion.'

'You are garbage,' Eve corrected. *Legion*. Cross had used the same term. Interesting . . . *Had Conroy dabbled in Satanism*, she wondered, *in witchcraft? And had the son been attracted to the same areas?*

Just how much, she wondered, *did Charles Forte know about his father's work? And how did he feel about it?*

'Computer, run Charles Forte of this city, formerly Charles Conroy, son of David Baines Conroy, all data.

Working …

As the information beeped on, she tapped her fingers on the desk and considered. The mother had taken her son to New York, which meant, Eve mused, that the boy had traveled back to attend the trial. He'd made the effort, likely over his mother's objections. Dropped out of college, second term. Studied pharmaceuticals. Very interesting. Licensed as a chemical drone, worked on drug cloning and manufacture. Moved around quite a bit, she noted. Like his dear old dad. Then settled back in New York, co-owner of Spirit Quest.

She leaned back, unconsciously rubbing her wounded throat. No marriages, no children, no arrests. She played a hunch.

'Medical data.'

Charles Forte, age six, broken hand. Age six, minor concussion, abdominal bruising. Age seven, second-degree burns, forearms. Age seven, concussion and fractured tibia.

The list went on through childhood in a pattern that made Eve's stomach clench. 'Hold. Probability of child abuse?'

Probability ninety-eight percent.

'Why the hell wasn't it picked up?'

Medical records indicate treatment was issued at varying hospitals in varying cities over course of ten years. No record of requested search through National Child Abuse Prevention Agency.

'Idiots. Idiots.' She rubbed her hands over her face, pressing hard on the headache now brewing in the center of her forehead. It was too close to home.

'List any psychiatric treatment or available psychological profiles.'

Subject entered Miller Clinic voluntarily as outpatient. Doctor of record, Ernest Renfrew from February 2045 to September 2047. Files sealed. No other data.

'Okay, that's enough to chew on. Save data, file Forte, Charles, case number 34299-H. Cross-reference, Conroy. Disengage when complete.'

She glanced up as Feeney stuck his head in her doorway. 'Cross just got sprung.'

'Well, it was too good to last.'

'You have anybody look at those cat scratches?'

'I will. Got a minute?'

'Sure.'

'David Baines Conroy.'

Feeney whistled, made himself comfortable on the corner of her desk. 'That's going back. Sick bastard. Cut his victims up when he was done with them. Kept the parts in a portable cold box. Had a trailer, traveled around. Preaching.'

'Preaching?'

'Well, that's not exactly the term. Set himself up as a sort of Antichrist. Lots of shit about anarchy, freedom to pursue carnal pleasures, opening the gates of Hell. That sort of thing. Figures he plucked most of his victims off the road. Itinerant LCs. At least three they pinned him on were licensed companions. Hookers have always been easy marks for psychos.'

'He was found competent to stand trial.'

'Passed the tests. Legally, he was sane. In reality, a real whacko.'

'He had a family.'

'Yeah, yeah, that's right.' Feeney closed his eyes to try to bring it back. 'I was still working Homicide then, and there wasn't a cop on planet who wasn't personally caught up by the case. Never did any of his work here, that we know of, but I remember he had a wife. Pale, jumpy little woman. Left him – before he got snagged seems to me. And there was a kid, a boy. Spooky.'

'Why?'

'He had his old man's eyes. Except they were dead, you know? I remember thinking we might be tracking him one day. In his father's footsteps. Then they ducked under the Privacy Act, and nobody ever heard of them again.'

'Until now.' Eve kept her eyes level. 'I'm seeing Conroy's son tonight. At a witch's coven.'

Roarke brought the limo. She'd been certain he would, just to annoy her. She'd have stayed annoyed if he hadn't seen that the AutoChef was stocked, Italian style.

Eve was wolfing down manicotti before they crossed the Jacqueline Onassis Bridge. But she shook her head at the burgundy he poured.

'I'm on duty,' she said with her mouth full.

'I'm not.' He sipped, studied her. 'Why haven't you taken care of that?' he asked, brushing gentle fingers over her throat.

'I got tied up.'

'Now, that's something we've yet to explore.' He smiled genially when she goggled at him. 'Just a thought. I caught the replay of your little tête-à-tête with Nadine on the way over to Central. I'm surprised you agreed to it.'

'It was a trade. I got my share.' She leaned forward, engaged the privacy shield between them and the driver. 'And I'd better fill you in before we join in tonight's festivities.'

She detailed the new line she was pursuing, then sampled one of the sweet, fat olives on the antipasto tray. 'It bumps him up a few notches on the list,' she concluded.

'The sins of the father?'

'Sometimes it works that way.'

He said nothing a moment. They both had reason to be uncomfortable with the theory. 'You know best, Lieutenant, but isn't it just as likely circumstances would push him to the opposite pole?'

'He knew Alice, he has knowledge of chemicals. Her grandfather had chemicals in his system, and she'd been hallucinating. The other two victims were ritual slayings. Forte belongs to a cult. I can't ignore the steps.'

'He looked remarkably unhomicidal to me.'

She poked through the antipasto, selected a marinated pepper. 'I once took down this little old lady, looked like everybody's favorite granny. She took in stray cats and baked cookies for the neighborhood kids. Grew geraniums on her windowsill.' Enjoying the bite, Eve chose another pepper. 'She'd lured a half a dozen kids into her apartment, and had fed their internal organs to the kitties before we nailed her.'

'Charming story.' Roarke slipped his plate into the holding slot. 'Point taken.' Reaching into his pocket, he took out the amulet Isis had given him the night before, slipped it over Eve's neck.

'What's this for?'

'It looks better on you than me.'

She narrowed her eyes at him. 'Bull. You're being superstitious.'

'No, I'm not,' he lied and set her plate in with his before he shifted and began to unbutton her shirt.

'Hey, what are you doing?'

'Passing the time.' His hands, clever and quick, swooped down to take her breasts. 'It'll take an hour to get there by car.'

'I'm not having sex in the back of a limo,' she told him. 'It's—'

'Delicious,' he finished and replaced his hands with his mouth.

She felt remarkably limber and relaxed by the time the limo turned onto a narrow country road. Here the trees were plentiful, the stars brilliant, and the dark complete. Half-denuded trees arched over the roadway, tunneling them in. She caught the glinting gold eyes of what might have been a fox as a shadow darted across the road and into the woods.

'Feeney and Peabody still behind us?'

'Hmm.' Roarke tucked his shirt back into his trousers. 'It would seem so. 'You're putting that on inside out,' he said mildly and grinned.

'Hell.' Eve struggled back out of the shirt, pulled the arms through, and tried again. 'Don't look so smug, I just pretended to enjoy that.'

'Darling Eve.' He took her hand, kissed it. 'You're too good to me.'

'You're telling me.' She slipped the amulet off, looped it over his head. 'You wear it.' Before he could object, she caught his face in her hands. 'Please.'

'You don't believe in it, anyway.'

'No.' She tucked it under his shirt, patted it. 'But I think you do. Your driver knows where he's going?'

'The directions from Isis are programmed in.' He checked his watch. 'By my calculations, we should be nearly there.'

'Looks like we're nowhere if you ask me.' She stared out the window. Nothing but dark, trees, and more dark. 'I'd rather be on my own turf. Hard to believe there's this much nothing less than two hours' drive from New York.'

'You're such an urbanite.'

'And you're not?'

He moved his shoulders. 'The country's an interesting place to visit for short periods of time. Quiet can be restful.'

'It makes me edgy.' They turned onto another winding road. 'And everything looks the same. There's no . . . action,' she decided. 'Now, you stroll into Central or Green-peace Park and you're bound to run into a mugger or chemi head at least. Maybe an unlicensed hooker, couple of perverts.'

She glanced back, saw he was grinning at her. 'Well?'

'Life with you has such . . . color.'

She snorted, strapped on her side arm. 'Yeah, like everything was gray in your little world before I came along. All that wine, women, and money. Must have been pretty tedious.'

'The ennui,' he said on a sigh, 'was unspeakable. I might have faded away from it if you hadn't tried to hang a murder or two on me.'

'Just your lucky day.' She caught the glimmer of lights through the trees as the car turned up a steep, rutted incline. 'Thank Christ. Looks like the party's already under way.'

'Try not to sneer.' Roarke patted her knee. 'It would offend our hosts.'

'I'm not going to sneer.' She already was. 'I want impressions. Not just of Forte, of everybody. And if you happen to recognize a face, let me know.' She took a small device out of her bag, slipped it into her pocket.

'Micro recorder?' Roarke clucked his tongue. 'I believe that's illegal. Not to mention rude.'

'I don't know what you're talking about.'

'And unnecessary,' he added. He turned his wrist, tapped a tiny button on the side of his watch. 'This one is much more efficient. I should know. I manufacture both brands.' He smiled as the car stopped at the edge of a small clearing. 'I believe we've arrived.'

Eve spotted Isis first. She was impossible to miss. The sheer, white robe she wore seemed to glow out of the dark like moonlight. Her hair was left long and loose, flowing over her shoulders. A gold band studded with colored stones circled her brow. Her long, narrow feet were bare.

'Blessed be,' she said and disconcerted Eve by kissing both her cheeks. She greeted Roarke the same way, then turned back to Eve. 'You're injured.' Before Eve could respond, she lay fingers against the scratches. 'Poison.'

'Poison?' Eve had visions of vicious nails dipped into a slow-acting brew that crept through the bloodstream.

'Not of the physical but of the spiritual kind. I feel Selina here.' Her eyes stayed on Eve's as she lowered her hand to Eve's shoulder. 'This won't do. Mirium, please welcome our other guests.' She spoke to a small, dark-skinned woman as Feeney's rattletrap of a car bumped up the road. 'Chas will see to your wound.'

'It's fine. I'll see an MT in the morning.'

'I don't think that will be necessary. Please come this way. It's unhealthy to have even this much of her here.'

She led the way around the clearing. Eve could see a wide circle formed by a ring of white candles. People stood outside it chatting, she mused, as they might at a mid-town cocktail party. Dress varied. Robes, suits, long and short skirts.

Twenty in all, by her count, ranging in age from eighteen to eighty with a mixture of race and gender. There seemed no spe-cific type. Coolers were stacked nearby, which, she supposed, explained why several members were sipping drinks. Conver-sation was muted, punctuated by the occasional laugh.

Chas turned from a folding table as they approached. He wore a simple blue unisuit and soft shoes in the same tone. He smiled, noting Eve's suspicious scan of the table.

'Witch's tools,' he told her.

Red cords, a white-handled knife. *An athame*, she thought. She saw more candles, a small brass gong, a whip, a gleaming silver sword, colored bottles, bowls, and cups.

'Interesting.'

'It's an old ritual, requiring old tools. But you're hurt.' He took a step toward her, his hand lifting, then pausing when

527

she aimed a cool, warning look. 'I beg your pardon. It looks painful.'

'Chas is a healer.' Isis curved her lips in challenge. 'Consider this a demonstration. After all, you did come to observe, didn't you? And your mate wears protection.'

And so, Eve thought, feeling the comfortable weight of her weapon, did she.

'Okay, demonstrate.' She tilted her head, inviting Chas to examine the scratches.

His fingers were surprisingly cool, surprisingly soothing as they played over her abraded skin. She kept her eyes on his, watched them focus, then flicker. 'You're fortunate,' he murmured. 'The result didn't equal the intent. Will you relax your mind?'

His gaze lifted from his hand, met hers. 'The mind and body are one,' he said quietly in that lovely voice. 'One guides the other, one heals the other. Let me ease this.'

She thought she felt warmth move through her, from the point where his fingers lay, into her head, down through her body, until a drowsiness seeped through. She jerked herself alert, saw him smile quietly. 'I won't hurt you.'

He turned, picked up an amber bottle, uncorked the stopper and dabbed clear, floral-scented liquid on his hands.

'This is a balm, an old recipe with modern additions.' He spread it gently, his fingers following the path Selina's nails had raked. 'It will heal clean, and there will be no more discomfort.'

'You know your chemicals, don't you?'

'This is an herbal base.' He took a cloth from his pocket, wiped his fingers. 'But yes, I do.'

'I'd like to talk to you about that.' She waited a beat, her eyes keen. 'And about your father.'

She saw the demand hit home in the way his pupils dilated, then contracted. Then Isis was stepping between them, fury glorious on her face.

528

'You've been invited here; this place is sacred. You have no right—'

'Isis.' Chas touched her arm. 'She has a mission. We all do.' He looked at Eve, seemed to gather himself. 'Yes, I'll speak with you, when you wish. But this isn't the place to bring despair. The ceremony's about to begin.'

'We won't stop you.'

'Will tomorrow, nine o'clock, at Spirit Quest, be suitable?'

'That's fine.'

'Excuse me.'

'Do you always repay kindness with pain?' Isis demanded in a furious undertone as Chas stepped away. Then she shook her head, aimed her gaze deliberately at Roarke. 'You are welcome to observe, and we hope you and your companions will show the proper respect for our rite tonight. You aren't permitted within the magic circle.'

As she swept away, Eve slipped her hands into her pockets. 'Well, now I've got two witches pissed off at me.' She looked over as Peabody hurried to her side.

'It's an initiation,' Peabody whispered. 'I got it from the big gorgeous witch in the Italian suit.' She smiled across the clearing at a man with burnished bronze hair and a million-watt smile. 'Jesus, makes a woman consider converting.'

'Get a grip on yourself, Peabody.' Eve nodded at Feeney.

'My sainted mother would be saying half a dozen rosaries tonight if she knew where I was.' He pushed on a grin to cover nerves. 'Damn spooky place. Nothing out here but a lot of nothing.'

Roarke sighed, slipped an arm around Eve's waist. 'Cut from the same cloth,' he murmured and turned as the rite began.

The young woman Isis had called Mirium stood outside the circle of candles and was bound and blindfolded by two men. Everyone, but for the observers, was now naked. Skin glowed, white and dark and gold in the streaming moonlight. Deeper in the woods night birds called liltingly.

Itchy, Eve slid a hand inside her jacket, felt the weight of her weapon.

The red cords were used for the binding of the initiate, leaving a kind of tether. As the ankle cord was attached, Chas spoke.

'Feet neither bound nor free.'

And there was unmistakable joy and reverence in his voice.

Curious, Eve watched the casting of the circle, the opening ritual. The mood was, she had to admit, happy. Overhead, the moon swam, sprinkling light, silvering the trees. Owls hooted – an odd sound that rippled through her blood. Nudity seemed to be ignored. There was none of the surreptitious groping or sly glances she knew she'd have seen at any city sex club.

Chas took up the athame, making Eve's hand close on her weapon as he held it to the postulant's heart. He spoke, his words rising and falling on the smoky breeze.

'I have two passwords,' Mirium answered. 'Perfect love and perfect trust.'

He smiled. 'All who have such are doubly welcome. I give you a third to pass you through this dread door.'

He handed the knife to the man beside him, then kissed Mirium. As a father might kiss a child, Eve thought, frowning. Chas walked around the postulant, embraced her, then gently nudged her forward into the circle. Behind them, the second man traced the tip of the athame over the empty space, as if to close them in.

There was chanting now as Chas led Mirium around the circle, as she was turned by hands after hands in a playful child's game of dizziness and disorientation. A bell rang three times.

It was Chas who knelt, speaking, then kissing the postulant's feet, her knees, her belly just above the pubis, her breasts, then her lips.

She'd thought it would be sexual, Eve mused. But it had been more . . . loving than that.

'Impressions?' She murmured to Roarke.

'Charming and powerful. Religious.' He slid his hand up and covered the one that still curled around her weapon, gently tugging it away. 'And harmless. Sexual, certainly, but in a very balanced and respectful sense. And yes, I see one or two people I recognize.'

'I'll want names.'

As the rite continued, she reached up absently to rub her throat. She found the skin smooth, unbroken, and free of pain.

As she dropped her hand, Chas looked at her, met her eyes. And smiled again.

Chapter Sixteen

Spirit Quest wasn't open for business when Eve arrived with Peabody. But Chas was there, waiting on the sidewalk, sipping something that steamed out of a recycle cup.

'Good morning.' The air was just chilled enough to have slapped color into his cheek. 'I wonder if we could talk upstairs, in our apartment, rather than in the shop.'

'Cops bad for business?' Eve asked.

'Well, we could say that the early customers might be disconcerted. And we do open in half an hour. I assume you don't need Isis.'

'Not at the moment.'

'I appreciate it. If you could, ah, give me just a moment.' He shot her a sheepish look. 'Isis prefers not to have caffeine in the house. I'm weak,' he said, taking another sip. 'She knows I sneak off every morning to feed my addiction and pretends not to. It's foolish, but it makes us happy.'

'Take your time. You get that across the street?'

'That would be a little too close to home. And to be honest, the coffee's filthy there. They make a decent cup down at the corner deli.' He sipped again with obvious pleasure. 'I gave up cigarettes years ago, even herbals, but I can't quite do without a cup of coffee. Did you enjoy the ceremony last night?'

'It was interesting.' Since the morning air was sharp, she tucked her ungloved hands in her pockets. Traffic, both street and air, was beginning to thin a little with the first commuter rush passing. 'Getting a little brisk to run around naked in the woods, isn't it?'

'Yes. We probably won't hold any more outdoor ceremonies this year. Certainly not skyclad. But Mirium had her heart set on being initiated to first-degree witch before Samhain.'

'Samhain.'

'Halloween,' he and Peabody said together. She shuffled her feet as he smiled at her. 'Free-Ager,' she muttered.

'Ah, there are some basic similarities.' He finished off his coffee, stepped over to a recycling bin, and neatly slipped the cup in the slot. 'You have a cold, Officer.'

'Yes, sir.' Peabody sniffled, determinedly blocked a sneeze.

'I have something that should ease that. One of our members recognized you, Lieutenant. She said she'd given you a reading lately. On the night, actually, that Alice died.'

'That's right.'

'Cassandra is very skilled and very sweet-natured,' Chas began as he started up the steps. 'She feels she should have been able to see more clearly, to tell you that Alice was in danger. She believes you are.' He paused, looked back. 'She hoped that you're still carrying the stone she gave you.'

'It's around somewhere.'

He let out a sound that might have been a sigh. 'How's your neck?'

'Good as new.'

'I see it's healed cleanly.'

'Yeah, and quickly. What was in that stuff you put on it?'

Humor flickered in his eyes, surprising her. 'Oh, just some tongue of bat, a little eye of newt.' He opened the door to a musical chime of bells. 'Please be comfortable. I'll get you some tea to warm you up since I kept you standing.'

'You don't have to bother.'

'It's no bother at all. Just be a moment.'

He slipped through a doorway, and Eve took the time to study his living quarters.

She wouldn't call them simple. Obviously, a lot of the stock from the shelves downstairs made its way up here. Large, many-speared hunks of crystals decorated an oval table and circled a copper urn filled with fall flowers. An intricate tapestry hung on the wall over a curved, blue sofa. Men and women, suns and moons, a castle with flame spewing from the arrow slits.

'The major arcana,' Peabody told her as Eve stepped up for a closer look. She sneezed once, violently, and dug out a tissue. 'The Tarot. It looks old, hand-worked.'

'Expensive,' Eve decided. Art such as this didn't come cheaply.

There were statues in pewter and carved from smooth stone. Wizards and dragons, two-headed dogs, sinuous women with delicate wings. Another wall was covered with odd, attractive symbols in splashes of color.

'From the Book of Kells.' Peabody lifted her shoulders at Eve's curious glance. 'My mother likes to embroider the symbols, like on pillows and samplers. They look nice. It's a nice place.' And it didn't give her the willies like the Cross apartment. 'Eccentric, but nice.'

'Business must be good for them to be able to afford the antiques, the metalwork, the art.'

'The business does well enough,' Chas said as he came back with a tray laden with a flower patterned ceramic pot and cups. 'And I had some resources of my own before we opened.'

'Inheritance?'

'No.' He set the tray down on a circular coffee table. 'Savings, investments. Chemical engineers are well paid.'

'But you gave it all up to work retail.'

'I gave it up,' he said simply. 'I was unhappy in my work. I was unhappy in my life.'

'Therapy didn't help.'

He met her eyes again, though it seemed to cost him. 'It didn't hurt. Please sit down. I'll answer your questions.'

'She can't make you go through this, Chas.' Isis slipped into the room like smoke. Her gown was gray today, the color of storm clouds, and swirled around her ankles as she moved to him. 'You're entitled to your privacy, under any law.'

'I can insist that he answer my questions,' Eve corrected. 'I'm investigating murder here. He is, of course, entitled to counsel.'

'It isn't a lawyer he needs, but peace.' Isis whirled, her eyes alive with emotion, and Chas took her hands, lifted them to his lips, pressed his face to them.

'I have peace,' he said quietly. 'I have you. Don't worry so. You have to go down and open, and I have to do this.'

'Let me stay.'

He shook his head, and the look they exchanged had Eve staring in surprise. It was baffling enough to speculate on their physical relationship, but what she saw pass between them wasn't sex. It was love. It was devotion.

It should have been laughable, the way Isis had to lean down, bend that goddess body to reach his lips with hers. Instead, it was poignant.

'You have only to call,' she told him. 'Only to wish for me.'

'I know.' He gave her hand a quick, intimate pat to send her off. She shot Eve one last look of barely controlled rage and swept out.

'I doubt I would have survived without her,' Chas said as he stared at the door. 'You're a strong woman, Lieutenant. It would be difficult for you to understand that kind of need, that kind of dependence.'

Once she would have agreed. Now she wasn't so sure. 'I'd like to record this conversation, Mr Forte.'

'Yes, of course.' He sat, and as Peabody engaged her recorder, mechanically poured the tea. He listened without glancing up as Eve recited the traditional caution.

'Do you understand your rights and obligations?'

535

'Yes. Would you care for sweetener?'

She looked down at her tea with some impatience. It smelled suspiciously like what Mira insisted on serving her. 'No.'

'I've added a bit of honey to yours, Officer.' He sent Peabody a sweet smile. 'And a bit of . . . something else. I think you'll find it soothing.'

'Smells pretty good.' Cautious, Peabody sipped, tasted home, and smiled back. 'Thanks.'

'When's the last time you saw your father?'

Caught off guard by the abruptness of Eve's question, Chas looked up quickly. The hand holding his cup shook once, violently. 'The day he was sentenced. I went to the hearing and I watched them take him away. They kept him in full restraints and they closed and locked the door on his life.'

'And how did you feel about that?'

'Ashamed. Relieved. Desperately unhappy. Or perhaps just desperate. He was my father.' Chas took a deep gulp of tea, as some men might take a gulp of whiskey. 'I hated him with all of my heart, all of my soul.'

'Because he killed?'

'Because he was my father. I hurt my mother deeply by insisting on attending his trial. But she was too battered emotionally to stop me from doing as I chose. She could never stop him, either. Though she did leave him eventually. She took me and left him, which was, I think, a surprise to all of us.'

He stared down into his cup, as if contemplating the pattern of the leaves skimming the bottom. 'I hated her, too, for a very, very long time. Hate can define a person, can't it, Lieutenant? It can twist them into an ugly shape.'

'Is that what happened to you?'

'Nearly. Ours was not a happy home. You wouldn't expect that it could be with a man like my father dominating it. You suspect I could be like him.' Chas's sensual voice remained calm. But his eyes were swirling with emotions.

It was the eyes you watched during interview, Eve thought. The words often meant nothing. 'Are you?'

'"Blood will tell." Is that Shakespeare?' He shook his head a little. 'I'm not quite sure. But isn't that what all children live with, and fear no matter what their parents, that blood will tell?'

She lived with it, she feared it, but she couldn't allow herself to be swayed by it. 'How strong an influence was he on your life?'

'There couldn't have been a stronger one. You're an efficient investigator, Lieutenant. I'm sure you've studied the records by now, run the discs, watched them. You would have seen a charismatic man, terrifyingly so. A man who considered himself above the law – any and all laws. That kind of steely arrogance is in itself compelling.'

'Evil can be compelling to some.'

'Yes.' His lips curved without humor. 'You'd know that, in your line of work. He wasn't a man you could . . . fight, on a physical or emotional level. He's strong. Very strong.'

Chas closed his eyes a moment, reliving what he was constantly struggling to put to death. 'I was afraid I could be like him, considered giving back the most precious gift I'd been given. Life.'

'You attempted self-termination?'

'I never got as far as the attempt, just the plan. The first time, I was ten.' He sipped tea again, determined to soothe himself. 'Can you imagine a child of ten pondering suicide?'

Yes, she could, all too well. She'd been younger yet when she had pondered it. 'He abused you?'

'Abuse is such a weak term, don't you think? He beat me. He never seemed to be in a rage when he did. He just struck out at unexpected moments, snapping a bone, raising a fist, with the absent calm another man might display while flicking away a fly.'

His fist was clenched on his knee. Deliberately, Chas opened

537

his hand, spread his fingers. 'He struck like a shark, fast and in utter silence. There was never a warning, never a gauge. My life, my pain, was totally dependent on his whim. I've had my time in Hell,' he said softly, almost as a prayer.

'No one helped you?' Eve asked. 'Attempted to intervene?'

'We never stayed in one place very long, and were allowed to form no attachments or friendships. He claimed he needed to spread the word. And he would snap a bone, raise a fist, then take me into a treatment center himself. A concerned father.'

'You told no one?'

'He was my father, it was my life.' Chas lifted his hands, let them fall. 'Who was I to tell?'

Neither had she told anyone, Eve thought. Neither had she had anyone to tell.

'And for quite a while, I believed him when he said it was just.' Chas's eyes flickered. 'And I certainly believed him when he told me there would be terrible pain and terrible punishment if I said anything. I was thirteen when he sodomized me for the first time. It was a ritual, he told me, when he bound my hands and I wept. A rite of passage. Sex was life. It was necessary to take it. He would take me on the journey as was his duty and his right.'

He picked up the tea pot, poured, set it neatly aside. 'I don't know if it was rape. I didn't struggle. I didn't beg him to stop. I simply cried without sound and submitted.'

'It was rape,' Peabody said, and her voice was very quiet.

'Well . . .' He found he couldn't drink the tea he'd just poured but lifted the cup, held it. 'I told no one. Even years later when they had him in a cage, I didn't tell the police. I didn't believe they would hold him. I simply didn't believe they could. He was too strong, too powerful, and all the blood on his hands seemed to add to it. Oddly enough, it was the sex that pushed my mother to run, and take me. Not the violence, not the little boy with broken bones or even the deaths I think she knew he'd caused. It was the sight of him kneeling over me on his altar, with the black candles lit. He didn't see her, but I did. I saw her face when she stepped into the room. She left me there, let him finish with me, and that night when he went out, we ran.'

'And still she didn't go to the police.'

'No.' He looked at Eve. 'I know you believe if she had, lives might have been saved. But fear is a very personal emotion. Survival was her only goal. When they arrested him, I went to the trial, every day. I was sure he would stop it somehow. Even when they said they would lock him away, I still didn't believe. I erased his name, and I tried to slip into normality. I took a job that interested me, that I had some talent for. And I allowed myself to get close to no one. There was a rage in me. I would look at a face and hate it because it was happy. Or it was sad. I hated them all for their unshadowed existence. And like my father, I didn't stay in one place very long. And when I found myself considering suicide again with great calm and great seriousness, I was frightened enough to seek help.'

He was able to smile again. 'It was, though I didn't realize it at the time, the beginning for me, taking that step, allowing myself to speak the unspeakable. I learned to accept my own innocence, and to forgive my mother. But the rage was still there, this hard, secret knot inside me. Then I met Isis.'

'Through your interest in the occult,' Eve prompted.

'Through my study of it, as part of my therapy.' He drank his tea now, and his lips were curved. 'I was angry and rude. Religion of any kind was an abomination to me, and I detested what she stood for. She was so beautiful, so full of light. I hated her for that. She challenged me to come to a ceremony, to observe much as you did last night. I preferred to think of myself as a scientist. I would go, I thought, to prove there was nothing in her faith but old words repeated by fools. Just as there had been nothing in my father's creed but an excuse to hurt and dominate.

'I stood back, separate, cynical, and secretly enraged. I hated them for their simplicity and their devotion. Hadn't I seen that same captured look on the faces of those who'd gathered to hear my father speak? I wanted nothing to do with it, with them, but I was drawn back. Three times I went back and watched, and though I didn't know it, I had begun to heal. And one night, on Alban Eilir, the Spring Equinox, Isis asked me into her home. When we were alone, she told me that she had recognized me. I panicked. I'd tried so hard to bury all of that, all of him. She said she hadn't meant from this life, though I could see in her eyes that she knew. She knew who I was, what I'd come from. She told me I had a great capacity for healing, and I would discover it once I had healed myself. Then she seduced me.'

He gave a short laugh, and in it was great warmth. 'Imagine my surprise when this beautiful woman led me to her bed. I went along like a puppy, half eager, half terrified. She was the first woman I'd had, and the only one I've been with. And on the night of the Spring Equinox, that hard, secret knot inside me began to dissolve.

'She loves me. And the miracle of that made me believe in other miracles. I became Wiccan, I embraced and was embraced by the craft. I learned to heal myself and others. The only person I've ever harmed in my life has been myself. But I understand better than Isis with all her insights, the lure of violence, of selfishness, of bowing to another master.'

She believed him, yet too much of his past mirrored her own for her to trust her instincts. 'You've gone to a great deal of effort to hide your connection with your father.'

'Wouldn't you?'

'Did Alice know?'

'Alice was innocence. She was youth. There were no David Baines Conroys in her life. Until Selina Cross.'

'And Cross is an intelligent and vindictive woman. If she'd discovered your secret, she might have used Alice, and others, to blackmail you. Would the members of your cult trust you if they knew your history?'

'Since that's never been tested, I don't have the answer. I'd prefer, certainly, to keep my privacy.'

'And on the night Alice was killed, you were here. Alone with Isis.'

'Yes, and we were here, alone, on the night Lobar was killed. You know I was on hand at the last murder, again with Isis. And yes.' He smiled slightly. 'I have no doubt she would lie for me. But while she would live with a murderer's son, she would never live with a murderer. It's against everything she is.'

'She loves you.'

'Yes.'

'And you love her.'

'Yes.' He blinked, and horror filled his eyes. 'You can't believe she'd have a part in any of this, beyond the fact that she loved Alice, cared for her as a mother would a sick child. She's incapable of hurting anyone.'

'Mr. Forte, everyone is capable.'

'You don't think he's involved,' Peabody said as they started down the outside stairs.

'There's history of aberrant behavior in his family. He has an expert knowledge of chemicals, including hallucinogens and herbals. He has no alibi for any of the incidents. He was associated with Alice, closely enough that she may have stumbled across the secret he's been hiding for years, and that exposed, could destroy his cult.'

She paused, tapping her fingers against the rail as she ticked off her mental list. 'He has good reason to hate Selina Cross and her membership, to want to punish them as he couldn't punish his father. He was on hand when Wineburg started to break, and could have easily circled around and killed him. That gives him motive and opportunity, and with his background, the potential for violent behavior.'

'He's made himself a decent life after a nightmare child-hood,' Peabody protested. 'You can't condemn him for what his father did.'

Eve stared out at the street and fought her own demons. 'I'm not condemning him, Peabody, I'm investigating every possibility. Consider this.' She turned. 'If Alice knew, and told Frank, his reaction might very well have been to demand she break off the connection. It's likely, following this line of speculation, that he confronted Forte himself, even threatened him with exposure if he didn't break off his influence. He was in Homicide when Conroy was taken in, and he'd have known and remembered every filthy detail.'

'Yes, but—'

'And Alice moved into her own place. She continued to work part time for Isis, but she no longer lived here. Why did she move out, away from here, when she was afraid?'

'I don't know,' Peabody admitted.

'And we can't ask her.' Eve turned back, started down the stairs again, then swore when she saw the boy leaning on her vehicle. 'Well, hell.'

She strode down, straight over to Jamie. 'Get your butt off my hood. This is an official vehicle.'

'An official piece of shit,' he corrected with a quick, sassy grin. 'The city puts you cops into recycled garbage heaps. A high-profile detective like you ought to have better.'

'I'll tell the chief you said so next time I'm in the Tower. What are you doing here?'

'Just hanging.' His grin flashed again. 'And I ditched the shadow you put on me. He's good.' Jamie tucked his thumbs in his pockets. 'I'm better.'

'Why aren't you in school?'

'Don't bother to call the Truant Brigade, Lieutenant, it's Saturday.'

How the hell was she supposed to keep track? 'Then why

542

aren't you terrorizing one of the sky malls like a normal delinquent?'

His grin spread. 'I hate sky malls. They're so yesterday. Caught you on Channel 75.'

'Did you drop by for my autograph?'

'You scrawl it on a credit slip, I could outfit this heap of yours and make it rock.' He looked past her toward the shop. 'I got a load of the witch through the glass. She's doing some heavy retail today.'

Eve glanced back, noted the customers browsing inside. 'You've seen her before.'

'Yeah, couple times when I tailed Alice.'

'Ever see anything interesting?'

'Nope. Everybody's always wearing clothes in there.' He wiggled his brows. 'A guy has to hope. I studied up on Wicca. They liked to be naked a lot. Did see the head witch kick a guy out of the shop once.'

'Really.' It was Eve's turn to lean on the hood. 'Why?'

'Couldn't say, but she was maximum pissed. I could see they were having words, and I thought she was going to belt him. Especially when he shoved her.'

'He shoved her.'

'Yeah. I thought about going in then, though she was a hell of a lot bigger than he was. Still, guys got no business pushing women around. But whatever she said had him backing off. Backing way off until he was backing right out of the door. And he went off in a big hurry.'

'What did he look like?'

'Skinny dude, five ten, maybe a hundred and twenty-five. Couple years older than me. Long black hair, red tips. Long face, with his incisors fanged. Red eyes. Light complexion. Turned out in tight black leather, no shirt, couple of tattoos, but I was too far away to make them out.'

He shot her a smile, grim around the edges. 'Sounds familiar, doesn't it? Last time I saw him, he wasn't looking so jazzy.'

543

Lobar, Eve thought, exchanging a glance with Peabody. The kid had given a solid and nearly professional description. 'And when was this? When did you see the incident?'

'The day—' His voice cracked a little, so he cleared his throat. 'The day before Alice died.'

'And what did Isis do after Lobar?'

'She made a call. Couple minutes later the dude she lives with came on the run. They talked for a couple minutes, real intense, then she put up the Closed sign and they went into the back room. Ticked me off,' he added. 'I could have followed the leather guy.'

'You want to stop tailing people, Jamie. They make you, they tend to get annoyed.'

'People I tail don't make me. I'm too good.'

'You thought you were good at B and E too,' she reminded him dryly and watched as his color rose.

'That was different. Look, the guy that was stabbed, he was right there, at Alice's viewing. It has to be connected, to her, to that Lobar creep, and I got a right to know.'

She straightened. 'Are you requesting the status of my investigation?'

'Yeah, yeah, right.' He rolled his eyes skyward. 'What's the status of your investigation?'

'Ongoing,' she said shortly, then jerked a thumb. 'Now, scram.'

'I got a right to know,' he insisted. 'Survivors of victims, and all that.'

'You're the grandson of a cop,' she reminded him. 'You know I'm not going to tell you anything. And you're a minor. I don't have to tell you anything. Now, go play somewhere else, kid, before I have Peabody here roust you for loitering.'

The muscles of his jaw tightened and jumped. 'I'm not a kid. And if you don't deal with Alice's killer, I will.'

Eve snagged his arm by the jacket before he could storm away. 'Don't cross the line,' she said very quietly. She kept her face close to his, forcing him to look directly into her eyes. 'You want justice, you'll get it. I'll by God get it for you. You want revenge, I'll slap you in a cage. You remember what Frank stood for, and what your sister was, and then you think it all through again. Now, get out of here.'

'I loved them.' He jerked his arm free, but not before she saw tears rush into his eyes. 'Fuck your justice. And fuck you.'

She let him walk because, though the language had been an adult's, the tears had been a child's.

'The kid's hurting,' Peabody murmured.

'I know.' So was she now. 'Tail him, will you, just to be sure he doesn't get in any trouble. Give it thirty minutes, until he calms down, then beep your location. I'll pick you up.'

'You going to talk to Isis?'

'Yeah, let's see what she and Lobar had to say to each other. Oh, and Peabody, watch your step. Jamie's a clever kid. If he made one of Roarke's men, he's likely to make you.'

Peabody flashed a smile. 'I think I can manage to tail a kid for a few blocks.'

Trusting her aide to keep Jamie out of trouble, Eve walked into Spirit Quest. The air swam with incense and the scented melted wax from dozens of candles. The October sun was strong and gleamed in shooting colors through hanging prisms.

The look Isis sent her held none of that exotic welcome.

'You've finished with Chas, Lieutenant?'

'For now. I'd like a few minutes.'

Isis turned to answer a question from a customer on a blend of herbs to enhance memory. 'Steep it for five minutes,' Isis told her. 'Then strain it. You'll need to drink it daily for at least a week. If it doesn't help, let me know.' She turned her head back to Eve. 'As you can see, this is a bad time.'

'I'll be quick. I'm just curious about the visit you had from Lobar here, a few days before he ended up with his throat slashed.'

She'd kept her voice down, but left her intention clear.

They would talk, in private, or in public. The location was up to Isis.

'I don't think I misjudged you,' Isis said quietly, 'but you make me doubt myself.' She signaled to a young woman Eve recognized from the initiation rite. 'Jane will handle the customers,' Isis said as she started toward the back room. 'But I don't want to leave her long. She's very new at shop work.'

'Alice's replacement.'

Isis's eyes burned. 'No one could replace Alice.'

She entered what appeared to be a combination of office and storeroom. On the reinforced plastic shelves were gargoyles, candles, sealed bins of dried herbs, clear stoppered bottles filled with liquids of varying hues.

On the small desk was a very modern and efficient computer and communication system. 'Jazzy equipment,' Eve commented. 'Very now.'

'We don't eschew technology, Lieutenant. We adapt, and we use what is available to us. It's always been so.' She gestured to a chair with a high, carved back, took another for herself, one with armrests shaped like wings. 'You said you would be quick. But first I need to know if you intend to leave Chas in peace.'

'My priority is closing a case, not the peace of mind of a suspect.'

'How could you suspect him?' Her hands curled around the armrests as she leaned forward. 'You, of all people, know what he's overcome.'

'If his past is relevant—'

'Is yours?' Isis demanded. 'Is the fact that you survived a nightmare to your credit or to your detriment?'

'My past is my business,' Eve said evenly, 'and you know nothing about it.'

'What comes to me, comes in flashes and impressions. Stronger in some cases than others. I know you suffered and were innocent. Just as Chas is. I know you carry scars

546

and harbor doubts. As he does. I know you struggle to make your own peace. And I see a room.'

Her voice changed, deepened, just as her eyes did. 'A small, cold room washed with dirty red light. And a child, battered and bleeding, huddled in a corner. The pain is unspeakable, beyond endurance. And I see a man. He's covered with blood. His face is—'

'Stop it.' Eve's heart was hammering, choking off her air. For a moment, she'd been back there, back in that child who'd crawled whimpering like an animal into the corner with blood staining her hands. 'Damn you.'

'I'm sorry.' Isis lifted a hand to press it to her own heart, and it trembled. 'I'm so very sorry. That's not my way. I let anger take over.' She shut her eyes tight. 'I'm so very sorry.'

Chapter Seventeen

Eve lurched out of the chair. There was no room to pace, to prowl, to steam off the dregs of memory. 'I'm aware,' she began coldly, 'that you have what is commonly called heightened psychic skill. HPS is still being studied. I have a report on my desk right now. So you've got a talent, Isis. Congratulations. Now, stay the hell out of my head.'

'I will.' Pity swam in her eyes and couldn't be blinked away. She'd seen much more than she'd expected or intended. 'I can only apologize again. Part of me wanted to hurt you. I didn't control it.'

'It must be hard to control it when you're angry. When you're threatened. When you see a weakness and can exploit it.'

Isis took a careful breath. Her system was still rocked, not only by what she'd seen, but what she'd done. 'It isn't my way. It's against the foundation of my faith. I will cause no harm.' She lifted her hands, rubbing her fingertips under her eyes to dry them. 'I'll answer your questions. You wanted to know about Lobar.'

'You were seen arguing with him here in the store, the day before Alice died.'

'Was I?' She drew her composure back, cloaked it over her. 'It's always a mistake to believe yourself alone. Yes, he was here. Yes, we had words.'

'About?'

'Alice, most specifically. He was a misguided young man, filled with a dangerous self-importance. He thought himself powerful. He was not.'

'Alice wasn't here, she wasn't working that day?'

'No. I'd hoped she'd spend time with her family, connect with them again through her grandfather's death. That was the primary reason I'd encouraged her to move out of here and into a place of her own. I'd asked her not to come in for a few days. Lobar expected her to be here. I don't believe he was sent, but came on his own. Maybe to prove himself.'

'And you argued.'

'Yes. He said that I couldn't hide her, that she'd never get away. She'd broken the law – the law that Cross and those who belong to her subscribe to. He said her punishment would be torture and pain and death.'

'He threatened her life, and you didn't tell me. I was here before, and I questioned you.'

'No, I didn't tell you. I considered it no more than a clash of wills, his against mine. He was no more than a pawn. I didn't require HPS to intuit that. He only wanted to upset me, to prove his superiority. His way of doing so was to describe, graphically, what he had done to Alice sexually.' She drew another breath. 'And he told me that I had been promised to him. That when I was taken in, when my power was crushed, he would be the first to lay hands on me. Then he told me what he intended to do and how much I would enjoy it. He invited me to sample some of his many talents then and there, so that I would see how much more of a man he was than Chas. I laughed at him.'

'Did he assault you?'

'He pushed me. He was angry. I'd deliberately baited him into it. Then I used it. An old spell,' she said with a flick of her hand. 'What you might call a mirror or boomerang spell, so that what he was sending toward me – all the darkness, the violence, the hate – was reflected back at him, and when reflected, enlarged.' She smiled a little. 'He left quickly, and very frightened. He didn't come back.'

'And you were frightened?'

'Yes, on a physical level, I was.'

'You called Forte.'

'He's my mate.' Isis lifted her chin. 'I have no secrets from him, and I depend on him.'

'He'd have been angry.'

'No.' Eyes level, she shook her head. 'Concerned, yes. We cast a circle, performed a rite for protection and for purification. We were content. I should have seen,' she continued, with regret shimmering in her voice. 'I should have seen that Alice was their goal. Pride made me believe they would turn on me, that they wouldn't dare touch her while she was under my protection. Maybe I wasn't as honest with you as I might have been, Dallas, because without my pride blinding me, I know Alice might still be alive.'

Guilt was there, Eve decided as she drove off to pick up Peabody. And guilt could lead to retribution. Frank and Alice had been killed by a different method than Lobar and Wineburg. The deaths were connected, she was certain, but the connection didn't mean they'd all been committed by the same hand.

She wanted to get back to Central, run a probability scan. There was enough data for it now. And if the numbers warranted it, she could go to Whitney and request the manpower for a twenty-four-seven watch on both groups of suspects.

Damn the budget, she thought as she fought traffic. She'd need a high probability ratio to wangle the expense of time, money, and manpower. But Peabody and Feeney weren't enough to keep round-the-clock tabs on everyone involved.

Including Jamie, she thought. The kid was looking for trouble. She believed he was smart enough to find it.

Peabody hopped in when Eve swung to the curb at Seventh

550

and Forty-seventh. Across the sidewalk, the rowdy noise and computerized warfare of a VR den spilled out of the open doorway. It nicked the ordinance on noise pollution, but Eve figured the proprietors were willing to risk a fine or two in order to lure in tourists and the bored.

'He in there?'

'Yes, sir.' Peabody looked hopefully at the rising steam from a glida grill. She could smell fresh soy burgers and oil fries. It was near enough to lunch to make her stomach yearn and her heart sink at the thought of facing the slop served at the Eatery back at Central. 'Do you mind if I grab something from this cart?'

Eve shot an impatient look out the window. 'Aren't you supposed to starve a cold or something?'

'I never could keep that straight. Anyway,' Peabody took a long deep breath through her nose, 'I feel great. That tea did the trick.'

'Yeah, yeah. Make it quick, and eat it on the way.'

'Do you want anything?' Peabody asked over her shoulder as she pushed out of the car.

'No. Snap it up and let's roll.'

Drugs, sex, Satan, and power, Eve mused. *A religious war? Hadn't humans fought and died for beliefs since the dawn of time? Animals fought for territory; people fought for territory as well. And for gain, for passion, for beliefs. For the hell of it.*

They killed, she thought, *very much for the same reasons.*

'Got two of everything,' Peabody announced and set the thin cardboard filled with food on the seat between them. 'Just in case. If you don't want it, I can probably choke it down. It's the first time I've had an appetite in two days.'

She bit into the loaded burger while Eve waited for a break in traffic. 'The kid led me on quite a route. Walked off his mad for ten blocks, caught an uptown tram, got off, headed west. And talk about appetite. He hit a cart on Sixth and downed two real pig dogs, and a mega scoop of fries. Hit another a block down for an orange Freezie, which happens to be a personal favorite of mine. Before he went into the VR den, he tagged this guy for three candy bars.'

'Growing boy,' Eve commented, and shot out like a bullet when she saw a slim gap in traffic. Horns bellowed in protest. 'As long as he's eating junk and playing VR, he should stay out of trouble.'

Inside the whoops and whistles of the arcade, Jamie sneered at the holograms battling on his personal screen. He listened to the exchange in Eve's car, courtesy of his earpiece, and the micro recorder and location device he'd planted.

Yeah, it had been worth the risk, he decided, diddling with the VR controls with his mind wandering. Of course, it hadn't been that much of a challenge. Not only was the cop car a rolling heap of refuse, but its security system was rinky. At least when it came up against the skills of the master of electronics.

Dallas wouldn't tell him what was going on, he thought grimly and destroyed the holo image of an urban tough. He'd just keep tabs on things his own way. And he'd deal with things his own way.

Whoever had killed his sister had better prepare to die.

Eve ran the probability program with mixed results. The computer agreed, by a ninety-six percentile, that the four cases were connected. The numbers dropped ten points when it came to tagging different perpetrators.

Charles Forte scored high on the index, as did Selina Cross. For Alban, she continued to run up against insufficient data.

Frustrated, she buzzed Feeney. 'I've got some data I want to download on you. For a probability scan. Can you see what you can do with the numbers?'

He wiggled his brows. 'You want them higher or lower?'

She laughed, shook her head. 'I want them higher, but I want it solid. Could be I'm missing something.'

'Shoot it over, I'll take a look.'

'Appreciate it. And there's something else. I'm running into blanks every time I try to access data on this Alban character. The guys in his thirties. There has to be more on him. I'm not getting education, medical, family history. There's no criminal record, not even an illegal zone stop. My take is he had it wiped.'

'Takes a lot of talent and a lot of money to wipe it clean. Something's always somewhere.'

She thought of Roarke, and the suspiciously limited data on record. Well, he had a lot of talent, she reminded herself. And a lot of money. 'I figured if anybody could find anything . . .'

'Yeah, flatter me, kid.' He winked. 'I'll get back to you.'

'Thanks, Feeney.'

'Was that Feeney?' Mavis bounced in, literally, on new air pump, stack-heeled, neon yellow sneakers. 'Shoot, you zipped off. I wanted to talk to him.'

Eve ran her tongue around her teeth. Mavis was decked out in classic Mavis style. Her hair matched her sneakers and made the eyes burn. She wore it in a spiral mass of curls that exploded up as much as down. Her slacks were glossy simulated rubber, dipped well below the glinting red stone in her navel, and hugged every curve. Her blouse, if it could be called that, was a snug band of material that matched the slacks and almost covered her breasts.

Over it all she wore a transparent duster.

'Anybody try to arrest you on the way in?'

'No, but I think the desk sergeant had an orgasm.' Mavis fluttered emerald green lashes and dropped into a chair. 'Great outfit, huh? Just off Leonardo's drawing board. So, are you ready?'

'Ready? For what?'

'We've got a salon date. Trina shuffled you in. I left the

message on your unit. Twice.' She narrowed her eyes at Eve. 'Don't tell me you didn't get it, because I know you did. You logged it out.'

Logged it out, Eve remembered. And ignored it. 'Mavis, I don't have time to play hair.'

'You haven't taken lunch today. I checked with the desk sarge,' Mavis said smugly. 'Before his orgasm. You can eat while Trina whips you into shape.'

'I don't want to be whipped into shape.'

'It wouldn't be so bad if you hadn't hacked at it again yourself.' Mavis rose, picked up Eve's jacket. 'You might as well come quietly. I'm just going to keep hounding you. Log out for lunch, take an hour. You'll be back and making our city safe by one thirty.'

Because it was easier than arguing. Eve snatched the jacket, shrugged it on. 'Just the hair. I'm not having her put all the gunk on my face.'

'Dallas, relax.' Mavis began to tug her out. 'Enjoy being a girl.'

Eve snapped out her log book to mark time, scanning Mavis's rubber clad butt bouncing along. 'I don't think that means the same thing to you as it does to me.'

Maybe it was the fumes – the potions and lotions, the oils and dyes and lacquers so typical in salons – but Eve found inspiration striking as she tipped back in her treatment chair.

She wasn't sure how they'd gotten her to take off her clothes, submit to the indignity of the body smoother, the facial, the poking and prodding. She had managed to put her foot down – her bare, now toenail-painted foot down – when the discussion had veered toward temporary tattoos and body piercing.

Otheise, she was a hostage, coated with goop, her hair covered with the spermlike cream Trina swore by. Privately, she could admit she was deeply terrified of Trina with her snapping scissors and green glop. That's why she kept her eyes shut during the procedure, so as not to imagine herself emerging looking like a Trina clone with frizzed fuchsia hair and torpedo breasts.

'Been too long,' Trina lectured. 'I told you, you need regular treatments. You got the basics, but you don't enhance, you lose the edge. If you came in regular, it wouldn't take so long to bring you back.'

She didn't want to be brought back, Eve thought. She wanted to be left alone. She suppressed a shudder as she felt something buzzing around her eyes. Brow shaping, she reminded herself and struggled to calm. Trina was not tattooing a smiley face on her forehead.

'I've got to get back. I've got work.'

'Don't rush me. Magic takes time.'

Magic, Eve thought and rolled her eyes, causing Trina to hiss at her. *Everybody was obsessed with magic, it seemed.*

She frowned, listening to Mavis chirp happily about a new body polish that gave the skin a gold glow. 'This is mag, Trina. I've got to try it full body. Leonardo would lap it up.'

'You can get it temp, and edible. Six flavors on the market now. Apricot's real popular.'

Potions and lotions, Eve thought. *Smoke and mirrors. Rites and rituals.* She opened her eyes to slits, saw Mavis and Trina huddled over a vial of gold liquid. *Mavis with her neon hair*, she thought with odd affection, *Trina with her pink frizz.*

Weird sisters.

Weird sisters, she thought again and sat up. Trina let out another hiss.

'Back down, Dallas. You got two minutes left.'

'Mavis, you said you used to run a psychic con.'

'Sure.' Mavis fluttered her newly painted neon nails. 'Madam Electra sees all, knows all. Or Ariel, the sad-eyed sprite.' She dipped her head, managed to look delicate and forlorn. 'I guess I had about six grifts on that theme.'

'You could spot somebody pulling the same grift?'

'Shit, are you kidding? From three blocks with sunshades on.'

'You were good,' Eve considered. 'I never saw you in that gig, but you were good in the others.'

'You busted me.'

'I'm better.' Eve flashed a smile and felt the glop on her face ooze. 'Listen; there's this place you could check out for me,' she began as Trina marched over and shoved her back into the horizontal. 'Both of you,' she added, eyeing Trina.

'Hey, is this a cop deal?'

'Maybe.'

'Frigid,' Trina said and pushed Eve back toward the rinsing bowl.

'You could scope it out.' Eve squeezed her eyes shut as water flooded. 'See if you can get the clerk – her name's Jane – to talk. Give me a rundown. They don't come clean with cops.'

'Who does?' Trina wanted to know.

'I want impressions,' Eve continued. 'You're interested in herbs, in mind expansion, love potions, sex enhancers. Soothers.

'Illegals?' It didn't take Mavis long to catch on. 'You think they might be dealing?'

'It's a possibility I need to confirm or eliminate. You could spot it every bit as quick as an undercover. And you could spot a grift. If they're hosing customers. If they're playing any cons. The money's coming from somewhere.'

'This could rock, Mavis.' Trina grinned. 'You and me, a couple of detectives. Like Sherlock and Dr Jekyll.'

'Decent. I thought it was Dr Holmes, though.'

Eve closed her eyes again.

Must be the fumes, she decided.

When she arrived home, Mavis and Trina were there, enter-

556

taining Roarke with their exploits. Eve scooped up the cat and followed the laughter.

'I bought this lotion to rub on,' Trina was saying. 'It's supposed to bring out the animal in men. Like pheromones.' She stuck her long arm under Roarke's nose. 'What's it do for you?'

'If I wasn't married to a woman who carries a weapon, I'd . . .' He trailed off, grinned. 'Hello, darling.'

'You could finish the thought,' Eve told him and dumped Galahad in his lap.

'I'll wait until you're unarmed.'

'Dallas, it was so, so decent.' Mavis popped up, waving her glass of wine so that the straw-colored liquid sloshed to the rim. 'I can't wait to get home and tell Leonardo. But Trina and I, we wanted to grab some nutrition, you know, and come right over and report. You should see all the stuff I bought.'

She started to dive into one of several shopping bags with the Spirit Quest logo. Eve resisted groaning and tugged Mavis's arm. 'Talk now, show later. I must have lost my mind, sending the two of you in there. I tell you,' she said whirling to Roarke. 'It's the fumes in those places. That's what makes people sit there and let themselves be shaved and painted and pierced.'

His eyes clouded briefly. 'Pierced? Where, exactly?'

'Oh, she wouldn't go for the nipple job.' Trina waved a hand. 'Said she'd zap me if I came near her with the jabber.'

'Good girl,' Roarke murmured. 'I'm proud of your restraint.'

Because her head was starting to ache, Eve poured herself a glass of wine. 'Did the two of you do anything in there but spend your credits?'

'We had readings,' Mavis told her. 'Genuinely iced. I've got an adventurous soul, and my narcissism is balanced by a generous heart.'

Eve couldn't help it; she laughed. 'You don't have to be

psychic to read that one, Mavis. You just have to have eyes. You did go in dressed like that, right?'

Mavis dangled her neon sneaker. 'Sure. Jane, the clerk, was real helpful, seemed to know her herbs. We judged her sincere, right Trina?'

'Jane was sincere,' Trina agreed, soberly. 'Kinda dull. I could fix her up with a couple sessions. A little high-lighter, some body work. Now, the goddess, hard to improve on that one.'

'Isis.' Eve sat up. 'She was there?'

'She came out of the back while we were doing the herb thing,' Mavis put in. 'I was saying how I wanted something to improve my performance level, boost my stage energy. See, when you're working a grift, you hang better if you believe the con. So if you can do true, it's mag.'

'I was looking for sex stuff.' Trina smiled sinuously. 'Stuff to attract men, lift sexual performance. And I said how I had this stressful job. Kept me tense and edgy. Over-the-counters just weren't cutting it for me. So I thought they might have something more potent, and I didn't mind the cost.'

'They had lots of blends.' Mavis took up the story. 'I didn't see anything off. Fact is, she said how drugs weren't the answer. What we wanted was the natural way. Like holistic.'

'Holistic,' Trina agreed. 'We nudged her, flashed credits and stuff, but she wasn't buying. Or I guess that would be selling.'

'The Amazon Queen went into the back.' Mavis picked up the story. 'Came back with this mix.' Hair flying, Mavis dug into her shopping bag, tossed the smaller, clear bag to Eve. 'Said I should sample it, and wouldn't charge me. She wants me to let her know if it worked for me. You can test it out, but I'd say it's clean.'

'Who gave you the reading?'

'Isis. She didn't look too keen when she came in.' Mavis tipped back her glass. 'We were playing it up, you know. I

558

went with the wide-eyed giggle act. Oohed and aahed a lot over the stock.'

Eve shifted her gaze to the shopping bags. 'I see you carried the act through.'

'I liked the stuff.' Mavis grinned, unrepentant. 'Then AQ, you know, Amazon Queen, she started to get into it. I had my sights on this A-one crystal ball, a green one. What did she call it, Trina?'

'Tourma-something.'

'Tourmaline,' Roarke provided.

'Yeah, right. Tourmaline. She steered me away, said it was for relaxing, for soothing, and if I wanted energy, I should go for the orange one. For, like, vitality.'

'More expensive?' Eve assumed.

'No, cheaper. Way cheaper. She said how the green one wasn't for me. She thought I had a friend who could use it, someone close to me who carried too much stress. But she should choose it for herself, when she was ready.'

Eve grunted, frowned.

'Then she gave us a reading. Mega. She said how she was glad we'd come in. She'd needed the positive energy. She wouldn't charge us for the readings. I liked her, Dallas. She hasn't got the eyes of a grifter.'

'Okay, thanks. I'll check out the package.' One way to make money, Eve mused, was to round up repeat customers. And a sure way to insure repeaters was to addict them.

'We got to make it.' Mavis was up again, gathering her bags. 'I bought this candle for romance. I want to see if it works. See you Tuesday night.'

'Tuesday?'

Mavis tapped her platform sneaker. 'Our Halloween party, Dallas. You said you'd come.'

'I must have been drunk.'

'No, you weren't. Nine o'clock, our place. Everybody's coming. I even tagged Feeney. See you.'

'Loosen up,' Trina advised as she strolled out. 'Wear a costume.'

'Not in this lifetime,' Eve muttered. 'Well.' She bounced the small bag of leaves and seeds in her hand. 'That was probably a monumental waste of time.'

'They enjoyed themselves. And you'll feel better once you analyze that mix.'

'I suppose. I'm not getting anywhere.' Eve set the bag on the table. 'I keep taking wrong turns. I can feel it.'

'Enough wrong turns, and you usually end up in the right place after all.' He leaned forward, set his hands on her shoulders, and began to rub. 'Mavis has a close friend who carries around too much stress.' He worked on the knots. 'I wonder who that could be?'

'Shut up.'

He chuckled, kissed the nape of her neck. 'You smell wonderful.'

'It's that goop Trina poured all over me.'

'She mentioned it. She said I'd enjoy it.' He sniffed her neck again, made her chuckle. 'And I am. She also said she managed to hold you down for a full body treatment. I'm to pay particular attention to your butt.'

'*She* certainly did. She tried to talk me into a temp tattoo of a rosebud on my right cheek.' She started to sigh, then bolted up, grabbing her ass. 'Jesus Christ, she had me on the table for ten minutes. You don't think she snuck one on.'

Roarke lifted a brow, then smiled slowly as he rose. 'I'll have to make it my job to find out.'

Chapter Eighteen

She had a rosebud on her ass, and wasn't happy about it. Standing naked in the bathroom, Eve adjusted the trifold mirror until she could get a good look.

'I think I could bust her for this,' she muttered.

'Decorating a cop's posterior without a license?' Roarke suggested as he strolled in. 'Felonious reproduction of floral imagery?'

'You're getting a big charge out of this, aren't you?' Miffed, Eve snagged a robe off the hook.

'Darling Eve, I thought I made it perfectly clear last night I was on your side of the issue. Didn't I do my best to chew it off?'

She would not laugh, she ordered herself as she bit down hard on her tongue. There was nothing funny about it. 'I've got to get some solution or something. Whatever they make to get it off.'

'What's your hurry? It's rather . . . sweet.'

'What if I have to go in for a disinfect? Or need to shower or change at the station? Do you know what kind of grief a butt tattoo's going to get me?'

He slid his arms around her, clever enough to get them under rather than over the robe. 'You're not working today.'

'I'm going in. I've got to check my unit, see if Feeney shot back some data.'

'And it won't make any difference if you do it Monday morning. We've got the day off.'

'To do what?'

He merely smiled, slid his hands lower to stroke her rosebud.

'Didn't we just do that?'

'It bears repeating,' he mused, 'but it could wait a bit. Why don't we spend the day lazing around the pool?'

Lazing around the pool? It had a certain appeal. 'Well, maybe . . .'

'In Martinique. Don't bother to pack,' he told her, planting a quick kiss on her mouth. 'You won't need anything but what you're wearing.'

She spent the day in Martinique, wearing nothing but a smile and a rosebud. That might have been why she was dragging a bit more than usual on Monday morning.

'You look tired, Lieutenant.' Peabody dug a bag out from her field kit, set two fresh cream donuts on the desk. She was still beaming over the fact that she'd gotten them through the bullpen without the hounds sniffing them out. 'And sort of tanned.' She peered closer. 'You get a flash?'

'No. Just got some sun yesterday, that's all.'

'It rained all day.'

'Not where I was,' Eve muttered and filled her mouth with pastry. 'I've got a probability ratio to run by the commander. Feeney worked some numbers, we're still pretty light, but I'm going to shoot for round-the-clocks on the top suspects.'

'I don't suppose you want my probability ratio on your chances of getting it. New interoffice came down this morning about excess overtime.'

'Fuck it. It's not excess if it's necessary. Whitney could play it to the chief – and the chief could play it to the mayor. We've got two high-profile homicides, generating a lot of media. We need the manpower to close them and turn off the heat.'

Peabody risked a smile. 'You rehearsing your pitch.'

'Maybe.' She blew out a breath. 'If the numbers were a few

points higher, I wouldn't have to pitch so hard. There are too many people involved; that's the problem.' Lifting her hands, she pressed her fingers to her eyes. 'We've got to run the name of every member of both cults. Over two hundred people. Say we eliminate half on data and profile, then we've still got a hundred to tag, check alibis.'

'Days of work,' Peabody agreed. 'The commander would probably spring for a couple of uniforms to knock on doors, sweep out the obvious noninvolved.'

'I'm not sure there are any obvious noninvolved.' Eve pushed away from her desk. 'It took more than one person to transport Lobar's body, strap him onto that form. And it took a vehicle.'

'None of the primes owns a vehicle large enough to have carried and concealed the body and the pentagram.'

'Maybe one of the membership does. We run names through vehicle licensing. Failing that, we start checking on rentals, vehicles reported stolen on the night of the murder.' She pushed at her hair. 'And it's just as likely whoever dumped him jumped a vehicle from one of the long-term lots, and nobody ever noticed.'

'Do we check, anyway?'

'Yeah, we check, anyway. Maybe Feeney can spare somebody in EDD to do some of the grunt work. Meanwhile, you get started, and I'll go begging to the commander.' She punched her 'link when it beeped. 'Dallas, Homicide.'

'I need to talk to you.'

'Louis?'

Eve cocked a brow. 'You want to talk about the charges against your client regarding resisting, you talk to the PA.'

'I need to talk to you,' he repeated, and she watched as he lifted his hand to his mouth and began to gnaw away his perfect manicure. 'Alone. Privately. As soon as possible.'

She lowered a hand, signaling Peabody to keep back and out of view. 'What about?'

'I can't talk about it on the 'link. I'm on my pocket unit, but even that's risky. I need you to meet me.'

'Come here.'

'No, no, they may be following me. I don't know. I can't be sure. I'm being careful.'

Had he made the shadow Feeney'd put on him, Eve wondered, or was he just being paranoid? 'Who might be following you?'

'You've got to meet me,' he insisted. 'At my club. The Luxury on Park. Level Five. I'll leave your name at the desk.'

'Give me some incentive, Louis. I've got a full plate here.'

'I think – I think I saw a murder. Just you, Eve. I won't talk to anyone else. Make sure you're not followed. Hurry.'

Eve pursed her lips at the blank screen. 'Well, that's incentive. I think we've caught a break, Peabody. See if you can sweet-talk Feeney into giving you an extra pair of hands from EDD.'

'You're not going to meet him alone,' Peabody protested as Eve grabbed her bag.

'I can handle one scared lawyer.' Eve bent down, checked the clinch piece strapped to her ankle. 'We've got a man outside the club in any case. And I'm leaving my communicator on. Monitor.'

'Yes, sir. Watch your back.'

The fifth floor of the Luxury Club held twenty private suites for the members' use. Meetings of a professional or private nature could be held there. Each suite was individually decorated to depict its own era, and each contained a complete communication and entertainment center.

Parties could be held there, of the large or the intimate nature. The catering department was unsurpassed in a city often preoccupied with food and drink. Licensed companions were available through the concierge for a small additional service charge.

Louis always booked Suite 5-C. He enjoyed the opulence of the eighteenth-century French style with its emphasis on the decorative. The rich fabrics of the upholstery on curved-backed chairs and velvet settees appealed to his love of texture. He enjoyed the thick, dark draperies, the gold tassels, the gleam of gilt on pier glass mirrors. He had entertained his wife, as well as an assortment of lovers, in the wide, high, canopy bed.

He considered this period to have embodied hedonism, self-indulgence, and a devotion to earthly pleasures.

Royalty had ruled and had done as it pleased. And hadn't art flourished? If peasants had starved outside the privileged walls, that was simply a societal mirror of nature's natural selection. The chosen few had lived life to the hilt.

And here, in midtown Manhattan, three hundred years later, he could enjoy the fruits of their indulgence.

But he wasn't enjoying them now. He paced, drinking unblended scotch in quick, jerky gulps. Terror was a dew on his brow that refused to be wiped away. His stomach roiled, his heart rabbitted in his chest.

He'd seen murder. He was nearly sure of it. It was all so hazy, all so surreal, like a virtual reality program with elements missing.

The secret room, the smoke, voices – his own among them – lifted in chant. The taste, lingering on the tongue, of warm, tainted wine.

Those were all so familiar, a part of his life now for three years. He'd joined the cult because he believed in its basic principles of pleasure, and he'd enjoyed the rituals: the robes, the masks, the words repeated and repeated while candles guttered into pools of black wax.

And the sex had been incredible.

But something was happening. He found himself obsessing

565

about meetings, desperately craving that first deep gulp of ceremonial wine. And then there were the blackouts, holes in his memory. He'd be logy and slow to focus the morning after a rite.

Recently, he'd found blood dried under his nails and couldn't remember how it had gotten there.

But he was starting to. The crime scene photos Eve had shown him had clicked something open in his mind. And had filled that opening with shock and horror. Images swirled behind his eyes. Smoke swirling, voices chanting. Flesh gleaming from sex, the moans and grunts of vicious mating. Dank black hair swaying, bony hips pumping.

Then the spray of blood, the gush of it, spurting out like that final cry of sexual release.

Selina with her feral, feline smile, the knife dripping in her hand. Lobar – God it had been Lobar – sliding from the altar, his throat gaping wide like a screaming mouth.

Murder. Nervously, he twitched the heavy drapes open a fraction, let his frightened eyes search the street below. He'd seen a blood sacrifice, and not of a goat. Of a man.

Had he dipped his fingers into that open throat? Had he slipped them between his lips to taste the fresh blood? Had he done something so abhorrent?

My God, dear God, had there been others? Other nights, other sacrifices? Could he have witnessed and blanked it from his mind?

He was a civilized man, Louis told himself as he jerked the draperies back into place. He was a husband and a father. He was a respected attorney. He wasn't an accessory to murder. He couldn't be.

With his breath coming fast and short, he poured more scotch, stared at himself in one of the ornately framed mirrors. He saw a man who hadn't slept, hadn't eaten, hadn't seen his family in days.

He was afraid to sleep. The images might come more clearly

in sleep. He was afraid to eat, sure the food would clog in his throat and kill him.

And he was mortally afraid for his family.

Wineburg had been at the ceremony. Wineburg had stood beside him and had seen what he had seen.

And Wineburg was dead.

Wineburg had had no wife, no children. But Louis did. If he was in danger and went home, would they come for him there? He had begun to understand during those long, sleepless nights, when liquor was his only company, that he was ashamed at the thought of his children discovering what he had participated in.

He had to protect them and himself. He was safe here, he assured himself. No one could get inside the suite unless he opened the door.

Possibly, he was overreacting. He mopped his sweating forehead with an already sodden handkerchief. Stress, over-work, too many late nights. Perhaps he was having a small breakdown. He should see a doctor.

He would. He would see a doctor. He would take his family and go away for a few weeks. A vacation, a time to relax, to reevaluate. He would break off from the cult. Obviously, it wasn't good for him. God knew it was costing him a small fortune in the bimonthly contributions. He'd gotten in too deeply somehow, forgotten he'd entered into the cult out of curiosity and a thirst for selfish sex.

He'd swallowed too deeply of wine and smoke, and it was making him imagine things.

But he'd had blood under his nails.

Louis covered his face, tried to catch his breath. It didn't matter, he thought. None of it mattered. He shouldn't have called Eve. He shouldn't have panicked. She would think him mad; or worse, an accessory.

Selina was his client. He owed his client his loyalty as well as his professional skill.

567

But he could see her, a knife gripped in her hand as she sliced it across exposed flesh.

Louis stumbled across the suite, into the master bath and, collapsing, vomited up scotch and terror. When the cramps passed, he pulled himself up. He leaned over the sink, croaked out a request for water, at forty degrees. It poured out of the curved gold faucet, splashed into the blindingly white sink and cooled his fevered skin.

He wept a moment, shoulders trembling, sobs echoing off the shining tiles. Then he lifted his head, forced himself to look in the mirror once more.

He had seen what he had seen. It was time to face it. He would tell Eve everything and shift his burden into her hands.

He felt a moment of relief, sweet in its intensity. He wanted to call his wife, hear his children's voices, see their faces.

A movement reflected in the glass had him whirling, had his heart bounding into his throat. 'How did you get in here?'

'Housekeeping, sir.' The dark woman in the trim black-and-white maid's uniform held a stack of fluffy towels. She smiled.

'I don't want housekeeping.' He passed a shaking hand over his face. 'I'm expecting someone shortly. Just leave the towels and . . .' His hand slid slowly to his side. 'I know you. I know you.'

Through the smoke, he thought through the cracked ice of fresh terror. *One of the faces in the smoke*.

'Of course you do, Louis.' Her smile never wavered as she dropped the towels and revealed the athame she held. 'We fucked just last week.'

He had time to draw breath for a scream before she plunged the knife into his throat.

Eve strode out of the elevator, bristling with annoyance. The reception droid had kept her waiting five full minutes while he checked her ID. He'd given her a hassle over taking her weapon into the club. She'd been considering just using it on him to shut him up when the day manager had bustled out full of apologies.

The fact that they'd both been aware he'd been apologizing to Roarke's wife rather than Eve Dallas had only irritated her.

She'd deal with him later, she promised herself. See how the Luxury Club would like a full-scale inspection by the Department of Health, maybe a visit from Vice to check out their LCs. She had strings she could pull to insure the management a couple of days of minor hell.

She turned toward 5-C, started to punch the buzzer under the peep screen. Her gaze flickered over the security light. It beeped green for disengaged.

She drew her weapon. 'Peabody?'

'Here, sir.' Though her voice was muffled against Eve's shirt pocket.

'The door's unlocked here. I'm going in.'

'Do you want backup, Lieutenant?'

'Not yet. Stay on me.'

She slipped inside, soundlessly, shut the door at her back. She kept to her defensive crouch, sweeping her weapon and her gaze through the room.

Fancy furniture, ugly and overdone in her mind, a rumpled suit jacket, a half-empty bottle. Drapes drawn. Quiet.

She stepped farther into the room, but kept near the wall, guarding her own back as she circled. No one hid behind the furniture, behind the drapes. The small kitchen was empty and apparently unused.

She stepped to the doorway of the bedroom, again crouched, again sweeping her weapon. The bed was made, heaped with decorative pillows and apparently hadn't been slept in. Her gaze moved to the closet, the firmly shut carved doors.

She sidestepped toward it, then heard the sounds from the

bathroom. Quick, heavy breathing, grunts of effort, a distinctly female chuckle. It passed through her mind that Louis might be having a quick roll with the LC of his choice, and she gritted her teeth in annoyance.

But she didn't relax her guard.

She stepped left, shifted her weight, and swung to the doorway.

The smell hit her an instant before she saw it.

'Jesus. Jesus Christ.'

'Lieutenant?' Peabody's voice, ringing with concern, piped out of her pocket.

'Back off.' Eve leveled her weapon at the woman. 'Drop the knife and back off.'

'Sending backup now. Give me your situation, Lieutenant.'

'I've got a homicide. Really fresh. I said back the hell off.'

The woman only smiled. She straddled Louis, or what was left of him. Blood pooled on the floor, splattered the white tiles, coated her hands and face. The stench of it, and the gore, was thick as smoke.

Louis, Eve noted, was well beyond hope. He'd been gutted and disemboweled. And he was busily being eviscerated.

'He's already dead,' the woman said pleasantly.

'I can see that. Put down the knife.' Eve took a step closer, gesturing with the weapon. 'Put it down and move away from him. Slow. Face down on the floor, hand behind your back.'

'It had to be done.' She slid her leg over the body until she was kneeling beside it, like a mourner over a grave. 'Don't you recognize me?'

'Yeah.' Even through the mask of blood, Eve had made the face. And she'd remembered the voice, the sweetness of it. 'Mirium, right? First-degree witch. Now, drop the fucking knife and kiss the floor. Hands behind you.'

'All right.' Obligingly, Mirium set the knife aside, barely glancing at it when Eve trapped it under her heel, sent it skidding across the room well out of reach. 'He told me to be quick. In and out. I lost track of time.'

Eve tugged her restraints from her rear pocket, snapped them in place over Mirium's wrists. 'He?'

'Chas. He said I could do this one all by myself, but to be fast.' She let out a sigh. 'I guess I wasn't fast enough.'

With her mouth thin, Eve looked down at Louis Trivane. No, she thought *I* wasn't fast enough. 'You copy that, Peabody?'

'Yes, sir.'

'Pick up Charles Forte for questioning. Do it personally, and take two uniforms for backup. Don't approach him alone.'

'Affirmative. Do you have the situation under control there, Lieutenant?'

Eve stepped back from the blood running in a rivulet toward her boots. 'Yeah,' she said. 'I've got it.'

She showered and changed before the interviews. The ten minutes it took was necessary. She'd all but bathed in Louis Trivane's blood before she'd released his body to the ME. If anyone in the lockers noticed the elegant little flower on her ass, there was no comment.

The buzz on the state of this particular crime scene had already swarmed through the station.

'I'm taking Mirium first,' Eve told Feeney as she studied the dainty woman through the one-way glass.

'You could take a break, Dallas. Word is, it was pretty rough over there this morning.'

'You always think you've seen it all,' she murmured. 'But you never do. There's always something else.' She blew out a breath. 'I want to do it now. I want to close this.'

'Okay. Duet or solo?'

'Solo. She's going to talk. She's on something . . .' Eve shook her head. 'Maybe she's just plain crazy, but I think she's using. I'm going to get her to sign for a chemi-scan. The PA doesn't like confessions given under the influence.'

'I'll order one up.'

'Thanks.' She moved past him, walked into the room. Mirium's face had been washed clean of blood. She wore a baggy disposable shift in police station beige. And still managed to look like a young, eager fairy.

Eve set the recorder, entered standard, then sat. 'You know I've got you tagged, Mirium, so we don't have to take that dance. You murdered Louis Trivane.'

'Yes.'

'What are you on?'

'On?'

'Doesn't look like straight Zeus, you're too mellow. Will you agree to a drug scan?'

'I don't want to.' Her pretty mouth pouted; her dark eyes sulked. 'Maybe later I'll change my mind.' She pursed her lips and plucked at the thin skirt of the shift. 'Can I get some of my own clothes? This thing's itchy, and it offends the eye.'

'Yeah, we're real worried about that right now. Why did you kill Louis Trivane?'

'He was evil. Chas said so.'

'By Chas you're referring to Charles Forte.'

'Yes, but no one calls him Charles. It's just Chas.'

'And Chas told you Louis was evil. Did he ask you to kill Louis?'

'He said I could. Other times I just got to watch. But this time I got to do it myself. There was a lot of blood.' She lifted a hand, studied it carefully. 'Gone now.'

'What other times, Mirium?'

'Oh, other times.' She moved her shoulders. 'Blood purifies.'

'Did you assist or witness other murders?'

'Sure. Death is a transition. I got to do this one. It was a very powerful act. I cut the demon out of him. Demons exist, and we fight them.'

'By killing the people they inhabit.'

'Yes. He said you were smart.' Mirium beamed at her out

of slanted black eyes. 'But you'll never touch him. He's too far removed from your law.'

'Let's go back to Louis. Tell me about it.'

'Well, I have a friend on staff at the Luxury. All I had to do was screw him, and that was okay. I like to screw. Then I slipped one of the master codes in my pocket. You can get in most anywhere with a master. I put on one of the maids' dresses, so no one would bother me, and I went right on in Louis's suite. I took him towels. He was in the bathroom. He'd been sick, I could smell it. Then I stabbed him. I went for the throat, just like I was supposed to. Then I guess I got into it.'

She moved her shoulders again, sent Eve a mischievous smile. 'It's kind of like punching a knife through a pillow, you know. And it makes this sucky noise. Then I cut the demon out of him, and you came. I guess I'd finished, anyway.'

'Yeah, I guess you had. How long have you known Chas?'

'Oh, a couple of years. We like to make it in the park, in the daytime, because you never know if somebody's going to come along and see.'

'How does Isis feel about that?'

'Oh, she doesn't know.' Mirium rolled her eyes. 'She wouldn't like it.'

'How does she feel about the murders?'

Mirium's brows knit and her eyes unfocused for a moment. 'The murders? She doesn't know. Does she? No, we wouldn't tell her about that.'

'So it's just between you and Chas.'

'Between me and Chas.' Her eyes fluttered, stayed blank. 'I guess. Sure.'

'Have you told anyone else in the coven?'

'The coven?' She laid her fingers on her lips, tapped them. 'No, no, it's our secret. Our little secret.'

'What about Wineburg?'

'Who?'

'In the parking garage. The banker. Do you remember?'

'I didn't get to do that.' She bit her bottom lip now, shook her head. 'No, he did that. He was supposed to bring me the heart, but he didn't. He said there wasn't time.'

'And Lobar?'

'Lobar, Lobar.' Her fingers kept tapping. 'No, that was different. Wasn't it? I can't remember. I'm getting a headache.' Her voice turned petulant. 'I don't want to talk anymore now. I'm tired.' She laid her hands down on her folded arms and closed her eyes.

Eve watched her for a moment. There wasn't any point in pushing now, she decided. She had enough.

Eve signaled a uniform. Mirium murmured sulkily as Eve slipped the restraints back into place. 'Take her down to Psych. Get Mira to do the evaluation, if possible; make a note to request permission for a drug scan.'

'Yes, sir.' Eve stepped to the door behind them, pushed a call button. 'Have Forte brought to Interview Room C.'

It occurred to her that she would like to lay her head on pillowed arms herself. Instead, she turned down the corridor into the observation area. Peabody stood beside Feeney.

'I want you in on this, Peabody. What did you think of her, Feeney?'

'She's whacked.' He held out his bag of nuts. 'Whether it's psych or induced, I dunno. Looks like a mix of both to me.'

'That was my take. How come she seemed so damn normal the other night?' Then she pulled her hands through her hair and laughed. 'I can't believe I'm saying that. She was standing naked in the woods letting Forte kiss her crotch.'

She lowered her hands, pressed them to her eyes, then dropped them. 'His father never used a partner. That was never hinted at. He worked alone.'

'So, he's got a different style,' Feeney said. 'Whacked or not, the girl pinned Forte.'

574

'It doesn't feel right to me,' Peabody murmured, and Eve turned to her with a mildly interested glance.

'What doesn't feel right, Officer?'

Detecting the light trace of sarcasm, Peabody lifted her jaw. 'Wiccans don't kill.'

'People kill,' Eve reminded her. 'And not everybody takes their religion seriously. Had any red meat lately?'

The flush worked up from under Peabody's starched uniform collar. Free-Agers were strict vegan and used no animal by-products. 'That's different.'

'I walked in on a murder,' Eve said shortly. 'The woman with the knife in her hand identified Charles Forte as her accomplice. That's fact. I don't want you to take anything but fact into that interview room. Understood?'

'Yes, sir.' Peabody stiffened her shoulders. 'Perfectly.' But she stood in place a moment longer when Eve strode off.

'She's had a rough morning,' Feeney said sympathetically. 'I got a quick scan of the first crime scene shots. It doesn't get any rougher.'

'I know.' But she shook her head, watching as Charles Forte was led into the room behind the glass. 'But it just doesn't feel right.'

She turned away, headed around the corner, and stepped into the interview room just as Eve was reading Forte his rights.

'I don't understand.'

'You don't understand your rights and obligations?'

'No, no, I understand them. I don't understand why I'm here.' There was puzzlement and a vague sense of disappointment as he turned his gaze toward Peabody. 'If you'd wanted to speak with me again, you had only to ask. I would have met you, or come in voluntarily. It wasn't necessary to send three uniformed officers to my home.'

'I thought it was necessary,' Eve answered shortly. 'Do you want counsel or representation at this time, Mr Forte?'

'No.' He shifted in agitation, tried to ignore the fact that he was inside a police facility. Like his father. 'Just tell me what you want to know. I'll try to help you.'

'Tell me about Louis Trivane.'

'I'm sorry.' He shook his head. 'I don't know anyone by that name.'

'Do you usually send your handmaids out to murder strangers?'

'What?' His face went white as he pushed himself to his feet. 'What are you talking about?'

'Sit down.' Eve snapped the order out. 'Louis Trivane was murdered two hours ago by Mirium Hopkins.'

'Mirium? That's ridiculous. That's impossible.'

'It's very possible. I walked in while she was cutting out his liver.'

Chas swayed, then sank onto his chair. 'There's a mistake. It couldn't be.'

'I think the mistake was yours.' Eve rose, wandered over, then leaned over his shoulder. 'You should pick your weapons more carefully. When you use defective ones, they can turn on you.'

'I don't know what you mean. May I have some water? I don't understand this.'

Eve jerked a thumb to Peabody, signaling her to pour a glass. 'Mirium told me everything, Chas. She told me that you were lovers, that you neglected to bring her Wineburg's heart as promised, and that you'd allowed her to execute Trivane herself. Blood purifies.'

'No.' He lifted the glass in both hands and still slopped water over the edge as he tried to drink. 'No.'

'Your father liked to slice people up. Did he show you how it was done? How many other defective tools have you used? Did you dispose of them after you'd finished with them? Keep any souvenirs?'

She continued to hammer at him while he sat, just sat, shaking his head slowly from side to side.

'Was this your version of a religious war, Chas? Eliminate the enemy? Cut out the demons? Your father was a self-styled Satanist, and he'd made your life a misery. You couldn't kill him, you can't get to him now. But there are others. Are they substitutes? When you kill them, are you killing him, hacking him to pieces because of what he did to you?'

He squeezed his eyes tight, began to rock. 'God. My God. Oh God.'

'You can help yourself here. Tell me why, tell me how. Explain it to me, Chas. I may be able to cut you a break. Tell me about Alice. About Lobar.'

'No. No.' When he lifted his head, his eyes were streaming. 'I'm not my father.'

Eve didn't flinch, didn't look away from the desperate plea in his eyes. 'Aren't you?' Then she stepped back and let him sob.

Chapter Nineteen

She worked him for an hour, relentlessly pushing, then backtracking, then shifting directions. She kept the death photos on the table, dealt out like grisly playing cards.

How many more, she demanded. How many more images of the dead should there be?

Through it all, he wept and denied, wept and was silent.

When she turned him over to holding, his eyes stayed on hers until he was led around the corner and away. But it was the look in Peabody's eyes that caught her and had her waiting until they were alone.

'Problem, Officer?'

Observing the interrogation had been like watching a wolf toy and tear at a wounded deer. Peabody drew a breath, braced. 'Yes, sir. I didn't like your interview technique.'

'Didn't you?'

'It seemed overly harsh. Cruel. Using his father, over and over again, directing him to look at the stills.'

Eve's stomach was raw, her nerves scraped clean, but her voice was cool, her hands steady, as she gathered up the stills. 'Maybe I should have asked him politely to please confess so we could all go home and get back to our comfy lives. Don't know why I didn't think of it. I'll make a note to try it the next time I have a murder suspect in interview.'

Peabody wanted to wince, managed not to. 'It just seemed

to me, Lieutenant, particularly since the suspect had no representation—'

'Did I read him his rights, Officer?'

'Yes, sir, but—'

'Did he verify that he understood those rights?'

Peabody pulled back, nodded slowly. 'Yes, sir.'

'Can you estimate, Officer Peabody, how many interviews you've conducted on homicide cases?'

'Sir, I—'

'I can't,' Eve snapped, and her eyes went from cool to hot. 'I can't, because there's been too fucking many of them. You want to take a look at the stills again? You want to see this guy with his guts spilled out all over the tiles? Maybe it'll toughen you up a little, because if my interview techniques upset you, Peabody, you're in the wrong career.'

Eve strode to the door, then whirled back while Peabody stood where she was at rigid attention. 'And I expect my aide to back me up, not question me because she happens to have a soft spot for witches. If you can't handle that, Officer Peabody, I'll approve your request for transfer. Understood?'

'Yes, sir.' Peabody let out a shaky breath as Eve's boots clicked down the corridor. 'Understood,' she said to herself and shut her eyes.

'A little rough on her,' Feeney commented when he caught up.

'Don't you start on me.'

He only held up a hand. 'Isis came in voluntarily. I put her in Room B.'

With a jerk of the head, Eve changed directions and pulled open the door of Room B.

Isis stopped her restless pacing and spun around. 'How could you do this to him? How could you bring him here? He's terrified of places like this.'

'Charles Forte is being held for questioning in the stabbing death of Louis Trivane, among others.' In contrast to Isis's raised and furious voice, Eve's was cold and flat. 'He has not yet been charged.'

'Charged?' Her golden skin paled. 'You can't believe Chas had anything to do with a murder. Trivane? We don't know any Louis Trivane.'

'And you know everyone Forte knows, Isis?' Eve set the file on the table, kept her hand on it as if to remind herself what was inside. 'You know everything he does and thinks and plans?'

'We are as close as it's possible for human bodies and minds and souls to be. There is no harm in him.' The temper drained out of her. Now her voice trembled. 'Let me take him home. Please.'

Eve met the pleading eyes straight on, forced herself not to feel. 'Did you know, being as close as it's possible, that he'd decided to get equally close, bodily speaking, with Mirium?'

'Mirium?' Isis blinked once, then nearly laughed. 'That's ridiculous.'

'She told me herself. She smiled when she told me.' Remembering that, bringing that image back, dried up any sympathy. 'She smiled as she straddled what was left of Louis Trivane, while his blood was smeared all over her hands and her face and the knife she held.'

As her legs went weak, Isis reached out blindly to brace a hand on the back of a chair. 'Mirium killed someone? That's impossible.'

'I thought all things were possible in your sphere. I walked in on her little ceremony myself.' Eve's fingers curled on the file, but she didn't open it. There was still pity, after all, for the woman who loved and believed. 'She was very cooperative, happily told me that Forte had allowed her to kill Trivane herself. Unlike the others, where she only observed.'

Using her hand to keep her balance, Isis stepped unsteadily around the chair, eased herself into it. 'She's lying.' There was a lance in her heart, quivering there. 'Chas has nothing

580

to do with this. How could I have missed this part of her?' Closing her eyes, Isis rocked herself gently. 'How could I not have seen? We initiated her, we took her in. We made her one of us.'

'Can't see everything, can you?' Eve angled her head. 'I think you should be more worried about your vision as it applies to Charles Forte.'

'No.' She opened her eyes again. There was misery in them, but behind it was a steel Eve recognized. 'There's no one I see more clearly than Chas. She's lying.'

'She'll be tested. In the meantime, you may want to rethink allowing yourself to be used as his alibi. He's betrayed your trust,' Eve said, stepping closer. 'It could have been you, Isis, at any time. Mirium's younger, probably more biddable. I wonder how much longer he'd have pretended to let you run the show.'

'How can you not understand what there is between us when you have it yourself? Do you think the word of some disturbed young woman would make me doubt the man I love? Would it make you doubt Roarke?'

'It's not my personal life that's in dire straits here,' Eve said evenly. 'It's yours. If you care for him so much, then cooperate with me. It's the only way to stop him, and to get him help.'

'Help?' Isis's mouth twisted. 'You don't want to help him. You want him to be guilty, you want him to be punished, because of where he came from. Because of his father.'

Eve looked down at the folder in her hands, the plain tan cover that hid the terrible images of terrible death. 'You're wrong.' She spoke quietly now, almost to herself. 'I wanted him to be innocent. Because of his father.'

Then she lifted her gaze, met Isis's. 'The warrant will have come through by now. We'll search your shop and your apartment. Whatever we find can be used against you as well.'

'It won't matter.' Isis forced herself to stand. 'You won't find anything to help you.'

'You're entitled to be present during the search.'

'No. I'll stay here. I want to see Chas.'

'You're not related or legally married—'

'Dallas.' Isis interrupted quietly. 'You have a heart. Please listen to it and let me see him.'

Yes, she had a heart. And it ached to see the plea in the eyes of a strong woman. 'I can give you five minutes through security glass.' As she wrenched the door open, she set her teeth. 'Tell him to get a lawyer, for God's sake.'

In the storeroom of Spirit Quest and in a workroom in the apartment above, were dozens of bottles and containers and boxes. They were filled with liquid and powder and leaves and seeds. She found organized records detailing the contents and their uses.

Eve ordered everything sent to the lab for analysis.

She found knives, carved handles and plain, long-bladed and short. She tagged a sweeper, ordered him to scan for traces of blood. Ceremonial robes and street clothes were scanned as well.

She blocked out the voices – sweepers never worked quietly – and went about her job with focused efficiency.

And there, under a neatly folded stack of robes kept fresh in a chest smelling of rosemary and cedar, she found the balled-up and bloody black robe.

'Here.' She signaled to a sweeper. 'Scan it.'

'Nice sample.' The sweeper snapped her gum, ran the nozzle of her shoulder unit over the cloth. 'Mostly on the sleeves.' Behind her protective goggles, the sweeper's eyes were mildly bored. 'Human,' she confirmed. 'A neg. Can't tell you much more with a portable.'

'That's enough.' Eve slid the robe into a bag, sealed and labeled it for evidence. 'Wineburg was A negative.' She looked at Peabody as she handed the bag to her. 'Careless of him, wasn't it?'

582

'Yes, sir.' Dutifully, Peabody stored the bag in her evidence kit. 'It would seem so.'

'Lobar was O positive.' She moved to another chest, hauled back the domed lid. 'Keep looking.'

Twilight had settled with its dim light and fitful breezes when she climbed back in her car. Since the tension was still simmering between her and Peabody, she didn't bother to speak but engaged her car 'link instead.

'Lieutenant Dallas for Dr Mira.'

'Dr Mira is in session,' the receptionist said politely. 'I'll be happy to log your message.'

'Has she tested Mirium Hopkins?'

'One moment while I check the logs.' The receptionist slid her gaze to the side, then back. 'That session has been rescheduled for eight thirty tomorrow morning.'

'Rescheduled, why?'

'The log notes indicate that the subject complained of severe head pain, and on examination by the physician on duty, was medicated.'

'Who was the physician on duty?' Eve asked through clenched teeth.

'Dr Arthur Simon.'

'Simon Says; figures.' Disgusted, Eve whipped her car around a slow-moving maxibus packed with commuters. 'He'll give you a double tranq for a hangnail.'

The receptionist grimaced in sympathy. 'I'm sorry, Lieutenant, but the subject was already medicated before her scheduled testing. Dr Mira is unable to proceed until morning.'

'Fine. Terrific. Ask her to let me know as soon as she's done.' Eve broke transmission. 'Son of a bitch. I'm going in to take a look at her, myself. Deliver the bags to the lab, Peabody, with a request for rush – for what good that does. Then you're off duty.'

'You'll interview Forte again tonight.'

'That's right.'

'Sir, I request to be present during interview.'

'Request denied,' Eve said shortly as she pulled into the garage at Central. 'I said you're off duty.' She shoved out of the car and walked away.

It was midnight and her own head was aching viciously. The house was quiet when she slipped in, dragged herself up the stairs. It didn't surprise her to see Roarke, awake and on the bedroom 'link. She glanced at the monitor as she passed through and recognized the young, eager face of one of the engineers assigned to the Olympus Resort.

It made her think of the last few days of her honeymoon. There had been death there, as well. Big surprise, she thought as she leaned over the sink and splashed her face with cold water. There was never any escaping it.

She toweled off, then walked to the bed to sit and remove her boots. When they hit the floor, the effort of undressing further seemed beyond her. She crawled onto the bed and lay across it, facedown.

Roarke listened to his engineer with half an ear while he watched her. He knew the signs, the shadowed eyes, the pale skin, the slow, deliberate movements. She'd worked herself to the breaking point again – a habit that both fascinated and frustrated him.

'I'll get back to you on that tomorrow,' he said and abruptly ended transmission. 'You've had a bad one, Lieutenant.'

She didn't stir when he straddled her and began to knead her neck and shoulders. 'I know there's been worse,' she murmured. 'I just can't think of when right now.'

'Louis Trivane's murder has been all over the news.'

'Goddamn vultures.'

He unhooked her weapon harness, wiggled it off her, and set it aside. 'A prominent attorney gets himself hacked up in an exclusive private club, it's news.' Competently, he worked his thumbs up her spinc. 'Nadine's called here several times.'

'Yeah, she's buzzed Central, too. I don't have time for her.'

'Mmm.' He tugged her shirt free of her slacks, and used the heels of his hands. 'Did you walk in on it, or was that added for entertainment value?'

'No, I walked in on it. Maybe if that idiot droid at the desk hadn't—' She broke off, shook her head. 'I was too late. She'd already opened him up. She was still working on him, like a kid with a science project. She implicated Charles Forte.'

'That's out, too.'

'Of course it is,' she said with a sigh. 'You can't plug all the leaks.'

'You have him in custody?'

'We're questioning him. I'm questioning him. He denies everything. I found physical evidence in his apartment, but he still denies everything.'

Denies, she thought, *while looking shocked, dislocated, terrified.*

'Oh shit.' She turned her head, pressed her face into the spread. 'Oh shit.'

'Come on.' He kissed the top of her head lightly. 'Let's get you undressed and into bed.'

'Don't baby me.'

'Try to stop me.'

She started to shift, then moved quickly before she'd realized her intent or the need. She had her arms around him, her face buried against his shoulder, her eyes squeezed tight as if to block out visions.

'You're always here. Even when you're not.'

'We're not alone, anymore. Either of us.' Because he thought she needed it, he lifted her onto his lap. 'Talk to me. You've got more than murder and evidence on your mind.'

'I'm not a good person.' She blurted it out before she could stop herself. 'I'm a good cop, but I'm not a good person. I can't afford to be.'

'That's nonsense, Eve.'

'It's not. It's true. You just don't want to see it, that's all.' She pulled back so she could look at him. 'When you love somebody, you can handle the little faults, but you don't want to see the big ones. You don't want to admit what the person you've attached yourself to is capable of, so you pretend it's not there.'

'What are you capable of that I'm blind to?'

'I beat Forte into pulp. Not physically,' she continued, dragging her hair away from her face. 'That's too easy, that's too clean. I ripped him to pieces emotionally. I wanted to. I wanted him to tell me what he'd done so I could finish it, close it away. And when Peabody had the balls to tell me she disapproved of my interview techniques, I trounced her. I sent her off duty so I could go back in and hammer at him again.'

He was silent a moment, then rose to turn the covers down. 'So let me recap. You walked in on a mutilation in progress, took the killer into custody, a killer who implicated Charles Forte in this and in other murders. This is a matter of days after you discover a mutilated body on your doorstep.'

'It can't be personal.'

'I beg your pardon, Lieutenant, but that's bullshit. To continue,' he said, coming around to unbutton her shirt, 'you then take Charles Forte in for interview, a man you suspect with good cause is responsible for several violent deaths. You play hardball, something which your aide whom you're training, and who, though highly competent, has considerably less experience than yourself in these matters, disapproves of. A police officer who did not walk into a room and find a woman gleefully carving a man into pieces. The news reports were quite specific,' he told her.

'And,' he added before Eve could speak, 'you then reprimanded your aide when she questioned your judgment,

586

subsequently sending her off duty so that you could resume your interrogation. Does that about sum it up?'

Frowning, she studied the top of his head as he bent to pull off her slacks. 'You're making it black and white. It's not.'

'It never is.' He swung her legs into bed, pushed her down gently. 'I'll tell you what it makes you, Eve. It makes you a good cop, a dedicated one. And a human one.' He undressed, slipped into bed beside her. 'And that being the case, it's probably best if I divorce you and get on with my life.' He pulled her close until her head cozied into the curve of his shoulder. 'Obviously, up till now, I've been blind to your hideous character flaws.'

'You make me sound like an idiot.'

'Good, I intended to.' He kissed her temple, ordered the lights to dim. 'Now, go to sleep.'

She turned her head so that she could smell his skin on her way to sleep. 'I don't think I can let you have that divorce,' she said on a sigh.

'No?'

'Uh-uh. No way I'm giving up the coffee.'

Eve arrived at her office at eight A.M. She had already been by the lab to harass them, which had, in part, cheered her. Her 'link was beeping with an incoming when she opened the door.

And Peabody stood at attention beside her desk.

'You're early, Peabody.' Eve moved to the 'link, coded in, and waited for the messages to dispense. 'You're not on for thirty minutes.'

'I wanted to speak to you, Lieutenant, before I came on duty.'

'All right.' Eve put the messages on hold, turned to give Peabody her full attention. 'You look like hell,' she commented.

Peabody kept her gaze steady. She knew how she looked. She hadn't eaten or slept. Symptoms, she knew that were embarrassingly similar to those she displayed when a love affair ended badly. And this, she'd realized during the long night, was worse than any breakup with a man.

'I would like to formally apologize, Lieutenant, for statements made after the Forte interview. It was insubordinate and incorrect to question your methods. I hope that my lack of judgment in this matter will not influence you to dismiss me from this case, or from this division.'

Eve sat, leaned back in a chair that creakily begged for lubricant. 'Is that all, Officer Peabody?'

'Yes, sir. Except to say—'

'If you've got more to say, pull the stick out of your butt first. You're off duty and off the record.'

Peabody's shoulders slumped slightly, but in defeat rather than relaxation. 'I'm sorry. Watching him fall to pieces that way got to me. I wasn't able to divorce myself from the situation and view it objectively. I don't believe – don't want to believe,' she corrected, 'that he's responsible. It tainted my viewpoint.'

'Objectivity's essential. And, more often than any of us want to admit, impossible. I wasn't completely objective either, which is why I overreacted to your comments. I apologize for that.'

Surprise and relief spread through her. Peabody found them both easier to swallow than crow and fear. 'Will you keep me on?'

'I've got an investment in you.' Leaving it at that, Eve turned back to her 'link.

Behind Eve's back, Peabody closed her eyes tightly, dug for composure. She took a breath, swallowed hard, and found it. 'So, does this mean we've made up?'

Eve slanted a look at Peabody's hopeful grin. 'Why don't I have any coffee?' She engaged the 'link, let her messages run. The first had barely begun when Peabody set a steaming cup at her elbow.

'Come on, Dallas, come on. Give me a break. I can go on with an update any time, day or night. Get back to me damn it. Just a couple details.'

'Not going to happen, Nadine,' Eve murmured and zipped through the next three messages from the reporter, all increasingly desperate.

There was a communication from the ME, with the autopsy report. Eve downloaded and ordered a hard copy print. Finally, a relay from the lab which verified the blood on the robe was Wineburg's.

'I can't see it,' Peabody said quietly. 'Why can't I see it? It's all there.' She lifted her shoulders, let them fall. 'It's all right there.'

'We charge him and book him.' Eve rubbed a finger up and down the center of her forehead. 'Murder one on Wineburg. We'll hold off on the conspiracy to murder on Trivane until Mira's done the testing. Have him brought up for interview again, Peabody. We'll see how many more we can pin to him.'

'Why Alice?' Peabody asked. 'Why Frank?'

'He didn't do them. They're not his.'

'Separate cases? You still think Selina's responsible for them?'

'I know she is. But we're a long way from proving it.'

She spent the day going over reports, filing her own. By noon, when she faced Chas in interview again, she was ready to try a different tack.

She studied his chosen representative, a young, sad-eyed woman who, by Eve's estimate, could barely be old enough to have passed the bar. She didn't bother to sigh as she recognized the woman from the initiation ceremony.

A lawyer witch, she mused. And wondered if that would be considered a redundancy.

'This is your chosen counsel, Mr Forte?'

589

'Yes.' His face was a sickly gray, his eyes shades darker. 'Leila has agreed to help me.'

'Very well. You've been charged with murder, Mr Forte.'

'I've requested a bail hearing,' Leila began and passed Eve some paperwork. 'It's scheduled for two P.M. today.'

'You won't get bail.' Eve handed the papers to Peabody. 'And it won't delay this very long.'

'I didn't even know the man who was killed,' Chas began. 'I'd never seen him before that night. I was with you.'

'Which puts you on the scene at the time, giving you opportunity. Motive?' She leaned back. 'You were there, you knew he was about to break, to talk. His blood wasn't the first to spill, was it, Mr Forte?'

'I don't know anything about it.' His voice quavered. He took a breath, laid his hand over Leila's as if for support. Their fingers linked and his voice came stronger. 'I've never harmed anyone in my life. It's against everything I believe, everything I've made myself. I've told you. I held nothing back from you, trusting you to understand.'

'Do you own a black robe? Natural silk, wrap style, floor length?'

'I own many robes. But I don't care for black.'

Eve held a hand out, waited until Peabody put the sealed garment into it. 'Then you don't recognize this?'

'It's not mine.' He seemed to relax a little. 'That doesn't belong to me.'

'No? Yet it was found in a chest in the bedroom of the apartment you share with Isis. Carelessly, perhaps quickly hidden under a stack of other robes. There's blood on it, Mr Forte. Wineburg's blood.'

'No.' He cringed back. 'That's not possible.'

'It's a fact. Your representative is free to study the lab report. I wonder if Isis will recognize it. It might . . . jog her memory.'

'She has nothing to do with this. Nothing to do with any

590

of this.' Panic had him lurching up. 'You can't suspect her of—'

'Of what?' Eve cocked her head. 'Of being an accessory? She lives with you, works with you, she sleeps with you. Even if she's just been protecting you, it puts her in it.'

'She can't be drawn into this. She can't be put through this. Leave her alone.' He leaned forward, resting trembling hands on the table. 'Leave her alone, Promise me that, and I'll tell you whatever you want to hear.'

'Chas.' Leila stood, put a firm hand on his shoulder. 'Sit down. Don't say anything else. My client has nothing further to say at this time, Lieutenant. I need to confer with him and request privacy to do so.'

Eve took her measure. The woman no longer looked young and sad-eyed, but cool and determined. 'There won't be a deal, counselor, not on this one.' She rose, signaled Peabody. 'But a full confession might get him a psych facility rather than a maximum lockup. Think about it.'

She swore under her breath once she was outside the room. 'She'll put a lid on him. He'll do what she tells him because he's too scared not to.'

Eve paced a yard down the corridor then back. 'I've got to get to Mira. She's bound to be done by now with testing. You contact the PA's office. We need somebody down here. Maybe if we have a prosecutor talk to his rep lawyer to lawyer, we can open it up.'

'Isis cracked him.' Peabody glanced back toward the door as they headed away. 'He really loves her.'

'There's all kinds of love, isn't there?'

'I don't get why he had sex with Mirium.'

'There's all kinds of sex, too. Some is straight manipulation.' She turned into her office to call Mira.

Chapter Twenty

Delusional, sociopathic, an addictive and easily influenced personality. Eve tossed Mira's report aside. She hadn't needed a psychiatrist to tell her Mirium was a lunatic with no conscience. She'd seen that for herself.

Or that she had obsessive leanings toward the occult, a low intelligence quotient, and a capacity for violence.

Mira's recommendation for further testing, and for treatment as a mentally defective might have been sound, but it didn't change the facts.

Mirium had butchered a man in cold blood, and would more than likely do her time in the quiet rooms of a mental health facility.

The truth testing hadn't been much more helpful. It indicated the subject was telling the truth – as the subject saw the truth. There were gaps and hitches and confusion.

Likely due, Eve noted, glancing at the drug scan results, from having a half dozen illegal substances bouncing around in her system.

'Lieutenant?' Peabody stepped in, waited for Eve to look up. 'Schultz from the PA's office just tagged me.'

'What's the status?'

'The lawyer won't budge. She's pushing for a truth test, but Forte keeps refusing. Schultz thinks she's stalling, says she wants forty-eight to study all the reports and evidence. It'll keep Fortc in since bail was denied, but she's insisting.

Schultz thinks Forte's ready to roll over, but she's keeping him on a short leash.'

'Schultz give you all that?'

'Yeah, well, I think he was looking to make time. Fresh divorce.'

'Oh.' Eve lifted a brow. 'And he likes a woman in uniform.'

'I'd say it's more like he likes a human with breasts at this point. Bottom line, he doesn't think we're getting any more tonight. The lawyer exercised her client's right for minimum break. Schultz agreed to talk more in the morning. He's headed out.'

'All right. Maybe it's best to give them both time to stew. We'll swing by Isis's place. May be able to shake her.'

'You've got it pretty well wrapped.' Peabody fell into step beside her. 'You'll be able to relax some tonight at the party.'

'Party?' Eve stopped dead. 'Mavis's party? That's tonight? Hell.'

'So speaks the party animal,' Peabody said dryly. 'Personally, I'm looking forward to it. It's been a shitty week.'

'Halloween's supposed to be for kids, so they can blackmail adults into forking over junk food. Grown men and women running around in dopey costumes. It's embarrassing.'

'Actually it's an old, revered tradition with its roots in earth religions.'

'Don't get started,' Eve warned as they rode down to the garage. She eyed Peabody suspiciously. 'You're not actually wearing a costume.'

'How else can I guarantee getting my share of candy?' Peabody brushed some lint from the front of her uniform.

The store was dark, and so was the apartment. No one answered the knock on any door. Eve considered, checked her watch. 'I'm going to stake it out for a couple of hours. I'd rather hit her tonight.'

'She's probably at the sabbat ceremony.'

'I don't figure she's in the mood for naked dancing under the circumstances. I'll stick. You can catch transpo from here.'

'I can stay.'

'It's not necessary. If she doesn't show in a couple hours, I'll head to Mavis's.'

'Like that?' Peabody scanned Eve's faded jeans, worn boots, and battered jacket. 'Don't you want to wear something more . . . festive?'

'No. I'll see you there.' Eve climbed back in the car, lowered the window. 'So, what are you wearing?'

'It's a secret,' Peabody said with a grin and walked off to catch a tram home.

'Embarrassing,' Eve decided, and settling back, engaged her 'link. The system put her through to Roarke at his midtown office.

'Just caught me,' he told her, and noted the edge of the steering wheel on the monitor. 'Obviously, you're not at home getting yourself ready for tonight's festivities.'

'Obviously not. I've got a couple more hours here, so I'll meet you at Mavis's. We can duck out early.'

'I can see you're already looking forward to an exciting evening.'

'Halloween.' She glanced over as a ghoul, a six-foot pink rabbit, and a mutant transexual crossed the street in front of her car. 'I just don't get it.'

'Darling Eve, for some it's simply an excuse to be foolish. For others it's a serious holy day. Samhain, the beginning of Celtic winter. The beginning of the year, the turn of it with the old dying and the new yet unborn. On this night the veil between is very thin.'

'Boy.' She gave a mock shudder. 'Now I'm spooked.'

'Tonight we'll concentrate on using it as an excuse to be foolish. Want to get drunk and have wild sex?'

'Yeah.' Her lips twitched. 'That sounds pretty good.'

'We could get started now. A little 'link sex.'

'That would be illegal over an official line. Besides, you never know when Dispatch is going to get nosey.'

'Then I won't mention how much I want to get my hands on you. My mouth on you. How exciting it is to feel you under me, when I'm inside you and you arch back, struggling to breathe and fist your hands in my hair.'

'No, don't mention it,' she told him as the muscles in her thighs tingled and went lax. 'I'll see you in a couple hours. We'll, ah, go home early. Then you could mention it.'

'Eve?'

'Yeah?'

'I adore you.' With a silky, satisfied smile on his face, he disengaged.

She blew out a long, slow breath. 'When am I going to get used to this?' she muttered.

The sex was mind-scrambling enough. She'd never thought of the act as any more than a necessary and mildly pleasurable physical release. Until Roarke. He could turn her dry-mouthed and needy with a look. But more was the hold he had on her heart in that firm, possessive grip that was alternately comforting and terrifying.

She'd never understood the demanding power of love.

Frowning, she looked back at the apartment across the street. Hadn't that been what she'd seen there? Power and love? Isis was a strong, powerful woman. Could love have blinded her so completely?

It wasn't impossible, Eve mused. But it was . . . disappointing, she admitted. For herself, she knew Roarke had spent much of his life skirting the law. Hell, she thought, he'd stomped on it.

She knew he'd stolen, cheated, finagled. She knew he'd killed. The abused child from the mean streets of Dublin had done what he'd needed to do to survive. Then had done as he'd liked to profit. She couldn't entirely blame him for either.

Yet, if he used his power and his position today to kill, what would she do? Would she stop loving him? She wasn't sure, but she was sure that she would know. And the code that she lived by wouldn't allow her to turn a blind eye to murder.

Maybe the code Isis lived by wasn't as strong.

And yet, as she sat in the dark with the sharp little teeth of the wind biting at her windows, she found she couldn't balance it.

Forte had all but confessed now, she reminded herself. Once she'd confronted him with the robe, with the evidence, he'd started toward surrender.

That wasn't entirely true, she thought. It was when she'd brought Isis into it that he'd changed directions.

Protecting her. Shielding her. Sacrificing for her.

With a new theme playing in her mind, she got out of the car, crossed the street.

A number of people wandered the street, many of them in costumes. Even as she stepped over the curb, a gaggle of teenagers rushed by, making enough noise to wake the dead. No one paid any attention to a lone woman in a leather jacket climbing the stairs to a dark apartment.

She stood on the landing a moment, scanning the street, the surrounding buildings. It was an area where people minded their own business, she decided. And wouldn't the neighbors be accustomed to seeing people – perhaps the-less-than-usual type of person – going up and into the apartment.

To test her theory farther, Eve tried the door. Finding it locked, she simply fished a master code out of her pocket. She had the door open in seconds and waited just outside it for the sound of a security alarm.

There was only silence inside.

No security, she decided, and resisted the temptation to go in. The average civilian wouldn't have access to a master, but there were other ways of popping unsecured locks.

Hadn't the apartment been empty the day before? With both Forte and Isis at Central, how easy would it have been for someone to slip in, to plant a bloodstained robe in an obvious place?

Eve shut the door again and stood arguing with herself. Mirium had implicated him. She'd said his name as she sat on the floor, blood still running from her hands.

Delusional, sociopathic, easily influenced.

Damn it. Eve trooped down the steps, back to her car. The evidence was there, wasn't it? Motive, opportunity. It was a fucking textbook checklist. She even had a confessed accomplice in custody.

An accomplice he'd been sleeping with on the side. Having sex in Central Park, using his influence to bring her into the coven right under his lover's nose.

It fit, she told herself. And that was the trouble. It slid so well into place it was as if someone had oiled the slot. All you had to do was leave out love – selfless, devoted, unquestioning love. Add that, and it scraped along the sides of that slot, screaming in protest.

If there was a chance it was a setup, and that she was being used to make it click, she was damn well going to find out. She considered calling Peabody, started to reach for her 'link, when she heard the scream. She was out of the car, her hand on her weapon, when she spotted the black-robed figure dragging a woman into the shadows.

'Police.' She rushed forward, drawing. 'Back off.'

He did more than that. He ran. When Eve reached the woman, she was lying facedown, moaning. Holstering her weapon, she crouched down.

'How bad did he hurt you?' As she rolled the woman over, she saw the glint of a blade. It was pressed, keenedged, against her stomach before she saw Selina's face.

'All I have to do is push, just a little.' Selina smiled. 'I'd enjoy that. But for now . . .' Her hand tapped against Eve's throat. She felt the pressure and the sting an instant before her vision blurred.

'Now you're going to help me to the car. Or it's going to look that way if anyone notices.' Smiling, Selina put her arms

597

around Eve, keeping close so it appeared she was being lifted to her feet. 'And if you don't do exactly what I say, your guts will hit the sidewalk and I'll be gone before you realize you're dead.'

Eve's head was swimming, her legs like rubber as Selina led her down the sidewalk. 'Get in,' Selina ordered, 'slide over.'

She found herself obeying dully, while a part of her mind screamed in protest. 'Not so smart now, are you, Lieutenant Dallas? Not so cool. We led you right where we wanted you. Stupid bitch. How do you set this thing to auto?'

'I—' She couldn't think. Fear couldn't get through the haze, nor could anger or training. She stared blankly at the controls. 'Auto?'

Her voice was enough. The vehicle shuddered, then hummed discordantly.

'I don't believe you're in any shape to drive.' Selina threw back her head and laughed. 'Give it the address. My apartment. We have a very special ceremony in mind for you.'

Mechanically, Eve repeated the address and stared straight ahead as the vehicle slowly slid from the curb. 'Not Forte,' she managed, struggling to snap back. 'It was never him.'

'That pathetic excuse for a man? He couldn't kill a fly if it landed on his dick. If he's got one. But he and that half-breed Wiccan are going to pay. You've seen to that, haven't you? They thought they could save poor little Alice. Well, so did her stupid grandfather. See where it got them. No one challenges me and lives. You'll find out just how much power I have very soon now. And you'll beg me to kill you and end it.'

'You killed them all.'

'Every one of them.' Selina leaned closer. 'And more. Many more. I enjoy the children most. They're so . . . fresh. I walked right in on the grandfather, used his weakness for females. Sobbed, told him I was afraid for my life. Alban would kill me. Then I slipped the drugs into his drink and I killed him. I wanted blood but, well, it was nearly as satisfying to watch his eyes as he realized he was dying. You've seen how the eyes die first, haven't you, Dallas? They die first.'

'Yes.' The mists were moving back to the corners of her mind. She could feel her legs and arms tingle as the nerves pumped back to life. 'Yes, they do.'

'And Alice. I was almost sorry when we had to end that. Tormenting her day after day was so arousing. They way she would jump at a cat or a bird. Druids. Easily programmed. We used the cat that night, had it speak to her with my voice. We were waiting for her, we had plans for her, but she ran into the street and killed herself instead.

'So we'll do to you what we'd planned for her. Here we are now.'

As the car veered toward the curb, Eve tested her hand, forced it into a fist. She struck out, backhanded, felt the satisfying connection with flesh and bone. Then the door was wrenched open behind her, hands clenched around her throat.

And the world went black.

'She should be here by now.' Though her apartment was filled with people and noise and wildly spinning lights, Mavis pouted. 'She promised.'

'She'll be right along.' Roarke managed to avoid being butted by a red-robed bull, lifted a brow at the manic call of 'Toro!' An angel spun by, desperately dancing with a headless corpse.

'I really wanted her to see what Leonardo and I have done with the place.' Proud, Mavis turned a quick circle. 'She'd never recognize her old digs, would she?'

Roarke scanned the magenta walls with their uninhibited splashes and streaks of cerise and periwinkle. The furniture consisted of heaps of glossy pillows and glass tubes. In keeping with the event, streamers of orange and black swayed everywhere. Skeletons danced, witches flew, and black cats arched.

599

'No.' He could agree with complete honesty. 'She'd never recognize her old apartment. You've done . . . wonders.'

'We just love it. And we've got the best landlord on planet.' She kissed him enthusiastically.

While he hoped her purple lipstick hadn't transferred to his face, he smiled. 'My favorite tenant.'

'Could you call her, Roarke?' With fingers tipped the same shade, she plucked at his sleeve. 'Just give her a little goose.'

'Of course. Go play hostess, and don't worry. I'll get her here.'

'Thanks.' She rolled off on glittery, red-wheeled shoes.

Roarke turned with the idea of hunting up somewhere quiet to make his call, then blinked at the apparition. 'Peabody?'

Her elaborately painted face fell. 'You recognized me.'

'Barely.' With a faint smile, he stepped back to take a full measure.

Long blonde hair swirled over her shoulders, down her back, over the tiny scallop-shaped bra that covered her breasts. From the waist down, she was encased in shimmering green.

'You make a lovely mermaid.'

'Thanks.' She perked up again. 'It took me forever to rig myself out.'

'How the hell do you walk?'

'I've got a cutout for my feet, the skirt of the tail covers it.' She wiggled back. 'Pretty restrictive to movement though. Where's Dallas?' She twisted her head to search. 'I want her to get a load of it.'

'She isn't here yet.'

'No?' Because she hadn't worn her watch, she peered down at his. 'It's almost ten. She was only going to stake out Isis's place for a couple hours then come straight here.'

'I was about to call her.'

'Good idea.' Peabody tried to ignore the prickle of nerves. 'She's probably stalling. She hates stuff like this.'

'Yes, you're right.' But she'd have been there for Mavis, he thought as he slipped into the corner. And for him.

When her 'link went unanswered, he bypassed security and called through her communicator. There was a humming buzz that indicated it was on standby, but it went unanswered.

'Something's wrong,' he said when he stepped back up to Peabody. 'She isn't picking up.'

'Let me get my bag, try her communicator.'

'I already tried it,' he said shortly. 'She isn't picking up. She was staking out Spirit Quest?'

'Yeah, she wanted to talk to Isis . . . let me get out of this costume. We'll go check it out.'

'I can't wait for you.' He pushed his way through the crowd as Peabody shuffled and looked for Feeney.

She thought it was a dream at first when she woke, groggy and hot. Her head spun, and when she tried to lift a hand to it, she found she couldn't move.

Panic rushed in first. Her hands were bound. He'd often tied her hands when she was a child. Tied her to the bed, clamped a hand over her mouth to hold in her screams when he raped her.

She pulled at them, felt the vague, faraway pain of the straps cutting into her wrists. Her breath sobbed out as she struggled. Her legs were secured as well, tied down at the ankles so that her thighs were spread.

She whipsawed her head, trying to see. Shadows shifted through the room, chased by the flickering lights of dozens of candles. She could see herself in a mirror, a wall of black glass that reflected images and light.

She wasn't a child, and it wasn't her father who had tied her.

She forced down the panic. It wouldn't help. It never did. She'd been drugged, she told herself. She'd been brought here, stripped naked, and tied to a marble slab like a piece of meat.

Selina Cross meant to kill her, and maybe worse, unless she could keep her mind clear and fight back. She continued to work at her wrist straps, twisting, tugging, while she forced her mind to focus.

Where was she? In the apartment, most likely, though she couldn't quite remember. The club would have been too dangerous, full of people. It was more private here, in this room. This room where Alice had seen a child sacrificed.

What time was it? God, how long had she been out? Roarke was going to be pissed. She bit her lip hard enough to draw blood to hold back the bubble of hysteria.

They would miss her, wonder about her. Peabody knew her last location, and they would check it out.

And what good would that do her?

Eve closed her eyes to wait for calm. She was on her own, she told herself. And she meant to survive.

The mirrored wall slid open and Selina, draped in an open black robe, slipped through. 'Ah, you're awake. I wanted you awake and aware before we started.'

Alban stepped in behind her. He wore a similar robe and the fierce, toothed mask of a boar. Saying nothing, he picked up a thick candle, set it between Eve's thighs. He stepped back, lifted an ivory-handled athame from a black pillow, then held it aloft.

'Now, we begin.'

Roarke opened the door of his car when his pocket 'link beeped. He whipped it out. 'Eve?'

'It's Jamie. I know where she is. They've got her. You have to hurry.'

'Where is she?' As he spoke, Roarke climbed behind the wheel.

'That Cross bitch. They've got her inside the apartment. Or

602

I think they do. I lost transmission when they got her out of the car.'

Roarke didn't wait, but pushed the accelerator and flew through traffic. 'What transmission?'

'I bugged her car. I wanted to know what was going on. I planted a transmitter. I heard stuff tonight. Cross told her to put the car on auto, go to the apartment. Dallas must've been drugged or something, because she sounded weird. And Cross said how she'd killed my grandfather and Alice.' His voice flooded with tears. 'She killed them both. And kids. And Christ . . .'

'Where are you?'

'I'm right outside their place. I'm going in.'

'Stay out. Goddamn it, you listen to me. Stay out. I'll be there in two minutes. Call the cops. Report a break-in, a fire, anything, but get them there. Understand me?'

'She killed my sister.' Jamie's voice was suddenly calm and cold. 'And I'm going to kill her.'

'Stay out,' Roarke repeated, swearing as the transmission ended. Digging for control, he called Mavis's, snapped out a demand for Peabody when the call was answered with wild laughter.

He was already pulling up at Selina's building when Peabody answered. 'Roarke. Feeney and I are heading to Spirit Quest right—'

'She's not there. Cross has her, most likely in the apartment building. I'm there now, and I'm going in.'

'Jesus, don't do anything crazy. I'll call for a cruiser. Feeney and I are on our way.'

'There's a young boy in there, too. You'd better hurry.'

With no weapon but his wits and his will, he rushed the door.

They were chanting over her. Alban had lighted a fire in a black cauldron and the smoke was thick and overly sweet.

603

Selina had discarded her robe and was now slowly rubbing glistening oil over her body.

'Ever been raped by a woman? I'm going to hurt you when I do it. So will he. And we won't kill you quickly, the way we did Lobar, the way we told Mirium to kill Trivane. It's going to be slow and unspeakably painful.'

Eve's head was clear now, brutally clear. Her wrists burned, slicked with her own blood as she continued to strain against the straps. 'Is this how you call up your demons? Your religion's a sham. You just like to rape and kill. It makes you a degenerate, just like any creep crawling in the gutter.'

Selina brought her hand back, whipped it down hard over Eve's face. 'I want to kill her now.'

'Soon, my love.' Alban crooned it. 'You don't want to rush the moment.'

He reached into a box, pulled a black cockerel out. It clucked and squawked, wings flapping as Alban held it over Eve's body. He spoke in Latin now, his voice musical, as he took the knife and sliced off the head. Blood gushed out, steaming over Eve's torso. Beside her, Selina moaned in ecstasy.

'Blood, for the master.'

'Yes, my love.' He turned to her. 'The master must have blood.' And very calmly, very quickly, he raked the knife over Selina's throat. 'You have been so . . . tedious,' he murmured when she stumbled back, breath gurgling as she grabbed at her throat. 'Useful, but tedious.'

When she collapsed, he stepped over her, removed the mask, set it aside. 'Enough of the pageantry. She enjoyed it. I find it stifling.' He smiled, charmingly. 'I don't intend to make you suffer. There's no purpose in it.'

The stench of blood was nauseating. Using all her will, Eve concentrated on his face. 'Why did you kill her?'

'She'd ceased to be useful. She's quite insane, you know. Too many chemicals, I suspect, in addition to a defective personality. She liked me to beat her before sex.' He shook his head. 'There were times I actually enjoyed it. The beating part, anyway. She was very clever with chemicals.' Absently, he ran a hand up and down Eve's calf. 'And I discovered with the right direction, the proper incentive, she was a clever businesswoman. We've made an enormous amount of money over the last couple of years. And, of course, there's the membership contributions. People will pay ridiculous amounts of money for sex and the possibility of immortality.'

'So it was just a con.'

'Come on, Dallas. Calling up demons, selling the soul.' He chuckled, delighted. 'It's the best grift I've ever run, but it's hit its peak. Now Selina . . .' He glanced down, idly rubbed a thumb over his chin. 'She became quite serious about it. She actually believed she had power.' He studied the sprawled body with something like amused pity. 'That she could see in the smoke, call up the devil.' He smiled again, made the ageless sign for lunacy by circling his finger at his temple.

A sham, Eve thought, *from the beginning, nothing but a long con for profit*. 'Most grifters don't add human sacrifice to the theme.'

'I'm not most grifters, and a few realistic ceremonies kept Selina in line. She developed a taste for blood. So did I,' he admitted. 'That I did find addicting. Taking a life is a powerful thing, an arousing thing.'

He let his gaze roam over her, appreciating the slim, subtle lines. Selina had been all lush curves, just on the point of overabundance. 'I may have you first, after all. It seems a waste not to.'

Everything in her revolted at the thought. 'You were the one who had sex with Mirium, you were the one who told her to kill Trivane, to infiltrate the Wiccans.'

'She is the most malleable of women. And under a little

605

chemical inducement, some posthypnotic suggestion, selectively forgetful.'

'It was never Selina. That's where I was off. You weren't her lap dog. She was yours.'

'That's very accurate. She was losing control. I've known that for some time. She did the cop on her own.' His mouth thinned in annoyance. 'That was the beginning of the end for this, and for her. He'd never have pinned us, and should have been left to fumble around until he gave up.'

'You're wrong. Frank wouldn't have given up.'

'Hardly matters now, does it?' He turned away, taking up a small vial and a pressure injector. 'I'll give you just a bit, to take the edge off. You're really quite attractive. I can make you enjoy it when I rape you.'

'There aren't enough drugs in the world for that.'

'You're wrong,' he murmured and walked toward her.

Roarke had to force himself not to enter the apartment at a run. If she was inside and in trouble, his rushing in could do her more harm than good. He closed the door quietly at his back. Since the security had already been bypassed, he knew Jamie had gone in.

Still, the movement at his side had him lashing out, grabbing at the throat.

'It's me. It's Jamie. I can't get into the room. They've installed something new. I can't bypass.'

'Where is it?'

'There, that wall. I haven't heard anything, but they're in there. They have to be.'

'Go outside.'

'I won't. And you're wasting time.'

'Then stay back,' Roarke ordered, refusing to waste more.

He approached the wall, running his fingers over it, ordering himself to be thorough, methodical, while every instinct in him screamed to hurry.

If there was a device, it was well concealed. Reaching into his pocket, he took out his daily log, tapped in a program. He thought he caught the distant wail of a siren.

'What is that?' Jamie demanded in a whisper. 'Jesus, is that a jammer? I've never seen one worked into a pocket diary.'

'You're not the only one who knows the tricks.' He began to play it over the wall, cursing it for being too slow, too inefficient. Abruptly, it emitted a low hum, beeped twice. 'There's the little bastard.'

As the door slid open, he crouched and, baring his teeth, prepared to spring.

She strained away from the injector, but it pressed against her upper arm, then just as quickly, was removed.

'No.' With a quick laugh, Alban, set it aside. 'Not for sex. That would be unfair to you and a blow to my pride. Afterward, I'll put you under deeply so you won't feel the knife. It's the least I can do.'

'Just kill me, you son of a bitch.' With a final vicious pull, she popped the strap, dragged one arm free, and shot her fist into his face. But when she reached for the knife lying beside her, it clattered to the floor.

Then, for just a moment, she thought the demons of hell had been loosed after all.

He came in like a wolf, with a snarl and a lunge. The force of Roarke's attack sent Alban flying back, sent candles flying to gutter out in pools of blood.

Rearing up, Eve struggled to free her other hand, and panic left no room for shock as she spotted Jamie. 'Hurry up, for Christ's sake. Get the knife, cut me loose. Hurry!'

His stomach was heaving, but he stepped over Selina's body, grabbed the knife. Keeping his eyes locked on her wrist, he hacked at the strap.

'Give it to me. I can get the rest.' Her gaze was locked on Roarke, the desperate struggle over the bloody floor. Fire was

607

beginning to live in the corner, growing from upended candle to hungry flame. 'There's the cops,' she said when she heard the siren. 'Go let them in.'

'The door's unlocked.' He said it calmly, flatly, as he moved to her feet to cut her ankles free.

'Do something about that fire in the corner,' she ordered as she scrambled down.

'No, let it burn. Let the whole damn place burn to the ground.'

'Put it out,' she snapped again, then leapt like a madwoman onto Alban's back. 'You bastard, you son of a bitch.' Even as she dragged his head back, Roarke's fist flew up and cracked against his face.

'Get the hell back,' Roarke demanded. 'He's mine.'

They rolled over in a violent tangle of limbs to discover only two of them were still conscious.

'Did he hurt you?' Roarke's eyes were still wild when he grabbed her arms. 'Did he put his hands on you?'

'No.' She had to be calm now, she realized, for he wasn't. She wasn't entirely sure what Roarke was capable of when he was in this state. 'He never touched me. You took care of that. I'm all right.'

'You were taking care of yourself, as usual, when I got here.' He lifted her hand, stared at the blood seeping from the abrasions on her wrist, and lifted it to his lips. 'I could kill him for that. Just for that alone.'

'Stop. It's part of the job.'

He was struggling to accept that. His jacket was ruined, a bloody mess, but he took it off and wrapped it around her. 'You're naked.'

'Yeah, I noticed. I don't know what they did with my clothes, but I'd just as soon be wearing something other than skin when the troops get here.'

She rose, discovered she wasn't entirely steady on her feet. 'They drugged me,' she explained, shaking her head to clear it as Roarke moved her away, eased her down to sit on a clear spot on the floor.

'Just get your breath back. I have to put out that fire.'

'Good thinking.' She drew a couple of cleansing breaths as he used one of the robes to smother the flames flicking along the floor. Then she shot to her feet, cried out. 'No. Jamie, don't.' She took the first running steps forward, but it was already too late.

Face white, Jamie got to his feet. The knife still wet with Alban's blood was in his hand. 'They killed my family.' His eyes were huge, the pupils pinpricks as he offered the knife to Eve. 'I don't care what you do to me. He won't ever kill anyone else's sister.'

She heard the footsteps rushing through the outside door, and following instinct, gripped the athame by the handle so that her own fingerprints were on it. 'Shut up. Just shut the hell up. Peabody.' Eve turned as her aide rushed in, weapon drawn. 'Get me something to wear, will you?'

Peabody's breath came out in three unsteady puffs as she scanned the carnage. 'Yes, sir. Are you all right?'

'I'm fine. Cross and Alban ambushed me, drugged me up, and got me here. They've both confessed to the murders of Frank Wojinski and Alice Lingstrom, Lobar, Wineburg, and conspiracy to murder Trivane. Alban killed Selina, for reasons I will detail in my report. Alban was killed during the struggle to contain him. It was confusing, I'm not sure exactly how it happened. I don't think it matters.'

'No.' Feeney stood beside Peabody, scanned Jamie's face, then Eve's. And he knew. 'I don't think it matters now. Come on, Jamie, you shouldn't be in here now.'

'Lieutenant, with respect. I think it would be best if you and Roarke went home and cleaned up. You're a little too in tune with the season, so to speak.'

Eve glanced at Roarke, grimaced. Blood and smoke coated his face. 'You look disgusting.'

'You should see yourself, Lieutenant.' He slipped an arm around her. 'I think Peabody has a point. We'll find a blanket. That should be sufficient to get you home without you freezing or getting arrested.'

She wanted a bath so desperately she could have wept. 'Okay. I'll be back in an hour.'

'Dallas, it isn't necessary for you to come back tonight.'

'An hour,' she repeated. 'Secure the scene, call the ME. Get that boy an MT. He's shocky. Contact Whitney. He'll want to know what happened here, and I want Charles Forte released as soon as possible.'

Eve tugged Roarke's jacket more securely around her. 'You were right about him, Peabody. Your instincts were on target. They're good instincts.'

'Thank you, Lieutenant.'

'Use them again. If that boy says anything that doesn't jibe with my brief statement of the events, ignore him. He's emotionally wrecked and in shock. I don't want him questioned tonight by anyone.'

Peabody nodded, kept her eyes carefully blank. 'Yes, sir. I'll see that he's taken home. I'll remain on scene until you return.'

'Do that.' Eve turned, started to button the jacket.

'By the way, Dallas?'

'What, Peabody?'

'That's a lovely tattoo. New?'

Eve clamped her teeth together, strode toward the door with as much dignity as she could manage. 'See?' She jabbed a finger into Roarke's chest as they walked down the corridor. 'I told you I'd be humiliated by that stupid rosebud.'

'You've been drugged, slapped, tied up naked, and nearly killed, but a rose on your butt humiliates you?'

'All that other stuff's the job. The rosebud's personal.'

Laughing, he swung his arm around her shoulders, hugging her close. 'Christ, Lieutenant, I love you.'